ABYSS

Unbound Book Seven

NICOLI GONNELLA

ıis is a work of fiction. Names, characters, places, and incidents either are the products
the author's imagination or are used fictitiously. Any resemblance to actual persons,
ng or dead, businesses, companies, events, or locales is entirely coincidental.

To my brother.
Because one time we crashed while tandem skateboarding down a hill, and you saved me and broke your own ankle as a result.
We'll ignore that it was your idea in the first place.

CHAPTER ONE

Fear the blackened skies and the mountains that fall; fear the breaking of chains. Fear the untethered demons you have loosed, that their collars may slip. Fear. For the Night descends.

-Seer Ceros, Primarch of the Invisible Eye

The Shining City of Amaranth was the gleaming core of the Hierocracy, the center of its commerce, and the beating heart of its Authority. Within walls that had never been breached were hundreds of thousands of people, all of them living and dying within sight of the alabaster towers of the Hierei—those that sat upon the Conclave, that bore a portion of its Seat and Seal in order to govern the vast breadth of the nation. The largest portion of that Authority, however, sat upon the shoulders of a single individual.

The Hierophant.

Built as a mountain of stainless white stone, the Hierophant's shining palace dominated Amaranth. Its soaring arches and impossibly thin towers were filigree upon the stout, brutal construction of ten thousand chambers. The sweeping grounds housed a veritable army of Priests, Paladins, Inquisitors, and all those who served the vaunted Three Orders. The Hierei were housed within the twelve towers that ran the circumference of the palace, each connected to the others by a series of vaulted arches that were both incredibly delicate and improbably strong...all of which lead to the grandest and tallest tower at the apex of the palace, which was surmounted by the grandest of all statues, and the Altar to the Light. The Tower of True Faith, it was called by some, though Kellis knew it by a different, older name.

En'Cridhe. The Star of Heaven. Kellis Faer, the Hierei of Calumb, Pax'Vrell, and Sao'thun found himself enraptured by its majesty with every approach. Even now, as he rushed across the whisper-thin stonework from his own tower, he could not help but appreciate the masterwork statues of Humans, their perfectly designed bodies lifting the exposed stairwell that spiraled around the Tower's circumference.

Yet, if one looked close enough, they would notice that not all of the statues were Human. A number of the huge statues were defaced, officially during a conflict in the Hierocracy's founding, but Kellis knew the damage was intentional. Faces and limbs were cracked and missing, but he had read the records and knew the secret histories the Priests kept.

A bell tolled, deep and loud enough to shake his Tempered organs. Kellis sped up, pressing his old bones as fast as he could to cross the distance above the Shining Palace, before ducking into the shadowed doorway at its end. Mana crystals dotted the walls, shaped into exquisite facsimiles of flame. Each one bloomed with a brilliant golden, magical light. Such light was said to expose the lies of the wicked or untrue before they could be granted an audience with the Conclave, but that was only superstition.

Not that we disabuse anyone of that notion, the Hierei thought with an inward smile. He took several surreptitious gulps of air in an attempt to calm his thudding heart. *Far easier to deal with supplicants when they are too afraid to lie properly.*

Down a winding corridor built of a gorgeous mix of white marble and golden filigree was a large door guarded by two men in milky-white armor and an eclectic array of vicious weaponry. The door was covered in ornate details, things Kellis no longer noticed, but which were suitably impressive to the masses: the Shining City and, above it, a figure of indeterminate features, radiating light like the sun itself.

The guards' eyes met Kellis', and a shiver of fear chased itself down his back. He refused to let it show. The High Guard only respected warriors, and while the Hierei was not of that number, he found that cowering did little to endear them to him. Still, he gave a tiny inclination of his head—the smallest recognition of their station—and was responded to in kind.

The door was ajar, and Kellis slipped through, the eyes of the High Guard following him.

Within was an antechamber that the Hierei walked quickly across, and he soon entered the wide, domed expanse of the Conclave. Within was more of the same: highly polished white marble, golden decoration, and dark, masterwork tables and chairs. Atop a raised dais, a throne of ivory, white jade, and deep, gleaming lengths of golden crystal sat empty, yet exuding an irrefutable sense of majesty. The room, normally filled with the Hierei, was empty save for three others.

"You are late, Faer," Hierei Mivun chastised in his deep voice. "Seventh glass sharp was the designation."

"My deepest regrets, Brother Mivun."

"The bells rang not a few heartbeats ago, Mivun," said the whip-thin Hierei Quist, her face drawn into a dismissive moue. "Leave off, and let us begin."

"I apologize to the esteemed Hierei, but the bells *ended*, that means it is no longer the advent of the seventh glass." Mivun rumbled discontentedly, his bulk shifting within his pale robes. "Precision matters in all things. It is the virtue by which Order is maintained."

"Order is nothing before the Strength to enact it," said Hierei Quist, her face creasing with disdain. "Precision, while vaunted, cannot match the conviction to advance."

"And conviction is nothing if the soul is not cleansed by Purity," said Hierei Lar, the pale robes of his station cut by a lavender sash. He frowned at them all. "This is not an argument worthy of our time, Brothers and Sister. The Night moves against us as we dawdle, speaking of Ideals."

"I could not agree more," said a new voice, one Kellis knew almost better than his own. A woman in pure white robes stepped from behind the throne with two of the High Guard at her side, a silver diadem on her brow and an alabaster staff in her left hand. "Order is maintained by Strength, Strength is maintained by Purity, and Purity finds its fullest measure only under Order. These are the Ideals by which I have built this nation, how I bound our Fates together under the auspices of the Pathless. It is by these Ideals that we still stand, free of the greater threats upon the Continent, and it is by them that we shall have victory before the Night."

As one, the Hierei dropped to a knee, even the ponderous bulk of Mivun. "Glory be to the Hierophant, Servant of the Remnant King, the Trackless Lord."

"May all your Paths shine under the light," the woman intoned. Kellis shivered at the simple, earnest compassion in her voice. "Please, stand."

They did, and the Hierophant looked to them all in silence for an extended moment. The woman was neither old nor young, comely nor haggard, though her hair was long and lustrous and her smile bright and unbroken. Lines crinkled the edges of her eyes, proof of her incredible age—for a Paragon to exhibit even that much meant she had lived far longer than all of the Hierei combined. They were only Grandmasters, after all, and were still mortal. Ocalla Marzul, Hierophant of the Shining City and Ruler of the Hierocracy was something far more.

"Lar, what news have you?" she asked, voice an ethereal mix of warm regard and cold command. "How fares the West?"

"It remains, as it always has, beneath your benevolent hand," Lar said with a deep bow. His lavender sash swayed with the movement. "But there has been unrest at the farthest reaches."

"You speak of the upstart? This...Autarch?" the Hierophant asked, and a chill descended upon the chamber. Kellis barely suppressed a shiver.

"Felix Nevarre. Yes. As I have mentioned before, my Inquisitors were in the area before this strange barrier was erected. They were searching for the Unbound, as you ordered us, and were set to capitalize upon some unique resources. The Foglands had opened up, and the treasures within that untouched vista are said to be as potent as anything within the Interior." Lar's voice stumbled as he caught the Hierophant's uninterested glare. "But, I uh, have not heard from a single one since the barrier went up. More Inquisitors were dispatched to the edge of it, halfway through the city of Setoria, but none have been able to penetrate it." Lar shook his head, and Kellis could hear the bare flicker of fury from the man's Spirit. "It is a potent working, fueled by a higher Tier of Authority."

Hierei Mivun tried to gasp quietly, but it was loud as a Smith's bellows. "Such a thing is not possible."

Kellis agreed. Not all Authority was created equal, not for Ages. Even the Seats and Seals upon which their own power was based was—for all its complexity—a butchered version of the processes of their forebears. The old ways were Lost, Ruined in Ages past and buried beneath the ever-growing mountains of time.

"Nevarre," Quist said, rolling the surname across her tongue. "The name sounds Wyvarren. Is there a House Nevarre on record?"

"Not that I have found," Lar admitted. "The Master Archivist is still looking, but we've precious little from Wyvarr due to the civil war last century. He's not of the Major Houses, of that we are certain."

"Then we simply let this act of rebellion go unchecked?" Maross said imperiously. He was very carefully not looking at the Hierophant as he vented. "It is asking for far worse from this supposed Autarch."

"Enough. Let us think on this. Quist, speak of the South. How goes the conquest of the Scorched Expanse?"

The woman quivered under that gaze and bowed her head. "I fear I, too, have unfortunate news. Contact with High Justiciar Haim has been...severed."

Kellis drew a sharp breath, as did everyone save the Hierophant. She only blinked slowly. "And the Regalia?"

Quist wet her lips and clutched her hands before her. "Lost."

Kellis reeled at the implications of Quist's words. To have lost a piece of the Pathless' mortal Regalia? Such an artifact was precious beyond measure, and Kellis was astounded it had been gifted to the Paladins of all people.

"So, your Paladins are dead," the Hierophant said.

Quist nodded unhappily. "It must be assumed so, your Eminence. No Ffen have been received, nor messages upon the Waystones in Ghreldan. For the moment, I must assume the Kel'lyv discovered the ruse and turned upon our forces. No other explanation makes as much sense."

The Hierophant nodded. "I agree. The Grandmaster of Desert's Fire has always been a rabid dog. I had hoped that the Paladins would be able to put him down, but he and his Territory were of minor importance. What of the Unbound?"

"They found him. A Minotaur of incredible Strength and some sort of necromantic ability." Quist's expression twisted. "But the creature has continued to evade my Paladins. His whereabouts are currently...unknown."

Silence poured into the Conclave, a thing alive and volatile. The Hierophant did not stare at any of them, but glowered upward, at the apex of the domed chamber where a hanging Mana crystal had been grown. The silence stretched and wavered, a steady, pulsing flex like the echo of his heartbeat. Sweat gathered at the nape of Kellis neck, clinging as if too afraid to drop for the noise it would make.

Quist stumbled through the silence, clearly unable to take it any longer. "I—I can send more men into the waste. I am already mustering another battalion to—"

"No," the Hierophant snapped.

The silence returned, heavier this time and edged in something so very close to violence. Kellis watched the Hierophant's fingers flex on her staff, hard enough to creak the Tier X stone it was constructed from and turn her knuckles white. All of them went still, too afraid to even look at one another.

She raised her staff and rapped it against the floor. A boom loud enough to shatter a Journeyman's eardrums ripped across the chamber. "What matters is corralling these wild Unbound. We have lost contact with Haim, meaning the Unbound likely overcame him. How, in such a short amount of time in that blasted desert, I haven't the foggiest. But that means he is too dangerous to bring in...for now. Instead, we must focus on those who have not yet amassed such power."

"The Gnome and the twins," Kellis said. "Unless you have word of the others?"

"Not yet. But you are correct. Quist, send a small contingent into the Expanse and dig around. See how Ahkestria has fended off my soldiers, and locate the Unbound but do not engage. Mivun, focus your efforts in the East upon the twins. I know you've had little progress, but I assume a battalion of Paladins and Inquisitors would aid your search?"

"It would indeed, your Eminence."

The Hierophant locked eyes with Kellis. "And Faer, you have tracked the Gnome down to a city along the Rimefangs?"

"I—I have, your Eminence. It is between three cities, actually," Kellis started, but was cut off.

"You shall have the resources needed to secure the creature; simply let the seneschals know of your needs."

Kellis bowed as deeply as his old bones could manage, forcing his Spirit to beat a tattoo of grateful relief.

"What of the Autarch?" Lar asked. "How would you like me to proceed?"

"I am unconcerned with this lordling's attempts at rebellion. Even he must know that the Path he walks is one that leads nowhere but the grave, which is why he maintains that barrier. Nevarre is of minor importance. Soon, so much will be changed."

"Then let us send the High Guard, your Eminence," Lar suggested. "They will make short work of the barrier and reclaim the Territory for you at minimum cost. The added Authority will only be beneficial in the face of our adversary."

The Hierophant pursed her lips before nodding. "A small contingent, same as the Paladins. Let it be done."

"As you will," Lars said, bowing gracefully once more. "This Nagast will fall before the end of the year."

The Hierophant waved a hand, dismissing the man's words. "As I have said, its re-acquisition is of minor importance. But...Faer."

Kellis couldn't help jerking slightly in surprise. "Yes, your Eminence?"

The Hierophant paused, tapping her lips with a slender finger. "Your situation is uniquely suited to testing our newest recruit. I would like you to take them with you when you return to the North." She rapped her staff once more on the ground, and a door opened somewhere behind the throne.

"Newest..." Kellis' voice trailed off as a woman was led into the room, her face hidden by a mask and her body covered in enough Master-Tier armor to assault a mountain. She was tall, far taller than any other who was present, but it was the unmistakable weight of her unveiled Spirit that was like a blow to the spine. Small shouts of alarm erupted from all the Hierei, until the Hierophant gestured sharply, and the pressure vanished.

"Unbound..." Lar whispered, astounded. "I had not known she was...ready."

"She is well-trained, her Skill levels advanced far beyond what my people can teach her." The Hierophant's hand clasped around the other woman's armored bicep. She was perhaps a full stride taller than the Hierophant, but just as slender despite the armor. "Imara is ready to truly experience what the Continent has to offer. Aren't you?"

"Yes," Imara said, but Kellis recoiled at the sound of her voice. "Yes, I wish to see it all."

Her voice sounded dead.

CHAPTER TWO

I—

He floated in gelid darkness, buffeted by currents he could not see. There was no thought, no memory or experience beyond the now. There was no him.

I am—

Then there was. Thoughts and phrases trickled into a space in the dark, a swirling configuration of whispered light and sound. Patterns formed from them, twisting around and through one another, weaving and knotting in the strangest of ways, until the whole of it ignited into riotous song.

I am the—

Memory flashed into place. Memory of a yacht, of lightning and a beach. Of forests and fog and monsters. Of a vault hidden in the earth, suspended behind wards and traps enough to kill the greatest of adventurers...and the creature within.

A terrible cry echoed into the dark depths. Cold fluid coursed around his patterns, pressing them down, deeper. The far-off bellow came again, and again, each time closer. He had no eyes, but he knew he shined brighter than anything else in the depths—a torch in the night, glimmering prey among the waters. Beneath, something *moved.*

I am the Un—

The thing was rising, a mountain made flesh, with teeth and eyes and in such quantities that all that he was froze as Memories of the vault stormed through his patterns. Of a creature born of blood and hunger and delirious madness. Of—

I am the Unending Maw, and I am relentless and inescapable. I am the hungry gullet at the end of all things!

NO!

A Memory—an instinct buried in his bones—surged to the fore, of refutation. Of stark denial of what *would not be!* A piece of him locked into place, and as it did, the patterns of light and sound solidified and rose to a tyrannical crescendo.

I. AM. NOT!

All that he was pulled inward, yanked from vast distances in the deep, until the patterns of his Mind were joined by new points of incredible starlight. Spirit formed, a nebulous curtain around him, a cloak of ephemeral energies that sunk into and expanded outward from his patterns. A split second later, the rest of him rushed close, until a solidity encased limbs he could finally feel, and senses emerged that were more than just transient impressions. His Body flexed and joined in the dancing interplay of Aspects, weaving among his Mind and Spirit as if it had never left.

I am Unbound! I am the Fiend! I am Autarch!

The entirety of him gathered, pressed together by sheer, unbroken volition.

I AM FELIX!

The behemoth rose, a screaming snarl on its mile-wide maw, and he met it.

And there was light in the dark.

Felix jerked awake to the sudden, thunderous sound of splintering wood. His Mind whirled, tossed from nightmare to a sudden drop as the bed he laid upon split. He fell unceremoniously onto hard, cold tile. Immediately, he pressed up from the ground, throwing himself back to his feet fast enough that the air made a keening noise in his ears, arms up and ready to fight.

Only to find himself utterly alone in a master suite half the size of a football field. What's more, his left hand was partially stuck in a splintering piece of bedframe, with sheets and mattress stuffing still floating down all around him.

"Oh," he muttered, more than a little embarrassed. "Glad no one saw that."

Felix pulled the wood apart as easily as ripping a thick piece of clay and disentangled his legs from silken sheets. He was wearing a short-sleeved tee shirt and gym shorts, for some reason, and they seemed particularly odd on his surprisingly muscular frame. His limbs felt weird, like they were too long for his body, and everything around him seemed off in a way Felix couldn't put a finger on. One thing he *could* see, however, was more concerning.

His arms were scaled.

The room he found himself in was far finer than any he'd stayed in before, and Felix quickly found an entire wall dominated by a mirror with a golden, scrolled frame. He placed himself in front of it and willed his Garment to remove his shirt. The magical clothing obeyed, and Felix held up his arms in front of him. Black as midnight, the scales covered him from fingertips to mid-bicep, turning from fine, glossy things on his hands, to more rugged and heavier as they extended up past his wrists. Small claws adorned his fingers, nothing as brutal as his usual talons, but very much not Felix's normal hands.

"What the hell?" His Sovereign of Flesh wasn't active, he could feel that, and as he inspected himself in the mirror, he was reminded that he'd changed even more than he'd realized. His feet were tipped with small talons and covered in scales as well, these extending all the way to his mid-thigh.

Sovereign of Flesh!

The Skill activated easily, and the scales vanished completely. Yet, the moment he ceased to run the Skill, the scales and claws returned. This...was just who he was now.

"Great," he muttered, twisting this way and that. More than the scales, the rest of his Body had undergone some significant remodeling during his Primordial baptism. His shoulders were wider, his limbs longer, and his general proportions were simply bigger. If he had to guess, Felix would have put his new height at six and a half feet tall, easily six or seven inches taller than before. "Not gonna complain about being taller, I guess."

He felt a little wobbly—all knees and elbows like a newborn foal—but that was fading fast. Energy pulsed in his center, threading through his veins like rivers of molten lava. Felix's muscles felt denser than ever, and his joints responded so easily to his movements it was uncanny. He'd figured he had a powerful Body before, but this new one was in another league.

He could feel the notifications waiting for him, things that must have built up during his time unconscious, paying back the Adept Temper he'd finally earned. He toggled them open.

Challenge Complete!
Congratulations!
You Have Extended Your Authority, Autarch!

You Are Now Lord Of Ahkestria And The Scorched Expanse!
ERROR!

Scorched Expanse Has Undergone Fundamental Changes!
Territory Reshaped...
Recalculating...

The Scorched Expanse Has Been Restored!
You Are Now Lord Of Ahkestria And The Leviathan Depths!

New Title!
Challenger's Crown I (Rare)!
By might and magic, you have prevailed against another Territorial Lord in a duel to the death. By defeating them, you have gained their Authority and added it to your own!
+Tier Upgrade For A Single Feature Of Your Primary Stronghold!

New Title!
Primordial Slayer (Transcendent)
+50% All Stats - You have killed a Primordial—

ERROR!
Primordial Undead!
ERROR!
Primordial Detected!
ERROR///!
Prim-#(#-$(%!!!
KZZZT!

You Have Gained 2 Levels!
You Are Now Level 59!
You Gain:
+40 to STR! +44 to PER! +44 to VIT! +52 to END! +48 to INT! +56 to WIL! +52 to AGL! +58 to DEX!
+40 All Harmonic Stats!
You Have 30 Unused Stat Points!

A glitch like static sizzled through Felix, then everything blinked back into order with a deep chime. System energy roared through his cores, echoing back outward into his Aspects in a cataract of power. Felix gritted his teeth, more than used to the sensation of leveling up.

He was blindsided, however, by a glut of information that flooded his potent Mind as the increasing weight of Authority pressed itself into the weft of his Spirit. It hurt a little as his Mind started to heat up, a scorching burn as new Territorial information drilled into him. Bits of ancillary knowledge floated up, things like tax rates and yield from the crystal mines, but they were fugitive concepts, fading just as quickly as they arrived.

The Authority, however, spread itself throughout his Spirit. It joined seamlessly with his extant Authority, a mantle that spread out to fill his giant room to the brim with an invisible, intangible potency.

Your Authority Has Grown!

As Lord Of Two Territories, You May Share A Single Specialized Benefit Of Your Primary Stronghold!
Choose One:

- **Tier III Forge**
- **Tier III Alchemical Lab**
- **Tier III Storage Facility**
- **Tier III Glyphworks**

WARNING!
Sharing Crafting Facilities Will Increase Production Speeds.
Sharing Crafting Facilities Will Also Increase Resource Loss.

Putting aside the annoyance of that Primordial Slayer Title he'd almost gotten—again—Felix focused on the things he could affect.

"Karys? Which should I do?" Felix asked, but the buzzing of his Inheritor's Will was absent. In fact, none of his weapons were anywhere in the large, palatial room, and Felix advanced his worry from sleepy confusion to mild concern. Even his vambraces and greaves were gone. Still, he was more than dangerous enough without armor or a blade. If he'd been captured by some Master or something, they'd realize their mistake soon enough.

Once he gave it a little thought, the decision before him wasn't so hard to make. He could pick Karys' brain later about other things, but to Felix there was only a single solution.

You Have Chosen To Share:

- **Tier III Storage Facility**

Due To Advanced Authority, Storage Capacity Has Doubled!
You May Erect A Single Beacon In Your New Territory!
Choose Placement.

A trickle of more information fed into his Mind, while at the corner of his vision the castle icon of his Authority Screen flashed at him. He toggled it open and quickly navigated to the Maps subsection. There he found two sub-categories, one labeled as Nagast and the other as The Leviathan Depths. He selected it. A half-fogged map of the former Expanse expanded before his eyes, with Ahkestria nestled a little north of its middle.

"Wow, that's...that's a lot," he said. "Almost as big as the Foglands...and it's mostly underwater now."

That would affect his Beacon placement a great deal. The Beacons were crystalline lamp posts that allowed people in his Stronghold to immediately store and retrieve supplies from his Storage Facility, and it was the precise reason he'd chosen it over one of his Crafting Halls. The benefits of increased production speeds wasn't worth losing more resources during crafting, not for him. Access to his Storage Facility from multiple Territories away? That would prove useful, for many reasons.

Felix checked his Status.

Name: Felix Nevarre
Level: 59
Race: Primordial of the Unseen Tide (Greater)*
Omen: Magician
Path: Cardinal Fiend
Born Trait: Keen Mind

———

Health: 9392/9392
Stamina: 8162/8162
Mana: 6746/6746

———

STR: 2404
PER: 2040
VIT: 1848
END: 1408
INT: 2080
WIL: 2512
AGL: 2222
DEX: 1940

———

BODY - Calamitous Dawn (Journeyman)
***Resistances*: The Song of Absolution (L), Level 87**

***Combat Skills:* Dodge (C), Level 70; Heavy Armor Mastery (C), Level 1; Blind Fighting (R), Level 59; Corrosive Strike (R), Level 73; Wild Threnody (E), Level 74**

***Physical Enhancements*: Armored Skin (R), Level 80; Relentless Resolution (L), Level 78**

<u>MIND - Fiendforged (Adept)</u>
***Mental Enhancements*: Deception (C), Level 34; Meditation (U), Level 69; Negotiation (U), Level 33; Bastion of Will (E), Level 87; Deep Mind (E), Level 75; Manifestation of the Coronach (E), Level 67; Chthonic Tribute (L), Level 86**

***Information Skills*: Alchemy (C), Level 49; Tracking (C), Level 34; Exploration (U), Level 66; Voracious Eye (E), Level 81; Aria of the Green Wilds (L), Level 86**

<u>SPIRIT - Eldercrowned (Adept)</u>
***Spiritual Enhancements*: Dual Casting (U), Level 56; Manasight (U), Level 71; Manaship Pilot (R), Level 22; Etheric Concordance (L), Level 82; Last Cry Of The Chthonic Host (M), Level 2; Sovereign of Flesh (T), Level 81; Unite the Lost (T), Level 51; Fiendforge (Un), Level 19**

***Spells*: Abyssal Skein (R), Level 70; Cloudstep (R), Level 50; Green Shaping (R), level 39; Invocation (R), Level 65; Oathbinding (R), Level 46; Shadow Whip (R), Level 48; Stone Shaping (R), Level 80; Sunken Ward (R), Level 1; Rime Shaping (R), Level 45; Mantle of the Infinite Revolution (E), Level 51; Arrow of Perdition (L), Level 46; Cardinal Flame (L), Level 84; Rain of Cataclysm (L), Level 72; Theurgist of the Rise (L), Level 82; Adamant Discord (T), Level 80**

Unused Stat Points: 30

<u>Harmonic Stats</u>
RES: 804
INE: 1248
AFI: 2446
REI: 972
EVA: 1228
MIG: 935
ALA: 1495
FEL: 2125

Hot damn.

Thunder rattled the window casements, and for the first time, Felix realized the light in the room had faded to a dull, dim gray. He could still see perfectly, but if the lighting were to be believed, night was almost upon him. He strode to one of the many tall windows and peered out onto lush, grassy grounds and thick with trees, each heavy with fruits and nuts. Beyond them, through the haze of driving rain, were tall walls made of bright orange stone. Even that color was leached, faded beneath the crackle and gloom of the storm above their heads.

"Maybe I'll wait on placing the Beacon, for now." Felix needed to figure out where he was and why he was there. Last he knew, he had been in the Tomb when the exhaustion of his Adept Temper had knocked him out cold. Now, his Map told him he was in Ahkestria again...and the open sky meant he was at the top, in the Risen Ward. "Whose mansion is this?"

The room gave him little in the way of clues, other than it was someone obscenely rich. That left the Matrons, Masters, or one of those merchant lords he'd heard about. Seeing as how he hadn't been chained up or collared, Felix was leaning toward his allies having somehow found him. With a minor effort of Will and Mana, his Garment shifted into a full-sleeve blue tunic, black, waist-length jacket, and dark trousers ending at calf-height leather boots.

There were three exits from the chamber, one leading to a huge closet, another to a long, tiled hall and smelling of water and soaps, and a third that was the most ornate of them all. That one he eased open and found a smaller antechamber, filled with sumptuous, well-padded couches and thick rugs. A fire burned merrily in a fireplace bigger than Felix, and all along the walls were framed oil paintings depicting bald, scowling men and severe-looking women. Atop one of the long couches and neatly filling it up was a mass of feathers and fur that he recognized.

Pit, Felix sent with a smile. The tenku snorted, clearly asleep, and Felix's smile grew before it froze. His friend was different than before, smaller and sleeker by a great deal. The tenku had always resembled a fox and raven mixed together, but now the black of his feathers and russet of his fur seemed to radiate a vibrancy Felix had never seen before.

He was naked, without his barding or saddlebags, and Felix could easily perceive small flashes of lightning coursing down his sides and pinions. In fact, his wings were changed, too, covered with a number of crimson feathers on the interior while his outer flight feathers were all a brilliant cyan. The sparks of electricity seemed to congregate on those far more than the rest.

The shape of Pit's head and sleek, glossy black feathers reminded Felix of Lord Wonderment, the raven-like Korvaa from the Void. *You've changed a lot since then,* he sent quietly. *We both have.*

A second, daintier snort caught Felix's attention, and he belatedly realized there was another person in attendance. Vess sat only a couple chairs away, covered in a thick blanket with her head propped up on a chair. Her mouth was open as she lightly snored, and her dark brown hair was mussed, but even so, she was beautiful. The firelight played off her dark skin, shining off a number of metal objects she cradled loosely against her chair. Weapons. His weapons.

“She’s been waiting here all night.”

"AH!" Felix shouted and skipped backward. He hadn't heard anyone else come in, and when he looked, Felix only found Pit sitting up and staring at him with his big golden eyes. "Pit? Who said that?"

"I did," Pit said in a high tenor. He sounded like a teenage boy, of all things, just without the cracking tone.

"Wha—you can talk?" Felix asked. This was blowing his mind, and when the back of his knees hit a chair, he sat down happily. "Since when?"

Pit lifted a wing, letting lightning crackle impressively along its length. “My Evolution. A'zek said it could affect many things about me...then you ripped apart a Primordial and shoved it through us.”

Felix paused. He *did* do that, didn’t he? “But you're okay? It didn't hurt you or anything, right?"

Pit trilled, his version of a laugh, same as it always was. "I'm fine. You worry too much."

"This is weird," Felix said, before lifting his hands to cut off Pit's frown. "Awesome, for sure, don't get me wrong. I know we could talk before, but doing it out loud feels a little nuts."

"It was...odd for me, too. Everyone reacted about the same as you when they found out." Pit trilled again, pleased. "The Fiend's Claw even started bowing to me. I liked that."

Felix frowned. The Fiend's Claw was his personal militia of sorts, and they had a distinct problem with hero worship. Still, it was hard to blame them; Pit was hard not to like. "What else changed in your evolution?”

"Take a look," Pit said and flexed a wing. A series of blue boxes rapidly appeared in front of Felix's face, each one more wild than the last.

"Whoa."

CHAPTER THREE

First Evolution: Primordial Stormwing!
You Gain:
+200 AGL
+100 DEX
+100 END
+75 INT
+50 WIL

New Level Up Bonuses!
+10 to STR, +9 to PER, +4 to VIT, +11 to END, +7 to INT, +10 to WIL, +20 to AGL, +20 to DEX Per Level!
+10 to AFI, RES, REI Per Level!

Skills Have Changed!
Bite (Common) Has Become Bloody Gnaw (Epic)!
Level Has Been Maintained!
Bloody Gnaw (Epic), Level 70!
Attack with a simple bite of your beak, but upon breaking their skin, you inflict a withering venom into their Body. Base damage has increased dramatically. Speed of effect and damage done will increase slightly per Skill level.

Rake (Common) Has Become Hurricane Rasp (Epic)!
Level Has Been Maintained!
Hurricane Rasp (Epic), Level 73!
Your talons have been imbued with the riot of stormwinds,

increasing the speed and damage inflicted by their assault. Speed increases per Skill level, damage slightly increases per Skill level.

Cry (Rare) Has Become Howl At The Dark (Epic)!
Level has Been Maintained!
Howl At The Dark (Epic) Level 64!
The Beast within you has emerged, and its howl is a fearsome thing to all prey. Inflicts the Stunned Status Condition in a large range, and even if resisted, all targets are afflicted with minor sonic damage.

Skulk (Common) Has Become Gloaming Shroud (Epic)!
Level Has Been Maintained!
Gloaming Shroud (Epic), Level 49!
Draw the shadows of the sun's setting and hide from the senses of all others. Can be extended to affect those within your flock, up to a maximum of Skill level divided by 10.

Wingblade (Uncommon) Has Become Dawn's Advent (Epic)!
Level Has Been Maintained!
Dawn's Advent (Epic), Level 74!
Summon the horizon's inevitable return, manifesting a large crescent blade of lightning, wind, and fire Mana to assault a target, burning through them like dawn's light through the Night. Size, damage, and speed of Skill increase slightly per level.

Frost Spear (Common) Has Become Tempest Fugit (Legendary)!
Level Has Been Maintained!
Tempest Fugit (Legendary), Level 74!
Coalesce the frozen fury of the storm into dire projectiles, and bring to them the rage of the heavens. With each impact, the frozen piece of lightning will burst and do extra damage.

Poisonfire (Rare) Has Become Mantle Of Tumult (Legendary)!
Level Has Been Maintained!
Mantle of Tumult (Legendary), Level 72!
A cloak of swirling winds and lightning hangs about your neck and wings, a tempest of your own making, striking at any foe within melee range.

Flight (Rare) Has Become Thunderwing (Legendary)!
Level Has Been Maintained!
Thunderwing (Legendary), Level 58!
Your speed has increased tremendously, enough that your acceleration tears thunder from the sky.

Skill changes flew at Felix, followed swiftly by an updated Status sheet for his Companion.

Name: Pit (Companion)
Level: 68
Race: Chimera - Primordial Stormwing Tenku

Health: 3083/3083
Stamina: 4489/4489
Mana: 4189/4189

STR: 506
PER: 584
VIT: 616
END: 847
INT: 764
WIL: 761
AGL: 1958
DEX: 1468

Bloody Gnaw (E), Level 70
Hurricane Rasp (E), Level 73
Howl At The Dark (E), Level 64
Gloaming Shroud (E), Level 49
Etheric Concordance (L), Level 82
Dawn's Advent (E), Level 74
Tempest Fugit (L), Level 74
Cold Resistance (C), Level 34
Mantle of Tumult (L), Level 72
Thunderwing (L), Level 58
Poison Resistance (C), Level 24

***Active Titles*:**
Survivor III
Butcher III
Unconquered
Face the Charge
Bulwark of the Innocent

Pactmaker
Work Horse
Blind Pugilist
Hero
Iron Will
Apprentice Magus
The Broken Path
Voidwalker
Indomitable
Unleash the Beast
Blessing of the Lost
Fatebreaker
The Shape of Fate II
Frostbane
Architect of the Rise
Cardinal (Major)
Save The Lost
Thief of Fate
Tyrant of Choice
Against Catastrophe
Tyros of the Unseen Tide
Stigma of the Chosen
Born of Will
Coronation of the Wild Song
Forge of Cardinal Thunderflame
The Call of Defiance
Transmuter of Burdens
Savant of the Green Wilds
Champion of the Halcyon
Sheltered
Challenger's Crown I

Pit's Harmonic Stats
RES: 135
INE: 110
AFI: 325
REI: 224
EVA: 255
MIG: 45
ALA: 132
FEL: 92

"Holy wow," Felix muttered, attempting to keep his jaw from the floor. "That's...that's a *lot* of change."

Pit warbled in agreement.

"You're a Primordial, now?" Felix asked, too floored to absorb it all.

"Just like you," Pit said, his tone bright and pleased. "Now I won't fall behind anymore!"

"Bud...is that how you felt?"

Pit shrugged and looked away. Felix gathered him up in a hug, and Pit cooed into his shoulder. "I'll never leave you behind, Pit. Alright?"

"Alright."

"I mean it, bud," Felix repeated. He let his friend go and held his newer, more slender shoulders at arm's length. He was still the size of a pony, and small pops of static electricity zapped his scaled hands. "I don't care if you're as big as a house or as small as a pup, you're with me. No matter what."

Pit didn't reply, just ducked his glossy raven head into Felix's chest. They stayed like that for a bit, Felix standing next to the couch, Pit rumbling contentedly into his torso. Things were strange and hectic, but Felix felt good and...and calm, for the first time in a long while. The storm raged outside, but around him, there was only the soft crackle of the fire.

His eyes drifted to Vess, still asleep despite their noise. She'd shifted into a different position at some point, and now her long umber hair hung over her face like a curtain, revealing only the tips of her nose and far cheek. He bit his lip as his Mind started to spool outward again, picking up on new worries.

"Were the others affected?" he asked Pit, meeting his friend's golden gaze. "Like you?"

"In a way."

Felix and Pit parted as Vess stood, stretching languidly and letting her blanket slide from her lap. She was wearing a pale orange silken blouse and voluminous navy trousers, both of which set off against her darker skin tone remarkably well. A dimple deepened as she smiled brightly and brushed hair out of her face. "I am happy to see you well, Felix."

"Me too," he said, then coughed. "You, I mean. Seeing you is nice."

"Mm." Her smile widened a bit more. "You are taller than I recall. And...scalier."

Felix immediately shoved his hands into his jacket pockets...only to discover he didn't have any. A frustrated burst of Will and Mana changed that, and he stowed his scaled fists. "Ah. Yeah. Consequences of my actions, apparently."

Vess tucked a wild lock of hair behind her ear. "I see. And you are...fine? You were out when Pit and your other friends brought you back."

"My other—Beef? Is he here?" Felix pressed his Perception up against the edges of the room, but the doors were warded for privacy. "Is he okay?"

Vess stepped forward, carefully resting Felix's weaponry against the chair she'd left. "He seemed well. The Lady Isla was taking a look at him, last I knew. He is...strange, though. Him and his little companion creature."

Hallow survived, too. That's good. "Don't be fooled by that big Body of his. Where I'm from, he's basically a kid."

"Truly? Remarkable. He was the only one strong enough to move you, despite his injuries. He seemed quite sweet." She lifted a hand and touched his jacketed forearm, causing Felix to flinch slightly. "May I see?"

Felix swallowed nervously. Somehow, she'd gotten so close without him noticing at all. *She can't teleport, can she?* He didn't fight as she eased his left hand out of his pocket and held it up in hers.

Vess peered closely at his knuckles and fingertips, and Felix felt her hot breath against the strangely sensitive scales. "They are shinier than I expected," she said.

"What?" he asked.

"Your scales. They are glossy in the firelight, and quite delicate." Her small hands, dark brown to his midnight black, twisted his hand over and ran across his palm. His palms were lighter by several shades, and the scales were intricate and tiny. "Beautiful."

"Uh," was all Felix could manage. He pulled his hand back, disengaging her light grip. "Uh yeah, I guess. It's something I have to get used to, regardless of whether I like them or not. Shoving a metric shit ton of Primordial Essence through your core has some side effects, apparently." He paused, blue eyes going wide. "You're not...?"

"Covered in scales?" Vess asked, laughing in that husky way she had. "No. I am much the same. Physically, at least. The rest of us haven't had a chance to speak much on it, but that Tier IV Link produced some drastic changes in all of us."

"Not physical?" Felix asked. "So did your Skills change?"

"They did." An expression flickered across Vess' face as she stepped back from him. Felix couldn't place it before it vanished into a businesslike calm, and she busied herself with her hair. It came loose quickly, her Agility and Dexterity proving their mettle as she combed and braided it in quick succession. "A great deal, in fact. You, Lord Autarch, have changed almost every one of my Skills to Epic or better."

"That's...good, right?" Felix ventured. "The Link didn't mess up your—shit, wait. You had specific Dragoon Skills didn't you? Did that progression get screwed up?"

Vess secured her braids into a single plait behind her head, tugging it into place. She took a quick breath and met his eyes. There was a vulnerability there, an uncertainty that made Felix's stomach turn over. "I—I do not know. The Memories I carry of my order are...they do not cover this. I need more time to be certain how they've changed."

Felix wanted to smack himself. He should have realized that before he'd offered up the Primordial Essence to her. "Jeez, Vess I'm sorry. I didn't think about that."

She raised a hand, cutting him off. "It is fine, Felix. You gave me the choice, and I accepted it. I bear the consequences of that action, not you."

He clenched his jaw, biting off any more words before they came out. He wanted to push his Affinity toward her, to inspect her Spirit and emotions, but he cut that urge off. With his level of Affinity, it was sort of like mind reading, and just as invasive. Even if he put his foot in his mouth, he'd rather just interact as real people instead.

Vess, meanwhile, had gathered herself up again and seemed entirely composed. "And you, Felix? Other than your scales and your...considerable new dimensions, has anything dire changed? Atar confirmed that the Grandmaster was after you. Did he find you?"

"He did." Felix frowned at the memory of it, almost happy to avoid...whatever was going between Vess and him. He could perfectly recall the Grandmaster collapsing beneath a rockslide and rising water. Aside from his fury, Felix felt a tight, acidic relish over the memory. "He regretted it."

"Oh." Vess paled a touch and stepped backward. "My apologies for bringing it up, Felix. It was not my intent to anger you."

Felix blinked at her reaction, only belatedly realizing that she was likely not pulling back on her Affinity. She had felt his remembered rage. "You—it's not you, Vess. It's everything. The masters and matrons and Pathless and everyone in power," he said, disgust on his face. Not for her, or even for the Grandmaster, but for himself. For what he'd been forced to do. "This world is broken."

"That is why you must fix it, my Lord."

Vess and Pit started, but Felix's hand was up and roiling with unreleased lightning. A man stood in an open doorway Felix had sworn was closed a moment prior. He was wide-chested and broad-shouldered, covered in a sort of blue-green armor, and bearing a huge, silvery chest in his hands.

On his back were a number of twitching appendages that looked like spider legs, each also encased in that blue-green armor. He smiled once he had Felix's attention, showing off a too-wide grin, many sharp teeth, and a set of glowing copper eyes. He set the chest upon the ground and dropped to a single knee before speaking. "The chest, as promised, my Lord."

Felix raised an eyebrow as his Voracious Eye activated. "You're...a

Yttin?" The man looked like a Human aside from the mouth, the eyes, and those wriggling, spider-like legs from his back.

"I am Eyxti, and yes, I am Yttin. Restored at last." Eyxti pressed his fist to his heart, and the chitinous legs at his back went still.

"Restored," Felix said, chewing over the word. "I didn't realize you were in need of...How?"

"That is something our shaman must speak to you on. He is waiting within his apartments at your earliest convenience. For now, we have brought the Platinum Chest, as we promised the Beast." He bowed again, still kneeling, in the direction of Pit.

"Beast, huh?" Felix said. Pit's sleek head had lifted imperiously into the air, reveling in the attention. "Platinum Chest. That's a system reward, and a big one. Why do you have one, and why would you give it to us? And stand up, please."

Eyxti stood easily. He was tall for a Human, and positively giant for a Yttin. At least how Yttin *used* to be. "When our people were first cast down, we were given hope. A Quest from the System itself to break the curse upon our lands and people, to restore them all to what once was. It was passed down from shaman to shaman for Ages, until yesterday."

"When I unleashed the sea," Felix finished for him.

Eyxti nodded and bowed, deeply. "Yes, Savior of the Deep."

Felix's lips twisted at the title. "Ah, don't, uh, just call me Felix. No one needs to call me savior. Okay?"

The Yttin stood hesitantly from his bow. "If that is what you wish, then I shall spread the word." He gestured to the Platinum Chest again. "Please open this at your leisure. Shaman Klzix is ready to receive you at any moment."

With that, the armored man slipped back out the door and vanished. Seconds later, a guard in leather and mail opened the door and looked around sharply. A badge on their breast showed five black slashes against a red and blue background. When they noticed Felix, Vess, and Pit staring, they gave a little hop of fright. "Oh! Lord Autarch, you're awake! Did you—did you see someone come in here a moment ago?"

Felix and Vess exchanged a glance. "Did you not?" he asked.

"Noctis' tits! They slipped right past us!" the guard spat. "Oh, ah, sorry my Lord. I should get the rest of my Talon to start searching. Did they hurt you?"

"No, it's fine. They were a friend," Felix said. "Just keep doing...whatever it is you were doing before."

The guard hesitated only a moment before snapping to attention and saluting, hand to heart. "Aye, sir!" They ducked back and closed the door behind them, sigils lighting up upon the door's surface as it clicked shut.

"They slipped right through privacy wards and a Talon of guards without notice," Vess said. "That is impressive."

Pit scoffed. "I could do that."

Felix ruffed his friend's head absently. "Of course you could. Seems like I have to talk to a shaman, soon," he said. "But first..."

He walked to the Platinum Chest, which was shimmering in the firelight. The Chest was four feet long by two feet wide and two feet tall. From experience, he knew System Chests were extremely heavy, so even that was another point in the Yttin's favor. With an easy movement, Felix lifted the lid and squinted against the rush of System energy that burst outward in all directions. Once the glittering gold and azure dust settled, Vess and Pit had joined Felix and peered into it together.

"A ball, a stick, and a hat?" Pit said derisively. "Boring."

"That is a scepter and orb of rule, Pit," Vess said. She patted Felix on the back. "And the last one is not a hat—"

Felix swallowed. "It's a crown."

CHAPTER FOUR

Without lifting any of the items from the Chest, Felix activated his identifying Skill.

Voracious Eye.

Name: Crown of Sea and Stone
Type: Raiment (Enchanted)
Lore: Made of hekite coral and purified water Mana crystal, the Crown of Sea and Stone is more than simple headgear. Crafted in the First Age for the founding Queen of Ahkestria, it, along with the Scepter and Orb, were symbols of her Authority over the seas of her Territory. The Crown is the pinnacle of the set, bestowing a measure of greater Authority over Ahkestria and the Leviathan Depths, specifically.

Name: Scepter of the Tides
Type: Raiment (Enchanted)
Lore: Made of cobalt and life-touched gold, the Scepter of the Tides is a symbol of Authority over the waves of the Leviathan Depths. Wielding it, the worthy bearer gains control over a portion of the sea around you, their rise and fall. While within one's own Territory, the effect is greatly multiplied.

Name: Orb of Plenty
Type: Raiment (Enchanted)

Lore: Made of purified water, life, and shadow Mana crystals, the Orb of Plenty is a symbol of Authority over the life that dwells beneath the waves.

Felix furrowed his brow. "A crown of Authority, a scepter that controls water, and an orb that...controls fish?"

"Hm," Vess hummed beside him. "Those are quite useful, considering our new situation."

"New situation?" Felix asked. Lightning flashed outside the shuttered windows, and gut-shaking thunder was right on its heels. "Right. The sea's worth of Mana crystals."

Vess nodded. "An ocean sprang up from the empty desert, flooding it entirely from the mountains to the lowest levels of Ahkestria. We...I am sorry, Felix, but we assumed you were the cause."

The metal of the Platinum Chest screeched as it deformed beneath his grip. Felix grunted and pulled his hands away, leaving crumpled impressions of his fingers. "Fucking Pathless. I started it, but the Coward pushed it outward in an attempt to drown me."

"Coward?" Vess asked.

"Yeah," Felix spat. His Mind returned to that dark space, the blasted terrain at the edge of things where the moons loomed close. He recalled their words—what they called the god of the Hierocracy—like they were etched into his skin, separate from his Born Trait. Felix doubted he'd ever forget them. "Remnant. Coward. Trackless. The guy has a lot of names. At least I'm not the only one who hates him. The gods aren't too impressed with him, either."

"Coward fits him," Vess agreed. "You have...spoken to the gods again? That makes it the fourth time now? I doubt few outside the Hierophant could boast of so many interactions with the Divine. And even then, I doubt it; the Pathless is notoriously close-mouthed."

"I'd like my life a lot more if the gods kept their noses out of my business," Felix said.

"The Pathless I understand," Vess said. "Worship of the Pathless is enforced among the nobility of the Hierocracy. My family has even commissioned a number of cathedrals to that worthless religion and has been forced to keep our devotion to Siva a secret. I cannot imagine a goddess as benevolent as the Lady of Fortune to be as vile as Vellus has proven herself to be."

"Siva." Felix could still see a silver moon in his Mind, a calm voice warning him of the others, and the deadly threat of Noctis and her unbridled rage. He took a small breath and wiped his hands on his jacket. "She...I'm not a big fan of any of them, if I'm being honest."

Vess opened her mouth before hesitating, shut it, and nodded. "Considering your experiences, I can understand that, I suppose."

"Hm," he said, as noncommittally as possible. The last thing Felix was interested in was debating religion, so he reached down into the chest and snagged all three items. He had to juggle the Orb a bit, but his high Dexterity meant that it was child's play. In moments, the Chest disappeared with a sudden inward *pop*...and a tiny trumpet blared in Felix's ears.

"That the hell...?" he said, before his eyes were assaulted by a huge, ornate notification. The thing was blue as all the rest, but the edges were bordered in gold and looked almost carved out of metal. Tiny waves marched around the edges of the notification, while figures in tiny boats moved through it all.

Hidden Racial Quest!
To Cleanse The Curse!
In Ages past, the whole of the Territory and its rulers were cursed in a war that shook the Continent. The sea was drained and locked away, while the Yttin were sealed into weakened, Untempered forms. To return the sea is to restore the Yttin, but you must defy the very will of those who cursed the Depths.

As The Primary Agent In Resolving the Quest, You May Claim Full Credit For Its Completion.
Rewards Include: XP, Titles, Platinum Chest
Warning: All Rewards Have Been Given To The Yttin People. Claiming Full Credit Will Remove Their Growth And Add To Yours.

Do You Wish To Claim The Full Credit Of This Quest?
Y/N

That's interesting, he thought a bit sourly. *System gave me the Quest after the fact, but in order to get anything out of it, I have to deprive the Yttin of their fair share?* "No, that's horseshit. *No.*"

You Have Rejected Full Credit!
XP, Titles, And Platinum Chest Will Remain With Original Recipients!

Felix shook off the faint rush of System energy and met Vess' gaze. "What just happened?" she asked. He explained, and Vess' expression tightened. "You could have stolen it from others? That is reprehensible."

"I thought so, too," Felix said. "As much as I'd love the experience, that feels—"

“Felix?”

He bent over, suddenly wracked with incredible pain. Sparks danced at the edges of his vision as the song within his cores rose to a terrifying crescendo. Pressure built, enough that it felt like his teeth and eyes would rip themselves out, and then it twisted and sank. Felix gasped.

Congratulations!
You Have Chosen To Walk The Path Of Beneficence!
Few Are They Who Step Along The Way!
Fewer Still People Who Hold Tight To The Path!

A Reward Has Been Given!

A symphony coursed through Felix’s veins and rang loud in his ears. Harmony was chased by the quiet insistence of Dissonance, just below the surface. But it wasn't experience that flashed across his notifications, nor Essence gifted by the System, but instead a heaviness settled into his core space.

It sank into the crimson-black expanse of his Divine Tree, into the spinning rings of his dual cores, and into the darkness that surrounded all of his Skills. Another ragged gasp was squeezed from Felix's lungs, as everything inside of him seemed to collapse and expand at the same time. Light crushed and bloomed, and fires roared along with discordant harmony, driven along a razor's edge until—

Significance Has Reached Acceptable Levels
Initializing...
ERROR.
Pillars Incomplete.
Process Aborted.

Felix fell to his knees like a puppet with his strings cut, and he panted fast and shallow as the sensation of crushing pressure receded.

"Felix! What is this?" Pit asked, his voice higher with worry.

"Felix what happened? Are you alright?" Vess was there, kneeling beside him. She pressed her cool hand against his forehead and hissed in sudden pain. "Your skin is burning!"

He could feel it, the heat coursing through his Body, but it wasn't uncomfortable. Not like the pressure had been. "I'm...I'm fine, I think. Just gimme a second, and I'll explain." Without another word, he threw himself inward, into his core space.

There, nestled within a vast expanse of darkness, were the collection of his Skills and cores. His Skills were humming globes of light and sound that revolved ever so slowly around his cores, like planets around two suns. Two cores, [Thunderflame Core] and his [Cardinal Beast Core] spun in opposition at the center of what appeared to be a blazing solar system. The cores were shaped as rings, stacked atop one another with their hollow middles lined up, and made of a slow, gelatinous flame —one blue-white and the other red-gold, respectively. As they spun, they ground into one another, releasing waves of discordant sound into the otherwise melodic harmony of his humming Skills.

From the center of those ring-shaped cores, there was an unstable abyss, darker than the void around them and pulsing with a distinct Need. A Hunger. One that, for the moment, seemed satiated.

That's rare, he thought. *And concerning. Maybe.* His Hunger had experienced some issues during the last few days, resulting in one of his most useful Skills being rendered worthless. Felix had thought it had recovered during his Tempering, but perhaps he'd been wrong. *I'll worry about that later.*

While the abyss of his Hunger dwelled within his hollow cores, there was another piece that rose from its immeasurable depths: a crimson-black growth that stretched upward on a stalk an eighth as thick as the abyss itself. This growth continued, reaching high above his little solar system until it branched into a thousand tendrils, much like a winter-nude tree. It quivered as he watched, thrumming with its own unique song.

The Tree is empty, damn. My Essence has run out completely, he noted. Normally, wisps of multi-colored light would collect in the Tree's branches, hanging from them like shimmering, abstract leaves. Sometimes, he'd even have Essence Motes or Memories cradled in the boughs. Now it was utterly bare. *Which means...*

He moved downward, willing his projected form lower at blinding speeds. Skills and his cores flashed by as he sank below them, down to where his thick, trunk-like Pillars supported his entire core space.

...I can't weave any more Pillars yet. Dammit.

The Pillars were woven of Essence, Mana, and significance. He had none of the first and plenty of the second. The last was more of a metaphysical supply, but one which Felix could tell he also had in spades. The whole of his core space was so much *more* than it had been just days before, as if it were truly real. He could feel the heat and buzzing rhythm of his Skills above, taste the strange, burning air, and as he drifted closer to his two Pillars, Felix could feel the slow and steady vibrations of his foundation.

All of that was a result of increased significance, which was like a weightiness or density imbued into the heart of his being. The greater your potency, the greater your significance, and as far as Felix knew, it helped fuel the upper stages of power.

As he understood it, a person who intended to advance beyond

Master Tier needed to weave all nine Pillars at the base of their core space. It would act as his foundation for advancement through Master Tier and into Grandmaster Tier...though he knew little beyond that. Those who advised him—Zara and Karys mostly—kept things from him due to the strange nature of advancement. To know too much was far, far worse than knowing nothing at all. Expectation, he'd been told, shapes reality.

Well, I was expecting to have enough Essence to weave the rest of my Pillars here and now, he grumbled to himself. *Should be easy. I've got the rest; I just need another Primordial to eat.* His Hunger rumbled, pulled slightly from its oddly sedate rest. *Oh, that caught your attention, did it?* It rumbled again. *We'll eat later. Go back to sleep.*

And wonder of wonders, it did just that.

Huh. With a minor flex of his Mind, Felix rose back into his physical Body and stood up. Vess and Pit both looked at him expectantly. "I guess I got a reward anyway, just not the one the Quest was originally offering."

"Truly?" Vess said, tilting her head in concern. She bit the inside of her cheek, which pressed a dimple deeply into the other one. "And that caused you to fall to the floor?"

"It gave me, and I'm estimating here, a butt load of significance," Felix said, letting a wry smile curl his lip. Vess closed her eyes and shook her head, but her worry turned to faint amusement. "So much that it kick-started something else. Another step in advancement, maybe." He wet his lips and looked at the warded door. "I need to talk to Zara. Karys, too."

"Good idea," Pit said around a mouthful of Scepter. "What about these?"

"Oh yeah, probably shouldn't leave those on the ground, huh?" Felix said, gathering the Scepter, Orb, and Crown in his hands. Uncertain what to do with them, he rolled his eyes as he remembered he had magic clothing on. Expending a tiny portion of Mana and Intent, Felix commanded his Garment to form a large pouch at his side. It grew from his belt, leather unrolling and stitching before his eyes, until it was a sizable pouch that could hold the Orb and Crown easily. The Scepter, he tucked into his belt.

"Ah, here, your weaponry as well," Vess said, gesturing. From where they leaned against a settee, three blades were cradled in a net of air Mana and levitated to his side. All three were remarkably different from each other. The first was his Blade of the Fang, a massive greatsword formed from the tooth of a pseudo-Primordial and consisted of a grip and the naked edge. No crossguard. It was detailed with numerous lines, dots, and other designs that weren't sigils, even though it was clearly enchanted.

Interestingly, it didn't seem nearly as big as it had before. It was still eight feet long, though, and he strapped it to his back with some effort, aided greatly by his Garment. It formed a heavy baldric across his shoulders and back for the weapon to hook right into. The second was his Inheritor's Will, a khopesh-like blade made of magical Crescian Bronze and imbued with all sorts of magical effects. It slotted into a specialized sheath that, again, his Garment formed in seconds. The last, however, was new.

"What is this?" he asked. *Voracious Eye!*

Name: Skyslain's Riposte
Type: Weapon (Enchanted)
Lore: Belonging to Tch'lys Skyslain, the last King of Ahkestria, the blade was a gift from the Nymean Empress. Made of Crescian Bronze and enchanted to grow at its bearer's command, it was a symbol as much as a blade. Its last use was as an anchor, a powerful spike to trap the deadliest of foes that had wrought an untenable ruin upon the kingdom. You have claimed and freed the sword, releasing it from its Ages-long duty.

"Right..." he said, trailing off as the memory of the Grandmaster's defeat rose again. He'd claimed the huge blade from the Tomb, and it had shrunk before turning into a thin spike that had pinned the bastard to the wall. Felix grinned and hefted the weapon, which had become an eight-inch dagger. "Glad to have you aboard."

Very faintly, Riposte quivered in his hand. Felix's eyebrows raised, and he swiftly stowed it next to his pouch. A new sheath slipped over it easily. "Thank you, Vess. Before I check with Zara, I should look into the others, too. Will you come with me? Us?" he amended quickly after a glance at Pit.

"It would be my pleasure," she said, her throaty laugh rising up again. "Come. Let us see the healers first, just to be sure. Your Minotaur friend was there, last I saw."

"Beef? Perfect." Felix offered his arm, and the heiress of Pax'Vrell took it with a smile.

CHAPTER FIVE

When the outer doors opened, Felix was greeted by the sight of six men and women garbed in chain and leather armor. A hooded cloak hung from their backs and looped across their shoulders and chests like a mantle, made of dark material that was one part purple to two parts gray. Emblazoned on it was that badge he'd seen before: a simple, embroidered circle of five black slashes against a red and blue background.

"Lord Autarch!" the nearest of them said in a strangled tone. It was the same one that had stepped in before, and he gestured frantically at the others. All of them fell to a knee. "Was your rest further disturbed?"

"No, nothing like that," Felix said, activating his Eye. "Lieutenant Errol. The Lady Dayne and I were just looking to uh, stretch our legs."

"Me, too," Pit said behind him. He was smaller, but even the size of a small horse was hard to hide.

"Him, too," Felix added, smiling at the guards. "Just keep on guarding the uh, empty room, and we'll be on our way."

"My Lord, we cannot do that. We are your guard. We go where you go." Lieutenant Errol's expression was steady, but his face was already awash in sweat. Felix uncurled his Affinity and felt the rapid tattoo of the man's nervous fear and a steady, frankly upsetting amount of awe. "We are the Fiend's Shadows."

Oh right. Them. Felix had gained himself an honor guard during their journey to Ahkestria. He'd forgotten about it, but they clearly hadn't. He spotted members of the Henaari Dawnguard, as well as a member from the Fist, Blade, Bone, and Arclight Legions kneeling before him. *A few missing...I wonder where they are?*

A nudge at his back made Felix realize he'd been just staring at these people. He smiled ruefully at Vess and her elbow. "Well, Lieutenant. Follow us, I guess."

Felix walked down the corridor. It was a dead-end passage leading to an arched threshold, through which another, far larger chamber was visible. The floor was tiled with beautiful, polished stone, all of it cut into small rectangles of varying sizes, and the walls were filled with tiny ridges and moldings that divided up the space with a pleasing complexity. It was clear that Felix had been in a suite of rooms, and knowing his friends and followers, it was likely the master suite. But whose? He asked Vess that, as they stepped into a large, almost circular room filled with low couches and a number of lounging guards.

"Oh, this is the former Grandmaster's mansion," she said with a small smile. "It was available and well-appointed, so we took it for our purposes."

A smile curled his lip as well, especially when he saw the Frost Giants leap to their feet...leaving muddy stains on thick, ornately woven rugs and splatters of blood across pale, broken furniture. "Good."

"Lord Autarch!" the two giants said, slamming a fist to the ground as they dropped to a knee. Beside them, and much smaller than their fifteen-foot frames, were four others: the remaining members of his Shadows.

"Stand, please. We're just taking a walk," Felix said, but he didn't stop. If he did, he worried that he'd get bogged down in another uncomfortable conversation. To his growing annoyance, the giants and others all stood and joined the rest of his impromptu procession.

"My Lord, if you please," said one of the Henaari, Maryk by Felix's Eye. The other Dawnguard—Waryn—was beside him, and they looked similar enough to be brothers. "Let us act as vanguard. If trouble should come for you, let us handle it first."

Felix opened his mouth to protest—he could very well walk through a house by himself—Vess' slight shake of her head stopped him. Biting back his words, he forced a smile. "Sure. Go ahead." The Spirits of the two Henaari literally vibrated with satisfaction as they turned and walked a touch faster than the rest, and Felix tilted his head down toward Vess. "Do they think I'm going to be attacked?"

"One can never be too sure," Vess said, patting his arm with her right hand. Her left was still entwined with Felix's, and he was happy to see she hadn't removed it. "Plus, they wish to aid you. A loyal retainer is one that feels needed, Felix."

He mulled that over as they moved through a series of interconnected hallways. The giants had some trouble with a few doors, but for the most part, the Grandmaster's former home was so ostentatious that it easily accommodated their fifteen-foot height and bulky weaponry.

Those two were, in fact, quite enthusiastic about guarding his back, and far more expressive than the stoicism he'd experienced with most of the Risi.

Felix made it a point of inspecting each of his Shadows, committing their faces and names to his prodigious memory. He'd yet to regret choosing perfect recall as his Born Trait, and doubted he ever would, especially as their way grew more and more labyrinthine. Thresholds and corridors passed in quick succession as Vess navigated them out, and it was only after walking for a solid five minutes that she revealed that it was all just part of the Grandmaster's apartments.

Jeez. This guy. Who needs this much house for one person? Felix could barely understand that; he'd have felt swallowed up by all the pointless space within hours. They'd passed three different dining rooms and no fewer than six parlors of some variety. *What's the point?*

Eventually, Vess led them to a large door made of thick, dark wood and inlaid with panels of glittering, silvery metal. Sigils were carved in looping patterns around the threshold, but the door itself bore only a single, convoluted glyph. Vess lifted a small silver rod, notched in several places and carved with faintly glowing lines—and she placed it directly on the glyph. Immediately, the array winked out, and the door split into two as it opened outward.

"Fancy," Felix said with a whistle. "That was a locking array?"

"Quite a complicated one, too. If we hadn't found this key, I doubt we'd have been able to enter these apartments," she said, tucking the metal rod back into a pouch at her waist. "It's inscribed with the counter array, allowing it to unlock the door without issue."

"That's...really cool, honestly. The sigaldry is beautiful," Felix said, running a hand across the darkened glyph. "Never thought I'd say that about a locked door."

"Well, there is a first time for everything," she said, a touch too quietly. Before Felix said anything else, she bustled through after the two Henaari. "If you wish to see the others, then the healing wing is where we should head next."

Felix followed silently, thinking entirely too hard on what exactly Vess had meant. For some reason, at their rear, Pit snorted musically.

The halls were different outside the Grandmaster's apartments—*his* apartments, Felix supposed—but far from decreasing the overly involved designs along the walls and floors, the rest of the mansion only increased the extravagance. Mana crystals dripped from every surface in the form of lighting sconces and decorative chandeliers. Fluted scroll-work was carved into stone walls, and golden frames held up richly painted landscapes of lush desert oases and torrid, burning altars. Each hall and chamber had alcoves filled with statuary in ivory, gold, and obsidian, each depicting Human men and women in fluid, utterly nude movement.

Contrasting the garish environment, at each room they passed, Felix spied a great number of ragged-looking families huddled around overstuffed couches and merrily burning hearths. Survivors of the mass sacrificial ritual, Vess had told him. They filled these rooms, too many to count but easily numbering in the thousands, and all of them haggard from their experiences. Servants dressed in black and gold hustled to and fro, bringing food to these groups.

But Felix could feel their Spirits recoil in disgust at the dirty, bloodstained garments they wore and the scent of unwashed flesh. Yet, when they caught sight of his procession, the servants all dropped into deep bows and curtsies, followed quickly by the more able-bodied among the commoners around them.

Emotions vibrated the air, rippling the many Untempered Spirits with awe and fear. A more complicated emotion thrummed within those they passed, something that mingled the two emotions and rose up, like a soldier at attention. It wasn't a negative emotion, but Felix couldn't quite parse its meaning. At any rate, he hadn't a clue what to say to them and only managed a tight nod as he passed through.

More and more survivors greeted his eyes as they made their way across the huge mansion. Families of tall, powerfully built Yttin were clustered together, looking far less comfortable in their temporary accommodations than the smaller Goblins, Gnomes, or even the strapping Orcs and Dwarves. Most of them were miners with the heavy muscles to go along with it, but more than half were children, the old, or the infirm. None were spared when the Grandmaster and Paladins sought to sacrifice them all for power. The poorest neighborhoods had been almost completely cleared out—and good thing, since Vess informed him that the sudden sea had flooded all of the lowest layers.

"The city was damaged by the Paladins' assault, terribly so," Vess explained as they stepped swiftly across a huge ballroom. Tents were set up there, each one holding three or four citizens, and Felix noticed that these didn't look as ragged as the survivors earlier. They were mostly dressed in finer cloth and brighter colors, and while many sported bandaged wounds and tired eyes, few had the wan cheeks and sallow skin of the miners.

Close by, a number of communal pots manned by black-and-gold liveried servants were ladling out fresh food. "The mid-levels suffered fire and axe before the rains came. In that way, you could say the rising sea saved them, at least. The Paladins were driven out by their sudden vulnerability, and the waters put out the fires...still, many people died before we could save them."

"But people helped," Pit added. "I saw it when we arrived. The gold armors and the white robes were helping."

"They...they did," Vess said, almost begrudgingly. "A small contingent of the Urge worshippers here turned against their leaders and aided our efforts to save those below. More still to hunt down the Paladins that couldn't escape anymore."

"The Paladins are still here?" Felix asked, feeling his temper flare up. *All these people... It's just like Haarwatch. Hurt because of zealots and monsters...and me.* "Where?"

"Would that we knew," Vess said, voice tight with her own frustration. "We've chased many down, but more always seem to turn up. Their ships were blasted out of the sky by the storms...not a single one survived the advent of the sea."

Almost to prove her point, lightning flashed through the large, twenty-foot windows on their right and Felix focused his gaze out the window. Manasight activated, a wavering bell in his ears, as the world around him burst into life. Vaporous threads of Mana swelled and bloomed, weaving into the solid shapes of the casement and glass before him. Beyond, white-green and dark gray gusts spun around and around, tearing through the sky like tiny, self-contained hurricanes as the clouds flashed and emptied themselves. Dark-blue water Mana rained down, following the wind, influenced by it, connected to it by tethers that Felix could dimly sense. The storm brightened, sparked again, as light blue and orange skipped across the clouds. Lightning raced toward flame, but was swallowed up by the wet and the dark.

It was a majestic tapestry of vibrancy. Of life itself, writ large and oh so small. A storm wasn't a beating heart, wasn't a brain turning thoughts to action and supposition, but it *was* alive. The Grand Harmony played through it like an instrument of wonder, and a distant warmth traced down Felix's cheeks. Then, among the wondrous, he saw the tiniest piece of it: an array of cloud and shadow and fire and force.

"There is a protection in the clouds, we are certain. Zara says it is benevolent, or at least of no concern to us, only to ships that dare ply the skies," Vess said.

Felix blinked, banking the burn of his Manasight until objects barely wisped with their hidden potency. "I see."

"Felix, are you crying?" Pit asked. He poked his head into Felix's large, scaled hands. In his new, more compact Body he barely reached Felix's sternum, though that was still taller than most Humans they'd met.

"A little," he admitted, scratching the tenku's head just behind his triangular ear tufts. "We've seen lots of bad things out there. Nice to remember that magic can be so beautiful, too." He looked to Vess, who was staring up at him with a gentle smile and warm eyes. He cleared his throat. "Ah, let's keep walking, yeah?"

She squeezed his bicep and pulled him onward.

The healer's wing was aptly named, as it occupied a full third of the gargantuan estate. More ballrooms, two amphitheaters, and a greenhouse had been dedicated to the care and treatment of the injured. If walking through the multitude of displaced masses hadn't been enough to cement his hatred for the former rulers of Ahkestria, seeing the thousands of wounded people would have done it. Many were suffering from severe burns and dehydration, a result of being exposed to entirely too much fire and heat Mana for too long, according to Vess. The heiress had been helping what patients she could, when she wasn't out fighting Paladins and watching over him.

Isla was running the show in this area, that much was clear to Felix. The faint chime of the vocalized Chant hung like tinsel in the air, glittering and heavy as it sank into the afflicted all around them. He wasn't familiar with it, but Felix assumed it was accelerating the healing process in some way when he saw a Goblin's nasty chest wound close up in a matter of seconds.

"Gross, huh?"

Felix looked up from the Goblin—now breathing far easier—to see a hulking mass of fur and muscle standing to his left. Beefhammer the Minotaur, formerly thirteen-year-old Michael of Earth, stood a touch shy of seven feet tall and bore two upswept horns on either side of his bullish head. He was wearing a belted green tunic that bulged strangely and brown shorts that stopped just shy of his bovine-shaped knees, both of which continued on into hooves.

"Beef," Felix said in relief. His smile froze when he saw the heavy bandages across the guy's right shoulder and arm. From the lumps under his tunic, it was clear the wrapping extended even farther than that. "Are you alright? Were you hurt like this in our fight?"

"Huh? Oh this? Nah, did this to myself," he laughed and smacked his right arm with his ham-sized left hand. His smile turned into a grimace. "Never better," he wheezed.

"That was foolish, Michael," said another voice. Female, it appeared to come from Beef himself.

"I told you not to call me that anymore, Hallow," he muttered.

"Hallow? Where is she?" Felix asked, looking around the room. His strange spirit summons had proven very useful in their battles together, not to mention being just really, really interesting. But he didn't see a single undead Risen around. "I thought all her Bodies got destroyed."

"They almost did, but—oh!" Beef swiftly forgot all about his pain and clapped his hands together, hard. He winced, but kept going. "I didn't get to show you this yet! Hold on!" The big Minotaur reached into his tunic and with some effort pulled free the bulging portion Felix had noticed. He carefully set it onto the ground, muscles straining and a thick vein in his forehead popping out. "There!"

It looked like nothing more than a bundle of clear, quartz-like crystals and lumpy earth. "Uh, what is it?" Felix asked.

"Right right, lemme do this," Beef said, and sent out a streamer of blackened-green Mana from his palm. The instant it touched the crystal lump, that same color completely infused the whole of it, until the bundle blazed with blackened-green light. "It's a Homunculus!"

"A what?" Felix asked.

The crystals stood up.

CHAPTER SIX

"Hallow? Is that you in there?" Felix asked.

The bundle of crystal and rock lifted a club-like hand and grew a single, luminous crystal where its thumb should be. "Yes."

"You like it? I ended up with this chunk of rock and crystal in my stuff when I was washed outta the Tomb," Beef explained as he knelt next to the Homunculus. The thing was small, barely three feet tall, but it was bulky and looked to weigh a fair amount. A solid column of luminous crystal made up its center, with chipped pieces of dark stone clinging to more crystalline bones like flesh. Its head was a half-dome lump of rock and branching crystals, but it retained the basic shape of a person. Sorta. "When I touched it, the whole thing sparked and sucked up some of my magic. So I figured, why not give it some? Turned out to be a good idea, and my Hallow Rise activated, splitting off a chunk of Hallow's...Hallowness into it."

"A large piece of me is now here," Hallow said in that faintly echoing, feminine voice. "Much more than in my other Risen. However, this is...comfortable."

Beef leaned in close to Felix and whispered. "She's never said stuff like that before. Been real weird, like she's growing." He grinned, and Felix noticed he had several missing teeth growing back in. "Like some sorta magic AI."

"You used to be able to summon around thirty to forty Risen at a time. How many can you manage now, while maintaining that Body?" Felix asked the Homunculus.

Hallow tilted her head, rocks grinding. "Perhaps ten. No. Nine Risen."

Pit whistled. "Steep cost," he said.

"Eh, worth it," Beef insisted. "She's got a core now. Never had that in any of the corpses, even the Multipede. It's that crystal through her center, and it can Evolve. Here." He flicked his fingers at Felix, and a blue window rotated into view before him.

Name: Hallow
Type: Homunculus
Evolution: Tier 0
Lore: Homunculus are rare creatures born of a confluence of factors that result in a Vessel of such purity that it may be moved by a Spirit of sure potency. Born as little more than a core and a hard shell to defend it, a Homunculus retains the ability to grow if it is nurtured properly.

"The Body's still pretty weak right now, but after using Hallow Rise on it once, it grew legs, arms, and something like a head," Beef explained. "I'm thinkin' if I keep fighting with the thing, facing down some monsters or Paladins or somethin', then she'll get stronger."

"Combat is difficult in such a form," Hallow added, lifting its nubby little arms. Suddenly, dagger-like needles of glowing crystal burst from its stony shell, like some sort of nightmare porcupine. "But the crystal proves quite sharp and durable."

She swiped her arm, and several projectiles shot outward, embedding themselves in a stone column thirty feet away.

"Impressive," Vess said, peering after the attack. "That sank a few inches into Tier II stone. Most Apprentices couldn't do that with an attack."

"See? Strong," Beef said, patting his bicep.

Felix knelt down and peered closer at the Homunculus. "Do you mind?" he asked.

"I do not," Hallow replied, and though Felix couldn't quite feel her emotional affect. She seemed...bored.

As Beef continued boasting about the possibilities of the Homunculus, Felix ran his senses over the construct. He assumed it was a construct, much like a Golem was, animated by some sort of advanced inscriptions and buried in the depths of the Tomb. The rising waters must have knocked it free, and it had ended up in Beef's hands. A simple, easy explanation...one that did nothing to account for the fact that the creature contained not a jot of sigaldry.

What? That's impossible. How's it functioning? It's made of Mana crystals and rock. He ran his fingers over its craggy surface, sliding them across razor-sharp protrusions of glowing crystal as his senses quested deeper. His expansive Perception could pick out individual grains of sand clinging to the rocky carapace and hear the faintest tapping as something inside the Homunculus expanded and shrank in steady succession. It sounded like a heartbeat, built not of meat and fluid, but silica and something else. There was a resonance to the Body, a familiar Dissonance buried beneath Beef's blackened-green magic and the earth Mana the Homunculus wore.

Felix's memory was entirely too perfect to miss it: the cadence was the signature of the Primordial of Withering Dust. Was it one of the "confluence of factors" that created the Homunculus? Felix's heartbeat sped up, as if readying him for a fight, but the Homunculus didn't suddenly sprout fangs and claws and attack him. In fact, as he pressed his Affinity and Perception to their limits, he found not a single trace of the flesh curse in the Homunculus. Apparently, when he had eliminated the curse previously, it had been a thorough job.

He stood up with a grateful sigh. *It's remarkably magical and strange, but it's not gonna magically infect everyone around it. It's safe.*

"Quite the amazing find, is it not?" a new voice asked. Felix looked up to see a small blonde woman step closer, her pale blue gown covered in a stained, once-white smock. Her hair was still up and immaculate, still bound by a silver circlet on her brow, as if she were some princess from a fairy tale. "When Michael brought it to me, I immediately knew it should be developed further. I imagine a...person such as he can truly take advantage of its strengths."

"Lady Isla. You seem in good spirits," Vess said with a slight inclination of her head.

"Were that I was better. The procession of wounded never seems to end. More and more people are being brought up from the lower layers with truly gruesome injuries." The Chanter shook her head as she cast her gaze across the sea of cots and robed figures moving around them. "The defectors from the Highest Flame have been quite useful. I believe their guilt drives them to excessive helpfulness."

Felix saw them, clad in white robes embroidered with golden and orange thread. A number of them had picked out the stitching on the flame that dominated their backs, so now it was an amorphous mess of orange, yellow, and golden lines. They were leaning across the sick and infirm, applying ointments and administering vials of various potions.

Pit, who had ranged a bit afield, sniffed a gooey-looking poultice one of them had just laid. He snorted, pawing at his nose when the acrid scent stuffed itself into his nostrils. Felix could admit it was nice to see not all of the Temple's adherents were so blind as their leaders, even if he also didn't trust them very much. From the way Isla was watching their progress, she didn't, either.

"And you, Felix? How goes your recovery?" Isla asked. "Last I knew, you were in the throes of some considerable System backlash."

"I'm fine," he said.

"Are you sure? Perhaps I should inspect your channels, to be safe," Isla suggested, lifting her hands toward him.

A burning annoyance flared in his chest, and the Chanter stopped, her face paling even further than usual. "I am fine," he repeated.

The woman licked her lips once and dropped her hands with a queasy smile. "Of course. How foolish of me."

"That's what I keep saying," Beef said, before loudly whispering to Felix. "I think she listened better when she was Naos."

Isla smacked him. "You seem quite fine, Michael. Has your masochism reached its end?"

Vess raised an eyebrow. "What is this?"

Beef blushed, though it was hard to tell through his thick skin. "Just been experimenting with Hallow's new form. She can shift her shape a bit, so I thought, why not have her be armor, too? Then I could hide the Homunculus Body until it's needed, and bam!" He slapped his hands together, hard enough that a wave of air kicked back the cots around him. People cried out. "Oh damn, sorry. Sorry!" In a much quieter voice, he repeated himself. "Bam. Surprise Hallow."

"And it is cutting you up? That's where your injuries are from?" Vess asked. When Beef nodded sheepishly, she laughed. "You two are very much alike. I once saw Felix shoving his arms into a basin of acid just to raise his resistance Skill."

"You saw that?" Felix hadn't thought anyone had been awake then.

"The smell was hard to ignore."

Beef put his fists on his hips, looking proudly at Felix. "It's a cool idea,right? Living armor and a hidden weapon?"

Felix nodded. He couldn't deny it. "It's *very* cool. Just don't hurt yourself too much."

"Eh, I'm like stupid sturdy now. After that Link thingy, most of my Aspects pushed close to Journeyman. I even Tempered my Body."

"You did? This happened after the battle?" Felix asked, his good mood fading. He could almost feel Isla's attention sharpening the longer they spoke. "How did you get an Essence Draught?"

"Pit gave me one of yours," Beef said. "We were on that Yttin boat, and I just couldn't hold it back anymore. Guy saved me, that's for sure. Though it was real nasty."

"One of...mine?" Felix asked. The only Essence Draughts he'd carried with him were the unattuned ones. The ones that weren't fit for anyone but him to use. "How'd that go?"

"Oh dude, it was rough. One time I broke into my dad's liquor cabinet and drank his favorite whiskey. This felt like that but, like, ten thousand times worse. Like glass in my throat and chest." Beef shuddered. "Hit me like a ton of bricks, too. After four of them, I felt wrung out, but it got me a new Body. Called the Savage Riot Body. Increased my Strength by 200 points! Even my Endurance and Vitality have gone over a thousand now, can you believe it?"

Felix could believe it. The Minotaur had a considerable advantage on his Body, and he'd been a great help in their battles together. But the kid was always lagging a bit behind, unable to keep up with the punishment and speed that Felix and Pit showcased. He might not be much faster now, but his durability had vastly increased. Frankly, Felix was relieved. Beef would be able to keep up with him in the future, and the Essence Draught hadn't just ripped his core space into pieces. While he hadn't the same advantages of constitution Felix did, nor a Hunger aiding the process of digesting such potency, he was Unbound. Apparently, that had been enough.

"What is truly interesting about this 'Link' that Michael speaks of, is that his Skills have also increased," Isla added. "How did such a thing come to be?"

"Oh yeah, Hallow Rise jumped like ten levels and Tempered into Journeyman, too. My first Spirit Skill to get so high," Beef said with palpable excitement. "I've got more Mana, too, though my Willpower didn't increase too much. That's a little strange."

"Hmm," was all Felix offered. He wasn't in the mood to explain anything to Isla. In fact, he wasn't sure that he trusted her all that much. The Chanter's order, the Cantus Sodalus, hadn't proven itself to him yet. He was still sore about Zara Marking him—essentially planting a GPS tracker on his Spirit—without his knowledge or consent. Felix had removed it, but he wasn't too quick to trust again...and Isla was a mystery. What she wanted was anyone's guess. "Beef, you mind if I take a look at your core space? I can make sure nothing too squirrelly went on when you Tempered."

"Oh, uhm. I'd, uh, nah. That's not something you have to do," Beef said.

"I mean, it's relatively easy for me," Felix said with a shrug.

"It is?" Isla said. "When did you learn to delve?"

"Here and there," Felix said, but kept his eyes on Beef. "You sure?"

Beef gave a wide smile. "Yeah. I'm sure. I'm totally fine."

The Minotaur's Spirit twisted, an atonal squeal that spelled out the lie. He wasn't fine, but Felix wasn't sure why. And with Isla right there, he didn't want to press the issue. "Alright. Let me know if you change your mind."

"Sure."

"Isla, where is Zara?" Vess asked into the brief lull in conversation. "We are seeking her out."

"Oh, she is off dealing with that hulking Reed and his soldiers. Why did you think there would be changes in young Michael's abilities?" Isla asked, undeterred.

"We fought a lot of enemies in the Tomb, not to mention the dead Primordial down there," Felix said. "Things were chaotic, to say the least. I just want to make sure everything went smoothly, and I have a little experience with checking core spaces. Besides, a Primordial's flesh curse is insidious, even if the thing was dead."

"But have you not conquered the flesh curse?" Isla asked. "You are able to cleanse it, after all."

Felix raised an eyebrow. "Where'd you hear that?"

Vess spoke up. "She aided us in distilling a portion of the Primordial's curse to use against the Highest Flame. She was told about your ability to cleanse our people of the curse." *And little else,* her gaze told him.

Felix nodded slowly. "Right. Well, I can cleanse it, which is part of why I want to inspect his core space. Making sure it's safe."

Beef waved his hands. "I'm fine. Better than fine. Hallow and I just finished rebuilding a whole crafting house. Took a while, but Hallow's got a new knack for stonework."

"I am pleased with the capabilities of this new Body," the spirit said. "I only wish to see how we fare in battle, Michael."

"Eventually. We've been banned from the Paladin hunt," Beef explained to Felix's questioning glance.

"You're too precious to risk against those fools," Isla said, patting Beef on the shoulder. "Both of you." With a swift motion, the Chanter discarded her stained apron and gathered up her fine blue skirts in a fist. "Now come. You said you were looking for Zara? I can take you to her."

With little else to do, Felix and Vess found no reason not to agree. Isla soon led them across the open amphitheater and down through a series of doorways. Pit, Beef, and a stumping Hallow followed behind them.

After a while, as the chambers kept coming, Isla began talking. She spoke of small things, engaging Vess in a conversation about the efforts at producing enough potions with their limited supplies, while Vess spoke on the continued threat of the Paladins. It was a back and forth that Felix let slide past him just as the doorways and corridors swept across his path. But ignoring the conversation only earned him a jolt of surprise when the Chanter addressed him.

"So, Felix, can you explain to me how you can cleanse the flesh curse of a Primordial?" she said, as casually as if she were asking about the weather. "It is an affliction that *no one* in the history of the healing arts has ever cured. I am simply amazed that you've found a way."

Felix wasn't sure how to answer that, so he simply didn't. He knew it made him come off as boorish and maybe even an idiot, not having some pithy come back to distract or divert the question, but he had nothing. His ability to cleanse the flesh curse was a function of his Transcendent rarity Skills: Chthonic Tribute, Unite the Lost, and most recently, Sovereign of Flesh. But answering with that would lead to more questions, such as where those Skills had been learned or what they could accomplish. Instead, as his own silence grew a touch too heavy to bear, Felix said, "What can you tell me about weaving Pillars and the Tapestry Stage that follows?"

Isla tapped her lips as if he hadn't ignored her and awkwardly changed the subject. "Ah, well. One requires anywhere between five and nine Pillars, and each one represents a piece of your foundation. Weaving them is quite important, especially weaving them well with Skills that have been properly Tempered with useful and potent Features. Most make it their purpose to Weave all of them once they hit Adept Tier, but few manage to complete such a monumental task. Typically, one is well into the Master Tier before their Weaving Stage has reached its end."

Felix perked up at that. "Really? Why do some have more Pillars than others?"

"A matter of Tempering and, to be honest, care," Isla said. "There are always those impatient to climb the steps to power, and it takes a long time to properly weave one's Pillars."

"I see," Felix said, glancing at Vess. She was watching Isla as if she were memorizing every word that came out of her mouth, and likely was; information like this was hard to come by on the Continent, even, apparently, for duchal heiresses. "And making your Tapestry is...?"

"A worry for Master Tiers," the Chanter said bluntly. "One cannot advance into Grandmaster without completing one's Pillars and beginning the weave of one's Tapestry. More than that, I cannot say."

"Because saying would influence the process," Felix said, nodding in understanding. Karys had said the same.

"What? No, because I have not yet reached that stage myself. I am only at the beginning stages of Master Tier, though my Pillars are almost completely formed."

Oh. That was surprising. The woman felt a lot more powerful than Felix, but he was only a few steps behind her in core formation. *Does weaving Pillars help so much?*

"From what Zara has told me, you are growing quite fast, Felix. Two Pillars already, and while still a Journeyman. That is remarkable...and foolhardy," Isla said.

"What? Why?" Vess demanded. "Felix is clearly stronger than many. He was able to defeat a Grandmaster, in his own Territory no less," she continued, expression more than a little heated. "Everything he is, he was forced into in order to survive or save the people around him. That is not foolhardy. That is admirable and noble and—" Vess suddenly cut off her words when she met Felix's gaze. A faint redness flushed the very tops of her cheeks.

Isla held up her hands, perhaps to forestall another outburst. "It is foolhardy because it invites disaster. Quick growth is the surest way to outpace your own foundation. This is why I've ensured Michael has had only steady gains throughout this past half year. All of you Unbound must be molded so that you do not extend yourself beyond reach of our ability to save you; that is one of the priorities of our Order.

"Grow too fast, and your foundation will not be solid enough to carry you into Grandmaster and Paragon." They came upon another set of double doors, these carved into complicated geometric patterns and plated with polished gold. Felix could faintly hear the sound of fighting on the other side. "For it is in those Tiers that you and your fellows will truly prove useful to the Continent."

She shoved open the double doors and walked out onto a wide stone landing. Above them, the storm roared, discharging lightning and a torrential rainfall that filled the night with a wet haze. The patter of water and crashing thunder nearly drowned out the sound of close to a hundred men and women engaged in a brutal, bloody fight, just feet below them.

The Chanter shook her head, as if the fighting were pointless. "Only at that point will you have the potential to *perhaps* stand up against the Ruin."

CHAPTER SEVEN

"Harn!"

A solid kick bashed open the stout, metal-clad door, sending it crashing into the wall. A slight figure lurched out of the gathering gloom, her grunts of effort barely audible over the roar of the storm. Stepping into the dim light of the smithy, Evie held tight to a length of crimson cloth she'd bundled over her shoulder. "Harn, get your ass out here and help me!"

"Mfah," said the battered stack of metal plates connected to the red cloth—a cloak. "Mmrah!"

Evie kicked backward with easy grace, catching the concussed warrior in the temple. "Go back to sleep." The cloak dragged even harder at her shoulder, but at least it was still. A rhythmic ringing sounded from farther within—the sound of a hammer on an anvil. "Harn? You there?"

The smithy on the old bald bastard's estate wasn't small, but still not so large that finding it had been easy. The grounds of the Grandmaster's *former* home were easily of a size on par with the Temple of Elemental Fire, and that place had been a damned maze. She'd found the forge in the sideways rain while dragging a bleeding Paladin behind her, and all because the stupid idiot had gone and started bleeding out...and Evie had run out of Healing Potions.

"Harn? You have any spare potions? This murdering dolt wouldn't stop with his fire sword, so I had to perforate his lungs a bit. Dunno if he'll last the trip to Isla so we can question him." Evie dropped the cloak, and the Paladin's armored legs hit the ground with a dull *thunk*. "Stop foolin' around and come out here—"

Evie's foot hit something hard, and it slid across the floor. *A mace?*

The entrance to the smithy was a showroom, housing a number of weapons mounted on the walls between the dim Mana lamps—but those were all fancy pieces. Jewels and inscriptions covered them, and more than a few were in warded glass cases. But the floor and low furniture in the showroom, where folks would expect to have a sit or lay down as they tried out their purchases, those were *covered* in weapons. Swords and maces and spears of all size and shapes were leaned against walls and couches and counters, each of them hammered out of what appeared to be standard steel.

"Where is everyone? And why are the lights out?" Evie picked her way over the weapons. All of them were unfinished, without leather or wood or bone strapped to their handles or hilts. As if Harn had smithed them all and just...tossed them to the ground. The hammering kept going, uninterrupted.

Beyond the circular expanse of the showroom was a thick counter where clerks would no doubt have stood to take her measurements and orders. Now it was empty and dark, like a drunk's smile. Most of the staff had fled the Grandmaster's estate, barely grabbing what they needed and fleeing into the city. Apparently, a great many were Oathbound to serve, and that compulsion faded with the gray mage's death—it was part of how they knew the bald fuck had perished before Pit and that Minotaur had come to confirm it. Now the smithy and lots of other parts of the estate were empty...but a flickering light and steady hammering emanated from the back rooms.

Evie slid over the counter with perfect, feline grace. Her Body had grown by leaps and bounds since Felix and his...whatever he'd done. Fighting felt easier than ever, so much that she'd been chasing down the feeling for almost two days, getting her chain soaked in crimson zealot. She hadn't thought of Harn, of the dangers he might face here when she'd been out.

The back of the counter was a wall filled with more of those special weapons, even a suit of full on platemail decked out in gold filigree. At the center, where the firelight ebbed and flowed, was a thick door. Wide open. Evie stepped through, hand at her waist, and ice Mana almost boiling out of her palms. *C'mon Harn. What's goin' on here?*

Through the door was a short passage, barely thirty strides long by eight wide, yet it too was filled with unfinished blades, hammers, and axes. A lot of axes, actually. There were three doors, one to the right and at the very end, but those were closed. It was the one on the left, the extra wide threshold that glowed with yellow-orange light, as if the Highest Flame had come again. Through it, Evie could feel an incredible wash of heat and noise, that steady hammering louder than ever. Through it, she could see Harn.

"Noctis' tits."

The man stood over a massive anvil made of dark brown crystal, silhouetted by the blazing forge behind him. Implements and tools hung from every available surface, including racks above and around him, and more weapons littered the edges of the chamber. Harn was bringing a dark metal hammer down atop a piece of glowing steel, sparks and bits of char flying as it impacted. It was a...shovel? No. No, Evie recognized it from all the near-identical versions around her. It was an axe.

"Harn, if you wanted me not to interrupt, you could've hung a sign or somethin'," she said over the din. The man didn't look up, didn't react to her voice. He just kept turning and flipping the steel, his hammer falling steady as a heartbeat. With every strike, a pulse of bright silvery Mana surged from Harn's tool and into the unfinished axe.

Slam and press. Strike and fold.

Mana massaged into the metal itself, but also...something else. An earthy scent lingered around Harn, but it was something Evie could *hear*. A deep noise that sounded like old water and heated dust, that smelled of violence and a baffling weariness. Harn's body was slick with sweat, his tunic stained, and his dark hair dripped over his vacant eyes. He hunched and brought down the hammer, rotating, flipping, working the metal. Never stopping.

"You're scaring me, you ugly bastard. Stop it!" Evie had finally crossed the distance—she was done with this spooky shit. She reached out a hand for his shoulder...but another pale hand grabbed her wrist. "Hey!"

"Don't." The owner of the hand stepped clear of some debris that had blocked Evie's sight, fully illuminated by the forge light. She was a short woman, Human but built almost like a Dwarf; all curves and thick arms. It was Palin, the tavernkeep, and her grip was as steely as her gaze. "He's almost broken through."

Evie's eyes widened in realization, and in doing so, she finally parsed the heavy, basso song that thrummed across her friend's broad shoulders. It rose in peaks and dropped into valleys in time with each shaping blow, caused by or perhaps causing the intense, mindless focus that had consumed the man. "He's Tempering?"

Palin nodded, and for some reason, she looked proud. And tired, covered in grease and several bandages herself. "Into Adept at last."

Evie was more than strong enough to contest the tavernkeep, but she let herself be led out of the forge. They crossed the corridor and entered the chamber on the right-hand side, which turned out to be a set of living quarters. Presumably for the prior, Oathbound smith. It was a homey little setup and, once the door shut behind them, far quieter.

The remnants of the previous occupants were obvious, with supplies and personal effects scattered all around. Some effort had been made to clean it all up, but there was such an abundance of *stuff* that it made little difference. A smallish bed was there, tucked against the back of the utilitarian space, and a finely crafted table and chairs stood in a dining area off from a small but functional kitchen...but most of the open chamber was overflowing with crafting materials. Stacks of ore gleamed in the lamplight, beside sealed barrels filled with unknown substances. Evie shoved at one, letting the four-foot cask wobble and slosh. *Something liquid. Mabye oil? Smiths use oil, right?*

"Excuse the mess. We've only been here a day, and most of that has been dealing with Harn's...issues," Palin said. She busied herself clearing off one of the handsomely crafted wooden chairs, lifting stacks of bone and Mana crystal in both hands. "My *muar* and *tuar* were helping me earlier, but they're all of them Untempered, and it's been a long day."

"Moo'er and too'er? What's that?" Evie asked, eyeing the proffered chair but not sitting. "And where are those Dwarves you work with?"

Palin smirked. "*Muar* and *tuar* are Dwarvish for, well, the closest approximation in the common tongue is 'uncle' and 'aunt.' They *are* my Dwarven workers, but they're also family."

"Oh," Evie said, feeling a little foolish. That had never stopped her before, though. "You look Dwarven. That makes sense."

This time the woman laughed, but it was a little bitter. "Ask my Dwarven relatives that. They say I'm too Human."

Evie wasn't so dumb as to chase that conversation down. So instead she focused on easier topics. "They're stayin' nearby? Your aunts and uncles?"

"Close enough to help, but far enough to stay out of the way. After all the excitement, being held prisoner, almost being sacrificed, they've had their fill of adventure for quite a while." Palin shook her head. "None of them ever had a head for this lifestyle; only my *muar* Tevuk even left to become an adventurer. Said he joined the Protector's Guild and everything, up in Hekail."

Evie frowned at the mention of the Guild. Another topic she'd rather not linger on. "How long's Harn been like that? And why's he *makin'* things?"

Palin sat in the cleared chair with a soft groan and massaged her thighs. "I don't know. Never heard of a Tempering like his, but he just said 'I need the forge,' and 'give me metal.' That's all before he sucked down those Essence Draughts and started hammering away. Since then, I've been making sure he has metal to hand, and clearing out the weapons he keeps churning out. It's been an exhausting day."

"He always liked smithin', I guess," Evie said after a moment.

"More than likes it. The man won't shut up about it. Only thing he talked about more than smithing was, well, you," Palin said.

Evie grunted in surprise. "Me? What for?"

The tavernkeep looked at her like she was daft. "He—you can't be surprised to know that he loves you like his own, right? The whole trip across the desert, he kept going on about your accomplishments. About how you fought some monster named DuFont and saved him from some sort of living armor? Honestly some of it seemed quite far-fetched, but then that's why I'm no adventurer."

"Huh," Evie said, turning the idea of it over in her Mind. "He said all that to you?"

Palin smiled, wide and soft, like she was remembering something. "He says a lot." The tavernkeep's smile faded when Evie grunted again. "What?"

"So, you two...you're a thing now, eh?" Evie asked. She narrowed her eyes at the tavernkeep, watching her as the woman's face sagged open in surprise. "Oh, don't bother denyin' it. Harn doesn't talk to people. Like ever. Maybe, if he likes you and thinks you might be useful, he'll give some advice or tell you if a boulder is gonna crush your head. But 'chat'?" Evie laughed. "No."

Palin stuttered a second longer before she focused on smoothing her skirts around her crossed knees. "Well, he intended on telling you himself. After. But yes. We have been...I suppose courting is the closest word. There isn't truly a phrase for 'spending time while fleeing from an undead army' is there?"

Evie snorted. "No, don't suppose there is." She stepped closer to the tavernkeep. "I'm happy for you, whatever you want to call it."

"Thank yo—" Palin started to say, but cut off as a span-length spike of ice pressed a finger-breadth away from her eye.

Evie stared down at her and held the Ice Spike close. "If you hurt him, I will bring such terror onto you that your Dwarvish ancestors will pull their mountains down on themselves, just to get away from me." She leaned her face down, until only the Ice Spike separated their gazes. "Understand me?"

The tavernkeep, though, gave glare for glare. "I don't plan on it, girlie. But if you put that in my face ever again, I'll box your fool ears."

Palin held Evie's gaze for several long heartbeats...until Evie dropped her Ice Spike completely. With a laugh, she slapped the tavern-keep hard on the back. Palin winced in pain. "Glad to see Harn's lady has some spine!"

"Was," Palin stammered, suddenly confused. "Was that a...test?"

Evie waggled her hand back and forth. "Eh. I wanted to see what you'd do. High-pressure situations reveal a warrior's measure, ya know? Harn taught me that."

"Really," Palin said, unable to stop her hand from touching her cheek.

Evie supposed it still felt cold from her magic, but could only shrug. With a luxurious stretch, Evie straightened her back and grunted in relief as something popped and cracked. "Now, how about you help me with this Paladin I left dying in your shop?"

Palin started. "Come again?"

CHAPTER EIGHT

The rain was pouring sideways as a brutal battle played out before them. Felix looked beyond Isla and the waist-high balustrade to a muddy field that had once likely been very nice. The battle involved members of the Fiend's Claw, the warriors he'd brought with him from Nagast, but it also contained a number of faces he'd never seen before. A great deal of them, in fact. Dwarves, Goblins, Hobgoblins, and Orcs outnumbered his Claw ten to one, all of them clad in ill-fitting mail and wielding heavy wooden clubs instead of proper weapons. The Claw weren't using naked steel, either...but that was about as far as their concessions went. As Felix watched, honed limbs met weak, untrained flesh, every strike laying out a club-wielding foe.

"What's the point of this?" Beef asked. "Are those guys Untempered?"

"They are," said a voice, serene and smooth as placid waters. Zara Cyrene, Naiad and Chanter of the Cantus Sodalus stepped up beside them. A small smile adorned a face only lightly touched by age, her ochre skin creased with laugh lines, and her aquamarine hair cascaded down her back in waves. She was clad in the dark black robes of a chorister, now accented with a belted purple sash around her waist. Felix raised an eyebrow at that. "A gift," she said, inclining her head toward Lieutenant Errol.

The sweaty Lieutenant sketched a hasty bow. "A well-deserved one. As I told you before, you are first among our number, Lady Zara."

"You're one of my Shadows now, too?" Felix asked.

"How else can I hope to keep track of your miraculous achievements? It seems that whenever I let you out of my sight, you annex another Territory." Zara's cool serenity turned warm, a sensation echoed through her Spirit—not that he trusted it entirely. She was Master Tier, likely at the higher end, and Felix had never been able to read the woman. She smiled as if she knew his every thought, revealing shark-like teeth. "Consider me glued to your side now. A shadow in name as well as title."

"Wait wait, why are your soldiers fighting a bunch of villagers?" Beef asked Felix. "That seems kinda villainous."

"They wish to join up," Zara stated. "A test was required. One-on-one instruction is always the most fruitful, but with so many looking to join the ranks of your Claw, Felix, it was decided a mass application must be devised."

"This is how they determine the rankings among the lowest of our military," Vess said slowly. "The newest, greenest recruits are pitted against the seasoned veterans, and talent will stand out. Or that's the hope."

"Like, just hope the good ones kick ass?" Beef asked before nodding. "Alright, cool. So like, the exceptional rise to the top. I like it."

Felix let out a long and judgmental "Hmmmm." His brow furrowed. "This doesn't seem like a good way to assess anyone's true capabilities."

"It is not. What if real aptitude is missed, or someone is turned away who would be useful in a role that isn't immediately obvious? I will admit to not being a fan of this practice, but it is an...acceptable method of establishing a baseline, if done properly." Vess' mouth tightened, and she pointed into the rain-lashed grounds with her chin. "And Darius knows his business."

Sure enough, Darius Reed, Chosen Hand of the Duke of Pax'Vrell and Vess' former guardian, stood stiffly at the far side of the conflict. The distance, even through the heavy rain and lightning, was nothing to Felix's Perception, and he watched as the man panned his gaze across the flailing combatants. It certainly seemed like the man had things under control.

Felix admitted to himself that their time in Ahkestria was, by necessity, a short one. Memory stabbed back at him, of Haim, the former leader of the Paladins, and what he said. "They are willing to leave Ahkestria?" he asked Zara. "To join up with someone they don't even know?"

She nodded. "They are. Many either have no homes, due to the flooding, the Paladins, or both. And it isn't just warriors; almost every single one of them has a family in this estate, mothers and brothers and fathers and sisters that they wish to care for. I have spoken to many, and they all share the same sentiment that burns in the recruits below. We have only been training them a few hours, but...can you not feel it, Felix?"

It was his turn to nod. Felix did indeed sense the harmonies weaving across the battlefield. Hell, he'd been feeling pangs of it throughout the entire compound. Fear in all its varieties, inchoate rage, and weeping sadness were the bulk of it, but more lay around their Untempered Spirits. It forced his jaw open as he peered closer at the untrained miners and poorest Ahkestria had to offer. Even as some struggled to rise from brutal, bruising hits, the ephemeral song did not stop. "Conviction. I don't hear a single note of doubt from any of them."

"Truly?" Vess asked. Her brow was furrowed and her nose scrunched. "I can only hear pain."

"An element not to be ignored, certainly," Zara said. She leaned over the well-carved railing, and a faint, humming glow manifested around her head.

Felix narrowed his eyes, but realized it was a weather warding inscribed in the railing and overhang itself. The warding was why the sideways rain did not touch any of those upon the landing. Zara was merely pressing against it without piercing it. "Pain is a catalyst. It leads to a great many things, most of them heinous, but growth is also accompanied by a necessary ache. We can either choose to embrace that ache or run from it and remain stagnant. These people were considered the dregs of Ahkestria, given only enough shelter and food to keep the mines operational. I am not surprised that they wish to join us, to join the banner that they saw freeing them. Even so far as defending them from their suddenly wrathful god."

"The Highest Flame wasn't a god," Vess said with a sharp tone. "But...she is right. We left an impression on them all. Especially Atar."

"Atar?" Felix asked. "What happened with him?"

"Change. Change at a pace that is quite frankly alarming, Felix." Isla said. She looked at Beef and his Homunculus, both of whom were looking awkwardly between Isla and Felix. "Michael was far from a Journeyman's understanding, yet he stands a third Tempered into the Tier after only a day in your presence."

"Oh yeah, I grew a ton," Beef said. "Why wouldn't I? We fought, like, an army of Paladins and undead, plus that big bone monster thing."

"What are you implying?" Felix asked, ignoring Beef's outburst.

Isla tilted her head and smiled. "That your presence is strengthening the others around you in ways that even I cannot understand. I have spent time enough around your allies to see that they are all of them balancing upon the cusp into Adept Tier, one of the hardest early bottlenecks to breach. The Grand Harmony is swirling about you, Felix Nevarre, in ways that being an Unbound is simply not enough to explain."

"Isla is correct, if a bit bold in her assertions in so open a space," Zara said, a tight admonishment in her tone.

"I am quite lucky then, that you erected a privacy ward the moment we arrived," Isla replied, her smile unwavering.

"Indeed." Zara pivoted, focusing on Felix. "What you have done...what you *are* has begun to have effects on those around you. A substantial number of your Fiend's Claw have reported strange notifications over the past day, ever since the Battle of the Flame concluded. Every single one of them have unlocked their Affinity and are hearing 'strange sounds' as they progress through their training. An astounding number, in any circumstance, to have unlocked a Harmonic Stat. That includes your Shadows, as well."

Felix glanced at his escort, most of them looking stoic, but a few with bright, eager faces. The two Frost Giants nodded along happily with Zara's words. "Ok. But what does that mean? Unlocking some Harmonic Stats is rare, you've told me that, but it doesn't mean anything by itself...does it?"

"Truly, you are from another world," Isla muttered. "To bear the face of the Grand Harmony, to unveil an entire subset of the System—that is a gateway to powers most mortal forces cannot begin to grasp. You have the beginnings of an army of Harmonically sensitive warriors, and I do not know how else they may grow."

Zara rolled her shoulders, as if casting something off herself, and a slight vibration Felix hadn't even noticed faded away. *The privacy ward,* he realized. She bade him to step up to the railing. "Felix, come here. Look at them. Extend your senses over them all."

He did. The battle was over, and folks in white robes moved among the injured while the uniformed members of his Claw helped other new recruits to their feet. They spoke and laughed and patted the battered recruits on the backs, welcoming them into the fold. Beyond the physical, there was a distinct vibration among that swirling sense of conviction; now that Felix knew what to look for, he spotted the difference right away.

All of those who wore the cloak depicting his Seal, a glyph of *lightning* and *fire* shaped into an eye and surmounted by a crown, all of them seemed to create ripples around them. Like rocks in a stream, forcing the waters to move around them; not quite shaping anything, but influencing things by their very existence.

"Do you feel them?" she asked.

"I do."

"Their Affinity is only the start, and they know it. The recruits can feel it subconsciously and are drawn to it, and to you. Time enough has passed to spread stories among them, and soldiers are ever so chatty.

They know of the Fiend, the Autarch, the man these warriors call their leader."

As if this was all planned, a ripple rolled out among his Claw, almost visible to Felix as each of them turned to see him. As the rain drenched them and ran rivers across the muddy field, every one of them went to a single knee, fist to heart and fist to earth. A swell of unspoken sound filled the air, a thunder louder than any storm to Felix's Affinity, as his Claw spoke as one.

"Lord Autarch!"

Holy shit. Felix clenched his jaw and swallowed, unsure how, or if, he should respond. Belatedly, the green recruits also fell awkwardly to their knees, mimicking the others with considerably less grace. Felix settled on a single, downward nod and tried to project a sense of approval and confidence.

Beside him, Zara chuckled.

"What?" he asked.

"It's a good effort, but unclench your jaw before you break a tooth," Zara said through her kind laugh. "But Vess' teachings haven't been in vain, I see."

Out of the corner of his eye, Felix saw Vess shift a little. Perception being strange as it was, he could pick out the smile that stretched her lips...just as he sensed the hobbling approach of someone else. Felix turned toward them and froze, his greeting halted by shock.

"Ah, hello everyone," Atar said, supporting himself on Alister's blue-clad arm and his thin, metal staff. "Felix."

"Atar," he said through his shock. "What happened?"

The fire mage's skin, once olive-toned, was now an unrelieved gray the color of cold ash. His hair was longer but just as curly, except it was an ethereal platinum blonde, only a shade or two from pure white. His eyes, however, were the most startling. Half-hidden by his hair, they burned like the embers of a banked fire, as if they would flare up at a moment's notice. He was a bit emaciated and stooped, and the hands that clutched at his staff and Alister's arm were not steady at all, but his snort of amusement ignored all of that. "Speak for yourself, lizard boy."

Felix held up his clawed hands and smirked. "Touché."

"Why are you out of your bed, Atar?" Isla asked, somewhat harshly. "You're still recovering."

"I told him that, but he refuses to listen," Alister said with the look of a longsuffering saint. "It was either help him or watch as he fell onto the floor and crawled his way out."

"Burning ash, I needed some time away from there. Fresh air, movement. Something," Atar groused before narrowing his eyes at the Chanter. "And you have no say in what I do. You're still new."

Felix bit his lip to keep from smiling too hard at that and tried to focus on his friend. "What happened?"

Atar licked his lips, opened his mouth and then shut it again. "Not here. Find me later. Shouldn't be a problem for you, since you got all stretched out. What, did you eat a giant, too?"

The smirk of amusement on Felix's face faded slightly as a game of word association flared across his Mind. Giants led to Frost Giants, which made him think of those within his Stronghold, held fast within the Mirk Enclosure spell he'd crafted weeks prior to protect his Territory. The thought arrived, an urgent nugget that had become buried since his fight. "Haim," he said, spitting it like a curse.

"The High Justicar? What about him?" Zara asked. "Pit told us of his defeat at your hands."

Felix waved his hands. "No, no. It's what he—he said that the Triumvirate was sending forces to Nagast, to tear down the barrier. The Hierocracy is coming for my Territory."

Zara's expression hardened, her mouth firming around her words. "I see. I had expected as such, but—Come. Let us retreat somewhere more suited to this conversation. All of us."

Felix didn't have a problem with that.

CHAPTER NINE

They settled into a room not far distant from the sparring grounds, Zara leading the way. It was ornately designed and cavernous, much as every other aspect of Kel'lyv's home had been, so much so that it dwarfed their company. The Chanters, Vess, Beef, Hallow, and Pit all claimed spaces around a large rectangular table, followed slowly by Atar and Alister. The thing was huge, ridiculously so, and once again made Felix question the Grandmaster's sensibilities.

"It's for show," Atar explained when Felix voiced his wonder aloud. Alister eased him into a high-backed chair studded with brass buttons. "My...former master cared only for power or the trappings of it. Anything else was beneath his notice."

"He was an ass," Alister said from Atar's side. "Through and through. I'm glad you killed him, Felix. I'm afraid of what I might have tried to do if he was still around." Atar gripped Alister's hand, the ashen gray stark against the force mage's pale skin.

"Where is Evie? And Harn?" Vess asked, looking around. "I have not seen either of them in a number of hours."

"Evie was leading some of the Talons after rumors of Paladins," Zara said as she settled into a round chair with a low back. She spread her black chorister robes out, draping them around her legs and chair. "Harn has been seen in the Grandmaster's personal smithy."

Felix smiled, unsurprised by either answer. While the huge table was mostly empty, the only other person they were missing was Darius, and he was busy overseeing the training warriors. He didn't sit, but stood at the far end of the table and cleared his throat. "Lieutenant, if you please, take the Shadows outside the chamber and wait there. Don't let anyone in without my permission, okay?"

Errol saluted, and all twelve of his honor guard slipped out the doors. The moment they closed, Zara lifted her hand, and a wash of aquamarine Mana vapor swirled outward in a ring. The ring expanded until it hit the edges of the room, where it flashed once before zipping upward to erect a privacy warding.

"Thanks, Zara. I suppose, before we get into everything, we should start from the beginning."

With as few words as possible, Felix sketched out the events of the past few days, starting with the first, disastrous fight against the Grandmaster. Some of it they already knew, such as meeting Isla in her guise as Naos or finally finding Beef. He told them of the Tomb beneath the sands, of the crystalline city built there and a vault very much like the Labyrinth in Shelim, containing a similar captive. He skimmed over the details on the fighting and glossed over the gut-wrenching terror he'd felt as he saw his friends cut down, but Felix lingered over the array the Paladins had been utilizing.

"That explains their power source," Alister said as he slapped the table. "The Paladins had a barrier around them, preventing us from doing any real damage to them. It was a protection spell like I'd never seen, and when I noticed the sigaldry relays on their Manaships, I simply thought it was some new, frightful design."

"New maybe, but it's not repeatable," Felix said, before frowning. "At least, I hope not."

"The knowledge that the Hierophant can drain and repurpose a Primordial's power is concerning," Zara said slowly. "Far more so than what the Highest Flame was doing. It, at least, seemed to have been designed to siphon the creature's power. That cage of complex arrays around the Primordial that you mentioned, Felix. That was clearly intentional, and had the Urge breached it to extract pieces of the dead Primordial, it would have broken apart, much like how you say it did when the Paladins altered it."

"That the ancient Ahkestrians and the Nym were involved in entombing the beast is no surprise," Isla said. She was drumming her fingers on the table top, her lips pursed. "Could more of their ruins hold hidden Primordials? *Could* this be replicated?"

"I don't think so. The catalyst of the entire attempt appeared to be an artifact from the Pathless. They called it a piece of the god's Regalia," Felix said.

Beef squirmed in his seat and opened his mouth, but Vess spoke over him. "That was what they promised the Grandmaster they would sacrifice to help the Urge," she said. "I *had* found it unlikely they would part with such a rare item."

"An artifact of Divine provenance is far more than rare. You're sure?" Isla asked. "Beef made no mention of this."

"Oh yeah, it was Divine," Felix said, remembering the visceral encounter he had with a man made of light. It had been brief, but intense. "A tiny fragment of the Divine, but still there."

"How could you tell the Divine from anything else, Felix? They are not baubles at a market."

"I trust Felix's judgment in this," Zara said, cutting off her fellow Chanter.

Isla gave the Naiad a look that Felix couldn't quite read before smoothing her features. "Of course. Then, if it was of Divine origin, the chance of them attempting this again is very slim. Correct me if I am wrong, but the rest of the Pathless' Regalia was lost some two hundred years ago, yes?"

Zara smirked. "Mysteriously so, yes."

Vess gasped. "No! The Attack On The Light? That was you?"

"The Cantus Sodalus, yes," Isla said proudly. "And it wasn't an attack. That's just propaganda. They were simply tricked, they just can't admit it—"

"We are going far afield," Zara reminded them gently. "Let us return to the task at hand. Felix. Please continue."

"Right," Felix said, and finished telling them the rest. Of the breaking of the array, both Paladin and Primordial, and the consequences. Atar chipped in with his version of events, too, which explained some of the changes in the mage. Felix had worried that their empowered Link had somehow totally changed Atar, but it seemed a good portion of it was a result of jumping into the heart of a burning Urge.

"I don't know why you have to repeat all this; I told them already," Pit said from Felix's side. The tenku was still more than tall enough that his head, while seated on the floor, was level with everyone else. He was clearly bored.

"Sweetie, you left out several large pieces," Vess said, giving Pit an affectionate scratch.

"Like talking to a child," Isla muttered.

A knock sounded on one of the doors before it opened a crack. Ulnar, an Orc, leaned his head in. "My Lord, someone named Fiammetta wishes to enter."

"Oh. Yeah, sure let her in," Felix said. Atar's explanations had mentioned her and how she'd helped out during Felix's absence, turning her back on her home in order to do the right thing. He had no problem letting someone like that into this conversation.

Soon after, a Faun woman—looking very similar to Felix's idea of a satyr—slipped through the doors. She wasn't wearing her usual white, gold, and orange robes and instead wore ones that were predominantly a dark blue and yellow. On her shoulder was a brightly colored kingfisher. "Hello. This...bird told me I was wanted here?" she said, a bit hesitantly.

The bird in question flitted from Fiammetta's shoulder and landed atop Zara's outstretched finger. "Thank you, Keru. Fiammetta, please have a seat."

The Faun made her way to the table and sat, positioning herself near Vess and Pit. Felix, meanwhile, finished the last of the details, including his somewhat accidental release of an entire sea.

"We had all assumed it was you, anyway," Atar said.

"Apparently, there was a curse that locked away the sea. It also affected the Yttin, reducing them to their tiny size and withered features. I'm sure you've all seen how they look now," Felix said.

"That explains much. Their sudden transformation took us by surprise, though I think many simply did not notice in the hectic hours after the Masters and Matrons fell," Zara said.

"So, the question is, what do we do now?" Felix looked at everyone at the table. "Haim mentioned that the Triumvirate of the Pathless had decided to send forces to Nagast. I know the Mirk Enclosure can only last so long, especially if a Grandmaster gets involved, but I also know it's still standing. My Authority Screen confirms it."

"Why not just leave?" Beef asked. "Job's done here, right? Finished the quest, got the loot, let's move on."

"That's the question. I have no interest in ruling here, though I hold the Authority. I'm thinking I should appoint another chancellor."

"A wise decision," Zara agreed. "The true question is, however, who would you trust in such a position of power?"

"It is worse than that," Vess added. "This city is in shambles. As I told you, Felix, the Paladins are still at large. A great number of them were stranded when the Storm Ward activated and brought down all of the Manaships, and now they're hidden in a hundred bolt holes. A number are Adept Tier, and the rest are all Journeyman Tier, far too strong for the general populace to defend against. Even the private guards of the Merchant lords are Journeyman, at *best*, and they have no interest in protecting the common folk."

"Ahm, if I may," Fiammetta said softly. Her face, lightly freckled with a wide nose and large eyes, swiveled between them all as if she wasn't sure where to look. "Apart from the Paladins, the city is also suffering due to its sudden...lack of leadership."

Atar wheezed in laughter. "Right. The Matrons and Masters are dead, and the Temple Knights aren't much better off."

They explained for Felix's benefit. Most who fought against them had died in the struggle, while the destruction of the Highest Flame turned the rest catatonic. Unable to move or do much more than breathe, they withered and died within hours as their cores slowly extinguished themselves. The Matrons and Masters had fared the worst, with a huge amount of their power tied to the Urge, but the Temple Knights had all been busted back down to Apprentice Tier, and many were still in bed recovering from their broken Tempers. Isla expressed some doubt that they would live, and those who did might never again attain the power they'd lost.

"The only ruling body that remains in Ahkestria is the Merchant's Council, and the nobility to a lesser extent," Fiammetta said. Felix could hear eerie, strained music from her Spirit, as well as sense a deep gulf of exhausted grief. She was not doing as well as she made it seem...and Felix was willing to bet a number of her Skills suffered deeply from the Urge's demise. "In the single day since the battles concluded, we have received close to fifty missives requesting an audience with the new Lord of Ahkestria."

"You think they'll fight for control of the city?" Felix asked.

Fiammetta nodded vehemently. "Absolutely. This city remains an economic powerhouse. The Mana crystals mined here are worth thousands upon thousands of crowns in the farther-flung areas of the Continent....though the lack of Manaship travel will hurt trade dramatically."

"Hm," Felix said, pacing at the head of the table. "So, in order to manage the powers of the city, we need a chancellor who can stand up to the merchants and the nobility. Not to mention their armed militias they have on their estates. Am I missing anything?"

"No that's about it," Alister said with a weak grin. "Anyone come to mind?"

"Maybe," Felix said, his Mind tracking down a hundred different paths. "But the question is, can I trust them to rule well?"

"Trust is good, but it is in short supply," Isla said with a sharp gesture of her hand. "What you need is someone you can predict and control."

"No." Felix rejected that out of hand. "I'm not controlling anyone. Not ever."

"I mean with market pressures or access to their riches," the Chanter said, as if it were the most obvious thing in the world. "It is how Authority is parceled out and fealty is maintained. The strong rule, and all others fall in line."

Felix's frown only deepened. "That may be how things have gone on the Continent, but it's not how it *should* be."

"Perhaps not, but you'd be hard-pressed to convince the noble Houses of that, let alone the Merchant's Council," she said with a shrug. "Authority, levels, and gold. It's all of it power, and without them, I doubt you'll long hold onto this Territory."

"Gold," Felix muttered. "Trade. The merchants relied on Manaships to transport goods, right?"

"That is correct. Sometimes, they would use overland transport, but the dangers of the Cursewinds was too great," Fiammetta answered. "Now...I suppose ships will have to be made."

"But that takes time, and are there any ship builders in Ahkestria?" Felix asked.

"I somehow doubt it," Atar said. "What are you getting at?"

"Trade. If they can't trade with the outside world, what if we bring the outside world to them. Sorta." Felix summoned his notification and flicked it at all of them.

You May Erect A Single Beacon In Your New Territory!
Choose Placement.

"This...this is brilliant," Alister said. "You'd have sole access to this city."

"Indeed, this will prove an effective way to hold the merchants and nobles accountable," Zara said. Her sharp-toothed smile was like a banner of approval.

Felix gripped the sword at his belt, his Inheritor's Will, and focused his Mind upon it. "Karys?"

The sword glowed, gathering drifting wisps of green-gold Mana vapor along its length, and a voice echoed out into the chamber. It sounded like nothing so much as a kindly old man. "Lord Autarch! Are you well? I have not heard from you in days!"

"I'm fine, Karys. I'm fine." Among them all, only Isla and Fiammetta had never seen him do this before, and their shocked expressions were pretty amusing. "We'll catch up a bit later. Right now, I have questions."

"Ah. How may I be of service?"

"How is our supply of healing potions, salves, and ointments?"

"At an all-time high. Aenea has had the alchemy team working double shifts to press their Skills to the next Tier. There is a great plenty to use in trade or charitable aid, not to mention the alchemical reagents we've collected. Harvesting has continued apace as well. Our stores are filling quite rapidly; it would do us good to unload some of it for currency or direct trade."

"It should help, I imagine, that my Chancellor will be one of the few with access to the Beacon," Felix said.

"I would say so, yes," Vess agreed with a grin. "Authority is one thing, but the merchants will understand this far better. In fact, gathering them to you before erecting this new Beacon would be wise. A direct link, showing them the Authority you and whoever you choose as chancellor would wield."

"I feel like gathering everyone up would take time, though, time we don't have. For a couple reasons." Felix continued pacing. "How are your supplies right now, Isla? Are we in dire need of healing potions?" Felix asked.

The Chanter took a moment to gather herself. The one-two punch of his Beacon and talking sword seemed to have rattled her, but she rallied. "My...abilities are mighty, but I have limits. We've been forced to portion out our healing supplies, though we've attempted to do so conservatively. Those who could heal from their trauma naturally are bandaged and given basic salves for Status Condition prevention, and that is it. Potions and more complicated alchemy remains in stock. For now."

Vess shook her head. "But many of the structures around Ahkestria have collapsed or have structural damage. Another storm surge, and we could see a wave of new gravely injured citizens. Would that wipe out our stores?"

"It would."

Felix nodded. "Then I'll summon the Beacon now. I don't care much about grandstanding, if it's at the cost of people's lives. The only real question is, where to put it?"

Fiammetta cleared her throat, not quite meeting Felix's eyes. "I have an idea."

Felix led the way into the inner sanctum of the Temples of Elemental Fire, followed by his Shadows and friends. In addition to the overcast gloom above, the blackened firepits and snuffed torches served to render the lavish edifice gray and drab. With their leadership dead or neutered, Fiammetta told him that the only remaining residents were the junior attendants and initiates, not yet dedicated to the Flame, but without any other place to go.

Instantly, Felix had spotted them, watching their procession through the pristine halls, and their fear was palpable to him. He felt torn as they had marched past them all. He and his people had turned their entire world upside down in a matter of hours, but their leaders and the Urge itself had been sacrificing people to gain power, and that was unacceptable.

Someone had to stop it, and Felix wasn't sorry that it had been them.

Within the inner sanctum, Felix beheld the ghost of a battle. Splintered and charred wood and stone was everywhere, the fine details of a place of worship rendered into chaotic debris. Swaths of melted stone surrounded the center of the room, dominated by what Atar said once was the Altar of the Highest Flame. It was a huge bronze basin, easily thirty feet wide when it was whole. Now, it was sundered, split almost in half, and as empty and dead as the Temple itself. Yet as Felix approached the nadir of the inner sanctum, he could feel something stir in the air.

"Felix..." Atar said, almost at the same time Pit chirruped in worry.

"I feel it," he assured them both. There was a remnant potency there, and it tasted of ash and char, mingled with the familiar, dissonant undertones of the Primordial of Withering Dust. Felix took a deep breath. Mana and Essence, baked into the brick and tile and bronze by countless generations of the Urge and its subterranean, sacrificial captive. Woven into that was the weight of that history, of unwilling sacrifices mingling with a sense of grievous burden. It was the invisible component that he'd sensed within Essence so many months ago, and which he'd only recently found the word for: significance. Time and emotion and the persistence of memory, all pressed together within the flow of Mana and physical matter. If the Grand Harmony wove reality out of Mana, then Essence was its counterpoint...and significance was the accumulation of both, somehow.

Felix drew back, afraid to get lost in the sensation of what he felt, and called to his people. "Stay back. I have to clear this."

Chthonic Tribute!

His Skill sounded, a roaring cry within his core that was picked up and echoed by the Hunger at its center. A ferocious eagerness and savage glee answered Felix's call, and the stone and tile before him was rendered into glowing dust. The basin resisted, but the leverage of Felix's Willpower, Intent, and his Hunger's dire Need proved too much for it. Soon, all of the metal, stone, and gemstones of the Altar were pulled into his channels, deposited into the branches of his Divine Tree. Everything that bore traces of the Urge's worship and power, Felix took for himself. It was a fair amount, though sadly not enough to weave a single Pillar. He pushed that thought away.

What was left was a bare patch of earth, dusty soil, and rock in the midst of crafted opulence. Felix channeled his Mana, sounding Stone Shaping and sculpted the bare, orange stone beneath the sanctum. He raised it, forming it into a wide, raised platform and climbed atop it. With a flick of his Will, his Authority Screen activated.

Do You Wish To Place Your Beacon?
Y/N

"Yes. Here is good," he said.

All at once, System energy surged inward, roaring across his Affinity and coalescing on a point just below the stone platform. Rock buckled and broke as a tall cylinder rose from the depths, shimmering with multi-hued light. Stone and crystal alike flowed like water, forming the cylinder into an eight-foot-tall lamppost. From the crystalline portions, the light shifted until it was a slow, alternating mix of red-gold and blue-white. The colors of his cores. With a final sound like a pealing bell, the Beacon finished forming.

New Beacon Placed!
Authority Strengthened!
Do You Wish To Access Your Storage Facility?

Yes. A part of his Mind and Spirit reached inward toward the strange connection between Beacons and Storage. The larger part of Felix, however, was aware of eyes watching him. Not his allies and guards, who were looking onward with expressions that ranged from awed to satisfied...but to the shadowed balconies and half-shut doorways around the inner sanctum.

"This is for all people. This is evidence of my care for this city, this Territory," he said on a whim, pitching his powerful voice outward to catch his silent audience. He accessed his Storage Facility, reaching into a storeroom thousands of miles away, and plucked out four five-foot cube crates. They materialized out of thin air, landing beside him with the sound of glass vials clinking against one another. "Isla and Vess, could you see to the distribution of healing items? If you need more, let me know. For now, I'll be the only one with access to this."

Vess nodded, her dimpled smile as bright as the sun, while Isla looked a touch overwhelmed.

"If you need help, just come and see us," Felix said, again speaking to the hidden attendants. "We won't turn anyone away."

He sensed several figures slipping back out, some running away, and contained a sigh. But the offer had been put out there. Felix stepped off the platform and clapped his hands. "Alright. What's next?"

CHAPTER TEN

Atar hobbled from the temple complex alone and deep in thought. All around him, his friends and allies moved past, hunched against the incessant rainfall, including Felix and his squadron of muscle. It seemed overkill to the mage, especially when the two Frost Giants trundled past, the ground shaking just a bit beneath their tread. Far more so when Atar thought on the power packed into Felix's much taller frame. He shuddered, and only partly due to the cold. The sight of Felix devouring the Altar of the Highest Flame had made him feel uncomfortable—it reminded him all too much of himself.

Atar coughed, and the wracking convulsion conspired against him. His shudder, weakened grasp, and the rain-slick stone sent his metal staff skidding away from him, and Atar stumbled...only to be caught by the warm grip of another.

"Atar! Are you alright?" Alister said, pulling the mage back to his feet. "You shouldn't have left by yourself. Here, take this."

Alister pressed a vial of medicinal restorative toward him, but Atar firmed his grip on his staff and turned away from it. "I'm fine, Alister."

"Of course you are," the force mage said, uncorking the restorative and holding it to Atar's mouth.

Brow furrowed, Atar huffed a breath that turned into another wracking cough. "Fine," he choked out and grabbed the vial. His partner was only trying to help, but that didn't mean Atar had to like it. He coughed again but kept it down, which meant Alister nodded and gripped Atar's elbow. Gently, and without making more of a fuss, the noble helped him walk down the thoroughfare.

The support was appreciated, and the quiet moreso, but it only sent

Atar's Mind tumbling deeper into thought. *How'd I even survive?* he wondered, and not for the first time. His memories were hazy. He'd told everyone that he'd leaped into the Urge's flames then fuzzed over the rest, ending with absorbing the flames of the Highest Flame with his evolved version of Strength Ignition. Atar hadn't mentioned the Tier IV Link that existed between Felix and his friends, if only because he still didn't know what to make of it, or how it had altered him so much.

you destroyed the me that was.

A ghostly flame kindled above Atar's shoulder, white with a glimmering crimson at its center. Only Atar could see it, evidenced by the many times it had manifested itself and remained unnoticed by all save for the mage himself. It hadn't any eyes or features, much as the Highest Flame itself, but Atar could feel its gaze on him like two tiny points of heat. "You deserved it," he muttered.

"What was that?" Alister asked.

"Nothing, just...thinking aloud," Atar said. Perhaps it was the tremble in his voice that hid his clumsy lie, but Alister didn't question it. The flame, meanwhile, vanished. Somewhat sullenly, if Atar were to judge such things.

Did I truly consume the Highest Flame? An Urge? That part was the most unbelievable to Atar. *That's Felix behavior, not me. But...if that weren't the case, how did I get my...passenger?* Atar wasn't sure if the ghostly white flame was a remnant of the former Urge or something entirely new. All he was sure of was that it was another symptom of his considerable distress.

During his time in the healing ward, Isla had worked among the injured, along with Vess, stitching wounds and applying poultices that had worked a lot more than they should have. The slight Chanter hadn't used magic that Atar could sense, but she utilized strange noises—subharmonics, she called them. They were what accomplished the healing, as far as the fire mage could understand.

Couldn't do much for me, though, he thought as he glanced down at his hands, still quivering from his coughing fit. They were unblemished—surprising for a man who'd been on fire—but the gray coloration was disfigurement enough. Earlier, he'd managed to snag a mirror from a dead man's kit and saw that his hair had lightened, and his eyes...his eyes were red, lit from within like banked coals.

It was a horrifying visage, and Atar found himself tucking his hood a bit farther over his face as he urged Alister down some less well-traveled streets back to the estate. Few were walking the roads after everything, but that didn't matter. It was bad enough that Felix and Fiammetta had to see him like this; he didn't need some ancient acquaintances perusing his new features. *Does everyone look like this after they die?*

His partner pushed back his hood and dabbed at Atar's forehead, where a small cut still bled a little. Atar groaned in annoyance. "Stop fussing over me, Alister. I'm fine."

"You were punched through the Altar of an Urge that you killed by your former teacher who is a Grandmaster, while being burned alive," Alister said, ticking off each ridiculous point on his good hand. "You are not fine, and you cannot convince me otherwise. Your fancy new Title might have changed you and healed the worst of it, but I'm not risking it. The Paladins are still about."

Atar smiled, not because of the danger in his partner's words, but because not once had Alister made a fuss about his looks. He hadn't flinched when Atar had climbed bloody and bruised out of the Altar's twisted remains, half on fire. Alister had simply beaten out the flames, pulled him to safety, and had been taking care of him ever since. What made his smile falter, however, was the reminder of his Title.

New Title!
Reborn (Legendary)
You have absorbed the potency and fire of an elemental Urge, claiming a large portion of its significance as your own. Due to your Link to a Primordial, the attunement of your core, and your Born Trait (Heart of Fire), you have been remade!
+100 Willpower, Intelligence, Intent.

The bonuses were extraordinary, but the Title itself was...suggestive. Atar didn't like thinking about it.

Almost as concerning, his Race had even changed in the wake of his confrontation with the Highest Flame. Now it read as "Human (???)" and he'd never heard of such a thing. But it meant his gains per level had changed, too. Instead of a set three free stat points per level, Atar now received four free stat points...and one stat point in Intelligence, Intent, and Perception. It was a significant boost to his potential, far more than he'd ever hoped to claim, and it was exciting. Less exciting, however, were the consequences of that change.

Alister pressed the back of his hand against Atar's gray forehead and tutted. "You're burning up again. Are you sure this is normal?"

"Feels normal. No Status Conditions, and my Health is at full," Atar said with a shrug and rueful twist of his lips as they stumped down the street. "Can't say any of this is normal, though."

His partner sighed. "Too true. It concerns me that neither Isla nor Zara can identify what is happening to you. I'd feel so much more at ease if we simply had some expectations to manage."

Atar agreed, but he only shrugged again. Even that was tough. The consequences of his change was more than a new Title and Race, it was affecting his Body itself. The Aspect hadn't changed but it felt on the cusp of it...after all, only a few more Skill levels, and he would Temper into Adept in two of his three Aspects, one of which was his Body. His Spirit was not far behind, leaving only his Mind trailing by a few more Skill levels. Adept Tier could mean everything would change once again, and Atar only hoped it meant for the better.

"I need to train, Alister. My Skills...they've changed as much as my skin and eyes. I need to know what I can do now. What to expect."

"What you need is rest," the noble insisted in that infuriatingly calm voice. "Do you think you can withstand the rigors of training?"

"...No," Atar groused, more than a little unwillingly. "I can barely walk. But that doesn't change the fact that soon we will leave here, and I need to know my capabilities."

"Perhaps gaining your Adept Tier Body will improve you. That is a thought I've had, but what if it doesn't? What if all of this," Alister said, gesturing at Atar's everything with his free hand. "What if it only worsens your condition?"

Atar tried to snarl in annoyance, but it devolved into a hacking cough. "Then so be it. I'd rather move forward than linger back in fear."

They paused, and Atar could sense Alister's conflicting emotions. *Hear* them. Low, staccato notes of worry and frustration intermingled with...grief. *Oh, Alister.* "I will be fine, you know. This can't stop me."

The force mage pursed his lips. "I don't like when you listen to my emotions. It's cheating."

"I call it creative communication," Atar shot back, smiling gently. His partner's worry transmuted into begrudging amusement. "I will be fine."

"Blood and ash, you will," Alister said. "If Yyero wants you, he'll have to face me down first."

Atar grinned.

"Come, love," Alister said with renewed vigor. He pulled gently on Atar's elbow, guiding him forward. "There are mugs of mulled wine and a plush seat by the fire beckoning to us. It would be a shame to keep them waiting."

"Hm." Atar kindled a burning white star above his free hand, and the white flame flickered around it, within it. He grunted before dismissing them both. "Wine sounds good."

"Felix? May I walk with you?"

Felix looked up from within the bristling embrace of his Shadow guards, his Authority Screen open in front of him. They had left the temple complex and headed back along the main roads to the Grandmaster's estate, and the guards apparently weren't taking any chances. Pit padded beside him, but it wasn't him who had spoken. "Make a hole, folks," he said as he closed his screens. Only then did they part to reveal Zara standing with a bemused expression. "Zara. Of course you can walk with me."

She stepped into the ring of armed guards with a quiet grace, very similar to the way Vess moved. She likely had a Skill for it, but he wouldn't have been surprised if it was something with the Chant. "They protect you well."

"I'm not sure why," he said the moment Zara erected a privacy ward. "I can certainly handle myself."

"Ah. Their loyalty is commendable, even if it is not necessary."

"Hm," Felix said, noncommittally. "What is it you need?"

The Chanter let the silence stretch several paces before she answered. "You do not trust me."

Pit trilled in amusement. "Nope."

"Pit," Felix said. His Companion only shrugged and padded forward, still close enough to touch, but at least pretending not to be interrupting the conversation. To Zara, he shrugged a single shoulder. "It isn't that I don't trust you. I will admit that I don't trust Isla, though. Your Cantus Sodalus, either."

"We are dedicated—"

"To your own causes," Felix said. "Every organization is, and here on the Continent, that seems to include an angle for more power. Can you say it isn't?"

Zara took a tight breath and expelled it through her nose. "I cannot. All of us chase after power. It is the way of the world. That does not mean I do not have your best interests at heart, Felix."

"Maybe. But agendas shift, and I cannot trust that your order will align with mine forever." Felix held up a hand, stopping Zara as she opened her mouth. "I agree that the Ruin is a threat. I agree that we need to get the Unbound away from the Hierophant and anyone else that would manipulate or use them. But that does not mean I will be delivering any of them into the Cantus' hands."

"I see. And I cannot fault you, Felix. Your introduction to this world has been as harsh as any I've seen, and troubles continue to pile atop your shoulders." Zara folded her hands behind her back and lifted her chin as they kept walking forward. "Would that I could ease those burdens for you, but the mantle of Authority is yours by right. As much as you may decry it, might does provide authority in all worlds. That you have defeated threats beyond your advancement—far beyond, in many cases—only speaks to the worthiness of your rule."

Felix frowned. "I find the idea of 'might makes right' to be short-sighted in the extreme, Zara. Of those in power that I've seen, few are what I would call kind, merciful, or wise. Everyone chases after power—for protection, for dominance, for all sorts of reasons that I'd simply boil down to selfishness. Yeah, I killed some Lords and monsters and a couple Primordials.

"Yeah, I took a bite out of a freaking *goddess*. But does that make me any more able to rule? More worthy?" Felix laughed, and it was like all of his sour disbelief and frustration escaped into the sound. Like a monster crawling out of his throat to bare its teeth. "No. I don't know the first thing about ruling, about this whole damn world. Yet here I am, piled high with more Authority than I can handle, and gearing up to go fight another war. To face off against an empire and gods and who knows what else. Fine. I'm game. But things are changing. I won't have 'mercy' or 'compassion' be called afflictions of the weak, and if my people are growing stronger by remaining within my influence, then they are damn sure going to follow my lead."

Zara was silent as Felix tried his best to calm down and simply breathed, letting the cool rains soak into his overheated skin. He realized he was literally steaming a little with each drop of rain that struck. The quiet persisted for a while longer, but Zara clearly had more to ask. He sighed. "What else, Zara?"

"The Primordial," she said, and this time she glanced outward at the guards around them, despite her own ward. "How did you defeat it? I noticed your explanation to the others left out specifics. Was that because of Isla and myself?"

"No, you've earned at least a little goodwill and trust, Zara. Isla has not."

"Did you...consume it, as before?" she asked.

"Nope. Couldn't."

Zara furrowed her fine brows. "What do you mean?"

"The part of me that's the most Primordial is a little patch of my core that I call my Hunger. Most of my consumed targets are rendered into Essence and stored within my core space, but when it's too much, I've had to either shove the overflow into my Hunger or share it with Pit," he explained.

"Hunger. Hm, and does this Hunger have a will of its own?" Zara asked.

"It does, or something like it. After my unsuccessful fight against the Grandmaster, it had finally reached a saturation point. The thing refused to take any more Essence in, which meant my core space began to act up, and my Chthonic Tribute wouldn't work right."

"I was unaware that could happen. Was it resolved when you Tempered to Adept?"

"It was," Felix said with a nod. "It seemed my Hunger needed its own upgrade, and it's apparently tied to my Aspects. Body most of all."

"Fascinating. But you said you could not consume it...so you had not completed Tempering when the Primordial was defeated?" Zara asked.

"Yeah. I had to get creative. Sovereign of Flesh to rip it apart, tearing free the flesh curse—which, by the way, was a Divine curse, I found out—then I had to divide the Essence and significance with some volunteers." Felix grinned as Zara's calm demeanor faltered. "What?"

"Divine? The flesh curse that spreads a Primordial's influence like a disease is caused by the gods?" Zara let her hands go and planted them on her hips. "How do you—no, explain that later. You divided the Essence and significance from a Primordial...with whom?"

"Those who wished to help," Felix said. Seeing Zara flounder a bit improved his mood quite a lot, he'd found. "I gave them all a choice."

Her eyes skipped to Pit...then in the direction they had both seen Atar leave.

"You didn't. Is that why—?"

"Sorta with Pit. He's actually a Primordial now, in addition to his new Evolution. But for Atar...I actually don't know why he looks like that. I wanted to press him more during his explanation, but he looks like he needs to take a nap for a few days. I'll ask him later. But yes. Him, Pit, Vess, Evie, Harn, and Beef all helped out by taking a portion of the Primordial of Withering Dust's power." Felix marveled at that a bit. Everyone had helped him, without hesitation or question. "I think they've all changed in some way, but other than Vess, I haven't had much confirmation. I still need to check out her core space, let alone the others."

"Yes, that should be a priority and something we can do together later this afternoon. I think resolving any lingering questions there would be the wisest course of action," she said. "How did you do such a thing? Other than Pit, who you share an extraordinary bond with, only Beef was nearby. The rest were literal miles away."

"Tier III Links. Tier IV now, actually," Felix said by way of explanation. When Zara's face remained just as confused, he sighed. "Damn, I was hoping you would know more about them. The connections that I've been sensing since becoming...this," he gestured at himself. "Well they kicked up a notch. Now the System is calling them Links, and I can apparently send power through them. Not sure if I can send more, though, like my Mana or Stamina or something. I recover those so fast, it might be useful if that were possible."

"Links. You are correct in assuming that I have not heard of them. So much has been Lost, but I have not heard of even the greatest of Sorcerers utilizing their Affinity in such a way. I believe you are right. It must be something to do with your Primordial nature. The Unseen Tide." She said the words, and Felix felt a sudden and faint pressure from them. It was gone in an instant, so fast that, had he not possessed perfect recall, he would have doubted it had happened. "And perhaps that can be used in our favor, to find the other Unbound. We must do the ritual again, and soon."

Felix nodded. "I'm all for that. The sooner we can find those poor people, the better off we all are."

"If you can continue to strengthen those Links, perhaps we may have a way to reach out across the Continent. Dreams and shared experiences are one thing, but direct communication would make our job far easier," Zara added.

"Later," he said. "If we can get this city stuff resolved, then we can get moving back to Nagast as soon as—"

An enormous sound ripped through the sky, like the bugle of a horn the size of a skyscraper. It even drowned out the constant thunder. What followed was a bloom of fire and light to the north, high enough to be visible over the six story mansions around them.

The guards pressed closer, weapons drawn. "My Lord! We need to move you off the street! Someone is attacking—!"

Lieutenant Errol turned and found Zara standing there, smoothing down her dark robes. She was alone, save for the crackle of lightning around her feet. "The Autarch has taken a personal interest, it seems." As one, the Shadows all looked up at Felix as he rose atop a pillar of brilliant, blue-white lightning, with Pit at his side. "I would suggest we follow. Quickly."

CHAPTER ELEVEN

"Step away from the Manaship!" Vess shouted over the whipping winds. Lightning flashed above them, and the rain was even more violent here, at the edge of the Risen Ward. She had left the Temples of Elemental Fire, intent on finding Evie among the streets, and had instead found this.

"The Pathless does not recognize your Authority, wench!" their leader crowed from the ship's steering. "And the Paladins certainly don't, either!"

Arrayed on the deck of a damaged Manaship were thirty or so Paladins, their crimson armor covered in oiled greatcloaks that streamed rainwater onto the broken planks. The Manaship was in bad shape, but to Vess' amateur eye, it had fared far better than most struck by the storm. Its mainmast had survived, but most of its sails and all of its lower guidance fins were torn to shreds. It was anchored at a skydock at the edge of the Risen Ward, an area typically heavily controlled and guarded, and Vess could see a number of crumpled bodies around the loosened moorings.

"They killed the retainers," Fiammetta said at her side. She held a pair of maces made of hissing yellow Mana, and they cast a visible brilliance onto the street around them. "House Iretus runs the skydocks here. They must have salvaged the Manaship, and the Paladins stole aboard."

"Where are you planning to go, Captain?" Vess asked, pitching her voice over the storm. "The sky won't have you, and it's sixty strides to the sea below. You are trapped here. Best for your men if you come quietly, or else I cannot promise you will all survive."

The Paladins hefted longswords menacingly, as if daring them to approach as their fellows loosed ties and what sails remained. None of them were sailors, that was clear. The captain, however, never dropped his gaze from hers.

"Fah! The promises of a betrayer aren't worth much, Vessilia Dayne!" the captain shot back. Vess flinched at hearing her full name. "Aye, we know who you are, heiress! Just as we know the Hierophant won't tolerate treason from her Dukes. So go on, play at fighting for these heathens. We'll be waiting for you back home, eh?"

Vess gripped her partisan hard enough that, were it not made of exceptional materials, she would have crunched it into scrap. The captain was goading her into attacking him—he was an Adept, while the rest of his Paladins were surely Journeymen. Rushing onto the ship would be exactly the wrong move. She knew that, but it didn't stop the insidious promise from wriggling into her Mind. *Father. Father, will you remain safe as I walk this path?*

"Burn it all, we will. And they'll watch as you..."

She let her Perception spread, absorbing what she could of the environment and blocking out the loathsome Paladin. The docks were ahead, a series of stone bridges into the thin air surrounded by large, warehouse-like buildings. The Manaship was only one of several such craft, though it was the only one that seemed at all functional. Closer to hand were the shops and taverns of a normally bustling district, now shut and shuttered against the constant storm and especially against their conflict. A few eyes peered fearfully from behind well-appointed sills or silken curtains. Those in the Risen Ward, even the laborers, were fairly well off it seemed. Other than Fiammetta, Vess was alone on the paved street.

Oh? As the captain of the Paladins continued threatening her, she focused on a small sound to her left. A scraping of leather against stone and the tap of a harness pulled her Perception further, tugging at her gaze until she found a grizzled older man standing in the upper stories of a nearby inn, half-hidden by thick drapery. Their eyes met, and he raised a finger to his lips before making handsign at her. <Archers above. Stall.>

He was wearing livery that matched the downed soldiers by the skydock. *House Iretus*. Vess' eye flicked up to the roof, where she sensed several dark shapes barely silhouetted against the cloudy sky. *At least five archers. All of them Journeyman Tier.*

They were drawing a bead on the ranting Paladin captain, but the man only had eyes for Vess' spear and the flashy lights of Fiammetta's magic. "—cannot hope to overcome us. Your godling is dead! And your city is next!"

"Ignore him, your Grace. What should we do?" Fiammetta asked through gritted teeth.

Vess kept her face carefully neutral. "We end them. How many of those weapons can you manifest?"

"Enough, but I'm drawing on my own Mana store now...the air is too wet and cold to pull heat from the air." The former Disciple shuddered, her voice a mix of annoyance and awe. "I've never seen so much water."

"Hurry, damn you!" The captain shouted again, his men still furiously fumbling with the ship's lines. "I can tell by your stricken faces that you do not wish to fight. Run and save your lives, heiress!"

"If you are so confident, Captain, then come and face me," Vess said, ignoring the hiss of alarm from Fiammetta. She sauntered forward until only thirty strides of dock separated them, her blue and white partisan held in a loose grip, as if she were unworried about the threat the man posed. "You are an Adept, are you not? Surely, you could best both of us with ease." Vess dropped into a stance, her feet finding the sixth Form of the Dragoons, her spear lifted up and wavering like a monster's stinger.

"You—! Fine!" he shouted, and with a single, overly violent yank, pulled free his own longsword. "I'll tear you to pieces, duchess or no, but first I'll let my men have—!"

"QOURRAHHH!"

The rest of the captain's words were drowned out by a sickening gurgle and guttural trumpeting. Vess drew back, stance abandoned, as a hunched creature covered in wet-slicked scales drove a short spear into the man's unprotected neck. It cried out, lifting its spear with preternatural Agility, and the Paladins all moved at once. Seven bolts of sizzling light tore through the air, striking the monster all at once and ripping it to pieces.

The guttural trumpeting didn't stop. In fact, to her horror, Vess watched as dozens of the monstrous fish people climbed aboard the Manaship...and the skydock itself.

"Your Grace!" Fiammetta shouted, and a shield of compacted yellow Mana blazed into being. A jagged spear crashed into it, skittering sideways and followed by two more. "There are twenty—no, thirty of them, at least! What...what are they?"

Elemental Eye!

Elemental Eye Failed.

Vess stepped around the heat shield and thrust her spear through the head of a charging monstrosity. It tore easily through its fish-like mouth, and it reflexively gnawed on the haft with jagged teeth. But its huge, bulbous eyes went glassy, and it sagged on her partisan and yanked it downward...just as another creature leaped into the opening.

Spear of Tribulations!

A Spear manifested out of air and metal Mana, woven so quickly and tightly together that the monstrosity impaled itself on it...and was launched back fifteen strides into two more of its kin.

"Solitary Tribulation!" she hissed, and the conjured weapon detonated into a storm of razor-sharp wind that shredded all three monsters.

Quick as its fellows, more Spears appeared in the air around Vess, floating above her shoulders like deadly, martial arms. She started for only a moment, realizing that her Skill had summoned not her usual seven Spears, but ten. Screams brought her attention back to the fight, as the docks before her filled with the horrid lizard-fish men. Fiammetta wielded her mace constructs in either hand, the heat type proving exceptionally effective against the monsters, but she was quickly being mobbed on all sides.

"Down!" a voice cried out, and both Vess and Fiammetta obeyed without thinking.

A rain of whistling arrows fell all around them, dozens of them, each one finding a fish-man through its head or chest. Bulbous eyes burst and thick, blue blood flooded onto the docks, but only some of the monsters were downed. Many barely paused in their assault, but instead grew more savage and feral, baring jagged fangs and abandoning their crude weapons to attack with tooth and claw.

Vess manipulated her Spears, spinning them into defensive arcs that kept the worst at bay as she fought back to Fiammetta's side. She shouldn't have worried, however, as the Faun was laying about herself with an impressive array of heat-forged weaponry that changed with every strike she made.

"Don't! You! Come! Closer!" she howled, each word punctuated by the bloody squelch of fish flesh pulping beneath her Skill. The smell of foul, baked fish was overpowering. "Burn me, you all stink!"

"Keep it up; we need to keep these creatures out of the town! Archers!" Vess called, parrying another crude billhook with her Spears. The men atop the inn loosed another volley, dropping several more fish men who tried to run deeper into the streets. "Sound the alarm! Get more men down here! Who knows where else they're coming up!"

Vess didn't wait to see if they complied. Instead, she let two more of her Spears burst, shredding a clutch of the enemy and driving a hole in their defenses...but they were swiftly plugged up with more foes.

I cannot end this without fighting properly, she realized and flared her nostrils. Within her core space, the mountains rang out in the ceaseless winds, and she embraced her new Skill. Dragoon's Footwork, Grace, and Wall Run had vanished. Under the influence of Felix's Link, they had all fused into one. Evolved.

On The Wing!

A rush of Mana and Stamina fled her immediately, funneled into the swirling patterns of her new Skill. Immediately, however, Vess' movements became more fluid and graceful, as if her Dexterity and Agility seamlessly combined into something far greater. Her Spears wove to her Will, but her Body moved almost without thought, Vess' partisan intercepting wild strikes with such ease it was like fighting children. She parried and countered, her riposte tearing through hearts and skulls so fast that her weapon was a blur.

Atop the ship, something exploded, ripping through the sky like a signal flare of light and fire. Bolts of golden radiance shot in all directions and far more natural-colored flames raced across unfurled sails. Somewhere close by, the bugle of alarm tore into the night, signaling the attack.

Yet Vess didn't care. Couldn't. Her core space resounded with the vibration of On The Wing, and it sent shivers of resonance throughout her entire being. Spear and partisan danced, haft and honed edge one with her hand, arm, an extension of her Body and Spirit and Mind. Within that sound, echoes of the Primordial Essence still lingered, expanding until the blue sky of her core space that swelled above her mountain temple opened into a deeper, chasmic darkness. Stars glittered in that expanse, each one a brilliant, multicolored gemstone. And there, drowning out the light of a silver moon, were two stars so brilliant, they sent pulses of light racing across the crags. Red-gold. Blue-white.

Tier IV Link Established!
On The Wing is level 76!
On The Wing is level 77!

A notification she'd seen more than once flashed by again, almost in time with that pulsing light. Connections and meaning chased after it, stark against the endless wind of her core space. Her Body spun and fought, and inside her Mind whirled, carried aloft on ancient wings. The Skill was flight—it was evading a dark fate in the dead of night as teeth closed around the throats of those too slow to flee. Of death on her heels, while life sang like fire in her blood.

The vibrations shook Vess, literally and metaphorically, plucking her soul like a lute string. Fury filled her—fury and a terrible, sourceless grief. She fed it into her thrusts, ripping through slimy flesh with each hit. The beasts were vicious and hit like a kicking Avum, but each of her strikes was catastrophic for them. Two or three fell with every sweep of her Spears, the shockwave of her thrusts sending others skidding backward and tangling their footing. It wasn't just her impressive new Skills and recent levels—Vess was tearing through this enemy far faster than anyone else on the field, Fiammetta, Archers, or Paladins. As their lizard-like snouts glistened in the fire and rain, she realized why.

Title: Draconic Slayer III (Rare)
You have faced and overcome your enemies, earning the fear and anger that your very presence elicits. You are the hunter; they are the prey. Boost damage against and reduce damage from the draconic Type by 30%!

Dragons!

She leaped, and On The Wing sent her soaring into the sky, synergizing so perfectly with her Born Trait—Exalted Vault—that it was like she took flight. A thin barrier of golden light surrounded the burning ship for a moment...before dark arrows shattered it to glittering pieces. More of the creatures screeched into the night, and a sudden secondary explosion lit up the Manaship, ripping the deck apart as the monsters were thrown back, and Paladins were thrown into thin air. Their screams faded swiftly into the roar of the storm and battle.

Draconic Stormfall!

Vess and all ten of her Spears twisted in mid-air, her leap frozen at the apex of momentum, before the wind itself howled at her back. As if a column of the tempest clung to her, Vess dropped back down into the mass of fish men like descending judgment. All eleven of her Spears hit the stone-paved thoroughfare in a ring around her, and the earth buckled before erupting into a vicious, razor wind cyclone thirty strides wide and twice that tall.

Draconic Stormfall is level 71!

You Have Killed An Unknown Monstrosity (x22)!
XP Earned!

For a brief moment, the force of her impact scattered the driving rain...before it and the macabre fall of corpse parts descended upon the battlefield. "By spear and Skill and magic's descent," she recited from memory. "We suffer no dragons to live."

Elemental Eye!

Whether because she defeated some in battle, or some other strangeness, her Eye pierced their defenses now. Yet she found herself just as confused as before.

Name: Fathom Hatchling

Type: Draconic (Manawarped)
Level: 45
HP: 1394/1443
SP: 1003/1127
MP: 400/400
Lore: Unknown

"Manawarped?" she repeated. "What is that?"

But her questions were pressed from her Mind, because more of the wretched creatures were climbing up the sides of the city as she spoke. Many clambered atop the burning Manaship as the few remaining Paladins sought to ignite its sputtering engine while dozens more emerged from the manicured lip of the topmost layer. Their claws dug into stone like softened clay, and hundreds of luminous fish eyes rushed at her with cold, predatory malice.

"SKREEEAWW!"

A mighty, shrieking screech sundered the air more completely than the thunder ever could, and in its wake came a shimmering crescent of blinding Mana. It sliced down from above and curved at the last second to cut a twenty-foot-wide swath through the Hatchlings. Bolts of lightning followed, frozen like spears of galvanized brilliance and shattering to a staccato, concussive beat of fish man screams and thunder. Pit dropped to the ground, landing in an easy crouch before looming tall before the now-hesitating Fathom Hatchlings.

"Come get some!" he growled.

"Pit! Is Felix—" Vess started, but was answered almost immediately.

A bolt of lightning forty strides across blasted from the heavens, shattering into the assembled Hatchlings and utterly eradicating them. Blood and flesh were turned to a horrendous black vapor in an instant, all of which swirled and streamed back upward. A dire typhoon that terminated in a man dressed all in black.

No, she realized. *Not dressed. Scaled. And not Felix.*

The storm above them went deathly still.

That's the Fiend.

CHAPTER TWELVE

Stone Shaping!

Dusty-brown Mana screamed from Felix's channels and slammed into the earth, spreading rapidly in a liquid deluge that did nothing to budge the strange monstrosities below him. What did affect them was when he claimed the very stone beneath their feet within the steel vice of his Will, and *heaved.*

Stone Shaping is level 81!

The entire roadway lifted at an angle, pressed upward so fast the fish men were hurtled from their feet...and straight off the cliffs. Gurgling screeches punctured the sudden quiet, the storm above him gone still, while bursts of razor-sharp winds tore apart the creatures he'd missed. Below his scaled feet, Vess and that Faun girl fought dozens of the fish men, deftly avoiding their jagged claws but starting to flag against the relentless onslaught. He could...feel it, their weariness, even without activating his Voracious Eye. That, he used on the monsters.

Fathom Hatchlings? Felix clenched his jaw. *They were a problem for the Nagafolk, not here. How did they—the flooding,* he realized with a sour wash of disgust. *Because I flooded the entire flipping desert. Shit.*

The Fathom, a threat that had endangered one of his sworn peoples —the Naga—were supposed to be in the Ghreldan Hills beyond the Stormeater Mountains. Not climbing the walls of Ahkestria.

Clawed, bony hands scrabbled over the low wall at the city's edge. More Hatchlings were coming, and fast, according to his Perception.

Felix's senses snaked over the lip of the city and beheld over a hundred of the loathsome creatures scuttling up the stone cliffs like spiders.

"No more!" Felix lifted his arm and sent more of his Mana rushing outward through the rain. Dusty-brown hit the edge of the city, turning the blasted and scored stone into tumultuous terrain. The wall and cliff itself, for twenty feet below, tore apart into shifting, liquid sands that fell apart beneath the Hatchlings' claws. Many dropped, shrieking, into the sea. He did not get kill notifications for them, but that didn't matter. His goal was to keep them out of the city.

Yet Felix's Perception informed him that more were spreading into the streets, at least two dozen. He reached out with his Affinity, touching upon their Spirits for a moment to figure out their goal—and he immediately recoiled in horror. The Hatchlings were bundles of rabid bloodlust and a cold, alien madness. That small glimpse of their emotions was enough for him; Felix could tell what they wanted, and it curdled his stomach and stoked his rage.

They just wanted to kill.

He gathered himself, but before Felix could reach for his magic, a wave of aquamarine light coursed around the nearest corner and into the path of the creatures. His Shadows, headed by Zara, discharged from the wave of Mana and straight into a charge. Lightning flashed, and acidic Mana gathered along sword edges and blunt weaponry, all of which descended upon the Hatchlings without hesitation. The Shadows were weaker than the Fathom spawn, but it was clear they had kept up with their training. Strike after strike hit the Hatchlings, driving them back and seizing the momentum of the fight.

To his other side, Vess and Fiammetta rallied alongside a number of men and women in an unfamiliar uniform. Regardless, they were drawing and loosing black arrows with remarkable Dexterity, drowning the Hatchlings in a volley of projectiles.

"Go! We have this!" Pit shouted from the air beside him, just before unleashing another Dawn's Advent. The huge, glowing crescent of power scythed through more monstrosities before burying itself into the street. "Go! Stop them!"

A few more Fathom spawn had managed to avoid his Stone Shaped obstacles, cresting the wall when Felix finally relented. "None of you are welcome," he said, and a basso rumble shook his words. "This is *my* city."

Adamant Discord!

His strangest Skill grasped at the connections between him and the monsters, represented by gossamer threads of light that only Felix could see. Intent and Willpower wove together, gripping the oddly dense connections and pulling them taut. Lightning snaked along the invisible threads, a consequence of Felix's manipulation, squeezing even more fearful cries out of the Hatchlings.

Adamant Discord is level 81!

Felix threw himself forward, weakening his own connections to the air around him and wrenching on the stone below, letting his immense body weight send him careening over the city's edge. All around the lip of the skydock, bars of crackling blue-white lightning snapped into existence, and the gurgling cries reached a panicked crescendo. Felix fell, and he dragged all of the monsters with him.

So many! Felix's eyes widened as he dropped, free-falling from on high and witnessing the absolute enormity of the Fathom swarm. He had sensed a hundred or so before, but there were over a thousand of the loathsome spawn, most clinging to the sea-slicked stone of the city plateau and more crawling out of the crashing waves with every second. Felix flared Adamant Discord, snatching his metaphysical link to those closest—perhaps fifty or sixty—with his woven Willpower and Intent, tethering himself to those still climbing with wrist-thick cables of lightning. He jerked to a sudden stop, his own weight and momentum not enough...until he focused on the sea.

He reached.

The Skill latched onto the distant water, and a bond wider than the horizon and brighter than the sun briefly and intensely blazed. Blinding lightning wreathed him and *all* of the Hatchlings, until Felix felt like he had frozen in time and space. With a rippling shockwave of force, the inertia burst, and Felix rocketed downward so fast a cloud of compressing air appeared and shattered before him. Felix hit the water, and above him, every single Hatchling was torn in his wake.

He knifed through the water, not so much a sinking stone as a sharp blade, thrust with violent intent. Bolts of radiant electricity arced in all directions, the murky, dark waters illuminated by the captive monstrosities. Felix hit bottom, his clawed feet finding purchase in the sandy floor hundreds of feet below, while all around him, a tree of barbed light collapsed. The Hatchlings smashed into the sea floor, just as he did, but with none of the grace or fortitude—they pulped, bursting like overripe fruit.

You Have Killed A Fathom Hatchling (x648!)
XP Earned!

Others piled atop the first arrivals, cushioned by the gruesome pile of their brethren, and survived. The lightning of his Skill winked out, plunging the sea into stygian darkness. Felix's Manasight picked things out easily, however, the deep blue currents, rigid dusty brown floor, and noxious rainbow hue of the Hatchlings moving as if painted by vaporous light. His Perception enveloped them all, those that fled and those that charged him with mindless, mad bloodlust.

Rimeshaping!

All around him, the sea crackled, frozen by the immensity of Felix's power. Mana surged from him, claiming the water as his own and multiplying the potency of his ice shaping Skill—Felix thrust outward in all directions. Thin, rapier-like blades of hardened ice spiked into monster after monster, reaping lives as easily as breathing. A hundred, two hundred, more.

MORE, his Hunger roared. ***MORE!***

The Fathom spawn died at his hand, every single one, until the murky waters were awash in ichor and rapidly decomposing bits of fat, muscle, and bone.

You Have Killed A Fathom Hatchling (x419!)
XP Earned!

Sunken Ward!

A newer spell unfolded from his channels, enveloping Felix in a sheath of shimmering blue energy that let him draw in a deep breath. The spell wasn't entirely necessary for him, as it protected folks from the cold and crushing pressure of deep water, but it also let him breathe underwater. And that was required for his next trick.

Chthonic Tribute!

Felix pulled in a titanic breath, sounding his Primordial Skill and commandeering every last bit of foul Fathom spawn for his own. All at once, the dire detritus turned to effervescent smoke and shimmering light before being drawn toward him en masse. Felix inhaled it all, sending the Essence hurtling into his core space, until his Divine Tree hung heavy with glittering power.

Sunken Ward is level 2!
Sunken Ward is level 3!

Rimeshaping is level 46!
...
Rimeshaping is level 49!

Only Felix remained in the deep dark. He turned, surveying the empty, frigid water all around him, almost hoping for another monstrosity to dare approach. Nothing survived, and Felix kicked off the sandy floor, speeding upward toward the surface once again. He emerged through a crashing wave, the vicious crest of which slammed him into the crystalline base of the city plateau.

"Oof!" he gasped, more surprised than actually injured. Quite the opposite, as his scales and claws had gouged furrows out of the glowing green-gold Mana crystals he'd fetched up on. They grew like hexagonal basalt, in pillars and branching clusters, all of them immensely thick and rising a dozen feet before changing to regular Tier III stone. Felix stood, bracing against the waves that tried to dislodge him again, and patted the crystal. "Thanks for the catch."

Much to his surprise, beneath his hand, he found a jagged tear in the crystal. More than that: there were a set of uneven slashes, each of them ten or fifteen feet long and a foot wide. He held out his own talons, curling them into a claw and eyeballing them against the slashes. Something very big had done this. Something very, very big.

An explosion of fiery light shook the sky, pulling Felix's attention just in time for him to see the massive, smoking hulk of a Manaship careen downward from on high. It hurtled dangerously fast, trailing smoke and flames like a funeral pyre, but slowed just enough at the last second to splash down into the sea. Shouts from above chased after them, and his own heightened senses picked out the cause: the Paladins were making a break for it.

"I am *not* in the mood for this," Felix muttered. He let his Sunken Ward die out, banishing the light blue glow from his Body, and seized the sky.

"Row! Put your burnin' backs into it!" Captain Jora shouted over the crash of waves. "This sea is wild but by the light of the Pathless, we'll tame her! Row!"

Constructs of light Mana, shaped into rough, oar-shapes swept out of the holes in the Manaship's hull. With only a single man to an oar, they moved far faster than he had expected; the benefits of Journeyman Tier Strength, Captain Jora supposed. He tried not to look into the raging whitecaps all around him, or show how uneasy the relentless motion made his stomach.

Flight aboard a Manaship was nothing like it, not unless you were fool enough to fly into a storm. Lightning cracked above them, its own form of relentless motion as the unceasing rain pummeled them. "Like the whole damn world is drowning," he muttered. "But not us. We'll be free of this place."

Ironically, they had only been able to escape thanks to those nightmarish monstrosities. When the wretched beasts had crawled up on the deck and stabbed him in the back—him!—Captain Jora thought it had been the end. But the Pathless provided for him, as He always had, and his men rallied against the twisted fish. Yet the Lord In White had been thorough with His blessings, for the creatures had immediately set upon the city defenders, distracting them from the Paladins and their flight. When the *Fiend* had shown up, Captain Jora had almost died of terror even as his guts had boiled with rage. The beast that had destroyed all of his brothers and sisters stood upon the thin air and called down stone and lightning like...like a god.

Not a god! he chastised himself, before offering a silent apology to the Pathless. *Not even a man. A monster.*

When the Fiend took action, that had been the Captain's time to move. The other defenders were too preoccupied with the swarm to bother watching them, and he had his men sever the last of the mooring lines and disengage the inscribed dock arm. With a brief prayer of guidance, they fell. It was only a god-given miracle that they had survived, that the Mana engine had ignited for even the briefest of moments. That had been enough for them to land the still-burning ship.

The waves pulled against him and the rudder as they rowed through the crests and troughs of waves the size of hillocks. There were huge holes in the Manaship, the sails were tattered, and the Mana engine dead, but Captain Jora felt a smile tug at his lips. They had escaped the death trap of Ahkestria and the influence of the wicked Fiend. All they had to do now was survive the journey into the Ghreldan Hills, where more of their people were waiting. There, they would finally be safe.

Lightning crashed around them, thunder and light appearing simultaneously and entirely too close. The ship dipped, sending massive gouts of foaming spray to either side of the gunwales. Captain Jora shielded his eyes and cursed. "Blasted Damnation! That bolt almost speared us all!"

"Believe me, Paladin. Had I wanted it to, it would have."

Captain Jora gasped and stumbled back. Before him, standing amidship as if he'd always been there, was a man. Other than his considerable height and wide shoulders, he looked entirely normal with shaggy black hair, sharp features, and a simple jacket and trousers. Yet his gloves arrested the captain's attention, strange and black and oddly...clawed.

"You," the captain said. His throat tried to tighten, but he shoved his words through it anyway. "You!"

"Me," he said, and his eyes *burned* with a cold, glacial light. His hands, tipped with talons, flexed, and lightning danced among them. "You were not allowed to have this ship, Paladin. I didn't say you could leave."

"You don't command us, just as your pretty little doxie doesn't, either!" Jora rallied his fears of this thing, shoving them behind the burning light of his clean, holy rage. "You're a charlatan and unworthy of the Authority you've stolen, Fiend. What have you done to the High Justiciar? What trickery have you pulled on this city?"

The Fiend sighed, and Jora detected a hint of weariness in it. Weakness. "Return this ship, and I promise I won't harm any of you. Stop all the violence and the weird, kinda racist hate speech, and we can talk. Find peace."

Jora laughed. He couldn't help it. "Peace was a Path the gods took with them. All we have now is Strength, and Strength does not bow down before false Authority!"

His Paladins, well trained to the last of them, struck. From all corners, a deluge of radiance descended upon the Fiend, enveloping him in fire and hardened light so quickly and powerfully that the entire Manaship bucked and groaned. Captain Jora poured his own power into a crackling javelin of Divine light, a Skill taught him when he gained his mantle of leadership. A heavy burden and privilege to smite those that would sully the world. He hurled it, and the upper decks detonated in a blaze to rival the wild tempest above them.

We got him! he crowed, but another javelin formed in his off hand. "Again! He's not dead yet!"

More and more Skills piled atop the Fiend, so much that Jora couldn't even see the man anymore. Yet unease grew, dwarfing his brief elation. There were no screams, no struggle. No System notification.

"Are you done?" The Fiend's voice was a basso thrum that resonated in the captain's chest, though it wasn't loud at all. Light and flames vanished from him all at once, sucked into his open maw as if he were devouring their power. Sapphire eyes burned not like ice but like twin, distant stars, and the captain's gut went cold in certain dread. "My turn."

Jora bellowed and pulsed with panels of hardened light that settled over his frame. A suit of armor, forged in Divine light. "Come, then!"

Lightning flashed, and Jora stumbled, gripping his midsection in wide-eyed disbelief. A black claw gripped him, tore through him. Shattered motes of light Mana drifted around them, fallen stars drenched in gold that dazzled him. Then the claw vanished, and the captain fell onto the wet, heaving deck.

The lights—all of them, everywhere—went out.

CHAPTER THIRTEEN

"Young Master! Young Master, where are you?"

The words were muffled and almost drowned out by the roar of storm and crackling fire, but he heard them. From within the heavy corpses of his former guards, Florian Iretus raised a bloody, shaking hand. Cold rain soaked him before someone with coarse leather gloves grasped it and heaved. The bodies of his guards fell away, and he cried out weakly against the chill deluge from the sky.

"Florian! You're alright!" His sister, Meina, pulled him into a tight embrace. She was just as blood-soaked as he felt, and twice as wet. "I feared the worst!"

"Young Master, thank the Highest you're alright," another voice said, before Florian heard the sound of metal against metal.

"Watch your tongue, Krin," said a far gruffer voice. Captain Landas, the grizzled veteran who led his father's men, had his hand firmly on the other guard's pauldron. "Or do you want to attract their attention?"

Florian followed the captain's gaze toward a pair of women. One was a Faun, common enough around the city, though the red hair was a touch less so. The other...the other was wearing bloodied armor of blue and white design, wielding a huge spear and directing a number of armored soldiers around the docks. All of them saluted and scurried off, quick to do her bidding—even the two enormous, blue-skinned giants. "Who is she?" he asked.

Meina had produced a thick woolen blanket from somewhere and was busy draping it around Florian's shoulders. She gave the women and their soldiers a quick, fearful glance. "A Duchess from the Hierocracy. She came with...with *him*."

At the last, Meina gestured with her head up, toward the Temple of Elemental Fire. Or what had been a Temple. Now, the bright beacon of their city had guttered out. There was little question in Florian's Mind about who his sister meant, and it sent a thrill of fear through his belly. "Why would she fight against the Paladins? The Paladins...! The ship!"

"Is gone," Captain Landas said, blunt as ever. He kept talking, even as Florian spun in an attempt to find the Manaship, as if he could conjure it from thin air. "The Paladins unmoored it and took it down into the waves. They're gone, lad."

The young master of House Iretus shivered in the cold, driving rain, less concerned with the pending Status Condition than with what his father would say. Florian had been given charge of the skydocks, and of this project in particular. To salvage one of the enemy's Manaships and retrofit it for sea travel. While the other Houses were scrabbling to arrange an audience with *that man*, they were taking action to ensure their merchants would have exclusive ownership of the seas. And now, it was all gone.

Did they die for nothing? Florian's whirling gaze forced him to once again confront the pile of corpses he'd been pulled from within—it was all he could do to keep his bile down. Men he'd known all his life were splayed across the ground, split and stacked like cordwood...all in an attempt to protect him. The young heir of House Iretus said a quick prayer—but he kept it silent.

Men had died for him today. He would never forget that. And while he was free of their stiffened grasp now, Florian knew the feel of them would linger on him for all of time. Their sightless eyes, clouded with death, their warm, wet lifeblood....

"Young Master? I would like to introduce you to Her Grace, Lady Vessilia Dayne of Pax'Vrell and Miss Fiammetta of Ahkestria," Captain Landas said in his gravelly drawl. "Without either of which, far fewer of us would still be standing."

Florian paled and stifled a gasp. He hadn't noticed anyone walking up to him at all, and now the two women were so close. "I-It is a pleasure to, ah, to meet you both."

The Faun's lips quirked slightly, but she inclined her head. The other, however, looked at him with upturned brows and soft, dark eyes. "Are you well? Is all that blood from you?"

"Me? N-no, I'm fine. My guards, they—"

"The guards of our House saved my brother, sacrificing themselves to the blades of the Pathless' dogs," Meina said, almost spitting the words. "Captain Landas, please recommend all your men here for honors from our father. You are all to be commended. As are you, your Grace."

"My efforts were paired to my associate, Fiammetta, and without

Captain Landas and his archers, I doubt we would have held them back long enough," Lady Dayne said modestly. She was like the captain in that way, Florian realized. The way her eyes kept scanning the battlefield as if looking for others to help—it spoke to her compassion. Not something the young man was familiar with in Ahkestria.

Is this Pax'Vrell so different? he wondered. *And what is she doing with this group of invaders?* It didn't make sense to Florian, but then, the world had become a confusing place in a short time. At least now things were quieting. The Paladins escaped, yes, but those horrible creatures were no longer threatening the city or House Iretus' property. "What of the fish men? Are they gone?"

"Aye, dragged to the depths of damnation by—" Captain Landas cut himself off, turning his words into a grumble. "Lord Nevarre stopped them."

"Truly?" Florian wasn't sure he believed it. Before he'd been buried, he'd seen the swarms of the monstrous fish men. They were powerful enough that their claws ripped right through his guards' Journeyman-Tier armor. To have one man face them, alone? All of them? That beggared belief.

One of those purple-sashed soldiers jogged up to them, a little too fast for his Apprentice Tier eyes to track. "Your Grace, there is no further sign of the Paladins. If there are any more in the city, they are not here."

"Thank you, Maryk. Please join the others and ensure no one was hurt in the nearby buildings."

"As you wish, your Grace."

The soldier jogged away just as speedily, and only after he had gone did Florian's eyes widen. *That was a Henaari.* Indeed, a good number of the soldiers weren't Human at all...a rarity within Ahkestria. Florian even saw a Goblin in mage robes. *Do Goblins even know magic?*

"If that's the last of the Paladins, I'll eat my boot," Captain Landas said.

"I agree that it is unlikely," Lady Dayne said with a sigh. She tucked her spear into the crook of her elbow and adjusted her armored gauntlets. "The Hierophant's forces have proven as invasive as a weed."

"Still. It sickens me to see any get away," Meina added. "After what they did here. And at the Temple."

Florian's father had told them what little was known of events the day prior, which was that the Paladins of the Hierocracy somehow invaded the city and attacked the Council Masters and the Matrons of the Temple. The Fiend and his forces had shown up during the conflict and ended it, but not before many had died, and That Which Burns guttered out.

They knew the Highest Flame was gone, if only because everyone who had once been given a Blessing were abed, recuperating after their cores suffered an immense shock. His own father, mother, six uncles, and three aunts were all stricken with fever and the shakes. Which was why Florian was here at all, managing this operation.

"The Paladins are a curse," the Faun said with considerable heat. Literally, as the air around her warmed by a fair margin. "If you see any more, tell us immediately. We are looking to expunge every trace of them from Ahkestria. We cannot let them get away again."

"I am not so sure that they did, Fiammetta," Lady Dayne said. She pointed out into the gloom that was rapidly progressing toward darkness. "Look."

Florian followed her gesture with bated breath, afraid to see more disgusting creatures rise from the depths of the strange, alien water. But at first, he saw nothing at all. The curtain of clouds and heavy rainfall made visibility trying at best, but...*There. Lightning, again.* The storms had not ceased since amassing a day ago, and all that time lightning had traced its contours, stalking the skies like a predator. *But nothing else. What are we supposed to be looking at?*

Shouts came then, and more pointing, but Florian could only squint against the gloom...until he realized the light show was not from the storm, but from a tattered and hulking shape floating through the sky. Streamers of blue-white luminescence shot off of it in multiple directions, but it was the relentless pummeling from the ward in the sky that drew out the details for him. It was the Manaship, flying back toward them despite the restrictions...and it wasn't stopping or crashing.

"Is...is he—?" the Faun started, before choking on disbelief.

"Yes," Lady Dayne said, and she shook her head with a smile. "Yes he is."

The ship drew closer, and Florian suddenly saw what most others had already spotted: beneath the ship, there was a figure, holding tight to the keel. Only, the Manaship's engines weren't engaged. Florian gasped, disbelief and awe warring over his Spirit. That lone figure was hefting the entirety of the Manaship on his back and lifting it through the sky.

"That's impossible," his sister said. "Unless...is he a Master Tier?"

Florian had no words, and could only watch as the ship came closer, and the man flew toward the docks, wreathed in blue-white electricity. Before he could land, however, a terrible flash split the sky. All of the rage of the storm raced down and hit the Manaship, as if punishing it for daring to fly. Everyone cried out, some blinded and others thrown physically back by the sheer force of the impact. Through dark splotches in his vision, Florian watched in stunned amazement as the man, the Fiend, caught the lightning itself.

And *ate* it.

The storm abated, perhaps as flabbergasted as the young master himself, and the Fiend landed with a mild grunt of effort. His sister rallied first, ordering their men to hustle forward and secure the damaged ship with enchanted mooring lines. Men and women scrambled up the sides, drawing nothing but an amused glance from the blue-eyed man, until they gave the all-clear. Then he shrugged the horrendous burden of wood and steel off his shoulders and into the prepared slip. Someone aboard had managed to get the Mana engine working, at least for a moment, enough to guide the ship into its lock before shutting it all down.

We have the ship back, he realized, belatedly. The information seemed unimportant, however, in the face of the Fiend's sheer...existence. *What is he? What does he want?*

The Fiend stood, watching it all happen with a grim expression on its face. His face. It was hard for Florian to consider the creature before him as a man, so covered in dark scales that he all but faded into the dark around him. Midnight black, save for the cyan markings swirling across his shoulders, visible through the rents in his tattered jacket. Holes that, as Florian watched, repaired themselves without seam or stitch.

"Who runs this skydock?" the Fiend asked. His voice was nothing special, just a man's voice, though his tone was commanding. Forceful.

"House Iretus," Captain Landas answered.

"And that's you?" When Florian nodded, the Fiend grunted. "How many other skydocks are there in Ahkestria?"

"Three others," Meina said.

The Fiend gestured to several men, similar to the ones the Lady Dayne had been ordering. "Explain to them how to find these skydocks. Stennar, Olias, I want you to marshal more of the Claw and check them out as well. Ensure that there aren't any more of these Hatchling creatures, right?"

"Aye, sir." The Hobgoblin and Dwarf saluted, fists to hearts, before leaning close to Florian's sister. She was quick, giving them House names and directions in only a few words, and soon the soldiers ran off, presumably to get more of this strange man's army.

"Now," the Fiend said, turning his bright blue eyes in Florian's direction before flicking toward the Lady Dayne. "What exactly happened here?"

"So they tried to steal the ship, and the Hatchlings showed up," Felix repeated, scratching his jaw. He hissed and pulled his finger back to see blood. His stupid claws were too sharp; they scratched even his toughened skin. "But we don't know how or why they appeared. Right?"

"Those are the basics. But I cannot believe it is a random attack," Vess said. "That many monsters, all of one type? And you saw large claw marks in the crystal? I have to believe this was planned."

"Planned? By who?" The older soldier looked at him with a steady, if tired resolve. He was a retainer for House Iretus, and apparently had helped a bunch in the conflict. Captain Landas was older and grizzled, someone Felix would have guessed anywhere between fifty and sixty-five years old, had he been on Earth. On the Continent, however, he could be closer to a hundred. "If we are being attacked by more than just these pathetic Pathless, then I would like to know. Sir."

"You remind me of a friend," Felix said with a grin, and waved off the concerned look the man's subordinates were giving them. "You helped us, so I'll gladly tell you. There are creatures called the Fathom that are a problem in the Ghreldan Hills. It seems they have decided to enter the Leviathan Depths as well."

"The Ghreldan Hills? How would they have gotten past the fortifications in the Caleph Pass?" That bit of insight came from the teen boy in fancy clothes. He looked overwhelmed by everything. "Tevin's Knights wouldn't simply allow them entry."

"My concern as well. Felix, we may have a problem in the Hills," Vess said.

For his part, Felix thought he kept fairly calm, for all that his insides were boiling with worry and regret. "We'll handle that soon. For now, are you fine? And you, Fiammetta?"

"We are well. Your aid was appreciated, as was that of your guards and Lady Zara," the Faun said. "Though...where did she go?"

Felix shrugged, but detached the case of Healing Potions at his waist. "Please pass these out among the injured. House Iretus included."

"Sure."

When Fiammetta took the potion case and started distributing its contents out, Felix caught Vess' eye again. "You're sure you're okay? You feel...I try not to pry, but it's hard. You seem troubled."

Vess wiped a bit of blood from her cheek, but her gaze was warm. "I truly am fine...or will be, soon. I need to process some things about our...connection. I would like to speak with you later. Perhaps this evening, in your apartments? I think I saw a particularly nice dining set or twelve there."

Felix smirked. "I think I could host a dinner for the whole city in those apartments, to be honest."

"Hm. Dinner sounds lovely. I am sure I will be famished by that point," she said.

"Oh, uhm, okay. Yeah, I'm sure one of those servant people—yeah, no worries. We'll talk then." Felix managed to spit out the words just as Vess walked away, a strange smile on her lips.

"Quite the woman to pursue, if I may say so, sir." Captain Landas' eyes hadn't missed a beat of that interaction, and Felix fought down a blush. "Though, I'd watch out for her father. Even in Ahkestria, tales of Duke Dayne's temper are legendary."

Rather than answering any of that, Felix turned to the young teen and a slightly older woman in her twenties. "You are of House Iretus, right?"

"We are," the boy said, pushing out his chest slightly. "I am Florian Iretus, and this is my sister, Meina."

He handed a Healing Potion to both of them, pressing it into their hands when they moved to refuse. "Take it. You'll need it. Tell me about your plans for this Manaship."

"Ah, we salvaged them from the Paladins, when the ward shot them down," Florian started saying, before his sister laid a restraining hand on his shoulder. He shook it off. "You think he won't find out, sister? We stole them. The plan was to rebuild them into proper Manaships for when this storm passes...but it seems that isn't happening, is it?"

"It's not," Felix answered, refusing to give more information. Not like he knew much.

Florian nodded. "I had feared as much. My plan, then, is to adapt them for the sea."

"Seaworthy craft, huh?" Felix said, looking back over his shoulder. It was still afternoon, but the constant downpour turned everything dark and occluded. The rain was coming down so hard it obscured anything beyond a few miles, even to his ridiculous Perception. Mist had risen above the sea as well, and the waves were extremely high. "A dangerous idea. Tell me more."

CHAPTER FOURTEEN

Felix leaned back, and his spine popped like bubble wrap. "Ouugh god, that's better!"

"I am unsure if that noise should come from a living body," Karys observed between bites. "Perhaps next time you lift an entire Manaship on your back, take time to stretch first."

They were sitting atop a glossy wall within Felix's Bastion of Will—a mental Skill within his core space—and his Chancellor was busy eating a small pile of greens that he called *caeliis* and insisted were delicious. Felix had tried them and thought they tasted like spicy cardboard, but kept eating them, regardless.

The sky was blue here, instead of gray and stormy, and the air danced with warmth and the fragrances of springtime. "Two things: it was like, barely half of a Manaship. Also, this isn't my real Body anyway, so I'm sure that was just my Mind's projection of my own stress. Or something."

Karys laughed, and his older Nymean face creased in a wide smile—so similar to a Human's, save for perhaps slightly wider eyes and sharper features. "The Body you project into your core space is you, just simplified into an incarnation to interact with your Skills and core. Or cores, in your case. It is a reflection of your Aspects, cast and refracted through the glittering pool of your own power. As above, so below." Karys popped another leafy stalk in his mouth and chewed, sighing through his nose.

Felix waved off the man's concerns. "I'm fine. Adamant Discord did most of the heavy lifting, and my Body is a lot more resilient now, since

Adept Tier came through. Like scary resilient. Those Hatchlings couldn't put a scratch on me, and the Paladins..." He trailed off, thoughts back on the Manaship earlier that day. Of the storm and the fire, and the end he had enacted. "They didn't stand a chance."

He pushed his Mind away from those memories. He did what was necessary, but it didn't mean he had to like it. Felix focused instead on a notification that had been lingering around his vision for a while now. But in all the hubbub of ships and fish monsters and the cleanup, he hadn't given it any attention.

New Skill!
Auroral Forge (Epic), Level 1!
The sun dawns and sets, but light is ever-present...and it is yours to forge. Precision, strength, and speed of manipulation increases slightly with Skill level.

The new Skill blossomed within his core space, a palpable feeling of warmth and light suddenly glowing in the distance. It was an orb of interlocking patterns as the rest, but farther away from his cores than any other Skill, being at level one. It was fairly large in size, though, bigger by far than the Sunken Ward Skill near it, perhaps due to its rarity.

"Hm."

"What is it?" Karys asked.

"Killing and devouring the Paladins earned me a new Skill. A light-shaping Skill." Felix lifted his hands and let the ability activate. Golden wisps of Mana flowed from his hands in amorphous, smoky blobs. "This must be what they used to make their light constructs."

"Another shaping Skill for your repertoire. You have quite the collection," Karys observed. "Have you considered combining them, or perhaps joining them together in a Skill Array?"

Felix had, just then, but even with a quick assessment using his Affinity, he was certain. Something was still missing. "It's not ready to combine yet. Just like before, when I got all the other shaping Skills, the pattern feels incomplete." He had previously learned a number of shaping Skills, all of which were immensely useful, not just for their power but their utility as well.

Stone Shaping, Rime Shaping, Green Shaping, and now Auroral Forge. Add in Cardinal Flame, which aided in controlling internal and external Mana—and, to a lesser extent, fire—and he had quite the assortment. Even Sovereign of Flesh was a shaping Skill, of a sort. "My only idea is to keep learning new Skills to hopefully combine them in the future. For now, maybe this Auroral Forge will be useful."

He flexed his powerful Will and fed the Skill a measure of his Intent, focusing on the shape he wanted. The amorphous glob of light straightened, flattening out at the end to form a long, thin spear. He felt the Skill quiver, trying to keep up with the force of his stats as it sang in a curious series of high chords.

Auroral Forge is level 2!
Auroral Forge is level 3!
Auroral Forge is level 4!

Each level up allowed Felix to pack just a bit more Mana into the spear, solidifying it a bit more. He flared his Manasight and Cardinal Flame, just to watch the process as it evolved. There was a spellform, created by the resonance of his new Skill and fed by his vast store of Mana. Each level up increased the complexity of the spellform, the pattern, and allowed more power to be added to the weapon. Eventually, it looked like a golden bar of light in his hands, shining almost too bright to look at directly.

Auroral Forge is level 15!
Manasight is level 72!

"Huh. I've never seen this much detail before." Felix held out the spear, now a weighted, tangible object in his hands. Not much weight, especially in his hands, but it had a heft to it that matched a standard polearm. "Is this how Skills have always worked?"

Karys nodded. "You have simply lacked the senses to parse it. Congratulations. A new realm of power has opened for you, Felix. With increased proficiency in shaping magics, you will find that your efforts at creation will only grow more complex and refined." He patted the glossy battlements beneath them with a dark brown hand. "Perhaps you will be able to increase the rank of your Stronghold again, if we incorporate your new Skill."

Felix gazed at the walls of his Bastion, currently underfoot. They were made of stone polished to an impossible shine, blue-black threaded with glimmering red-gold veins, much like his Stronghold in Nagast. The walls spread outward, forming a hexagon that was easily the size of the Grandmaster's estate in Ahkestria.

It was, however, mostly empty.

The middle portion, the inner bailey, was a field of lush green grass and wildflowers. He had even noticed some woody shoots rising in places, growths that looked like they would soon become trees. At the center of it all was a large, hexagonal tower that rose twice as high as the walls, and was surmounted with a large silver spire that was threaded through with a dizzying array of shimmering cords. Like a needle, stuffed to bursting with enough yarn to gag a hobby shop.

He let his gaze skip over those threads. They were an entirely different can of worms he had to deal with later.

Each face of the hexagonal tower was marked with the convoluted pattern of a Skill, each one different and all of them tied to his Bastion of Will by a process that Felix still didn't really understand. This was what Karys meant when he said Skill Array: a network of Skills woven together in Harmony to effect a greater potency. And his Skills were plenty potent already. By manually activating multiple shaping Skills, Felix had crafted the new walls of his Bastion from scratch, somehow improving the Skill itself...if he could manage to combine all shaping Skills into an Array, what else could he create?

"It's tempting, but my Affinity keeps flagging strange dead notes when I consider the Skills together. My gut says wait." Felix pivoted, letting the spear of light dissipate and discarding thoughts of his Skills and their growth. For now. "Tell me about the Stronghold. What's new?"

"Ah." Karys dusted off his hands and stood. At his feet, the bowl of greens vanished into the air. "To business, then."

The air before them distorted, blocking out the view of distant forests, rolling hills, and the spray of an acid-green sea. A blue box edged in golden scrollwork filled the space, large enough to count as a billboard sign back home. His Authority Screen.

Karys reached up and scrolled, flicking past several options. "I had intended to share these with you sooner, but your distance from Nagast means your Authority Screen will not populate properly. Thankfully, that is not an issue within your Bastion—had you the time, we could have done this sooner."

"I would have done lots of things, if I had time," Felix said, a touch irritated. "Issues continue to pile up. Ahkestria needs to be sorted out, this attack on Nagast has to be mitigated, and now these Fathom creatures. Not to mention all of the problems in my own party. The Link I established with them is doing...things to their core spaces. I could *hear* it on Vess—hell, anyone could see it on Atar's face."

"Well, to your second point, I have reached out to Lady Cal, and she is not aware of any incursion into the Territory. Luckily, one of the Manaships Lady Zara acquired was just leaving to the border when I reached her; she sent a missive with a few of her Haarguard and expects word from Setoria within the week. Faster, if they catch favorable winds."

Felix quirked an eyebrow. "When did you call Cal? I just told you like an hour ago."

"I was once a Paragon, Felix. Though I no longer hold the power I once had, there is a great deal of skill still in these old bones."

"You don't have bones," Felix pointed out but winced a moment later.

"Not strictly true. While I may no longer look as I did in life, the mechanical Body you gave me has a skeleton." Karys folded his robes a bit closer around his false, old form. A phantom of who he was now hovered around his shoulders: a golden giant made of metal and magic, with two eyes of burning flame. Then it faded, and there was only the tired old man. "I am...reduced, but it is better than my Eidolon Body, frozen in place by rot and the passing Ages. And it is beside the point. My Mind and Spirit are my own, and holes in my memory or not, I can still accomplish great things."

"I don't doubt it, Karys. I'm sorry. That was just rude," Felix said, scratching his jaw. Here, at least, his hands were human and without claws. "Please. Continue."

"Very well," Karys said, and returned his attention to the Authority Screen. "Your Stronghold has grown with the arrival of settlers from Haarwatch and Setoria coming in relative droves. The housing has spilled out of the original walls and into the forest beyond, which we have had to clear quite a bit of—but don't worry! Kikri, that Elven archer follower of yours, she and a number of Elven arrivals were able to shape the forests back, without harming a single leaf. The song of it," Karys closed his eyes, and a smile returned to his face. "It was beautiful. The Green Aria is a balm to the senses."

Felix absorbed the information Karys was relaying at the same time he went over the general details for his Territory. *One of my Territories*, he thought with no little disbelief. *It's...changed so much.*

Authority Screen
Territory - Nagast

General Overview

- ***Current Residence*: Nagast**
- ***Residence Rank*: Stronghold, Rank II**
- ***Allied Population*: 2,489 Henaari, 59 Risi (Frost Giants), 44 Hoarhounds, 2 Chimera, 437 Humans, 113 Half-Orcs, 64 Elves, 37 Dwarves, 14 Gnomes, 115 Hobgoblins, 233 Goblins, 16 Korvaa, 44 Orc, 5 Half-Elves**

Factions

- **The Risi**
- **The Henaari (Night Talons Tribe)**

Affiliated: Wallwalkers

- **The Henaari (Skyborn Tribe)**
- **The Henaari (Featherwalk Tribe)**
- **The Henaari (Thundercry Tribe)**
- **Nagast (New) (Varied)**
- **Fiend's Legion**

Arclight
Blade
Bone
Fist

"Whoa, that's a *lot* of new people," Felix said, alarm creeping into his voice. "Do we have enough resources for everyone? Food? Shelter?"

"We do. More than enough. When the second Henaari tribe began arriving, the Night Talons put themselves into high gear. The Farwalker wished to stay in our good graces, and he offered to establish an official organization for his builders. He calls them the Wallwalkers, because of course he does, and they have been working night and day to help design and build additions to your growing town.

"The Green Singers joined with them, using their gifts in tandem and truly cutting down on the time required to erect reasonable housing." Karys sighed, obviously pleased. "This, of course, meant that the Night Talons Tribe remains the dominant tribe among the newer Henaari arrivals."

"But where did all the Henaari come from?" Felix asked. "The rest you explained, and even that I can't quite believe, but the Henaari are wanderers. Why would they come to the Foglands?"

Before Karys could answer, a tingle shuddered through Felix's spine. Above them, one of the many cords of effervescent light twanged, plucked hard as if by a massive, curved claw. It was a dark cord, edged in shadow as much as light, and the moment Felix's attention fixed upon it, the sound of faint, sharp cawing reached his ears. *The Endless Raven.*

"I believe you have your answer. The Urge the Henaari worship must have sent word to its people. What precisely that word was, not even the Farwalker has deigned to reveal. And I've asked." Karys pursed his lips, not angry so much as thoughtful. "It is not malicious, of that I am certain. I trust the Farwalker and his inner coterie.

"The other tribes...ah well, they have not posed any sort of threat and have also rushed to prove themselves useful. I have taken the liberty of engaging their Skills to continue responsibly harvesting the forests and valleys beyond our own, and for the more martial-minded to delve into the Steelgrave Domain with the Frost Giants. It has progressed well. Our stores of raw ore and varied reagents for alchemy have grown by the bushel."

"Wow," Felix breathed. He was impressed. "You've really got a handle on things."

Karys fixed his robes, picking imaginary pieces of lint from his chest. "I appreciate the acknowledgement, Felix. Were that our crafting was going so well. Without our Masters, even with the interim replacements, the Stronghold cannot progress as quickly as it might. It would be nice to reach Tier III before anything untoward happens with the Hierocracy. When do you think you shall return?"

Felix sighed. "Not soon enough. If only I could simply pick a chancellor for the Territory and leave. But you know the deal there."

"Mhm, indeed. Do you have a candidate?"

"Not sure. I have to do some poking around here, ascertain a few details, but I'll hopefully have it wrapped up quickly." Here Felix hesitated and gazed up at the threads in the sky again. He could pick out six that stood apart and were bunched together, far more sturdy than the vast majority of others, almost sizzling with unexpressed intensity. "But...I'm worried about my friends, too. Will you look more into the Links, like I asked?"

"Of course. I will scour my memories, but as I told you before, the substance of your power confounds me. Your Primordial nature influences your core space in strange and increasingly complex ways. Links, such as you are describing, are not a part of the standard advancement." Karys tapped his lips and swiped closed the Authority Screen before them. The view of dark forest and distant, crashing waves was stark without the translucent blue window in the way. "The Fathom. These are the creatures the Naga asked you to eliminate?"

"Yeah. Same name, at least. Can't believe that's a coincidence," Felix said.

"Hm. And they were draconic creatures?"

"That was their Type, yeah. Looked more like gross fish monsters. Like those things you find at the bottom of the ocean, all slimy bits, teeth, and big, pale eyes." Felix's lip curled, recalling their defeat...yet the image of them swirling around him in the dark water was haunting. "I'm not a fan."

"Nor should you be. Draconic Type creatures are dangerous, not just because of their growth potential, but because the lesser ones do not often work alone. They are rigid in their hierarchy and will bow to those of their Type possessed of a greater advancement."

"Oh shit," Felix said, softly. "Are you saying the Fathom are dragons?"

"I do not know." Karys shook his head. "I am saying that you need to tread carefully when you finally return to the shadowgate in Haestus, Felix. There may be more danger there than you realize."

CHAPTER FIFTEEN

Felix stalked the halls, followed close by a grumbling Pit. "Yes, we'll get some food in a second," he muttered at the Chimera. "We have to do this first, alright?"

"Fine," Pit said, sounding anything but.

"I saw you, Pit. You ate two of those Hatchlings."

Somehow, despite having a beak, Pit managed to pout. "They tasted like sour feet."

Felix let slip a soft chuckle but didn't stop his march. The opulent halls of the grandmaster's mansion oozed by, his power walk more akin to a steady jog thanks to his beefed up Agility. His Mind, however, was turning over the things Karys had said a few minutes prior.

His Stronghold had grown. The Offensive rating had risen from a measly 5% to a whopping 52%, and his Defensive rating from 40% to 61%, thanks in large part to the influx of warriors. Almost two-thirds of the new residents joined the ranks of his Legion, and their training had been nonstop, thanks to Rory and a few other former Guild trainers. Rory had come to visit for a while, but according to Karys, the Dwarf had chosen to stay on and help whip the Legion into shape. Felix had grinned at that—he remembered all too well the brutal methods that Rory employed—if they listened, the Legion was almost guaranteed a substantial increase in ability.

The other facet of that increase in offense were the ballistae that Atar and Alister had been working on before they left. Hector and the apprentices had been able to make several prototypes of the inscribed siege weaponry, each one designed to absorb ambient Mana and throw it back as bolts of force.

As it stood, the things were absolutely massive, requiring a wagon and crane to move them about, and their operation wasn't so smooth, either. Large stores of Mana were necessary to fire them, as the siphon arrays were entirely too limited, for reasons Felix didn't understand. If they returned, Atar and Alister could look into them, and a great many other issues.

At Felix's order, Karys was getting people ready for war. Neither of them believed High Justiciar Haim had been lying when he'd told Felix of the Hierocracy's plans; why would he? The man had been confident in his success at the time, and frankly it was what they had all been expecting since the System had declared Felix as Autarch. Karys was meeting later with the heads of the various Factions to mobilize their forces out of the Stronghold and back toward Haarwatch within the week. Felix hadn't wished to wait, but he doubted resolving the issues in Ahkestria *and* a journey back to the Shadowgate would be done any sooner.

To that end, Felix's swift movement through the halls came to a sudden halt as he beheld a tall, wooden door layered with a ludicrous amount of Mana crystals. The type varied wildly, forming a mosaic from a certain distance that Felix could appreciate: a figure stood atop a rock, holding aloft a bundle that was clearly a crown, scepter, and orb while waves crashed at their feet.

Standing before the door were seven Yttin, all of them around six feet in height and muscled like swimmers beneath their chitinous armor. The armor in question was ridged and spiked in places, covering their chests, arms, legs, and head with an imposing, crustacean look. They varied in hue from greenish blue to bluish-purple, generally, though one of them had a deeper reddish hue, like a lobster. The crab-like legs on their back, also covered in segmented chitin, hung loose against their shoulders like a curled up spider, until they spotted Felix. Then they flared outward in alarm.

"Halt, traveler. You encroach upon..." one of the older Yttin said, before his mouth dropped open in shock. "Lord Autarch. I apologize. I did not see you—"

Felix waved off the man's words, just as Pit prowled from behind. "I was moving kinda fast around the bend. I sneak up on people all the time. Is your shaman available? I would like to speak with him."

"For you, Autarch, he is always available," the Yttin said. The other guards pivoted smoothly, and the crystal-laden door opened to reveal a sumptuous apartment filled with, of all things, plants. "Please, enter. Shaman Klzix is just beyond the dream pool."

"Uh, thanks," Felix said, and walked past the Yttin. He stood a good half foot over the tallest of them, which was a weird experience he hadn't grown used to yet. "C'mon, Pit."

His Companion followed, giving the Yttin a cheerful chirp of greeting. A warmth spread among the guards' Spirits as they passed, a clear fondness for the Chimera, then the doors closed. A chill wind breezed across Felix's shoulders, but he shrugged it off. "Made friends while I was asleep?"

"They have a nice boat," Pit chirruped. His tufted ears twitched. "Why is there a pond here?"

Somewhere along the line, the tiled flooring had turned to soft, slightly glowing moss. The walls were lined with more Mana crystals, most of them a soft green-gold, and they grew along the geometrical architecture of a large, domed chamber. Above them, a pale blue crystal hung, festooned with growing vines and flowers, swaying in a warm breeze that smelled of honeysuckle and lilac. They stopped, booted feet and furred paws at the edge of a softly babbling stream that extended from one of the ornate walls and down into the center of the chamber, where it formed a pool at least thirty feet wide.

"Ah, be welcome, Lord Autarch. Be welcome to the dream pool." A Yttin with a handsome face and a too-wide smile greeted them from across the pond, his soft body not covered in armor but loose, flowing cloth.

"Klzix. You look different," Felix said, then gestured to the greenery all around them. "What is all this?"

"The usurpers to the Cerulean Throne destroyed much. Very little of our ancient city remains, and what little does is hidden in mansions and behind walls and tiny armies." The shaman ran a finger through the pool, and the water clung to him like glowing paint before evaporating. "This is something old, something that I believe the Grandmaster of the Desert's Fire chose to construct his home upon."

"Something that once belonged to the Yttin," Felix said, grasping at a truth that danced around his recent interactions with the transformed people. Things the shaman had mentioned to him a long time ago, in the sands. "*You* used to rule Ahkestria, didn't you?"

Klzix chuckled. "We did, when the tides were high and the waves at their fiercest. The crystalline groves and fecund jungle were like a green blessing beneath the bluest of skies, all of it under the reign of our kings and queens."

"Until you were cursed," Felix added. He considered using Rime Shaping to form a bridge across the pool, but that felt rude. Sacrilegious, almost.

"Until we cursed ourselves," the shaman corrected him.

"What? Why?" Pit asked.

"Explain this curse to me," Felix asked, trying to keep his tone respectful. "I don't really understand what happened to your people. Your messenger with the Platinum Chest mentioned some of it."

"Ah yes. And did the Chest prove worthwhile? It is the least we could do for our Savior." Klzix raised a hand, forestalling Felix's objections. "It is clear the name causes you some distress, but it is what you are, Felix Nevarre."

"The contents of the Chest don't feel like they are mine, Klzix. If your people were rulers of Ahkestria, then it seems they belong to the Yttin." Felix pulled the crown from the pouch at his waist, and it glimmered in the soft light from above.

"The Crown." Klzix sighed before shaking his head. "Let me tell you the tale, then, Felix Nevarre. Decide then how you wish to proceed." He shifted himself and ran his fingers through the luminous pool again. "What do you know of the godlings of the Realm?"

"Godlings. You mean Urges?" Felix asked.

"Yes. Long have they dwelled among the Continent, many of them intangible spirits, feeding off of us but causing no ill effects. Even now, nascent Urges walk the world, growing and changing with every passing moment. They are as sure as the dew upon the Weavings, clinging to the warp and weft of the Realms, no matter how it changes shape." One of the shaman's appendages, clad in white wrappings, reached out and drew a glowing line atop the water.

"They are...travelers between Realms. The Mind of the gods give them a spark of life while the Minds of mortals give them shape. Long before the Highest Flame was That Which Burns, it was an idea, a mote of significance in the endless dark. Then it found followers, mortals that eased it from Thought to Action, from Mind to Body. They fed it, kept it stoked through the dark."

"And when it ran out of fuel, it demanded sacrifices," Felix growled, his lip curling at the thought of it. "Disgusting."

"I wholeheartedly agree. Yet, to them, they are simply acting as their natures dictate. Some are more heavily influenced by their source than others, though only a few are able to garner strength from the merest mention of their purpose. Pit told me of Urges that died at your hand, horrors that fed upon the worst inclinations among mortals, inclinations that no doubt kept the Urges alive for Ages. Godlings are ideas given shape, and ideas are so very hard to destroy." Klzix tilted his head, and tawny hair cascaded across his face. It did not obscure his glowing copper eyes, however. "Until they met you. A man that is more than a man. A Devourer."

"He said that, huh?" Felix frowned at his Companion, who just looked back at him with wide golden eyes and a happy expression, as if waiting for praise. Felix could only roll his eyes. *So much for secrets.* "What's your point?"

Klzix's other appendages reached out, each one inscribing a glowing line atop the pool's surface. Mana swirled in Felix's senses, flowing toward the water and pulling the bright lines deep within it. In moments, the water lightened, until Felix swore he saw shapes flickering beneath. "It was not the first Godling to lay a stake upon this Territory. Far from it. Long ago, before my grandfather's grandfather was anything more than a whisper of lineage, there was a massing of such creatures."

The flickering increased, now furious, as if describing the vast shapes of creatures Felix couldn't begin to identify. "A battle that became a war between the Withered and the Godlings' dark leader. The Treacherous One, a creature of secrets and hidden depths."

The light darkened at the center, as if the dream pool had become a window into a dark, smoke-filled tunnel. Felix almost felt like he'd fall in if he stared too long...yet he couldn't pull away. "The Withered? You mean the Primordial of Withered Dust?"

Klzix nodded. "Yes. In the most ancient of our stories, the Withered was our protector against the predators of the depths. The Treacherous One suborned the glorious Leviathans, turning them against the Withered, taking their name and steeping the waters in darkest ichor." The water fully darkened, flooded with black blood...before it cleared to show a strange, long shape twisted upon itself. A sudden golden crown stitched itself atop the twisted mass, filling the waters with a sickly radiance. "The Leviathan Urge was graced with a bounty from the heavens, and with it the Treacherous One confused us, convinced us that the Withered was our enemy. We...struck down the Ancient One, smote it with magic and steel and the gifts of our allies. It was severed and entombed. Trapped for all eternity."

Images of wave and wind spiked through the waters, followed by rupturing earth and descending lattices of crystals. A vast, amorphous shape was trapped, thrust through with a flash of bronze, and sank away into the abyss.

"Too late, we found out the lie. The Leviathan Urge bore an emptiness inside of it, a vastness poised to end us all, to entrap all of our people within its unbearable visage." Klzix's voice broke, and a deep grief welled up from his Spirit. In the waters, something huge slithered by, bearing a face that was cloaked in shadow. "We should have died then, wiped from the Continent as surely as if we'd been Lost. Yet the Withered...it managed to drain its own significance and power upon one last move."

"Your curse," Felix said, and Pit chirruped at his side.

"Yes. The sea itself drained away, slaying the Leviathans of the depths, and the Treacherous One fled before its unrestrained might. The Queen made a choice to take the curse upon herself, to halt its spread. The royal family joined her, and soon all of our people stood as one, to stop the calamity from unfolding. It worked. The curse was stopped, spreading no farther than the borders of our Territory...and in return, cursing our people to a life of the wandering wretch. Reducing us, in Mind and Body, so that we could not even struggle against it.

"All we had to hope for was the Quest."

"Right." Felix shook himself from the vision in the pool. Already, the water was darkening again, the illusion of its tale fading. "The Quest. You received that after?"

"We did. The Quest was passed down among the shamanic line, passing from eldest to youngest in an unbroken tradition. Each year we sought our penance in the sands, each year attempting to keep our people alive long enough to see the curse broken. There was no sign, however, until the two of you arrived."

"Were the gods involved?" Felix asked. The golden crown and the light it radiated was awfully familiar to him.

"Yes. The Withered and the Treacherous One. Their clash is what—"

"No, no. The Divine gods, not Primordials and Urges. Like Noctis and Siva and all of them?" With each successive name, Felix watched understanding flit away from the shaman's face. "Do you not know of those gods?"

"We do, but they are not our gods. They were not present at the creation of the Yttin, nor the Leviathans that sustained our way of life for Ages beyond memory. Those came from the Ancient One. From the Primordials."

That was new. Felix hadn't heard of anyone worshiping the Primordials before, mostly because everyone kept insisting they were extinct. "Okay, but the golden crown. You said it was a bounty from the heavens. From the Divine?"

"Perhaps. It is an old story, and I have recited it, enacted it, as it was taught to me many decades ago." The shaman shrugged and stood from the pool with an effortless grace. His body was far more lithe than the bulky guards. A priest, not a warrior. "The truth of a story lies not in its facts, but in its essence. It's Spirit. And the Spirit can hold far more than the Mind or Body."

Felix tried and failed to keep the scoff from escaping his mouth. "The spirit of a story isn't going to help me solve the issues in front of me, Klzix. And this still doesn't answer why you would give up these artifacts." He pulled free the scepter and orb to join the crown in his hands. Felix could literally feel them buzzing with power, each one so charged up, it was a wonder he wasn't electrocuted.

"We do not deserve Authority, Felix Nevarre. We who failed the Withered, who failed ourselves, cannot hold the crown again. Will not." The shaman smoothed his robes, each of his back appendages tugging and draping cloth. "This is a stance held by all of the Yttin. Bred into our hearts by an Age of desolation and sacrifice. We have witnessed the end of our old world."

He bowed to the tenku, almost folding in half. "We thank you, Savior and Beast alike, for what you have done in ending this curse. In returning the sea and our treasured Bodies to us. You have ended our old world, blackening the skies and letting the sands flow as blood. We are free of our shackles...and would pledge ourselves to you once more, Autarch."

You Have Lost A Faction!
The Yttin (Beastsworn) Have Abandoned Your Fledgling Nation!
-25% To All Positive Relations With Yttin!

Congratulations, Autarch!
You Have Recruited A Faction!
The Yttin (Beastsworn) Have Joined Your Fledgling Nation!
+50% To All Positive Relations With Yttin!

"Let us know what you wish us to do," Klzix said from his deep bow. "You have only to ask, and the Yttin shall obey."

"Uhm, alright," Felix managed, unsure of what else to say. "But servitude isn't what I had in mind." He grasped his hands tight around the artifacts, unsure whether to clench them in anger or throw them up in disbelief.

Klzix straightened, more than a little hesitantly. "Servitude is all I fear we have to offer, Lord Autarch. We are capable warriors, sailors, and craftsmen. We are nimble and strong, and we offer all of that to you."

Felix looked around the chamber, at a bit of a loss. "Right. I'm glad you've decided to follow me, because that makes this next part far easier. I need a Chancellor."

Klzix lifted his arms and backed up a single step. His face was stricken. "My Lord, we are not worthy of rule. I cannot—"

"Worthy? That's stupid. *You* didn't do anything," Felix said, and this time he did activate his Rime Shaping. The surface of the pool flash froze, and Felix trod across it with crunchy steps. "Your ancient ancestors made some bad calls, and everyone paid the price. That's not on you." He reached out and placed a hand on the cringing shaman's shoulder. "Listen. I don't need you to rule, but Ahkestria is your ancestral home. I would see that its native people hold the reins while I'm not here."

Klzix couldn't quite meet Felix's eyes. "We have erred in the past, my Lord. Why would we not err in the future?"

Felix shrugged. "People fuck up. I do it all the time. That's how you learn to be better, right? I've heard a lot about what the Yttin once were," Felix said, staring until Klzix met his eyes. Copper and blue shone in the dark. "But tell me, who do you wish the Yttin *to be*?"

The shaman blinked and opened his mouth. "I—"

A vile, burning surge flashed across his senses, and Felix snapped his hand out instinctively. His scaled fingers closed around a sudden, deadly projectile. A blade, hissing with poison Mana...stopped mere inches from the shaman's neck.

"Killer!" Pit let out an ear-piercing shriek. "Sworn!"

CHAPTER SIXTEEN

Pit's words barely registered before the doorway of the chamber was thrown open, and a patch of swirling darkness shot out into the light.

"Stop them!" Klzix shouted, recoiling from the dagger in Felix's grip.

"No! Don't engage!" Felix flared his Agility and ripped across the dream pool, shattering the thick layer of ice behind him, but not before the guards tried to close with the dark cloud. To them, it was no more than a shadow, but Felix could see the being's insanely swift moves as it wove through the Yttins' grasp. A thin, flexible blade slashed around them in a whirlwind of strikes that the guards had no defense against. They all fell in a spray of dark crimson blood.

The shadow took off.

"No you don't! Thunderwing!" Pit screeched, and *blasted* past Felix, streaming afterimages of crackling lightning. "Mantle of Tumult! Howl at the Dark!"

An ear-piercing cry filled the corridor, stabbing at Felix's toughened senses, and it wasn't even aimed his way. The shadow, on the other hand, stumbled and crashed into an alcove filled with delicate pottery. Pit was on the assailant in an instant, a veritable storm coursing over his sleek Body while lightning spat from his wings and tail.

"Hurricane Rasp!" Black talons ripped through rug and stone, missing the dark assassin by inches. Their thin blade flashed upward, arcing toward Pit's neck. He let it glance harmlessly off his Master Tier barding and lunged for the kill.

"Sanguine Caul!" the shadow croaked out, and a thick, bloody wrapping slashed across Pit's face and helmet, binding to it.

"Ahh!" Pit reared back, clawing at his beak and eyes, and the assassin slipped from his grasp. In a fraction of a second, they were up on their feet and running.

Until Felix tackled them through a wall.

They screamed, and Felix growled, yet both of their voices were drowned out by the absolute clamor of falling masonry and shattering support beams. They hit the ground and rolled, pulverizing a couch and end table inside yet another parlor. Felix fetched back onto his feet only a breath before the assassin, which was plenty of time to marshal his Skills.

Adamant Discord!

Lightning stabbed between them, flashing back and forth like a strobe light, while the shadowy figure was wracked by painful seizures. Felix's Will clamped down atop them, a vise of Mind and Spirit, while his Body walked cautiously forward. The assassin's Body was still obscured by a misty sheath of shadow Mana, so tight and thick that nothing more than a vaguely humanoid shape could be made out. Even the lightning failed to illuminate it.

"Who are you? Why are you here?" Felix asked. "Your Agility and Dexterity seem to be really high, so you didn't miss me. You were aiming at the shaman. Why?" The shadow didn't answer. They only struggled harder against the riotous pain and Felix's indelible grasp.

"Fine, be that way." Felix reached forward and grabbed the figure by their neck. "*Chthonic Tribute.*"

All at once, the shadow around the figure fled, sucked completely within Felix's channels. The shroud of darkness was ripped apart, revealing lacquered body armor and a half mask that was entirely familiar. Eyes of milky white stared at him balefully, and their squared chin was thrust forward in challenge. Felix clicked his tongue. "Sworn. You were right, Pit."

"Of course I was," his Companion answered, picking his way across the rubble. His forepaws were crimson with vibrant Mana, and his helmet and beak were caked with hardened, fleshy strings. "I know that cold steel smell."

The Sworn were an order of assassins for hire, though their job might not always be to kill. The only experience either Felix or Pit had with the order was Ilia, a Sworn assassin he'd faced off against. She had been formidable, but this one had very nearly outrun Pit *and* himself. At their current, frankly overpowered level of advancement. If neither of them had been there, then this person could have killed any number of people under Felix's care.

"What is your name, Sworn?" he asked, and his grip loosed on their larynx. A little.

The Sworn's mouth opened, but instead of teeth and tongue, their insides were just an utter void. A breath vibrated up through Felix's clasp, rattling out of the assassin's dark craw like a corpse's final scream. What came out wasn't a sound so much as a wave of pressure that squealed against Felix's senses. He jerked backward, his grip unmoved, but the Sworn wasn't done.

The yowl ripped its void-filled mouth, tearing its cheeks and jaw like paper to reveal a greater darkness within. Fissures appeared, crazing their flesh and dark armor, as the dissonant tenor of its cry tore it apart.

Warning sparked along his Affinity, told in twisted song, and Felix threw the Sworn back, into the nearby fireplace. With a concussive blast, the assassin ripped apart, exploding into dissonant tremors. Jagged tongues tore through the stone mantle, eating it away in a flash, leaving nothing of the Sworn but a fading pillar of smoke.

Pit trilled in distress, his brilliant wings outspread and crackling with various strings of light. "Where are they?"

"Gone," Felix said. He stepped closer to the fireplace, close enough that he winced from the deep fissures. They were harsh and atonal, not unlike the touch of Primordial but also very different. More...acrid. "I don't even think that was a real person. Look." He waved his hand through the plume of smoke. "Mana. Essence. I think...I think we need to talk to Zara about this." Guards piled into the room, a mixture of Felix's Shadows and more of the Yttin. Shaman Klzix was among them, looking pale but otherwise composed. "You need to get somewhere safe. This assassin wasn't sent for me."

"What? For me? Why?" Klzix traded glances with his fellow Yttin, but all of them seemed confused and more than a little perturbed.

"Because, as far as everyone is concerned, you lead the Yttin. And I have a feeling that folks' memories aren't as short as they like to pretend." Felix was guessing at that, but his Mind teased out several potential scenarios, and it felt the most likely. "The Sworn don't just kill people for fun. They're paid. That means they have a client, and that client wants you dead." *And they didn't attack until I asked you to be my Chancellor,* he finished silently. No need to spread that around yet.

"They...they fear us so much?" Klzix's voice was awash in confusion and a touch of strange wonder. "We have done nothing."

"You represent change," Felix said. "This is your moment to choose who *you* wish to be, Klzix. You heard my offer. I will expect an answer in the morning." Not waiting for a response, Felix nodded to the Yttin guards and his own Shadows. "See that the shaman is kept safe until I send for him, okay? Maryk and Waryn, get Lady Zara and Atar and Alister."

"At once, my Lord. Where shall I send them? Here?" the Henaari asked him.

"No." Felix wiped his hands off against his trousers and stepped away from the fireplace. "Have them meet me at the library."

Evie stood atop the rain-slicked rooftop and cursed in time with the rainfall. "Bloody burning ash and broken teeth. Damn nightfall. Ain't no moons to see, ain't no Paladins, and now we're huntin' damn ghosts."

"Calm yourself, kid. And tone it down. Not gonna find shit if you scare 'em all off."

Evie' scowled over her shoulder through the moonless dark and curtains of rain. Lightning crawled across the sky, reflecting briefly off a shorter man in an oilskin cloak. "Glad you're feelin' better enough to sass, Harn. But we're not gonna find any of 'em. You know how the Sworn work. They're not popping up then sticking around."

"They failed at their job," Harn pointed out. His face was covered by his usual frog-mouthed helm, making his tired voice echo faintly. He was a bit shaky still, having just emerged from his forge trance not two glasses past. He'd pressed full on into Adept, though, and Evie held that was worth any amount of discomfort.

Two new axes hung at his waist, the final, ultimate expression of his Tempering at the smithy. Evie wasn't sure what had happened to the old ones but also didn't really care. The new pair were Adept-Tier weapons, shaped with a bearded blade and a vicious spike from the back, the metal folded with so much Mana that they almost glowed in the dark. "Sworn don't abide failure. They'll keep comin' 'til they get their man. That's why we're out here."

"I know that." Evie glanced over the rooftop, eyeing the other members of the Fiend's Claw who had joined them. The more agile of the Blades and Fists followed her, making up their hit squad. Felix had asked Evie to head up a team to hunt down the assassin he'd dispatched, and she'd jumped at the chance. She'd taken out one Sworn before, but it was never too late to add another notch on her belt. However, she hadn't expected a surge in the ever-present storm. "Still. Couldn't handle killin' one shaman. This is overkill, ain't it?"

"Not if they're as strong as Felix suspects," Harn said. They were both talking quietly enough that the rain covered most of their words. Someone in Journeyman or Adept Tier focused in Perception might have heard them, but the chance was low, and they had sight lines in almost every direction. He glanced over the edge of the roof, into the warren of alleys below. "A projection ain't somethin' everyone can do. It's a specialized Skill set, and I've only ever heard about it in stories. Sworn who use it don't usually get caught in the act, let alone thwarted. That crab man is lucky Felix was there."

"Yeah, well, the weather sucks, is all." Evie flashed several handsigns over the edge of the roof and waited three heartbeats. A patch of darkness raised blue fingers the size of her head and signed back. "Ari is saying we should move from here. What do you think, Harn?"

"Callin' the Frost Giant Battlelord by his first name? That's good." Evie scowled, harder than ever, but Harn only laughed and patted her gently on the back. "You can't go around clutchin' hate too long. Glad to see you movin' on."

Evie only stared at him, Willing the armored fool to change the subject. She wasn't certain *how* she felt about the Frost Giants any longer. Harn was right, though, and the hate had thawed a bit since Tempering her Body. It hadn't completely gone away, and Evie still felt intensely uncomfortable being around them too long, but she had found some common ground with Battlelord Ari and his men in recent days.

They had accompanied her and Vess on many of their hunts for the Paladins and had saved her life once or twice. She made sure to save theirs right back, and more often for good measure, just so the scales balanced right. Now the giants had followed her lead and joined her newest hunt. Ari and his contingent were cloaked in the biggest oilskins she'd ever seen, looking like someone put a tarp on a boulder. They stalked for beans, but Evie could admit they were quieter than most Untempered. Most.

When Evie didn't respond at all to his probing, Harn sighed. "I suppose we move on. Let's shift closer into the district. I imagine the Sworn is staying somewhere fancy. Their kind like their nice things."

"Fine. We move then," Evie said, and made the signs. Behind her, the Talon stood from relaxed, readied crouches and loped across the rooftops. Below, large patches of wet darkness slipped forward, ghosting down the alleyways near the skydocks. "You comin', old man?"

"Aye, I am," Harn grumbled. His fingers traced idly across his axes, as if he were eager to use them. "Let's hope we find them before they find us."

Xavi slid down the flooded thoroughfare, his boots well and truly soaked. He was thankful that he still had his oilskin, though the wind had tried to snatch that from him a time or two as well. The cloak was all that kept his prize safe and dry, and without his prize, Xavi knew he would not be believed.

Splashes sounded from further up the street, followed by curses and whoops as his fellow messengers ran their own missives to their masters. Unlike Xavi, they dashed through the moonless dark, seemingly careless of the rain and treacherous streets. *Why are they so cavalier? Don't they know what they have?*

Xavi had seen them all receive one, the same as him. The man who gave it to them was strange and terrifying, and said that they had to protect the prize, to make sure each and every one made it to their masters within the glass. Xavi hadn't questioned it; he feared being late, for what it might mean. For what the man might do to him.

So the messenger stuttered into a run again, his boots squishing unpleasantly with every step. At least he was close to his master's mansion, and in a few more heartbeats, he'd reached the imposing gate. Xavi banged on its iron exterior, his fist aching from the exuberance of it. "Manny! Manny, let me in!"

A small panel slid to the side with a metal-on-metal shriek. "Burning ashes! Who's knocking at my gate at this hour? Xavi? That you?"

"Yes, sir! It is! Can you let me in?"

Manny shook his head, and while Xavi couldn't see more than his eyes, he knew his thick, drooping mustache was wobbling with his head. "No no, can't do that. No one in or out after nightfall. Master's orders."

"Manny, sir, please! Tell the master that I have a missive for him. From the Autarch!" Xavi practically begged the guard, trying to say everything with just his wide, limpid eyes. It was a look that had often gotten him second helpings in the lesser kitchens, and sometimes worked to get him into places he shouldn't be. This, however, was not such a place. He needed to deliver the prize, and he was running out of time. "Please!"

Manny groaned and rolled his eyes. "Fine, just stop with the Avum eyes, ya manipulative bastard!" The gate clanked and squealed as Manny pulled it open enough for Xavi to squeeze through. "In ya git!"

"Thank you!" he shouted, bolting past Manny and into the servant's entrance of the mansion. Quick as a flash and not stopping to chat with the servants in the gathering hall, Xavi stripped off his oilskin and tossed it onto a wooden peg. He barely stopped to adjust the collar of his mussed-up shirt, or to change his waterlogged boots, and instead tracked a squishing trail of rainwater with every second step.

Eventually, he came to the outside of the dining chamber, where the sound of boisterous laughter and soft music filled the air. Two more liveried guards were there, dressed down but bearing their weapons. Xavi met their eyes and nodded. "Message for Master Rellest. From the Autarch," he repeated.

The guards traded a look and waved him through.

Inside the chamber were several dozen guests, all of them regulars to the master's parties. They were scions of the various noble and merchant Houses in Ahkestria, the cream of the crop and future ruling elite among the City of Embers. Or they had been, Xavi gathered, before the monster showed up and changed everything.

Xavi navigated his way through the crowd, moving swiftly until he came upon a long table bearing many ornate chairs. At the head of the table, engaged in a story he was telling, was Master Rellest.

"Sir? I have a missive, a gift, from the Autarch. Sir," Xavi said. He'd never said that much to the master before, not in his entire life, and he felt proud to have gotten through it so smoothly. He held up the prize and found that his arms only trembled a little bit. "He sent me with this."

A hush fell over the crowd, and Master Rellest stared at Xavi's hands with the strangest expression. Almost as if he was afraid the thing was going to come to life and attack him. Which was ridiculous; there was no chance his master was thinking such a far-fetched idea. The prize was a small sculpture of a muscular man with long limbs and strange claws, all fashioned by an unnerving magic. Xavi had seen the statues being created, one at a time, and couldn't believe how smooth the thing felt.

"The Autarch made this himself. I—I don't know how," Xavi admitted into the quiet. He'd never felt comfortable with long silences. He lifted the statuette and showed his master the large, round bottom of it, where words were inscribed. "It says, 'Dawn. Temple square. All are invited to the raising of your new Chancellor.'"

Xavi's Master went beet red as he heard the words, and a wrenching sound filled the air. The silver goblet in his hand dropped to the table, crumbled out of shape and leaking red wine like blood. "Sir?" Xavi asked.

"Assemble our people. All of House Rellest," his master said in response. Much to Xavi's surprise and worry, his master sounded...shaken. "The Autarch commands our presence at dawn. Be ready.

"All of you."

CHAPTER SEVENTEEN

Zara reached out and fixed Felix's collar with her thin hands. "Remember to keep their gazes. They are used to the powerful lording over them, but all nobles are jackals. They will pounce if they sense weakness."

Felix brushed her hands away and Willed the Garment into proper shape. With a snap of rippling cloth, his formal jacket shaped up around his neck, dipping just at the front where a half-circle was cut out of it. The thing was made of a rich green fabric—silk, he thought—and embroidered up the sleeves and shoulders with elaborate vines and leaves. He'd been shown a number of formal clothing options by the mansion's servants, and Felix had just chosen a set at random, studying it a moment before copying it all with his magical clothing.

They were standing in an antechamber off of the inner sanctum of the Temples of Elemental Fire, surrounded by gilded finery, sculpture, and polished architecture. His honor guard surrounded him, blocking exits and windows, and beyond them were several Talons of the Fiend's Claw, all waiting on his orders. Closer to hand were his allies and friends, most of whom were poring over a pile of dusty tomes they'd dragged with them from the library. Felix checked himself in a huge, ten-foot mirror again and nodded in satisfaction. "Good enough. Zara, you're describing literally everyone I've met on the Continent that had even a smidgen of power. I know how to deal with them."

"Hm," was all she said. "The Houses Voru, Wuan, Perevor, and Rellest command the greatest power in the city. They hold the reins of the Merchant's Council, setting prices for the city's goods and other such details. As such, they will be the ones to watch out for and the ones who have the most to lose by what you plan."

"Which is mad, I don't mind saying," Isla chipped in from the side. She was wearing a diaphanous pink gown that faded into a dark purple at the flowing end of the skirt, while a set of delicate silver jewelry hung around her neck and down both of her arms and wrists. They looked more like avant garde armor than anything else, and Felix could practically feel the Mana radiating off of them. They were defensive measures, he was certain. "Your choice of Chancellor is sure to rile all of them against you. Why not choose among their number? It would lead to a smoother transition."

"Because I don't know them, and because I can't trust them," Felix said. He was tired of this conversation, one that had been repeated for the last six hours.

Isla scoffed. "And you know and trust this man? You only met him a few days ago!"

"Enough," Felix said, putting an edge to his voice and gaze. Isla opened her mouth to continue despite his glare, but she glanced at Zara and snapped it closed. "Thank you. Guys? Have you found anything yet?"

Off to the side, Pit lifted his head from a large atlas, dust clinging to the feathers around his beak. "You know I can't read, right?"

Felix rolled his eyes. "Just look at the maps, and it'll update my Authority Screen. I wasn't really talking to you though, bud. Atar? Alister?"

His mage friends were also in the stack of books, piled haphazardly on what was once an altar of some sort. Alister massaged his lower back as he carefully turned another whisper-thin page. "No records of the ancient line of Yttin royalty. Yttin? Yttish?" He shrugged, clearly tired from the all-nighter Felix had kinda, sorta forced on them. "Either way, the old borders aren't drawn up anywhere."

"And there are no histories or records that reach back farther than the last thousand years," Atar added.

Zara placed her hands on her hips, surveying Felix's outfit one last time before nodding. "I am not surprised. The victors often determine what is and what is not the history of a people. In this case, those words were crafted by the Humans who ruled Ahkestria after the curse was placed upon the Territory. I doubt they much cared about the Yttin's side of things. My apologies, Shaman Klzix."

"No apologies needed for the truth, Chanter Zara. Our fall was neither comfortable nor short enough for self-deception to survive in our hearts," Klzix said from within his ring of armed guards.

"Are we beginning soon? Dawn is just about upon us," Fiammetta pointed out from the side. She was dressed in a flowing robe of blue with a sash of bright yellow, colors representing Felix and her own core attunement, she'd said.

In fact, all of them were dressed up, with Zara's black chorister robes covered in a blue-green shawl, Atar and Alister's mage robes looking cleaned up and repaired. Beef wore a sturdy, quilted blue jacket and some flowing pants over his bovine legs. Vess, too, was decked out in a flowing set of robes cinched tightly over her white-enameled armor, leaving her limbs free to move. Her dark brown hair was done up in a series of thick braids, all of them drawn into a tight bun. Colored beads and ornamental clips were woven into her braids, blue and green and white and violet among them. Their vibrant color was particularly striking against her deep skin tone and dark eyes. Like everyone else, she seemed tense.

Vess peered out of the large double doors. "The square is nearly filled with people. Did you send an invitation to everyone in the city? I see more than the nobility out there."

"I did," Felix said, shifting his shoulders a bit. The jacket was a touch tight across his chest, but the Garment quickly adjusted. "I need them all here. Everyone I can get."

"Hm," was all she said, and returned her gaze outside.

Is she mad that I missed our dinner? he wondered for the hundredth time. *Maybe I can just check. Just for a second.* The thought came and was snuffed out instantly; Felix still refused to use his Affinity on her. It was an invasion of her privacy...though he admitted he had no issues scanning his other friends' Spirits. He pushed that line of logic away, as well. *I'll just talk to her...Later.*

The only people who weren't immediately in attendance were Evie and Harn, and he knew why. "Alright. Let's begin."

The alabaster double doors opened with a stentorian boom, and a flood of black-cloaked warriors marched outward. The crowd murmured and gasped, and Felix's Affinity caught snippets of strained vibrations as they rippled across the assembly. Row after row of the Fiend's Claw stepped out onto the raised landing before pivoting smoothly to the right and left, until they filled the double stairwells to either side. They were followed by an equally large contingent of Yttin warriors, all of them wearing chitinous armor, sea-green tunics, and bearing simple halberds. They stepped in concert with the Claw, taking up position right behind them, much to the crowd's surprise.

Behind them came Felix himself, flanked and trailed by his own train of friends and followers. He stepped forward, attempting to convey a sense of authority and solemnity. What he was attempting had to go off without a hitch, otherwise the whole city would turn on itself. *I made the right choice*, he reminded himself. *The only right choice.*

Felix stopped at the ornamented balustrade crafted of white stone veined with gold. The entire square outside the main structure of the Temple of Elemental Fire was composed of the same gold-veined white rock, though the veins congregated in swirling, circular patterns around the edges of the square itself. Felix could just make that out, barely, through the press of the crowd.

It was easier, he found, than focusing on the many faces of anxiety, fear, and outright awe. He knew those were masks, especially on the more affluent crowd members dressed in finery and surrounded by retainers. Their weapons had been taken before they were allowed to enter the temple grounds, but all of them had a way of standing that made it clear what they really were.

He flared his Affinity, sending it sprawling across the mass of people. As before, it was rippling with so many emotions that only chaotic noise was the result. Drilling down toward the nobles near the front, Felix could sense guilt and anger and more than a little envy, but it was scattered. Diffused by the sheer number of people and all of their strong emotions mingling in Felix's ears.

C'mon. Which one of you. He kept scanning, even as Zara stepped up and began talking. *I know you're here.*

"We are gathered today to witness history being made once again in Ahkestria," Zara said. Her voice was light and kind-sounding, yet its impact reached every corner of the square and likely beyond. "Twice now the Autarch Nevarre has saved your people. Once when he defied the Master's Council and the Matrons of this Temple, all of whom had planned to sacrifice their own citizens to the Highest Flame.

"In his name, we defeated them, smote the Urge that sought your demise, and drove the Paladins of the Pathless that dared darken your skies. The second was when the Autarch personally battled and defeated Grandmaster Kel'lyv, earning him the Authority to claim this Territory. Both of those events will be remembered in your annals for Ages to come, but today marks a moment of renewal and rejoicing. When the ancient meets modern, and tradition is upheld to bring forth a new destiny."

Zara turned to Felix and bowed at her waist, a motion repeated by his friends, while every single one of his warriors saluted, fist to heart. Felix stepped forward, and a raucous cheer took up from the back, where the common folk were located. He grinned, and at his side, Pit trilled in interest. He was tall enough to see over the railing, which meant his dark, armored form was easily visible to everyone else as well. A number of the retainers frowned, while still more among the commoners cheered.

Felix raised a hand, asking for silence, and it fell in stuttering stages. Then he raised his other hand, and in it he held the Crown of Ahkestria. This time, the strangled gasp came from the nobility.

"I see some of you recognize this. The Crown of Ahkestria, ancient artifact of the original, true rulers of this Territory. The Yttin." He grinned as more gasps and hissing whispers let loose among the audience. *Chew on that, nobles.* "With it, I choose Shaman Klzix as my Chancellor, to act in my stead and to be my right hand within this Territory.

"Shaman," he said, gesturing him closer. Klzix took two steps forward, his face calm but his Spirit bubbling with unease as the barrier of Yttin warriors parted around him. Felix had practiced this next part, getting most of the words from Karys' somewhat rickety recollections. "Do you make this choice willingly? To take up Authority and responsibility for those under your care?"

"I do," Klzix said. The unease turned to a shaky euphoria as his eyes flicked outward to the crowd and back to Felix. "I have chosen to take up this burden willingly and without coercion."

Felix smiled, and he lifted the intertwined circlet of coral and crystal in his hands. "Then kneel, Klzix, Shaman of the Beastsworn Tribe. Kneel and—"

"The light denies you! HUAAH!"

A flash of sizzling light blasted toward them both, but Felix threw up his arm, absorbing the hit and turning his sleeve to ash. A deafening shout ripped through the square, propelled from lungs so mighty that a few of the nobility were bowled aside. From that gap, dozens of figures poured through, all of them casting aside shimmering, enchanted cloaks to reveal thick, crimson platemail.

"Kill the monster!" their leader cried. "Kill them all!"

Blades of fire erupted as panicked screams seized the crowd, yet before they could advance much farther, they were met by Blade and Fist and Bone.

Chaos erupted.

The Claw clashed with the blazing swords of light while Felix's Shadows shielded the landing from a barrage of golden Mana bolts. "Enough! Go! Take down the Paladins!" Felix ordered. Lieutenant Errol nodded, but only half of his guard joined Vess and Beef as they leaped into the fray.

"My Lord! Take cover!" Errol threw himself forward as a flash of darkness descended from on high.

Time slowed to Felix's Perception as his hefty Intelligence and Mind kicked into high gear. He saw the darkness, identified them as thick arrows the size of spears, all roiling with a corrosive Mana that was a mixture of shadow and poison types. There were twenty of them, all fired from the rooftops around the square where he'd stationed a number of guards. Felix's senses spread, streaking across tiles and spires and parapets, feeling the dead...and the dire enemy that performed the deed.

Chthonic Tribute!

Felix flung out his hands and his Will at the same time, catching two of the massive black spears in his hands while the rest...the rest dissolved into harmless vapor and were devoured.

Lieutenant Errol blinked up at him owlishly from the ground, his arms still raised defensively. "Sir? Are—are you alright?"

"I'm fine," Felix said, before growling and snapping the conjured spears in half. They crumbled to nothing. "But they won't be."

He focused on the Sworn, threading his awareness outward even as they readied for another volley. He could feel them, hear them through his Affinity, though every one sounded the same. That was the thread, the through-line between their false Bodies. A repeated refrain that connected them all to one another and led all the way back to a belltower...behind and above Felix.

"Got you," he hissed, and he accessed his Authority.

Greetings Autarch!
What Song Do You Wish To Sing?

Sing the Song of Fallen Skies, he commanded the System.

He hadn't spent his entire time in the library the night prior after all. A good portion of his time had been finding and claiming the Seat and Seal of the Leviathan Depths. Felix raised his hand, and a complicated swirling pattern of light formed in his outstretched grasp. It was echoed above in the churning supercell looming over the Territory, multiplied a hundredfold, layers upon layers of complicated sigaldry shifting and aligning all in an instant.

KRAKOOOM!

A blast of incandescent lightning hurtled from the sky, shattering the belltower with a single blow. Masonry and the copper dome of it detonated in all directions, but Felix tracked a form through the blinding haze. A figure on fire yet wreathed in darkness jerked its arms.

Before Felix could react, a wall of aquamarine Mana flowed over the shaman and Zara, who had stepped forward. An arrow twice the size of the others had plunged into her shield, punching half its length through it before stopping. Felix met Zara's shocked eyes. "Behind you!" she shouted, just as a second arrow clipped him in the side.

"ARGH, fuck!" he gasped. "Sovereign of Flesh!"

Scales sprang up from his skin, shredding what remained of his fine cloth as it appeared. Felix grabbed at his side, but the wound had already healed, and he deflected another massive arrow from the pain in the ass Sworn. It clanged from his fists, unable to penetrate that, at least, even if he couldn't see them move. "Damn things are moving too fast. Evie!" he shouted, and let his Adept lungs loose. The air rippled from the force of it. "There!"

Cardinal Flame!

A pillar of red-gold flame appeared above the Sworn's dark shape, even when it dodged backward in an attempt to hide. Felix grinned as a single spike of ice shot up into the air in acknowledgement and turned back to his guard. "Get the Chancellor out of the line of fire. I'll shield you all. Go!"

"Yes, sir!"

CHAPTER EIGHTEEN

Lightning blasted from the sky, striking the rooftops and shattering clay tiles again and again, but the shrouded Sworn dodged them all. The lighting was powerful, but nowhere near as strong as the one who had demolished his hiding place.

The monster has control of the Storm Ward, too? How? Mikhail slipped over the tiles, the coating of oil Mana on his boots allowed him to glide as if on ice. Another bolt of lightning arced downward, but it found only empty architecture. *Rellest, you bastard! You held out on me!*

The Kindred held only the loosest of presences in Ahkestria, but Mikhail had been contracted by some nervous, hand-wringing nobles to track down and kill whoever this Autarch chose as Chancellor. The trick was to do it before anyone got invested with any Authority. It was unknown how much the Autarch controlled, just that he had somehow defeated the Grandmaster for it and claimed the Territory. Likely by some trickery, instead of strength.

He wasn't the one who destroyed the Urge and the entire council of Masters. From all the intel Mikhail gathered, the Autarch hadn't even been around. Still, if Mikhail struck too late, after the Chancellor was invested, there was no guarantee of completion. The protection from the Authority, especially here where the Seat was undoubtedly located, would fuck it all up.

The poisoned blade had been his solution, thrust from the shadows. The Autarch, for all his supposed power, hadn't been able to see through his Shroud, so following the man had been a simple matter. Then, he'd led Mikhail right to the new Chancellor-to-be. It had been perfect. The throw was precise and powerful—it should have slipped by the Autarch's notice and punched right through that Yttin's throat.

Mikhail hissed in pain as another bolt of lightning careened into him, rolling from the blast and trailing tendrils of his disrupted Shroud. *Yyero's ass!* The bolt had charred the outside of his left arm. *This cursed storm!*

That the Autarch had stopped Mikhail's blade was one thing, but then he and his nasty little Chimera chased down and *caught* his Mannequin? That was concerning. He'd had to detonate it prematurely, but even that hadn't been enough to harm the man. But this? Authority claimed and the storm being wielded as he caught Mikhail's Master-Tier arrows? The man was strong. Powerful.

So Mikhail ran.

The enormous greatbow in his hands was dragging him down, despite his Master-Tier Body, but the Sworn was loath to give it up. He aimed another shot on the run, funneling Mana through his palms and into the greatbow as an arrow made of shadow and poison formed on the string. He released but didn't stop to see if it hit. His aim was perfect...the true problem was this Autarch's defensive abilities.

Get off of me! Mikhail swiped at the flame above his head, but only got burned for his efforts. It refused to dissipate, following after him like a loyal dire hound, marking his position for all and sundry. As one of the Sworn, Mikhail had a number of ways to escape such tracking magics, but none of them were pleasant or easily performed. He sent a pulse of Will and Intent along his active Skills. *Get off the roof. Rush the target!*

Mikhail felt the Mannequins move, firing one last shot at the Yttin shaman before half of them leaped down into the chaos of the crowd. Lightning chased after them all, but Mikhail couldn't worry about their wellbeing. They would be expensive and time consuming to replace, but what he needed now was a distraction. He—

A chain lashed onto his path, writhing up and into the Sworn's face. Mikhail dipped and twisted, popping under and up into an aerial somersault while bringing his greatbow to bear. He fired, but an axe of silver deflected his conjured arrow into a nearby chimney, which burst and collapsed under the impact.

"Damn, ya have some muscle in all that dark, eh?" A gruff voice spoke up from within a bulky set of armor, complete with a strange, elongated helmet. "Almost tore my axe outta my hand."

"Watch him, Harn," said a second figure, the one with the chain idly spinning in her hand. She looked the flexible sort, someone Mikhail would normally steer clear of; his powerset was best against slower enemies. Except...one of them barely had her feet in Adept Tier, and the other was freshly minted. Mikhail could practically smell the Essence Draught on his breath.

"You think you two are enough?" Mikhail asked, letting his Shroud distort the waves of his voice. It came out thick and deep enough to kick up the loose stones on the rooftop. He threw down his greatbow. "I am a High Adept. You cannot harm me."

The Sworn didn't wait for them to reply but burst into motion. His blade, Whisper, leaped to hand and lashed out just in time to meet the wave of silver fire from the armored goon. Mikhail surged through them, Whisper slashing and tearing the flames to shreds, before meeting the warrior with a powerful thrust knee. It took him in the chest and hurled the warrior onto his ass, prone and unable to defend against Whisper's whirling thrust.

CLANG!

Blade met chain—no, a *shield* formed of chains. Perception burning, Mikhail skipped backward just as the shield burst into a series of bladed tendrils...but couldn't avoid them all. Two latched onto his sword and arm, tangling with his Shroud and pressing hard into his lacquered armor.

"Ah ah," the girl said, wagging her finger at him. "We dance first, yeah?"

"Fine, *child*." Mikhail spat the words and flared his Shroud. The threads of shadow Mana thickened and slickened, prizing apart the jagged chains and slipping his arm and blade free. The chains whirled backward, returning to the floating shield. "You may die first."

Murk Transposition!

Beneath their feet, shadows oozed from the clay tiles, crawling onto one another until they'd formed a simulacra of a man. A Mannequin. Three of them, in fact, all of a size with the Sworn and possessing a large portion of his stats. He grinned, though the soon-to-be-corpses before him couldn't see it. He'd always enjoyed this part. "Focus on the brute. I'll handle the girl."

———

Beef kicked a Paladin's chest in, relishing the crunch and clatter of their armor on the ground. "Eat it, nerd!"

You Have Killed A Paladin Of The Pathless!
XP Earned!

Awesome. Just a few more, and I'll level up again, too. Beef surveyed the battle, an easy task at his seven-foot height, but all he saw was chaos. About forty Paladins had formed up in the square, holding shields sparkling with golden radiance and long spears of hardened light. Around them were the black-cloaked Claw members and a few of the blue-cloaked Yttin warriors, all of them engaged with the Paladins. Magic burst and exploded, Stamina Skills flared, and weapons were brandished. All while the nobles and commoners alike were pressing themselves into the edges of the square, probably hoping no one killed them with a stray Skill.

Damn. Gotta end this. Can't have them get hurt because of these jerks. Beef firmed up his grip on his great maul and swung it. The necrotic, blackened green light flared as it bashed another Paladin into the flagstones. "Didn't think I saw you, huh?" Beef said to the struggling warrior zealot as he walked past them. "I got eyes in the back of my...back. Hallow!"

A series of razor-sharp crystal darts fired from his lower back, taking the Paladin across the face and neck.

Your Homunculus Has Killed A Paladin Of The Pathless!
XP Earned!

"Wow, good aim," he said over his shoulder. Hallow's strange, rocky form tightened against Beef's midsection before releasing itself with a heavy jolt. "Oof, you're still so hefty."

"I am made of stone and crystal, Michael," Hallow's feminine voice echoed back at him as she landed. "Watch out. The commoners are in danger."

"What? Oh shit!"

Ahead, two Paladin Adept Tiers unleashed streamers of glittering fire onto the crowd. Beef charged, bashing through a few unfortunate nobles on his way, but pulled on his limited Mana all the while. "Chitin Construction!"

A shield of insectile armor formed from nothing, big enough to cover Beef's entire Body, and he interposed himself into the flames. The fight was turning, and the Paladins were attempting to run.

"Ruak tu falla!" a mammoth voice screamed, and Beef laughed. "Warriors! Shields!"

Six Frost Giants, each twice his height or more, stepped out of the fray, and planted huge black shields in the way of the Paladin Adepts. Ice Mana swelled and crackled across the ground, racing toward the Pathless zealots. Their flames guttered out, and several screamed in sudden, frostbitten pain.

"Leviathan bone shields?" Beef said to the giant nearest him. "Impressive!"

"Made by Commander Harn himself," said the giant, and he unsheathed a huge, bone-crafted warhammer.

"Aw that's so sick," Beef muttered. He wasn't jealous. He could make his own stuff, anyway. "Let's bring the pain!"

"Advance!" shouted another giant warrior, and they moved forward as one.

More fire and spears of light assaulted their shield wall, but they held long enough. Beef glanced behind him and noticed that hundreds of commoners and nobles had flooded into their shadow, huddling in the safe zone created by their shields. Many were wide-eyed with fear and only a few had any wounds, but they caught Beef's eye like a magnet. "Hallow?"

"Yes, Michael?"

"I want you to try the barrage thing." Another blast of fire made him grunt and stagger, the entire shield line buckling slightly. "Now, please!"

"Of course." His Spirit friend rolled forward, forming into a segmented ball of coarse rock and smooth crystal small enough to slip between their shields. She popped up, just on the other side. "Firing now. Silicate Barrage."

Screams sounded, followed by a sudden slackening of attacks. A notification window popped into Beef's view.

Your Homunculus Has Killed A Paladin Of The Pathless (x12)!
XP Earned!

Your Homunculus Has Gained 3 Levels!
+21 Endurance
+15 Strength
+12 Vitality

"Oh, I love this!" Beef shouted in glee and threw his entire weight into his advance. The giants took up the charge. "Flatten 'em!"

———

"Hah!" Mikhail huffed an annoyed breath. "You're quite fast, girl."

"You're just slow," she shot back, though her face was a mess of cuts and blood. The girl had put on quite the show already, but now she was limping and nursing at least two broken ribs. He stood there, assessing as she followed her attack up with another blast of icy chains. They tried and failed to catch onto his Shroud. "Tch. Your cloak is cheatin', assassin."

"Tactical advantage, child." Mikhail blurred forward, his flexible blade bending around the girl's shield of chains. The thing tried to latch onto him again, but he'd learned the timing of it. The Sworn produced a final burst of speed and felt his Whisper blade catch flesh. He *twisted.*

"Ahh!" she cried out and fell.

Across the roof, his Mannequins piled onto the armored warrior, holding his arms down despite the blaze of his silver flame. "Evie!" he shouted.

"Worry for yourself," Mikhail hissed through his nearest Mannequin and manifested Whisper in its hand. He thrust, cracking a hole in the man's armor. Handling them in two separate fights was a challenge, but not an insurmountable one. He pulled back—

"Ragh!" the Sworn shouted as a shard of ice plunged into his face. It couldn't break his skin, couldn't even bruise him, but the sheer wretched cold was enough to break his concentration. "You petulant infant!"

"Descent of the Bestial Barbarian! Withering Raze!" The armored warrior erupted with sudden potency, breaking through the weakened grip of his distracted Mannequins. In seconds, one of them was bisected by a blazing silver axe, and another had lost its arm.

"Seems like you're falterin' there, assassin," the girl said from behind not one but three floating shields. She could barely stand, but her primary weapon whirled in the air above her, a stinger waiting to strike. "I thought you were almost Master Tier?"

"Fine. Neither of you were my target, and I was going easy on you. Enough of that. I will show you the meaning of pai—" Mikhail's words died away as his gaze was drawn up. Up into the sky where the thunderous clouds were joined by a terrifying new appearance.

A towering wave the size and approximate mass of the entire *city* had reared into the sky. It rose, higher and higher, until it seemed to touch the clouds and spark a raging tempest of lightning through its expanse. Mikhail's heart was clenched by the twin jaws of disbelief...and terror. The wave hung there, partially curled over itself like a threat. A deadly promise.

"Stand down."

The words shook the air, quaking it and tearing away even the constant rain from the sky. Everything went silent, and the Sworn tore his gaze away from the impending disaster and glanced down at the Temple doors. There, the Autarch stood with a single arm upraised, holding a scepter that scintillated with streamers of Mana, as if he had captured the sun and held it in the palm of his hand.

This isn't Authority, he thought. His Mind was struggling to comprehend the sheer scope of Mana on display. To control such a volume of water would beggar entire Territories! *What is this? What is this!*

"Stand down," he said again. His face was calm, but his eyes burned brighter than the artifact in his hands. The words shook dust and debris from the rafters and archways, even knocking a few weaker individuals to their knees. The man's Spirit joined in the effort, and even Mikhail felt his knees weaken. "I hold Authority over this Territory, and it is absolute. Stand down, or all of it is over. I, for one, do not need *two* Territories."

He's bluffing, Mikhail determined. *He has to be. He'd never—*

Click.

A cold void opened up in the Sworn's chest as he felt the equally cold metal of an elision collar around his neck. He gasped, seizing as his core space rebelled against the confinement, while his Aspects recoiled from the vile inscription in the collar. His Mind and Body quailed, and this time he truly fell to his knees. *No!*

"Night night, asshole," the girl growled before her heavy chain-shield crashed into his face.

The fighting had stopped, but Felix was so damn *pissed*.

In his hand, the Scepter of the Tides hummed like his old sedan when he'd pushed it past ninety miles per hour. It was hot from the strain of holding the massive wave, and Felix felt just about scraped raw. It had taken every ounce of his Mana to conjure the thing, and thankfully the Scepter acted as a massive focus, enhancing the effect, or else the threat wouldn't have worked at all.

The Paladins were hemmed in, many of them dead, but not all. Above the square, on the rooftops, Harn gave him handsign confirming the Sworn had been caught as well. Felix had figured as much, since the assassin's strange shadow duplicates had all burst into nothing seconds prior. They had done it.

Yet as Felix's eyes drifted over the square, as he noticed more than a few dead bodies of innocent bystanders, rage kindled in his chest. Blood was still dripping from his claws as he shifted his stance and his burning glare onto those nobles and commoners still alive. He felt dire emotions echo in their Spirits, but Felix was past caring. The scepter dimmed, and the wave receded from view...but none of their memories, as he'd hoped. The nobles he saw were alternating looks at Felix and the sky in equal horror.

He raised his hands, gesturing for silence, and it fell like an executioner's axe. Someone started sobbing.

"I take attempts on my peoples' lives as deadly serious," he said into the quiet. The rain resumed, and its soft pitter-patter was the only other sound. "I will not suffer a threat to live. I can guess why, I can guess who, but I don't need to do that. Because I will find out. And all those responsible will learn that there are a great many things worse than death."

Felix gestured, and the doors to the Temple opened once again. Zara, accompanied by a ring of Yttin guards, escorted the shaman back to Felix's side. They were all on edge, the shaman most of all. "Under my Authority, I name you Chancellor and gift to you the estate of the former Grandmaster Kel'lyv. Do you accept?"

"I-I do, my Lord."

A notification popped into Felix's view, confirming his selection, and he acknowledged it and moved on. The crowd had gone stone silent.

"I grant you use of these artifacts, the Raiment of the royal line of Ahkestria, a gift that you yourself bestowed upon me. The Crown of Sea and Stone, which will grant you greater Authority over this Territory in my name." He placed the crown of intertwined coral and water crystals atop Klzix's head and watched as the Yttin's copper eyes ignited with a sudden understanding.

Felix pulled a crystalline orb from his side pouch and proffered it as well. "I give you the Orb of Plenty, to increase your Authority over that which dwells beneath the waves of your Territory. And I give you the Scepter of the Tides," he said, and this time, the crowd gasped, much as Felix had hoped. The artifact that had just commanded a mountainous wave that threatened the entire city was handed over to another. Just like that. "With which the very seas will be at your command."

"Thank you, my Lord. I will guard these treasures with my life," his new Chancellor said.

"You will use them," Felix corrected and made sure his words were loud enough that everyone could hear. Again, the air rippled with the force of his voice, though he kept it to a low roar. "As Chancellor, you will use these artifacts to keep this Territory safe. For everyone."

"Yes, my Lord," Klzix said, before dropping to a single knee in the way his soldier had started doing.

Felix smiled, but it was forced. "Stand up and face them," he instructed the shaman before turning one last time to the crowd. Klzix at his side, he surveyed them all. The commoners were bundles of cautious excitement, while the nobles looked on with fixed smiles and more than a few sodden brows. "People of Ahkestria! Welcome your new Chancellor, Earl Klzix, Shaman of the Yttin and my right hand in Ahkestria and the entire Leviathan Depths!"

The cheer was half-hearted, but it was enough. Felix released his hold on the Storm Ward, and let deafening thunder roll as rain poured down from above.

CHAPTER NINETEEN

"You gave up the artifacts? For what possible reason would you do such a thing?" Isla's voice echoed off the high, vaulted ceiling of Felix's apartments—not quite a shout, but she certainly wasn't being timid with her annoyance. "Those artifacts were priceless and powerful and—"

"And only of use to me while remaining in this Territory," Felix snapped. He rounded on the diminutive Chanter, turning away from the servants who had gathered before him. "I could use them to enhance my Authority and powers a bit outside of the Leviathan Depths, but they are more useful *here*. With my Chancellor." He turned away from Isla and her startled pout. "He needs them more than me."

A notification flashed in his vision again, and he suppressed it for a moment in favor of meeting the eyes of a dozen startled servants in black and gold livery. "Go and speak with Commander Reed. He needs help with provisions and equipment transfer."

The servants nodded in unison and left faster than Felix expected—their Agility was quite high for being Untempered. Behind him, Isla was still grumbling, but Felix sensed Zara's cool demeanor like a chill cloth against his neck. "Isla. Go and assist the healers and see to it that the transition is as smooth as possible. They will need guidance, with you leaving."

"Hmph."

Felix didn't watch, focusing instead on the storm outside, but his Perception picked up Isla stomping away in a huff. Zara stepped up next to him and peered up at the clouds. "That was poorly done, Felix. Isla is tempestuous, but she is a good resource for you."

"You think I should trust her with my decisions before I make them?" Felix asked, raising an eyebrow. "No. Not doing that until she gives me a reason to believe she has my best interests at heart. I don't even like how close she is to Beef."

"She is Cantus Sodalus, Felix. I trust her with my life," Zara said.

"And, in this case, you'd be trusting her with *my* life," Felix pointed out. "I'll be the one doling out trust, thanks."

"As you wish." Zara was a blank page to his Affinity; her ability to master her own emotions was amazing...and another reason why Felix felt he couldn't quite confide in the Naiad. "I believe I already know, but can you tell me *why* you put on such a display today?"

Felix grunted. "Because the powers-that-be here need to remember that I'm here, even if I'm no longer around. Yttin in Authority was going to be an uphill battle, but at least now, with the threat of the Scepter—and of me—people will maybe think twice before turning to infighting."

"Hm, a credible tactic...and a common one in the politics of the Continent. It is an approach the Hierophant excels in."

Felix drew in a sharp breath, but he wasn't surprised. Not really. He could still see it, the memory of himself standing bloody and armored before the terrified crowd, forcing them to listen. To obey.

Even worse, he had received a new Quest immediately after. The first one in ages.

New Quest!
The Path of Empire!
Many are the benefits of empire, and many are their enemies. Secure a total of 4 Territories under your banner and gain a reward worthy of the ancient emperors. Beware, for the higher you climb, the greater the winds that will attempt to force you from the Golden Path. Unification may be your destiny, but violence is your birthright. Gird yourself, Felix Nevarre!
2/4 Territories Secured
Reward: XP, Title(s), Advanced Authority, Varies

The Quest description suggested more and more conflict in his future. That wasn't a surprise. He was on a collision course with the Hierophant, and sooner or later, they would impact. Felix wasn't looking to add Territories to his collection; he was, at best, a reluctant leader. Yet, when all the options he came up against were sacrificing their people for their own gain, how could he do much worse?

Violence is my birthright...Felix wasn't a fan of that line. Before coming to the Continent, he'd never been very contentious, not in any aspect. Sure, there was the fight on the yacht, but he hadn't started that. A distant specter of anger at those idiots rose up in him, a sure sign of how unbalanced he was feeling. *Haven't thought about them in a long time. Or Gabby. Or Mom. Gah, that's enough of that.* He shook himself and focused on the second notification, the one he'd been putting off.

Territorial Boundary Warning!
Boundary Has Been Reshaped By Recent Developments!
New Rivers Have Been Established With The [Ghreldan Hills]!
Do You Wish To Send Inquiry To Neighboring Territory?

An inquiry? Like how I could call Haarwatch from the Stronghold? He tapped his lips and selected *Yes.*

Establishing Connection With Authority Bearer...
...
Error, Authority Splintered.
No Bearer To Contact.
Inquiry Failed.

Felix asks Zara about it. "Zara, what's an Authority Splinter?"

"Hm? Where did you hear of such a thing?" The Naiad looked suddenly alarmed. "Was it after you named your Chancellor?"

"What? No, it's because of this," Felix said and sent her the warning message. "I tried to send the inquiry, but the Seal couldn't establish a connection."

"An Authority Splinter is when a Territory has been divided among many rulers. It is something that has happened in many places, and the Ghreldan Hills are notorious for it. Its Princes have cut up their Seat and Seal into nine relatively even pieces, and each one wields a small fraction of the Authority you have at your command. It is enough to control their lands, their people, but not truly enough to keep them safe. For that, they must rely on their Knights or other outside forces."

Felix grunted. "Sounds like a great place. So, I can't reach anyone because they don't have enough Authority to receive the call?"

"Essentially, yes. You bear an ancient version of Authority, Felix. Your Seat and Seal in Nagast is more complex than any I have ever had the honor of witnessing. A master painter compared to a child's finger painting. It has likely afforded you a greater Authority than others of similar stature."

"So I've gathered," Felix muttered. It had allowed him to challenge the Grandmaster for Ahkestria, he was pretty sure. "Well, if it's not working, we'll just have to see what the big deal is when we get there. I want to leave by nightfall. With luck, we'll hit the Caleph Pass within a day, two at the max."

"I'll see that your soldiers are ready to leave," Zara said, inclining her head.

"Thanks." Felix's gaze snagged on Vess from across the chamber, and as Zara walked out of his apartments, he strode closer. Vess was directing a number of servants out of various doors, all of them taking things at a run. "Hey."

"Are you alright?" she asked, immediately.

Felix blinked, thrown more than a little. "Am I—? I'm fine." He spread his arms, showing his unbroken silk jacket. "See? Not a scratch on me."

"You and your clothes heal from scratches," she pointed out, just as the last of the servants scurried off. "Your plan worked, but I saw you after. Felt you. You did not like doing it."

Felix grunted. "You've been practicing your use of Affinity on me?"

Vess blushed, which darkened her already dusky skin. "It is a poor habit I have developed, I will admit that. But my concern is not misplaced. You hurt."

He shrugged. Felix wasn't sure *what* he was feeling, except overwhelmed. "I'm tired. Tired of being stuck here, and of the way people flock to power and squirm under its weight. Tired of being...I've killed a lot of people, Vess. I've come to terms with that. There wasn't much choice at the time, and I don't regret it exactly...but I'd," Felix groped for the words as he stared up into the vaulted ceilings.

"I'd like to stop, someday. Explore the world, maybe. Go to sleep without having to figure out how to fight a country of zealots, the gods, and some eldritch brainwashing abomination." Felix sighed and let the emotions coiling around his heart dissipate. He breathed in and out, slowly. "I'm sorry about last night. You wanted to talk, and I got caught up with," he gestured. "Everything."

"Apology accepted, Lord Nevarre. I cannot say I was pleased, but upon learning the cause, well, some things cannot be avoided." She smiled at him, one of her cheeks dimpling. "I would be quite unreasonable to assume otherwise."

"What a life. An assassin ruined my day," Felix said, then grinned. "How about we ruin his?"

Vess smile widened, showing off her million-watt grin. "A grand idea."

"The death toll was minimal," Vess told him as they jogged lightly down a set of steep stone steps. The air was distinctly cooler now, as if they had slipped through some invisible boundary beneath the Grandmaster's estate. "I wish none had fallen, but we could not reach everyone in time. Those few that suffered less-deadly injuries were treated quickly. Our people made it quite clear that the healing salves and potions came from you and the Chancellor."

"Yeah." Images of the dead flicked across his perfect recall. He shoved them aside, for now. "The healing is good. He'll need all the goodwill he can get. I assume the potions impressed?" Felix ducked beneath an archway at the final landing, the door clearly made for shorter people.

Vess followed without an issue, her height being just shy of six feet tall, a full half-foot lower than Felix. He still found that weird. "They did. I could pinpoint a number of covetous hearts and calculating gazes. I ensured the healers gave out the potions in the presence of the nobility."

"Even better. They'll see how good our products are, and that'll lead them right back to the Chancellor." Only a couple of his Shadows hung around them, and they moved smoothly to open a heavy, iron-banded door in advance. Vess and Felix moved through with a nod of gratitude. "Maybe he won't have to threaten everyone, like I did."

They drew abreast of another door, this one manned by six guards: three of the Claw and three Yttin in chitin armor. All of them saluted, fist to heart. "Lord Autarch. Do you wish to see the prisoner?"

"Yeah. I have some questions." The guards didn't hesitate but unlocked the door rapidly. A metal key in their hands lit up, six of them in fact, and a complicated scrawl of sigils appeared atop the metal door. The sigils rotated, spinning like a combination lock before depressing with a loud *clunk*, the sigaldry vanishing in a chaotic puff of vapor.

The door was opened, revealing a wide cell with nothing save for a single metal chair...and a man in chains and a simple, silver collar.

"Been wondering when you'd come around," he said through a full beard. "Autarch."

"Sworn." Felix bent his neck to get into the room, but once inside found he had more than enough space to fully stand. "Or should I say Mikhail Nesben?"

The bearded man looked far different than he had in their prior encounters. He had been stripped of his lacquered armor, his black half-mask, and every weapon they could find. In fact, he was completely naked, which was a bit of a surprise.

"So, you got someone good at Analyze. Did you get my level and Tier in that scan, too?" He smirked and jangled his chains. His arms were bound behind him, connected to his legs by more chains that were bolted to the floor. "I've been at this a long time. You won't break me before I die."

Felix closed the door behind them with a firm pull. "I never said I was gonna kill you. That would defeat the purpose of my visit."

He stepped closer, and the Sworn laughed. "Not going to kill me? Then I'm on easy street. Torture doesn't work on us, Nevarre. We're inured to it from *birth*."

Vess produced a glowing silver spear, hovering it in the air level with the man's eye. He yawned. "Hold still, Sworn. This will only take a few minutes."

"What will—?" The Sworn's words were lost to a ragged gasp as Felix's hand clamped over the top of his head.

Oathbinding!

Adamant Discord!

The world *exploded* into light.

Lightning crackled in vibrant arcs, and a silver radiance infused the very air. All around Felix, once-invisible strands manifested. At first, they were everywhere, connected to everything; walls to floor, stone to stone, air to their lungs. Relationships of meaning, described by forces Felix still couldn't grasp, but he could see them regardless. Too much. Felix narrowed his focus, flaring his Affinity. The random connections dwindled, fading from sight as those specifically connected to the Sworn came into clearer focus.

Felix cast out his Intent like a fishing line. A lasso of his need to know. *Show me.*

A brilliant silver thread appeared, thick as his thumb and coiled tightly around the Sworn's chest. Felix followed it with his eyes, activating Manasight as his Affinity traversed the length of the connection through walls and ceilings and muddy ground. It emerged at the edge of his range, still heading somewhere into town.

"Hm, not quite," he muttered, and removed his hand from the Sworn's skull. The man's voice returned to him in a stuttering scream that he mastered moments later. Felix reached down and shattered the chains holding the man in place before grabbing him by the arm and hauling him to his feet. "I need to get somewhere higher."

"W-what are you—what did you do to me?" the Sworn asked, stumbling behind Felix like a dazed child. "My head...my chest...I..."

Felix quirked an eyebrow up, but his strange "thread-vision" saw the silver connection twisting tighter around the Sworn's chest. It was constricting him like a snake.

"I—I can't b-breathe!" the Sworn gasped.

"Felix?" Vess asked.

"It's not me," he said, before looking closer at the silver cord. Complicated knots had formed across its length, redoubling with every passing second, and likely had been since he started observing it. *Is this a warding? A trap to prevent their people from revealing too much?*

"The connection is changing. The Oath you gave. Who did you give it to?"

"N—not gonna—tell! Can't!" The man was looking purple, his face and upper chest darkening as air stopped flowing inward. His neck bulged with veins, and his mouth opened uselessly.

"No," Felix growled. He reached out, coating his hands in his Intent and attempted to take hold of the connection. His hands passed right through it. "Dammit! *Adamant Discord!*"

Felix had never attempted to manipulate an Oath link before, but he hoped it wasn't any different than grabbing at the air or earth. It was, and yet it wasn't. The silver cord fought against him, writhing away from the electric touch of his Skill, but Felix applied all of his Intent behind his effort...and this time his hands grasped it tight. He pulled at the cord, allowing the Sworn to take an abrupt breath, before looking at the complicated knots securing the connection. They were woven in eye-bending loops that defied description, folded around and through itself. Frustrated, Felix wrenched his hands in opposing directions.

The Sworn's scream was deafening, but the System rang out in equal fury. A bell tolled, vast and deeper than anything Felix had ever heard. So deep, it felt like his soul was being shaken apart.

New Title!
Chain-Breaker (Unique)!
You have proven yourself dedicated to violating the very laws of Creation, and in so doing have voided an Oath of another through sheer force of your monstrous Will.
+Skill Evolution

Potency surged into Felix's core space, a tight hurricane from the System itself, slamming through his dual cores and into his Oathbinding Skill.

Pain followed. It rivaled anything he'd experienced before, and his Song of Absolution did nothing against it. Blinding anguish, transcending his skin and bones and elevating somewhere ephemeral. Felix was scattered, pieces of his Mind hurled in all directions as ribbons of silver light bloomed.

...threads...

The light tarnished. A slashing, retributive force pressed against his pieces, snapping threads between claws of purest white.

Oath Of The Nagafolk Is Sundered!
Benefits Lost!

Oath Of The—

Felix grappled with the threads, holding them tight out of instinct. His Will and Intent clashed with another, far more wrathful one. Still, other threads strained, fraying as the peerless agony spun outward in ever widening circles. A scream tore out, and Felix had no clue if it was him or not.

Abruptly, it ended. The vibrational pattern shifted, twisted into a complex and menacing sound an entire octave lower. Felix panted, drenched in sweat, as a notification popped into existence before him.

Oathbinding Has Evolved To Skein of Fate (Legendary)!
Level Is Maintained!

Skein Of Fate (L), Level 46!
You have broken the bonds that Siva holds most dear. Not only on yourself, but on another against their Will. You carry upon your shoulders a dire potential, one that others will not be pleased to witness. Be wary, for to weave the Skein of Fate is to invite calamity, Felix Nevarre. Bonds can be formed and broken at Will, ease of creation increases with Skill level, ease of breaking them increases slightly with Skill level.

"That...that was bad," he said, while the silver cord in his hands writhed like a viper. It, at least, was still whole.

"Felix!" Vess cried out, and batted the Sworn from his grip.

The man fell, his skin bubbling into liquid smoke as his final scream filled the chamber. He hit the stone floor and shattered, his form turning to blackened smoke that Felix instinctively grabbed and consumed. When it cleared, all that was left was a single collar of dull silver, spinning slowly on the floor.

"What in Siva's name just happened?" Vess asked.

CHAPTER TWENTY

"And he just died?" Evie asked.

"I assume it was a condition of his Oath. The Sworn have their name for a reason," Vess said with an elegant shrug.

"What I don't understand is how that led us here," Harn grunted softly. He held up a glowing, green-gold crystal and turned it this way and that. "Or what this is."

Vess plucked it out of Harn's hands. "It is a rudimentary device fashioned by Zara. With the Chant, somehow. She took the Oath cord from the Sworn and trapped it within. Now it is a dowsing stone, keyed to the other end of that Oath."

"That's what you said before, but I don't see how that thing can track an Oath. Didn't think that was possible," Harn said.

"A great many things have been overturned in my time with you all," Vess said softly. She too couldn't resist holding the green-gold crystal up in the air and admiring its shine. It flared with a minute amount of light whenever she pointed it northeast, toward the walls ahead, and it was like the sunset trapped in a jar. The mansion they'd come upon was near the skydocks, well in the Merchants' District, and upon arrival, Vess had immediately sent out several Dawnwalkers to assess its defenses.

Harn shrugged and hefted his second axe. "Those scouts need to get back here fast. I'm fixin' to kill some Pathless today."

"Hear, hear," Evie cheered, quietly.

Vess could feel the woman's bloody excitement echoed in the Talons behind them. Everyone was keyed up after the attack and Felix's display, though they kept their heads covered and out of sight. The alleys in the

Merchant District were plentiful, but they were broad and well-maintained; not the easiest of places to hide a company of soldiers. Vess let her Perception play among the crowd, catching snippets of whispered conversation despite the tense atmosphere and dour, rainy weather.

"These merchants are scum. Worse than the Guilders back home..."

"Fiend'll teach 'em. You'll see."

"...don't stand a chance. Captain Aren and Commander Harn took out the shadow bastard that fired on the Autarch."

"The Sworn. Heard he was a Master Tier, too."

"Sure, but that don't mean nothin' to them. The Autarch eats Master Tiers for breakfast, and his commanders do the same. S'what I'll do, when I become a captain. Take on a whole horde of Adepts, not let any of 'em pass."

"...see her? She was a whirlwind in the crowd. The Lady Dayne slayed a grip of Paladins, her and her flyin' Spears..."

"That's Dragoon work, that is. Passin' rare, they are."

"Gods, but she's bleedin' beautiful—ow! What's that for?"

"Ain't for you to be gogglin' at. Lady Dayne's a higher class of person than some Blade."

"Oh and an Arclight's so much better? Mages ain't half as smart as the lot of ya pretend, ya know..."

Vess pulled back on her Perception, a flush creeping across her cheeks. She had long grown used to being referred to by passersby during her time in her father's house, and training within the ranks of common soldiers had hardened her sensibilities to the...ribald tongue that most warriors bore. No, what clung like thick, foul medicine in the back of her throat was something else entirely.

Dragoon work. Is it, though? She held a hand to her middle, roughly above her core space. *Am I?*

The Dawnwalkers stole up to them, dropping stealth Blessings close enough that Vess jolted in surprise. "Milady. The way is cleared."

Vess clenched her jaw and held up the crystal once more. It glimmered, brighter than ever. "Then it is time to knock on the door."

"Why is everyone in such a hurry, ma'am?" Xavi asked. Something sensational must have been happening, because everyone he knew was running about like madmen.

The round and kindly Mrs. Hetch looked at Xavi as if he'd grown another set of horns atop his Faun head. She snapped at him, in a manner that he was quite unused to. "Don't ask questions, boy. Just keep your nose down and go back to the stables. Please. You'll be safe there!"

Mrs. Hetch bundled Xavi out the door and into the southern courtyard. The door slammed behind him and was bolted shut—he could hear that through the thick, imported wood. The rest of the courtyard was abandoned, as if no one dwelled in the immense Rellest Estate at all. That didn't surprise Xavi overmuch. Few came this way. All the southern courtyard contained was the secondary stables and a gate out onto the streets.

Now, Xavi *loved* the stables. He loved the Avum and the rare khedor, even if it had scary teeth and big claws. He loved the saddles and the feed, even mucking out the stalls wasn't so bad, not compared to descaling the cauldrons in the kitchen. Xavi shuddered as he crossed the flagstones. He was a runner first and foremost, but the Estate put him to work in whatever way they needed him. Parents dead, no other family to speak of, he was happy enough to have a roof over his head and two whole meals a day. There wasn't a lot he wouldn't do for some square meals.

The stables were just as quiet as the courtyard, free from all the hustle and bustle inside the manor. The Avum looked up from their stalls, a variety of beautiful plumage on display. From green to a golden sheen, these were some of the finest birds the little Faun had ever seen before. It almost made up for the fact that he'd been shoved out there, away from whatever excitement was going on inside.

Stuck out here, no one to talk to but the birds. And I think I saw a sword! Xavi kicked a rock that had wandered into the stables, sending it careening into the painted walls. The khedor snarled. *I already missed all the commotion down at the Temple today. I can't believe I'm missing this, too!*

A rattling *whomp* shook the stables with enough force to tear open a wall. Xavi ducked and hollered, bracing himself against the cobblestone floor and wooden posts. A second burst of heat and light made the earth lurch again. He fell onto his face, bruising his chin and driving his teeth into his tongue.

"Hurry! To the stables!"

The shouts mingled with the pain in the Faun's head, rolling around each other until Xavi could force himself up onto his knees. Over the blasted out wall slats and piled up feed sacks, he could see that the manor was on fire. Of the ten windows he saw, six were belching a thick black smoke, and two of those were being licked by the tongues of vivid orange flame.

Men hustled into the stables, shoving open the heavy doors with ease, yet their faces were all streaked with soot and sweat. Xavi was rattled, but he recognized the first person. *Master Rellest!* The master of the manor was followed by a number of men and women, all Humans, who Xavi had seen around the manor before. Except now they wore dark cloaks that did little to hide their blood-red plate armor. *Paladins!*

Fear gripped the Faun, and he froze behind the feed bags as Master Rellest and the others stomped farther inside.

"Mister Hob! Mister Hob, I have need of you!" Master Rellest shouted into the loft, but there was no answer. "Burning ash, what a time to run and hide. Faithless servants. Faithless!"

"Merchant, we need to leave now. I'll have my men saddle your Avum," the lead Paladin said. A tall, bald man that Xavi had seen once or twice in the parlor, his hand never once left the sword at his waist. "We cannot tarry."

"I know that!" Master Rellest snapped. At the same time, his gaze fell onto Xavi's hiding place and it widened in recognition. "Little deer boy! Come here!"

Xavi froze, but a wide hand clamped onto his arm and hauled him to his feet. Master Rellest was grinning, but it was off somehow. Xavi's heart hammered in his chest, and he couldn't speak through the clenching of his lungs. He could barely hear over the roar of his heartbeat, and when he did, it made no sense.

"...get these saddled for us. I need the khedor ready to ride," Master Rellest said. His affable grin slid away and flattened. "Now, boy."

Xavi couldn't stop staring. At Master Rellest. At the Paladins. The Master shook him, so hard he bit his tongue again. "Go! We need to leave! Now!"

"Merchant! Forget this fool boy and your favorite mount. You'll run, if you have to!" The leader of the Paladins was already mounted up on an Avum, and half his men were, too. Another explosive boom shook the manor. A huge, tearing crash came from outside the stables, followed by a wash of arctic cold. "The Fiend's men are coming!"

"Worthless child!" Master Rellest bellowed and threw Xavi away. Propelled by Apprentice Strength, Xavi's slight body arced through the air a solid fifteen strides before he landed in a rolling heap of limbs and bruises. He tried to scream, to cry out, but the pain was too much to bear. All he could do was watch in breathless horror as his Master grabbed an unsaddled Avum and all but throttled it in his efforts to get onto its back. "Ride!"

The earth thundered, and not with the step of the Avum. That arctic cold seeped into Xavi, deeper than the chill of the rains, until he saw strange, crystalline patterns of ice form in the cobbles. Rellest and the Paladins ran to the back gate, but behind them emerged a handful of immense giants, all of them surrounded by a whirling sphere of white flecks and raging flames.

"There! Secure him!" one of the giants called out, its voice almost too deep to understand. Xavi laid upon the freezing ground, unable to move, only watch as their enormous tread ate up the short distance.

"Diurnal Reach!"

Bolts of golden light speared from the gate, crashing into the giants and driving a few back with pain grunts and grievous wounds. Xavi watched, helplessly, as one of them took a bolt to the knee and tripped. Their shadow covered him entirely as they fell, and though he tried, the Faun was as frozen as the ground itself. He could only watch as death dropped atop him.

"Chains of the Protector!"

A shield of swirling metal Mana flashed into existence, a magic that made Xavi's heart soar as it deflected the fall of the injured giant. Another, smaller giant ran to their side, helping them up and giving them a sort of jug of glowing liquid. The shield held, however, until a green-skinned man leaned over the boy.

"You alright?" he asked, the words sounding funny through the small tusks in his mouth. "Geir, is Hapdir—?"

"He shall be fine. Go, Loquis. The others need your help," the smaller giant said. They were already helping the injured one into a sitting position.

More of those light bolts blasted across the courtyard, but they hit a shield made of crackling light...and another shield of conjured metal. "Don't dawdle! We almost have the weasels!" A slender woman landed among them, and the shield moved to her gestures, blocking more of the light bolts. Her hair was rain-slicked against her head, and her skin was flushed and bloody, but she was grinning like she was having the time of her life.

The green man mumbled something and ran forward, accompanied by an absolute herd of armored soldiers, all of them wearing a flashy purple sash. The bolts stopped, and the lady warrior banished her shield. She looked down at Xavi, and her grin grew wider as she dropped a glowing red vial onto his lap. "Take this, kid. And stay safe!"

Xavi's lungs finally unclenched, just in time for the strange, beautiful lady to leap away. "T-thank you!"

But she was gone, joining the dwindling fray at the gates just as Xavi saw the two-faced Master Rellest fall to his knees. He was confused and frightened, but he couldn't blink as the Paladins were brought low, and blood ran red in the gutters. All he could do was clutch the glowing vial to himself, a tiny remedy for the ache in his chest.

Vess strode among the collared and shackled prisoners, making an inventory of exactly who they had taken. The Rellest manor hadn't put up much of a fight, not when confronted by the Fiend's Claw. Vess had been fairly impressed to see how smoothly the Claw operated now. Many of its flaws had been smoothed out and their fractious nature reforged into something resembling a functioning army, even the small portion they had taken for the strike force. *Darius' and Harn's doing, no doubt.*

It meant that none escaped the net they'd tossed atop the manor, certainly not the culprits. A fair few of their prisoners were servants and retainers, all of them guilty of attacking the Claw with their Skills. Most of them were likely innocent of the larger plan, but Vess was not taking any risks. All of them were restrained and collared. Thankfully, they had found a goodly number of elision shackles in a deep storeroom at the Grandmaster's estate during their cataloging efforts.

"Repeat yourself, Paladin," Harn grunted from the side.

A man in crimson plate, chained and kneeling on the ground, grimaced at the axe held near his face. "I *said* that we were promised safe passage from this Pathless-forsaken city if we killed the new Chancellor."

"By whom?" Vess asked.

"House Rellest," he said. "And *her*."

Vess followed the man's acidic gaze toward a cowled woman kneeling among the prisoners. At a gesture, one of the soldiers marched over and threw back her hood, revealing a face that was at once old and young, and hair of a vibrant red. Vess flared her Analyze, but the woman's details were blocked. She was strong enough that the shackles only sealed away her active powers; she clearly had a potent Temper. "Who are you?"

The woman stared at her, pride etched into every inch of her face. "I am Matron Lavelle, high seat of the Elemental Fire and devotee of the true ruler of this city." She tried to make a gesture, but the shackles turned it into a pained shrug. "And these unfortunate fools forced me into aiding them in exchange for my life."

"Liar!" the Paladin shouted.

"Enough!" Vess did not have the patience for their bickering. A Spear hovered just under the man's chin, lifting him as high as he could go without standing. "You will be silent unless spoken to. Do you understand?" The Paladin grunted something close to an affirmation, but Vess was already moving back to the Matron. "You. Speak."

"I demand an audience with the Autarch," the Matron declared, her pride not smudged at all by the rain matting down her copper tresses. "I claim the right to Plead Before Authority."

Vess couldn't see any menus, but the moment those words left the Matron's mouth, she heard the System make an almost audible trill in her Affinity. She was, of course, familiar with the right; it was something allowed to all members of a System-certified city, and Ahkestria qualified. The Matron looked positively smug at the annoyance on Vess' face, which drove her scowl deeper.

"Fine," she said after a moment. "Right acknowledged. On your feet, all of you."

The Claw pulled every shackled prisoner upright, even the unconscious Lord Rellest. The Paladin fumed. "Where are you taking us?"

"To do as requested. We go to see the Autarch," Vess said before glancing at the Matron. Behind her, the Claw began to march the lot of them out of the gates of the burning estate. "For better or worse."

Vess took small comfort in feeling the Matron's shackled Spirit tremble at those words.

CHAPTER TWENTY-ONE

Vess led the march away from the smoldering ruins of the Rellest Estate, through the wide thoroughfares of the Risen Ward without a care to be quiet or cautious. Her strike force was at her back, leading two dozen Paladins in chains and twice as many servants and retainers, and the thud of boots and rattle of shackles was enough to wake the dead. Just as she intended.

Porticoes filled with well-dressed nobles at every mansion they passed, while laborers and workers came to the windows at shops and crafting halls, all of them staring with wide eyes at their procession. Soon, the bravest of them joined the march, trailing behind like a caravan's train, their curious chatter soon drawing even more to their fold. By the time they reached the skydocks, it was as if half the city followed in their wake.

Vess led them down into the even broader avenues around the docks, pressing through a madhouse of activity. Laborers wearing the livery of House Iretus hauled wagons of stone and sodden sand to the edge of the city, where a large scaffolding had been erected around the broken length of one of the skydocks. Others clustered around a large Manaship, now mostly repaired, where a familiar figure stood upon the quarterdeck and blazed with Mana. The laborers halted, and Felix's bright blue eyes fixed on them almost immediately. Vess' Perception allowed her to see his tight frown as he cut off his spellform.

"Company, halt!" Harn commanded, and their procession ceased. "Prisoners, forward." Claw members hauled on chains, pulling the near hundred prisoners upward, until only Vess, Evie, and Harn stood before them. The crowd and Claw remained at their back.

A sharp retort cut through the afternoon air, and Vess found Felix standing beside her. He was back to wearing his dark blue jacket and green tunic, and the lot of it was smudged heavily with dirt and some sort of shiny grease. Vess looked down in time to see a surge of dusty-brown Mana patch over the small crater he'd punched into the road. Felix noticed and smirked. "So, what's this?"

Vess held up the green-gold crystal and waggled it. "We found them."

"All of them?"

"Everyone who was at the Rellest Estate. That's him there," Vess said, pointing out a man that was only just being woken up now. "Zevan Rellest. Merchant and minor noble. We found him attempting to escape from us with a group of Paladins, and more than a few of the man's people attacked us during detainment."

"Why are they here, then? Why not take them back to the jail cells?" Felix's gaze took in the prisoners, then the crowd beyond them. "Why the show?"

"Because I demanded to Plead Before Authority," the Matron said loudly again.

Felix grunted sourly. "Matron of the Highest Flame. Still standing."

Members of House Iretus, soldiers now, appeared from the dock buildings. Beef did as well, wiping his hands with a large rag, a curiously furtive look on his bovine features. Captain Landas himself sidled up to Felix and looked ready to spit at the Matron's feet. For her part, the Urge-worshiper remained stoic—even her Spirit was a calm, steady tone.

Felix swiped at something, likely a message from his Authority Screen informing him about the right to Plead. His frown deepened. "Say your piece, then."

"I am innocent of all accusations, my Lord." The Matron's voice was high and proud, a fine match for her ageless features. She lifted her chin a touch more. "I was forced into compliance by the wretched Paladins of the Pathless and bound by Oaths to Lord Rellest."

An explosion of sound came from the prisoners, though mainly from the Paladins themselves. "Bullshit! You contacted *us!*"

Felix raised an eyebrow, but the Matron was unfazed. "Would you believe their word? Their twisted god has turned them against everything that is decent and honorable. They attacked and razed our city! It is *they* who orchestrated the recent attacks, *they* who coerced me into providing them aid and support."

"She lies," rasped another voice. Vess saw Lord Rellest stand on shaky legs, bound in chains and collared. "That bitch found me, told me exactly what to do and how to do it. *She's* the one who hired the Sworn, who masterminded all of this!"

The green-gold crystal vanished from Vess' hands, plucked by Felix as he strode forward and held it aloft. He stepped to the Matron, who only slightly flinched at his approach. The crystal shimmered several shades lighter, pulsing with an inner light. The arrogant tilt of her chin twitched, faltering just slightly. "Hm," was all he said.

He moved on. Trailing next down the line of Paladins, Vess watched the crystal fade in vibrancy, as if each step took him farther away from its target. Until the opposite happened, and it slowly began to brighten. The Paladins, as if in contrast to the Matron, were almost shaking as they stared at Felix's impressive size and sharp, black talons. He, however, ignored them. Then he reached Lord Rellest. Vess had been convinced the crystal had glowed bright for the Matron, but now it positively blazed. As if Felix held a mote of pure sunlight, the crystal ignited into an incandescent ball that flickered wildly.

Lord Rellest's face screwed up in confusion. "What is the meaning of this, Lord Autarch? Is this blinding lightshow for simple theatrics, or are we proceeding with a proper handling of justice? That woman enslaved my entire household! I'd have her chained and hung from the Council portico by sunset! I—"

"Stop," Felix said. His words weren't loud, but it silenced the merchant lord as if he'd screamed. "Even if I didn't have this, which shows the origin of the Oath the Sworn gave, I could hear the lie in your Spirit. Your fear outweighs the false outrage you've mustered up, and not even your...Journeyman-Tier Deception can convince me otherwise."

Rellest opened and closed his mouth several times, but all that came out was a jumble of vowels. "Ah. Uh. But I—"

"When I removed this Oath from the Sworn," Felix said, talking over the man. "His body crumbled to ash. What do you think will happen when it's returned to you?"

"You cannot be serious, my Lord! I—"

"Let's find out."

There was a sound like shattering glass, and the light of the crystal winked out...before a vivid cord of silver manifested in its place and wrapped viciously around Lord Rellest. The man had a moment to scream but was too shocked to utter a word. And then it was too late; the silver cord slithered across his chest and neck and mouth, its ephemeral glow proven to have true heft and weight as it dimpled his Tempered flesh and thick clothes.

"Mercy!" someone cried from the crowd. "Have mercy!"

Vess watched with grim satisfaction as the man turned red, then purple before collapsing to the ground. The silver cord thickened and turned a fetid black as the merchant's bulk was rendered down to nothing, his flesh collapsing in on itself within his voluminous garb, until he stopped moving entirely.

"All choices have consequences," Felix said.

Felix's face was a thunderhead, and his Spirit lashed in a strange, circular anger. Vess couldn't parse it, but it was just as intense as the crystalline light and as dark as the thread that coiled like a well-fed snake before him. He reached out and seized the cord with his dark hands, and everyone around him backed up as far as they could.

"This is your reward for betrayal. This is what comes from caring only for power and prestige and titles piled atop your name." His eyes flashed, glowing so bright in the gloomy afternoon it was a wonder those closer were not burned. The writhing cord turned to smoke, pulled inexorably into Felix's channels. "I did not come to Ahkestria to ruin your lives, and I certainly didn't come to kill your council or your god. I arrived in peace and was met by suspicion, violence, and betrayal. So no. I will not be showing mercy today.

"Your turn, Matron."

The woman blanched and tried to take a step backward, but was arrested by Harn and Evie.

He stalked across the square, violence written large across his stance for anyone with a Mind to think. The Paladins, however, proved their true nature. As one, the two dozen warriors of the vaunted Pathless surged forward, throwing off the restraining hands of the Claw around them for only a moment. Enough for them to attack the Lord Autarch with gauntleted hands and the crushing grip of their Tempered Bodies. Vess blinked, too shocked at their stupidity to catch all of what transpired, for in the next instant, several bystanders in the crowd were thrown back as the wind whipped into a mighty gale...and Felix stood, hair swaying, exactly where he had before.

And every single Paladin was dead.

"I told you," he growled, and Vess wasn't sure who he was speaking to: himself or the crowd. "No mercy."

Relentless, the Autarch stepped to the Matron, whose disbelieving gaze could barely tear itself away from the Paladins' bloody corpses. "You're strong. To have survived your Urge's fall, you must have had a significant amount of power outside of your Blessings." The aloof expression on her face melted as she gasped in sudden pain. Felix's head tilted. "A hall of clouds and the brilliant sun. It's dimmed, but it still burns bright enough."

The red-haired Urge-worshiper stared at him, aghast. "Y-you can delve, too? Who are you?"

"I'm the only chance you have. I give you a choice, one that the Paladins gave up when they chose to attack just now. One that Rellest forfeited by contracting the Sworn in the first place."

"A choice," she echoed, disbelief loud in her Spirit.

"I will always give a choice, but only once. I'm too tired to dance with you and those with eyes bigger than their stomachs." Felix pulled his hooked blade from his waist, leveling it at the Matron's neck as if preparing to anoint her...or perform an execution. "Serve my chosen Chancellor without guile or ulterior, self-serving motives. Serve the people, *all* the people, of Ahkestria and this Territory. Bind yourself to an Oath. Or die."

The Matron swallowed, loudly. "A choice between incarceration or death? That is not much of a choice, *Autarch*."

"It's the only one you'll get," he said levelly.

Silence stretched over the square. The crowd did not whisper, the soldiers did not shift or scratch, and few even breathed. There was only the rumble of thunder and the constant patter of drizzling rain. Until stone scraped, and the Matron fell to a single knee.

"I will serve, Lord Autarch," she muttered.

"Yes," he said. "Yes, you will."

The next few hours went by with far less commotion. Less drama, at least. Felix was frankly just happy that he hadn't been required to kill anyone else.

Breathe, he murmured inwardly. Meditation sang in his core space, not his most powerful Skill but useful for the boost it gave to his regeneration. It was also useful in how it helped him steady his Mind, even after a day like the one he'd had.

The memory of dead Paladins splashed across his thoughts, vivid thanks to his Born Trait. He shied away, not squeamish so much as hateful. He hated killing them, and an unreasoning anger kicked back to life in his chest. He had done it to prevent worse from happening to the people of Ahkestria and of Nagast. No Paladin could escape to tell them what happened there. Only then could they remain safe.

The nobles of the city and the rulers of the Hierocracy were equally power-hungry, proving themselves willing to simply take and take and take, until nothing was left. Until the weakest were used up, rendered into fuel for their own advancement.

So Felix wouldn't let them. At every turn, he would deny them all.

The Matron had accepted his offer, and when he extended it to the retainers and servants of House Rellest, they, too, took the knee. Now, all of them were under an Oath of Willing Service, as the System had dubbed it, binding all of their advancement to the fulfillment of the Oath and remaining faithful to the spirit of it.

He had considered tying their lives to the Oath, but that was both too far and not enough. But their power? The very lever by which they held themselves higher than others? All of them, and the Matron especially, cared more for their advancement than their lives.

Oaths... Their very nature had dragged at him since the Sworn had died. Not to mention another brush with what he could only assume was the goddess Siva. His loss of the Nagafolk's Oath had rattled him at first, but after consulting with Zara, he realized it shouldn't be too detrimental. He'd proven he was a powerful ally back when they had entered Haestus Temple, and the Deepking would be an idiot to disregard that. The fact that some force had tried to break more of his Oaths had been even more concerning. If he focused on them, he could feel some of his old ones pulling in strange ways, especially the ones connected to his friends.

Those are useless now, he realized. Those oaths were made long weeks back, when he had wanted to keep his Unbound nature close to his chest. He wasn't shouting it from the rooftops now, either, but it had spread far enough that it was, at best, an open secret. What's more, he trusted his friends, yet he kept them bound in Oaths that would break their Skills and levels if they violated it? It wasn't fair, and it wasn't necessary. *I release you all.*

The Oaths to his closest friends dissolved as soon as he made the decision, the tension in them going slack before vanishing entirely. Unlike his Skein of Fate, this wasn't a breaking. As owner of the Oaths in question, he could release them whenever he wanted.

His other Oaths—those of allegiance and loyalty—weighed on him if he gave them any thought, but they were a minor thing. Zara said that increased Authority meant that his tolerance for Oaths was greatly increased, and where a simple shopkeep would find their Spirit crushed under the weight of a dozen Oaths, Felix could expect a far higher limit.

And I'm sure I'll need it.

He had gotten his people moving back to the estate to finish packing up what they needed. He'd met with Klzix and explained his new aides, but for the most part let his Chancellor take charge of things back at the Grandmaster's—ah, the Chancellor's Estate. Klzix had a number of tasks he had to accomplish, not the least of which was communing with the Seat and Seal beneath the former Grandmaster's lowest basement.

All of which freed Felix up to continue aiding Beef and House Iretus with ship construction. Now, however, they were ready. Finally. So, as the sun set on the overcast horizon, he took a moment to escape from everyone.

Just breathe. He settled into Meditation again, focusing on relaxing his Body and Mind. He was balanced atop a piece of scaffolding, listening to the rumble of thunder and the cry of sharp-voiced seabirds. The smell of freshwater filled everything; the air, his lungs, the sky. He tried to sink into it, to simply *be* for a while.

"Felix!"

He cracked open his eye, and saw Beef sitting on the scaffolding stairs below him. "Yeah?"

"Can I talk to you?"

Felix took a single, measured breath and rolled backward off the thin scaffolding and into the open air. He grabbed at the sky with a tether of Adamant Discord, slowing his descent with a flash of electrical discharge, and landed lightly on the flexible stairwell. Well, lightly for him. The entire structure was made of chitin, thanks to Beef, which flexed a lot more than wood, and thanks to his considerable weight, the whole thing rippled like the sea below them.

"Whoa!" Beef said, grabbing at a support beam to steady himself. Felix stood from his soft-kneed crouch, tilting his hips in time with the swaying scaffolding. "How heavy are you?"

"Have you seen any scales on the Continent?" Felix asked.

"Oh. Uh, no. I guess not." Beef suddenly snapped his fingers. "No, wait! I have. You could use those wagon scales I saw on the other side of the docks! You can't weigh more than a wagon, right?"

"Beef. What's up? I'm..." Felix wanted to say *tired*, but admitting that felt pointless. Of course, he was. They all were, especially after the last few hectic hours building their fleet. Beef himself was slicked in sweat that smelled more of Mana Potions than Minotaur stink. "What's up?" he repeated.

"Hey, so the ships are ready. I finished the last mizzlemast or whatever just now."

"Mizzenmast," Felix corrected offhand. "Are you okay? I know using Chitin Construction is draining for you."

"What?" Beef puffed up his chest. "I've never been better! Plus, I've got these beautiful boys," he said, patting a hard case at his hip. All but two of the glass potion bottles were empty. "I can go all day with these."

"Not all day, but they help," Felix said. *Less and less each time, when you drink them in a row.* "But good. Glad you're alright. We have a long way to go tonight, and I'll need you to be alert."

"Alert? For what?"

"More Fathom spawn, if my luck holds out," Felix muttered. He scrubbed his face with the heels of his hands. The hard edges of his scales felt nice on his skin. "Is that what you wanted to talk to me about? Finishing the ships?"

"No. I mean yes, but also...also no." Beef took a breath, his big, chitin-covered chest expanding like a bellows. "I think—"

A high, intense call sounded into the air. It was loud, piercing in a way that had nothing to do with his ears, and filled with such vivacity that Felix felt his exhaustion retreat just a touch. He looked up and away from the docks they'd built below, away from the fleet of ships, and up the crystal-laden cliff of Ahkestria. Zara stood there, along with his many, many peoples.

They were ready.

"Finally. God damn it. Finally." Felix slapped Beef on the back, excitement welling up in him. "C'mon. It's time to leave this damn city."

CHAPTER TWENTY-TWO

Zara brought down the Claw first, those who had traveled with him into the unforgiving Scorched Expanse and had fought their way across its sands. They were changed now, more confident but also closer. Felix could feel it, a burgeoning sensation in the back of his Mind—bindings that only those tested in battle seemed to forge.

Skein of Fate is level 47!

Interesting. Like Oathbinding before it, as well as Adamant Discord, Skein of Fate allowed him to sense the connections between people. Where Oathbinding had been laser-focused on sensing oaths, and Adamant Discord was a potent mess of everything, Skein of Fate seemed somewhere in the middle. He had no clue what to do with it, though, and shoved the revelation aside for later. For now, there were stairs to reinforce.

Stone Shaping!

Rime Shaping!

Green Shaping!

As people started streaming down, the stairs creaked and swayed, the entire scaffolding not built for so many at once. Felix's Mana shot from his channels, a thickening liquid that shimmered in his Manasight. Dusty-brown, green-gold, and purple-white intertwined in a chaotic mix that punched into the cliff face of Ahkestria's edge and anchored itself way, way down atop the crystalline crags below. Pillars of slick, blue-black stone rose up, forming beneath the tread of his followers as they traversed the stairs, dragging nearly half of his considerable Mana total into its construction. But, in only a handful of seconds, the scaffolding had become something more permanent...even if it wasn't all that pretty to look at.

Green Shaping is level 44!

Rime Shaping is level 50!
Journeyman Tier!
You Gain:
+7 INT
+7 WIL
+7 DEX

Gotta work on my artistry, I think, Felix mused as his people marched down the almost Brutalist structure. It was all sharp angles and squared-off pillars; even the buttressed supports connecting the stairs to the cliff face were simple and thick. *At least it's sturdy.* Felix took a breath as his Mana regeneration kicked in. He could feel it being drawn from the air around him, an almost pressure at each of his Mana Gates. "Beef, you all packed?"

"Yeah. Moved all my stuff down here when we moved the boats from the skydocks down to the dock-docks." Beef paused, scratching his jaw. "Never said that out loud. Sounds stupid. Sea docks doesn't sound much better. Boathouse sounds fancier than it is. What's that other word? Jetta? Worf?"

"Just docks is fine, I think," Felix said through a smile. He was tired and beyond ready to leave the city, but Beef reminded him of Earth every time he spoke. He appreciated that. "Oh, what did you want to tell me?"

"Hm? Just—" Beef clenched his jaw and shuffled his feet, before tossing his head, like a real bull might have done. "Nevermind. I'll go check the boats and make sure I didn't miss any parts of the hulls."

"Alright." There was a weird tingling around the Minotaur, his Spirit bucking before it settled into a dull sort of disinterest. Felix would have found it weird had he not remembered being a teen himself. Disinterest and lack of communication were hallmarks of the experience.

As it was, Felix didn't have the energy to shake out whatever was bugging the teen Minotaur, and he let him plod away as more folks began piling onto his newly built stairwell. Behind the Claw came the new recruits, at least five *hundred* of them by his quick estimate, each and every one wearing rudimentary or salvaged armor from the Grandmaster's estate. Felix stood aside as the first of them drew close, thinking.

Zara passed him with a sedate nod, while the men and women behind her saluted fist to heart and continued onward, most of them torn between staring at him and staring at the stairwell that had formed beneath their feet. The entire structure hugged relatively tight to the cliffs, switching back and forth with wide, squared landings before ending at a series of jetties that stabbed out into the rollicking waves of the Leviathan Depths. Ten ships were arrayed below, large, galleon-classed structures that Felix now doubted would hold his new soldiers, let alone the civilians and families that followed in their wake.

And follow they did—at least twice as many men, women, and children toddled after his armored soldiers, and they were far less shy about gawking. At the stairs, at the ships, at the crashing waves themselves. But not Felix. Unlike the soldiers, there was a melody of fear from the adults' Spirits, and it made Felix's inside squirm. Most wouldn't even lift their gazes when they passed his standing place on the stairs, and a few even huddled their children closer, away from him. He almost had time to wonder at their reaction when he caught whispers from their number.

"...keep your eyes down. Do not meet the Fiend's gaze. He is dangerous."

"...killed that man. That noble, right? Ripped him apart and ate his bones in front of everyone..."

"...just caught those black spears, like they were nothin'. Pulled up that sea like it was his own trained beast, too. Can't trust a man so powerful."

"...ain't no man. Not with claws like that, not with eyes that burn like that bleedin' storm."

Felix clenched his jaw and tried to let it all wash over him. *Just breathe. It's fine.* The sound of the surf was loud, but not loud enough. *You did what you had to do. Right?*

The clatter of boots against stone drew Felix's attention upward, and he saw a company of armored Yttin march behind the civilians. There were another hundred of them, each armored in sea-hued chitin and bearing their set of extra limbs folded against their backs, while long glaives were held in the crooks of their arm as they marched along. Klzix was at their head, with Fiammetta at his side, a pensive smile on his face as he met Felix halfway down.

"Lord Autarch. I am sad to see you leave so swiftly, but it is remarkable what you have achieved in such a short time." The shaman gestured to everything around them, including the breakwater Beef and Felix had brute forced out of fallen crystals and conjured rock. It had been Florian's idea, and had at least cut down on *some* of the waves of the sea. "I am honored to stand for you while you are abroad, my Lord."

"Don't worry, I'll check in regularly. My other Chancellor and I have this trick that...well, you'll see," Felix said with a smile he only half meant.

Apparently, Yttin senses were better than Felix assumed, because

Klzix's copper eyes flashed between Felix's face and the retreating backs of the civilians. His face pinched in something close to annoyance, and the cloth-bundled appendages on his back writhed. "They do not appreciate what you have done for them. Do not blame them, Autarch. Their Minds are too consumed by dread of the unknown to be reasonable."

"I don't blame them," Felix said truthfully. He didn't. They weren't wrong about what they said, what they feared. "They've been through a lot."

"Do not let yourself lose sleep over it, my Lord," Fiammetta said. The Faun was dressed in an ornate, predominantly orange silk battlerobe marked with a burning blue eye across the front panel. The symbol of House Nevarre, he'd been told, established by Zara in the official records of Ahkestria. It was very similar to the symbol on the cloaks of the Fiend's Legion. "There are always those who fear that which they do not understand, and the weak cannot know the realities of the powerful."

"No. They do." Felix huffed a tight breath and tore his gaze from the civilian's descending forms. "They're all too knowledgeable about the powerful and what they can do. That's why they're afraid."

Felix simply had to prove he was better than the Kel'lyvs and DuFonts and Archons of the world.

"C'mon, let's go the rest of the way down. The docks are wide enough to hold everyone." Felix didn't wait for them to follow, simply started walking. Fiammetta and Klzix did a little hop and run to catch up to him, while the rest of the Yttin followed at a steady march.

Pit flew high above the city, careless of the whipping winds and crackling sky. He gloried in it, in fact, his new form reveled in the rush of energies that coursed through his flesh. Lightning thundered from on high, striking at him and siphoning away into his Mantle of Tumult that wreathed him.

Mantle of Tumult is level 73!
Thunderwing is level 59!

The Primordial Stormwing cut through the air at incredible speeds, his shriek of joy lost to the winds of his passage. Rooftops flashed below him, the bright, crystal encrusted structures dimmer in all the gloom of the Storm Ward. People crowded the streets, rich and poor mingling as they all pushed closer to the skydocks, where a great cacophony arose as folks pressed against the chest-high wall.

Pit flapped, channeling air Mana through his feathers with such great ferocity that he kicked up cloaks and hats in the throng below, until he shot out over the edge of the city itself. Thick, blue-black stairs clung to the edge, leading down to the wet expanse of stone where ships rolled in the waves. People boarded them, wobbling on deck as they hustled to and fro, so far below Pit as to seem like ants.

"So many people," Pit said to himself in wonder. He had spent many days now in large cities, places so different from the forests of his home. Following Felix had given him a great many experiences with crowded spaces, and most of it had been quite uncomfortable. But now... "Now I'm small again. I...I can go anywhere."

That fact pleased Pit almost as much as the evolution of his Skills and core. While he wasn't as small as he had been when Felix had first found him, the tenku was happy to be only the size of a large Avum instead of an entire wagon. He'd sacrificed some of his brute force and ability to soak damage, but in return, Pit had gained a great deal more speed and flexibility, not to mention his amplified magical prowess. With his smaller size, even on a boat so crowded, Pit wouldn't feel so out of place. He gave a happy little trill that was lost in the storm and flew closer.

The ships grew in size as he descended in a lazy spiral, as did the people. Felix was there, a presence that Pit could find in a dark room with his eyes shut tight, and he was speaking to a large group of others. They were dressed in that odd uniform the shipbuilders wore, and at their front were the child and older child that led them. *Iretus*, he recalled. *Florian and Meina.* Pit had been putting extra effort into remembering others' names, now that he could speak. It was proving harder than he had anticipated. He had the Intelligence for it, but something about strangers made him bored.

"...as thanks for their contribution to our efforts, we are granting House Iretus the first Storm Pass," Felix was saying. He handed something to that Klzix, a round piece of metal, and the shaman brought it before a kneeling Florian. The little boy took it reverently in his hands. "That is to be bloodbound to three captains of your choosing. It will key them to the Storm Ward and will allow their Manaships to fly through it at will. I imagine that will help House Iretus get back on its feet."

The child was dumbfounded, and Pit could sympathize. To be allowed flight again, even after being grounded by a few days by the Storm Ward? Pit would have whooped for joy, had it been him. In fact he did, just a little, shrieking out to celebrate little Florian's return to the sky. Faces turned upward, and Felix grinned as Pit banked low around them, his wings and Mantle a crackling thunder around the Manaship below.

"I do not know what to say," Florian stammered. He clutched the metal disc to his chest. "Thank you, Lord Autarch."

"The amount of work your people put in during the last day? It's been nuts. I can handle a lot, but your engineers and shipwrights kept pace despite everything I threw at them. I'm willing to pay for good work, and I imagine that Pass will pay plenty," Felix said.

Klzix also spoke up. "And, in recognition of your newfound mobility, we would speak more in the coming days about our plans for this city."

"It would be my honor," Florian said, giving a little bow.

Pit flapped his wings, sending out a shower of sparks as he flew over other ships in the fleet. Beef was leaning over the side of one, talking to a giant Multipede clinging to the hull at the water line. Zara sat on the bowsprit of another ship, her eyes trained on the horizon, while Isla lounged at her back, watching all of the ships instead. Harn and Darius hustled about, each of them yelling instructions to the soldiers about something Pit didn't care to listen to, while Alister and Atar meandered about, running their hands over the hastily crafted ships. On the last ship, Evie and Vess were chatting atop the crow's nest. They waved at Pit as he passed, and Pit chirruped happily at them.

The people streamed everywhere, placing their small bundles and belongings in the various holds before wandering the wide decks. It felt like the busy marketplace in Haarwatch, all those months ago, when he'd sat in Felix's Spirit and stared out at the world. Now Humans and Orcs and Dwarves and all sorts stared and pointed at him, children laughing and running along the decks as he passed. Pit loved it all.

Hollering started soon after, a joyful, boisterous noise from the ships that was soon echoed by the multitude up in Ahkestria proper. Hands waved, on ship and city streets, bidding a sudden farewell to those leaving and those staying. Sails unfurled and snapped open in the wind, lines were tightened and tied, and the distinct tang of magic began to whirl up from the ships. One by one, each of the retrofitted Manaships began to mobilize as their rudimentary Mana engines roared to life.

Pit circled back until he was at the flagship once again and tucked his wings. He dove from the sky, flaring his wings outward only moments before he landed in a graceful clatter of paws and claws, right next to Felix on the quarterdeck.

"Hey there, bud! Ready to set sail?" His Companion's face was bright and happy, an expression Pit felt was getting rarer in recent days. He chirruped his agreement, and Felix reached out to rustle between his triangular ears. "Me, too. Me, too." He whistled, high and piercing, louder than the roar of the storm and the engines. "Alright, everyone! Weigh anchor and set sail!"

And in a soft voice only Pit could hear, Felix murmured. "Let's go home."

CHAPTER TWENTY-THREE

"The first step is often the hardest," Vess told him as they balanced atop a thin mountain peak. She stood next to him, balancing on a single foot while keeping her eyes closed and her breathing steady. "Empty your Mind."

"What, like literally?" Felix asked. Ten feet below the flat top of their mountain peak, the clouds hung thick as a carpet. So thick he imagined he could walk across, it if he wanted.

Vess cracked open a single eye and smiled. "I am teaching you as I was taught. Empty all your wants and needs and urges from the pitcher of your Mind, leaving it hollow and unsoiled."

"Alright," Felix said. "I am pretty good at Meditating."

Felix closed his eyes and lifted himself up on a single leg, copying her. His sense of balance, even in his projected form, was impeccable. Projecting himself into Vess' core space had felt easier, too, a task which required him to activate and maintain the use of several skills. His boot shifted in the dirt with a soft crunch, and he emptied his Mind.

Or tried to, anyway.

Breathe.

Thoughts of the last day flitted through his head, of sailing across the Leviathan Depths. It had rained more often than not, providing them with more fresh water. The water of the sea had turned decidedly brackish and a touch acidic, despite being inland and away from the immense world ocean.

Focus.

Felix marshaled his Mind, emptying it once again. Yet it didn't last.

Thoughts oozed between his fingers, no matter his Willpower and Intent.

Fish. Fishing. The sound of the water rushing past them. While they had plenty of food stores, that wouldn't last them forever, and they had to focus on fishing to ensure their soldiers were fed. It was a challenging task at first. Felix had thought he'd have to dive into the water and find food for them, or something more drastic, but the Yttin that accompanied them were more than capable fisherman. Apparently, while living in the desert, they had frequented the oases dotted around the Expanse.

Felix was surprised there were even fish at all, considering the sea had been desert no less than a week ago. But just as the Yttin surprised him with their prowess, so too did the waters. The oases had clearly been divested of their denizens, forced to join the seas. There had been a lot of monsters in those oases, and the deep waters likely delved far deeper than Felix knew.

Focus. Emptiness. A sense of quiet began to form as he chased the thoughts away. Felix hardened his Mind against further intrusions, but the problem wasn't the outside, it was the frenetic energy within. His overactive Mind spewed out thoughts like water from a geyser, and he wrestled them back over and over…but streams slipped through.

The image of standing atop the forecastle, wind streaming in his hair and spray on his face stole through his Mind. The fishing resolved, Felix had taken a selfish moment to enjoy simply being there, standing on a ship on an alien world. He had imagined he was simply traveling. Exploring. Felix wanted to do so much more of that.

The place he found himself was included in that exploration. Vess' core space. It was majestic and beautiful, a series of mountain peaks rising above the thick cloud cover, each peak a Skill while a chill, gale-force wind whipped all around them. At the center, somewhere, was a temple dedicated to the order of her mother, the Dragoons, containing the coolest-looking core he'd seen: a dragon statue so realistic it seemed like it could leap to life at any second.

Thoughts kept slipping. The emptiness wobbled.

Are there less mountains than before? Had she consolidated some Skills? Felix's eyes snapped open. *Did I change her core, too?*

Fully and finally, the emptiness fled. It popped like a bubble within his tumultuous Mind, and Felix let out an annoyed grunt. "This is harder than it should be."

"Emptying your Mind of needless thoughts requires more than stats to accomplish." From beside him, Vess was standing with her arms cupped together and one leg entirely folded atop the other, which was extended straight down. "The greater the Temper, the harder this is to accomplish, as your Mind is stronger, faster, and more obstinate.

Rigidity follows Tempering, and the flexibility required is easier for those with less established potency."

"Is it impossible for an Adept?" he asked.

"Not impossible. I have seen those of higher advancements make changes to their core space visualizations. It is simply very hard and requires more than brute force." She opened a single eye. "It requires technique."

Felix tried not to grumble. He had perfect recall and a Mind that hadn't failed him in a great many terrible situations. He could think up dozens of potential responses to threats in an instant...but completely quieting it? No. Apparently not. Not even when he Meditated did he accomplish that so much as relaxing himself.

Maybe that'll work. He sat down on the gritty summit peak of Vess' visualized mountain and folded his legs beneath him before engaging his Meditation Skill. *Something has to.*

Yet, a clutch of moments later, Felix groaned in frustration and fell backward until he was just staring up at more thick clouds.

"Perhaps discussing the whole of the process will help?" Vess asked, grinning down at him.

"Blergh."

She chuckled. "The goal is to clarify your core space and add as much detail as you are able. To do it, you must empty your Mind and then, in that emptiness, you visualize your core space. All of it that you can...hold it in the palm of your hand."

Vess put her own hand out and atop of it a tiny replica of cloud-covered mountains manifested. It looked odd. The temple at her center was too big, comparatively. Yet, before Felix could ask, she closed her hand, banishing the example.

"From that point, you can begin making changes to the space as a whole. It is far easier that way than moving span by span across the breadth of it." Vess helped Felix to his feet. "Will you try it again?"

Felix did try it. Over and over.

He was able to hold the emptiness for longer, perhaps a whole minute, but it always collapsed. Every. Single. Time.

"Maybe this just isn't for me," he said into the chill breeze. He'd laid down again and was watching the clouds swirl about in distant eddies.

"Nonsense. You have slain Primordials and Urges. I do not think you will be defeated by some peace and quiet," Vess chided him.

"Peace and quiet aren't for me, either, I don't think," Felix said after a moment. "Not anymore."

She sat down next to him, graceful in her full armor as always.

"More nonsense. You are a leader now, that is true, but that does not preclude you from peace. I think, instead, that you are so used to conflict that quiet feels dangerous."

"That's…not wrong," Felix admitted. He peered up at her. "Is that pulled from personal experience?"

Vess frowned, just a touch. "More than a little. My childhood was perhaps more hectic than most. Training in war and tactics and governing has consumed much of my life." Her smile emerged, a sun from behind clouds. "I learned to find my peace where and when I could."

"You're better than me," Felix said, still gazing into the sky.

"Simply more experienced." Vess leaned back but looked forward. The wind howled and roared, whipping at their imagined clothes. "Finding one's center was always a core tenet of the Dragoons."

Felix sat up, something finally clicking in his head. "Your core space. Where is your temple?"

Vess didn't answer him right away, only sighed before making a single, commanding sweep of her arm. In the distance, the cloud cover shifted and fell like a cascading waterfall. From the veil came a huge mountain peak, at least twice the size since the last time Felix had seen it, fully dominated by an immense temple that…was very different.

"Are those dragon wings?" Felix asked.

"I believe so, yes," Vess said in a quiet voice.

Her temple, the core, had been altered from a sedate, almost monastic temple into what looked like the fossilized corpse of a massive dragon. Instead of stone, it appeared to be made of gold and silver and gleaming blue gemstones, pillars and tiled roofs worked into the shape of a skull and chest and pelvis. Its huge, bat-like wings were raised up and spread, cloth of gold spread across like sails that rippled ceaselessly in the wind.

"I fear the Dragoons would have a great deal to say about this," she said in that same quiet tone.

"How—was it the Link that did this?" Felix couldn't believe it had enacted so much change in her. "Is this what you meant about your Skills changing?"

"Yes. My core space is but a reflection of the changes I have undergone. More than a few Skills have…evolved."

"Into what?"

Vess stabbed at the air and swiped at him, sending a blue screen rotating into Felix's vision.

Dragoon's Footwork (Epic), Grace (Common), And Wall Run (Uncommon) Have Become On The Wing (Legendary)!

Pierce The Sky (Rare) Has Become The Fang of Havoc (Legendary)!
Dragon's Descent (Rare) Has Become Draconic Stormfall (Legendary)!
Wyrmling's Call (Rare) Has Become Matriarch's Lament (Legendary)!

"Whoa," was all Felix could manage.

"Indeed. And that is not all, Felix." This time, Vess pointed upward, and at her command, the overcast sky cleared to reveal a dark vault of stars. "Our newfound connection has changed so much."

The sky was dark, though the ground all around them was lit as if by daylight, and twinkling among the false stars were a familiar pair of lights. Too far to be moons or suns, but entirely too large to be a coincidence, Felix gawked at the red-gold and blue-white light. "Is that…are those my cores?"

"From your description of them, I had guessed so." Vess pushed a breath through her nose. "Felix. Why are your cores in my sky?"

"Uh." Felix reached out, questing with his Cardinal Flame toward the distant celestial bodies. It was a vast, incomprehensible distance, but it was there. He could feel them, a strange twin sensation in his gut and the senses of his Cardinal Flame. "The Link. The Tier IV Link I—we strengthened with the Primordial's power. Did—did this happen to everyone?"

"I do not know. Evie has remarked on her own Skills growing, and Harn progressed into Adept. Atar…well, he is changed certainly, and perhaps not only by that foul Urge, either."

"Well, I was planning on touching base with Atar soon, anyway. I'll make sure to talk to everyone else. If they've seen such dramatic changes to their Skills and core spaces, that might be a problem."

"I am unsure how they might have been affected. The Primordial's power seemed to alter the substance of my Skills and not merely their function." Vess shook her head. "My Skills were designed to fight all manner of monstrosities, but especially draconic foes. Now, I find my Skills so closely aligned with them it is unnerving. On the Wing is the least of them. Matriarch's Lament…"

"Is there a problem with having dragon-styled Skills?"

"A great many problems, yes." Vess suddenly had her partisan in hand and was leaning on it. Clutching at it. "Long ago, after the Ruin devastated the ancient empires and so much was Lost, the world was steeped in monsters. Even more so than now, the land and sky were dominated by beasts of incredible size and ferocity.

"Dragons were among the worst and most vicious, their following Type hordes sweeping entire Territories clean of mortal life. Humanity and the other Races were pushed to the brink of extinction. Bands of warriors fought out small spaces of peace among the savage violence, but those villages were almost always overrun.

"That was when the Dusk Dragons came.

"I do not know why, but they decided to help us. They trained an order of warriors to better fight off the hordes of monsters, gave them skills based upon their own techniques. These were the first dragoons."

"I thought you said your Skills were more touched by dragons *now*?" Felix asked.

"They are. The skills passed down in my order carry the touch of the Dusk Dragons still, but they have been changed. Modified by generations until the Dragoons had perfected a weapon against the monsters, especially those in the sky. Eventually, even the Dusk Dragons turned on us, falling to infighting before a faction of them attacked our people. After their defeat, all draconic Types were considered anathema. The order grew, and our region was stabilized. The rest is history."

"If they betrayed your order, why is your core a giant statue of a Dusk Dragon?" Felix asked.

"I was taught that just because a few chose poorly it does not invalidate the legacy of their mentorship. My mother taught me that. Others would disagree." Vess stood, grinding the butt of her partisan into the stone as she faced the wide expanse of her changed core space. "That, however, is not a Dusk Dragon. It is of no breed with which I am familiar. My seniors would still be aghast to see this, however, and I cannot escape that. The ritual for final acceptance into the Dragoons will reveal all of…this."

During their talk, more clouds had parted, the lumps of cottony mist falling to reveal the changed Skills. Felix drew in a sharp breath. They were no longer unified by her deft attention to detail, instead they were darker and craggier—looming peaks that suggested violence, rage, and a soft, crippling melancholy.

"They feel…why do they feel so sad?" he asked.

"I do not know," she admitted. "There is a story baked into them, a tale that tingles at the edge of my Affinity."

"Or a memory," Felix suggested. He could feel a tingling point of friction buried in those peaks. It was moving, shifting through the pattern of its song, but it was there. He pointed it out. "If you can capture that, hear it, then maybe you can figure out why this is happening."

"I know why it is happening, Felix. I simply wish for it to stop. If it continues, I—I fear I will never be a Dragoon."

The light of his dual cores flickered above them, and the looming mass of the dragon temple hung over them like a stormcloud, gold and shining in their weak light. Felix opened his mouth, raised a hand…and lowered it. What could he say?

Without warning, the mountains shuddered and lurched. Felix gasped, turning just as a tsunami crested the furthest peaks and crashed into them both—

—throwing them from their trance and slamming the both of them back into awareness.

"What the hell?" Felix shouted.

The ship lurched again, dropping twenty feet as it rode down the trough of a massive wave. Someone screamed, clinging to the side, as Felix and Vess flailed slightly before landing atop the slickened chitin-deck. A swift Shadow Whip shot out, latching onto the Claw member's failing grasp and pulling them to safety.

Vess manifested ten silver Spears as another shuddering tremor hit the ship. "You! What is going on?"

"Monsters! Starboard side!"

From behind, the lashing tendrils of blue-black slime whipped up and onto the Manaship's railing, hauling up the bulk of a massive, fish-like mass of scales and slime. A dozen pale, burning eyes stared in malicious rage, and a crocodilian mouth opened wide and *screamed*.

CHAPTER TWENTY-FOUR

"On The Wing!"

Vess blasted past Felix with all the fury of a hurricane. Spears flashed, all ten at a time, sticking into the monster's sticky, grasping tendrils. It roared, more in defiance than pain, just in time to catch the woman's partisan directly to the roof of its alligator-like mouth.

"Ten Tribulations," she hissed, and twisted her spear.

Explosions of air and metal rocked the ship, tossing more of the scrambling crew backward as the monster reeled back in mortal pain… before falling limp back into the sea.

"Damn, Vess," Felix said, before the boat shuddered again. "Damnit. They said monster*s*, didn't they?"

"Indeed," she said with a grim smile.

Another oozing tendril of croc-fish slapped up onto the railing of the Manaship, soon followed by six more, all of them hauling up a toothy maw and blank, glowing eyes.

Voracious Eye!

Name: Fathom Draktopus
Type: Draconic (Manawarped)
Level: 72
HP: 2003/2003
SP: 1413/1722
MP: 865/865
Lore: The Fathom touches the abyss, and it has answered. Writhe upon the waves, writhe with the rage of dragons.
Strength: More Data Required

Weakness: More Data Required

"Draktopus? Are you serious?" Felix said as they chambered aboard. "Fathom spawn! Tier III! Everyone! Get back from the edge of the ship!"

Roughly equal to the strength of a Journeyman-Tier warrior, a Tier III monster was extremely dangerous by itself, let alone in a group. The Yttin crew scrambled up the rigging while his Claw brandished their various weapons as if ready to leap into the fight at any second. But they held back, which is all Felix needed. "Lady Dayne, I believe it is my turn."

Her Spears were manifesting around her once again, and her grim smile quirked to the left. "As you wish, Lord Nevarre."

Cardinal Flame!

Red-gold fire streamed from his channels, igniting the dark, wet air as the ship continued on its rollercoaster journey. They hit the Draktopi all at once, igniting six of them with the paralyzing, ravenous flame. They froze in place, battling against Felix's Willpower with no effect. "Ranged attackers! Ready!"

While he could kill them quickly with his fists, his people needed the levels. His Claw summoned the glow of their Mana and various Skills, holding crackling lightning, frigid ice, and more burning flame.

"Fire!"

All at once, they unleashed thirty different attacks all aimed at six immobilized targets. The impact was enough to rock the boat yet again, the smell of burning and freezing and charred ozone overcome by the splash of foul ichor. But the croc-fish weren't even at half health.

"Again!" Felix commanded, holding onto their Bodies easily with his Skill. Their attacks hit, but the wounds already inflicted began to heal over as he watched. *Damnit!* At least the Claw would get credit for the kills. *Adamant Disco*—!

Before the song of the Skill fully engaged, Vess blurred past him, hair streaming and her partisan held low to her side. More than speed, her new movement Skill was as if each of her limbs were slipping through an entirely different space, her movement like greased lightning sizzling atop a cast iron skillet. She stepped and was two steps farther than Felix had anticipated, an echo of her old Dragoon's Footwork.

Another Draktopus leaped over the burning six and was met with a blurring silver Spear to its face. Vess arrived like a whirlwind. It smashed an oozing tendril at her midsection, but Vess could not be touched, dancing away faster than Felix had ever seen. As she gracefully twisted through the monster's lashing strike, a pair of spectral shapes blossomed from her back.

Are those...wings? Draconic wings did indeed trail behind her, burning bright for only an instant before they lost cohesion, flickered once, and faded into smoke. *She wasn't kidding about the connection to dragons.*

A warning flare smeared across Felix's Perception, and his concentration wobbled ever so slightly on his Cardinal Flame. He turned, finding the nearest Claw member, and shouted. "More are coming! At least fifteen! Focus behind us!"

Without questioning or hesitation, the Claw members spun and launched lightning bolts and arrows into the Draktopi that leaped from the sea. Most did not penetrate their strange mix of scale and slime, but his soldiers were all at high Apprentice or low Journeyman. Their hits were enough to send several backward, unharmed but slowed.

Violent explosions tore up the Draktopi that Felix held immobilized, and he let go of the spell entirely. The creatures immediately began moving to attack, but Vess did not relent. Felix left them alone, confident she would handle them without him, and focused instead on the creatures still oozing up the port side of the heaving ship. It was still heaving as the waves grew to greater proportions, lifting them high into the sky before they rode down from the crest at ridiculous speeds.

"No!"

"Pava!"

Two oozing, dark blue limbs smashed into the Claw ranks, too fast for any of them to react. Many fell, bowled over like pins, while one was dragged up and into the air. A dark-skinned Human woman dangled while she swung her sword wide, each strike shearing through the ooze but unable to sever it before it reformed. It lifted the woman up, over its gaping, toothy maw.

Felix tensed to move, but before he could, a bovine cry blasted away the driving rain, and Beef hit the Draktopus like a freight train. The tendril was blasted apart by the Minotaur's immense, armored Body, and its jaws smashed shut by the descent of his glowing great maul.

The woman fell, screaming in rage, but Felix was there, catching her in his clawed arms. She landed, light as a feather, her curse-filled diatribe cut short. "Ash and bones—Lord Autarch!"

"Pava," he said, accessing that bit of his Mind that housed his Born Trait. Perfect recall was very helpful. "Go back to your Talon, form up, and focus on keeping the monsters from assaulting the ship."

"Aye, my Lord!"

She ran off just as Beef rose from the ground, half his legs and chest covered in vivid blue ichor. The split skull of a Draktopus lolled on the deck beside him. "How many more?"

"A great deal," Hallow said, peeking up from under his cloak. "I sense at least five more in close proximity to the ship. Shall I engage?"

"Engage away," Beef said.

In the water, just over the side of the ship, a massive Multipede the color of bone rose up, churning the water as it closed with the pod of monsters that were attempting to attack the ship. On his shoulder, Hallow grunted. "They are quite strong en masse. I could use some help."

Beef hefted his hammer and looked to Felix. "Want to smash some crocs?"

"Happily," Felix said.

"Hallow!" Beef thrust his arm forward while a rocky, crystalline mass crawled from his shoulder to his bulky forearm. "Fire!"

Five-inch-long shards of blackened green crystal sprouted from Hallow's Homuculus and fired all in the same few seconds, peppering the croc-fish with tiny projectiles that punched through scale and slime with ease.

In the water, Hallow's Multipede form thrashed about, wrapping around several of the Draktopi at once. Their ooze arms flailed, but were unable to escape the strength and length of the undead mega-insect. At the same time, the storm descended in the form of Felix's screeching Companion.

"Tempest Fugit!" Pit shrieked, and frozen lightning fell atop the struggling Draktopi.

Pit Has Killed A Draktopus!
XP Earned!

More frozen lightning dropped out of Pit's wide, glowing wings, blasting off portions of their regrowing hide but not killing them. The ship lurched once more as sticky ooze tendrils slapped into and began climbing the sides.

"Felix!" Beef hollered, his maul busy splashing through the dark tendrils.

Adamant Discord!

The song of his Skill sang bright in Felix's veins, igniting the chaotic mess of threads that made up the world. In moments, he seized a connection with the sky, and from the sky, he grasped the Fathom spawn. Lightning sizzled along the connections, the friction caused by the leverage of his Will too much for the atmosphere. Plying his Strength against the sky itself, which in turn was lashed to the Draktopi, Felix pulled with everything he had. His muscles screamed at the effort, but Felix didn't relent.

Lightning struck in rapid succession directly onto ten Fathom spawn, their long, eel-like bodies writhing madly in pain as they were all lifted entirely out of the water. "Beef! Claw! Hit them!"

Crystalline darts, lightning bolts, icy shards, and streamers of brilliant flame shot outward, plastering the monstrosities with pain if not immense damage. Apart from Hallow's crystal darts, the electrical side effect of his Adamant Discord was doing greater harm than all the rest.

Damn things are a real threat. We have to kill them all. His Claw was doing their best, but they couldn't finish this fight. *It has to be me.*

"Fang of Havoc!"

Vess hurtled into the sky, shooting up sideways and ahead of the ship while her partisan led the way. Around her, Felix saw the cloudy backdrop flicker and stream in a distinct teardrop shape, before her momentum halted entirely.

"Draconic Stormfall!"

Like a comet of judgment, Vess dropped from the sky and back onto the deck of their leading ship. The impact drove the prow down, cutting deep into an approaching wave and sending a massive spray of sea water onto the deck…just as a rolling wave of thunder exploded in all directions.

Felix hunched against the waves and the chunked pieces of Fathom spawn, only barely managing to split a tendril of Shadow Whip and save a few of the Claw members swept away by the dip of the careening ship.

Shadow Whip is level 49!

"Vess!" Felix shouted through the strain. The Draktopi were hurt, but they were also very angry. Holding them had begun to hurt even his muscles. "Vess!"

His friend stood amid the ruin of draconic muck and ichor with her spear sunk halfway through the deck. She looked up, more than a little dazed. "I—I did not mean—I did not know it would spread so far." She blurred across the gore-covered boards, grabbing and hauling more of the Claw from beyond the railings where they clung. "I am sorry."

Felix's Perception caught more shapes moving nearby. Below them, in fact, and rising fast. "More are coming! Vess, hold them off!"

Her head turned just as the first of the Draktopi breached the surface of the heaving sea and hurtled up toward the ship. "I shall do more than that, Felix."

Cardinal Flame scorched the monsters in his Adamant Discord, baking their flesh even as more frozen bolts and crystalline darts tore regenerating chunks from their hides. "What are you doing?"

"I am ending this. Matriarch's Lament!" Around the heiress, a massive, spectral dragon formed that raised its long, fanged snout into the air and began to croon. A deep, mournful cry echoed out, a lament of unremitting loss that seized Felix's heart in the grip of terrible and inconsolable grief; and Felix wasn't even the target.

The monsters were hit so much harder.

Dozens of shapes bobbed up from the depths, each of them unmoving and listless, as if they had simply given up all attempts at attack and even movement. The song hung in the air, thick and heavy and incredibly sad.

Beef and Hallow ran across the deck, seemingly unaffected, while Felix's Spirit reeled from the awful, beautiful vibrations. Darts and chitinous projectiles flew at the impaired Fathom spawn, but Felix's eyes were on Vess. She had fallen to her knees, spear forgotten at her side.

"What the hell was that?" he asked her.

Vess didn't answer. Instead, as Beef and the crew and Claw started cheering, she shuddered and stood.

"Vess?"

Beef rushed up to him, shouting in savage glee. "We killed them all! Did you see it? Hallow's Homunculus got another two levels!"

"Yes," said the craggy creature atop Beef's shoulder. Her voice was warm. "I am pleased."

Felix didn't respond to them, instead trying to reach Vess as the Claw and Yttin crew rushed across the deck to clean it all up. By the time he navigated the press of people, she had vanished.

"Also Felix, I—uh, I need to speak with you," Beef started. "Felix? What's going on?"

He spun in place, ignoring the call of his Minotaur friend, until he could spot the retreating head of dark brown hair through the cheering crowd.

"Felix!" Suddenly, a stomp rang out, the report loud enough to be a gunshot back home, and nearly strong enough to rip through the deck itself. Felix turned, eyebrows up. Beef held out a trembling fist. Within was a small bundle of chitin that hung from his fingers. Something about it pulled at Felix, something he couldn't believe he hadn't noticed before.

Something Divine.

"We need to talk. Now."

CHAPTER TWENTY-FIVE

Claw and crew scrambled across the decks, their celebrations of victory spoiled by the continued storm. The seas kept on heaving, and lines and sails needed tending. Felix had sent Pit winging off into the rain to check on the other ships, but so far, they seemed untouched. The Fathom spawn had attacked their boat and only their boat.

Why, though? Were they just hungry? Opportunists? Felix tapped his lips as the muck and bright blue ichor was swept from the deck. Pieces of the Draktopi were even still twitching, a motion distinct from the swaying of the ship, as if they were reaching out...toward Beef. *What?*

Beef was still there, a few feet away from Felix, holding his clenched fist out before him. It was trembling almost as much as the Fathom pieces. "Felix, please. I—I can't do this much longer."

"Right. Follow me."

Felix led the Minotaur into the captain's quarters. His quarters, according to the crew. The room was as wide as the Manaship and half that in length, so forty feet by twenty give or take a few inches, and for all that space, it was mostly empty. Building a dozen Manaships in the span of a day and a half—even with most of the parts and the expertise of shipwrights—hadn't given them the time to furnish the ships at all. At best, there was a wide bed and a chest of drawers at the foot, both of which were grown into the floors and walls wherever they met them.

Once the doors closed behind them, Felix turned and held out a hand. "Can you let it go?"

Beef was sweating now, and the knuckles on his hand were pale and bloodless. "I'm trying to. It's like my hand's not listening...even—even holding it out is taking a lot." He grabbed at his fist with his other hand, straining to move even a single finger. "I can't!"

Divine strains of music were spinning through the air, harder to ignore now that they were in close quarters. Felix clenched his jaw. "It's protecting itself." He reached up, but the moment his claws came within a foot of Beef's fist, it jerked upward.

Beef gasped, and veins of gold began to pulse through his ruddy fingers and forearm. His eyes widened, amazement piled atop the physical pain. "It's afraid of you."

Adamant Discord!

Felix had a guess at what Beef held, but once the connections of the world were highlighted by his Skill, he knew it for a certainty. A vibrant, pulsing cord of connection extended toward Felix from the thing, golden and thicker than the object itself. He and the hidden object had a history, after all, and connections were all about meaning and relationships. It also had a stranglehold around Beef's arm, which was why his veins were lighting up with Divine power, and a corona of gold hovered around the Minotaur's head.

"Hold still," he warned.

"Quickly! It's ah! It's like needles are crawling up my arm!"

Felix flared his Skill, igniting a minor burst of lightning as the connection solidified and hardened, somehow transitioning into an object that his Will could now grasp freely. Forging a cage of Intent around the chitinous envelope and backing it with his Willpower, Felix hauled back on the cord with every ounce of stat he could put behind it.

With an underwhelming, sizzling *pop*, the envelope slipped from Beef's hand and clattered to the floor.

Adamant Discord is level 82!

Beef fell back as thunder boomed between them, hitting the deck so hard the whole room shook. He grabbed at his forearm, which was a mess of blood. "Ah damn it! Shit!"

Felix crouched low, just over the small object, but his eyes were for his friend. "You okay?"

"Fuck!" Beef swore a couple more times, but quickly ran out of gas, then he was just breathing through his teeth. "Yeah. Healing is...yeah, it's happening slowly. Did you have to rip open my arm when you did that?"

"It was crawling into you, already had a little before now, but it was getting worse fast. How's your head?"

"It—" Beef paused, mouth open. "It feels good. Better, but I didn't know it felt bad before now. What did you do?"

"I had to tear out the thing's influence, and it was affecting your

Mind, I think." Felix peered down at the thing, which was starting to smoke a bit. "How did you find it?"

"I don't remember—wait, no, I do." Beef screwed up his face, furrowing his brow and closing his eyes as if reaching way, way back into the vault of his Mind. "I found it in the water. Days ago. When we were coming out of the Tomb, and the ocean rose up around us. It...it wanted me to keep it secret." He shuddered. "It had me hide it away, I can remember that now. Just like how I remember trying to tell you about it three different times...but it kept fogging things up. Distracting me."

"What was different this time?" Felix asked. The chitin was fully eaten away by the burning now, and he waved his hand rapidly to clear the smoke. A scrap of dingy, off-white cloth sat there, utterly normal aside from the threadbare patterns of gold on it. "How were you able to tell me about it?"

"I think...I think when Vess did that dragon call thing. It shook something loose in me." Beef clambered back to his bovine feet, but didn't come any closer to Felix or the scrap of cloth. "What the hell is it?"

"A piece of the Pathless' Regalia," Felix said and picked it up with his clawed fingertips. Beef hissed in warning, but the thing was utterly inert. It hung between his fingers like...well, like cloth. "Looks burned a little. Probably from when I blew it up before."

The Regalia had been used as the catalyst of an array that had been designed to siphon away the powers of a Primordial. It would have rendered the Paladins invincible, even their weakest members, and who knew how long it would have lasted. When he stopped it, the whole array had detonated and led to a great many problems. *Story of my life,* he mused. "It feels diminished, compared to last time, and not just in size."

"Burnt up or not, that thing is strong," Beef said with a shudder. "It was messing with me this whole time, and I couldn't even remember it! This is a Divine thing?"

"Yeah. Part of the Pathless' Regalia, a cloak or robe maybe, which I assume the Hierophant has access to in order to furnish her Paladins with this. I wonder how many, though." Felix rubbed his fingers over the cloth, feeling tiny jolts of energy spark across its length. It was painful, but nowhere near the level it would need to make him drop it. Small tendrils tried reaching out to him, but they found no purchase on his Aspects. He grinned. "I wonder what would happen if I used this to track down all the pieces of the Regalia and destroy them? It worked on the assassin."

"Ooh, that's a cool idea. Knock them on their asses for once." Beef laughed at the idea and shook his fist. Blood splattered on the floor. "Ouch, that still hurts."

The Divine were simultaneously intriguing and repulsive to Felix. They were gods, supposedly, but they were more like monsters in everything but name. His few encounters with them had always ended with horrifying results, typically featuring him barely escaping their incredible strength. Questions remained, however: who were the gods? What is their purpose? Could he find out through the Regalia, at least a little?

Felix stood, still frowning. The gods disliked him, hated him in the case of the goddess Noctis. She had tried to kill him, last they had "met." Felix couldn't say he was in any hurry to repeat that particular experience.

"I can remember more now," Beef said quietly. His head was tilted in thought. "Every chance that thing got, it wanted me to leave. Head north."

"Back to the Hierophant," Felix said. "Makes sense."

Beef shook his head. "Not just that. It didn't want to be found, but it was...excited when I held it. It...it knew I was Unbound. It called me out, by name." He shuddered hard, and more blood spilled onto the floor. "It's why I knew in my gut I needed to get rid of it. I've read enough books to know that some faceless object 'wanting' things is a pretty good reason not to listen."

Felix held it up. He could feel the Intent that Beef spoke of, and for someone with less advantages, it would have probably overridden their Mind quite easily. Felix was frankly impressed that Beef had resisted it at all. The thing was insidious, the Intent squirming through the Mind to convince you that it was *your* idea to do as it wished. And right now, all it wanted was to get as far away from Felix Nevarre as possible.

The Call of Defiance is active!
+25% Willpower When Contested By A Foe Of Divine Or Greater Advancement!

Against him, however, it wasn't even a contest. Felix quashed its Intent as easily as stepping on a bug...well, a big bug the size of a cat maybe. It was a fragment of a fragment of the Divine, after all. As the insistent Intent within it flickered out, all that was left was a small, infinitesimal spark buried within its folds. Within him, his Divine Tree rustled in agitation, resonating with the spark. "A fragment of Divinity," he said.

"A fragment of an asshole," Beef muttered.

Felix chuckled. "Yeah, that's been my experience." Felix lifted the scrap of Regalia and inspected it in the light of a Mana lamp. "Last I saw this, it just about blazed with light. Still," he said, hefting the oddly heavy fabric. "There's quite a bit left."

"What?" Beef asked.

Felix ignored him, more focused on the Regalia and the odd reaction his core space was having to it. The thing was giving off vibrations, subtle ones, but his Divine Tree was picking up on them easily. The Divine spark was so little, but it was enough to kindle the interest of two facets of his core space. Both wanted it, but the Divine Tree could only quiver at him, grasping ineffectually without a Will of its own...and his Hunger was waiting.

On him.

Feed us, it whispered. Across the breadth of their fleet, he felt Pit's attention turn toward Felix in concern. *Feed us. Grow strong.*

Felix shoved the scrap of cloth into a pocket, willing the Garment to form a zipper and closed it shut. Pit trilled in approval.

His Hunger quietened with a grumble, and the Divine Tree ceased its more frantic swaying...but with the Regalia no longer to hand, Felix felt something else in its place. It had been tethered, sorta, to the artifact, but now it hung in the air and wrapped around his attention like a coiled snake. It was a thread, colored ebon-gold, thick as the one he held to Beef, and it stretched off to the north.

He touched it with his Affinity, or tried to; it shied away like an opposing magnet each time he drew close. The ebon-gold light that emanated from the metaphysical connection barred his touch, but it echoed something he had felt in the Regalia. A spark of the Divine.

What the hell is this?

"Felix?" Beef asked.

He refused to relent. Felix recognized the connection now, having seen it within the bundle of Links in his Bastion. When he'd been hunting down Beef, this had been the one other connection that had shone brighter than his, and just as now it had fled from his touch. It was undoubtedly a Link to another Unbound. If it was showing itself as he inspected the Regalia, then he *needed* to know why. It squirmed, but Felix bent everything he had into seizing it tight.

Adamant Discord!

Skein of Fate!

Got you!

"Felix, what is going onnnnnnnnnnn—"

Sound stretched and bent while the world around him faded into streaks of riotous color, until he felt like he was bridging a vast divide between here and a place impossibly distant. Time smeared just as space and sound, until Felix no longer knew how long he held onto the Link, no longer could remember why he cared, only that he must not let go. *Hold on!*

The world cracked. Once, twice, until a web of fissures filled the smearing colors of reality and the soundless void. Until everything shattered.

And Felix was somewhere else.

"Are you quite sure you are well enough to travel?"

The voice of a kindly old man was the first thing Felix heard. Then, reality flowed back together, a jigsaw puzzle reassembling itself, and he could see a rustic town in the middle of tall, snow-capped mountains. The streets were filled with people, Dwarves mostly, and the houses were all built in an odd style he'd never seen before. Like interlocking cubes iterated over and over again until they formed complex structures that rose three or four stories all around him. Geometric patterns were worked into the cubes, leaving nothing bare but the cobbles beneath their feet.

He stood there, bodiless as he always was in these visions, though he could pivot and move around the area to an extent. Among the crowd was an old man in white robes, looking in his direction with such fearful intensity that Felix was worried he'd actually been transported there.

"I require no coddling, Hierei Faer. I need only serve." This voice was strange to Felix's ears, female as if strained of all emotion and personality. Like a corpse given voice. "What is the problem you have encountered?"

Felix looked at her, but instead of a person, he only saw a figure dressed in enough plate armor to put Harn to shame. She was taller than Felix, somewhere close to seven feet tall, and just as wide. The armor was patterned with sharp edges and hard angles, covering her so completely that not a speck of skin or hair could be seen. She flexed her hands, spiked gauntlets bending around the hilt of a sword at her waist. One of *many* weapons that covered her person.

Goddamn walking armory, he thought. *She's gotta be the Unbound. By why does she sound so weird?*

The old man swallowed nervously, the loose skin of his neck rippling, and sweat dotting his bald pate. "As always, Imara, please call me Kellis."

"What is the problem you have encountered?" she asked again.

"We are waiting while the Dwarves determine if they will let you into their city," the robed man said. The crowd ahead of them was murmuring, and quite a few cast looks back on the man and Unbound. "The Hierocracy is not well liked here."

"And if they decided against us?" Imara asked in that dead voice.

"Then we cannot fulfill our mission. The Gnome, whoever he is, will be lost among the peaks."

Gnome? Wait. Did he say Hierocracy? Felix spun, taking in the man's robes again and noticing a distinct sunburst pattern across his chest, embroidered in thread of gold. *Is he a priest of the Pathless? Why is she with the Pathless?*

"That is unacceptable." Imara was moving before the old priest could respond, pushing through the throng as if they were children instead of solid slabs of Dwarven adults. Shouts followed her, pained and outraged in turns, but the armored mountain didn't stop for a second until she reached the very front of the line, where twenty Dwarves in heavy mail stood outside a massive doorway carved from the side of a mountain. "You. Open the gate."

Felix followed after her, pulled by the magnetism that had drawn him to her in the first place, and he saw as the Dwarven guards traded disbelieving looks. "Ye the one with the old priest?" one asked.

"Open the gate," she repeated.

The priest in question was shouting at her back, unable to get through the crowd. "Imara! Imara no!"

"Yeah, she's the one. Naught else like her on this range, bleedin' giant," another guard said.

The first held out his axe, a simple but very stout-looking weapon. "Ye cannot pass. Not until the Hinterlords decided on it, aye?"

"My mission cannot be stalled. You will open the gate, or I will open it for you."

"Listen here, lassie. If ye take a single step further, ye will find the might of all the Giathban fall on ye. Unnerstand?"

Imara heard him, but it was clear she did not care. She stepped forward anyway, and the priest's shouts only redoubled. A series of riotous explosions went off: beams of sizzling heat followed by huge, concussive blasts. The guards had thrown up large, boxy shields that protected them, but the crowd was thrown back on their rears, even from twenty feet away.

Imara, however, remained standing. Her armor glowed at the edges, but Felix knew she was unharmed.

"Stand back!" the lead guard shouted, but Imara took another step. "Men! Grab yer weapons! We teach this one a lesson!"

All twenty of the Dwarven warriors rushed forward, shields and axes to hand. Imara only walked.

"Imara! Stop, now!" the priest shouted, far closer now. "We have other ways!"

The woman ignored him and unleashed her Spirit.

Everyone around them was blasted backward, save for the priest. Their Bodies seized, unable to move as the physical manifestation of her

Spirit swept them entirely out of her way. Even Felix, who was merely a witness projected across a Link, felt the heavy weight of it. It clawed at him like a malevolent creature, trying to tear away his Willpower and burrow deep into his own Spirit. The image of things flickered and faded like a television with bad reception, but Imara marched to the gates of this mountain city and unsheathed a thick club at her waist. She swung. A crack splintered across the face of the mountain door.

"Imara!"

She swung again. And again. Each time, Felix's connection thinned, until he could only parse the haziest of details. He witnessed the gates fall and an army arrayed against this Imara.

All Felix felt, at the end, was concern for the army.

Then reality shattered one last time.

CHAPTER TWENTY-SIX

"—eeeeeelix? What's going on?"

The world reassembled his vision first, leaving Felix standing with a single hand outstretched, still clasped around a fading ebon-gold thread. Beef was in the same position as before, mouth still finishing his earlier words.

"A vision," Felix explained as the thread vanished entirely. He rubbed his fingers together as the sounds of the sea returned to him, along with the creaking of ropes and sails.

Beef's mouth hung open. "A vision? Like a prophet?"

"No, not like that," Felix said, letting his hand drop to his side. "It's the same thing I did when I would see you. The same thing you were doing when you dreamed of me."

"Oh dang, you can control that?" Beef looked immediately excited, all his concern over the Mind-controlling Regalia gone. "Can you teach me?"

Felix shrugged. "No idea. But we need to talk to Zara first."

"Zara? Why? What did you see? Who did you see?"

"A problem."

Zara wasn't located on the flagship, as Beef and Vess were. She had chosen to travel in the next ship in line, likely because Felix had refused to let Isla travel along with him and Beef. Before they left, he tried to find Vess—ostensibly to include her on the situation, but also to check in on her. She was in her room but didn't answer when he knocked.

Felix and Beef left on their own.

The seas were still violent, the rains still constant, but both had slackened to an extent after their battle. It made riding atop the chitinous back of Hallow far more palatable at least, though it was only a minor act of Strength and Dexterity to keep balance atop the creature's shifting plates. The Multipede clambered up the side of the next ship, almost frightening the soul out of a Yttin crew member, and the two of them disembarked.

"Sorry about that. Do you know where Zara is?" Felix asked a panting Yttin woman. She swiftly dropped to a knee but did not answer him. Turns out, she didn't need to.

"Looking for you," Zara said. She walked easily along the deck, her gait uninterrupted by the waves. "I saw Pit streak past us right after the light show you all put on. He would not stop to answer my questions, so I would ask you: What happened?"

Beef grimaced, and Felix just kept walking past the Chanter. "We all need to talk."

Moments later, the three of them were ensconced in the captain's quarters on this ship. They were smaller than Felix's, as he rode in the largest Manaship, but they were just as empty of furnishings. Zara didn't even have a chest of drawers, instead having to make do with strange racks that secured a number of banded crates. Felix was tired, though, and he seized the water Mana in the air and twisted it to his purpose.

Rime Shaping!

A chair of ice formed between the cracks in the floorboards, rising up to meet his descending backside. Felix sighed in relief. "Endurance and Strength out the wazoo, but sitting down still feels good."

Zara raised an eyebrow, and Beef looked at him enviously, so he quickly made chairs for them both, explaining the details of their fight against the Fathom and after, the details of the Regalia.

"And it still contains a spark of the Divine?" Zara asked. "Might I see it?"

Felix hesitated only a little, but Zara's Perception couldn't be fooled. Her mouth tightened, even as he unzipped his pocket and handed the scrap of cloth to her. "Careful, it—"

"Ouch!" The Naiad jerked her fingers away and up to her mouth as a golden jolt jumped from the Regalia. "It is defending itself?"

"Yeah. Doesn't want to be touched by us, I assume. Me especially."

"Does it not hurt you?" Zara asked. She could see the golden light zapping against his scaled fingers. "Or does it not penetrate your new hands?"

"It does. I just don't care," Felix said with a shrug. "I've been hurt by a lot worse than some static electricity on a dishrag."

Zara's brow, furrowed with thought before, smoothed out, and her expression turned curiously soft. "Do you wish to talk about it?"

"What? No. I'm fine," Felix said. He held out the Regalia again. "Take it."

Instead of reaching for it, Zara let loose a trilling whistle that echoed far louder than it should have. Harmonies unspoken by her voice spread outward from her throat, and a hand of ghostly blue-green light reached out and cradled the Regalia in its oversized palm.

"That's so cool," Beef whispered.

Zara used her conjured hand to twist and tilt the cloth every which way. "It is giving out a piece of song itself. A tempting vibration that rattles against my teeth. You felt its Intent, yes?"

"We did," Felix said. "It wants to get away from me, is about all I've gathered."

"That it does. There is a layer of...disgust. Stranger and stranger. You've made an impression on the Pathless, I think."

"That's me, making friends wherever I go."

"Indeed." The ghostly hand rotated once more, displaying the embroidered patterns on the off-white fabric. "I believe this was once part of the Pathless' outer robes, based on what I've learned over the years. The Priesthood wear robes of a similar design—a sign of respect, they claim." She shook her head, as if worrying at something else. "There is more to it, however. The vibration it's sending out is pulling at things. People. Creatures. I was wondering why the Fathom were attacking us."

"So the Fathom are being drawn to it?" Felix asked.

"It is likely." Zara said.

"Across miles and miles of desert and mountains and stuff?" Beef asked. He glanced at Felix. "I thought you said it was weakened?"

"The ritual the Paladins attempted was as loud as anything upon the world's Harmonies. The sheer amount of Dissonance unleashed by the Primordial's awakening and the Pathless' aborted array would have been heard across multiple Territories," Zara explained. "It will draw others, I'm sure."

"Is Ahkestria safe, then?" Felix asked. A spike of alarm jolted along his spine. "Or will more Fathom spawn come looking?"

"Unlikely. Felix did not lie, Beef; the Regalia is weakened, but it is still a point of significance that drags along the Grand Harmony. Anything with the proper senses will sense it within a certain distance. It is unmistakable now that it cannot hide itself inside your Spirit."

"Hiding in my Spirit?" Beef's bovine face was as pale as Felix had ever seen it, turning an odd grayish-brown.

"The Regalia was burrowing into your Spirit and Mind, and only left your Body for last, when Felix attempted to take it."

"Burrowing?" Beef asked in a small voice.

"Mhm. You already gleaned its intentions in your Mind, but it seems like it was also cloaking itself within the noise of your Spirit. You are...uniquely qualified to host the artifact," Zara said. She tapped her lips with a cleanly manicured finger before walking to one of the secured crates along the side of the room. "But I believe I can find something better."

"What does that mean?" Felix asked. "'Uniquely qualified.' Because he's Unbound? Or a Minotaur?"

"It's because his Spirit is hollow." The door slammed open. Its internal locks slid aside as easily as if she held a key, and Isla stood framed by a flash of lightning. She walked in, closing the door again with a faint splash of green-gold liquid Mana. "Such a conference, and I am not invited? For shame, Zara."

"You were busy casting after the Fathom spawn," Zara said cooly, unruffled by the other woman's sharp tone. "I would not bother you for such stakes."

"Anything involving my Unbound charge concerns me," Isla all but snapped. She calmed visibly as she beheld Beef's worried expression. "Are you alright, Michael?"

"That's—yeah," Beef said, sounding exhausted suddenly. His arm had mostly healed, and the color had returned to his complexion. "I'll be okay."

"Tch." She leaned into the enormous Minotaur, checking his eyes, ears, even his mouth. For what, Felix hadn't a clue, but she seemed mostly satisfied. "You should not be on another ship without me, Michael. You could get into more trouble than you can escape. For instance, *that*," she said, pointing at the cloth Zara still held suspended with her phantom hand. "That would never have found you, had you stuck by my side."

"But you left to help Zara and the others. And Felix wanted to see the Tomb, and if we hadn't done that everyone would have died. Right?" Beef looked at Felix like a man casting for a lifeline. "Right, Felix?"

"Of course you're right," Felix said, giving his friend a comforting pat on the shoulder. Isla, however, got a harder glare. "He's doing fine on his own, Isla."

The diminutive woman pursed her mouth. "I was charged with finding and mentoring him, Felix. I cannot do that if I'm relegated to another ship."

"You'll do it just fine where you are."

"But—"

"Enough," he snapped, unleashing just a touch of his Spirit. It roared outward, like the door she had opened to the storm, and he shut it swiftly—but the impression remained.

Isla gave Felix a tight, unwilling nod. "As you wish."

Zara walked back to the group carrying a number of thick slabs of crystal, each a different hue. "This shall allow us to escape the significance of this piece of Regalia. I recall you saying the Paladins used a similar method to contain it?"

"Oh yeah. They had a little crystal container to hold the thing. When it was closed, I couldn't even sense its presence," Felix said. "You can recreate that?"

"Not exactly, no. It is likely they had the use of some Divine sigaldry to mesh with the Regalia's specific vibrations. I do not have such tools at my disposal." She set the crystals out into the air, and a new hand branched out of the ephemeral one that held the sparking fabric. With four pieces laid out, she brandished a stylus. "But I can make an approximation with some old-fashioned sigaldry and the Chant."

Beef and Felix both leaned in closer, curious to watch the woman work. Isla, for her part, stood silently outside their circle, tapping her foot impatiently.

Zara's hand was steady as she sang a soft, insistent melody just under her breath. The first two crystal lengths were pressed together, and Mana flared where they met, sealing together. But not entirely. The Naiad followed that action up with a series of criss-crossing inscriptions, lines rather than sigils or glyphs, each one a perfect circle above the join. She repeated it, again and again, until all but the last of the crystalline pieces were affixed to one another.

With deft movements and a lilting song from her lips, Zara shifted the entire structure over as her phantom hand dropped the Regalia into its hollow interior. It sparked wildly as it fell, the branches of golden light almost like claws, but it slipped easily into the crystal container.

Felix realized he was holding his breath and let it go, feeling just a bit silly. *What did you expect? No. You know what you expected. An explosion, a monster attack. Something.* The end cap was lifted by more ephemeral hands and moved to the last opening. *But this is working. I can barely hear it anymore.*

In fact, all the noise had stopped.

Felix stood up, but the floor was gone, as were the walls and the ceiling. He was alone in a vast stretch of darkness that was entirely too familiar. The Void extended in all directions, endless and featureless, and the only sound was his quickening heartbeat.

But that, too, changed.

The crashing sound of rushing water filled Felix's ears, and for a moment, he wasn't sure where it was coming from. It was sourceless and everywhere, as if the black skies were opening above him and letting loose a wild cacophony atop his head. It wasn't water, but pure sound. Harmony, threaded through with clanging, atonal streams of Dissonance. It was similar to the way his cores produced their songs, but far more unbalanced and chaotic, as if someone were simply mashing instruments together to see how much noise they could produce.

A door to a burned and blackened sky sat before him, a gate the size of a mountain and no bigger than a speck, all at once. The roaring noise raced toward it, screaming into its threshold like a river of howling rapids careening toward a precipice. Felix could feel their attention tilt, not yet aware of him, but their vast incomprehensibility damaging for him to even glance at sideways. Through the gate, their shapes morphed and rumbled, shifted into moons that were chained among the blackened heavens, each overflowing with surreal emotions too complex for Felix to understand.

Title: The Call of Defiance is active!
+25% Willpower When Contested By A Foe Of Divine Or Greater Advancement!

With all of his Willpower, he fought against the pull of that river, until the gate faded. Until its rumbling was only the thunder overhead, and before them all sat a crystalline tube, perfectly sealed together and marked with a dizzying array of glyphs and sigils across its facets.

Theurgist of the Rise is level 83!

He was in his icy chair, allies around him, none of them seeming the least bit concerned. Felix had a feeling none of *them* had just almost walked in on the gods for the second time in a week.

Zara sat back, stylus limp in her hand and face sweating. "The Regalia is sealed, and we are safe from its influence, at least for a time. It is done."

Yet Felix had the distinct feeling that things had just begun.

CHAPTER TWENTY-SEVEN

With the Regalia locked away, Zara was assured that the Fathom spawn would leave them alone entirely, save for perhaps chance encounters. He was told that draconic Types—the weak ones, at least—were notoriously cowardly, and their fleet represented a significant threat. Felix was still worried about the Fathom following the beacon lit by the Paladins' previous ritual, but there was little he could do except warn Klzix through his Bastion of Will.

That had gone off without a hitch. While contacting the Yttin Chancellor had been a chore of finding the right Link at the right time and momentarily strengthening it, Karys had assisted Felix in the endeavor. Now he had a somewhat reliable way to communicate among his two Territories, even if he had to wait for Klzix to fall asleep.

Ahkestria warned, ships protected, and everyone on the lookout had done a great deal to put Felix's Mind at ease. The gods thing was a worry, but it was one he was firmly determined to leave for Future Felix. As their ships sped across the heaving sea, he turned instead toward long overdue tasks. His friends, and the effects of his Tier IV Links with them.

Atar was meant to be first, though convincing the man to let him peer at his core space had been a chore in and of itself. To put him at ease, Felix started with Alister instead. The force mage had no reservations about Felix stepping into his core space; far from it, the man was happy to have someone to talk to about everything. While Alister had not been part of Felix's newly forged Links, he was essentially a baseline that he would compare to the others.

"Oh, wow," Felix said, his visualized projection standing atop a wide, white marble platform. He quickly realized that comparing Alister's inner workings to the rest might prove...difficult. "This is amazing."

"Really?" Alister said, surprise and pleasure rolling from his Spirit. Interestingly, Felix found it was far harder to mask one's emotions within your own core space. "I had thought it would seem...plain, compared to the others you have seen. Atar's, for instance?"

Felix laughed. "Atar's was beautiful and detailed, but this is another level entirely. Is that a machine of some sort?"

At the center of the spherical room was a contraption made entirely out of thick columns of blue force Mana. Plinths of white marble connected to it from most directions, forming a narrow set of support structures that encased the slowly spinning contents. It was a strange cross between a mechanical clock and a gyroscope. Gears and wheels made entirely of blue force Mana were accompanied by white marble discs and blocks, all of which were rotating around one another in a steady dance.

"Yes! You know of them? The only records I ever had were the Mana engines in the Guild Archive, and those were nearly a century old. Ancient records of an even more venerable technology." Alister walked forward, his blue-hued shoes tapping against the lightly veined marble flooring. The mage's entire projection was blue, from his clothes to his skin and hair, as if he'd crafted himself entirely of his attuned Mana type. As he reached the platform's edge, he pointed toward the circular walls around them. "This entire structure I based off of the diagrams of Vilas Tern. They were recovered from a Second Age ruin, preserved instead of Lost. One of only a handful of others like it."

"Who?" Felix asked.

"The Pagewright of the Violet Tower? Of the Lucent Towers in Levantier? Ah, right. Unbound. I imagine you've not had many chances to read up on local geography, let alone magical theory."

"Not really, no. A few books here and there. Found some nice maps in Ahkestria and took some books with me when I left. I was pretty sad the Eyrie got knocked down before I could access its Archive."

"Me, too. I loved those stacks," Alister said with a blue smile. "Oh, here! It's starting!"

A steady hissing filled the air of the circular chamber, like the inside of a white ball that was angrily deflating. But, instead of collapsing, the walls opened up entirely, revealing a network of blue gears and pistons behind the marble paneling. Like the isolated platform they stood upon, the entirety of the spherical room was made of white marble, veined very lightly with blue, and the curved panels all pressed inward in time with the core mechanism. Ripples of stone and force-made machinery rolled through Alister's core space, each piece of the outer wall shimmering and humming with a unique vibration to Felix's ear.

"Those are your Skills?" he asked.

Alister nodded. "Yes. They shifted depending on their levels, of course, but that is where the majority of my Skills reside."

"And now they are moving because...?"

"Because my core is releasing its regulated stream of Mana, which is in turn being taken up by my Skills and distributed evenly among them. When I am actively using a Skill, such as...now." A piece of the wall moved closer to the center, flowing with the elegant machinery but remaining nearer the blue-hued gears and chugging pistons. Waves of force Mana burst and spread, bathing the marble edifice and collecting in a series of apertures on its surface. "The Skill draws closer, and the core, which is moving and drawing in more Mana from my channels there, which in turn are pulling in Mana through my Gates."

"Pulling free force Mana from the environment outside," Felix said, nodding along. "That's a clever visualization. It's like a force pump and generator combined, drawing in your power and distributing it out among your core."

"I was actually inspired by Tern's depictions of ancient ethericraft. Precursors to the Manaships we're riding upon now. Far more advanced than these, in fact," Alister added with an apologetic smile. "Sorry."

"Don't be. I only required that we have enough ships to house our people and enough sails to keep it going. The Mana engines weren't part of the deal originally, but House Iretus have some very talented shipwrights."

"Indeed. The simple thrust the engines are providing is remarkable, though I imagine it's quite expensive to maintain," Alister said. "You're using Mana crystals to fuel it?"

"Yeah, though this ship I'll power myself when needed. The others are going through a lot of wealth whenever the engines are fired up, which is why having proper sails was a requirement." Felix sighed, less concerned with the monetary worth of his vast store of Mana crystals than with the potential they represented for their crafters. He hoped they'd be able to keep most of them.

Alister winced. "You're burning gold to propel us along. That is quite astounding, Felix."

He shrugged. "The engines are meant for emergencies. I'd rather lose all my money than risk anyone's life unnecessarily."

Alister was silent after that statement, releasing only a soft hum of appreciation and pride that Felix shut out of his senses. The two of them stood there a bit longer, watching the mechanized motions of Alister's core. After perhaps fifteen minutes, Felix had sussed out a pattern that appeared to play through the space, but only when the mage wasn't activating any Skills in particular.

The core would build up with Mana, and once it reached a certain amount, that was when the walls opened up and pressed inward. The Skills would prioritize themselves based on size: the largest lingering the longest near the core while the smaller pieces of carved marble would flit in circular patterns around the larger ones. The Mana would spread out, depleting over the course of another few minutes, until the Skills all returned to the spherical walls. Then the process would begin again.

"This is fascinating," he said at last. "Truly unique from the others."

"I'm glad I measure up," Alister said with a laugh. "Though, I admit to being surprised. I am not nearly as interesting as a noble Dragoon or an Urge-Blessed fire mage."

"Alister. You built this whole place out of half-guessed diagrams in tomes four times as old as you are. That's impressive." Felix stretched, though he didn't need it, before slapping the force mage on the back. "Thanks for allowing me to visit your space. When you are ready to Temper, I'll help guide you, if you want. My Fiendforge has proven pretty useful to Evie and Atar, at least."

"That would be my honor, Felix," Alister said.

"Great!" Felix clapped his hands. "Next up is Atar, then."

Transitioning to Atar's core space was simple, though taking Alister with him was next to impossible. Felix had hoped that it wouldn't be too hard, considering how he'd pulled Klzix into his Bastion...but apparently it required more than brute force to enable such a thing. True, real connection had to exist, and while Alister and Atar were in a relationship, it still didn't have the juice of a System-established Link.

Part of that, perhaps, was how hard Atar fought against the whole idea of it. He'd agreed, but his Spirit was clearly unwilling, providing a serious amount of friction to the entire process. Felix had eventually given up on the task entirely, resorting to stepping alone into Atar's core space, something that the fire mage only fought back against once before accepting it.

As he landed, Felix could see why.

Where before his friend's core space had been a sleek temple or library filled with burning braziers, black surfaces, and golden sigiladry, now it was a blasted crater. Far different than Alister's complex machinery or Vess' transformed mountains, Atar's core space looked like it had been hit by a meteor. Ash fell from the sky, which was filled with dark smoke that rose constantly from something just out of sight. Everything smelled burnt, and the scoured and pitted stone beneath his feet was so hot Felix was surprised it wasn't molten. "Atar?"

"Here."

Felix turned, and it took all of his bodily control not to take a leaping step backward. Atar was a bundle of charred bones, bound together with thin bands of cloth. Barely. His charcoal skeleton looked likely to fall apart at the merest hint of a breeze, and the only thing that seemed sturdy about him was the odd white fire, edged in bright crimson, that filled his ribcage and skull.

"This is what happens when you tear out the root of yourself," Atar said. His blackened jaw worked soundlessly for a moment, and the flames of his eyes darted around the broken space as if unsure where to look. "I...I know I look a horror. It has worried at me since I awoke. The only comfort I hold is that the same thing happened to all of the Flame's followers."

"I heard many died," Felix said quietly.

"And more wished for death's embrace," Atar said, and his jaw closed with a snap. "The pain was incredible, and were it not for my...special circumstances, I don't think I would have endured it." He held out his arms, waggling his charnel fingers. "I barely did."

"Yet you're free," Felix pointed out.

"That I am. I know we've barely talked on it, but the Link that you established—strengthened, whatever—I think it was all that kept me living through the Highest Flame's depredations. It was the only rope off a very deep precipice, one I, in my arrogance, thought I could handle alone." Atar shook, his bones quivering before he hugged his burning chest tightly. "I couldn't. Without that Primordial strength, I would have been burnt to a crisp, and the Flame would have limped on."

"The story I heard on everyone's lips is how you killed the Urge," Felix said.

Atar clacked his jaw again, this time in annoyance. "I know what they're saying, and it's not true, not really. I dealt the finishing blow, I absorbed the thing into my channels and blasted out my core space, but it would have survived, had it not been for you cutting off its primary source of sustenance."

"Tomato, potato," Felix said. "What does it matter? You're still alive, and the Urge is gone. I call that a win."

Atar hesitated before shrugging. "It means a great deal and also very, very little. My Skills have been scattered across my core space, drowned in dust and ash, and even my core has been swallowed up." He ran sharp fingers across his sternum, through the licking flames within his chest. "I salvaged this, my core flame, in order to keep my visualization stable. I had been hoping that I could rebuild it all from around this base...but it is slow going. The pain, it doesn't stop."

Felix stepped closer to his friend and smiled. "That's why I'm here. To help."

Atar's flame eyes flickered in a blink. "What of checking the others? Evie and Harn and your Minotaur friend? Vess?"

Felix only let himself pause a second before waving the mage's words off. "Based on our speed, we've half a week until we reach Caleph Pass. I can spare the time. And Vess has taught me a bit about visualization techniques that should prove useful here. So, what do you say?"

Atar smiled. Cautious joy and, oddly, shame wafted off of him thicker than the heat waves from his flames. "I would appreciate it."

Felix didn't spare the time to hunt down his friend's feelings. The part that mattered in that moment, above all else, was action. Felix was getting pretty good at that.

"Fiendforge," he whispered, and felt the core space tighten. Smoke billowed, bulging sideways as his Will and Intent clamped upon the whole of it, while in his hands he manifested two brilliant red-gold flames. "Cardinal Flames. You ready?"

"As ever."

Felix reached up before slamming his hand into the stone at their feet, sending wave after wave of lambent red-gold energy threading through it all. "First things first: we need to find your core."

CHAPTER TWENTY-EIGHT

Felix's main responsibility was holding the core space together. As it had before, his Fiendforge acted as a vice grip around Atar's visualized world, clasping it tight and keeping the pieces of it from splintering further. That wasn't a concern in the beginning stages, as above all else, Atar had to find the core itself.

The two of them hunted through the ash-filled, blasted terrain for at least an hour before Atar located the once-massive altar. It had been utterly buried in ash, and the flame suspended above its tilted bowl was nearly choked out entirely. The flame was a pale yellow-orange, closer to a torch than a bonfire. Seeing it made a number of things more clear, namely the length of Atar's recovery.

Without a properly working core space, his very Aspects were impacted, reducing regenerations on all fronts. Moreover, Atar revealed that his channels felt clogged as well, packed with more char and ash from the fallout of his confrontation. Clearing said impurities was a challenge that had to be tackled before any sort of reconstruction could be engaged in, and Atar set to it with gusto.

Atar's charcoal skeleton sat itself next to the cracked and tilted core, employing his own visualization technique. Felix watched, fascinated, as the pressure on his Fiendforge shifted subtly. The mage's methods were superficially similar to Vess', primarily in that Atar cleared his Mind and sent his Perception outward to make changes. He grabbed at and squashed each bit of debris and detritus that had piled up around them. Unlike Vess, Atar did not form a miniature facsimile of his core space before him, and Felix thought he noticed a significant lack of fine control because of it. Regardless, after another hour of slowly gathered momentum, Atar rendered large swathes of the core space clean and clear, ready for Felix to add in his own efforts.

Using his Skills in other people's core spaces was difficult to a certain degree, but mostly it was that Felix was limited in what permanent changes he could affect. He could create a huge statue of himself and Pit, detail it until it looked as lifelike as possible, but the moment he stopped feeding it Mana, the structure would crumble apart. Only Atar had Authority over himself, which was as it should be...but Felix could pave the way.

Stone Shaping is level 82!
Mantle of the Infinite Revolution is level 53!

By utilizing Stone Shaping on Atar's visualized bedrock, he could shift the cracked expanse into a solid whole. He did so, discussing the efforts with Atar as they went. They found his progress went faster when he also applied his Mantle of the Infinite Revolution, heating up the ground so that he could pull and shape the savaged stone with only mild difficulty. The bedrock, once cratered with devastation, was whole once again, marked here and there with small mounds to represent Atar's Skills. Fine as it was, Felix strained to hold and keep it from deteriorating right back into its old state. That was where Atar came back into play.

Essentially presenting a mock-up design, Atar flowed after, utilizing his techniques to copy the template Felix had laid out. It turned out that having a visual representation of what he wanted was extremely useful, allowing his Mind to focus on exactly what was needed rather than worrying at the process. The bedrock turned from a dark granite to a smooth, glassy obsidian as Atar finalized the initial changes.

Fiendforge is level 20!

After that, they began to map out the sigaldry that once dominated Atar's core. Due to having seen most of Atar's previous setup, and because that had been well within the thirty-day limit of his Born Trait, Felix could have faithfully replicated the majority of the old design. The question became whether or not they *should.* Atar was more heavily involved there, guiding Felix through what he desired and following right behind him each step of the way. It took some doing, hours of it, but eventually the obsidian flooring was gilded with elegant, golden inscriptions.

Manasight is level 74!
Invocation is level 66!

"Atar, these sigils don't make a lot of sense," Felix pointed out. "Your last core space had a lot of complicated bits to it, but the pieces I understood were pretty clear."

"They won't for a while, I don't think. This is a framework at best," he said with a desolate tone that didn't match his angry expression, such as it was. "You're right, my old setup had a great deal more clarity and complexity. Until I've fixed more details here, that much work will be pointless."

"Why?"

Atar clacked his jaws, as if considering his words. "Changes. If they happen, and I don't doubt they will, I will need to move fast. I am affording this opportunity only by the nature of my severed bond to the Highest Flame...and by my Title."

"Your Title?" Felix turned so he was fully facing the man. "You didn't mention a Title. From defeating the Urge?"

"From surviving it. Or not surviving it, as it turns out." Atar lifted a skeletal hand and pushed at Felix. A blue screen rotated into his view.

"Reborn?" Felix read on, his eyebrows slowly climbing up his forehead. "'Due to your Link to a Primordial and Nascent [Unknown], the attunement of your core, and your Born Trait (Heart of Fire), you have been remade!' What? The Primordial is me, but what's this Nascent [Unknown] bit?"

"I haven't a clue. Honestly, I had hoped you would be able to explain that."

"Sorry to disappoint." Felix bit at the inside of his cheek, thinking. "So, the surge in significance plus being 'reborn' has granted you some, what, flexibility in redesigning your core space?"

"That is my theory, yes. Everyone knows that one must solidify one's core space well before they reach Master Tier, or else be locked into less than ideal patterns of visualization. It can, and has, affected those attempting to advance into Master and beyond." He drew his knobby knees inward, toward the flames in his chest. "I am rushing headlong into Adept. I can feel it gathering around me, Felix. The Skills are in disarray here, but the power they took from the Urge was...it was a lot. Too much, almost."

"I know the feeling," Felix said before sighing and throwing up his hands. "Well, it's just another thing. We'll get it fixed as best we can and keep moving forward. Any other surprises, though? The Link I established with Vess threw some curveballs at her, and I'd rather face yours head-on if we can."

"No. That's it," Atar said. He hugged his knees a bit closer to his chest and laughed. "That's enough, I think."

"Mm." Felix could hear it, though. The lie. It tingled in the air between them, an atonal burr along Atar's complicated Spirit. "Alright. Just let me know."

"Of course."

At that point, their attention shifted to the man's core directly. Felix was told to hold back as Atar focused the entirety of his Willpower and Intent. Unlike the spaces around them, cores were not something you wanted another person's influence over, for various vague reasons Atar couldn't be bothered to explain. So, Felix watched and maintained the hold of his Fiendforge.

After a few aborted attempts, Atar successfully managed to reshape the altar that housed his flickering core flame, turning it from a wide, shallow brazier and bowl to a tall, rough-hewn cage of obsidian. Golden sigaldry crawled up its straight sides, marking out the cylindrical edges of the plinth that lifted the cage to approximately chest height. Within, the yellow-orange flame flickered and danced, as dim as ever.

"Now the tricky part," Atar muttered and shoved a fist into his own chest. The white flame gathered onto Atar's hand, and when he removed it, the majority of it came along for the ride, leaving only the barest glimmers still pumping with the man's skeletal ribs. Atar wheezed, clearly in pain, but did not hesitate to slip his burning hand into the obsidian cage. The moment he did, the yellow-orange flame flared up as if it had just been fed a huge helping of kindling. The white fire, however, was too strong, subsuming the warmer light and replacing it entirely.

"Wow." Felix watched the core flame brighten and expand, swirling with some sort of inner motion. It almost looked like wings for a moment, before the crimson-edged fire spun outward into a hollow ring. Except for being less dense and only one of them, it was basically a color-swapped version of his own core rings. "It worked."

"Haah, you...you doubted?" Atar asked between heavy breaths. His brittle hands held at the bars of his cage, while his much-dimmed eye fires tracked the swirling motion of his new core flame. "I am...the greatest...fire mage in Ahkestria."

"Technically true. We killed most of the others," Felix said with a chuckle. Atar glared at him, which only increased his amusement. "Alright, alright. I will say, the idea of a cage is interesting. Can I ask why?"

"I...do not entirely know why," Atar admitted. "We are all shaped by our perceptions and expectations, unconscious or otherwise." There was a harsh burr in his voice, different than before. More raw. "My Intent did this...my pain did this."

"Atar. You've rebuilt your core from the brink. I would call that a win, no matter how you slice it, dude." Felix walked around the cage-like core, while the odd flame expanded and shrank, as if flickering in the wind. "Plus, it looks pretty cool."

"Cool? Right. You've used that idiom before." Atar's charcoal skeleton gave the obsidian cage a wary look. "I suppose it holds a certain aesthetic."

"There you go!"

"Perhaps, if I..." Atar trailed his hands across the crude expanse of glassy stone, his voice turning to a series of nonsensical murmurs as his concentration narrowed significantly. Each pass of his hand did something, changed a bar or plane or join, until the cage was no longer quite as crude. By the time the man stepped back, breathing heavily through his gaping ribs, the cage and plinth upon which it stood had changed. Before, the design was rough and almost accidental, as if a cage had sprung up out of nature. Now, it appeared as if a craftsman had put conscious design into them. Not a great craftsman, per se, but there was a burgeoning artistry that even Felix could appreciate.

Atar stumbled, but Felix was there, supporting his friend. "Huh. Nice job. That had to take a good amount of mental energy. How much juice do you have left?"

"I think...I think I can handle one last detail."

"Skills?" Felix asked.

"Skills."

All the places where they had marked out the sigaldry, where Felix had built up tiny mounds in a spiraling path around the core, they lit up. Every single one of them. Then, from the mounds burst thickened slabs of obsidian, rough and unpolished and absolutely covered in golden scriptwork.

Felix's Fiendforge quaked, for once struggling to hold tight as Atar's core space wriggled and flexed with abandon. He bore down, pressing the splitting sides of it closer and closer, until the very air shook all around them. The monoliths kept rising, a veritable Stonehenge emerging from the polished black and gleaming gold. They rose like thunder, a rampaging herd of elephants until they rumbled to a sudden, lurching stop.

Fiendforge is level 21!

Atar fell to his knees, and his legs shattered on impact. Dust and charred splinters scattered all around them.

"Whoa!" Projection or not, Felix grabbed hold of his friend's Body and pulled him back up, not even caring that the white flame might burn him. It did, scorching his projected flesh like chicken under a blowtorch, but Felix ignored the pain. "You okay?"

For his part, Atar maintained he'd be fine, given some more rest. So, the two of them took some time, sitting within Atar's core space and recovering their spent faculties. By the time Atar had recovered, he'd rebuilt himself new legs, these a healthy off-white color in contrast to the burnt matchsticks that was the rest of his projected Body. Apparently, it was easier to visualize a new projected Body when one's core space was actually functioning as intended.

"I can walk, at least. That is enough to keep refining what we've started." Atar's blackened skull fixed Felix with an expressionless stare, but the man's Spirit vibrated with a sense of gratitude, relief, and no little embarrassment. "Felix. I—"

"Don't mention it. We're friends. A team." Felix grinned. "It's what we do."

Atar looked at his own feet as a cocktail of confusing emotions boiled up within him. It was too much to parse at a glance, and Felix didn't care to try. Like the lie earlier, he trusted Atar enough not to pry. He started walking away, dusting off his pants from the lingering specks of ash. "C'mon. Next check-up is Evie."

"What? Come with you?" Atar chuckled. "That shouldn't be possible. I've no Skill at delving people's cores, same as Alister."

"Ah, but much as I like him, we all have something Alister lacks."

"What—" Atar's eyes of flame expanded in realization. "The Links."

"Got it in one. Let's go pay our favorite chain fighter a visit."

CHAPTER TWENTY-NINE

It took all of ten seconds to find the tight grouping of Links that were Felix's closest friends, bundled atop his Bastion of Will. They were easily distinguishable from the myriad others that threaded through the silver needle atop his tallest tower, more vivid and thicker than almost all the others. Each shifted through various hues, though one was generally predominant, along with a soft, insistent vibration that *felt* like each of them.

White-green was Vess. Silver-brown was Harn. Blackened green was Beef. Pit's was mostly a black and crimson, threaded with electric blue, while Atar's was white, yellow, and flashes of vivid, bloody red. The last, Evie's, was a purple-white with woven threads of brightest silver and deepest blue.

He grasped it gently, and a thrill rolled through his consciousness. *Evie?* Startlement rolled off the Link, but no words. *Evie, we are ready.* Surprise faded into annoyed acceptance, and Felix smirked. In moments, he returned to Atar's core space, rising from his Skill in a confusing procession of flickering visualizations as Felix followed the connecting streamer of his Cardinal Flame. With a dizzying twist, his projected form, shorter and entirely Human-looking, landed beside Atar's mostly charred skeleton.

"Where'd you go?" he asked.

"Just needed to give her some warning. We took too long on your core space." Felix offered his arm to the mage. "Ready?"

Atar grumbled but looped his elbow with Felix's. "Will it hurt?"

"Not a clue."

Cardinal Flame!

Adamant Discord!

Skein of Fate!

His evolved Mana manipulation surged, singing through his own channels before streaming into Atar's. Blue-white and red-gold, the power swirled around them both, separate and alienated from the new-grown monoliths and spitting flames. It buffeted them, tossing Felix's hair about like a windstorm, but stilled at his word. His "thread-sight" expanded, focusing still on the purple-white Link that was stark in his Mind as his mouth opened. He spoke.

"Evie Aren."

Not so much a door as a hole punched into the stone wall before them, and the warm darkness of Atar's core was suddenly inundated with a chill breeze and the sound of rippling waters. Unwilling to risk it failing, Felix stepped forward, almost dragging Atar behind him.

The moment they entered, the hole sealed itself, leaving Felix and Atar standing in frigid, ankle-deep water.

"Gah, what is this?"

"Right. Word of warning: it is very chilly in here," Felix said. "More so for you, I think. You're practically skin and bones."

The flames in Atar's skull rolled in exasperation, and Felix chuckled before setting out in a steady, distance-eating stride. Evie's core space was one of the widest he'd seen, though it was nowhere near as detailed as Vess' or even Atar's old setup. Everywhere they looked was flat, shallow water pockmarked by the constant, gentle barrage of rain. The horizon was fogged, but toward the center, the water and rain became more and more agitated. Ice gathered, solitary floes at first but soon becoming thick icebergs that swayed and crashed into one another as the water deepened, and the waves escalated. "It's quite a bit tamer than the last time I was here," Felix remarked.

"*This* is tame?" Atar's new-formed off-white feet scrabbled for purchase along the sloping iceberg they climbed. It wasn't a difficult ascent, but the rollercoaster movements made it jarring for the mage. "Though it fits! Difficult terrain for a difficult woman."

"You're one to talk, SkelAtar."

Both of them looked up to see Evie standing atop an iceberg of her own...though it could more accurately be called a chain-berg. A flotilla of writhing chains formed a platform beneath the woman, a surface just flat enough to accommodate her slender form. She appeared fashioned from colorized ice herself, but metal gleamed across her arms and neck, as if she were wearing a thin layer of armor.

Atar sputtered. "W-what did you call me?"

She ignored him and graced Felix with an arch stare. "You're late. I've been waiting for hours."

"Things came up," Felix said, but didn't offer any explanations.

Atar's secrets were his own, after all. "Thanks for being available for this. Since I woke up, I haven't been able to stop thinking of how my Links may have affected all of you."

"Yeah well, I can't complain. Actually, I could, but that'd be a shit move, so I won't." She moved to the side, and more chains rose from the bulk below, flattening and weaving together to form a wider platform. "C'mon. I'll take you to see the show."

"The show?" Atar asked.

Felix shrugged and stepped aboard, followed soon by the fire mage. The mobile chain platform stopped and reversed direction, sending arcs of chill water firing around them. "Onward!" Evie cried out, and without buildup or preamble, the crude craft *rocketed* across the waves.

"AAAAH!" Atar screamed as he lost his footing.

Evie reached out casually and grabbed him by his forearm, fingers slipping between his crispy radius and ulna bones. She grimaced as she set the hyperventilating mage back in place. "Ugh. I know this isn't my real hand, but don't make me do that again."

On his hands and knees now, clinging tightly to the uneven platform, Atar only shouted again as they descended another rolling wave.

"You think he'd be used to this by now," Evie muttered at Felix. "Ships've been doin' worse than this for days."

The chain-fashioned conveyance slipped through the other obstructions, always finding a path through the increasingly crowded water, no matter how narrow. The body of her craft thinned and widened by turns, always taking up just enough space to get by, while their platform was kept high and safe out of reach of the rest. It went so smoothly, in fact, that Felix simply enjoyed the speed and wind in his hair. It also allowed him to study the sky instead.

While the general design of her core space was the same as previous, the interplay of her Skills was markedly different. Before Evie's Skills had been isolated balls of chain, many of which were iced over by the troubles of her Temper. When he'd left, that ice had broken and thawed into balls of floating water, each surrounded by rotating tangles of metal. That remained, but now the sky was a complicated net of chains, all of them shifting and clinking as they moved from Skill to Skill in great arcing patterns.

Felix even spotted a few off-color chains among the plethora of standard steel. They ranged from a deep blue to a purple white, but they weren't everywhere. Mostly, they congregated around the largest and most complex-looking knots, chains contorting into convoluted loops and whorls that never once stopped moving.

Unlike Atar's space, which needed building up to really get a good look at things, it was clear which rarity of Skills were being represented. Just like with his own core, it seemed the size and complexity directly correlated to the level, Temper, and rarity of the Skills in question. They had already passed the few Common Skills she possessed, and above were Uncommon and Rares, their construction featuring more and more of those colored chains. Felix wasn't entirely sure what their purpose was...not until they drew closer to Evie's core, and the rain intensified into a punishing deluge. Their flotilla slowed.

Atar had stood up by this point, and the rain hissed against his superheated skeleton. "Can I say, Evie, I am not a fan of your core space."

"I'm sure yours is pure sunshine, Skelly Boy, but we all work with what we got," Evie shot back absentmindedly, devoid of any heat. "Some of us have more in the way than others."

Felix pointed. "Evie. Those colored chains are all extending from the mists. Do they—"

"Connect to my core? Absolutely, they do. Tempered links, Harn calls 'em."

"Clever," Felix said, tracing the linkages as they disappeared into the thickening rain and heavy mist barrier ahead of them. "This barrier is still here, though. I thought you had worked through that?"

"Ah," was all Evie said, and it contained a knotted bundle of emotions.

Felix left it alone because, through the veil of rain and mist, he spotted a Skill he couldn't mistake. Evie's Unique Skill, Chains of the Protector, that she had intuited or perhaps inherited from the memory of her sister, Magda. It was a kite shield, woven from steel and purple-white chains in knotwork that reminded Felix of Celtic artistry. It was also bigger than the ice floe they rode upon, easily fifty feet tall and half that wide, and as they approached, the shield grew larger and more threatening...before Evie waved her hand. It unraveled around them, creating a sudden corridor of chains that blocked the rain and led them farther into the mists.

Evie smirked. "I think I got a handle on this, now."

Felix grinned right back, pleased as hell. Atar only grunted sourly as the mists swallowed them up.

They traveled in the purple-white corridor for a time, the mist so thick that it was similar to flying through a cloud bank. Felix's Cardinal Flame spread around him, a tether to this place as much as the Link was, eating away his Mana almost as fast as he could regenerate it. Still, it afforded him a greater perception of the area, even if his eyes were swathed in cotton, and when the flotilla ground to a lurching halt, he wasn't surprised. Atar made a weird noise in the back of his throat, but he held on and immediately started grumbling.

"C'mon!" Evie leaped forward, into the thinning mist. "Almost there!"

Felix offered a hand to Atar, but the mage shook his skull. "No, I can do this."

"Alright. See you down there." Felix leaped after Evie, free-falling through the cloudstuff before landing with a resounding crack atop thick, crystal clear ice. Evie looked at him, then at the ice, frowning at the deep fissure he'd put into it. Felix shrugged.

"I thought you could fly in core spaces?" she asked.

"I can. But you're showing us around. I didn't want to be rude and jump ahead of the tour."

"Hmph," Evie said before narrowing her eyes in concentration. Beneath his feet, the ice trembled before jabbing together like icy jaws. Evie panted after, the effort taking something out of her. "Well, don't keep breaking my stuff, if it pleases yer Majesty."

"Please. Call me Mr. Majesty."

Evie snorted, but her amusement fouled when a bundle of dark bones rocketed out of the mists behind them. White fire streaked with bloody crimson flickered across his entire Body, but it allowed Atar to land with surprising grace on the surface of the ice. He also melted a giant hole in it. "Noctis' tits, Atar, you're ruining the place! And stop grinning!"

"I'm a skeleton, Evie. This is my face right now."

"It's a dumb face."

"Children. Now's not the time, we—" Felix stopped as the wisps of mist faded from before them. "Oh wow."

Evie strode up, irritation suddenly forgotten as she spread her arms extravagantly. "Behold! My core!"

When last Felix had seen her core space, it had metamorphosed from a towering structure of chains and ice into a whirling, weaving circle of chains and elemental power. The ever-spinning loop remained, but the linkages had grown astoundingly complex. Water, ice, and metal all wove through one another in labyrinthine patterns, a knotwork that was as beautiful as it was intricate, all radiating the blinding glow of incredibly dense Mana.

Above the knotwork ring, clouds swirled like a hurricane's eye, pouring rain down in thick curtains that were being absorbed entirely by the core. The rest was hurled outward into the mists and beyond. The ground was still ice, fully frozen, but smoother than it had ever been and crystal clear.

Felix could see dark water below them, as if he were staring through glass, and only the aura of dire winter that arose from it indicated it was anything else. While smooth, as the ground reached the center, it rose in huge, elegant waves from all directions, merging seamlessly into one another to form a series of mountainous peaks. Six lifted up, just barely missing the swirling ring, while in the center the highest peak soared just enough to pierce the very center of the serpentine core.

"Burning ash, this is beautiful," Atar whispered.

Evie, to Felix's utter surprise, blushed. "Thanks."

No longer dazzled by the amazing complexity of her core space, Felix spotted the differently colored chains spread thick against the swirling stormcell above them. Purple-white, deepest blue, a burnished emerald, and even some few glowing silver were among the chains that spread from the edges of the knotwork core toward the mists. "Why are the mists still here, Evie? I thought that...issue had been solved."

The warrior shrugged a single shoulder, as if the thought hadn't really occurred to her. "Just is, I suppose. Seems like a good thing, keepin' my core safe from everythin' else. It did a number on that Primordial gunk you sent my way, too."

"What? Really?"

"Oh yeah. The moment I accepted, it started pourin' in, carrying all that dry, sizzling heat with it." Evie grimaced as if she'd swallowed something nasty. "It didn't have much flavor, but it burned fierce. Almost melted my ice, ya know?"

Shit. Felix looked around once again, worried he'd missed some glaring issue. "But...the mists protected you from it, entirely?"

"No, not entirely. But it blunted the edge, let me get in there and do somethin' good with all that Essence. I fed it into my core, piece by piece, fixin' up that storm you see and addin' more streams to my ring."

"Did it affect your Skills?" he asked.

"Like Vess, you mean?" Evie shook her head. "Only sorta. Though for the better, I think. Wanna see?"

"Of course."

Evie flicked her hand, and a screen appeared in front of both Felix and Atar.

Stealth (Common) Has Evolved Into Gloomstalker (Epic)!
Level Is Retained!
Gloomstalker (Epic), Level 70!
Time in the shadows has earned you the blood that streams from your chains, and few of those you stalk live to tell the tale. Even those of higher Tiers have difficulty spotting you, at least at first. Damage done while hidden moderately increases per Skill level, chance of remaining hidden from superior senses increases slightly per Skill level.

Mental Resistance (Rare) Has Evolved Into Barbican's Gate (Legendary)!
Level Is Retained!

Barbican's Gate (Legendary), Level 73!
Your Mind has survived encountering the primeval Essence of a dire creature more convoluted than any you have experienced before! It was only a glimpse of its shadow, but the walls of your Mind have been shored up, rendering them impenetrable to similar attacks. Increases the effect of your Willpower and Alacrity a moderate amount per Skill level.

Unconventional Tactics (Uncommon) Has Evolved Into Minds Of The Mad (Epic)!
Level Is Retained!
Minds Of The Mad (Epic), Level 68!
You have glimpsed into the heart of something vast and incomprehensible, but your Mind has survived and grown for its experiences! While unknowable to others, ancient memories have seeped into your core, influencing the way you fight and engage with enemies. Others will find your movements confusing and erratic, but they are simply blind to the truth of combat. Understanding increases slightly per Skill level.

Commander's Shout (Uncommon) Has Evolved Into Grim Fervor (Epic)!
Level Is Retained!
Grim Fervor (Epic), Level 40!
You are not a commander or captain to lead at the front. You are a dire shadow, a deadly arrow fired into the midst of your enemies. As you appear among two or more allied enemies, an instance of A Crisis Of Faith is applied to up to 20 targets, and an instance of Harrowing Thews is applied to yourself for each enemy in range. Effectiveness of Status Conditions increases slightly with Skill level, range of effects increases slightly with Skill level.
A Crisis of Faith - Reduce Willpower By 10% For All Enemies In Range
Harrowing Thews - Increases Your Strength By 0.05% Per Enemy In Range

Ice Spike (Uncommon) Has Evolved Into Rimefang's Wrath (Epic)!
Level is Retained!
Rimefang's Wrath (Epic), Level 50!
Rage sings its song along the path of Ages, and you have taken it up. Mana coalesces around your hands to form twin, clawed gauntlets of dark, jagged ice. Penetration and sharp-

ness of claws increases moderately per Skill level, hardness of ice increases moderately per Skill level.

Night Eye (Common) Has Evolved Into Frenzied Vigilance (Legendary)!
Level Is Retained!
Frenzied Vigilance (Legendary), Level 65!
You have glimpsed the chaos in the Essence of a Primordial's very being and have emerged changed. Your sight now functions in darkness and light with equal ease, but also spots the strains of Dissonance that linger within the Grand Harmony. Be wary, for to stare too long at such wildness is to invite chaos into yourself.

"Holy hell." The changes were sweeping and varied. None of the Skills that his Fiendforge had previously influenced had been affected, yet the many were still touched by the Primordial's Essence, and Felix wasn't entirely sure he loved the pattern he saw. Stealth had become Gloomstalker, which appeared to enhance the damage Evie did while unseen and simultaneously decreasing the chance of those in higher advancements from spotting her.

Useful and not too worrying, which was the same story for the next one. Mental Resistance had evolved into Barbican's Gate, which appeared similar to Felix's Bastion of Will, enhancing the potency and power of Evie's Mind by engaging her Willpower and Alacrity more fully.

That was the end of the good news. Next up was Unconventional Tactics, which made him laugh at first glance. It definitely accounted for Evie's particular brand of combat, but now it had been supplanted by Minds Of The Mad. The name itself was worrying, but the description was worse, indicating that pieces of the Primordial of Withered Dust had seeped into her core and was even now influencing her Mind. Passively, it seemed, but how would that play out?

Commander's Shout, once giving a nice boost to regeneration and Endurance, had been wiped out completely. In its place was a much more self-centered, offensive focused Skill that scaled up depending on how many enemies Evie was fighting.

Felix grumbled at the change, but had to admit it fit her brand of combat far better than the rarely-used Commander's Shout. Ice Spike was the same, turning from a relatively weak ice dagger into two conjured gauntlets of ice. That was useful, a powerful alternative for when she was stuck too close to an opponent, but the comments on rage made him hesitate. Night Eye's evolution to Frenzied Vigilance was worrisome, too, especially at the mention of her perceiving Dissonance directly.

"Good, right?" Evie said, a wide grin on her face.

"It...it is. I'm just a little worried about the effect of some of those Skills," Felix said. "Minds of the Mad and Frenzied Vigilance seem particularly...not great."

"Oh, psh," Evie waved off his concern. "They're fantastic, you just gotta appreciate their quirks, is all. Mind you, I still haven't had much time to practice 'em. Hope to change that soon, eh Felix? You can oversee all the new stuff, if we can get a couple spars in. I think my Rimefang's Wrath could do a number on those scales of yours."

He let himself grin, pushing away his apprehension. "Sure. I'm down for that." Worrying, his mother had told him, was borrowing trouble. He had enough at the moment, anyway.

"I would appreciate some sparring, once I've sorted my core space some more," Atar said. "Alister hasn't shut up about the training you two did back in the Yttin's Warren."

"Fine with me, Atar. We'll set something up soon, then." Felix looked at Evie's core one last time, committing as much of it to memory as he could. It was far more stable than Atar's, and more detailed in some ways than his own. Evie didn't need his help at the moment, so he sent his convoluted awareness down through her core into Atar's, and back into his own. He emerged, his friends none the wiser, a new Link firmly in hand. "We've more places to visit today, however. Next up: Harn Kastos."

The ice and mist punctured, and a familiar hole was bored through the fabric of space. A shimmering light, metallic and scorching hot bloomed through the opening, sizzling against Evie's ice and melting huge swathes of it.

"Hey!" she shouted, but Felix grabbed both of them and rushed them through.

CHAPTER THIRTY

A hammer fell, and a bell tolled deep and wide. Felix felt his guts shake with the force of it, driving a soft, surprised "huh" from his lungs. The others reacted quite a bit differently. Evie buckled at the waist, her icy body splintering as chunks sloughed off an underlying framework of chains. Atar leaned heavily against a rough stone column, his left arm and shoulder blasting back into greasy soot. Neither made a sound, even as the impacts continued; both were too focused on maintaining their projections to do anything else.

"Harn!" Felix shouted, a little panic in his voice. "We're here!"

The hammering didn't stop, but it suddenly quietened, as if cotton had been shoved into all their ears. All around them were immense stone columns, roughly hewn from the flagstone flooring and extending high into crawling smoke and velvet shadow. Silver firelight flickered through, only partially lighting the forest of columns, so that it appeared they were in an endless cavern of the things.

Harn appeared, hustling around the corner of a thick pillar, his projected Body moving smoothly and soundlessly in the vast chamber. For once, the man wasn't wearing a single piece of armor, but instead his skin itself was metallic, segmented around the arms and midsection, pitted and scratched but utterly solid-seeming. Harn smiled, and even his teeth were metal, each one forged of a dark iron.

"Sorry about that, kids," he said as he tromped closer. "My core is a bit energized these past few days."

Slowly, Atar and Evie stood, the former sooner than the latter. Atar's arm had reformed, and though it looked thinner than previous, it was at least a proper bone color. He offered a helping hand to Evie, whose icy neck and face was only just reassembling into frosted planes of ice and metal.

"Thanks," she muttered. "Harn, you twit! You just about split my skull!"

Harn grunted, his smile wilting. "I said sorry. 'Sides, ain't your real Body, anyway. And it looks like both of ya could use the practice at visualizing your projections. Be more like Felix, eh?"

Both Atar and Evie shot Felix a glare, but he only rolled his eyes and started walking. "When you agreed to show me your core space, you said you wanted me to see something specific, right?"

"Hrm." Harn held out a hand, guiding Felix down a path between more of the rugged pillars. "Come this way, all of you."

The cavern was silver-lit, yet the light remained warm despite its cool color. It was...there was a bloom in the air, as if the shadows couldn't quite gain purchase on anything. The edges of the pillars were soft, only sharpening on their darkest sides, and the light increased the closer they walked toward the center. The columns were in neat, orderly rows, but the shadows kept moving. At first, Felix thought that was because the silver flame, still unseen, was shifting about...but was quick to notice the pillars themselves were in motion.

"Cool, yeah?" Harn said with an iron grin. "C'mon closer! Haven't had a chance to show off since Evie was down here."

"What?" Felix glanced back at the frosted woman. "You've been in his core before? I thought that Skill was hard to learn?"

Evie shrugged, sending a flurry of ice down onto the ground. "I dunno. Old man just yanked me into his core once to show me how Visualization Stage actually works. But it was different then."

"Lotta changes since Haarwatch," Harn confirmed with a pleased grunt. "She has an internal Mana Skill called Beyond the Pale, helps with lots of things, but mostly improving the Visualization and Actualization Stages."

"Oh, didn't know you had a Skill like that, Evie," Felix said.

"Got a lotta things. Folks don't ask me much, do they?" Evie raised an eyebrow at the three of them. "I'm quite impressive." Atar opened his dark jaws, but she shot him a glare. "Not a word."

Wisely, the mage closed his mouth again.

Felix ignored them. "Okay, so internal Mana control, that makes sense. But how could she have seen *your* core space?"

"That's more complicated, and expensive. Takes a little ritual to set up beforehand and uses up a good portion of monster cores to fuel it." Harn led them closer, the rotating rings of columns now only feet away. "If I'd known you had the ability to do this, I'd have waited. Save some gold." Evie smacked the man, and he chuckled.

Huh. Neat. So maybe I can *get Alister into Atar's core space, if we adapt the ritual. Would that help him progress and recover?* It was worth a try. "Harn, remind me to get the steps to this ritual from you later today. I have some use for it."

"I'll have Pit ferry it to ya."

"Appreciated."

They came to the first of the moving columns, which were all installed on a wide, circular platform. It was around twenty feet wide, with each column taking up the majority of that width, and had double the space between each pillar on the platform. It wasn't always moving, but it shifted to their left as they watched, the empty space ahead of them now filled by a rough-hewn column.

Harn reached out and patted its side. "Pretty proud of myself for finalizing all this. Took some thinkin', but it's comin' together."

"It's really cool," Felix admitted. Each time they heard the muted sound of a struck bell, the columns moved one placement to the left. *Clockwise*, Felix realized. *It's like a giant clock.*

Now that they were in the central portion of the core space, Felix could see a vaulted ceiling supported by well-formed arches and a series of open balconies ringing the upper level. Tall, slitted windows opened up into a cool daylight, but their light did not penetrate the darkness of the lower level, only serving to highlight the stark difference. Instead, all of the light at their level was produced by the gargantuan hammer and anvil at the very center of all things.

"Are those made of crystal?" Atar asked.

"Yeah. Nagast and Ahkestria have influenced me more than I realized," Harn said with an indulgent grin. "Used to be simple steel."

Easily the size of a two-story building, the hammer came down atop a far larger anvil with the sound of an incomprehensibly vast bell, and silver radiance flared and shot outward in all directions. Both hammer and anvil were made of opalescent crystal, multi-faceted and multi-hued yet immaculately constructed.

With each hit, the hammer dropped onto a ring of liquid silver Mana that flowed around and across both tools. Liquid Mana would splash, chunks sent outward in flashes of silver light before becoming reabsorbed by the flowing ring...but Felix also spotted the anvil itself morphing in strange ways. A sort of depression kept forming and changing between hammer blows, a cavity of strange, esoteric shapes. "What is that?" he asked.

Harn grinned so wide that Felix swore he could see iron molars. "My drop hammer forge. Turns out smithin' is useful in many ways. Leastwise for me."

As they watched, the hammer rose up, and from within that flare of silver flame, Felix spotted a semi-solid shape flung outward into the core space. It wasn't a sigil or glyph but appeared similar, and it hurtled into the ring of columns as they boomed into a new position. That was when he first noticed the panoply of weapons and armor that littered the space. There was probably three hundred feet between them and the anvil, but the esoteric shape zipped between pillars and splashed into a pair of huge axes fit for a giant. Mana burned across them once before fading just a touch.

"So many weapons," Atar said. "What are they?"

"Skills. Each one a Skill or at least part of one," Harn said.

"Part of one?" Felix could see hammers, axes, swords, staves, shields of various styles, and armor of all makes. They varied in complexity and size, much as all Skill representations he'd seen, but his Perception picked out incredibly minute designs worked into every one of them. "How can you have Skills in parts?"

Harn shrugged. "How do you breathe? I just do."

"That's...fair. I guess no one ever said a core space had to make sense on a physical level," Felix said at last. "I suppose it's all just symbolic representation. It works so long as it works for you."

"You got it," Harn agreed. "My armaments have always been my Skills; they've just gotten a bit more complex since I advanced."

"I was about to mention that," Atar said. He was leaning over a stave formed of gold and glittering rubies. "These are incredible, Harn."

"Well, thank you, Sparky. That one is part of my Parry Skill, believe it or not."

Atar's eye fires flickered. "But it is a stave made of gold and gemstones. Why would you ever want to parry with something like that?"

"Weapons are tools, even the fancy ones. Tools are meant to be used."

Felix kept his eyes moving, flicking from place to place as the hammer and anvil kept working. The columns shifted over and over, the pattern of their clock-like movements growing more complicated the farther in they went. Each movement brought new armaments—new Skills—nearer to the core while others shifted further back. It was complex and strange, but no stranger than any of the others. It reminded him of Alister's the most, though there was a definite sense of low-tech about Harn's core. More brawn and sweat, less cerebral conceptualizations.

Yet, for all the details in the armor, anvil, and hammer, the cavern and pillars remained rough and almost poorly designed. They were little more than natural formations in an ill-lit cavern too vast to spot any significant details, save for right above the core itself. Was that because of their Link? Had the Primordial eroded parts of his core space? Felix asked Harn that directly, but was surprised at his answer.

The man laughed.

"No no, that Link of yours has done me good," he said. "It's what boosted the changed size and design of my hammer and anvil. When I crossed over into Adept, finally, I used what was left to reinforce the essential pieces you see all around. Finer detail, sharper edges, polished surfaces. I feel twice as strong as before you did your thing below the sands."

"Did your Skills change?" Felix asked. "Everyone else's did."

"Oh, aye. That they did. Want to see them?" Harn didn't even wait for acknowledgement, just swiping his Skill notifications toward the three of them.

Raze (Rare) Has Evolved Into Wrath Of The Twin Fangs (Legendary)!
Level Is Retained!
Wrath Of The Twin Fangs (Legendary), Level 80!
The memory of violence has stolen into your Aspects, of jaws the size of mountains crashing upon hapless prey and obliterating all that they were. Mana imbues your slashing weapons with destructive might. Cost decreases slightly with Skill level, damage and penetration increases moderately with Skill level, and attack speed increases moderately with Skill level.

Brawler's Physique (Common), Unarmed Mastery (Common), Block (Common), Parry (Common), And Resistances (Acid, Fire, Cold, and Pain) Have Combined And Evolved Into Forgesteel Skin (Legendary)!
Level Is Retained!
Forgesteel Skin (Legendary), Level 76!
As a Smith, you have forged armor and as a warrior you have worn it, but the wild fury of Primordial potency has shown you a new truth. You are the bulwark, the armor itself. Steel and flesh are one. Reduces all incoming damage by a moderate amount per Skill level, Stamina consumption reduced by slight amount per Skill level, weight is increased by a moderate amount per Skill level.

Heavy Armor Mastery (Common), Armorsmithing (Common), Weaponsmithing (Common), And Mana Folding (Rare) Have Combined And Evolved Into Panoply Of the Halcyon Defender (Legendary)!
Level Is Retained!
Panoply Of The Halcyon Champion (Legendary), Level 77!
Metal has bent to your hammer and arm, but now all that

you forge will bend to your Will and Intent. Weapons and armor all but spring from the font of creativity at your hands, Mana imbued in every inch of material worked. Increases rate of crafting higher rarity weapons and armor per Skill level, moderately increases amount of Mana that can be folded into a crafted armament per Skill level, reduces rate of failure slightly per Skill level.

Descent Of The Barbarian (Rare) Has Evolved Into Colossus Of The Everflame (Mythic)!
Level Is Retained!
Colossus Of The Everflame (Mythic), Level 81!
Your rage knows no bounds, and Strength flows in its wake. Silver flame sparks within your soul, flowing through your axes and enhancing the savage brutality of all your attacks, bypassing standard Fire Resistance. Speed and damage increases greatly per Skill level, heat and damage of silver flame increases moderately per Skill level. Restricted to axes only.

"Yyero's rotten ass! Mythic rarity. That a step above Legendary, even." Evie clucked her tongue at Harn's smug smile. "Been holding back on us, huh?"

"Just waitin' for a good reveal."

"The rest are all Legendary, too," Atar noted. "Though they're a bit too...stabby for my tastes. Quite good, regardless."

"A crafting Skill as well. You're right. The Link did right by you," Felix said. "Is that because you have a greater handle on your core space?"

"Yes." Harn's answer was firm and without question. "All that Essence was purposeless. I could feel it when it flooded in. If I left it hanging around, it'd find something to burrow into. Guide it, though...Even I'm still surprised at how good it shook out."

"I heard you were in a trance for a whole day during your Tempering," Felix said. "Because of all this?"

"In part, yeah. The Mind strain alone was enough to lay me out for hours after, but luckily I had a forge at hand." His grin returned. "Always easier working out a problem with some heat and the right tools. Haven't had the chance to stretch my new Skills out, though. That Sworn was the nearest thing to a real opponent, and I was stuck fightin' his damn copies," Harn growled. Evie laughed, a touch triumphantly, and he gave her the sour look of an annoyed uncle. "The cavern and pillars, though...that's how I want it."

"You...want it to be undefined? I thought greater power was found through specificity and detail?" Felix furrowed his brow. It went against everything he'd heard up until then.

"Sure. Solid details are what pushes you up the ladder, but too much and you're stuck, right?"

"Stuck. What do you mean?" Atar asked.

Harn ran his gaze over all three of them. "Right. You're all advanced enough to think on this and actually have it be of use. Fluid visualization." All of them stared at him blankly, and Harn sighed. "By keepin' parts of your core space vague, you leave room for yourself to expand and evolve. Grow."

"But...I thought advancing was concerned with forming a strong, unyielding foundation and building each step in the same way. Are you saying that approach is entirely wrong?"

"Ain't wrong, Felix, so much as it's just...it's limited." Harn's bright silver tongue ran over dark iron teeth in contemplation. "Think of it like fightin'. You don't just stand there and let a man wallop on ya, right? No, you move, bend, and dodge. You create space around yourself, claim it as yours, but it's open for the movements you might have to make."

"That...that makes a lotta sense," Evie said. "Way more than Zara's drivel about singing clouds or whatever."

"The Grand Harmony aren't singing clouds, Evie. And you know it's not drivel," Atar said in a lecturing tone. "If you paid better attention, it would all make sense to you."

"Eh, I know what I know. Anyway, I'm better at the whole Affinity thing than you." She smiled, and ice crackled across her cheeks. "Ooh, mad about that, huh? I know, cuz I can hear it."

"*Any*way," Felix said, interrupting them. "How'd you figure this out, Harn? And why can we know now? Zara has been insistent on not telling us things for fear of 'exerting undue influence' on the process."

"It's something Magda came across. She held to it pretty rigorously, though she didn't get to advance much further than low Journeyman Tier." He grasped Evie's shoulder and squeezed, but her icy face remained remarkably impassive. "Her core space was defensive, of course, but she maintained that blank spaces within it were meant to evolve once she achieved higher rarity Skill evolutions."

"She couldn't possibly have been planning for that," Atar said, disbelief thick on his tongue. Felix blinked. *Huh. He grew a tongue at some point.* "Despite what Felix's experience displays, it is a rare thing indeed for a Skill to combine and evolve so effortlessly. She would have had to work for *years* to make such a thing happen."

"And she had been. Couple of her favorite Skills were almost there, she just needed a bounty of monster cores to make it happen. Which...which we didn't get 'til after. It's a real shame she never finished.

Woulda been a sight to see." Harn sighed, and a soft, chill breeze rolled through the too-warm confines of his core space. "Zara, though...she ain't a bad broad, all things told, but I trust her order only a little more than a snake. At least a snake's honest. You always know when they're about to strike."

"I don't like Isla," Evie said.

"You—" Atar shook his skull. "For once, we agree. She seems more the snake than Zara. The Naiad has fought by our side for months, at least."

"I'm not a fan of the woman, either, but she's an ally for now," Felix said. "All we can do is move forward. I want all of you to focus on improving your core spaces and training your new Skills. Chances are we're returning to a war. Best if we had five new Adepts ready to meet whatever challenges come to call."

"Six, if we can get Alister over the hump," Atar pointed out.

"Seven, if you count whatever Pit did. Does Evolution count?" Evie asked. "Oh, and that Beef boy. He's like two warriors wrapped up in a fursuit."

"Right, right. We've got options. But I don't want to leave anything to chance." Felix watched them all, meeting their eyes one by one. "Take the rest of the day. Training starts at dawn."

CHAPTER THIRTY-ONE

Within his spacious captains' quarters, Felix had made something of a nest for himself. After a few experiments, Green Shaping had proven the most effective for building creature comforts. The ice chairs from before had been fine, but a cold butt after hours of core diving wasn't a fun experience.

Unlike Stone and Rime Shaping though, Green Shaping couldn't simply fabricate plant life where there was none—that seemed to be a result of the type of Mana it affected. Stone was earth Mana, Rime was ice Mana, and both of them could be fashioned entirely out of his own stores in the rare event when he didn't have the raw materials to hand. Green Shaping, however, was control over *life* Mana, which was fairly nebulous as a concept. Growing things, suffusing them with further life, *that* Felix could manifest directly from his channels. Straight up manifesting wood and vines and stuff was beyond the Skill's scope.

Mana, Felix had learned, was a product of the Grand Harmony. It composed all of the Corporeal Realm, not just infusing things but as an intrinsic part of them. Felix could see it with his Manasight. A simple flex of the Skill showed Mana floating around him in rivers of vapor, the walls and floor and air itself filled with it.

There was a bit more to reality than just Mana, such as Essence, but in this case, Mana was all he was concerned about. With each moment, more of it was absorbed into his Mana Gates, which functioned as apertures and a sort of filter for most people; nine of them in the palms, elbows, knees, feet, and one at the base of the skull. For them, it kept non-attuned Mana types from entering their channels.

For Felix, that was a nonissue, as his Unbound nature made all

Mana types compatible with his core. Mana types, like the Grand Harmony itself, were all just a spectrum of vibrations, after all. When he activated one of his many Skills, their song sent shivers of Mana through his channels, the end result being the manifestation of the Skill itself. In the case of Green Shaping, that meant he could pour out life Mana bent on growing and shaping plant life.

All he had to do was find a bit of wood.

That had been a chore, but thankfully a chore he could assign to one of his many followers. Wood was rare in the desert, though Felix doubted that would remain the case, what with the new abundance of fresh water. Turned out, there were a few wooden objects they'd taken from the old Grandmaster's house. So now, Felix sat upon the remains of three small statues: one of a woman holding a sword, another of a man with a book, and the last of a fat, pig-like creature, lying on its back.

It was pretty cute. Each one was carved of ancient wood, but all contained tiny pieces that drank up the life Mana he provided, growing new shoots from their otherwise hardened forms. These he bent with his Will, growing the shoots into wide branches that formed a roughly circular bench. Additional branches split off, many of them going down to the deck and growing in between the chitin boards to secure it all. Foliage sprouted along the tops, a thick, moss-like greenery that was pretty comfortable to lounge on.

Once he was sure it could handle their combined weight, Felix settled in, making an effort to relax his shoulders and neck. "Alright, Pit. Our turn next."

"Yesss!" The fur pillow behind him rumbled in delight. Pit was sprawled along the rear of the circular bench, nestled close to Felix's back. The pleasure that had radiated off the Chimera once he realized he would fit had been nearly palpable, and now it shifted toward a more enthusiastic glee. "I can't wait to show you everything!"

Felix smiled, and cracked a single eyelid. Pit's beak and bright golden eyes hovered by his knee, quivering in excitement. "Close your eyes and breathe deep."

"Okay, okay. Got it." Pit did as instructed, screwing his eyes shut and laying his triangular ears against his skull. "What was next? Right. Breathing in." He sucked in a breath like a bellows. "Out." It came out, just as harsh.

"Just like back in Nagast," Felix reminded him. "Hold still."

Cardinal Flame!

Felix swooned, his Mind cast backward and down, thrown along with his Mana into freefall. His control meant it twisted, coursing into his Companion's Mana Gates and snaking through his channels in a blink, a flash of thought. Unlike his other friends, Pit was different.

Chimeras were different, somehow. A Race but with monstrous features, such as a monster core as opposed to a core space. A solid, spherical core that sat heavily at the junction of all his channels, where Pit's power radiated outward. Functionally similar to a core space, but fundamentally different.

Or so he thought.

Felix landed with flexed knees in the center of a verdant forest, to the babbling sound of a distant river and the incessant noise of animals, insects, and beasts. "What the hell?" Before, when Felix had inspected Pit's core, he had visualized it as a solid lump of magical material crackling with lightning. Now...now, it was so very different. Felix spun in a circle, eyes panning everything he could, from the ancient trees to the distant mountains and the endless, summer-blue sky. "What the hell is this?"

"You like it?" Pit landed nimbly next to him, having no trouble with the thick canopy and looming trees. The tenku was perhaps the size of a terrier, similar to how he'd been when they had first entered Shelim.

"You're *tiny*."

Pit hopped twice and spun in a quick circle, lightning trailing after his bushy fox tail. "I *know!* Isn't it great!"

Felix knelt down, and Pit rushed into his arms, trilling in joy. He ran his hands over Pit's feathers and fur, feeling the alternating textures and thick warmth from his projected Body. "You've packed a lot of detail into your visualized Body, bud. This is a really good job." Pit warbled at him, head still nestled against Felix's neck. "And this place...is this the Foglands?"

His Perception unfurled, rolling through copse and grove, meadow and field. The forest he'd gotten to know so well back in his earliest days on the Continent was here, and even the River Eile was there, with its enormous river lilies dotting the edges. Which meant the distant babbling was, in fact, the waterfall Felix had once taken a ride down, quite unwillingly. *If I go that way, will the Stronghold be there, as well? How faithful is this recreation?*

Felix almost started walking toward that direction when his Perception snagged on something different. Something changed from his memory of the forest. "What is that?"

Pit squirmed out of his grasp, and Felix let go. The tenku glided to the ground on small wings, his feathers shimmering with blue, black, and crimson. "I'll show you!" He dashed off into the underbrush.

Following more sedately, Felix kept his Perception unfurled, examining everything he could. The detail was stunning, though not nearly as good as the armor in Harn's space or anything in Vess'. Now that he was looking, Felix could tell the leaves were all the same teardrop shape, even the big ferns that dotted the underbrush.

Wind rustled those same leaves, but it didn't always move them the way it should, or even the branches. Instead, some were so rigid it was like they were made of stone. His Perception delved into the earth, and while the surface was springing and covered in loam, it all solidified into hardened rock only a few inches below his feet. Little details, mostly, but added up, they broke the illusion of a true forest.

Still really impressive. Felix followed the tiny Pit through the underbrush, tromping atop flowers and fronds that sprang back up, unharmed by his passage. *And that smell. So familiar.*

The scent of sharp spice wafted on the breeze, somewhere between pepper and coriander. Felix remembered that smell and the first time he had encountered it. The tall, bulbous trees it came from were in a discrete grove, separated from the other Fogland trees by a tiny rivulet. He had first found Pit among a grove very similar to it, hiding in the mangrove-like roots from the sharp claws of the Seven-Legged Orit. Except, there were far more of those trees than Felix could recall, and as Pit led him in the center of the grove, he realized why.

"See?" Pit said, proudly. His wings stretched out, barely four feet, tip to tip. Beyond him was another of the fat, mangrove-like trees, except this one was ten times the size of the others. It was, on closer inspection, several trees braided into one and was at least thirty feet in diameter. "My core!"

"Pit," Felix said, astounded. The tree was far more detailed than the forest, like looking at night and day. Ivy-like leaves spiraled down from looping branches, alongside hanging moss wafting in citrus-infused gusts of wind. The bark was smooth but ridged, the turn of the thick trees interrupted by long, raised cords, and all of the trees (at least ten of them) were meshed so completely they appeared to have grown into one another.

There was no telling where one tree ended and another began, save for at the very top, nearly fifty feet up, where a perfectly circular space was cleared. The trees grew around it, as if forbidden to touch the glowing object at the center. It was a smaller version of the red-black core he'd once sensed, fashioned from swirling liquid into the shape of a four-pointed star. "This is amazing."

Pit shrieked, a sound of joy mingled with unbridled enthusiasm. He ran forward, flapping his wings excitedly. "Did you see? Did you see my star core?"

"Yeah. Yeah I did. Seeing how you've somehow developed a core space, I expected a ring shape, like mine. This," Felix paused, memory jolting him. "Your core looks like a Nymean star."

Pit's eyes widened and dilated, gold vanishing beneath deep pools of black. "Whoa. What does that mean?"

Felix walked a slow circumference of Pit's tree core. "I wish I knew." He ran his hand through the lower branches, fingers just brushing the edges of hanging moss and leaves. There were patterns there, hidden in the weft and weave of threadlike stems formed something more. There was more, too, a secret vibration that hummed against his fingers. "These are your Skills," he realized. "You have Skills and a core space. What does that mean?"

Pit tilted his head, clearly confused. "I've always had a core."

"Not like this. I'm assuming it happened during or since your Evolution, right?"

The tenku nodded with a happy chirrup. "I've been waiting to show you."

Felix's hand reached for the next Skill, one he believed was Poison Resistance, and paused. He looked down at his friend. "Why were you waiting? Why not show me sooner?"

Pit shrugged his tiny shoulders. "You were busy and stressed. This isn't that important." He warbled in surprise when Felix's hand came down to scratch the top of his head.

"You're always important, bud. And this is remarkable, but confusing." Felix withdrew his hand and placed it on his hip. Suddenly, there was a sword there, though it hadn't been with him the whole time. The hooked blade, his Inheritor's Will, glimmered with green-gold energy. "Karys. I need to speak with you."

The green-gold glow intensified, expanding and separating from Felix until it formed a hazy man shape a few feet away. A dark-skinned, slightly wrinkled face emerged, then a body all wrapped in odd, ceremonial robes stepped out of the glow. Karys, in his full Nymean form, bowed deeply to first Felix and then Pit. "My Lord Autarch. How may I help?"

"I didn't interrupt you or anything, right?"

Karys waved a slender hand. "Merely the more boring parts of logistical management. Your army has mobilized. I have already sent a ship full of Legionnaires back toward Haarwatch."

"Oh dang. Then I won't keep you too long." Felix gestured all around him. "What do you make of all this?"

Karys looked around, his bright green eyes livelier than his aged appearance suggested. "A core space? I had expected your Bastion. To summon me into another's core space would require...this is Pit's, I assume?"

"It is."

"Fascinating." He ran an age-spotted hand over a particularly low-hanging vine. "You have done well, Pit."

The Chimera puffed up in pride, throwing his tiny chest out. Felix grinned. "He has. My question is...well it's more confusion. Last time I saw, Pit had a monster core, not a core space. After his Evolution, he now does. Is this...normal?"

"Ah yes. Your Evolution. Stormwing Tenku, yes? And a Primordial on top of that, just as your Companion. Hm." Karys tapped his lips in thought.

"He even has a tree as part of his core. Like me. Does that mean anything?" Felix asked.

"It could mean the visualizations you harnessed within your core space are influencing his through the Companion bond. Perhaps. Or perhaps it is simply a case of independent discovery. This," Karys paused and looked around. "This *is* Nagast, after all, is it not?"

"Yup!" Pit said excitedly. "Home!"

"Right. And your home well before Felix ever found you, yes?" At Pit's nod, Karys spread his hands. "There we have it. His core space is a recreation of his home. As our visualizations are predominantly subconscious, at least at first, to have it resemble something so close to heart is a natural occurrence."

Felix huffed an amused breath. "My core is the cold depths of space. That's not exactly home sweet home for me."

Karys shrugged his wide shoulders, still surprisingly built for an old man. "Not even the greatest scholars among the Nym and Geist knew all the secrets of core space formation. Perhaps being an Unbound affects your visualization process?"

Felix waved off that line of thought. "I'll deal with my own stuff later. What about his core? It isn't a sphere *or* a ring shape. It's—"

"A Star," Karys breathed. His green eyes grew large before the Nym gasped in sudden pain. He threw his hands up, grabbing at his skull. "A Star!"

"Karys!" Felix grabbed the man as he sagged to his knees, but before he could really be worried Karys stood back up. "Uh, what was that?"

"Memories," the Nym panted. "The holes in my memories have not progressed...in a long while, not since...you granted me a new Body...but I found more. Oh, Mercy Upon High, I found more." Karys shuddered in Felix's arms, only once, before he gently pushed away. "I am fine. It is simply an...existential agony to find the raw edges of my Mind."

"Jeez, Karys. I'm sorry. I didn't know it hurt you to remember..."

"Think nothing of it." Felix's Chancellor took a deep, fortifying breath. "I did, however, recall one thing. We Nym called the Chimera the Children of Harmony, the Guardian Beasts, and, most appropriately it seems, the Wardens of the Stars."

"Wardens of the Stars?" Felix glanced at Pit. The tenku was growing more pleased with every new title he heard. "As in the Nymean Stars? Found in literally every piece of Nymean art and ruin I've encountered?"

"The very same. I...cannot recall the how or why, but Chimeras are linked to it all." He jabbed a slender finger at the four-pointed core. "Their very cores have something to do with it."

"Huh."

"Chimeras are beast and mortal, Monster Type and Race all at once. They bridge two worlds, and while I cannot recall the meaning behind it, their nature is a fusion." Karys put a hand on Felix's shoulder and extended another to Pit's upturned face. "A bond between realms."

CHAPTER THIRTY-TWO

Karys left soon after that, his other duties proving to be more pressing than he had let on. He parted with a new timeline: "The last Manaship will depart in six days. If we wish to defend our Territory, you must make it back by then."

That was even later than Felix had originally supposed. By his estimation, they would reach the Caleph Pass in three more days, then it was a relatively quick overland journey to Haestus Lake and the Naga nest below the waves. With the compression that traveling the Shadowgate brought, they would reach Nagast with days to spare.

Plenty of time to focus on self-improvement.

Pit set about exploring the limits of his core space and seeking out ways to improve. Felix asked to help, but the willful tenku wished to do it alone, and Felix didn't press the issue. Pit was determined.

Instead, Felix found a familiar cavern within Pit's core space. He immediately recognized it by the overgrown vines that hung long to obscure its entrance, identifying the cavern as the one they had ventured into just before falling into the Archon's Domain. There were differences, of course, just below the surface. The cave was shallow and far too close to the river—Felix remembered exploring for hours before reaching it in the past—and the shadows inside were thick and strangely textured. Familiar in a way that had little to do with distant memories.

As Pit was busy walking the length of his core space, Felix entered the cavern, almost swimming through the dense darkness until the very floor fell away. Then he was falling too—no, flying—soaring across the dark expanse while lights ignited into burning bonfires of red-gold and blue-white light.

He had found the Link between their core spaces.

Felix glanced backward. Behind him, drifting away, was the Skill Etheric Concordance. For a moment, it was shaped like a long, narrow cave before it flickered and shifted back into a swirling ball of light and sound. *Makes sense that my bond Skill would serve as transport between our core spaces.*

This was the only route he'd encountered between his friends' Linked cores that didn't require Felix to punch a hole into things. Felix didn't even feel the strain of his Cardinal Flame as he entered his own, not required to bend himself backward to jump between cores. In fact, as he traced the connection of Mana back, it was a straight line from the Skill to his visualized Body, as if he'd never even stepped into Pit's channels. *Huh.* He cut off its use.

The illumination from his core rings dominated the area, distant as they were, but closer to hand were his numerous Skills. Not as many as he once held, certainly, but quite a lot compared to his friends. He drifted closer, pivoting his visualized Body in circles to fully take in the strange wonder of his own inner world. Seeing all of his friends' core spaces had given him a new perspective on things, namely on how *vast* his appeared to be, even as it remained significantly more nebulous.

It's all so spread out. Everyone else had a compactness to their core, except maybe Vess. She's an outlier, though. All that early training in visualization was surely responsible for the growth of her mountain range. Compared to the others, even Atar and Alister, she had a leg up in terms of time and resources. *Maybe being Unbound has something to do with it.*

He had tried to gain access to Beef's core space, but the teen Minotaur had flat-out refused. Perhaps it was because of his recent exposure to the Regalia, but Felix had an inkling it was more than that. Beef, more than anything, seemed terribly nervous. Why was an issue he'd worry about later, but it was something he had to tackle, if only because experiencing another Unbound's core space could give Felix greater insight into his own.

For the moment, Felix floated. In the past, he had used his Intent to sharpen the details of his core space, and he did so again. The dark became clearer and less gritty, while the light became brighter and more vibrant. The ribbons of red-gold and blue-white light gleamed against the black, vivid lassos securing his Tempered Skills to his dual cores. Skills shone, and their songs soared through the expanse, while above, the nebula of Essence glittered like multi-hued gemstones ground to dust. The Divine Tree trembled, but didn't change overmuch, and the pillars below merely grew more stark against the inky sky.

"Hmph," he grunted. His Intent and Willpower, powerful as they were, could only sharpen what was already extant. And then, only to a point. As an experiment, he tried to change the color of his nearest Skill

—Aria of the Green Wilds—from a rich, verdant green-gold to a dark wine red. The Skill flickered, color blooming inside its turning patterns like a bloodstain...before it vanished, returning once more to its original coloration. "I can change things...but everything just reverts to its original state. What if I use Fiendforge?"

He activated the Skill, and in the distance nearer his cores, what resembled an enormous gas giant began to hum. The Skill was Unique, an ability he'd formed after taking on the Omen Paths and all the dangers within it, and its size and complexity reflected that. Easily twice the dimensions of his highest-leveled Transcendent Skill, Fiendforge was an intricate ball of thrumming lines, waveforms turned and bound into an orb-like pattern and colored like a burning sunset.

The humming increased in pitch as the familiar pressure clamped down around everything, locking it firmly into its unbreakable crucible. Again, Felix applied his Intent and Willpower, directly attempting to change the color of the Aria of the Green Wilds. The bloody red persisted for longer this time, but just as before, it faded as his attention slackened.

"Changing things outright isn't possible, at least not through sheer brute force." Felix floated, basking in the multifarious jewel lights around himself. Brute force wouldn't work—which meant real skill had to take its place.

Felix righted himself, stood upon a single leg, and breathed.

Three hours later, Felix's Mind roared with unending flashes of thought and memory, spoiling his eighth attempt. A disgusted growl ripped from his visualized throat, and Felix slammed his Will against the dark around him. Lightning crackled, bursting along his blue-white ribbons as brilliant serpents, just as red-gold fire twisted atop its own threads.

"Fuck!" he shouted, loud enough that his Fiendforge quivered and flexed. "What am I even *doing*?"

He could be training his Skills, practicing sigaldry, alchemy, any number of things. Instead, he was sitting in an imaginary world, meditating upon an even smaller imaginary world, hoping to make both imaginary worlds slightly better. Felix ran his hands across his face but jolted when his fingernails cut bloody lines across his cheeks. He glared at his nails, now blackened talons, and a smaller scoff of distaste slipped out. "You followed me into here too, huh?" Felix checked his feet, and sure enough, they were the same: scaled and clawed and in proportion with his new, much larger frame. "Great."

His failed attempts to clear his Mind were annoying, but what truly ground Felix's nerves was the sensation that he was not in control of himself. For all his strength and power, he couldn't get a handle on Vess' technique. It was like his Mind was rebelling, shoving intrusive thoughts into the shreds of calm he could only barely manage to wrestle into existence. The claws and scales were just icing on the cake.

Many thoughts had pushed their way into his head during the prior three hours. From worries about their schedule to the risk of monster attack on their ships and Ahkestria, it was hard to shut it all off. Impossible, even. But, more than anything else, more than his fears and anxieties about the days or months ahead, Felix's thoughts kept returning to one single point: *What do I want?*

It was a simple question. For a long time, what he wanted was to be safe. Then the goalposts shifted, and it became about keeping his *friends* safe. From there, he became concerned with protecting a city, then a Territory. Again and again, the goals shifted, the metric by which he determined success constantly slipping further and further ahead. Now Felix rode at the head of a fleet of Manaships, dead set on stopping an incursion of Hierocratic forces into his Territory. He rode to war.

What do I want, though?

Karys and others had described a core space as a reflection of your unconscious needs, shaped by connotations, instinct, and deep-seated desires. The start of the process was always an instinctive leap, a subconscious jumping off point where so much was guessed at and intimated. Yet, by the time his channels were formed, his core space, however small, would have taken its first steps into the Visualization Stage. Felix had turned the burning heat of his Fire Within and ignited a core that flared with fire and crackling lightning...and from there, his Skills expanded, sorting themselves around it like planets around a sparking sun. It carried on from there, growing stranger and more arcane as Felix fought and triumphed over—or at least survived—all that attempted to end him.

If his core space represented his desires, his true goals beyond thoughts and surface motivations...then what the hell did this mean?

"It's a solar system. But that's so damn broad." Felix let his Perception unspool, cloaking the vast expanse of his core until he could sense every part of it. Above everything, he had a huge, galactic tree that spread its branches out into a nebula of glimmering dust and lights that hung from it like leaves and fruit. Below that, the burning sun had turned into two fiery rings, within which a terrible, hungry abyss lingered.

Still farther down were his pillars, woven of roots and shining core stuff. Felix could even make more of them, and he should in order to firm up his foundation, so he could step into Master and beyond without issue. "But should I? How can I build more foundation when I have no clue where I'm going with all this?"

Vess had said it was harder to enact visualization changes as one grew more powerful, and Zara had confirmed it. To advance, they both maintained, was to affix yourself, becoming rigid and potent at the expense of flexibility and change. He wasn't a fan of the idea, and Harn suggested something else that had either been left out of his tutelage by accident or design: that leaving an edge of unknown in your core space was possible, even preferable, in order to retain the flexibility to enact changes in your core.

Felix certainly had a bounty of unknown infusing his core space, namely in the thick, textured darkness that surrounded everything. It had always felt pregnant with purpose to him, even in its earliest stages, as if anything could walk out of the dark and into the light. And that, above all things, felt right to him.

"Out of the darkness," he muttered, still slowly rotating above his many Skills. "Into the light. Why does that feel...important?"

He had a path, one he had forged by dint of his own achievements and titanic Willpower. He'd wrested his very self from the dark, shoving himself back into existence during his trippy time among the Omen doors, and now walked the Path of the Cardinal Fiend. Yet, since that occurrence, Felix hadn't stopped to consider what that Path might mean.

The Fiend was a name. A persona he'd earned and learned to embrace, to a certain extent. It was the Felix that could be ruthless and unflinching when the hard decisions came up. He was not always a fan of the Fiend, were he being entirely honest, but Felix could recognize that it was necessary at times. Cardinal, on the other hand, was tied to his Primordial nature. A gift, one could say, from the Maw and its interference in his life.

Felix looked at his center, where the tree, rings, and pillars sat resolute among the rotating dance of his Skills. The cores were the [Thunderflame Core] and [Cardinal Beast Core], one an evolution of his power and the other a concentration of all that made him Primordial. Where they met, ring atop ring, they ground into one another and produced waves of glorious song and harsh, unremitting cacophony. Harmony and Dissonance, ever present within him. Beyond it was his abyss, his Hunger, another relic of the Maw, while the tree was a Divine root he'd stolen and allowed to grow, anchoring his pillars and cores together.

So should he chase that? A world tree upon which to build himself? *No,* came the answer, quick and decisive. That wasn't him, as much as he liked nature. Felix liked to think he was violence and compassion in roughly equal measure. He was devoted to magic and to thwarting those who stood in the way of his people.

Inheritor.

Autarch.

Scion of the Unseen Tide.

All of it was building to something. *But what?*

He focused on his Skills, floating like planets around the sun of his dual cores. A solar system with a black hole at its center. *Hm. Black hole. Do I lean into that? A ring of light, surrounding the collapsing event horizon of a monstrous point in spacetime that devours everything. It's almost* too *fitting.*

Then his Bastion of Will caught his eye. The center of his one and only Skill Array, the Bastion looked like a collection of intersecting vibrating lines that, if he squinted, could appear to be a green-ish planet. Around it, the other pieces of his Skill Array floated, orbiting the Bastion like moons...except unlike moons, they were all nearly the same size. Some even larger.

It was a tiny model of the rest of his core space. The Skill Arrays had strengthened him, bolstering the abilities of all Skills contained within it. Felix hadn't noticed a huge difference, but then he hadn't had the spare moment to pay too much attention.

Should I arrange for more Skill Arrays? What else could I group together? And could he just make them more like planets? Moons? *A black hole core, surrounded by the ever-shifting revolutions of countless celestial bodies. Is that...is that what I want?*

He pondered and floated. No longer posing or posturing. Just breathing. Felix attempted once again to empty his Mind.

It was hard. Harder than many things he had attempted. Just as in Vess' core space, his efforts were constantly interrupted by his busy, anxious thoughts, as well as by the hum and clash of Harmony and Dissonance. They sang to him, crooning at every possible instant, a battle that would never end.

Yet, in his blank-eyed floating, Felix realized he had wandered close to his cores. The song grew heavy and unavoidable, a riotous glory in his consciousness...until it began to dim. A hush settled over it all, and Felix jolted to full awareness. He realized, quite quickly, that he was standing above the abyss. His Hunger.

It had been curiously quiet, not pushing or prodding Felix save for its desire to consume the Regalia. And now, just above it all, Felix could tell the noise of his being did not quite penetrate its dark depths. "Hey."

His Hunger was silent, but Felix could feel it...orienting on him.

"You eat Essence and Mana, skin and bones, pieces of gods...What else can you eat?"

Feed Me. Find Out.

Felix hesitated for only an instant before he shrugged. "Worth a shot."

He drifted closer, lower, and the noise of his anxious thoughts faded. His enhanced Intelligence increased the speed of his cognition, and it still chugged away, but now it was held at arm's length. An invisible wall had been erected between Felix and all of the things that animated him. He floated farther.

His thoughts did not come to him slower, but like the Harmony and Dissonance, it was like music half-heard in another room. It grew...heavy. As if it were trying to escape the event horizon of his Hunger.

A black hole, came the thought, the space between words vast. *Huh.*

Felix coasted closer, until the burning blaze of his cores was below him, and he stood at the very cusp of the deeper dark. There, his Mind quivered as the Hunger inside him gleefully roared to life. Thoughts vanished, tumbling from his grasp before they could form, falling down into the dark....

Yet his hands began to weave, a performance he'd attempted so many times before that it had ingrained itself into his muscle memory. Except, this time, Felix was able to pull a small ovoid from the void around him, speckling it with bright lights and spinning flame, bisecting it with a tree and pillars and the firmament of dazzling, multi-hued dust.

His core space, in miniature.

Felix's Mind was divorced from his thoughts, his memory perfect despite his walled-off Intelligence. Perhaps that would have ended the experiment before it began, but his Born Trait was Perfect Recall, and there were few places more rooted in him than his core space.

He tweaked the miniature ovoid, casting his Will and Intent across it like a blanket. Around him, the dark rippled and flexed, and the Divine tree, so close, shimmered. Its crimson bark smoothed and shone, turning oh so very crystalline. Elation fluttered across Felix's gut, but he didn't pay it any attention, focused only on the ovoid.

Below, the abyss trembled, its velvet expanse shifting as his thoughts and emotions were swallowed wholesale. It *quivered.*

CHAPTER THIRTY-THREE

"Faster!" Beef shouted, laughing over the swells. "Faster!"

Felix cut through the Leviathan Depths like a knife, his long, lean Body all but made for physical exertion. Like Beef, he was smiling as the waves rose beneath them. It was thrilling to push himself, to find out everything his Adept Body could achieve. Almost thrilling enough to distract himself from the murky waters below. Evie was to the side and rear of him, splashing with speed but little skill; it was enough to keep up, at least.

"Hah! I've practically reached the boat! You're all so slow!" Beef shouted back at them, turning so that he was doing an almost leisurely backstroke. His horns rose up out of the water, tiny masts that echoed the Manaships they were all chasing.

Evie shouted something waterlogged and exceedingly angry before her flailing kicks went into overdrive. She pummeled the rolling waters with her fists and feet, kicking up a spray like a turbocharged manatee before shooting off after the Minotaur. She'd done something similar earlier, when they had first started the Endurance training. But, Evie being Evie, she had run out of steam fairly quickly.

Since then, it had been a back and forth between the two, both egging each other on with insults and wounded pride. Their competition was both amusing and effective at draining them both of Stamina, putting greater and greater strain on their Endurance. Felix, meanwhile, had lingered near the middle since they'd started. In the last two hours, he'd only approached Beef when the kid started getting too cocky. Like now.

Instead of swimming atop the oncoming swell as the others were,

Felix dove into it, plunging beneath the roiling surface with sure, implacable strokes. The endless crash and roar immediately silenced, resolving in a gelid, muffled vibration he could only feel with his limbs. Darkness expanded before him like an open door, darkest blue tinged with the faintest of purples as swirls of deepest water and almost-ice flowed in tireless currents. He swam as an arrow flew, cutting through the water with only a moment's pause.

Fish and monsters alike lit up in Felix's Perception, a sphere that encompassed hundreds of feet in all directions. It was easier to spot things under the waves, much to Felix's chagrin—there was living flesh, and there was the sea, and little else between. His Mind idly tagged the position of anything that dared come too close, while he fought to keep his imagination from conjuring worse in the fathomless depths.

As he swam toward the struggling forms of his friends, he was reminded of his Hunger, and of his efforts the night prior. The abyss inside of him was quiet, much like the Leviathan Depths, and had proven quite effective at clearing his Mind of idle, anxious thoughts. In turn, that had allowed him to finally affect some lasting changes to his core space. Felix had decided to lean toward the idea of a black hole, at least in the abstract; his Hunger was at the center of his most effective abilities, after all.

After firming up the structure of the Divine Tree—changing its trunk from strange, crimson bark to a glassy, far stronger crystalline substance—he had expanded on the idea of his Hunger pulling things toward the center. Slowly but surely, currents had formed within his core space, swirling and slow at first, drawing in the gritty detritus that lingered in the textured darkness between his Skills.

When Beef had shaken him out of his trance, he had effectively devised a self-propelled cleansing system for his core, one that even now was slowly clarifying the once-murky gloom. All in all, it had been a productive night. Using his Hunger to dull the frenetic churn of his Mind had been a great idea, one that Felix was eager to attempt again soon.

First, however, he had to show these kids who was boss.

Above, Beef swam with steady, powerful breaststrokes, and Evie was right behind him with the fastest doggy paddle Felix had ever seen. The rearmost ship of their fleet was looming a mere hundred yards out, and the two of them struggled mightily to be the first to reach its hull.

Without Skills or spells, Felix undulated his Body and kicked with all the Strength at his disposal, sending himself ripping through the waves like a rocket. He blasted past both of his friends, exploding up and out of the surface of the sea and straight into the air.

"Not fair!" Beef shouted, followed closely by Evie's garbled curse.

Felix landed nimbly atop the Manaship's deck, drenching several unsuspecting crew and Claw in seawater. Their alarm turned to bemused excitement as they realized who had landed on their ship, but Felix's grin was for his friends alone. He leaned over the railing and waved at them, affecting a bored expression. "Oh, hi there. Were you swimming, too?"

A forward-thinking Yttin sailor tossed a rope ladder over the side, and Felix gave him an appreciative nod. The man's armored appendages twitched in surprise, and he bowed before retreating to a gaggle of his fellows, all of whom gave him solid slaps on the back and wide, sharp-toothed smiles. Evie clambered up the ladder, her diatribe on Felix's lineage only broken up by her wheezing gasps. "Good for nothin'...muscle-brained...idiot...shoulda...known...you'd cheat."

She flopped bonelessly to the chitin deck, followed closely by the hulking form of Beef. He at least was able to stand, though he was blowing harder than a bellows. His shaggy fur dripped onto the deck like a tiny rainstorm, soaking Evie's prone form in even more water. "Hey! Stand over there! You smell like the inside of a Guilder foot locker."

"At least I can still stand," Beef said, tipping his snout upward and putting his hands on his hips. "I've got Endurance for days!"

Just at that moment, the ship hit a wave and dipped, and Beef's legs buckled instantly. He fell to the deck face-first, hitting with a wet *splortch,* like a sodden shag carpet. Evie's laugh was high and giddy, followed soon after by Beef's rueful chuckle.

"Ah, you're not so bad for a walking steak," Evie allowed, still flat on her back.

"Yeah. You're cool, too," Beef said into the deck before rolling onto his side. "Never seen someone doggy paddle as fast as you, either. That was awesome."

"Doggy paddle? What's that?"

"How're your gains?" Felix interrupted before that conversation could go awry.

Evie lolled her head toward him, still unable—or perhaps unwilling—to sit up, let alone stand. "Smaller than a foundling's lunch. All that...all that effort for two measly stat points." Water splashed up onto the deck as the ship rode through another cresting wave, soaking her further and finally forcing her upright. "Blech. And you monsters. Just swimmin' out here like fish."

"Two points of Endurance at your level and stage of advancement is great progress," Felix said encouragingly. "That's why we jumped in the water in the first place. I wasn't exactly chasing our ships for the fun of it."

It had been fun, but that was beside the point. Felix and Beef had devised a few ways to train themselves that were a bit more interesting than sparring on deck. Among other dangers, sparring could lead to injured bystanders. At least in the sea, they only risked themselves if more Fathom spawn attacked.

"I didn't earn any Endurance points, but I did get six whole levels in Swimming," Beef said. He was in an unsteady crouch, his shaggy fur still drizzling on the deck. "Getting close to Apprentice Tier on that one. Pretty sick, not gonna lie. I thought I'd reached my Skill cap back when this was all sand."

"Really? If you stick around, this one will have it so you're embarrassed to show anyone your Skill list," Evie said, jerking a thumb at Felix.

"And if you're lucky, you'll consolidate them all," Felix added.

"Consolidate? What, like combine Skills?" Beef whipped his head back, flinging dripping fur off his wide eyes. "You can do that?"

"With some help, yeah." Felix tapped his chin. "Hm. I've got some good ideas on new Skills you can get. How're your resistances?"

Beef shrugged. "Eh. Could be better. Got Pain, Fire, and Heat." He hesitated. "There are more?"

Felix grinned. "Lots more."

"Bah," Evie said, climbing to her feet. "You two carry on. I've had enough of bein' wet and cold. I'll go find Vess. I'd rather get beat down by that spear nut than train with two Unbound."

Felix's smile froze a bit on his face. "Is she sparring?"

"Yeah. Kicking the snot outta some of the Claw, from what I heard this mornin'. Before I went with you, she was knockin' 'em down faster than they could line up."

"Tell her...tell her I hope she's okay."

Evie, for her part, didn't snort or smirk at him. She just looked over the prow of the ship, as if they could both see her around the swell of keel and sail. "She doesn't seem like she is."

"Did she talk to you about it?"

"Nah. But I can tell. We women got wiles an' shit." Evie waggled her fingers for emphasis.

"My dad always said women have better emotional intelligence from a younger age," Beef said. "Which, uh, I gotta be honest: I don't know what that means."

"Sounded real smart. You sure you're not a mage? You're so wise." Evie snorted at her own dumb joke. "Well, don't you worry about what us women are up to, Mr. Fish. You just focus on that swimmin'. You need the practice."

"Who was it that was shouting a few minutes ago? 'I'm drowning! My legs are cramping! Ah!'" Beef did a fair imitation of her, flailing on the deck like a drowning bear. His sodden fur flung arcs of chill water in all directions before he devolved into a snorting giggle, too loud for a normal Human's chest. It cut off with a curse as icy chains suddenly solidified around his chest and arms, the hair freezing into solid, blocky chunks. "Shit! That's cold!"

"It's to help you keep afloat, ya great big monster," Evie muttered.

"Enough, you two." Felix glared at them both. "No Skill use on each other, except for sparring. Got it?"

Evie rolled her eyes, but nodded. Beef did, too, though it was hard to tell through all the shivering. He at least was able to smash the largest chains of ice with his meaty fists. Evie clucked her tongue. "All that muscle, wasted on a buffoon."

She fled across the deck before Beef even responded, too preoccupied with warming up his chest and arms. "Gah, that was cold as hell!" He glared down the length of the ship, where Evie soared through the air in an impossible, Born Trait-assisted leap. "She's been hanging around those Frost Giants too much. Ice Queen. For real."

Felix put a hand on Beef's shoulder. It was very cold. "Careful what you say there, Beef. She just about froze you solid because you irritated her. You don't want to be on Evie's bad side. For real." Beef glanced at him, but didn't reply, only shrugging a single shoulder before slowly standing up. "You want to continue swim training?" Felix asked.

"Suppose so," Beef muttered, then brightened considerably. "Oh hey! I just got Cold Resistance!"

Felix laughed. "Perfect! We'll train that, too."

"Sorry, what?"

The next several hours was a new kind of hell for Beef as Felix forced the teen to push his Body in new and agonizing ways. Swimming was predominantly an Endurance activity, but outpacing a fleet of Manaships? That involved his Strength and Agility in ways that the Minotaur hadn't quite explored. Felix made him swim to the end of the fleet before doubling back and doing it again, while using Rime Shaping to freeze the water around the teen until his lips were blue and chattering.

It all paid off, of course. They were Unbound, and this sort of low-level training was easy—not that Beef could tell. The kid nearly cried when Felix finally allowed him to climb back up onto the flagship, but he was the proud owner of two Apprentice-Tier Skills: Swimming and Cold Resistance. They'd even put some headway into getting Pain Resistance a higher level, though it had stalled out in the early forties. The numbing effect of the cold eventually counteracted that particular plan.

Still, Felix wasn't a jerk. He conjured a mote of Cardinal Flame and asked a passing sailor to bring them some of whatever the cooks had made that day. So, as Beef rested his aching bones and bruised muscles, they were each brought a large stoneware bowl of steaming hot stew and extremely hard bread, both of which were prepared from Tier II monster materials that seemed to sizzle with their own exotic seasonings. It was spicy and tangy, while the broth was salty and fulfilling. It was goddamn delicious, even the hardtack.

"Rest. You heal up fast like me, so we can keep going after a good meal." Felix wolfed down his stew between sentences, chomping right through the hardtack as if it weren't harder than some bricks. *The benefits of Adept teeth.* "Have you thought about what you want to do?"

"...Do?" Beef asked around a mouthful of stew. "Like, a job?"

Felix waved a hand. "No no, just a general idea of goals. I know you like magic, so do you want to follow that path?"

Beef nodded vigorously. "Yes. A hundred percent. Magic is so OP, it's ridiculous! Even the best hammer doesn't stand a chance against a guy who can move things with his mind."

"I can't argue there, but I'm sure there's something to be said for a purely physical build. Harn kicks a whole lotta ass."

"Harn's cool and all, but he can't take down a hundred monsters with a gesture like you can." Beef shoveled another mouthful of stew into his face. "Like, you made it rain *acid*, man. That's so sick."

"That's why you chose necromancy?"

"Hell yeah, dude. It's a force multiplier, provides excellent control options, and lets me be my own tank." Beef set the stoneware bowl onto the ground, now fully empty. "It's the perfect setup to do some solo grinding."

"But you're not solo anymore. You're part of a team, now."

Beef just shrugged. "It keeps my options covered, though."

"I guess. It's your core space, after all." Felix gave the teen a sidelong glance. "Speaking of core spaces: do you feel comfortable showing me yours yet?"

"I dunno," Beef hedged, a familiar embarrassment crawling across his Spirit and bovine face. "It's not like...cool, or anything."

Felix tilted his head. "Who said they had to be cool?"

"Me?" Beef shrugged again, a touch surly. "Everyone? All those soldier guys've been talking about core spaces nonstop since we started sailing. Everyone has these neat ideas about their cores, about how it all comes together with their Skills and stuff. Just seems so much more interesting than what I have."

Felix smiled gently. "You're comparing yourself to natives who know how this world works. You've been here less than a year."

"So? You've been here the same amount of time, and you've probably got like, a super magical lightning storm as a core thing." Beef deflated a bit more, and Felix could almost see the small thirteen-year-old boy inside of the hulking Minotaur. "I'm...I'm not that good at all this. Games are great. I'm a pro at games...but this is all real. It's too real, you know?"

"Yeah," Felix said and reached out until he grasped the big teen on the shoulder. His hands were big but barely covered the furry teen's deltoid. "I know exactly what you mean. But if you're not comfortable showing your core, then I won't push. We can focus on combat training next." Felix caught sight of a friend stepping out of the lower decks and grinned. "How do you feel about magic duels?"

CHAPTER THIRTY-FOUR

Atar rubbed his temples and sipped slowly at a Mana Potion. It didn't do much to ease his headache, but at least it kept the Mana deprivation at bay. The roar of the crowd didn't help much either.

"Ooh!"

A wince swept through the throng as a man was hurled into the shimmering barrier, sending ripples of light across the sigaldry's edge. Mana drained from the formation, spent by the impact, and Atar focused on channeling more Mana into the sigils to keep them active. The man—a Blade—tried to stand, but fell back onto his face, defeated.

"Who's next?" Evie shouted, reeling her chain back around her hands. The dull silver weapon moved like a living thing, twisting around the woman's arm and shoulder with a purpose.

Evie stood in the middle of a wide circle they had cleared on the third ship in the fleet, the outside marked by a barrier formation Atar had inscribed into the chitin boards. A mass of people hugged the edge of it, most watching with enthusiasm but a few bearing arms and armor with an excited air about them.

They were all there to fight, testing themselves against the elite of the Fiend's people. Vess had been out earlier, laying waste to any Claw members that dared face off against her, but she'd either grown bored or had a breakthrough. She left three glasses prior, right before Evie arrived, soaking wet and filled with a need for violence. The Claw had obliged.

Lens of the Magus is level 77!
Sigaldry is level 72!

Atar grunted as a final bit of Mana poured from his palms and into the circle, reigniting the failed portion just as the unconscious body of the Blade was dragged away. As annoying as it was to act as a Mana battery for the barrier formation, it was a form of training for him, as well. While Evie exhausted herself against challenger after challenger, he had to keep updating the barrier formation on the fly, adapting to the Skills and stats of the fighters quickly.

If any one of them proved too powerful for his array, they would pierce it and break the entire thing apart. On the plus side, the entire structure was a derivation on the field array he'd composed back in Nagast, and it was far more efficient now than previously. Even without Mana Potions to top him off, Atar was fairly certain he could keep up a similar barrier against Journeyman-level attacks for at least half a glass.

"We challenge you, Chainmaiden."

Evie spun to face a number of Yttin sailors, all of them stripped to the waist and bearing their long, trident-like spears. "All six of you?"

"Alone, we cannot hope to win. But together, we are stronger," the Yttin sailor said, and his wide mouth displayed dozens of sharp, triangular teeth. "Together, we shall triumph."

Evie shrugged, and the tightly coiled chain slipped off her shoulder like water, pooling on the deck with a heavy *clank-thunk*. "Sounds fair. I've been moppin' the floor with the rest of you. Let's make it interestin'."

Atar focused and opened up a hole in the formation directly in front of the six Yttin. They nodded at him in thanks before stepping through. Their broad chests were all covered in thick armor that varied between red, blue, and violet that thickened visibly as each of the sailors prepared. Wide plates of knobby and spiked chitin swelled their frame, until the Yttin were all hulking brutes covered head to toe in impressive natural armor. The extra appendages on their backs grew as well, turning into sharpened spears and huge, prehensile pincers.

"Twin's teeth," Evie swore. "Does that hurt?"

"No," their leader rumbled, his voice no less loud for the fact that his face was entirely covered by a chitinous mask. "It is our Born Trait, unique to our Race yet lost to us for many Ages. Now we claim it once again. You shall see that it is as fearsome as it appears, Chainmaiden."

"Yeah, yeah." Evie twisted her arm, and her chain rippled across the boards. "Prove it."

Atar leaned forward, interested to see if the warriors could best his annoying ally. They moved deceptively fast for their size, and from the way they shook the deck beneath him, Atar assumed they did not weigh as much as someone in metal armor would have.

Indeed, when the first two engaged with Evie, she turned their blows aside with relative ease. She didn't even use her chain, relying instead on her thickened vambrace and some sort of Parry Skill. When the other four closed the distance, however, things changed. The armored appendages moved independently of the Yttin's arms and legs, attacking from strange and complex angles that Atar had trouble noticing before they landed. Evie was forced to bob and weave, all thoughts of Parrying set aside for pure Agility.

Evie was laughing. "More! Faster!"

Yttin claws slammed down with tremendous force, missing her by a hairsbreadth each time, while she dodged between their huge Bodies with wild, impossible motions. She was like smoke or water, meeting their Strength with an Agility so high they couldn't land a single hit against her. Frustration danced across their Spirits as the Yttin's strikes became more and more forceful. Atar could sympathize with them.

"Tooth and Claw!"

As four of the six Yttin attacked, Evie's chain suddenly constricted, locking all four warriors' claws into a bundled mass of metal links. New, jagged spikes and blades erupted from the weapon, forged of Mana and Stamina, cutting deeply into their chitin armor and forcing an agonized howl from their throats. Horrifyingly, the chain began to rotate, spinning its mess of blades against the appendages and spraying chips of chitin and thick, orange ichor in all directions. Atar gagged as pieces of their limbs fell to the deck with a wet *thud*.

"Grim Fervor!" Evie shouted.

Mana Gauge is level 39!

Colorful bands of Mana vapor gathered around Atar's wrist as he held it up. Within the barrier, Mana was flowing through the air, a mixture of ice and metal in addition to water mixed with life Mana. Ice and metal were predominant, though, filling up the space with itself, asserting a dominance that Atar could hear as the Yttins' Spirits quailed.

She's inflicted a Status Condition. One that...affects their Willpower? The sensation in their Spirits wasn't one Atar had encountered often. It felt like a fluttering in the chest, sounding of quiet noises in the dark of an old home. *How does that help her? She doesn't have anything that capitalizes on reduced Willpower, does she?*

Reduced Willpower or not, the Yttin raged, pain apparently fueling them as their armor redoubled in size. The ichor stopped flowing, resealed beneath chitin claws as first two, then all six of the warriors advanced. If they were afraid of Evie, they gave no sign, and their thrusting tridents moved like lightning. Evie evaded most of them, slipping through their rain of blows unscathed until the last two. The only two uninjured, they appeared to let loose with all the Strength they could muster, bringing their tridents down on Evie like an avalanche.

She caught both of their strikes, one in each hand. Force exploded downward, splintering the decks and sending a wave of pressurized air rolling through the crowd. Folks gasped, then cheered as they realized the Chainmaiden was virtually unharmed.

"What the hell? I thought she was low in Strength?" Beef said from behind the mage. Atar jolted, half turning until he could see the Minotaur looming behind him. At his side was Alister and Felix. Alister gave him a little wave.

"How long have you all been here?" Atar demanded. He hadn't even felt them approach, though he could identify their noisy Spirits now. Beef was a battering ram, a loud shout in a quiet room, while Alister was like a softly trickling hourglass, smooth and steady. Felix...well, Atar couldn't sense Felix much at all. The Unbound had grown increasingly opaque to his senses, even his Harmonic ones.

"Minutes at best," Felix said. He nodded at the ongoing battle, where Evie was now brandishing her chain with increasing vigor. It crashed against the Yttin, splintering their armor wherever it struck. "How many people has she fought?"

"A lot. This is the most at once, though." Atar said.

"Hm. Grim Fervor is working well for her, then," he said. All of them looked curiously at Felix, and he shrugged. "Her new Skill. Reduces the Willpower of her enemies while boosting her own Strength in relation to how many are arrayed against her. She's probably better off fighting outnumbered."

"Bet she couldn't handle me, then," Beef said, flexing.

"Hm," was all Felix said, but Atar heard an entire speech in the word. Silly as the bull was, Atar saw a lot of himself in Beefhammer...and he wasn't fond of the comparison. There was a vulnerability in his bovine expression, one that Atar would have been aghast to see in the mirror.

burn him. burn them both. they are unbound. they will fuel our fire for generations, atar.

The Flame hovered at the edge of his vision again, but Atar did not look at it. Others couldn't see it—he had tested that on Alister—but they could see Atar react to it...and the last thing the mage wanted was the others to think him mad. "Shut up," he whispered.

"What?" Felix asked. The man wasn't even looking at Atar, but he could almost feel Felix's attention bend toward him.

"Nothing, just worrying at a...problem."

"Oh. Ok."

Luckily, the fight was taking up a good deal of Felix's attention for whatever reason. Still, Atar tried to keep his breathing even and his Spirit at ease. Controlling one's emotions was far harder than it seemed, despite what Chanter Isla had told him. Alister sat next to him, placing a comforting hand on his knee as they watched the fight progress. "The formation is impressive, love," he said, admiring the sigaldry. "You're holding it easily enough?"

Atar shrugged, carefully veiling his Spirit still. "It's Mana-hungry, but not terrible. With enough power, I believe it could stop Adept Skills for a short time."

"Did you try to incorporate the crystals yet?"

"No. That needs to be experimented on a smaller scale." Atar shuddered. He could imagine what a backlashed array this size would do to them all. "No need to hurt anyone."

"Lady Isla hasn't given you any further pointers on sigaldry? I thought she was to help on this?" Alister asked with a frown.

They'd both been getting extra lessons from the Sorcerer during their journey, and while she had provided some solid insights into the Grand Harmony, Atar would have much preferred to learn from Zara. Isla was quite dismissive of nearly everyone who wasn't an Unbound, and he'd had to sit through salvo after salvo of questions on Felix's history and character. It had gotten to the point that he'd started avoiding the woman outright. "No. She's been unwilling to teach me any further. Says my 'enthusiasm for the craft is lacking.'"

"You mean she wasn't getting enough information on Felix," Alister said, low and angry. He ran a hand over his dark locks before grabbing Atar's hand in his. "You're right not to trust her. Don't give her anything."

"I don't plan on it." The woman's questions had started innocuous, but it was clear the Chanter was trying to assess Felix for...something. "Have you mentioned it to him?"

"No. Have you?"

"No." Atar glanced up, seeing Felix several strides away and intently watching the fight. Evie was a whirling dervish in the circle, and two of the six warriors were down on the ground. He jolted, but his fear was replaced by soothing relief as he saw their chests rising and falling. A small flare of Analyze indicated their Health was rising slowly. *Burning ashes, Evie. Take it easy.*

"Then we should tell him. Tonight, after dinner." Alister squeezed his hand. "Alright?"

"Alright."

From within the circle, a sudden burst of purple-white lightning flashed across the space. The final four Yttin fell to their knees, Bodies limp yet hanging suspended by ghostly chains about their limbs and chests. With a sharp, exhausted gesture from Evie, the chains vanished entirely. That, however, wasn't the strangest bit: it was Felix, who stood poised at the edge of the barrier and was staring directly at Evie. *No. Not Evie. Her chain.* Atar pursed his lips. *Why?*

"Drop the shield, the fight's over," Evie said. She jogged over to the Yttins' side, pulling several Health Potions free from her pouch. Several Yttin came close to help their brethren, and she tossed the bottles to them. "Make sure they take these. That was a good fight."

They bowed and immediately uncorked the Potions and administered them.

you could have bested them all. they are nothing.

The Flame was very annoying, Atar had discovered. It wanted him to grow, no matter the cost, and just like its predecessor, it desired *fuel.* Atar had determined that the Flame was not the same as the Urge he'd somehow absorbed, but it carried many similarities. Mostly, it wanted to burn, bright and hot and furiously for all the Continent to see. The vast majority of its communication with the fire mage were requests for fuel or to somehow exhibit their power in a public forum. Like these sparring matches. Atar had refused. While he was feeling better, his recovery was far from complete.

Interestingly enough, the Flame had been affected by Atar's Link with Felix. While mostly it was a quivering tongue of flame, sometimes it manifested as a bird, a small one with only the roughest shape of wings. That was why he'd formed his new core into a cage, in the hopes that he could restrain the Flame within it. The plan had worked, sort of. The thing could still manifest around him, but it felt...leashed. Held tighter, at least.

People began dispersing as Evie left the confines of the formation, many of them moving away quickly as Felix arrived at her side. They began talking in low tones, the Autarch gesturing excitedly.

you cannot ignore us forever, atar. we sit in your heart. we know you desire the sky as much as we. to blaze.

Atar pinched the bridge of his nose, feeling his headache getting worse. He almost gasped in surprise when soft, warm fingers pressed against his temples and began to massage them gently. "You're pushing yourself too hard, love," Alister said. "You need rest."

"I've had enough. I need to fix myself," Atar said, and perhaps with more heat than he intended. The massage stopped for a second before resuming. "I—Alister, I have to rebuild it all. My core space is still in shambles, and these changes to my appearance and my Race...I need time. And we're going to fight soon. Worse, we're going to war, probably. I cannot—I cannot be a liability."

Though Atar couldn't see him, he could envision the annoyed amusement on Alister's face as he took several measured breaths. "Fine, you giant idiot. We keep walking the razor's edge together. Can you hold the barrier alone? Or should we get some of the Arclight Apprentices in to help?"

"No, no, I have it. It's been doing wonders for my Sigaldry and Lens of the Magus Skills." Atar sighed, enjoying the massage. "But I should take a break for a bit."

"Alright. Take that break now, because we'll need the barrier back up soon."

"Why?"

Alister laughed. "Because Felix wants me to fight our new friend."

"What?"

"Alister! Get ready!" Beef shouted from near Felix and Evie. He was doing a series of odd lunges and bends, flexing all the while. "I'm gonna crush you into paste, wizard!"

Atar blinked and looked up at his boyfriend in confusion. "What in Avet's black teeth is a wizard?"

CHAPTER THIRTY-FIVE

"Calm down, Beef," Felix said to the Minotaur's flexing back before focusing back on Evie. "Sorry. You were saying?"

Evie shrugged. "Just that I'm startin' to settle into these new Skills. The ones that evolved back in the Warren, mostly. The newer ones are a bit stranger."

"I noticed you using Grim Fervor."

"Yeah, that one's a treat." Evie flexed her arm and slapped her bicep. "You see me in there? It ain't much of a boost, but it got me imaginin' fighting in a big battle, like we did at the Nest in Haarwatch. I'd really see some gains then."

Felix could well imagine it; they had been forced into unfavorable odds many times. "It's a great Skill for you. What I was wondering most about was the last Skill. What did you call it?"

Evie made a silent 'O' with her mouth. "Bonds of Dominion, Legendary rarity. Evolved from Chain Mastery."

"A weapon Skill?" Felix scratched his neck. "It was...those spectral chains, that purple light...what was that, then?"

She shrugged. "Don't got a name for 'em. But I can feel them, you know? Hoverin' around us even now. Links in chains that just haven't been forged." Evie laughed. "Sounds foolish, I know. But they say the rarer the Skill, the stranger it all gets."

"Do they? That...makes a lot of sense, actually." Felix's weirder Skills were all higher rarities, all of them proving less straightforward than Running or Long Sword Mastery. "I only asked because the way it functioned reminded me a lot of my Adamant Discord Skill."

"Really?"

"Really. Adamant Discord lets me grab at connections between things—like myself and the air or a monster—and manipulate them. Pushing and pulling, mostly. But you're using them to bind and restrict, which is extremely interesting. I assume the purple light was your ice attunement shining through?"

"I assume so. Looked the same as my old Ice Spike spell, anyway." She toyed with the spiked chain, now securely wrapped around her waist. The weapon was cleverly enchanted to shrink when not in use. "You think we can spar a bit, then? See how far we can push our Skills?"

Felix grinned. "I'm down. We can try later tonight. First, I have to oversee Beef and Alister, here."

While they'd been chatting, a shimmering aperture had opened in the barrier formation. Beef and Alister were already inside, the latter carefully adjusting his azure robes while the former was nervously toying with his maul. Beef was talking, and from the amused expression on Alister's face, he'd dropped the bravado from earlier. "—gotta get better at magic. I'm like, really good at hitting things and getting hit, but I want to do big AoE spells like Felix. You know? Do you have any AoE spells?"

"AoE?" Alister asked. He tightened the sword belt at his waist and checked his rapier in its sheath.

"Area of Effect. Like, uh, like a big wave that can take out a city."

"That was due to the artifact Felix held, not a Skill he has," Alister pointed out.

"I know that!" Beef huffed a breath at the mage, forceful enough that it blew Alister's hair back. "But yeah. That."

"Well. Why waste words? I can simply show you what I can do." Alister unsheathed his rapier. It gleamed in the dull, storm-clouded daylight. "Shall we begin?"

"Oh! Yes." Beef hefted his maul up onto a shoulder and concentrated. To Felix's eyes, blackened green Mana swirled from the teen's palms, elbows, and base of his skull—his Mana Gates—before solidifying into a blocky breastplate and pauldrons, further increasing Beef's considerable bulk. The maul and armor alike leaked blackened green vapor, rising off his Body like steam.

"Listen up!" All eyes turned to Felix as he shouted loud enough to be heard over the crashing waves. The Claw and Yttin sailors who had turned away stopped in their tracks. "This is going to be a fight of magic. A wizard's duel, as it's called where I come from. That means Spirit Skills only, alright? First one to fall loses. You both ready?"

"Quite."

"Hell yeah."

Felix reached into the air, grasping at the storms that crackled above them and *pulled* with Adamant Discord. A bolt of lightning flashed. "Begin!"

"Seismic Shatter!" Beef roared and stomped the deck so hard it *rippled.* But no, it wasn't the deck, but a wave of earth Mana that blasted outward in a cone shape. It tore across the circle toward Alister, who simply stood in its way, rapier raised in guard position. It crashed against him, a jagged wall of conjured earth...just as Alister slashed downward. The Mana parted, splitting to either side of him before dispersing entirely. "Hey! What was that!"

"It's called finesse, Beef." Alister twisted his rapier and raised it into guard position again. "I'll show you. Grand Impetus!"

A single, savage thrust of Alister's rapier shot forward. It was fast even to Felix's eyes, likely assisted by a couple meta Skills, and a bar of force Mana crossed the circle in a blink. Beef stumbled backward, almost falling to his ass before recovering. When he stood up, he stared incredulously at a wide hole bored through his chitin breastplate.

"Whoa." Chitin flowed over the hole, patching it over. "You're good."

Alister grinned. "I try. Bring everything magical you have against me. I am ready for it."

"Alright. You asked for it!" Beef thrust his maul down toward the deck, and a flood of blackened green Mana poured out of it. "Chitin Construction!"

Within the cleared circle of the formation, the entire deck heaved and split apart. This time, it was no illusion of earth Mana, but the literal boards come to eerie life as Beef's mastery over chitin asserted itself. Alister cursed, dodging away as strips of jagged chitin shot out from around his feet.

"Pillars of the Domineering Sentinel!" Alister shouted, calling up glowing columns of blue force Mana from belowdecks. He leaped atop them, hopping from one to the next as more and more of the ship whirled around him. "Grand Impetus!"

This time, his rapier thrust was intercepted by a moving mass of gray-brown chitin. It was destroyed, but the blow didn't reach Beef at all, and the teen Minotaur laughed through gritted teeth. "Bet you didn't expect this!" He shouted, and Felix was unsure if it was in pain or effort. The swirling accumulation of chitin pulled together, forming into the biggest hammer he had ever seen; easily ten feet wide at the head and twenty feet long. It blazed with necromantic Mana. Beef held onto its end, muscles straining, and swung.

An explosion of blackened green and brightest blues filled Atar's formation to the brim. Vapor and dust described the full dome of the barrier, while aftershocks sent rippling tears through its sides. Atar shouted, glowing almost white as he poured his Mana into the sigaldry to keep it steady. Felix took several steps forward, but by then, the dust had cleared and the barrier stabilized.

"Yyero's entire ass," Evie said with a whistle. "Beefy boy is a menace."

The entirety of the sparring circle was torn apart, the rooms below decks exposed, and only the deck beams and stanchions were available for footing. The hammer that Beef had forged from his Mana and available chitin was already falling apart, its blaze of blackened green faded to a dim ember, and Beef himself was standing on shaking legs. Alister stumbled, his shield flickering and dissolving into the faintest of smoke.

"Damn," he said, leaning heavily against an exposed beam. "Couldn't get away in time."

Beef was panting, but managed a laugh. "Hah! Told you...told you I had good...good magic—"

Without another word, the immense Minotaur slumped forward. He fell, crashing through several hammocks, much to the dismay of the Yttin crew that scattered before him. Alister straightened and dabbed a measure of sweat from his forehead. He found Felix's gaze and gave a half smile. "I suppose that means I win?"

Felix sighed, heavy and deep. Beef had a long way to go.

Beef was a hard one to shift, weighing several hundred pounds and all of it dense muscle. It took Felix himself to lug the guy out of the tangle of hammocks and splintered beams. Felix felt bad for the damage and apologized to the Yttin sailors, but they had only bowed and thanked him for his assistance.

Once they were on the deck, it took three entire Mana potions to bring the Minotaur back to consciousness, and only just. Beef had driven himself hard, pressing deep into Mana deprivation with that last attack.

"You're strong," Alister said as Beef leaned woozily against the railing. "That was an impressive shaping Skill you had there. You would have broken my defenses, too, if you had enough Mana left."

"Didn't though," Beef grunted, his voice raspy. He was cradling his skull in two thick hands. "I feel like I'm gonna splint in half."

"Well, you hit your limit. That just means we have to push past it and train up your Willpower and Resonance." Felix started cataloging some new training regimens for them both. "I dunno how easy it'll be to boost them to a reasonable level, though. Atar, Alister. You both have Skills meant to give you more magical oomph, right?"

"We do," Atar answered from the edge of the circle. He was staring at the busted-up innards of the Manaship with a frown on his face and, for a moment, Felix thought he saw his pale white hair flicker like flame. *Odd.*

"Think you can teach Beef some of them?" Felix asked, and the two mages shared a look.

"Teach me? Teach me what?" Beef's voice was rough, but excitement bounced across his Spirit. "The ranged stab you did? Can you teach me the ranged stab thing?"

"We'll teach you Focus," Atar said, firmly. "And Meditation. That will start you off, at least."

Beef's expression fell. "Those sound like boring nerd Skills."

"Dude, you told me you spent most of your days inside, playing MMOs." Felix patted the teen on the shoulder. "You're a nerd, too."

"Damn. Rough."

Felix chuckled and helped Beef to his feet. Just as the mages started talking to him, outlining their training plans, Evie jabbed him with her elbow. "Ow," he said reflexively.

Evie made a face. "That didn't hurt, you ass. Look." She nodded her head at the prow of their ship. Beyond it, to where an ochre-skinned woman stood with her arms crossed over her black robes. Sea-green hair flowed wildly in the wind as she pointed at Felix and crooked a finger. "What do you think she wants?"

Felix sighed. He had an idea, though he wasn't sure how she had found out. "Rain check on that spar?"

"Sure, sure. If you're going to talk to Chanters, make sure you don't let that Isla ask you too many questions. I swear, she's half tick for how deep she buries herself in everyone's business."

A smirk quirked Felix's lips. "I'll keep that in mind. Beef," he called behind him. The Minotaur was standing in a huddle with the two mages, looking a bit overwhelmed. "Fix that hole before you go with Alister."

Beef looked at the half-shredded hammer and thick, peeling strips of chitin he'd ruined. "Ugh, sure. Sure. Hey, wait, where're you going?"

Felix gestured vaguely toward the ship ahead of them. "Autarch business."

"Oh. Uh, have fun?"

"Mm." Felix flared his Will and Intent, capturing the song of his Skill and sending it sizzling out of his channels. He grasped the air and leaped.

"Useless!"

The clatter of the bulky, metal-shod book was mostly swallowed by the plush carpet and thick, hanging tapestries. Both had been liberated from the grandmaster's ostentatious estate, though Vess was unsure who had taken them. Just as she was unsure who had outfitted her room with a wide bed and a wardrobe, all of which took up a remarkable amount of space on the otherwise cramped vessel. Yet her Mind was not on the spacious chamber or creature comforts she'd been provided; it was instead lingering upon the covers of the metal tomes, now glinting dully in the overcast light of her sole window.

Skill Books. Three of them gifted to her by Darius at the behest of her father, and all detailing the strange and esoteric paths toward gaining the Skills of a true Dragoon. She had been studying them, learning from them all during their trip across the desert, but their secrets had been kept from her; the Skills shown in the books were for advanced eyes only, impossible to achieve without a full set of Adept Aspects. In fact, she hadn't taken a look inside their covers since the seas had returned, since the battle in the temple...since the change.

Fearing what the changes in her core space and Skills might mean, Vess had avoided looking at the Skill Books. She had, instead, chased after distraction, fighting more and more of the relatively weak Claw members. Vess had tried to enjoy teaching them Sword and Spear Forms, just as she had before, but it was not the balm it had once been. Her Mind too anxious and Spirit unmoored, she had fled the sparring circle. She needed answers. She feared what she might find.

Now, staring at cast-metal covers featuring the graceful, deadly form of the Dusk Dragons, she realized it had happened. Her fears had been made real. The Skill Books were as useless to her as any Untempered off the street. Though she was not yet Adept, there had always been a tingling something, just at the edge of her awareness, when she studied the Books. That was all gone. The words did not dance in her Mind nor resound in her limbs, not as she was told they would. They were only dry ink upon dusty paper.

She could not become a Dragoon.

Is this because of Felix? The thought kept resurfacing, uncharitable as it might be; Felix had established this strange Link with her, after all. It was his core space that hung in the sky above her core, his influence that had...changed her. The Link was strong, unbreakable perhaps. Yet even if it were breakable, would she make such an attempt? *If it returned my Skills to the way they were? I…*

The Link with Felix was strong. She could feel his presence like the shine of the moonlight over her shoulders, and it...was not the worst of sensations. She reminded herself that she had chosen to accept the strengthened Link of her own volition; he had asked, and she had answered. She would do so again, given the chance. *He would have done the same for me.*

Vess took a breath, closing her eyes and steadying her Mind and

Spirit as much as her Body. She could feel her Skills swirl within her chest, the bizarre new peaks easy to spot among the detailed uniformity she had cultivated for all her life. They were a collection of hot coals, burning at her with frozen winds and unfamiliar emotions. There were songs in that wind—alien notes she had never before heard—full of longing and fear and anger. It chafed at her, tore against the stability of Vess' Spirit with every beat and measure. She—

A rapping at the door broke Vess' concentration, and she glared at the intrusion before her Perception picked up just who it was. "Come in."

The narrow door opened soundlessly, and a slight woman in a blue gown and pale blonde hair stepped gracefully into the room. She looked like a queen, and Vess had seen her fair share of nobility. "Lady Dayne. I am so glad to have found you."

Vess swallowed and took another surreptitious breath to steady herself. "Lady Isla. To what do I owe the pleasure?"

"Ah, this is simply a social call. I was wondering if—Oh. Oh, my dear." Isla's small, delicately featured face pinched in pained concern. Her bright eyes raked over Vess as if stripping her soul bare. "Something clouds your Spirit, child. Do you wish to talk?"

"I—" Vess' words tangled in her throat as her eyes once again landed on the discarded Skill Books. "Yes. Yes I would like that."

CHAPTER THIRTY-SIX

"We need to speak about this," Zara said and placed a crystalline container atop the smooth chitin table between them. Felix and she were seated in chairs within Zara's quarters, a place she'd immediately marched off to before he had even landed. He shifted in the chair, not looking at the glimmering crystal and its burning sigils, but the thing refused to move.

Bolted in. Right. Felix settled on folding his arms instead. "I thought we were done with this?"

"As did I, at least for the moment. But then I found this, haunting among the crystal matrices." Zara waved her hand over the container, which looked remarkably similar to a huge tank shell, were it made from multi-hued crystal. A sound rolled outward from her gesture, and a sudden haze appeared above the crystal, from which Zara plucked a single, quivering strand. It shimmered in brilliant but faded ebon-gold.

"Right. That." Felix took a breath. "There's something you should know..."

Felix outlined his vision of the strange, armored woman in the company of a Priest of the Pathless. Zara went pale, cursing in what sounded like several languages, none of which were familiar to Felix. He got the gist, though.

"You're sure it was a priest?" she asked him, finally.

"Positive. I saw a few of them back in Haarwatch. Those robes are pretty distinctive."

"An Unbound...they have an Unbound under their thumb." Zara leaned onto her elbows and placed her hands over her mouth, and for once, Felix felt her loosen the hold she had on her Spirit. It trembled.

"We always knew this might happen. Feared it. If she is as powerful as you say, then we must move faster."

"Faster? You mean collecting the other Unbound to us?"

"Perhaps. But I meant convening the Cantus Sodalus."

"Convening—like calling a meeting?" Felix raised an eyebrow. "How? Where?"

"My order makes it a point to not stay in any one place for too long. The superstitions against Sorcerers burn too bright. But we have ways of conversing over distance."

"You've said that before. How?" Felix asked.

"A special artifact, resonance, and a pool of liquid Mana mingled with our Marked blood." Zara held out a hand, and a familiar symbol appeared above it, etched in glowing blue-green lines. Mark of the Cantus Sodalus. "If you still held my Mark, you could do it, too."

"Pass," Felix said, not breaking eye contact with Zara's pure blue gaze. "No one Marks me against my Will, Zara."

"That is—" Her gaze hardened, yet she looked down, back at the crystal container. "Of course."

A moment stretched between them, weighted down by the past. By mistakes. Felix breathed through his nose, forcing his heartbeat to slow, to calm. "I thought that connection had fled after I saw the vision...why's it still here?" Felix asked.

Zara gestured again, and the thread appeared. The ebon-gold coloration was almost transparent now, a faint wash against the shadows. "It barely is. I only found it because of a certain resonance with you. And Beef."

"Resonance how?"

"Your Aspects, at their base, all have a unique vibration. With enough practice, you can begin to hear it, but understanding it is a task that would take many lifetimes, even for one of us."

That was interesting, but certainly not pertinent at the moment. Felix filed it away for later. "And how were you able to dredge it up? Every time I go near this one, it—" Felix reached out, and the ebon-gold cord squirmed away before vanishing completely. "See? Without my Skills, it runs from me."

"Curious," Zara murmured. She made that inaudible music once again, but the cord did not come back. "And it is truly gone now. Fled." She pondered a moment longer before apparently remembering something. "And why didn't you tell me of this sooner? We spoke soon after you found the Regalia on Beef. Why not then?"

"Isla."

It was all Felix said, but it was effective as a gag in Zara's mouth. She huffed a sharp breath, though. "Isla is trusted, Felix. My superior trusts her, as do others of the order. Why can't you?"

"She rubs me the wrong way. She's pushy. Any number of things, but really it's just my gut," Felix said. "And I've learned to trust my gut whenever possible. At this point, however, I'm more concerned with what that priest may have done to the Unbound woman. Her voice was just...it was a dead, flat sound. No emotion or life to it."

"If she was as powerful as you say, then the Hierocracy would have trained her...and they are brutal. I can only imagine what must have been done to this poor woman, but I imagine she is powerful. If her Spirit affected the guards to a Mountain City like that, she is not a force to be trifled with by any except, perhaps, a Grandmaster. If she is like you, then even that is not enough." She tapped twice on the table. "Tell me of the Dwarves. Their armor, the details on the gates. Anything."

Felix recounted everything he could, though putting it all into the right words was difficult. "And their armor had these geometric squiggles on them, across the chest."

"Was the armor dyed? Or cast of a particular color metal?"

"Uh, yes. A brassy color, but the center of their chest was a red with a white series of zig-zags on it," Felix recounted.

"The Redspine Clan, then. They control a number of cities in the Rimefang Mountains. Hard to determine which one this might be, at least from what you saw. The good news is that they are far to the north of us."

"How far?" Felix asked. "Do we have to worry about them finding us?"

"About as far as it is possible to be without stepping into the Hoarfrost," Zara said. "It would take us an entire year to reach them, were we to fly upon a true Manaship."

The Hoarfrost. That's where the Frost Giants had come from. "That's...that's really far," Felix said finally.

"It is. The Continent is quite massive, and even the Hierocracy only skirts the edge of its grand breadth."

Felix had been told that the Continent was huge, but this was a scale he couldn't fit his head around. How big was the planet?

"What I do not understand is why they are in the mountains." Zara said, either not noticing or ignoring the expression of consternation on Felix's face. "The Rimefangs are far away from Amaranth and only tentative allies with the Hierocracy. Trading partners only. To unleash such violence upon them would do more harm than good."

"They're hunting, clearly," Felix said. Zara raised her eyebrows. "What? It's obvious. If she's that volatile, why use her on allies? I'd be using her to do the same thing we're doing. Finding more Unbound."

"Ruin and Damnation," she cursed. "You're right." She slammed the table. "We need to perform the ritual again."

"Agreed. Do you have what you need?"

"I do."

Felix stood up. "Then let's get started."

Back in his Stronghold, Zara had performed a ritual to hone in on the connections Felix held to his Unbound brethren. It had allowed him to focus on Beef, finding him among the deserts of the Scorched Expanse. It had been a disorienting experience akin to his Memory delving, but Felix had plenty of practice at this point.

Sigils and glyphs were drawn around him, radiating in an array of concepts that Felix still only partially understood. Sigils for all three Aspects were there, along with the standard elements and more arcane markings. It was huge, and took Zara a solid hour to set up. By the end of it, Felix sat in the center with his legs folded and concentrated. He dropped down into his core space, falling into his Bastion and landing atop the tower there within seconds.

The silver needle atop his tower shone bright, bundled with all the connections he had ever established. They grew by the second as new, barely visible cords threaded through far brighter strings...and somewhere in their center were a number he'd found before. He thought of home, of Earth, and a bundle of cords were suddenly there, vibrating with a handful of familiar melodies. They burned him as he reached for them, and Felix gritted his teeth through the pain. First and thickest was the ebon-gold cord, but it fled him, as it always did. Next came a cord of blackened green and sandy brown—Beef's—but he discarded that one.

C'mere, you. The other six strands flashed with opalescent hues, each singing in a key once removed from the others. The first two were twined around each other, bright green-gold and purple-black in a complicated braid, while the next was a pale blue mingled with gold and sepia. The fourth cord was a murky, virulent green and bloody red, while the fifth was an iridescent white, like clouds across a blazing sunset. The last was hidden at the bottom, squirming almost as much as Imara's, and was a deep, dark brown, bordering on black.

He gripped them all, seizing them between his two hands and holding them tight. His Bastion lurched once, twice, three times before Felix was ripped into the distance, and everything became a series of streaking lights. A gulf opened up beneath him, a distance of vast, incomprehensible enormity as barriers of light shattered against his Willpower and clutched Intent. Razor-edged shards sliced at him, at his hands, and Felix ground his teeth so hard he felt two break. He held on as the world became a hurricane of light.

He was swept into a jungle of thick foliage, hot and steamy against his skin, to find two small creatures running along thick, moss-covered branches. They were almost identical, save for coloration, and appeared to be some sort of reptilian dog. *Horned reptilian dogs*, he realized. Mottled brown fur covered them both, but scales shimmered across their necks, faces, and limbs as they ran. One was golden green and the other a purple-black, and as he watched, the ground thundered with others.

Crudely armored men mounted atop massive boars came down the jungle path, trampling underbrush as they leveled short bows against the fleeing reptiles. "Kill them! First one gets half the loot!"

The bandits whooped in savage glee, firing a salvo of arrows that burst into flames, ice, and even lightning. Each and every shot, however, was met by a tangling whip of growing vines, catching or slapping the projectiles out of the air. Felix could trace the Mana use back not just to the green-gold lizard-dog, but also the purple-black one. Flowers of darkest purple bloomed along more vines that the boars ran across, ripping them apart to release clouds of noxious green pollen. The rear-most bandits clutched at their necks and faces, suddenly unable to breathe, before they and their violent-looking boars collapsed onto the ground.

"Poison! Damn Kobolds're usin' poison!" one shouted. "Spread out! Don't breathe!"

Felix grinned. The Kobolds were still running, almost out of sight by that point, but Felix felt his vantage point shift to follow them. *They* were Unbound, just like him. He could literally feel it.

Yet, as soon as he did, the world blurred once more, and Felix stumbled. When he righted himself, he was standing in...a library. *Oh wow. This is nice.*

All around him were books and shelves, some of which weren't even on the floor, but floating in the air like in a dream. The walls, what he could see of them, extended up so high Felix wasn't entirely sure there was a ceiling. Books and scrolls and tomes covered every conceivable surface, even the bottom of the dozens of balconies that dotted it all. And before him, seated atop a marble plinth with her legs crossed and eyes closed, was another Unbound.

She had the head of a deer—a doe, he supposed—and large, branching antlers. Robes the color of the sky and banded with silver and a muddy brown color across the sleeves and chest were draped across her broad, muscular form, and heavy forearms more commonly seen on warriors or smiths rested gently along the spine of a closed tome. More books floated around her, missing her antlers by the tiniest of margins as they floated on delicate traceries of blue Mana. *Force, mingled with some metal and...sound Mana, apparently. Interesting. What are these books?*

That was all he got, however, because once more, the world blurred.

His hand ached and burned, a phantom pain perhaps, or a memory of the cords that fought against his grip. Felix's step forward to grasp a book ended with him half-submerged in thick, god-awful-smelling muck.

"Oh gross," he grunted, pulling himself free with some effort. The muck didn't cling to him, but it did resist his efforts to climb out of it, somehow. It was distracting enough that he barely noticed the huge yellow eyes that watched him from only feet away. By the time Felix fully noticed them, the figure had emerged from the muck like a rising titan, filling the space of the strange, cramped tunnel he had found himself within. "Uh, hi there."

The figure didn't speak, only lunged with its huge, toothy maw open. A whirlwind of sensations accosted Felix, but there was no pain, just more blurring as the connection spun onward.

Okay. Not looking forward to meeting that one. Felix steadied himself, lights still streaming in a dizzying display around him. *How'd he even see me? I'm not there.*

The world resolved itself to a clifftop, where the world was apparently sheared in two. Below Felix, the cliff fell for what looked like an eternity, until silver clouds swallowed the flat plane of split earth. Music sounded close by, high and bright like a concerto of woodwinds alone, and the rushing wind increased in speed.

Over a hundred figures swooped low over the cliff, coming from somewhere above and behind Felix, to dive down into the silver clouds in a cascade of brilliant feathers. So many colors, ranging from emerald green and deep purple to lemon yellow and royal blue, many of them attached to a single pair of wings in a wild show of plumage. It wasn't until the figures rose back up and out of the silver clouds that he realized that they weren't birds at all.

They were people.

Specifically, they looked like Elves on a serious diet. Slender and sharp-featured, it was no wonder why their wings lifted them so easily. Felix also spotted trails of air Mana flowing around each and every one.

Which one is the Unbound, though? It was a massive flock of them, all flying in sync like it was a dance, their combined plumage forming colorful patterns in the sky that only heightened the trilling sounds of Harmony Felix could hear. Their spiraling flight was almost hypnotic, and he barely noticed that the world once again blurred into motion. Only the faint burning in his hands reminded him, and Felix jerked to a sudden stop at the edge of yet another precipice. This one, however, was within the dark earth, where only the faint, bioluminescent light of weird mushrooms dotted the walls.

"Now where am I?" he asked.

There was a snuffling in the dirt and stone, and without another warning, a creature emerged as if walking out of a pool of water. They were small, barely three feet tall, and with skin that looked like it had been burned or was very, very dirty. Felix blinked. Or...their skin *was* dirt, as eyes as bright as jewels panned around the narrow cavern.

This must be the Gnome, Felix thought. *Weirdest Gnome I've ever seen.*

As he watched, the Gnome jolted before running and diving down, back into the solid stone. It parted for them like water, swallowing them completely just as a glowing ball of golden light approached the crevasse. An armored figure was there, strapped with enough weapons to furnish an army and trailed by a hand-wringing old priest.

"Imara," Felix muttered.

The woman stopped, and in a motion faster than Felix could perceive, unsheathed and thrust a long sword straight through his chest. His hands and chest burned, scorching him like never before as everything around him dissolved into streaks of glimmering light.

"—what was that?" the priest asked.

"Nothing. A ghost."

The voices turned to dust, and Felix was thrust away as the world shattered once again.

CHAPTER THIRTY-SEVEN

"Felix, stop!"

Felix heard nothing but the roar of discordant harmonies, felt nothing but the searing heat against his hands and chest. The ritual tore apart, the layers of sigaldry flaring and burning out as the entire array collapsed under the weight of his charge. Potent energies ripped at him, slashing harmlessly at sudden black scales, but slicing his Garment to shreds. He landed outside the formation, hissing in pain and tearing at his shirt. The rest of his Garment was rent, revealing that the glowing cyan markings upon his chest and arms had turned a virulent, burning crimson.

W-what? The pain faded quickly, red turning to purple then blue, until there was only the phantom memory of its burning. Felix ran his claws over his naked chest, but instead of tenderness, he found only hale flesh and diamond-hard scales. *How the hell did she sense me?*

The array broke down, devolving into a screaming mess of feedback and flaring, multi-hued lights. Zara hissed, the sound itself infused with a musicality that cut through the cascading dissonance like a knife. The lights faded, smothered by her Will, the very markings upon the floor scrubbed and slashed through in mere seconds. It was over so fast that his Garment hadn't even managed to reconstitute itself, only just dragging itself back up his legs into the semblance of ragged pants. Felix hunched, rubbing at his chest, as Zara approached.

"Avet's darkened eyes, Felix. What was that? Why did you sever the ritual?" she asked.

"*I* didn't," he explained, before going into a breakdown of all the figures he saw through the haze of his connections. "...and when I was looking at the last, the Gnome I think, that armored Imara showed up. She's clearly hunting for him."

"And the priest?"

"He was there, too. But, Zara..." Felix licked his lips, the memory of it still forcing his heartbeat to speed up. "She heard me. Sensed me. I was hooked onto the Gnome, but *she* reacted and stabbed me through the chest." He gestured to the scorched room and now-faded sigils. "That's why this all happened."

Zara paled. "Damnation. Did none of the others react to you?"

"One did. The big lizard guy, though I didn't see much of him except his eyes. He attacked me the moment I showed up." Felix grimaced. "He was in some nasty place. Sewers, maybe. Still, when he attacked, it just forced me onward to the next connection, and it didn't hurt."

"Perhaps it is a thing of the Unbound. You are preternaturally gifted with the Chant, Felix. If they have pushed their abilities as far, then it is not unreasonable they could sense a glimmering of the harmonics that you were exploiting. I will have to speak with Mauvim and seek her counsel."

"Mauvim? Your boss?" Felix asked. She hadn't mentioned much of her organization, other than there was a network of Sorcerers out there.

"My friend and superior in the Order, yes. We speak through the artifact I mentioned to you." She straightened her robes, dusting pieces of charred chitin from her shoulders. "I hope that you will join me when I next speak to her."

"Yeah," Felix said. "I'd like that. Where's the artifact?"

"Here, in my quarters, but engaging its power atop water is an impossible task. The interference of the waves disrupts the delicate harmonics of the ritual. We will have to wait until we've weighed anchor and found solid land again."

Felix nodded. "Right. Two more days 'til landfall, at least that's what the Yttin suggest. We can take a short pit stop in Bogfeld. I promised those Menders I'd talk to them about selling healing supplies."

"A wise transaction. We can resupply and move toward the Shadowgate quickly from there. But," Zara held out a hand, halting Felix as he stepped toward the exit. "These visions of the Unbound...Felix, I believe it is wisest to hold that information close. The less that know of their appearances and their relative locations, the better."

"Even Isla?" Felix asked. It was part jab and part genuine curiosity. He didn't like the lady, but Zara had insisted time and again that she was trustworthy. "Shouldn't she know?"

Zara scowled, bearing her shark-like teeth. "Even her. I cannot risk the Unbound, not if the Hierocracy already has one and is actively hunting the rest."

"That's fair. I'll keep my mouth shut. When we talk to your boss, we can figure out the best way forward." He resumed his walk, only pausing at the door as a hard emotion welled up in his chest. It burned, like stubborn rage and tired, immutable conviction. "Just be aware, I'm going to do what is best for my people. And that includes the Unbound. Understand?"

"I do," she said, and her scowl eased into something softer, more earnest. "But remember, Felix, I am tasked with your care, as well. The Unbound are our hope, and you are...a friend. I would be a fool to squander that."

"Hm," Felix grunted, unsure how to respond. So he gave her a half-nod and pulled open the door. "You would be."

Despite the constant storm and ceaseless swells, the journey proved to be mostly unremarkable. No more monsters accosted their fleet since the Regalia was sealed, and even the waves weren't so bad. The Manaships thrummed along, their engines drawing just enough power to augment the sails, going faster than most cars, by Felix's estimation. All of that quiet meant more time to train...for everyone.

Darius and Harn pressed the Claw hard in the days that followed. While Beef continued the swimming regimen Felix had devised, soon Giants and Henaari and Legionnaires of all stripes were in the water with him, pushing their Bodies to the limit. It became a game at a certain point, a race much as it had with Beef and Evie, with the fastest swimmers then engaging in a waterlogged spar atop the nearest ship. It ran them all ragged, even Beef, but none could deny the effects.

Skill levels rose by the handful. New Skills were learned, polished, and pressed into Apprentice Tier or beyond. Atar continued to improve as well, joining in on some of the sparring as he wrestled with his core space and new Skills. More surprising was Alister, who had developed a few Harmonic stats and even evolved his Greater Force Shielding into Rampart of the Unyielding Vow, an Epic-rarity Skill. It was potent, too, and far less costly to maintain in addition to being remarkably effective against melee fighters. More than once, Felix witnessed an entire Talon turned aside by the force barrier, their charge blunted while Alister fired off a pinpoint barrage of Grand Impetus.

The evolution was an unexpected event, but Felix made sure to keep an eye on Alister's core space after that. Not just his, either. The Claw as a whole were slowly evolving their Skills. Felix made it a point to use Fiendforge on every single one of them, inspecting their cores and attempting to monitor the connection he'd formed with them all. It wasn't so blatant as the Links with his closest allies, but there was a glimmering to all of their core spaces, no matter how varied they were.

Red-gold and blue-white light lingered, just out of immediate sight, limning the edges of cores that were represented by waves and clouds and swords and once, horrifyingly enough, by a giant statue of *himself.* It was a huge one, cast from some greenish metal and surrounded entirely by weapons half-sheathed in the earth. Felix had made sure to keep clear of that particular Claw member.

A number of the Claw even combined their Skills, fusing things like Dodge and Acrobatics and Running into the Uncommon rarity movement Skill, Nimble Stride. Felix was there, utilizing his Fiendforge both for the experience but also to ensure nothing went wrong. The combinations and evolutions went off without a hitch, things that normally took an array and monster cores to fuel, all drawing on the ineffable connection they had to him. Felix could feel a small speck of significance flee him every time it happened, small enough that he barely felt it compared to the total weight within his core. To the warriors and mages of the Fiend's Claw, however, that speck hit them like a damn truck. Each and every one of them was laid out for hours after the event, and most were shaky for hours after.

"It's like swallowing the sky," one of them had muttered before passing out. Felix had only been able to shake his head and move on.

Get used to it. You'll need to face worse than that if you keep following me, he thought. He almost said it, but common sense caught up with him. He bent himself to his tasks instead.

Fiendforge is level 21!
...
Fiendforge is level 32!
Apprentice Tier!
You Gain:
+Decrease Significance Consumed In Forging!
+5% RES
+5% INE

He pushed himself hard, training alongside them all. He made time to spar with Evie, as well, and did not hold back. Evie wanted it no other way, though she complained when he defeated her every single time. Complaints turned to practice, however, their sparring continuing long into the first night. She managed to tangle him up a couple times...until Felix shattered her Chains of the Protector and defied her Bonds of Dominion, until it was all Evie could do to simply keep up with him. Felix stopped holding back. It helped none of them, and he needed to learn how to fight at his highest capabilities.

Relentless Resolution is level 79!

Chains sliced and slashed at him, ineffectual against Felix's scales, just as Evie's armor was pointless against his talons. Blood and sweat filled the sparring ring, but a grin never left Evie's bedraggled face, even when her Health dwindled closer and closer to zero. She would only swig a Health Potion and come back at him. She even managed to hit Adept Spirit while using her new Spirit Skills. By the end of their long hours sparring, all she required was her Mind, and she would fully Tier up into Adept.

More than once, Felix tried to practice with Vess, but she appeared to be avoiding everyone. She was either holed up in her room or in one of the ships' crow's nests. Whenever he spotted her, he could sense a rawness to her Spirit, enough that he shied away, unwilling to break her solitude even for training. From the little she'd mentioned to Evie, she was clearly still upset about her Skills and the Dragoons. That was his fault, he knew, and that knowledge burned at Felix. Yet there was nothing he could do, not according to Zara, as the Links he was forging were entirely new territory for even her.

So Felix distracted himself.

Their approach toward the Pass and Bogfeld beyond reminded him of the book he'd been given. *The Vicissitudes*, by Pagewright Vilas Tern, the same guy that Alister had hyped up in his core space. The book, however, was not about Manaships or ancient machinery. Instead, it was a dry academic tome of some sort. The words were hard to make out due to the overly flourished hand that had produced it, but it had a lot to do with the moral functions of power. It was a surprise to see, considering the attitudes of...just about everyone Felix had encountered in the Continent.

Alister was surprised to see it, too, and wasn't shy to say so when the mage spotted Felix reading on the stern deck. "Where did you get that?" he asked, mouth agape.

"A gift from the Prioress of the Menders." Felix raised an eyebrow at the mage's continued shock. "Why?"

Instead of explaining, Alister held out a trembling hand. "May I see it?"

"Sure." Nonplussed, Felix handed it over. Alister immediately began to comb through it, checking the back and front until he gasped. "What? What's going on?"

"Vilas Tern! The premier Pagewright of the Violet Tower in Levantier! This is a first edition, written in his *own hand!*" Alister practically gushed before he closed the tome reverently and handed it back. "And it is one of many books that was banned by the Lucent Towers themselves."

"Banned? For what? All I can tell is that it talks about morality and governance. Ah, right," Felix interrupted himself. *Of course.*"No one wants to hear about that, do they?"

"Indeed they don't. Tern is a controversial figure, though he remains to be held in high esteem for his work on the Manaship. This particular tome, along with others, were not as well-received. Nations outright banned him and his circle from entering their borders, and the backlash on the Lucent Towers was remarkable."

"Yeah." Felix looked at the table of contents, noting the entries. "'The Argument For The Dissemination Of Titles' and 'Treatise On The Functions Of The Omen' sound dangerous, if you're an asshole who controls information."

Alister paled. "Little is known about the contents of that book, save for dedicated collectors. Simply suggesting that everyone share how they receive specific Titles would be enough to cause an uproar, let alone frank discussion of what an Omen might mean and the advent of an Omen Path." Alister shook his head, awe and worry warring for space in his Spirit. "These are secrets everyone keeps close to their chest, for to reveal them would—for many—feel like they were weakening themselves."

"Hm, and yet, information fuels subconscious preconceptions," Felix said, mostly to himself.

"It does. Some scholars suggest that the reason the guilds and societies of the Continent maintain secrets is to protect us from the wrong sort of knowledge." Alister scoffed and spat over the railing. "Knowledge is knowledge. I'll not let others determine what I can and cannot peruse...not if I have the power to do something about it."

"Want to read it after me?" Felix offered.

Alister just about lit up. "Yes! If you don't mind?"

He didn't, obviously. Felix read through the book fast, his Perception and Intelligence working with the potent formation of his Mind to devour the information it contained. The grammar was archaic compared to a few of the other books he'd read, and the jargon was a bit unfamiliar in parts, but it was by and large understandable. There was nothing inside it that Felix found terribly controversial, but it was nice to see someone else contemplating the same ideas he had, ideas that Zara had continually told him were impossible to implement in the Continent.

Felix had been told that certain things about advancement could not be conveyed, as it would shape their growth, spoiling their potential. The book claimed that many others used the exact reasoning to squash any and all information on gaining and maintaining power through the System, and Felix thought it was just as bogus as Tern apparently did.

He couldn't really gainsay the remarks about advancement; Felix trusted that Zara, Vess, and Harn were all telling him the truth, but surely there was a line. What else were the guilds and societies and organizations good for? They provided training in specific ways to build their members up, whether it was a crafting apprenticeship or a mage's guild, secret Skills and Titles that would give their people an edge over others.

Why couldn't he do the same? Just more...expansively?

So, aside from the violence and exhaustion of spars and training and Fiendforging, Felix set part of his Mind to worrying at that obstacle. In what felt like the blink of an eye, two entire days passed...and the shouts from the crow's nest came.

"Mountains! Stormeater Peaks five leagues distant!"

Felix thought it remarkable that no one had spotted them sooner, but the answer to that revealed itself as they drew closer. The Stormeaters were proving true to their name as a line of pitch-black clouds boiled against their sides. Each dark cloud was a calamitous thunderhead, and lightning screamed across them while torrential rain and fist-sized balls of hail crashed into the water and mountains in a veil of violence.

"Burn me, *that's* what the Storm Ward is doing?" Atar asked. "It's obscuring the Pass entirely!"

The Storm Ward was a tangible presence, at least to Felix, and his Authority Screen pinged at him. He could feel his influence weave through the clouds, and following that feeling, Felix sent his Intent snaking up and into the hidden sigaldry far above. His Authority trembled once before strengthening, like a flexed muscle. With a single raised hand, Felix parted the storm entirely.

"Blind gods..."

"...with a wave of his hands!"

Mutters and shouts rippled across his ship, and more likely sounded down the fleet, but Felix found his Authority curiously tenuous, perhaps because it was the edge of his Territory. Regardless, he had to place a considerable amount of his concentration on holding the storm away, allowing his ships to pass through it unmarred.

He could not say the same for the Stormeater Peaks and the Caleph Pass.

"What happened here?" Evie peered over the railing, taking in the enormous rents in the once-smooth walls of the Pass. "Looks like a monster clawed through it."

Felix's eyes, however, were on the water itself. It lapped against the highest point of the Pass, a patch of stone and soil that had once held a massive wall that Felix had conjured from the earth. The wall had been smashed to pieces. Some rubble had been tossed toward the sea, but the vast majority of it was collapsed inward toward the Ghreldan Hills and Bogfeld.

"The sea." The worry that had been coiled in his chest unfurled. "The sea pushed through the Caleph Pass." *Is that what the Territorial Boundary Warning meant?* he wondered.

A Spirit blazed above them, and Felix felt its sudden terror as if it were his own.

"Monster sighted! Monster sighted!" the Yttin lookout shouted.

A wave lifted from the waters ahead of them, as tall as their ship, twice as wide, and crested with a forest of vicious, razor-sharp dorsal fins.

And it was coming straight for them.

CHAPTER THIRTY-EIGHT

Voracious Eye!

Name: Fathom Depthwurm
Type: Draconic (Manawarped)
Level: 92
HP: 15943/15943
SP: 10003/11248
MP: 8301/8439
Lore: A corrupted version of a true lindwurm, the Depthwurm has been immersed in the warping influence of the Fathom until it has been irrevocably changed. Able to command many of its lesser brethren, a Depthwurm is a dangerous foe to face, especially within range of its Den.
Weakness: More Data Required
Strength: More Data Required

"Hold tight!" The wave washed over his flagship at the same time Voracious Eye's info did, and Felix dropped low as the entire boat was soaked, bow to stern. "Adamant Discord!"

A blast of lightning sang into existence between Felix's outstretched hand and the approaching nightmare. It seared into Felix's vision, slamming through the water and into the scaled hide only fifty feet from their deck. The Depthwurm screamed and twisted away from the attack, its long, serpentine neck lifting entirely from the water as its voice turned from muffled screech to a bone-shaking bellow. It was easily fifty feet tall and twenty wide, and that was just the part of its Body above the water.

Not one but *two* heads writhed at the ends of that neck, both shaped like arrowheads given sentience and hatred for all things.

"Blind gods, it's a Tier V," Atar said from behind him.

Felix could only nod in mute agreement. If Tier 0 were the same as a Beginner-Tier warrior, then Tier V was something like a high Adept or low Master Tier. The comparison wasn't entirely one-to-one, but Felix could feel a significant well of power in the serpentine horror's Body. Not even his Adamant Discord stopped it, and Felix was shoved back a dozen yards as the Depthwurm continued to advance. "Everyone, open fire!"

His Claw, many of them on deck for the approaching Pass, now unleashed a flurry of Skills and spells. Bolts of lightning and shadow and fire and acid arced outward along with a volley of arrows infused with flickering vapor. The Depthwurm reared back at their approach, but the attacks hit and shattered against its blue-clad hide, doing nothing. It bellowed again, and this time it was like a thousand car horns attached to a squealing speaker, and it sent a burr of Dissonance crawling across Felix's brain. All at once, the waves *boiled*, churning to reveal the approach of dozens, no *hundreds* of Human-sized shapes hurtling across the water.

Voracious Eye!

Name: Fathom Hatchling
Type: Draconic (Manawarped)
Level: 45
HP: 1443/1443
SP: 1100/1127
MP: 400/400
Lore: The least of the Fathom spawn, the Hatchlings are fish-like humanoids that are aggressive and cruel. Like all Fathom spawn, they will toy with their food before eating it, often keeping their prey alive for days before consuming them.
Weakness: Vulnerable to heat and fire. Agility and Strength reduced when sufficiently dried
Strength: Agility and Strength increased while in the water, and large eyes see easily in dark, stormy conditions.

Felix had apparently killed enough of them to gather details on their weaknesses and strengths. It was all stuff he'd noticed but didn't actively think on, but Voracious Eye was good at compiling all that information in a useful way.

"Hatchlings! Coming in fast! Pit!" Across their bond, Pit focused on him. He was two ships back, surrounded by shouting sailors and anxious

Claw members. "Pit, get the ships to move up. We have Hatchlings incoming!" He sent the image of them swarming forward through the bond, and he felt his Companion surge into action, shouting out orders to the people around him. "Everyone! Refocus! Take down the Hatchlings!"

The volley of spells and projectiles were redirected into the water, and there was such a mass of monsters that every one hit something. The creatures were strong, though, and they did not die easily, even to high Apprentice Tiers.

Rain of Cataclysm!

Undulating tides of liquid Mana surged from Felix's channels, invisible to the normal eye, but as viscous as oil to his own senses. It changed from a sparking, fiery blue to a thick, virulent green as it flooded the sky, filling the air around his ship in only a few seconds. Its song rose in a crescendo, the chords coming faster and tighter, furiously played against his Affinity until the spell hit its height...and burst into sudden violence. Droplets of acid rain fell from the cloud, each one driving downward with all the force of an executioner's axe.

You Have Killed A Fathom Hatchling (x23)!
XP Earned!

Hatchlings died in droves, but the spell took too long to set up; already, there were more climbing up the sides of their ship, and others that swam around, rushing at the others in his fleet. *The Claw will have to deal with them.* Felix couldn't hold the spell too close to the ships, or else he risked killing his own people. Worse, holding Adamant Discord and Rain of Cataclysm pulled at his concentration, not normally an issue for him...except that he was also still holding the storm above them at bay.

This is pointless. Felix dropped Adamant Discord, firming his Intent upon his Authority and the cloud of acid rain. The last thing they needed was for a lightning-infused hailstorm to drop on top of them all. The Depthwurm could dive below the surface; they couldn't. "Beef! Evie!" he shouted as he spotted his friends. "On me!"

As Hatchlings crested the railings to meet sword, club, fist and spell of his people, Felix surged into the sky on a bolt of light. Behind him came a bovine bellow and a harsh, higher-pitched laugh as Evie soared up in his wake. She winked at Felix as she approached, her Body rising atop the winds as if she weighed nothing. Below, Beef splashed powerfully into the water, smashing his great maul down around him.

"Evie, lock it up," Felix ordered.

The grin on her face grew wider, and there was murder in her eyes as she uncoiled her chain and suddenly fell like a rock. "Bindings of the

White Waste! Chains of the Protector!" she shouted, laughing all the while.

Icy links tore from the water, wrapping around the massive Depthwurm like coiling snakes. White frost climbed across its scales, and the water began to freeze in large chunks, forcing another shriek from the monster's twin maws. They snapped up at her as she fell, fangs and pink tongues lashing toward her...only to run nose first into a twenty-foot-wide shield. It held only a moment before the Depthwurm's Strength, but when it broke, it turned into a mess of glowing chains that wrapped themselves around one of its two snouts. It recoiled, wrenching its neck backward in alarm as its jaw was suddenly tied shut, distracting it just long enough for Evie to fall into range.

"Bonds of Dominion! Tooth and Claw! Reap the Maelstrom!" Skills tumbled from her tongue as Evie turned into a whirlwind of motion. Silver, purple, and a deep blue flashed, her chain blades doubling in size and speed as they sliced into and through scales as large as her own Body. Dark ichor poured free, and the Depthwurm shrieked in rage and pain before its free head twisted on itself and darted toward its enemy.

"No you don't! Circle of Slam!" Came a hearty holler, before the Depthwurm was forcefully jerked to one side. Water erupted far below, where Beef clung to the monster's swimming Body. He was soaking wet with sea water and blood in equal measure. "Chitin Construction!"

Spikes of dark chitin shot from Beef's maul, embedding themselves into the Depthwurm's hide. It barely flinched...until Beef slammed them home with a second swing of his hammer, piercing scales and flesh alike. The monster screeched and dove its free head down at the bloody Minotaur...only to find a slab of ice rising out of the water and into its face.

Felix grinned, still hovering a hundred feet in the air. The Rimeshaping had been enough to give Beef a chance to climb up his impromptu spike stairs, slamming more and more into the monster's hide as he climbed its length. The twin heads chased after the two of them, Evie and Beef, and for the moment, they were fine.

Below, the other ships had pulled forward, and surprisingly, the horde of Hatchlings was being handled. A shield of bright blue had formed atop the waves, forcing many of the Fathom spawn into attacking one ship, upon which was a man glowing with white fire. Atar stood on the ship's prow, white hair looking like fire itself as he hurled stars of incandescent heat at the monstrosities.

The water was now literally boiling, bubbling and steaming as the fire mage's powerful Skills cooked the Hatchlings alive or burned through them entirely. Zara and Isla were there, wielding flashy powers like conductors of an orchestra, each hand gesture ending dozens of Fathom spawn. The Frost Giants were out in the water itself on rafts of ice, axes and spears moving with power and precision as they mowed through their foes. Arrows and ranged Skills of many stripes descended, supplementing the damage Felix still continued to do with his Rain of Cataclysm.

The Depthwurm moved, its huge bulk displacing gargantuan waves that crashed into the ships below. His friends were hurled free, both of them sent spinning into the foaming spray shortly before a thick, spiked tail slashed upward out of the water.

Right toward the ships.

No! Felix dropped with a final burst of Adamant Discord. The Storm Ward surged, fighting against his distracted Authority, squirming to continue functioning as it was designed. Felix couldn't pay it any mind, and instead flared Adamant Discord again and *pulled* with every ounce of Strength and Willpower he had.

Felix plummeted like a comet, fists outward, and hit the Depthwurm with the momentum of a very heavy man falling at above terminal velocity. The creature was tough, so its scales barely split as Felix hit, but its entire Body was hurled backward, folded in on itself as it was driven backward into the sundered cliffs of the Caleph Pass.

It sounded like a hundred Fourth of Julys all at once, a titanic blast of concussive force that shattered stone and toppled knotted, wizened trees that dotted the peaks. Felix and the Depthwurm rolled, its immense Body crushing and scraping against the cliffs, smashing him into the incredibly hard stone with every frenetic undulation. Rocks tumbled and crashed, scrub tore free, and the Storm Ward crackled in an imitation of anger.

Wild Threnody!

Arrow of Perdition!

Felix yanked out his hooked sword and channeled the power of his Skill through it and his own clawed fist. Both cut into the Depthwurm's scales, sending it rolling with greater ferocity, but Felix didn't pause. He stabbed deep, digging with his left hand until ichor and innards began to fall atop him like a vile, boiling stew. The Fathom spawn scrabbled against the mountains, cracking the rocks even further, but it could not dislodge him. Felix fell, sword and claw tearing a mighty gash into the Depthwurm's neck, until he hit the thicker protrusion of its torso. Flanked by its clawed paws, he immediately could sense the thrumming vibration of its heart...and its monster core.

He started digging.

Ichor and offal spilled out, drenching Felix and staining the rocks. The Depthwurm went ballistic, heaving its bulk across the cliffs in an effort to shake him free, even clawing at its own chest, but Felix batted its awkward attempts away. He glowed with azure and golden light, a clarion song that drove him ever deeper, even as the flesh began to rapidly heal itself. Regrowing muscle threatened to push Felix out, right into the waiting, dual jaws of the beast...but chains of ice and ghostly light snagged into its limbs and neck, while a huge Multipede crawled atop its snout and bound it shut once more.

"Where's Felix!"

"Inside, you lummox!"

"What?! GROSS!"

Given respite from the Depthwurm's violent movements, Felix put his friends out of his Mind. With his Strength and Agility, he moved like a wood grinder, going so far as to sheath his Inheritor's Will and focus entirely upon his talons. He burrowed deeper, a sense of déjà vu tingling in his memories of the time he fought and killed the Larval Ravager.

And, just as then, creatures began to writhe from within the innards of the Depthwurm, parasites that were wurms themselves. Tube-like and filled with teeth, they lunged for him without warning, but Felix burned them all as he switched to channeling his Rain of Cataclysm through his Wild Threnody. Mantle of the Infinite Revolution turned, igniting Felix's form with red-hot flame that cauterized the flesh around him, slowing down its healing as he tore deeper. Deeper. Until it was there. The monster core, shaped as a huge black pearl, lumpy and misshapen and glowing with a brilliant light.

More of the parasites surged, coming from all directions. It was all Felix could do to keep the Depthwurm from regenerating, fight off the parasites, and keep the Storm Ward at bay. His Mind trembled, the weight of Authority far greater than activating a dozen Skills at the same time. It was clear: if he wanted to land the killing blow on the monster's core, he needed to drop his hold on the Storm Ward.

Adamant Discord!

Lightning tore outward, back along the path he'd carved, and wrenched the lot of it wide. Gooey innards parted, newly healed flesh tearing again, until he could see the dark stormclouds above them. Alone, he'd have to choose the death of an enemy over the safety of his people. "Vess!"

But he wasn't alone.

From the sky where he'd felt her presence, a blazing spear of howling wind tore down and into the Depthwurm's guts. Even as the reopened wound tried to heal, Vess tore through it, blasting downward to hit with the impact of a damn bomb. Felix threw up his arms, skin covered now in full scales as her Draconic Stormfall *shattered* the Depthwurm's core.

You Have Killed A Fathom Depthwurm!
XP Earned!

The parasites all died, the flesh immediately stopped its hectic healing, and Felix dropped every Skill he held before reaching out and claiming it all.

Chthonic Tribute!

Around them, Vess and Felix, the gargantuan creature turned to greasy, light-filled smoke. It streamed into him while his Hunger rumbled in happiness, and his Divine Tree blossomed with new, vibrant Essence foliage. Body now gone, the two of them dropped several feet onto a blasted and scraped rock shelf, barely jostled by the transition from monster guts to wind-scoured cliff face.

"Hm," she started, wiping a bit of smoke from her partisan. It flowed over toward Felix and was pulled into his mouth. "How did you know I was there?"

"How did you know I was?" he asked.

Vess' lips quirked, as if she were fighting down a smile. "Thick of battle, fighting the biggest and worst monster, hip-deep in trouble? Where else would you be?"

Felix laughed. "Fair." He ran a hand through his hair and reminded himself again that he needed a haircut. At the very least, his Tribute had removed all the nastiness that had been in it. "I'm glad you showed up, though. Really. That strike was—"

Your Enemy's Essence Has Been Digested!
Memory Detected!
Do You Wish To View?
Y/N

CHAPTER THIRTY-NINE

"At least it is offering you a choice, now," Vess said.

"At least there's that," Felix agreed.

"Hey! You guys okay?" Beef landed on their narrow rock shelf with a stumbling grunt. His maul was a broken stump in his hands and trailed a haze of necromantic Mana. "Did you...did you explode it from the inside?"

"More or less, yeah," Felix said. "You good?"

Beef's fur was a matted mess, but most of it looked like dark ichor and not blood. He thumped his breastplate with a fist. "Me? I'm invincible!"

"Yeah?" Evie landed beside him with far greater grace; like a bird, almost. Her chain was coiled neatly around her waist again. "I saw a Hatchling stab you in the mouth while riding your horns like a Goblin on an Avum."

"What's an Avum?"

"Gah! My only weakness," Evie said, tutting. "You're too stupid to insult."

"Hah! Wait—"

Ignoring them, Felix looked out over the crashing sea and his fleet of ships just beyond. The decks were awash in magical projectiles, but the waters were almost empty of Hatchlings. "Looks like they're mopping up the rest just fine, but let's be sure. Beef, Evie. Go clear 'em out."

"You—Oh, aye aye, cap'n," Beef said with a mock salute. He nudged Evie, maybe a little harder than he should. "Race you down, tiny?"

"Avet's eyes, I'll beat you twice."

Felix smiled as the two leaped from the cliff face and down into the tumultuous sea. He sat with a small groan on the uneven ground. "I'm gonna check out the Memory. Watch over me?"

Vess shifted, planting her spear. "Can you keep holding off the harsh edge of the Storm Ward?" The wind teased her hair out of her thick braid, and she tucked it back absently.

"I think so. I'm not running any other Skills, with the System or Chant. A Memory dive shouldn't be too much to handle."

"Then, of course."

"Thanks." Felix wanted to say something more, ask her about her core space and how she was feeling...but instead, he just closed his eyes and mentally selected *Yes.*

Perhaps because of his Adept Mind or simply ease of use, the process happened fast. The world faded into a deep monochrome gray then rippled before bursting into a thousand shards of light.

The shards revealed a black expanse, similar to his core space but more akin to the Void itself. Felix flexed his Willpower, and the black shattered, too, unveiling a wild array of Depthwurms, thousands upon thousands of them all stacked atop one another like the world's weirdest conga line. Each one, he knew, was a Memory fixed at some point in the Depthwurm's timeline. There, at the center, was the Depthwurm with its chest burst apart; its most recent Memory. Its past snaked backward through, over, and across every conceivable inch of the space, until Felix was swimming in a mess of scales and twinned heads.

Felix drifted through the Memory space, idly wondering where it was even stored now that the monster was dead. He had a feeling it was somewhere inside of himself, which was interesting for several reasons, but he didn't let it distract him. He focused, feeling about with his Affinity just as he shaped his Intent: *why were the Fathom waiting here?*

An ephemeral feeling drew him onward, strengthening with every Depthwurm iteration he passed, until he came upon a version of the creature that only had a single head and seemed a touch smaller. Bracing himself, Felix reached out and grabbed hold.

—flicker—

Felix opened his eyes, curiously standing exactly where he had been before: on the rocky shelf at the edge of the Stormeater Peaks.

"Huh."

Below him, the waters were in even greater turmoil than before, rising far higher, too, as they rushed violently through the Caleph Pass. There was no dry land, no hump of stone and soil, just a continuous, raging river driving forcefully into the Ghreldan Hills. Swimming through that river, however, was the Depthwurm. Upon its serpentine back, just out of the rushing waters, were two dozen or so Hatchlings. They clung with webbed claws to the Depthwurm's numerous dorsal spikes, even as the huge beast began to climb up one of the opposing peaks.

"What are you doing?" Felix muttered to himself.

The Depthwurm kept climbing, only stopping when it had reached a deep crevice, where it proceeded to claw and scrape at the rock. The Hatchlings all hopped off at that point and joined in on the digging. In short order, the crevice had been ripped wide open into a wide cavern that the Depthwurm shoved its wedge-shaped head into, wriggling itself further and further as Hatchlings carried off smaller bits of stone. Eventually, the thing disappeared entirely into the mountain, just as the skies blackened with billowing clouds.

Felix shaded his eyes against the sun, but the glare vanished as sigils replaced the blue expanse of sky and began to rotate. The clouds spewed from the arrays until there was a roof of thunderheads above him, and driving rains followed soon after. "Storm Ward."

He figured the Depthwurm was looking to evade the lightning and hail that soon pummeled the peaks...but as time flowed onward, hours turning rapidly to days, the creature emerged. This time, it had its second head and carried hundreds of Hatchlings upon its back as it dove into the tossing sea. Waves proved little obstacle for its powerful muscles, and the Fathom spawn shot off into the distance, yanking Felix's consciousness with them. Time blurred again, light rising and fading as days turned into a solid week...and Ahkestria itself rose before them.

"This is where they came from." Felix chewed his lip as the Memory began to flicker and fade. A hum dropped into his hearing, high to low, a thready pitch even without the boom of remembered thunder. The last he saw before it all winked out was the Depthwurm pushing off the crystalline base of Ahkestria, leaving deep scars in the otherwise potent material.

—flicker—

Felix opened his eyes, and for the last time, he sat upon the rock ledge above the Leviathan Depths. His attention wobbled, disoriented ever so slightly, and his grip on Authority slipped. Just a touch. The storm boomed, and a wave of hail and rain fell from the sky, forcing Vess to leap back with a curse.

"Ah! Sorry!" Felix clamped down on his Authority, steadying his grasp and reopening the corridor between the Pass and his fleet. "Trouble on the dismount. Oh."

A notification trilled, popping into view.

New Skill!
Ephemeral Evocation (Epic), Level 1!
You have learned through trial and error how best to steal

into the Memories of others, pulling details from their Minds that even they might have forgotten! Increases chance of salvaging Memories from a consumed target. Bonus to Intent when searching through Memories. Increases time spent within Memories in exchange for greater detail.

Felix let a smile stretch his lips, more pleased than he could say. His ability to glean Memories from those he'd consumed had long been a strength of his...but actually garnering a Memory was not a sure thing. This, however, was promising.

"What is it?" Vess asked. "Did you find what you required?"

"I think so. Also got a new Skill." Felix explained the Skill, briefly. Vess looked suitably impressed, but pivoted to stare at the opposite end of the Caleph Pass. "What?"

"The cavern it made. Now that you mention it, I can feel a...heat emanating from high up on that peak." Vess pointed with her spear before jabbing it back onto the stone. "I thought nothing of it before, but now I am certain it is their home. We must finish these draconics off, quickly."

"Agreed."

"It's a Den," Darius said, standing atop the lip of stone. He, Vess, Felix, and Evie all stood atop another rocky ledge, and a number of the Fiend's Claws, too. "You see the membrane?"

Felix did. A shimmering barrier stretched across the cavern's opening, almost invisible except when it caught the light at just the right angle. It reminded him viscerally of a Domain's entrance, and he said as much.

"That's because it is one...or will be, anyway." Darius ran a hand along the edge of the opening before rubbing his gauntleted fingers together. He grimaced in distaste. "A Den is the first stage of a monster congregation. Monsters sacrifice one of their number, stealing their core and nurturing it with resources until it grows large enough to shroud their home in a filmy barrier."

"The weight of it dimples the world, and the shroud builds up to keep it separate from the Corporeal Realm," Felix muttered, half to himself. He could feel a heaviness near the cavern's entrance, though it wasn't anything spectacular. "So, a Den is the first stage. Then Nest?"

"Den, Nest, Lair, Domain, in that order," Darius confirmed. "Though there is no rule saying a sufficiently powered core could not skip from Den to Lair. The only prerequisite seems to be the core resource of choice and monstrous population."

"More monsters, bigger worries," Evie said succinctly. "It's what Mags used to say."

"Apt, if a touch vague," the Hand allowed. "From the looks of this barrier, this Den was approaching somewhere around the halfway point. I don't think we fought nearly so many monstrosities down there, so I'd have to guess that more are inside."

Disgust at the Fathom spawn rose up in Felix—disgust and a tired anger. Felix let his Cardinal Flame billow outward, wreathing his hands in red-gold flame. "Fine. Then we flush the whole cavern."

"Wait!" Vess pressed a hand to Felix's chest, as if to stop him. He could have walked right through her gesture, but he stopped. "You read the Lore on the Hatchlings, yes? The System marked them as cruel, and that it toyed with their food—"

"Keeping their prey alive for days," Felix finished, his memory twigging onto the Lore entry. "Shit. You're thinking they have prisoners?"

"Snacks, as they would see it. I cannot believe they have not raided nearby settlements," Vess said. "And Bogfeld is just beyond the Pass."

"Blighted Night," Evie cursed quietly.

Felix wrestled down another surge of anger, this one cleaner and brighter than the tired thing he held previously. "You're right. Shit. We need to send people in, hunt them down, and rescue anyone they can. I'll lead the first team—"

"No can do, Blue Eyes," Evie said. "Remember when we all jumped into Haarwatch's Domain, and it got all shifty on us? You really think this little Den can handle me, let alone you walkin' through it?"

Months ago, they had entered a Domain on the verge of breaking apart. It had, eventually, but even stepping across its threshold had put undue strain on it, and that had been far stronger and reinforced with Guilder arrays. "What if it does? I thought a Domain breaking apart just meant the monsters were let loose. These monsters already can come and go as they please. So what's the difference?"

Darius folded his arms, still staring at the whisper-thin barrier before him. "Shrouds work strange. Rules of the Continent don't fully apply in there. A Den is gonna have the weakest effect in regards to that, but we can still expect some spacial warping. Break that, and the monsters will get alerted, but who knows what happens to the people inside."

"Shit," Felix growled. "Then what do we do?"

"We need to send a few Talons into the Den. Most of them are Apprentice Tier and won't disturb it too much. Those Hatchlings are tough, but they're a manageable hurdle." Darius looked at Felix, his expression an odd mix of impatient and awkwardly subservient. He was waiting for Felix's order.

"Alright. Do it." It pained Felix to put his people into danger when he couldn't be there...but he had to admit the Claw had grown by leaps and bounds. They had handled themselves well only twenty minutes prior, and all of them had topped off their store of potions. They were ready.

"Talon Leaders, forward!" Darius shouted, and six men and women of various Races stepped up. The Hand quickly explained the situation to the Talon Leaders, all of whom maintained serious, even grim expressions while Felix witnessed their Spirits soar in excitement.

Felix surveyed them, battling the conflicted emotions in his chest. He held them tight, careful to reveal nothing to their burgeoning Affinity stats, but couldn't help grinding his teeth. He felt like a wooden marionette, barely held up by the flutter of nerves in his gut and a stiff, pasted on look of vague approval.

It was enough to fool the warriors, at least.

Soon enough, the six leaders led their Talons forward and into the cavern. The barrier flexed and parted for them until they were all swallowed by the Den.

"And now we wait," Vess said through a frown.

The waiting took an entire two hours, and Felix was driven by anxiety to do *something*. So, he got the sailors and remainder of the Claw to begin crossing over the Caleph Pass.

The Pass, as he'd noticed before, rose up higher than the waves of the Leviathan Depths, providing a tall barrier against the sea. It rose up at the center, stone and soil mingling, and was also an impossible obstacle to their heavily modified Manaships. The Yttin crew, however, had ideas on how to surmount the issue, ideas that involved ramps, pulleys, and an entire crew's worth of Strength. Here, the Frost Giants proved their worth yet again, shouldering much of the burden of dragging the somewhat stripped down Manaships up the chitin-constructed ramps.

They had only pulled a ship halfway up the hill when the first Talon member emerged from the Den. Felix was so relieved to see that the first group had returned intact that he failed to recognize that the team were carrying piles of weapons and armor. Most of it was scuffed and dented, but all of it had a similar design to it, one that tickled at Felix's memory. Far more pressing and alarming were the people who followed *after* his Claw.

They were haggard and bloody, but most were walking under their own power. The few who weren't were laid out between two Claw members, grievously injured but alive. Goblins and Gnomes were perhaps the predominant prisoners, and from the reports the six Talon Leaders began to convey, it seemed the Den was a confusing maze of narrow tunnels. Bringing the taller Races into such places made little sense, especially if the Fathom spawn preferred to keep their food alive.

They bustled around, handing out Health Potions to those suffering the direst of wounds and Stamina potions to many others. Shock was thick on many of their Spirits, but perhaps Zara or Isla could do something to remedy that. They began the long process of ferrying folks down the cliff face to the ships below, while Felix turned over the glimmering blue jewel in his hands.

"—we killed the last of them, we believe. Our Perception was not enough to penetrate through the Den, but at the end,we were not quiet. I imagine any remaining foes would have rushed out to engage us, seeing how they are little more than mindless beasts," the burly Orc leader said to them. "My last man is inside with the core now, Lord Autarch. If you wish, we can retrieve him?"

Felix nodded along with the report, his Mind split along several thoughts. The last comment, however, caught him up. "He has the core? As in, the Domain Core?"

"He does. It is a Den core, water attuned. Do you wish for us to remove it?"

Darius met Felix's eye and nodded. "If there is no one left inside, then I suggest we do so. Removing the core will cause the shroud to collapse. Essentially, the same thing that would happen were you or I to walk through it."

Ahh. "Right. Then if you please," Felix said.

The Orc saluted and used the handsign for "removal" to one of his subordinates. They jogged back into the Den, returning in a few moments with a Hobgoblin woman carrying a fist-sized, deep-blue jewel. The thing glimmered in the half-light as the sun began to set, clearly potent for all its diminutive size...and behind her, the opening of the cavern flashed with a brilliant light before collapsing entirely on itself. Rock cracked and boomed, the cavern mouth spitting out streamers of dust, but soon it all settled.

The Hobgoblin passed the gemstone off to Felix, who took it with a great deal of interest. "Good. You all did a great job. Getting this many people out...I'm impressed. Go with them and see that your people rest."

The Orc saluted, as did the others, before all of the remaining Claw members began the winding trek back down the cliffs. To Darius, Evie, and Vess, Felix held up the gemstone Core, idly flaring his Voracious Eye.

Name: Den Core Of Abyssal Waters
Type: Domain Core
Lore: A low-tier monster core that has been converted into the beginning stages of a Domain.

"How does it grow?" Felix asked.

"Through the consumption of resources. Mineral, organic, it depends upon the Type. This is an aquatic Domain Core. It draws power from water and those that reside within it. Perfect for these Fathom," Darius said.

"And convenient for them that a sea simply sprang up out of nowhere," Felix growled. Evie took the Core from him gently and started peering at it. He let her. "These guys are getting on my nerves. They seem entirely too ready to pounce on this development. How?"

Evie hefted the Core in her hands. "They were fightin' the Nagafolk, yeah? Maybe things ain't going so well as that Deepking said they were."

"They must be eradicated," Vess stated, as if it were the only truth in the world. "They are clearly expanding. We cannot let them prey on any others."

"We must also return to Nagast," Darius added. "Zara would agree with me. War is coming to your Territory, Felix, something far worse than a couple attacks from some lizards. Draconic or not," he said, holding a hand out to his former ward.

"Draconic Types are a disease. They will spread, rapidly, if they have not already," Vess stated, real heat in her voice as she faced down against Darius' surprised expression. "I will not let them continue. I cannot, not if I am to uphold the Dragoon's vows."

"Vows that do not bind you, outside of the order as you still are."

"All prospective Dragoons must live by the vows as if they had already taken their Oath," Vess said. "You know this. I will not abandon them for convenience."

"It just means we need to hurry," Felix said, interrupting the two of them. Vess seemed truly angry. "Let's just make it to Bogfeld. We can regroup there."

CHAPTER FORTY

"Damnation." Zara rubbed at her wrists, feeling the chafe in her channels. "I envy your healing abilities, Isla. Supplementing the Chant for Skills is a rough endeavor."

Isla, looking more regal than some queens Zara had known, gave a simpering smile. "Your praise is as welcome as it is rare, Zara."

"Tsk, come now. Is this still about the boy? Felix would not have taken to you, even if I had lavished you with praise." Zara packed away another sachet of herbs. They stood within Zara's chambers on the third ship in their fleet, packing away the paraphernalia of healing. Now that the worst wounds among the Claw and Yttin sailors had been mended, it was time to move. They were settled well within the border between the Leviathan Depths and the Ghreldan Hills, just beyond the wall of rain, hail, and lightning that marked the now-resumed Storm Ward. The first and second ships were still in the process of being dismantled and hauled up the rise of the Caleph Pass, but theirs would be next.

"You could have tried," Isla sniffed. "I'd have liked some respect, even if I could not have his loyalty. But that boy stinks of disobedience and malcontent. He is trouble, Zara. I do not know why you have been so lax in his training."

Zara stiffened, her annoyance well-hidden to the eyes of those who passed, but Isla could read her as few others could. "You question my ways, when your own charge has been languishing within the deserts for over half a year?"

"Michael may be underleveled and below Tiered for the challenges ahead, but our circumstances required care." Isla shoved a bag of used potion bottles into a hay-filled crate. "We had the desert, undead, then the Hierocracy's minions to contend with. What vile forces did your Felix have to face?"

A shark's grin split Zara's face. "Enough."

Isla sniffed, this time in frustrated disappointment. The woman was fishing for information about her charge, asking all around the fleet about him in multitudinous ways. Zara could tell her, reveal Felix's secrets; it would be to one of her order, after all. Yet, some measure of Felix's caution had seeped into Zara. The Autarch was unwilling to give Isla a span lest she take a league, and Zara would honor his wishes.

Soon, we will talk to Mauvim, and he will see the truth of things, she assured herself. "But it is not a contest. There is no prize for enacting our duty, Isla. When we meet with the Cantus at Eventide, the measure of success will be whether we have saved the Unbound from the Hierophant or not. All else is...childish."

"Childish? To wish strength for those who we seek to thrust into the flames of contention? For one so old, your naivete would be charming, were it not so worrisome."

Zara's jaw clenched. Isla had always been good at pointing out Zara's weaknesses. Perhaps it was the healer's training she favored for all of her long life—she always knew just where to jab the knife. "Some call it naivete, others call it faith."

"Ah yes. Those robes are no idle costume for your Mask, are they? You truly are a chorister of Avet." Isla sighed, as if defeated. "You're right, I suppose. Only...the Ruin *is* coming. They must be ready to face its wrath."

"They will be," Zara assured her friend. She rested a long-fingered hand atop Isla's narrow, rather bony shoulder. "We are in a promising position with Felix. As Autarch, he has access to some rather remarkable resources, which shall make gathering the rest of the Unbound far easier."

Isla frowned. "What resources? Is that why you allow him such free reign?"

"He, as all others, has a Choice in all things. He faces those consequences, as we all must, but Felix has proven himself capable of snatching victory from the jaws of defeat."

"Hm. And here? All signs indicate the emergent sea did great damage to the Ghreldan Hills. That was his Choice as well." Isla stepped away from Zara's comforting hand. "I'd rather not see my charge make such rash decisions, not if I could stop him. Guide him."

"Guidance isn't coercion or control," Zara said. A familiar, angry heat burned at the back of her throat. "It is trust."

A sharp, rapid knock interrupted them. "Ah, Lady Zara?"

The two Chanters stopped their quiet conversation as the familiar, mustachioed face of Lieutenant Errol pressed into the room. The man was red-faced and sweating, an uncommon look for someone of his Temper. Zara raised an eyebrow. "Lieutenant? What is it?"

Errol swallowed twice before he could speak. "It is the Autarch, my Lady. He's gone."

Zara could feel Isla's gaze, the weight of her smug grin enough to sink their ship. She ignored it and focused on the Lieutenant. "Tell me everything."

From the top of the Pass, Felix could see the fortification that had once straddled the Ghreldan end of it. Like the wall that Felix had Stone Shaped into existence, this construction was also torn asunder, and it was alarming to behold. Towers and blocks the size of houses were tumbled down, strewn further back like a giant's toys. More worrisome, however, was that just beyond the fortification, the ripple of water lapped at its gates.

"This looks...bad," Pit said from beside him.

"Yeah." A pang of guilt stabbed at Felix. "We need to see more. C'mon."

The efforts to move the ships up the slope of the Pass was proving arduous at best, and while his magics could have sped it up a bit, there was a certain amount of anxiety that started to press against Felix's Mind. From the System, he knew something had changed the physical boundaries of the Leviathan Depths, establishing "new rivers" in the Ghreldan Hills. From the Depthwurm's Memory, he had seen the Caleph Pass flood so completely, it might as well have been one of those new rivers. It was guilt over the consequences of his actions that drove him forward, alone save for Pit.

He needed to know.

The Pass was steep and winding, and Felix took it at speed. A tiny cloud of dust kicked up in his wake as he descended, feet a blur and Pit flying just to keep pace. He came to a skidding halt, however, at the start of the old fortifications. The way was clear enough, the well-constructed keep now a hollowed-out shell. The waters Felix had unleashed had clearly swept much of its construction away, even all the way down to the foundations in places. At the midway point in the fort, well before they even reached the water, they spotted Bogfeld.

Or what was left of it.

The town was located less than a mile away from the Pass proper, connected by raised roadways and drawbridges, but all that was gone. Water was in its place, with only a number of the tallest trees rising above the placid waves. The town itself had been built on a sloping piece of raised terrain and had been fully walled. He supposed that was the only reason some of it still stood. Approximately half of the town was still submerged, with the far side only showing the tops of roofs peeking out. The flooding stopped around midway, where the slowly elevating ground resolved into some of the nicer homes and structures.

"Half the town's been flooded out." Felix peered into the water, its surface murkier than the Leviathan Depths. Bits of bark and vegetation filled it so much that even his Perception had a hard time seeing to the bottom.

"More than that," Pit pointed out, nodding his head toward the Low Side, where pieces of masonry still peeked above the water line. "Look. Something clawed through those walls. That Depthwurm paid Bogfeld a visit, too."

He was right. The more Felix looked, the more he could see signs of a struggle. A big one, too. Char marks on the stone, pillars of ice that still hadn't thawed, many of them hidden in the High Side streets. Those streets were as empty as the flooded ones, and at first, Felix thought it was because they were hiding from any further monsters. He was wrong, however, as he made out the two largest structures, both of which were largely untouched by flooding…but extremely marred by the telltale signs of monster attack.

"The Priory still stands," Felix remarked, pointing at the castle of the Menders, an order of healers dedicated to helping everyone. His eyes could make out robed individuals rushing about, as well as a number of people in roughspun clothes bearing spears. "Looks like they took in people, too."

"But that…what is that?" Pit asked, pointing at a squat fortress at least half as large as the Priory. It was also bustling with people, though more of them were armored in dull iron suits. "I don't remember that last time."

"Those're Knights," Felix recalled. The armor was distinctive, Chevalier's Armor, each inscribed and ancient and passed down by their families. "I don't remember seeing their fortress before...but the Menders had me a bit distracted back then."

As far as Felix could recall, this portion of the Ghreldan Hills was controlled by Prince Tevin, one of several rulers who fought over the Territory almost constantly. Felix hadn't had much experience with the Knights or their master before—the Paladins had been throwing their weight around at the time—but they weren't held in high esteem. Lazy brutes, he recalled them being labeled, but a sight better than the Paladins, at least.

"So, what do we do?" Pit asked. "Looks flooded and...and bad. Do we go back?"

Felix shook his head. "No. We need to talk to the Menders and even those Knights, maybe."

"Why?"

"Why what? Why talk to them?"

"Yeah. Seems like we can't do much by ourselves. But we've got lots of healing items back on the ships." Pit let out a contemplative warble. "If we help get the ships through the Pass, we can help more." He paused, his large golden eyes unsure. "Right?"

Felix sighed. "You're not wrong. Zara and the rest will get the ships over here soon enough. With my help, maybe a little bit sooner. But I have to see. Let's just check, then we can come back and help the ships."

The tangle of treetops obscured much of the sight lines from the fortress to Bogfeld and its two sanctuaries, but enough of the area was rendered wide open by the flooding. Sneaking was going to be a task, even with Abyssal Skein; there was only so much hiding he could do when they had to splash around to get anywhere.

At that moment, however, Pit let out a warning trill. "Someone is coming. A...boat? Two people."

Felix found them easily enough. From his vantage just inside the cracked fort, he could make out two people in a wide, shallow boat moving carefully among the trees. The setting sun glinted off of their Bodies, though only one of them was fully kitted out in Chevalier's Armor, while the other was wearing a patchwork set that was as dented as it was rusty.

The Knight stood in the prow of the ship, a long spear held poised above the waters, like a man trying to fish in a river. The one behind him was looking haggard and sipped slowly at a glowing blue vial as he held onto the boat's tiller. Water splashed quietly but consistently behind them, like a small outboard engine from Earth.

From where Felix stood, it was unlikely the Knight would see him or Pit as they passed, and he made a quick decision. Before he could rethink it, Felix strode from the broken fort, down to the waterline. Pit let out a surprised squawk as Felix began to wave his hands. "Hey there! Hey!"

The Knight zeroed in on him immediately, though it took their little boat a solid thirty seconds to make its way over to them. As it did, the Knight lifted the long spear and braced it against the pronged prow, aiming it straight at Felix's chest. "You are standing upon the sovereign property of Prince Tevis. Who are you, and why are you here?"

The man's voice was deep, resonant, and slightly echoey from behind his full helm. The dark metal and filigreed design made him look almost sinister, and the spear leveled at Felix's heart didn't help matters. "My name is Silas Veil, and I'm just a traveler who got caught up in a storm."

Deception is level 35!

Felix felt the Knight flare some sort of Perception Skill or information-gathering Skill, felt its effect press against the effects of his Veiling Amulet before sending back only what Felix Intended. The man nodded slowly, head tilted in such a way that Felix was sure he was reading some sort of Analyze notification. "Alright, Mr. Veil. These lands are more dangerous than ever right now, so I would ask you to come with us to the Redoubt. You can find shelter, food, and most importantly safety from the vile creatures that crawl out of this muck."

"Creatures, huh? What kind—" Felix started to say, before he was interrupted by a sudden crescendo of gorgeous music. Soon after, a small crimson puppy ran into view, yapping all the while. It was no larger than a terrier, with large paws and somewhat ungainly legs, but looked terribly familiar.

"Oh! A dire hound pup! I can't believe you have one!" the mage said with sudden, intense affection. Pit—for who else would it be?—ran to the mage and accepted some very enthusiastic pets. "He's so young, too! I hear the younger you find them, the better. Easier to train obedience, ya know?"

"Hm, the last part doesn't sound familiar," Felix muttered. Golden eyes shined innocently from the dire hound's face. "But yes, he is mine. And I am his, I suppose. Do you mind if we both climb aboard?"

"Come. The sooner we are back at the Redoubt, the better." The Knight looked to the west in concern. "Night is coming on fast, and the beasts are far more active in the dark."

CHAPTER FORTY-ONE

"Here, lad. You and that pup, climb up," the Knight said, making space on the boat. "We must be away and in the Redoubt before the sun sets, but first we gotta finish our patrol."

Felix eyed the boat skeptically, worrying at his own weight for a bit. Pit, ever the enthusiast, leaped aboard immediately with his ungainly puppy legs. The mage laughed as the boat rocked side to side. "Maybe not as wildly as your friend, though."

Adamant Discord sang within him, pulling ever so slightly upward on his connection to the air above. It wasn't a strong connection, nothing so great as to generate the strange magical friction that resulted in brilliant azure lightning, but enough that Felix felt his weight shift. He took a cautious step forward, it felt as if he were tensing every muscle in his body at once while also feeling a little floaty. Felix reached out and grasped the gunwale of the shallow boat before taking a leap of faith...and a literal leap, right into the center. He landed with a light tapping, and only a minor splash as the shallow-drafted craft slapped into the water.

"Careful, boy," warned the Knight. Felix held up his hands in mute apology.

"Are...what is up with your hands?" the mage behind him asked.

Your scales and claws! Pit sent alongside a thrill of alarm.

Acting swiftly, Felix Willed his Garment to fashion black leather gloves, slightly scaled for texture. His Mana dipped, but the formation was near-instant and hopefully hidden by his body. Felix turned and held out his hands to the mage, as if proud to show them off. "Oh, these? Killed some big sand lizard out in the wastes. Broke my butcher blade skinning it, but made some good gloves out of it."

Deception is level 36!

The mage scratched his head, revealing slightly pointed ears beneath his hood. "Huh. That's some fine stitchin'. My nan did some good seamstress work, years back, though I never got a proper handle on it."

"It's a good Skill to have," Felix said with a smile. "I'm Silas. Never got your name."

"Mage Venali. He's Knight Tandagh."

"Quiet, both of you," Tandagh warned from the front. His spear was still resting on that elevated prong, but now he angled it toward the water as they pushed forward. "Things are stirring."

Felix and Pit both peered over the sides of the boat, eyes focusing on the murky depths. He could make out tons of debris, uprooted trees, and unsettled soil for the most part, but smaller, brighter shapes flitted among them. Fish of varying size and shape, but nothing to be worried about yet.

Mmm, fish. Pit licked his doggy jowls. *I'm hungry.*

Felix rolled his eyes. *You're always hungry. I see you've picked your [Chosen Form] then?*

A measure of joy trickled along their bond as Pit sat his small rear end in between the seats and panted. *Yes! I like this one.*

Felix smiled. *Me, too.*

The barding his Companion wore, now fully Masked by his [Chosen Form], gave him a couple of benefits aside from simple protection. The first was that the barding would change size with him, so that Pit need not ever worry about outgrowing his armor. The second was due to its construction within the Smithy in Nagast, beneath the boughs of the Spirit Tree, which granted increased protection from a foe's Spiritual pressure. The last was altogether more arcane and strange: the Mask of Echoes IV.

Name: Abjuration Barding
Type: Armor (Enchanted)
Tier: Master
Lore: A set of heavy armor designed exclusively for Pit, Companion of Felix Nevarre. Scales of exotic metal form a powerful barrier against harm, and the sleek design hugs tight to Pit's chimeric body, covering his legs, neck, back, and chest. An attached helm completes the set, and all of it is a unique red-gold coloration thanks to the bond between

Companions. An enchanted gem has been placed just below the gorget of the barding, a Stone of Alloyed Refrain, and it confers several bonuses. The armor has gained the ability to alter in size to fit its wearer, as well as masking the physical form of the one to which it is bonded. The armor must be bound by blood to a single user.
Chosen Form: Unknown
Mask of Echoes IV - Once bound by blood, the Stone will allow the wearer to appear as a [Chosen Form].
Chanter's Intent I - The Harmonic Song of a Chanter was used to enchant this item, and it bears their Intent. +10% Effectiveness of Mask of Echoes.
Chanter's Inversion I - Addition of Dissonance to invert the item's properties, hiding them.
Spirit Smithed I - A Unique enhancement, bestowed by a Forge that has been directly influenced by an Elder Spirit Tree. Increased resistance to Spiritual pressure given by those of greater Temper.

Like the enchanted Stone that had first granted Pit a Dire Hound form, this had a similar function. The main difference was that Pit could have chosen anything to mask his physical form...and had decided on a puppy. Felix found it hard to be mad about, though, as Pit shoved his hound head beneath Felix's dangling hand.

"You're a tall one, ain'tcha?" Venali said from behind. "Don't see many folks wandering the Hills or the Expanse...'specially not now that a Night-cursed sea has come up outta nowhere. You're only Journeyman though, huh? Pretty low to face the undead alone."

Sitting next to Pit, Felix settled his thick, sandy-brown cloak around himself. "It wasn't so hard as all that. Big rule is to stay active during the night and hidden all day. You might have to deal with the occasional creature at night, but during the day is when the Cursewinds start to blow...or it was, anyway. Things changed out there...here, too, I noticed," Felix said, gesturing to the water and broken fortification they were leaving behind. Their path looked to be an arcing circle around the ruined perimeter of Bogfeld, but for now it was through mostly thick, tree-clogged waters. "What happened here?"

"A wave as big as the sky dropped on us," the Knight grunted. "Crashed through the Pass and ripped apart the fort there before flooding the whole damn Province."

"It kept going, too. For days," Venali added. "I have lived in the Ghreldan Hills my entire life, the Land of a Ten Thousand Lakes, and I have never seen so much water. I cannot understand what happened in the wastes to make such a thing possible. The scouts even say the entirety of the desert has become a *sea*. Is that true?"

"It is," Felix said, suppressing a wince. "Did anyone survive the fortification breaking apart?"

"No, and good riddance," the Knight said, a growl in his deep voice. "Only those Paladins were in there, and they got what they deserved."

That was something of a relief. Felix had finally realized that the Paladins—as the Inquisitors before them—were not worth feeling guilty over. Not that it stopped him from feeling bad, at least a little. All the Willpower in the world couldn't quell his anxious Mind, after all.

The trees cleared as Venali pushed them out into the open expanse of water, though they clung to the edges. "Safer near the trees. Harder to maneuver, but..." The mage let his words trail off as he focused on the tiller in his hands. A very simple inscription had been carved into its wooden surface, nothing more than a basic *siphon* glyph paired with *force* and *water* sigils. It was sucking Mana straight from Venali's channels and converting it into thrust, but from a quick glance, Felix could tell the transfer rate was abysmal. A ton of the mage's Mana was being lost, wisping up from the sigaldry before it ever made it below the waterline.

They arced further outward, eventually reaching a point where Felix had an unobstructed view of the Low Side of Bogfeld, fully the opposite end from the Redoubt of the Knights of Tevin. That structure was bathed in the golden-orange light of sunset, same as the Priory, and small fires had bloomed along both of their walls and watch towers. "So who runs the Redoubt?"

"Knight Commander Etriska Lavin," the mage told him, and Felix could detect the faint beat of admiration across the Half-Elf's Spirit. "She's the reason so much of Bogfeld survived. Her and the Menders."

"Menders are good folk, if a bit...misguided," Tandagh said.

Felix wanted to ask about that, but he had other priorities. "The Priory, right. I see their castle survived the flooding, too. How...how many people died?"

"Too many," Tandagh said. His Spirit was bedrock solid, but a thready chord of sadness played at its center.

Venali spoke up when the Knight remained silent. "The wave caught us during market day, so at least most folks were in the town walls...the problem was the town walls didn't hold. Lost as many folks to the collapse as we did drowning, and that's before the monsters came."

"Monsters," Felix repeated. "What exactly are you looking for out here? What comes out at night?"

Venali shuddered. "Nasty things, Silas. Fishmen with claws. Dragon eels the size of trees. And once...once a Depthwurm. Ain't sure where they come from, 'cept the abyss below."

Tandagh grunted. "I saw a few come down the Pass, but not for a while. Mostly, they come from north and east. And it's why we need quiet. The beasts like to hunt at night, and I can't fight more than a handful at a time."

That's where Haestus Lake was...where the Deepking said the Fathom resided. Felix didn't believe that was a coincidence at all. *So the flooding allowed the Fathom to escape the lakes, to spread outward and into the Hills.* That guilt clung to his chest, persistent as ever, and heavier with every passing breath.

The ship slowed, not that it was going particularly fast. "Mage. Hurry up. I don't like the look of this grove we're nearing."

Venali tipped the last of his blue vial down his throat, grimacing the entire time. "I'm trying. But there are only two of us and too many patrols to man, Tandagh. I need rest, proper rest. Or at least better tinctures. This one tastes like boiled socks."

A scream tore through the gathering gloom, high-pitched and infused with a primal terror. Felix spun toward it, flaring his Perception, but was only able to make out the sounds and impressions of something struggling in the water in a distant copse of waterlogged wood.

"What is that?" Venali asked, his face pale.

"Someone with bad luck," Tandagh growled. "But it's too soon. The sun won't be down for another half glass."

"We should go find them," the Half-Elf suggested, already turning their boat toward the sound.

"Are you crazy, mage? You're almost outta Mana, and proposin'...what? That I go in alone and fight an unknown number of unknown monstrosities?" The Knight gripped his spear hard but shook his head. "As much as I want to, that's a bad call. We finish patrol, head back to the Redoubt."

"Move." Felix picked up the mage and rotated, setting the confused Half-Elf into the middle of the boat before sitting back against the stern wall. "And take this." Felix shoved a glowing blue bottle into Venali's hands. The mage and Knight both looked down at it in wide-eyed surprise. "You both better hold onto something."

Felix grabbed the tiller and focused his own Mana through it. Sparks flew, and Mana burst in a wave behind them that shot them forward across the waters. Venali shouted, nearly falling overboard, only to be saved by the stout Tandagh, who settled them both into the hollow at the prow of the craft.

Like Felix had surmised, the transfer rate was horrible, wasting fully half of what he was pouring into the construct, but it did its job. Felix wove between trees and hanging vines, threading the ungainly ship with a Skill he'd had little time to practice in recent months.

Manaship Pilot is level 23!

He dodged through trees and the odd block of masonry, weaving across the water and leaving only a riotous spray behind them. The Knight and mage shouted at first, but after a while, they merely braced themselves; one sprawled entirely at the bottom of the boat and the other still clutching onto his heavy spear.

The screaming continued, the sound growing more frantic as it went on. Then it went silent as violent splashes increased, just as their boat slipped through a copse of trees. At the center of a grove, a woman flailed in the water, barely getting her face above the surface as *something* swirled around her.

Pit immediately tried to dive in, but Felix quickly killed his connection to the tiller and grabbed his friend by the scruff of his neck. "Wait. Look."

The others stood, all of them watching the woman flail in the water, reaching toward them with every stroke and yet...not moving. She wasn't quite right, either. At first blush, in a panic perhaps, she appeared Human. But the longer they lingered at the edge of the grove, the more Felix could spot the strangeness. Her skin was too pink, her eyes too exaggerated, and her slicked back hair seemed to wriggle on its own.

"Blighted Night," Venali whispered. "What is that thing?"

"A trap," Tandagh growled.

The woman, never once ceasing her screams that *still* reverberated against Felix's Affinity with true terror, rose up out of the water. Her dress flopped to her sides, the murky liquid no longer hiding the way it spread and flapped like fleshy gills. A thick, pulpy tentacle filled the bottom of the "dress," lifting the thing up higher as the waters swirled and exploded upward. A dozen more tentacles ripped through the air, each one angled at their small boat.

Cardinal Flame!

Red-gold fire hit the creature and skipped off, the limning fading after less than a heartbeat, though the burning nature of the spell did send a few tentacles recoiling. Thankfully, Tandagh snatched up his spear and inscribed a wide circle before their boat at the same time.

"Aegis of Iron!" The remaining tentacles smashed into the circle, which instantly transmuted the air into a massive plane of dark metal. Sigils glowed upon the edge of the huge disc, but each one burned out with every strike against it. "Venali!"

"Y-yes! Bottomless Quagmire!"

Newly restored Mana thundered from Venali's channels, fully half of it pouring into the spellform that sank around the rising mass of tentacles. The water went from translucent haze to a thick, impenetrable morass that clung to the beast like sticky mud. Immediately, the creature's attacks faltered as its efforts turned toward escaping the strange spell.

Voracious Eye!

Name: Bog-Lure
Type: Beast
Level: 55
HP: 9984/9984
SP: 3388/4327
MP: 92/233
Lore: A Bog-Lure is an uncommon threat in the Ghreldan Hills, and normally only seen in the deepest areas where they are known to grow to immense size. Utilizing a magical form of mimicry, the Bog-Lure grows an appendage to appear as a mortal Race and emits an intermittent scream in order to lure its prey into its clutches. They do not move fast, so avoiding them is easy, so long as you do not enter within range of their strong tentacles. If caught, prey is pulled into the water to be devoured by the jaws just below the surface.
Strength: More Data Required
Weakness: More Data Required

"Nasty," Felix muttered. Judging by the flickering of Mana he could see, Venali's Bottomless Quagmire was fading fast, and Felix doubted the Knight could maintain his odd shield for long. *Don't attack, Pit. We're not trying to give away all our secrets right now.*

Ugh. Fine.

The smart thing to do was to pilot the boat out of the copse and just never enter it again...but that was a temporary solution. What if the thing kept growing? Would it eventually threaten the town? Felix could kill it in any number of ways, most of which were very flashy and counter to his purpose. So he settled on simple and hidden, instead.

Stone Shaping!

Rime Shaping!

With the others preoccupied, it was easy for Felix to shove his left palm into the water to obscure the *torrent* of Mana that poured from his channels. It speared downward, sinking into the earth more than thirty feet below them, until all the ground around was seized by Felix's Will. The water froze into spikes of jagged ice, each stabbing through the central stalk of the Bog-Lure, while the stone and soil itself began to pull inexorably downward. In seconds, the lure itself disappeared beneath the waves, pulled deeper and deeper as Felix reshaped the very earth beneath it. And then, with a final flex of his Will, it was gone and the stone solidified.

You Have Killed A Bog-Lure!

XP Earned!

"Damn good job, son," Tandagh said, slapping Venali on the back. The mage only stared at his hands, as if disbelieving what had happened.

"I'm impressed," Felix admitted, and it wasn't even a lie. Both the Knight and mage had acted fast and with level heads during the unexpected attack. "Now I know why you were chosen for patrol duty."

"Ah no, it's just because I can pilot the boat," Venali admitted. "But I have been practicing against the beasts...though I've never seen one of them before. A Bog-Lure, was it?"

"Aye. I've seen them, but not anywhere near a settlement, though." Tandagh lifted his visor and spat into the water, as if clearing his mouth of something nasty. Felix was mildly surprised to see he had the purple-green skin and short tusks of an Orc. "We need to report this to the Knight Commander. Bog-Lures aren't anything to take lightly." The Knight looked to Felix, suspicion and curiosity playing across his Spirit. "Mr. Veil. If you wouldn't mind, I think my mage is spent."

"Not a problem," Felix said, careful to breathe heavily, as if he, too, had just exerted himself. "Glad to put my back to this grove, that's for sure."

Tandagh grunted, and Felix guided them out of the trees and back toward the Redoubt.

CHAPTER FORTY-TWO

"Dunno how I killed it, honestly," Venali was saying as Felix guided them over the submerged forest. The boat was unwieldy, and the sigaldry had proven to be even worse than Felix had suspected; his Mana was spilling out into the water through the rudder. "Bottomless Quagmire isn't something that kills often. Especially not aquatic monsters."

"Thing had a mouth," Tandagh said. "You choked it out. Sometimes it ain't complicated."

"I guess. Gained a level from it, anyway." Venali lifted a hand, swiping as he accessed his Status screen. "What do you think, Mr. Veil? You clearly have an abundance of Mana. Should I put my points into Willpower or Intelligence?"

"Oh, I'm sure you know how best to develop yourself," Felix deflected.

The Half-Elf glanced at Tandagh then back at Felix, lowering his voice below the constant splash of the boat. "We Lotuses don't have the same luxury of tradition that our brother society has. Please. Any advice would be appreciated."

The earnest plea wisped across Felix's senses, and Pit barked once as if in encouragement. "Uh, sure. You're a Half-Elf right?"

Venali nodded. "I am. The Elven portion of my heritage is several generations back, but you know what they say. Half-Elves breed true."

"Of course. That *is* what they say," Felix said, focusing his gaze on the water ahead. It gave him the advantage of not lying directly to the mage's face. "I don't know many Half-Elves, though. Can you tell me what your level-up distribution is like?"

"Oh, yes. I understand not being sure. Not all Half-Elves are the same, I know. But with my Elven ancestor being outside three Human generations, the effect is a bit diluted. So, I gain one point in Endurance and Agility each level, and I also earn two free stat points to spend as I see fit." Venali snapped his fingers, as if remembering something. "Ah, and my Omen is The Emperor, so that's another two points for Vitality and one point each for Intelligence and Willpower."

Felix rubbed his chin, marking down another Omen in the running list he had in his head. "Emperor. Not bad."

"Yes. Perhaps the only reason I was selected for the Gallant Lotus Society." Venali tapped his breastplate which, although pitted, was not nearly as ill-kempt as other parts of his armor. It gleamed as if polished, and upon the center was a lotus flower stamped into the metal and painted green-gold. "We're traditionally trained as support for the Knights Ghreldan, and as such, we offer Skills that establish control, abjuration, and healing to a lesser extent. We were taught to focus our stats in Intelligence to increase the effect of our magics, but the resulting lack of Mana in our reserves is always a concern. With Willpower being provided through my Omen, why, the old trainers couldn't snatch me up quick enough."

A mixture of pride and frustration sang across Venali's Spirit...and expression. The man was either not interested or not capable of masking his emotions. In all honesty, Felix was starting to like the guy. "Alright. Well, I always advocate for more Willpower. Not only does it deepen your Mana pool, but it allows you to contend with a target's resistance to your spell. A spell that paralyzes or stuns is much more effective when you can quash the enemy's opposing Willpower directly."

"That is...but what of the benefits of increased cognition and greater impact through higher Intelligence?"

Felix shrugged. "It's useful, I'm not gonna say otherwise, but if you had to pick one? I'd pick Willpower every time."

Of course you would, Pit scoffed across their bond.

Quiet, you, Felix sent back.

"Hmm." Venali didn't seem entirely convinced, but his Spirit hummed appreciatively. "I thank you, Mr. Veil. That gives me something to think on."

"Quiet, and flare your Perceptions. You'll have all the time you need to think back at the Redoubt," the Knight said. He was standing again, holding his long spear in that odd stand attached to the prow. "Watch for Bog-Sprouts. That's the danger now."

Bog-Sprouts, it turned out, were the juvenile form of the Bog-Lures. Mostly harmless, they appeared to be large lily pads but speckled with a dark brown across the green in a distinctive pattern. They came upon six of them as they moved, and each time, Tandagh expertly pivoted and thrust his spear through their centers. The things would explode into movement, thrashing for all of a second before they expired, and immediate wisps of black smoke began to boil up from the water.

Juvenile or not, they apparently offered some good experience, because after the last one was killed, Felix heard the telltale trilling of the System from the Knight. The guy had leveled up, though he didn't mention it.

Why not have Venali fire shots at the Bog-Sprouts, too? Does the mage not have a ranged attack? Or was the Knight just hogging all the XP? Tandagh seemed a nice enough dude, but he'd encountered more than enough people who abused their power to get more power. What was far weirder was Venali's answer.

"Oh, no. Ranged offensive magic? That is pointless. The Knights are to engage in melee; the Lotuses are to simply control the field. Mixing the two would result in a great many injuries," he said.

"I...guess that makes sense." Truthfully, Felix had only a few in-passing lectures from Harn and Darius about field battles. Nearly all of his experience had been as a lone combatant or part of a small team. "Wouldn't even a simple ranged attack like Sparkbolt be an easier way to earn experience, though?"

To that, Venali only shrugged, though it was hesitant. "It is how the Lotus operates."

"I see."

Over the next ten minutes, they completed the final stretch of their patrol, though the shadows were stretching longer and longer. An eye was kept for more monsters, and Felix kept his Perception spread in search of any Fathom spawn. He did not spot any, though parsing anything through the chaotic, tree-choked waters was very hard.

Thick-limbed creatures that looked to be a cross between a hippo and an ape appeared near the end of things, swimming in peaceful pods at least twenty strong. Tandagh instructed him to swing wide, and Felix didn't argue; the creatures were all Tier III monsters according to his sense of things, and if they were anything like the hippos from back home, Felix wanted nothing to do with them. Hippos were vicious.

"A Bog-Lure so close to town, Hippotons grazing within sight of the walls...the patterns of the Wilds have been thrown completely," Tandagh spat.

Venali caught Felix's gaze. "Predators are getting hungrier by the day as prey dwindles. Hippotons are vicious, but they are prey for some of the nastier creatures out there. Like the Naga," he added with a shudder.

"The Knight Commander will know how to proceed."

Tandagh's tone was firm as bedrock. Spirit, too. Venali, however, was clearly uneasy, which only escalated as the shadows of the distant hills finally draped the waters. Below, Felix could sense movement. The waters churned, debris clogging his Perception, but something was coming. A lot of somethings.

Felix increased their speed, and the boat spat out a thick cloud of Mana as it jolted forward.

"Hey! Careful, wanderer! You—!"

"Knight Tandagh, look!"

The Orc's words stopped as he witnessed what Felix had sensed coming. The Hippotons were busy clambering up the branches of a stout tree, while all around them the water *boiled* with sudden fins and spines.

"Faster. Go faster, wanderer," he croaked.

Manaship Pilot is level 24!

More and more of Felix's Mana was wasted, blasting through the crude sigaldry and into the water behind them. Felix knew he wasn't being kind to the craft, but he didn't much care. The prow lifted, forcing Tandagh to shove his own weight forward to keep it level, and Felix didn't slacken their speed. Behind them, oozy appendages lashed out of the water and onto the Hippotons, drawing deep, honking cries of agony.

Draktopi. At least six of them, and more coming, too.

When can we kill them? Pit asked. His haunches quivered, as if winding up to leap out any second.

Soon enough. Felix could handle them himself, but there wasn't a reason to do so yet, not if he was going to keep a low profile. He still had things to learn, and his ships weren't through the Pass yet. *Let's see what's going on with these Knights first.*

Pit flopped back into the bottom of the boat, his floppy, puppy dog legs hitting with as much sullen annoyance as he could muster. *Fine.*

Felix reached down and ruffled his big ears.

Soon enough, they left behind the sounds of grisly chewing and interrupted honks and came up to the walled expanse of the Redoubt. It was at the far end of High Side, where Bogfeld lifted up on its odd plinth of stone, and the walls of the town surrounded it. Up close, the walls were in rougher shape than Felix thought, with chunks missing where teeth or claws had latched onto them.

There were also char marks and patches of ice so thick they were being chipped off by several workers with sledgehammers. The Redoubt itself also looked far larger than he'd estimated, and what Felix assumed was a small fort for a dozen or so Knights looked fit to hold hundreds. Tandagh guided Felix around the outside, to the rear, where a series of docks had been built.

"Had to make some sort of access to the outside," he explained. "Only way we can keep patrolling the area, keeping it as safe as we can."

Felix had dropped his speed and now was basically coasting until the hull smacked lightly into the side of a short dock. Tandagh hopped out and grabbed a mooring line, wrapping it once around a spar before pulling taut. "Out. Quicklike."

Felix, Pit, and Venali followed, hopping with easy grace from boat to dock. Once everyone was out, the Orc Knight reached down, grasped the gunwales and, with a grunt, lifted the whole dinghy above his head. Water streamed down all around them, beading impotently against the Knight's armor. "Can't let the monsters break our boats. We don't got so many as we can waste 'em. C'mon."

A fast walk down the short dock led them to a stone platform and iron-bound door, which opened for the Knight with a simple flash of light. Manasight traced it to the Knight's breastplate and the door itself, and his Affinity heard a paired chime as they went off. *Magic lock. That's never not cool.*

More Knights flanked the inner door, and they gave Tandagh a nod as he passed. They ignored Felix and Venali, though one was surprised to see Pit. Tandagh handed off the dripping boat to a pair of women off to the side, where a number of small boats were stacked. Both were dressed in thick leather jackets and aprons, each with a lotus worked onto the chest. "Tiller needs work. Started smellin' funny halfway 'round the town," he muttered by way of explanation, before leading them all through a second gate and into a curving hallway.

Before the gate shut behind them, voices crept into Felix's Perception.

"...this is charred! Sigaldry's ruined!"

"Too much damn Mana. How fast did they need to go?"

"Damn Knights."

The gate closed off any other sounds, and Tandagh led them up a winding set of stairs that branched multiple times. After several dizzying turns that Felix memorized just to be on the safe side, he was led into a wide courtyard that was at least the size of a football field and absolutely chock-filled with people. Carts and stands were everywhere, the air above covered in hanging lines filled with brightly colored flags snapping in the wind, while countless noises and delicious smells settled on them like a physical weight.

Food! Pit sang through their bond. *So much food! Can we get some? Can we?*

"Welcome to Bogfeld Redoubt, Mr. Veil." Venali gestured expansively to the cheerful chaos in front of them. "You arrived on a good day. It's the middle of Lightsfall, and we've managed to salvage enough from the town to celebrate."

"Lightsfall?"

"That's right, you were in the wilderness for a long while, huh? Yeah, the rainy season is coming fast." The mage paused, grimacing. "I'd have guessed it was here already, but that flood...who knows how that happened?"

"One of the many things I need to report to the Knight Commander," Tandagh announced. "Mr. Veil, you mind stickin' with Gallant Venali? I'm sure Lady Lavin will wanna speak to you later about the Expanse."

"Sure." He'd intended to speak with her eventually anyway, once things got moving. "I've no problem with that."

Tandagh grunted and lifted his visor to smile at them both. "Good. I'll be back shortly."

The Knight cut through the edge of the crowd and headed up a set of exposed stone stairs before vanishing among another set of armored folks.

Venali clapped his hands. "Well. Would you like me to show you around, Mr. Veil? Perhaps a meal?"

"That sounds great," Felix said.

FOOD! Pit crowed and took off into the crowd. The mage gave him a concerned look that Felix waved off.

"Don't worry. He's easy to find." Felix gestured ahead, and the two of them started walking. "He'll be at the nearest food stall."

FOOD!

CHAPTER FORTY-THREE

Kelpie Pie Consumed!
+5 AGL, VIT
Duration: 15 Minutes

"A buff? Huh." Felix chewed appreciatively and stared at the saucer-sized meat pie in his hands. "This is really good. What's a Kelpie? A type of fish?"

"Don't know the Kelpie?" The cook they'd just purchased from leaned over the stall counter and smacked a grease-stained etching of a half horse and half fish creature. It wasn't particularly well made. "Shapeshifter, Elemental Type. Real common in the Hills, but you gotta catch 'em before they can get to land. Unless you like the taste of sour horseflesh!"

Felix slowed his chewing and looked down at the flaky pastry in his hands. A sheen of brown and blue infused the fillings, only faintly occluding the flaky meat. "Really."

Voracious Eye!

Name: Kelpie Pie
Type: Protein/Carbohydrate
SubType: Elemental (Water/Earth)
Lore: Baked by Skilled hands, this dish is fortified by the essential Mana of the Kelpie, an Elemental shapeshifter that changes form depending on its contact with water. Effects have been increased due to applied Cooking Skill.
Effect: +5 Agility and Vitality for 15 Minutes

"Never had food good enough to give me a stat boost," Felix said.

"S'cuz you haven't seen a Journeyman Tier cook, that's why!" The man behind the counter flourished his hands, one of which was covered in flour, and the other held a chef's knife. They quickly went back to kneading dough and chopping vegetables, fast and accurate, and the man wasn't even looking. "If you travel north to Prince Garin's lands, you'll be able to find Adept Tier chefs, as well! They're the best in the Territory, by far! Some say they can boost three stats at once by more than ten points!"

The man's boisterous words had actually drawn a crowd—on purpose, Felix didn't doubt—and they all murmured excitedly before hastening forward to buy one for themselves. By and large, Felix had spent time in some of the more rural portions of the Continent, and had little experience with the potential wonders the Continent offered on a wider scale. Except Ahkestria, of course, but he hadn't had any real chance to experience that city. Felix idly wondered if there were high-Tiered cooks back in the city...and if he could arrange to have dishes sent through his Beacon.

"What do you think, Pit?" At his feet, Pit was basically vibrating with joy. His thin, Masked tail whipped back and forth fast enough to make a sound, and his tiny jowls oozed with drool. Two pieces of wax paper were on the ground, smeared with grease and little else, and Pit let out a warbling bark. Felix laughed. "It seems we both like them. Can I have another six?

"If the Gallant is payin', then I don't mind none at all!" the portly cook said with a hearty laugh. In a few short moments, the man slid another stack of greasy pies into Felix's hands. "I'll just send the bill to yer commander later."

Venali winced but didn't stop them as Felix fed all but one to his Companion. Watching both of their Status screens closely, Felix was disappointed to see that the buff stacked neither effect or duration. *At least it tastes delicious.*

"Do you think you're full?" Venali asked. "You and your...your Pit?"

"Good for now," Felix said with a burp, and for the first time noticed one of the people in the crowd paying. The sign said the pies were a full silver penny, but he hadn't any real idea what that was worth. Apart from the fact that he only barely understood Hierocracy currency, let alone the Ghreldan Hills', Felix hadn't had to pay for...anything in a while. "Huh. I feel a bit bad letting you pay for us all this time. I can pay myself, if you need—"

"No no, don't think of it, I offered," Venali said with a weak grin. "I make enough as a Gallant to offset it all."

"Uh huh," Felix said before fishing around in his pocket for some loose coins. He kept only a few in some hidden pouches he'd Willed into the lining of his jacket, but hopefully it would be enough. He pulled out six silver swords—he had only a few copper stones, ten silver swords, and like two golden crowns—and placed them into the Half-Elf's hand. "Does this cover it?"

Venali gaped at the silver before trying to shove all but one of them back. "M-more than enough! I cannot possibly take all this."

"Eh, keep it," Felix said with a shrug. "It'll make up for the other stuff Pit ate, too."

"A-ah, alright then."

The Half-Elf mage had been leading Felix and Pit on a tour of the courtyard and festival events when Pit had stopped (again) at a food stall. The Kelpie Pies were the fourth such stop they'd had to make, and the first one that had more than just fish or fried water reed. Everything had tasted delicious, if heavily spiced, and the pies had been the best.

Children rushed around them, way more than Felix had expected, all giggling and chasing one another. The tenku was happy to join in, letting out trilling noises as he nipped playfully at some little Goblin girl's heels. She shrieked in delight. Older folks watched on, small smiles on their lined faces that only lasted so long as the children were in view.

Then their expressions—and their Spirits—deflated like leaky balloons, revealing an undercurrent of distress and tension that Felix could read, even without his Affinity. Robes and dresses and tunics were torn or only hastily repaired, eyes were ringed with a darkness caused by more than lack of sleep, and more than one body was wrapped in bandages.

For how fast people healed on the Continent, Felix had to assume those wounds were very recent—only a day old at most. Knights prowled the walls, a number that increased as the sky darkened into deep twilight. More than once, sounds far beyond Redoubt had reached Felix's ears: screams and splashes, though not from any Human throat.

Monsters. They're in the town itself. The broken walls in Low Side had told the tale, and as he reviewed them in his memory, Felix recalled more than one sizable hole bored straight through. *Monsters got in, people ran to higher ground to escape.* He looked around, doing a quick count of the crowd. "Venali, how many people escaped the initial flooding?"

"We call it the Troubles," the mage said, gesturing Felix to keep his voice down. A few people shot them gaunt, thousand-yard stares and Felix grimaced in apology. "And not nearly enough. The water was bad, but it was the monsters that caused the real problems. That Bog-Lure, for instance; it's not the first thing to come washing out of the deep Hills, and it won't be the last."

"Oh aye, me caravan was swept away by some sorta bird-fish," a bespectacled man said. He was at their feet and slurred a little, and Felix jolted in surprise, having mistaken him for a mound of trash at first. He was wearing a ragged blanket over his shoulders and had an assortment of random junk spilled out onto another patchwork blanket in front of him. The man gave both Venali and Felix a sharp glare. "Had feathers and all, but fins, too. Strange thing, and stranger still will come."

"Alright," Venali said carefully, before beginning to walk away. "I'm sorry for your troubles, sir."

"We'll all be sorry soon, mark my words."

"The Knights and the Gallants will protect us, don't you worry, sir," the mage said, still stepping slowly away. He gave Felix a pained, somewhat exhausted look before addressing the junk merchant again. "Just hunker down a bit, sell your...wares...and we'll get it all sorted out."

"The Knights! Hah! And the Gallant aren't any better! Weak! All of 'em!" The junk merchant was yelling now, though he didn't stand or jump or point wildly. "What about those snakes? Hm? What's the Knight Commander gonna do about them? They ate my cousin!"

"Snakes?" Felix asked, interest piqued. "What sort of snakes?"

"Huge ones that come prowlin' outta the water, hungry as a Primordial and twice as mean. My cousin saw one the size of a mountain range that came up just south of here before it swallowed him and his entire village!"

"And how did you hear about this?" Venali asked.

"My cousin told me!"

"The one who died?"

"The—wait, don't try and trick me! He knows what he saw!" The junk merchant stabbed a single, gnarled finger at the mage. "You Gallants are all the same! Thinkin' you're too good for us, too smart with all your fancy magics and high Intelligence. Some of us had to invest in Endurance for a livin'!"

At that point, the Knights in the crowd were noticing things. The junk merchant was raising such a stink it was hard to avoid, though everyone around them was doing their level best to ignore him. Grief and fear rippled through the crowd like a bad smell, or a lilting melody in a minor key that drove everyone away. It was strongest of all in the merchant, and the man had tears dangling from the corners of his eyes. He'd clearly been through a lot, and the last thing Felix wanted to see was him hauled off for disturbing the peace or whatever. "Hey, Berek, listen."

The junk merchant looked up at Felix, surprised. "You know my name?"

"Who doesn't?" Felix smiled and spread his hands. Anyone with Analyze would have, but the guy was too upset, and a little too drunk, to think straight. "I also believe you. You're talking about the Naga, right?"

"Yes! Exactly! The serpents what linger in the deeps. They woke up same time as this flood came on!"

"Those are myths—" Venali started, but Felix cut him off.

"Myths come true all the time," Felix said. "When was the last time you saw a desert flood?"

"I-I suppose you have a point, Mr. Veil. But the Naga are bedtime stories to scare children."

"My cousin saw 'em! I told you!" Berek the junk merchant repeated. "And I'll keep shoutin' it 'til someone listens!"

"Berek. We're listening. Truly." Felix said. "When I'm done with the Gallant here, I'll come back and I'll listen to your whole tale. Start to finish. Alright?"

Berek squinted up at him, and Felix noticed the man's glasses were half an inch thick and cracked. "And you believe me?"

Felix only nodded.

"Fine. But you'll listen to all of it!" Berek said, half threat and half request.

"Of course," Felix said and mentally swiped away the notifications that popped up. "Stay outta trouble."

Negotiation is level 34!
...
Negotiation is level 37!

Felix led a stunned Venali away, into the crowd and out of the upset merchant's eyesight. He soon found Pit running in circles around a tall, thick pole that was being painted by several dozen children. A number of colored ribbons hung limp from the top, unmoving in the hot, humid air.

"That was astonishing, Mr. Veil," the mage said after a time.

Felix shrugged. "Hm? Oh, no it wasn't. Just had to defuse the situation a bit. Plus, I do want to hear what he has to say about those Naga."

Venali led him a bit farther down, until they came into a quieter section by the inner wall, where a wide, wall-mounted fountain burbled into a deep basin. The spigot was shaped like a scaled lion of some sort and layered with a heavy green patina. "The Naga are tavern tales. They don't exist, but plenty of the Hillfolk think they do, so the point is moot, I suppose. They'll report just about anything as Nagas in the waters, sending the Gallants and Knights running all over the Hills in search of rumors and fables."

"You don't think they could be real?" Felix asked. *Garox and the Deep-king are going to be so surprised to hear they're fake.*

Blech. Snakemen are unnerving, Pit sent to him as he rolled in the dust. His rusty coat was thick with gray-brown dirt, and he kept working it in farther.

Be nice. They're...not friends. Allies.

"There are a great many things located on the Continent that I have no handle on, Mr. Veil, but the Hills are where I've grown up. I have never seen a Naga before, and I never will." Venali snorted. "To hear the Hillfolk talk, a Naga encircles the whole of the world, end to end, biting its own tail within its mountainous jaws. Pure, idle fancy."

"Hm," Felix said, as noncommittally as he could. A part of him envisioned such a beast, and he begged the universe for it not to be true. Knowing his luck, Felix would have to fight it.

"I didn't mean to be short with the fellow. Honestly, the last few days have been rough on us all. That particular rumor drives me a bit mad, I admit. It's an excuse or false alarm put out to the Knights so often it's become a joke. The Naga stole my cattle. The Naga ate my kids. The Naga sank my whole village." Venali paused, taking a seat at the edge of the wide basin. "That one actually happened, though it turned out to be some young girl who discovered the Whirlpool Skill, somehow. We snatched her up quickly for training...after we gave her a stern talking to, of course."

"Been wondering about that, too. I've seen plenty of the Knights wandering around, but not a lot of Gallants," Felix said.

"Ah, yes. Well. The Gallant Lotus is a brother society of the Knights Ghreldan, as I said, but we are not afforded the same...luxuries as the Knights." Venali gestured vaguely before folding his hands on his lap, his rusty pauldrons squeaking a little. "Most of us are water mages of some stripe, though there are life mages among us as well.

"Once, we had an academy, best in the nine provinces, but now we all learn what scraps we can from the old, retired Lotuses in the Prince's third citadel, northeast of here. Villa Tevin, they call it, and there are only a handful of instructors. Most of the time, the younger, untrained mages are foisted on us out here in the Redoubts for field training. All in all, we've weaker, more common Skills, fewer Tempering opportunities, and few sure ways to get Titles. Not for lack of trying, mind you!" The Half-Elf laughed, blinking as if just realizing something. "Why am I telling you all this?"

"I've got one of those faces, probably," Felix said with a gentle smile. "Don't worry, I won't tell."

"It's not anything people don't already know. I'm just surprised I'm dumping this all on you. Nice as you are, Mr. Veil, I barely know you, so I apologize."

Felix only shrugged and offered a short laugh. "Venting to strangers is the best. You get it off your chest, and the stranger leaves, never to return. It's a great deal."

"True enough." Venali sighed. "All the Gallants are weaker than the average Knight, but we have our specialties. That is why we focus so much on support and battlefield control, Mr. Veil. Direct attacks do not work well for our society."

"That makes sense. Work with what you have, and all." Felix looked up, studying the stars as they started to peek out among the clear western sky. The night spread out above them like a dark shroud, slowly smothering the pinks, oranges, and yellows of the fading east. The sounds of roaring and splashing had faded a bit, likely due to the Knights firing a few volleys of arrows every handful of minutes. Curious, Felix stretched himself out, sounding his Affinity and Perception both toward the outer walls.

Huh. He tried again, but got the same result. *That's interesting. That's a* lot *of wards.*

The Redoubt wasn't huge, and Felix certainly couldn't encompass the whole thing with his senses at once, but just within his range, he spotted six wards. The unsurprising ones were worked into the walls themselves, designed to kick back anything that tried to climb them. He could even sense the monster cores buried deep within them, banks of them all tied to an impressive-looking array of some design. The details were fuzzy, of course—he'd have to get a lot closer to check them out fully—but Felix no longer wondered how the fortress had repelled waves of monster attacks.

Other wards, however, were far more subtle. Felix probably even missed a few within his range, they were so quiet and unobtrusive. One was above them in the central, squat tower. He could just make out the edges of something blocking Perception Skills, like a fuzziness in the air. But there was another, located farther down beneath them that was so strangely out of place that it was like a single dead, gray tooth amid a perfect white smile.

What's down there? Pit asked. *I can't smell anything.*

Felix stared a bit longer, attempting to work his senses beyond the shroud, to no avail. He stared so long that the mage was now peering at him curiously. "What are you doing?" he asked.

"Being nosy. What's beneath us?"

Venali's face paled, like someone had drained him of all the blood he had. "How did you—"

Above them, the large, heavy bells began to toll.

CHAPTER FORTY-FOUR

"What's that about?" Felix asked, but before Venali could answer, a younger man in ill-fitting armor clattered around the corner.

"Gallant Venali! The Knight Commander has ordered us all into convocation!" The man was sweating through his mail and looked both terrified and excited. "Someone's coming through the Pass!"

"What?" Venali stood and walked quickly to the other mage's side. "Who?"

"Dunno! But listen! They've got at least one ship!"

Venali looked to Felix, eyebrows raised. "A ship? A Manaship? It flew through the storms?"

"Definitely a Manaship, but not one I've seen. This thing wasn't even flying."

They made it through with the first ship, I guess. The crowd were all staring up at the central tower of the Redoubt, where those bells were still pealing, and Knights hustled through them toward the various stone stairways. Several Knights and Gallants were standing atop the walls and pointing to the south. Toward the Pass. "Manaship on the water, huh. How'd they get through the Pass? That was dry when I walked it."

"I'm curious about that as well," Venali admitted. "Please, Mr. Veil. Stay here, and I'll return as soon as I'm able."

"What about that thing I mentioned?" Felix glanced meaningfully at the ground. "What is it?"

"A source of strength." The other Gallant was all but pulling on Venali, urging him to move. "That is all I can say, Mr. Veil. I will return!"

The mages ran off, angling toward the central tower along with a great many other armored folks. Amidst it all, the people were huddling in small clumps beneath awnings and around small braziers, holding onto each other. Pit ambled up to Felix, his jaws stained by some stolen snack. "What are we doing now? Back to the boat?"

"Menders! Menders this way! The Knight Commander bids you to join our convocation!"

The voice wasn't loud, certainly not enough to cut through the worried murmuring of the crowd, but Felix's Perception caught it easily enough. It came from the other side of the tower. "Menders, huh? Perhaps we should be in on that meeting, too."

"Why?" Pit asked.

"I need to speak with the leadership anyway. And I don't want them to attack my ships." Felix looked up the sheer wall behind them, judging the distance. "How high do you think this is?"

"Fifty feet, maybe. I thought you wanted to be sneaky?"

"Don't worry," Felix said, patting the smooth stone wall. "I've got a plan."

Alessa Kartez, Prioress of the Blessed Fen and leader of the Menders, mopped her brow with a damp handkerchief. The night was hot, as they always were in the Hills, but the vast waves had increased the humidity to unbearable levels of late. Even if the Troubles had not brought such bloody mayhem to their doorsteps, the wet alone would be enough to drive her insane. Now the bells had begun to toll, and the Knight Commander had summoned them to speak. Stress piled atop sweaty, sticky stress.

"Bright gods, the conditions these poor people are left in are atrocious," one of her Menders complained. "Those tents are barely enough to deal with a quarter of the injuries we saw today."

"We are all of us short-staffed and overwhelmed," Alessa said, careful to keep her voice level. They were rushing up the steps of the battlements with as much haste as her small Gnome legs could manage, but she refused to arrive anywhere in disarray and out of breath. "I am happy that the Knights chose to work with us at all. To invite us in their Redoubt is a gesture of acceptance I would not have expected."

"It was either that, or let their people die of fleshrot and nettlebane," someone said. "Their Gallants may have talents in water and life, but they are no healers."

"And now they order us to attend this meeting? To drop our cases and rush into their tower fastness?" Dahria, one of her oldest friends and most talented Mender shook her head. Her matronly features were sunken in worried disbelief. "To not even send a litter for the Prioress. It is a scandal."

"Hush, Dahria. It is fine," Alessa assured her, and all the others listening. "I've lasted through four Knight Commanders and two wars. A few steps will not be the end of me."

They hit the third landing within the fortress complex and took a sharp left, following the young Gallant guide who was only a dozen paces ahead of them. He jittered from foot to foot, impatient for them to catch up. Alessa offered a calming smile to the boy. "It is just ahead, yes?"

"Yeah?" he said.

"I imagine you're needed elsewhere. You needn't wait on us, child. We can find our own way." The boy hesitated once more, and the Prioress made a shooing motion with her hands. "Go on. We can walk down a simple corridor."

A grateful grin flashed across the Gallant's pimpled face before he took off, tearing around a bend in the hall and vanishing. Diana frowned after him. "Off to prepare for a fight, no doubt."

"Perhaps. If this new arrival intends harm, then we should all prepare for the eventualities of battle." Alessa looked to her Menders, thirteen strong women clad in the formal robes of their order. All of them were weary, but none of them hesitated to throw themselves into the chaotic aftermath of every clash that had occurred over the past week. She walked a touch faster. "I only hope the Knight Commander's fervor for protection does not arouse conflict where it can be avoided."

Dahria made an agreeing sort of noise from the back of her throat, and all the Menders followed the Prioress down the short, curving corridor. They passed three intersections, but their goal was the central tower, where the Knight Commander held court beneath the shroud of her impressive wards. All Redoubts had such protections, a feature that made their fortresses all but impregnable and held deeply secret. In the past, Alessa had made quiet inquiries on their wardings in the hopes of providing the Priory with similar protections, but all she had ever received for her trouble was a scathing rebuke from the previous Knight Commander. Perhaps she could have pressed in the decades since, but the wisest course was almost always cautious.

A hand suddenly extended before the Prioress, halting her in her tracks. "Prioress. Wait. Something is in the hall before us."

Alessa tucked a lock of white hair behind an ear, peering through the curtain of protective hands. Ahead, sprawled on the square-cut tiles of the Redoubt hallway, was a russet-colored puppy. She clucked her tongue. "A Dire Hound pup, unless I miss my guess. Injured, too, it looks like. Hardly a looming threat, Dahria."

"Why is it here, though?" the Mender asked.

"Dire Hounds are popular pets. Could have wandered off from one of the refugees. Or perhaps a Knight or Gallant has a soft spot for the creature." Alessa ducked beneath her subordinates' barring arms, eyes locked onto the limping pup. Mana surged up from her core, spinning tightly behind her eyes with a tingling sensation. "He has the Bleeding Status Condition, though it is Minor. Hi there, little one."

Slowly the Prioress approached the Dire Hound puppy, extending a bare hand for the creature to sniff. His growl cut off and he snuffled at her hand, taking a single, appreciative lick before butting his entire head into her palm. The Prioress let out a single, breathy chuckle. "Yes, it's alright. I don't mean you any harm. *Fine Fettle.*"

Mana swirled from her core of lambent light, flowing from her channels with a puff of deep and comforting warmth. Instantly, the hound's wound stitched itself closed, the blood ceasing its flow, and the pup experimentally extended its hind leg. When it touched the ground without issue, the beast barked once before jumping right into the Prioress' arms.

"Oh!" she cried out, half-surprised and half-delighted. "Why, hello there."

"Prioress! Is it hurting you?" Dahria stepped forward, concern in her face warring with wary amusement.

"No no, of course not." The Hound was half her size, but she couldn't help but hug him a little tighter. He was adorable. "I think he doesn't wish to be left alone, however." Uncannily, the beast nodded its head before burying his snout into the crook of her elbow.

"Do you wish us to take the creature?" Dahria asked.

"No, it's fine. Let us just continue on our way. We cannot hold up the Knight Commander any longer." The Prioress swept forward, ignoring the sputtering protests to put the hound down or transfer him to one of them. Instead, she marched down the curving corridor and right up to the pair of armored Knights that stood to either side of a heavy, steel-strapped door.

Without a word, the sigils within the Knight's breastplate flashed, releasing some sort of lock in the door allowing it to swing inward. "Go ahead, Honored Prioress."

"Thank you." With the Dire Hound pup still in her arms, Alessa stepped into the Knight Commander's inner sanctum.

"I can't believe you had me cut you, Pit." Felix stood within Pit's forest core space, the sound of insects and chittering creatures sounding off in the distance.

"It worked, didn't it?"

"It did. Just don't ask me that again. I don't like seeing you hurt, especially not for one of my plans."

"You worry too much. The tiny lady healed me." A ripple of pleasure trilled across their bond just as a sharp wind rustled the trees around Felix. "Oh, and she's *good* at petting."

Felix rolled his eyes. "Glad you're having a good time. Now just focus on the meeting, please."

"*Fine.*"

"Calm down, little one. You're safe," the Prioress muttered to the hound in her lap. It was clear the pup had been traumatized by something, as he kept jolting whenever anyone moved a bit too fast or suddenly around them. "I will protect you," she said.

The beast settled down, soothed by her words or gentle petting. She didn't blame the pup for being uncomfortable, though she was surprised; it had not reacted in the slightest as they had passed through the harsh wards the Knights always produced. While the powerful tingling had thrummed through *her* entire Body, sizzling just under her flesh, the Dire Hound pup hadn't twitched. To see it now so anxious was both surprising and not; they were surrounded by powerful, Journeyman-Tier Knights and Gallants. To remain impassive under such circumstances would have strained credulity.

The convocation was filled with Knights and Gallants both, at least thirty of them in full armor. They were seated around a depressed area of the room. Each sat upon tiered benches leading down toward the center, where several armored individuals stood beside a thin, crystalline growth.

Knight Commander Lavin. The Knight acknowledged the Prioress with a simple, perfunctory nod as she scanned the room. *You look as tired as I feel.*

The Knight Commander was a Human woman, common among the Knights, and only of middling height for her kind. Aside from a single braid of golden thread over her left shoulder, there was little to identify the woman from another Knights. She gestured at one of her armored fellows, and they stood with great speed.

"Now that everyone is here, we may begin. As you might be aware, someone has just piloted Manaships from the Caleph Pass." The woman who stood had auburn locks tied into a series of complicated braids. The Prioress knew her as Knight Covain, second only to the Knight Commander herself.

"Ships, plural?" someone asked.

"Yes. Scouts have confirmed that, as we speak, ten modified Manaships are in the process of being hoisted through the Pass." Covain shook her head, disbelief clear on her face. "Scouts have also confirmed that each ship is packed with soldiers, bearing a strange emblem upon their breasts. One we have not been able to identify, as of yet."

"Hoisted? And what, exactly do you mean by 'modified'?" Dahria asked.

"They are somehow dragging the Manaship across the dried stretches of the Caleph Pass. How is unclear, as our scouts have been unable to get any closer. And by 'modified,' I mean only that these Manaships are not operating the same way a normal craft would; they sail upon the water, not the sky."

"Strange," Dahria said, again pitching her voice so that the entire assembly could hear her. "Are they damaged?"

"By the storms, you mean?" Knight Covain shook her head. "Not that we saw, but there is only one ship fully within the waters outside the Caleph fortress. Our scouts' Perception Skills are good, but they are not infallible. That they have arrived through the Pass at all would suggest they have found some way of bypassing the deadly stormwall on the other side, not to mention the monsters."

The murmur of light conversation rippled across the assembly. While the Menders' concerns had been with the people in Bogfeld, the Prioress was not unaware of the goings on along the Caleph Pass. She knew of the storm that never seemed to abate, as well as the dangerous monsters that dwelled on the Expanse side of the Stormeater Peaks.

"That is another thing. How did they escape the notice of the monster Den?" Asked an older Gallant, a woman with silver streaked liberally through her dark tresses. "I assume that, if these visitors had been followed by a swarm of those Hatchling creatures, you would have mentioned it. That you haven't is both encouraging and alarming. Who are these people?"

"A question we plan to see answered," the Knight Commander said, taking the center stage from her second in command. "Knight Tandagh, where is the traveler that you brought to us?"

An Orc spoke up from the side, hands folded neatly behind him. "Ma'am. He is down below, kept occupied by the festival."

"And he traveled through the Pass as well?"

"He did. We found him today, just outside the Caleph fortress."

"Is he associated with this new group, then?" the Knight Commander asked.

Tandagh looked a bit uncomfortable with bearing the Knight Commander's scrutiny so long, but he soldiered on. "That is...uncertain, ma'am. If he is, then it can only speak to the quality of their character. This traveler helped us defeat a Bog-Lure and its Sprouts we found just outside the town walls, and then proceeded to pilot the slip through monster infested waters. Gallant Venali can attest to it, but he was nothing but helpful."

"A glowing commendation of these strangers, if he proves to be part of them," Knight Covain said.

"Unless he was a plant, designed to worm into our good graces," said another Knight, an older man with sagging jowls. "Can we not question him?"

"A good idea. Gallant Venali?" the Knight Commander said, and a man with slight, almost delicate features stood from a mass of others. "Go find this Silas Veil and bring him back to us."

"Ah."

The sound was soft, but the impact was felt throughout the entire convocation. Knight Commander Lavin looked up, meeting Alessa's eyes with a deep frown. "The Knights Ghreldan acknowledges the Priory of the Blessed Fen. Thank you for joining us, Prioress Kartez. Did you have something you wished to share?"

"I do." The Prioress leaned forward, her arms full of a very curious hound, but her attention was wholly on the Knights around her. "I recognized that name. A man of that same name visited Bogfeld around a month ago."

"A month ago..." Lavin stroked her chin. "Was that not when parts of your Priory were damaged by a reckless discharge of Skill?"

"It was."

"And when the Paladins of the Pathless were assaulted in the Caleph fortress?"

"I do believe they occurred within a day of each other, yes," the Prioress admitted. "Whether they are related or not, I am unaware. But I do know that a man going by the name Silas Veil did us a great service, and I would be remiss in not mentioning that debt."

"I understand," Lavin said, though she sounded skeptical. "We shall add that to the list of details we can ask this man about, once he arrives."

"Huh," Felix said, tapping his fingers against a tree. "Gonna be hard to find me, I'm thinking."

"What are you going to do?" Pit asked, his disembodied voice echoing around them. "They seem on edge."

"Easy. I'll take a walk," Felix said.

"What?" Pit asked, but it was too late...Felix was already gone.

CHAPTER FORTY-FIVE

Felix slipped from Pit's core space and into the odd darkness that existed just beyond. Such a place existed outside everyone's core, though few were aware of it. Zara had explained that, but it was Vellus who had first shown it to him. It took a twist of his senses to achieve, but in yet another blessing from his Born Trait, he easily recalled how Zara had accomplished the same effect not three weeks ago. Remembering and doing were separate tasks, of course, but Felix's Intent and Will—the essential stats behind core space shenanigans—were up to the task.

It was a strange experience, doing it with his entire self. In fact, existing within Pit's new-formed core space physically had been odd. Before, Felix had simply floated in a weird shell of amorphous light, viewing things through some metaphorical aperture into Pit's own eyes.

Was that how it had been with Pit, all this time? He wondered that as the dark enveloped him. It tugged at his skin, sharp enough to cut, were Felix not made of sterner stuff, and even then, it seared him like friction burns as Pit's core space dropped away from him. Silence encompassed all, muting sounds Felix hadn't even realized he'd been hearing. Like shoving his head beneath the ocean as a kid, fighting to stay in place as the waves swept overhead...and the murky depths were a deep, unknowable threat.

Focus. He put his Intent and Willpower behind his thoughts, pushing at them in the same way he had between his and Atar's core space days prior. *Link Walk. No, that's a dumb name for it. Linkstep. Nope, also stupid...but I don't have a better name for it.*

Felix shunted his focus toward Linkstepping again; however, instead of a hole being immediately punched into things, a tunnel into Atar's core, the world resisted. That was the only way he could describe it. Reality pushed against his efforts, not like a brick wall but an elastic sheet. It stretched and stretched, dimpling with the combined force of his focus...but never breaking.

Damn it. This is probably because I'm physically here, right? I can only Converge with Pit due to our shared Skill, and none of the others have it. Felix had hoped their Tier IV Links would suffice in the same way it had with just his traveling Spirit. Still, the idea burrowed into his brain the more he thought on it; was there a way to accomplish such a thing? Could he teach Etheric Concordance to his friends and use that to basically teleport around, Body to Body?

It seemed unlikely, but then, little was known about the Companion Pact he and few others had established. *Maybe that's the secret to the Shadowgates. Did someone take the idea of Links and build it outside of a person's Aspects?*

The idea was a fire in his Mind, but Felix didn't have time for it. Not then. Instead, he shifted his efforts: if Felix couldn't travel directly to his friends, then perhaps a message would do.

Harn and Palin stood atop the prow of the first Manaship across the Caleph Pass, gazing out into the flooded landscape. Night cloaked the Ghreldan Hills, but it couldn't hide how completely everything had changed.

Yttin sailors bustled atop the lines, fixing sails and tightening spars or something now that they were no longer being manhandled across the dry grounds of the Pass. Claw members hustled about as well, following the orders Harn had set out before stepping away: they hadn't a clue as to the monster disposition in the Hills, not anymore, and the Claw should be ready to battle at a moment's notice.

For now, though, Harn stood with Palin as she stared in disbelief all around them.

“Broken heavens,” Palin said between soft gasps of almost-tears. "My home, my tavern. All of Low Side...gone."

Harn held the woman close and was thankful that her stature was shorter than his. It let him tuck her close to his chest as she grieved, placing his scarred chin atop her crown. It let him hide his scowl. He could *hear* her sorrow, and it was the worst sorta music he'd ever taken in. He didn't like knowing something could do that to her, something he couldn't stop. "Did all of your family come with you when you joined our caravan?"

The half-Dwarven tavernkeep—former tavernkeep—pulled back from his armored chest and dabbed at her eyes. "Yeah. That's about all that's keeping me from tearing into that mess myself. But my patrons?

The old men and women that came every morning to play cards, sip cool ales, and talk? Their homes are there, sunken in that muck. Did they make it out? Did anyone?"

"I can see movement at that fortress on the far end, and that healer place," Harn said, squinting into the distance. The dark night made it difficult, but Yyero's moon was rising over the hills, and the skies were clear. He had heard bells ring out from one of the structures not too long ago and had been keeping a close eye on the fortress ever since. It sounded too much like a rallying cry to make Harn all that comfortable.

"The Knight's Redoubt and the Priory. The Menders would have tried to save everyone they could, and the Knights," Palin let her words linger as she bit a lip in thought. "The Knights aren't all dicks, but too many that chase levels and Temperings find their way into their ranks. I never much trusted them."

"Knights, Paladins, Guilders. All the same, on one level or another," Harn agreed with a grunt. He didn't exclude himself from that list; he'd made a career of hunting for the next level, pushing himself and others as hard as he could go. He still felt that urge, the drive toward the peak...but it felt different now. His hand tightened around Palin's waist, and she let out a small yelp. "Everythin' you care about is here, yeah? Your uncles and aunts came with, and you've got all the recipes for your food and drink memorized, don't you?"

"I—I do," she said, turning her head up to look in Harn's eyes. They were deep and dark, big enough to get lost in, had he the Mind. And he did.

"Then there you have it," Harn grunted. "Problem solved. You'll come with me, back to Nagast."

She kissed him, and this once, Harn didn't mind the music.

"Hello? Hello? Hello, did this work?"

Harn hissed in pain. The sudden voice was louder than any screaming monster Harn had faced, so resonant he felt it shake his very bones. Palin gripped his shoulders, staring at Harn in terror. "Harn! What's wrong?"

"Harn! It's you! It *did* work!" The voice paused. "Was that Palin? Oh shit, did I interrupt something? *Oh no.*" The voice dropped down to a whisper, quiet enough that Harn could stop flinching. "*Did I—were you—?*"

"Felix," Harn said, firm as he could. "Stop talkin'. The answer to that question's no, and before I ask how in Yyero's blighted ass you're doin' this, I need to ask you to *talk quieter.*"

"Oh." The whispering continued. "Is this better?"

"Some. You don't have to whisper just...just don't scream at me." Harn rubbed his temples and gave Palin an annoyed glance.

"What's happening? Fel—the Autarch is talking to you?" Palin looked around, spotting nothing but the crew atop the bustling Manaship. "How?"

"That's what I'm wonderin'," Harn grunted. "You can't hear him?" Palin shook her head. "Then it's probably some magic bullshit. Is it, Felix?"

There was a laugh, but a soft one. "Yeah. It's magic bullshit."

Harn just nodded. He'd had enough experience with things to know when to stop gawking and start asking the proper questions. "Where'd you go, and why're you in my head?"

"I'm in the Knight's Redoubt right now, and I've got important news."

"Your minders are right pissed about you leavin', you know. That Isla came stormin' after you, but I stopped her. Told her you can roam as you please, and you ain't the type to just leave us for no reason." The kid went quiet for a bit too long. "Felix? What's goin' on?"

"You're being watched, and not by me."

Harn's gaze snapped up, his Perception flaring as his various Skills immediately surged into readiness, just at the cusp of activation. "Who? Where?"

"Dunno the where, but it's the Knights Ghreldan, maybe some of their mages. The Gallant Lotuses, they're called." Felix's voice paused. "Their Knight Commander is having a big meeting right now about you guys crossing the Pass. Did you hear the bells?"

"I did."

"That was why. They only saw one ship so far, but that'll change, and I honestly don't know if they're gonna get violent when they realize just how many of us there are."

Harn squeezed the hafts of his axes, thinking. He took in the cliffs that extended from the Stormeaters, and the forests that had become tangled waterways. There were a great many places to hide. "Hrm. We'll find 'em and deal with 'em."

Felix's voice sharpened, a weight settling into it. "Don't kill anyone, Harn. They just seem scared and tired."

Harn just grunted in agreement. "Why? Because of the flooding and the Den? Did you tell them we cleared it out?"

"I'm...sorta undercover right now."

"What?"

"Sneaking. They don't know I'm here. But it's more than the Den; there's monsters all over the waters that come out at night. I've seen a swarm of Draktopi already, and more are infesting the city itself. We have to get rid of them, too."

"Hrm. Might mean there's another Den nearby, or maybe a Nest." Harn grunted and checked how loose his axes were in their sheathes. "Or worse."

Palin's gaze hardened. "You mean there're more of them? Those nasty, noxious fishmen?"

"Aye. I'm imaginin' a great deal more." To Felix, Harn said, "What's the scheme?"

"Okay, it sounds crazy, but it'll totally work."

"Hrm."

"—cannot find him, ma'am."

That caught the Prioress' attention. The Dire Hound pup was restless in her arms, poking his snout in just about every direction while the Knights argued quietly among themselves. The entire time their messengers had been gone, the pup had been whimpering and fidgeting, and at first, she had assumed the beast had another injury. Her Skills showed no such thing however, and no matter how often she petted his silken fur with calming strokes, he refused to settle.

Where could Mr. Veil have gone?

At the other side of the room, the furtive whispers between Knights stopped. Knight Covain stood and tapped the crystalline rod that drove through the middle of the chamber. A series of sparks shot out, curling into vaporous Mana that seemed wan and too thin; the Prioress' Lifesight could track the life Mana in the crystal's discharge, but the other elements were invisible to her. She leaned forward, clutching a trace tighter on the Dire Hound as she witnessed the miracle of the Knights' fortifications.

A flat plane of blue light manifested before Knight Covain and the Knight Commander, and from that plane rose mountains and trees and blocky structures. *It's a map,* she realized. When the trees began to sway, and the blue surface rippled with miniature waves, the Prioress opened her mouth in a moue of surprise. *A* living *map.*

In her lap, the Dire Hound stopped whimpering and went very still. She couldn't blame him. It was *fascinating.*

"It seems our potential informant may have been a spy. They have gone missing from the Redoubt, though no one reports seeing his leaving," Knight Covain reported. She looked to the Prioress and her Menders. "Do the representatives of the Blessed Fen have anything to contribute? Perhaps this Veil's capabilities?"

The Prioress could practically feel Dahria narrow her eyes. "Watch your tone, Knight. Are you suggesting we are hiding things from you?"

"I am not suggesting. I know you are. What does this Silas Veil have to do with the deaths of over a dozen Paladins of the Pathless?"

"I assure you, Knight Covain," Alessa interrupted, flaring her Diplomacy Skill for all it was worth. "If we had pertinent information to share on Mr. Veil's abilities, we would have already done so. What or how he is related to these newcomers is unknown to us, but I will say that he had companions when he came to the Priory. One of which was a Master Tier."

"*That* is information we sorely require," Covain snapped.

"Ward your tongue when you speak to the Prioress, *Knight*," Dahria hissed.

"You—"

"Enough," the Knight Commander said, cutting them all off. Lavin glared at everyone, Knights, Gallants, and Menders alike. "We've no time for squabbling. Send word to the scouts, have them message the flagship under a white banner. I'll not have bloodshed where we can avoid it."

Covain swallowed her anger, and it looked painful. "Ma'am, that would make us look weak. What if they are a threat?"

"If they've a Master Tier among them, they *are* a threat. What matters is how we deal with them," Lavin said, her voice firm. "Send the message."

"Aye, ma'am."

However, even before Covain could nod to her attendants, the projected map began to flash with an eerie crimson light. At almost the same time, a second set of bells began to ring. This time they were accompanied by a sound that set the Prioress' teeth on edge. A watery bellow she found all too familiar after days of struggling against them.

"Rot and damnation," she swore and heard the same from a dozen throats.

Monsters were attacking.

CHAPTER FORTY-SIX

Where have you been? Pit screeched. It inundated him the moment he slipped from the darkness and into Pit's core again, a wind that bent trees and sent insects and small creatures scurrying.

Felix flinched as he landed on the soft, leaf-strewn ground. *Whoa, calm down. It's been like ten minutes. What's wrong?*

It felt...bad. You hurt when you left, and I didn't like it. Pit took several gulping breaths, and the wind died down. Outside, Felix could feel him shifting his paws on the Gnome's lap before finally settling down. *What did you do, exactly?*

Made a phone call. Felix landed among the trees of Pit's core, and through the hollows in the twisting trunk he could see the arguing forms of the Knights and Gallants. Pit was still sitting in the lap of the Prioress, and he was staring out at a map of some sort that had been projected into the center of the room. *Oh, that's neat. Looks like the map my Stronghold can make. Does that mean this place is classified as the same thing?*

Pit gave a warbling shrug.

Probably does. Hm, can you get closer?

Pit laughed inwardly, hiding the reaction with a shake of his jowls. Felix felt a small hand pat his doggy head. *This lady is holding really tight.*

Alright. He could make out a good amount of detail, still. The Redoubt itself was composed of four towers of varying heights, easily identifiable by the darker striations on the dun-colored stone. The walls around it were two fold, with a smaller inner wall around the towers and another, even taller one around the outside of the fortress. Felix was familiar with the former, as he and Pit had scaled it in order to get into the meeting, but the full extent of the outer wall was illuminating.

A solid quarter of the Redoubt was connected to Bogfeld and its own mostly wooden walls, while the remainder of the structure jutted out into what was once a small plateau. Now it was a peninsula, surrounded on three sides by water and the bush-like tops of trees. This also meant, however, that, if there were still threats in the town, then they could reach them through the dry streets of High Side. In fact, a few red blobs were somewhere off in the city itself, ambling aimlessly among the flooded residences and broken shopfronts.

How can we fix this? That was the thought that kept running through his head. Felix knew, without a shadow of a doubt, that the reason for Bogfeld's "Troubles" was his actions. Sure, *he* hadn't set off the chain reaction that unleashed an entire sea into the Scorched Expanse, but it wouldn't have happened had Felix not been there. *No. Instead, we'd have an army of unstoppable Paladins doing whatever they pleased. Interfering was the right decision, I know that.* Felix leaned against the braided trunk of Pit's core tree, pressing his forehead against its rough bark. *But I have the power, and we're ahead of schedule by a day or so. I can help.*

While Felix committed the map to memory—noting all the features he could of Bogfeld, the Redoubt, and some of the Priory—Knights argued with the Menders, talking back and forth about how they wished to deal with the "intruders." He was both surprised and delighted when they came to the excellent decision of sending out someone to parlay with his people. Felix was just about ready to reach out to Harn and change the plan, when the bells began to toll again.

His angle wasn't great, sitting in the Prioress' Gnomish lap, but he could parse out the layout of the fortress around them as well as the growing series of red blobs that were amassing at the northwestern wall. The creatures had simply appeared out of nowhere, and their numbers were increasing rapidly.

The Knights scrambled, Covain and the Knight Commander taking the lead and directing their captains on where to go. Gallants followed after, the Knights' poor cousins, with Mana swirling in their channels. The Menders around him stood, one of the last to leave the chamber, but Felix paid them no mind; because, for a brief second, a deeper, darker red marker had swelled beneath all the others before vanishing. The Prioress stood, holding Pit softly around the middle, and afforded Felix a final look into the projected Mana map. He didn't see the deeper crimson again.

Pit. We need to get out there, Felix sent. *Now.*

Got it.

"How shall we assist, Prioress?" Dahria asked for the rest of the Menders. The lot of them had their inscribed staves out, the sigils already glowing with green-gold Mana.

"Have the triage tent moved to the center of the northern courtyard, away from the western walls." Alessa jabbed her tiny hand at some rushing Knights, halting them in their tracks. "You and you, assist my people in moving the sick and injured along with the tent."

"But—"

"We are—"

"Your citizens are wounded and in danger of death," she snapped, and despite the Knights both being towering Humans, they cowered beneath her glare. "You will aid your people, or I'll see to it your Knight Commander strips you of your rank this very instant."

"Go. Do as she bids."

The Knights jolted, noticing the figure to the Prioress' side and knuckled their foreheads. "As you will, ma'am." They rushed out, followed by the majority of Alessa's Menders as watery roars filled the air outside the warded threshold.

"Thank you, Tris."

"Your healing is worth a great deal more than your ire, Alessa." The Knight Commander looked after her Knights, more of which were running from the warded chambers. The ground quivered as monsters still attacked. She frowned. "I hope we will not have need of either today."

"As do I," Alessa admitted, brushing a lock of white hair from her youthful face. "We shall do our best, regardless."

The frown deepened on the Knight Commander's face. "Why are you holding a Dire Hound pup?"

Alessa smiled, still holding the russet Hound in a cradling carry. He twitched, his legs kicking a bit as he growled at the ruckus outside. He seemed riveted on the door. "A stray I found in your tower. Do you recognize him?"

"No, but the kennels are often full to bursting, and with all the refugees," Tris' face tightened as the words trailed off. "Still, it should not have been allowed inside. I'll speak to the Captains and find out who was on guard duty."

Alessa grimaced, trading a brief look with Dahria. "Come now Tris, surely no one needs to be reprimanded for a single stray—"

A tremor *shook* the entirety of the tower, sending Alessa crashing into the Knight Commander just as the projected map burst into blinding light.

"Blighted Night!" Tris exclaimed at the same time. A wave of foul, unearthly buzzing tore through the chamber, its dire passage tearing sparks from her ancestral armor. More than one of her Knights fell back as their breastplates burst into brilliant, emerald flame. "Fire! Gallants, suppress!"

Alessa, however, fell to her knees, and the pup in her hands kicked with a sudden, *terrible* Strength. It landed several strides away, and the Prioress watched in dawning amazement as its fur wisped into static electricity. That buzzing washed against it, almost visible, rippling its russet fur into...feathers?

"Damn it," the Hound said.

"What?" Dahria said, almost dropping her stave.

"What?" the Hound asked, before gasping. "Whoops!"

Run, Pit! A voice from nowhere shook through the Prioress harder than the beast's discordant bellow. *Now!*

Covain shouted. "That's no Dire Hound! Monster! Monster in the chambers!"

"Good idea!" the Hound—Pit—shouted, before taking off like a loosed arrow. A flurry of Skills chased after the beast, from shadow jaws to water lures to even small crossbow bolts, and all of them missed. They weren't even close, the beast dodging each and every one of them with an erratic grace that Alessa couldn't track.

Covain was screaming. "Close the door! Trap it!"

Run for it!

Alessa winced; the voice was screaming at the edge of her Perception. A Knight just on the other side of the door slammed a gauntleted hand into a series of red-lit glyphs. The array was crushed, and a thick, steel door dropped from the ceiling with all the finality of an executioner's axe.

And with a burst of lightning, the small beast *ripped straight through it.*

"Wow! That hurt!" Pit shouted, trailing pieces of clinking metal from between his feathers. "You didn't say it was gonna hurt!"

You ran through a steel door, dude! Yeah! It's gonna hurt.

Armored Humans and Orcs and Hobgoblins leaped for them, but Pit was too fast. Skills smashed stone tiles and fluted columns, missing him by entire strides in most cases. The real threat ended up being the Gallants, who kept throwing patches of sticky stone or conjured trip wires in front of him. Pit actually had to try to avoid those.

"Gah, I thought the mages were bad!" Pit chirruped in annoyance. "And what was that back there?"

It felt like Dissonance! Felix growled. *If there is another Primordial around here, I'm going to lose my shit. Find a window and jump out. We need to get free.*

"Stop, creature!"

A man in rusty armor stood before them, blocking their path forward at the edge of the long corridor. A wide, arched opening was just beyond him, and Pit could see the chaos unfolding just outside the walls. The lotus on his breastplate gleamed in the torchlight. "Halt! Or I'll stop you!"

Pit didn't stop. More Knights were rushing from behind, hurling spears and arrows all imbued with Skills at his back. So, the tenku did the only thing he could, accelerated to incredible speed and body slammed straight into the Half-Elf mage.

"WAA!"

Together, tenku and mage tumbled out of the arched window. Venali screamed, but Pit's back burst as his Mask finally fell away. Huge wings erupted outward, his Body resuming its pony size and regal, perfect head...and just for fun, Pit borrowed a little something from his Companion.

Hey! Those are my—!

"ARMS!?" Venali screamed, as black, scaled appendages materialized out from Pit's underbelly and seized him by his polished breastplate.

Mantle of Tumult!

"Whoa, stop screaming, please," Pit said. Lightning spun off of his true form like a storm cloud. "It's very loud."

"Wha-but, what?!"

"Oh, those? Those are my Helping Arms!"

You're welcome.

"AAAAAAAAH!" was all the Half-Elf managed.

"Ugh, the screaming." Pit banked around the towers, still dodging the volley of glowing arrows that chased after him. But, if he had been quick on the ground, he was greased lightning in the sky. "I'm gonna drop you off, Venali."

Gently, Pit.

"Yup!"

Pit slalomed through projectiles, Mana swirling around his crackling wings, before diving down toward the festival grounds. People were running, terrified of the monsters at the gates and now shouting in alarm at Pit's descending form. There, among the stalls and wagons, was a displaced mound of hay where children had been playing. Several of them ran from it, scurrying into the worried arms of their parents, but thankfully Pit sensed none remained in the pile. "Dropping you now!"

"Waiiiiiiit!"

Felix's arms released the mage at Pit's urging, and Venali only let out a brief wail before he tumbled unceremoniously into the pile of hay. With a mighty flap of his wings, Pit arced back upward. He could see beyond to the city on their left and straight ahead where the waters churned like rapids. Creatures with dark scales, brightly glowing eyes, and lashing tentacles slammed against the fortifications. It was almost fully night, but they were easy to see for Pit, let alone for Felix.

Let's go to work, Felix sent. Pit screeched in response, an affirmation and joyous battlecry in one. In an instant, they flew over the walls, gathering greater and greater speed...and bounced hard off of a prismatic shield of Mana.

"SKREEEAAWW!"

Pit fell onto the battlements, slamming into the stone hard enough to crack it, and the storm shroud around himself burst in a cascade of vibrant light. Knights and Gallants were everywhere, converging on the spot with Agility that belied their bulky armor, and they surrounded the Chimera with drawn weapons and menacing expressions.

"Do not move, creature!"

Pit let out an apologetic trill. "Sorry, Felix. I thought we'd go right through."

"Kill the beast," snarled a Knight, holding aloft a halberd that glowed a vibrant blue and stepping forward—only to be dazzled by a flash of light…and a hooked blade at his throat.

"Anyone who touches him will die," Felix said softly, and carefully flexed his Spirit. It spilled outward like a slap in the face, driving the breath from everyone within a hundred feet. "Put up your weapons. All of you."

The halberd and other weapons retracted, Mana vapor vanishing as Skills deactivated. Pit let out a cheerful chirrup and regained his feet. "Good choice! We're mighty, you know."

"Pit."

"What? We are!"

A seismic bellow blurred the air, forcing every single one of them into a wincing flinch. From the waters just outside the shimmering shield rose a massive creature of vile proportions and dozens of oozing, goopy limbs. Water and its smaller brethren fell from it like foul debris, and Felix whipped his hooked sword away from the guard. "Get those weapons back out, folks. And open a hole for me. We got a monster to slay."

"I can't do that!" Halberd-man sputtered.

The oozing tendrils smashed into the barrier, sending flecks of red crazing across the shield and shaking the battlements beneath them. Felix shrugged. "Unless you wanna fight it alone."

The young Knight dropped his halberd and fumbled with a glowing brooch. An array of floating sigils manifested from the item, shining with the same glow as the shield.

"Smart man." Felix held his hooked blade in one hand and brandished a short dagger in the other. As the Knight twisted the brooch, an iridescent gap opened in the shield before them. "Pit! That's our cue."

CHAPTER FORTY-SEVEN

The gargantuan serpent beast roared as the shield opened, huge jaws agape and wet tongue quivering, but Felix and Pit gave it little time to act.

Adamant Discord!

Shadow Whip!

Felix changed his mind, resheathed his weapons, and they flew out of the Redoubt with all the speed and subtlety of cannonshot. The monstrous *thing* barely had time to rear back and they were before it, thick Shadow Whip stretched taut between the two of them. Lightning flashed, and they passed through, clotheslining the serpent-like creature hard enough to snap its head back.

Spittle and blood shot into the air as its massive jaws snapped shut, Felix's second Shadow Whip coiling about its knobby snout with as much Strength as he could put to bear. Its severed tongue flipped up and out, a fountain of thick, amber-colored blood. With a grunt, Felix landed on its back, which was covered in barbed spines three feet in length, but his metal-shod feet shattered those closest and landed firmly on its slick scales.

No, not scales, he realized, kicking through another barbed spine that cracked like wood. *Bark.*

Voracious Eye!

Name: Slaughter Nettle
Type: Plant (Manawarped)
Level: 98
HP: 20299/20299

SP: 13149/15958
MP: 3485/3485
Lore: A Slaughter Nettle is a rare evolution of the Bog-Lure, and just as violent as its name suggests. Born in thick marshland, it incorporates fibrous plant matter into its form, growing larger with each piece of the Green Wild it subsumes.
Strength: More Data Required
Weakness: More Data Required

Manawarping again! Up close, it really did look more like a plant than a real monster, though it had those same blue, oozing tentacles that the Draktopi had on them. He could see the goopy material wrapping around the creature's lower Body about twenty feet below them, but above that was thick, ridged bark, thorny branches, and moss-wrapped tendons of creaking wood. All of it formed into the shape of some sort of serpent that reminded Felix heavily of the Naga. *Is the ooze the cause of the Manawarping?* He hadn't seen any on the Hatchlings or the Depthwurm.

Watch out! Pit cried.

Those oozing blue tendrils exploded out of the water and slashed up at Felix, nearly slapping him free of the Nettle's back were, it not for the flurry of frozen projectiles. Jagged spears of ice rained from above as Pit strafed across the Nettle's position, and each spear burst upon impact, flash-freezing parts of the ooze even as electricity danced across the rest. The ice didn't last long, but it locked them up for a few seconds, at least.

More Draktopi down here! And the Knights are firing! Pit reported, whipping in tight circles just out of the Nettle's reach. *Draktopi are crowding the shield, and it's flashing like mad!*

Felix could see that, even around the bulk of the Nettle. Waves of color were flowing off the Redoubt's shields, blues and greens now, but getting lighter and warmer as the monsters kept attacking. *Focus on the lesser beasts! Keep the people safe.*

Got it!

Pit flew off, and the shrill zip of arrows filled the air. They hit hard, so hard that even from the other side, Felix could feel them impact the creature's wide, tube-like torso. Quagmires and paralyzing bindings formed around the oozing tendrils and the Draktopi that still flailed against the Redoubt's shields. There were dozens of the crocodilian squid beasts jetting through the churning waters, but many were being cut down by the Knights and Gallants on the walls, filling the already murky water with dark ichor.

"Ready! Fire!"

From atop the wall, Felix sensed a potent salvo coming from the assembled Knights, but he had no chance to do anything but hang on. A screaming bundle of raw heat slammed into the monster and engulfed it, so searing it set Felix's tunic ablaze. He gritted his teeth against the pain. Frankly, he was surprised it cut through his resistances at all, but it was clearly enough to hurt the Nettle, which vibrated so hard Felix nearly fell off, even with its throaty roars muted by the Shadow Whip.

Rime Shaping!

Ice Mana surged downward from Felix's feet, shaping a trail of hoarfrost along the Nettle's vegetation before impacting the sizzling goop of its tendrils. It hit the water fast and hard, crashing into the surface and freezing chunks of the monster's appendages in place. The tops of the tentacles had some mobility, but Felix held onto the Shaping, trying to send more and more to crawl up the beast's limbs. All the while, arrows and strange, arcane spells crashed into it and the lesser Draktopi below. Between Felix holding it tight and Pit attacking its tendrils, the creature was well locked down and an easy target for the Knights.

Yet it wasn't defenseless.

With an almighty lurch, the Slaughter Nettle fell backward, hurling its serpent Body into the water and a huge stand of thick-branched trees. Felix held on, summoning his battle form and clinging tightly to his Shadow Whip as he was slammed down onto branches and trunks, shattering them and the ice before plunging into the depths.

Everything went silent, yet rushed all the same. The Nettle landed atop him, writhing and twisting with all the malicious glee of a crocodile, grinding Felix into the rocky ground at least twenty feet below the waterline. Rocks shattered beneath them, tearing what was left of his tunic and pants to shreds and carving deep furrows into his scaled back while dirt and debris clouded his vision. Even with the protection of Armored Skin and his Sovereign of Flesh, Felix couldn't stop the damage, only repair it, and his Essence stores were burning up with the efforts to boost his healing.

Felix dropped Shadow Whip and dug his talons into the Nettle's bark, tearing chunks of oozing sapwood with every movement. His boots retracted into armored rings around his ankles and freed the talons there to kick and claw as well, until Felix burrowed an entire damn hole into the creature's back. The Nettle was still grinding itself against the lake bed, but he was out of the way now, and finally his Sovereign of Flesh was able to catch up on the damage to his Health.

Felix! The flagship is coming in fast! Pit sent to him, sounding out of breath even in his Mind.

Great. Wait! Yes! Great! Felix fumbled at his waist, awkwardly pulling free a small dagger. *Tell them to head toward me! Full speed!*

Okay!

Felix could sense Pit fly away, but he put it out of his Mind and instead focused upon the dagger. *Alright, you. Let's hope you still work.* Slick sapwood and rank water was all around him, and below was scraped-raw bedrock. With all of his might, Felix slammed the dagger up, pommel first into the Slaughter Nettle. *Grow!*

Mana surged from Felix's channels, a rushing torrent that soaked into the grip of his Skyslain's Riposte like water into sand. In response, he was thrown so fast and so hard that it was all Felix could do to hang onto the dagger's crossguard as the blade hit the bedrock, stopped, and kept growing in the opposite direction. The entirety of the Nettle was hurled upward at speed as the power and growth of the Skyslain's Riposte shoving it bodily from the water.

Just in time for the Manaship to ram right into it.

"Take it down!" Harn bellowed, and the Fiend's Claw responded with a cry that sent the water skittering away in waves. Felix scrambled out of the Nettle's wound, his massively grown dagger now wedged straight *through* the Nettle's center mass. Getting that out would be some work, and with the absolute hurricane of Skills that were slamming into the beast all around him, Felix wasn't willing to take the time. He hopped out of the shallow wound and yanked himself upward, grasping the thorns along the Nettle's back with every vaulting pull.

Far below, oozing tendrils whipped up from the water, smashing into the prow of the ship and sending a number of the Claw stumbling back. In an impressive feat of athleticism, Alister ran forward, sliding along the slick deck on his knees as Mana rushed outward from his hands and head, forming a massive shield nearly forty feet in width. The next strikes slammed down, but they rebounded with a crash, leaving smears of its bubbling ooze behind.

"Use the shield! Beef!" Harn shouted, before leaping up onto the edge of the force shield and running along its top. More tendrils slashed after him, but Harn was too fast, springing over them before taking a final jump straight onto the Nettle's rough Body. His axes slammed into the creature's bark skin with twin thwacks, followed only seconds later by the oversized form of Beef and his massive great maul.

The Nettle swayed, and from his higher vantage, Felix could see the Redoubt's shields flashing in deep oranges and reds. A high-pitched whine had entered the battle, barely audible over the fray, but increasing in volume with every handful of attacks. For some reason, the Knights were standing back, no longer attacking, despite the danger. Felix could sense a number of Perception Skills being trained on him specifically, but very few even seemed to care about the monsters. The Draktopi were thinning out, but there were still at least twenty going absolutely rabid at the base of the fortress. Sooner or later, the shield would fall.

Pit! The Draktopi!

On it!

His Companion flew low, sweeping right over a number of the Claw's faces and shouted something. Thirty of them split off, heading to the port side of the ship and unleashing their ranged attacks against the Fathom spawn in the water.

Below, silver fire and washes of dark gray chitin started to overwhelm the Slaughter Nettle. It was proving to be very strong, though; even after being stabbed through and pummeled with magic, its Health was only at around half.

"I'm not done yet," he muttered, and unsheathed his curved khopesh. The bronze blade glimmered with magic as he activated Wild Threnody, sounding the sour strains of his Corrosive Strike until the entire sword was dripping with virulent green liquid. Mana congealed onto the blade like a second skin.

Wild Threnody is level 75!
Adept Tier!
You Gain:
+10 WIL, INT, END

Ignoring the notification, Felix struck downward onto the monster's angled neck. Acid ate through vegetation and moss, sizzling over the vines and cutting deep furrows into its sapwood. Again and again, each swing biting deeper than even his talons had, each swing swelling with more acidic Mana. Tendrils reached up, slapping at him where he hung, forcing Felix to dodge among the thorny protrusions on the Nettle's back. But Wild Threnody sang in him, an untamed music that spiraled through his channels and pumped like the drumbeat of war. Mana was his to command, to shape, and it burned through his Mana Gates and surged across the face of his Inheritor's Will.

Wild Threnody is level 76!
...
Wild Threnody is level 80!

Something inside him rang out, a massive gong struck by the world's largest mallet, and the Skill *shifted.* A new pattern surged into place, smoothly adding onto the old Threnody as the Mana within him shot from his channels with more force than ever before. Again, two tendrils whipped up, but this time instead of running, Felix pivoted and slashed...sending two crescents of sizzling acid Mana flashing outward. They severed the tendrils with a sizzling pop that made the Nettle shriek into the sky.

"Oh, I like this," Felix said with a grin.

"What are they doing, ma'am?" Knight Covain asked.

"You can see just as well as I, Yani."

Knight Covain could, in fact, see what was going on, the problem was that she couldn't believe it. The strangers had sailed their Manaships toward the monstrosities that had besieged them and, not hesitating in the slightest, had *rammed* their crafts into its side. The ship was greatly damaged, but none seemed to care, and instead figures in armor and dark cloaks had begun raining destructive Skills atop the monster horde. Even more unbelievable was the one that had somehow infiltrated their fortress in the first place. According to her Knights, it was a man, but the creature she saw laughing atop the Slaughter Nettle was not a man at all.

You Have Killed A Draktopus (x27)!
XP Earned!

You Have Killed A Slaughter Nettle (Manawarped)!
XP Earned!

She grunted in surprise over how...little XP she felt settle into her core. The majority of it came from the Draktopi, of which they'd outright killed more than a few. From the Nettle, however, she barely felt a trickle. "Gallant Quin. What was its Health?"

"Over ten thousand, ma'am. My Analyze couldn't get a full read on its totals, just its current when I joined the wall and...and the foreign combatants had already done a number on them." A woman with dark orange eyes stared out through the shields, to where the strangers were gathering just atop the downed Slaughter Nettle. "It is remarkable."

"Indeed," Knight Covain said. They had not put through even a portion of that amount of damage, despite the opening Sunder Blade that the Knight Commander had sent out. That was part of why she'd halted their offensive, once she had seen the two enemies engaging with one another. "Hold yourselves ready," she said again. "Skills at bay."

She did not know what to expect from these strangers. They were too strong. As Covain watched them kill the last of the Fathom spawn, her guard did not ease. *That man. Someone who could stop these creatures, almost single-handedly, was—*

Another Gallant stepped forward, tapping his heels and saluting at the Knight Commander. "Ma'am. The...he is requesting entry. Again."

Covain gripped her sword hard. She hadn't noticed the man move from atop the dead Nettle, but he was there, *floating* before their shields like some sort of ghost. His entire Body was covered in dark, tight-fitting armor, and blades at his waist dripped with gore...but his expression was mild. He waved.

"Let him in," the Knight Commander ordered.

"Ma'am," Covain warned, but the Commander only held up a single finger. Covain clenched her jaw, forcing her protests back down.

The armored man floated through the gap in their shields. The whining from them increased in volume only a short while before fading as the gap closed; the shields were still damaged but would repair themselves in time. The man landed atop the wall, his feet sizzling a bit with miniature blue-white lightning, and he gave a wide smile to everyone. "Hi. Sorry for barging in earlier."

"Is that what you call infiltrating a private convocation?" the Knight Commander asked, her voice far more...comfortable than Covain liked.

The man winced and ran a clawed gauntlet up and through his hair. Covain wasn't sure how, but the armor *flexed* as he did so, moving with his Body. "Ah, well. I was worried you were going to attack my ships."

"They are yours?" The man nodded once again. "Who are you?"

"Oh!" He stuck out his hand. "I'm Felix—ah dang, one sec." Covain nearly dropped her sword when the armor on his entire Body just...vanished, turning into skin and hastily repairing clothes. He put out his hand, this time entirely scale-free. "I'm Felix Nevarre, Autarch of Nagast and the Leviathan Depths. Nice to meet you."

No. Not a man, Covain thought with a quiver of fear.

A monster.

CHAPTER FORTY-EIGHT

A plume of dust tore into the sky above the stepped plains, visible for leagues to any who cared to look. At its head, four loping creatures ran with tireless legs that blurred in the washed-out winter sun. The mountains were behind them by a bare half-league, and the curious, uneven terrain stretched ahead of them, seemingly without end. Seated atop the creatures were four figures in smooth, milky white armor and thick, fur-lined capes that streamed behind them in billowing folds.

"It is colder than I remember," one at the side said. She was wider than the rest by a full handspan, and a massive mace made of red-gold orichalcum hung from her saddle. "I do not like it."

"You don't like much, Mace," said the warrior to her left. She was far more slender across the chest and waist, though her powerful legs gripped the racing lizards beneath her saddle. A spear made of the same red-gold metal was sheathed near her stirrup. "You were complaining about the heat near Amaranth, too."

"That spitfire mountain makes everything too hot. And these plains are colder than a Dragoon's bedside." The one called Mace laughed; she laughed even harder when that orichalcum spear flashed up at her neck, stopping a hairsbreadth away from her skin. "Oh come off it, Spear. Don't pretend to hold affection for your old order."

The spear dropped, resheathed beside the slender figure with nigh-invisible speed. "It is a matter of honor, Mace. One never truly leaves the Dragoons. Do not besmirch them."

"Hm."

The other two were somewhere between Mace and Spear in build, though the one with the golden longsword strapped to his waist was stockier than the gangly figure holding open a book. The man with the sword shook his head and guided his mount around an oncoming protrusion of stone. Such natural obelisks were all over the stepped plains, some claimed as a result of an ancient conflict between elementals in the distant past. "Spear. Mace. Focus on the task at hand. We are nearing our destination."

"Of course, Sword."

"As you wish."

The one known as Sword nodded to himself and urged his basilisk forward. There was no snow on the ground, despite the frigid temperatures, for which Blade was grateful. The basilisks were not as fast in snow, preferring the hard-packed, rocky soil of their southerly homeland, but they were still incredibly fast beasts. Bred for Agility and Endurance, it was said a basilisk could run down an Agility-focused warrior of the same Tier and still have enough energy to kill them with their barbed and poisoned tails. *Savage creatures, tamed by our hands. As it should be.*

"Ah."

"Tome?" Sword asked, looking to the thin man on his right. He was gazing into the sky, his face hidden by the same smooth helmet they all wore. Sigils glimmered briefly across its surface. "What do you sense?"

"Tier III flyers coming in fast from the west," Tome reported before turning his attention back to the pages on his oversized book. "I count two hundred. Likely the flock that has been threatening the Manaships."

It took a few moments, but soon they could all perceive the flying monsters that were diving from high above. Sword sighed in annoyance. "Good. Then we can eliminate them, so our forces can move from the mountains. Spear? Take care of the trash, if you would."

"Very well."

The avian beasts burst into flame as they dove, the air screaming from around their outstretched pinions. Large meteors formed in the monsters' talons, swirling with molten stone, and their hateful, malicious Spirits pressed down upon them all. The basilisks kept running, their hooded eyes never once straying upward or otherwise responding to the monsters' dire Intent. Sword, Mace, and Tome all rode forward, equally unconcerned as their companion raised her long, orichalcum spear.

"Shatter. Let Fall The Heavens."

The moment the words left Spear's lips, Sword could feel the Mana surge outward, practically flooding the sky as two hundred pikes manifested; each one above a single avian. Spear thrust viciously forward, and as if in mimicry, the conjured pikes of air stabbed downward with all the force of a collapsing mountain. Horrendous shrieks pierced the heavens, only to end in a wheezing death rattle as each and every monster was struck low, their flaming bodies slamming into the plains before them. None of the warriors slowed, the basilisks evading them like the falling debris that they were.

Spear sniffed. "Barely any experience at all. I would have expected more from the creatures the Inquisition and Paladins had such trouble with."

"Manaships function on a very delicate balance of Mana types. The injection of a new, foreign type in large enough quantities is enough to damage a sigil-engine," Tome informed them all. "Admittedly, our Manaships are well-shielded and penetrating deep enough through the hull to even reach the engines is a tall order—but the risk is still there. That is why they waited behind us."

"Informative, as always, Tome," Sword said, a wry tone creeping into his voice.

"I don't remember askin', though," Mace said, blunt as her choice of weaponry. "But the way is clear, yeah?"

Tome tilted his featureless helm, going so far as to partially close the silver-wrought book for which he was named. After a long pair of moments passed, he nodded. "No other accumulation of beasts are nearby. At least none that would threaten our Manaships."

"Good. Send the signal, then," Sword ordered. He had been assigned lead on this mission, though all four of them held the same rank within the illustrious High Guard of the Pathless.

"It is done."

"Mm. Spear? If you would. I do believe these lizards need to show their worth, no?"

There was a glee in Spear's voice that could not be hidden by her faceless visage. Sigils sparked rapidly across her helm. "Aye. *Winds of the Valley Serpent!*"

Another wash of chill, bracing Mana hit their party, and all at once, the speed of the basilisks increased tenfold. The creatures let out a surprised hiss but leaned into the sudden boost, their frills extending along their head, back, and limbs acting as stabilizers as they ran and leaped across chasms and small, descending cliff faces.

The stepped plains were devoured beneath their pace, and by the time the sun was setting along looming mountains ahead the team rode into the dilapidated walls of Setoria. A massive wall of fog split the horizon, rising so high that it blocked the light of the setting sun so completely that entering Setoria felt like riding into the Night itself.

Sword eyed the wall, attempting to push his Perceptions through its opaque surface and failing. He growled, radiating a displeasure that sent crowds of people scattered from their path, their dirty, hunger-worn faces staring after them like fools. Sword identified a number of Inquisitors among them, their pristine crimson cloaks hard to miss, especially when they scrambled to salute once they realized just exactly who was riding into their presence. It was petty, perhaps, but he always found the veneration a fair bit intoxicating and couldn't help the secret smile that stretched his lips.

Their mounts were blowing and trembling, but Mace laughed as they drew abreast of the largest contingent of Inquisitors. "Redcloaks! Rejoice! Your salvation is here!"

An awed cheer went up, and Sword heard a number of them exclaim about the majesty of the High Guard. As was proper. He lifted his hands, demanding silence. "My brother speaks true! We have come to lead you against this upstart despot and to reclaim the lands he has stolen from the Hierocracy! A battalion of Paladins and Inquisitors rides just behind us and will touch down in a few short hours."

This time, the cheering was deafening as Apprentice and Journeyman Tier lungs shook dust from the nearby eaves. Over the din, Sword used his much stronger Master-Tier voice to bellow. "Ready your blades, and steady your hearts! This vile barrier will fall by midnight!"

The Rimefangs were on fire.

Kellis Faer, Hierei of Calumb, Pax'Vrell, and Sao'thun stared into the smoke-choked sky and could not help the feeling of despair that crawled across his old heart. Since their forced entrance into the Halls of the Hinterlords and subsequent...subdual of the Giathban warrior caste, the Unbound Imara had torn a swath of destruction across the whole of the mountain range. It wasn't until the Hinterlords acquiesced to her demands for access to their deepest vaults that she stopped her wanton destruction.

The Gnome had proven wily and more than capable of evading even Imara's might. Owing to some strange magic the creature had learned, it could vanish into the stone as if it were water, and it seemed to require neither food nor water as it ignored their baited traps. In fact, the hunted Unbound proved to be more clever than expected, utilizing Imara's impatience and quiet rage against her time and again.

> *...in the latest skirmish, the Gnome led Imara into the castle fastness of Hinterlord Klagg Orskellig. His unique gifts let him bypass the excessive wardings on the castle, and Imara followed suit straight through the barricaded portcullis and gate. The Gnome remains at large, while the damage done to Castle Orskellig and the Hierocracy's reputation is equally devastating.*
>
> *It is with a heavy heart and humble insistence that the Unbound known as*

Imara should be confined to the Shining Palace until better strictures are in place to guide her willfulness.

Blessed In The Light,
Hierei Faer

Kellis finished his missive to the Hierophant and carefully folded it before drizzling a deep pool of wax atop its edge. With the ring upon his pinky finger, he pressed that wax with the symbol of his Authority: a tower topped by three stars.

"*Call Minor Messenger*," he muttered into the wind. The Skill spread from him, moving in a way that Kellis swore was like ripples in a pond. It was perhaps a fanciful way of viewing the activation of his power, especially considering his core was attuned to light, which everyone knew moved in straight beams. Fanciful or not, it did not hinder the efficacy. A pure white songbird alighted on the sill of his window, briefly fluffing up its feathers before hopping inquisitively toward him. No words were exchanged, but a vague pulse of Intent flowed across their sudden bond. *Need?*

Kellis handed the missive wordlessly to the songbird, and it picked it up in its beak with the gentlest of motions. A single quirk of its head was all the Hierei got before it flew off once more, letter in hand. Or beak, as it were.

The Hierei looked out after the songbird, tracing the peaks that still had not been extinguished. Imara wandered the forested hills and cliff faces, hunting after the elusive Gnome with the single-mindedness of a Dire Hound. It was both the most foolish thing Kellis had ever seen, and the most frightening.

That woman could level an entire kingdom, given enough time. He feared only a Grandmaster could stand up to her, and warriors of such caliber were few and far between. Kellis pursed his lips, sending his Perception Skills questing outward after the Unbound, tracing the Mark on her Spirit. He could sense her two leagues distant, her own Spirit horrifyingly flat despite being engaged against a horde of Tier III beasts. *At least her violence is aimed at monsters, this time.*

The impact of the Hierophant's personally trained Unbound was unmistakable, and the repercussions of her choices would echo for longer than he cared to admit. The Hinterlords were aggrieved and incensed. Their attitudes toward the Hierocracy more foul than ever, thanks to Imara's actions in chasing her target. The neighboring Clans had even taken up arms to prevent the woman from forcing her way through their mountains, as well. They did not know they stood no chance against Imara's Strength; not even Kellis himself could contend against the forces that woman could bring to bear.

Yet action must be taken.

Kellis slipped a second sheet of rich vellum from his satchel and placed it perfectly atop his borrowed desk. At the same time, he sent his Mana expanding outward from every one of his Mana Gates until a crystalline sphere formed around his desk and person. Sigils briefly flared along the sphere's surface, symbols denoting *silence*, *hidden*, and *dream*, among others. They locked into place, rotating as each sigil slipped into an array forged entirely on the spot...without a true Skill behind it at all.

Dipping his quill into an ink pot, he adjusted his long sleeves with all the care of someone who routinely wore pure white. Then, when all was in place, he began to write.

Mauvim of the Hidden Song.

I seek an audience.

CHAPTER FORTY-NINE

You've Fully Consumed A Monster Core!
You Gain:
+1 STR
+1 PER

Pit warbled contentedly to himself, happy with his harvest. So many monsters had died within the waters around the Redoubt that the waters looked like they were on fire, with all of the black smoke that steamed from the surface. Finding and getting to a corpse before it broke down had been easy when the field was filled with them, but as the hours passed and fewer beasts dared charge their position, Pit found it harder and harder to catch the cores before they broke apart completely. The black smoke tasted awful, and twice he had a core trash itself in his mouth. Disgusting.

He clawed up onto a boulder that once sat atop a low hill; now only the peak of the oblong rock was above the waterline. Pit shook himself, shedding droplets from his fur and feathers before stretching his wings wide in the waning moonlight. A bare half sliver of Yyero's light hung above the rocky horizon, but it was more than enough for his evolved eyes to pierce the night. Pit could make out all eight of their Manaships that were now anchored near the Knight's Redoubt. "Close, but distant enough so they can't stab us in the back," as Harn had put it.

Eight of their ten ships had been moved across the Caleph Pass, with the last two still in progress. The how of it didn't make much sense to Pit, except that Beef had worked with the Chanters and the mages to create a sort of moving platform of chitin and water. Sigils were involved, and Pit never really understood that stuff. He left all that to Felix.

Felix, meanwhile, had gone and had a chat with that Knight Commander lady. And that nice Gnome, too. They'd been talking for hours—the whole time Pit had been fighting and eating, in fact—leaving everyone else outside the walls of the Redoubt. Most of his friends were here now, though most stayed on the boats. Only Vess had stepped out, mostly to fight, though also to inspect a few of the more prominent Fathom spawn. She had been concerned that the Slaughter Nettle was so similar to the Depthwurm, as she had heard it described quite differently in her studies.

"The Fathom corrupted creatures to make them more draconic," Vess had said to Pit. "A plant Type had been made into a serpent with oozing tendrils, and bark shaped into a facsimile of scales. Obscene."

The Fathom spawn were also rotting slower than others, perhaps due to the water, though both Pit and Vess were unsure. Vess had wanted to ask Isla, but the woman was hanging back at the Pass along with Zara. So, instead, she'd had Pit haul a few of their carcasses out of the water and onto the ship for inspection and observation. Pit had done so, though he'd grumbled the whole time. He had been hungry, after all.

They'd had plenty of opportunity for more, as it turned out. The monsters had resumed their attacks not an hour after the Slaughter Nettle had died, rushing from the depths in a swarm. Throughout the night, they had fought them back, Felix's Claw taking on the brunt of the assaults. The Knights and Gallants provided the occasional strike from behind their shields but little more than that.

Pit had simply shrugged and joined in the fray, happy to keep the experience to himself.

All kinds attacked, not just Fathom spawn, but there were always a handful with every wave, and they were always more powerful. Pit still wasn't the best at reading their Affinities, not like he was with Felix, but amid all the rage, he detected fear and pain. Like the Fathom spawn were spurring on the others. So on they came, relentless and unending for hours.

The Claw was good at killing, though. So was Pit. He'd heard more than a few of them exclaim at a new level, and Pit himself had earned two, boosting all of his stats up once more. He now sat at level sixty-nine.

Nice. He settled back on his haunches, checking on his Skills. They were leveling well, though his focus had been on his ranged and flight Skills more often, lately.

Bloody Gnaw (E), Level 73
Hurricane Rasp (E), Level 74

Howl At The Dark (E), Level 68

Dawn's Advent (E), Level 77
Adept Tier!
Gain:
+10 INT, WIL, DEX

Tempest Fugit (L), Level 76
Adept Tier!
Gain:
+15 END, VIT, INT

Cold Resistance (C), Level 39
Mantle of Tumult (L), Level 74
Thunderwing (L), Level 65
Poison Resistance (C), Level 32

Dawn's Advent and Tempest Fugit had earned him twenty-five points in Intelligence, ten in Willpower and Intent, and fifteen points in Resonance and Dexterity. Surprisingly, Poison Resistance had also leveled, netting him a simple three points in Endurance, Vitality, and Strength. That, coupled with his leveling bonus, had his core humming with System energy, thrumming through his channels with an electric glee. It was enough that Pit wanted to dive back down and hunt for more cores to press his Skills that much harder.

He held himself back, though, as the Knights atop the nearby walls started to make moves. His bond to Felix brightened suddenly, as if he were a sun passing from behind a cloud; a sensation no doubt linked to the wardings in that strange command chamber, Pit surmised. Making logical connections like that had become a great deal easier for him, now that he'd evolved, just as it had been a bit easier not to panic when Felix faded slightly originally.

Felix? All good? he sent.

All good. A sensation of vague annoyance accompanied the words from his Companion, but that vanished quickly. *How did the fight go?*

Pit sent him a bundle of sense memories, a trick they'd learned long ago, encompassing the highlights of the fight. At least, as far as Pit was concerned. *Fight went well. We won. I don't think any of the Claws died.*

I hope not. A pause. *Can you go get some people for me, bud?*

Pit tilted his head. *Who?*

Atar. Zara. Alister. And as many of the Arclights as you can. I'm gonna need some help.

Pit crouched low before leaping upward, a blast of air Mana sending water away from his boulder in a hectic crash as he shot into the sky. He angled himself toward the Manaships. *Help with what?*

Just some civil engineering.

The dawn was coming quickly and with it, a miracle.

Or so Mr. Veil promised. Or was it Nevarre? His names were as numerous as his apparent titles.

Mage. Warlord. Autarch.

That had been a surprise to the Prioress, but the expression on the Knight Commander and her second's faces had been almost worth it. They all recognized his true name, of course; Alessa doubted anyone of any importance had forgotten the abrupt message from near on a month back. Of a new Lord laying claim to a Territory that existed on no one's maps.

The last part had been a bit of a frustration for her scribes. The Menders prided themselves on their records, and though most of it was dedicated to the healing arts, they still had substantial tomes written on the various Territories around the Ghreldan Hills. Far from exhaustive, they still covered at least ten Territories in their annals, but none bore the name of Nagast.

A mystery, and far from the only one. Such things seemed to spring wholesale from Mr. Nevarre's shadow, such as how he manifested such deadly armor at will, or the manner of artifact he bore that allowed his clothing to change at a moment's notice. The man had gone toe-to-toe with the Slaughter Nettle, thrown into the water under its immense weight, and emerged virtually unscathed. And oddest of all: rumors pointed to the fact that he and that Dire Hound were somehow tied together. That he...emerged from the Hound during its mad flight from the Knight Commander's chamber. A Hound that now resembled those fabled rumors of a Chimera.

"A remarkable man. What does he intend to do now?" she wondered aloud.

"Save our town, he said," Covain sneered at his back as they walked toward the outer walls of the Redoubt.

"I heard his words, Knight Covain. I simply wonder at the Intent behind it."

Covain grunted and Alessa raised her eyebrows in surprise; that was as much agreement she'd ever gotten out of the woman. "I'll admit, his forces have helped us. My Knights are clear on that. But to be so arrogant as to single-handedly save our town...from what? The depths themselves?"

"Something like that."

Covain started, her hand gripping her pommel hard enough to creak the Journeyman steel. Mr. Nevarre was dozens of paces ahead of them, already at the walls and gazing out toward the half-flooded remains of Bogfeld. Alessa swore she could see the hint of a smile before he turned, and his expression returned to one of calm consideration. "Who leads the Gallant Lotuses?"

"I do," Covain said. "Beneath the auspices of the Knight Commander of this Redoubt."

"Alright. Can you loan me as many as you're able to?

The details on the Autarch's plan had been vague, and in fact, he had gone silent a number of times during their conversations, only to resurface a time later with strange assurances. Honestly, Alessa was not sure what to make of the man, except that he seemed earnest and willing to help them. He also seemed equally unwilling to accept payment for his actions, whatever they ended up being.

"Might I have your word, your Oath, that they will not come to harm?" the Knight Commander asked, stepping forward from somewhere behind the Prioress and her second.

"Nothing I do will hurt them, I swear," he said.

"Not by action or inaction?"

"I swear on my power and Authority," Felix Nevarre said, and the world *hummed* in response. Alessa watched, aghast, as Tris winced beneath the sheer weight of that Oath. How much Authority did this man hold? "You...are you okay?"

"Fine, Mr. Nevarre." Tris straightened, and the impassivity of her office settled across her features again. "I have your Oath. You may have all the Gallants who wish to aid you."

"Thanks. That should make this a sight easier," he said. "I'll need them all in the city in the next quarter glass. Sound good?"

Covain nodded. "It shall be done."

Soon, the Gallants stood within the square outside the Redoubt's city gate, at least two hundred of them. They were joined by more than three times their numbers from the Autarch's ships, all of them wearing armor and cloaks emblazoned with a blue eye upon the back. A symbol of House Nevarre, Alessa supposed.

But a part of her wondered at that. What House holds so many soldiers, all of them trained in the magical arts? Her gaze lingered on the ships, the last two of which having joined their brethren over the last short while. Life Mana surged among the ships, evidence of hundreds, perhaps thousands within. *Does he travel with his entire House? Why? And from the disastrous Expanse?* He had been close-mouthed about what happened in the desert, only telling them that Ahkestria had survived and that an impossible ocean now filled the entirety of the Territory. *What other wonders does this man have hidden away?*

She soon found out.

Two men in robes—one in a blue a few shades darker than her own, another in black—walked among the Gallants and Nevarre's mages, dragging inscription tools in the stone beneath them. A trail of bright Mana was left behind, blue and red-tinged white, forming into a complicated series of glyphs and sigils that Alessa could not follow. The Priory did not use sigaldry, apart from the most common of sigils, not out of disdain but a lack of education—learning sigaldry was a Skill that could only be leveled under the influence of a major guild, after all.

The Priory of the Blessed Fen was independent, and as such, relied far more on the time-proven traditions in their herbalism and practical medicine, with a bit of alchemy on the side. So when a city-block-wide array suddenly lit with wave of shimmering Mana, Alessa was just as astounded as all the rest.

"W-what are they doing?" Covain asked. "The Gallants look to be in pain."

"That's a siphon array at their feet," Tris offered, nodding down into the square. "They're getting their Mana drawn on to power the larger formation. Standard operating procedure for Protector's Guild forces when using large-scale sigaldry."

"Fascinating. But what is it doing?" Alessa asked. She also made a mental note to ask the Knight Commander how she knew about the Protector's Guild. They were a major one, but their presence wasn't well felt in the Hills.

"Look," Tris said, pointing at the far end of the High Side. "Can you not feel it?"

There, the waterline that defined the flooding damage of Bogfeld was rippling as if a great wind was pushing it back. Soon, that rippling manifested into looping swirls of aquamarine light, and each loop twisted and coiled, pressing harder against the water itself until it began to creep backward with greater and greater speed. Before long, the tide had risen into a wall of liquid twenty feet high, shoved back along the streets of Low Side until it splashed into the outer wall of Bogfeld...and out of the town entirely.

"Master-Tier magic," Alessa breathed. *But who cast such a thing?* She had seen no one.

"Is that what the formation is doing? Does that allow them to mimic a Master Tier?" Covain asked. Alessa couldn't tell if the woman was horrified or excited by the prospect. "Imagine what we could do with such power..."

"No. That is not the purpose of the formation," the Knight Commander said. "I think...I think this has just begun."

By the gods, the woman was right.

Felix Nevarre walked into the streets, just beyond the range of the formation, and pushed his hands down into the streets themselves. He shattered cobbles with his fists, but didn't flinch, and instead, a vast presence unfurled from around him. Dark brown glimmering with green-gold and deepest blues pressed visually before them, forcing Alessa to blink in order to understand what she was seeing. Her Skills allowed her to view life Mana, and she recognized its green-gold radiance, but the other two were not among her attuned elements. He was wielding three different Mana types, all at once, so powerfully that *everyone* could see them manifest as a cloak that hung around the man.

Covain pointed, looking more and more like a gawking schoolgirl. "The walls! They're repairing!"

Tris gritted her teeth, her hands shaking on the edge of the battlements, and not from nerves. "Not only the walls."

A rumbling filled the air as minute explosions rocked the town; small things, but loud, as the ground itself shifted *upward.* The Autarch hunched, that presence of Mana pouring into the earth once more as the ground shifted again. And again. Now, the formation wrapped about his feet, sigils forming as if by themselves upon the cobbled streets, until the gathered payload of siphoned Mana was sent hurtling into him as well. Through him.

Span by span, stride by stride, the town of Bogfeld lifted from the waters, until every inch of it was a dozen strides above the waterline. Alessa could only watch, speechless and immobile.

"Incredible," Tris whispered.

Covain ran a dry tongue across her lips and shook her head. "A miracle."

CHAPTER FIFTY

Felix pulled his hands out of the shattered cobblestone beneath his feet, wincing at every movement of his Body. With a final shove of his Will, he Stone Shaped the sigaldry back out of the ground around him, effectively sealing off his access to the siphon formation. He sagged in relief immediately.

He'd only intended to use Stone Shape to gradually raise a portion of the town by reinforcing the small plateau on which the settlement had been built. It turned out, however, that the pillars he made to ratchet up the bedrock layer just crumbled underneath the sheer weight. So, Felix had to reinforce them, make them of sterner stuff as he'd learned to do with his Stronghold and Bastion of Will.

It hurt—*so much*—but in a way that wasn't physical, at least not entirely. He'd lost track during the process, but the amount of Mana that had funneled through him dwarfed any working he'd done to date. All of his Aspects were burning like ill-used muscles, but it was a manageable strain, one he'd handled before and knew would be gone before long.

In all honesty, Felix was proud of himself. Lifting an entire town was *ridiculous*, and though he was sure he could do it, he hadn't anticipated having to weave four Skills at once for that long. He'd even managed to use the Chant to do it, too, not relying on the System's activation to access their power. That was the real achievement. That and the Skill levels.

Stone Shaping is level 82!

...

Stone Shaping is level 85!

Green Shaping is level 45!
...
Green Shaping is level 62!
Journeyman Tier!
You Gain:
+6 INT
+6 WIL
+6 PER

Rime Shaping is level 51!
...
Rime Shaping is level 63!

Auroral Forge is level 16!
....
Auroral Forge is level 27!
Apprentice Tier!
You Gain:
+10 INT
+10 WIL
+10 VIT

He'd even managed to incorporate his new light shaping Skill as well, though it had only been in brief touches. Felix could sense them, here and there, threads of hardened light that he'd woven into the tops of the newly-made walls, now twice as high and a glossy blue-black where the red-gold veins didn't glow. It was kinda cool.

I could make street lights with this combination, he mused, trying to think of anything except the ache in his veins. *Glowing stones. Hmm.* Ideas tumbled through his Mind, but none really settled. There was a good deal of Mana in his core that hadn't been his originally, and it was really distracting. Not as distracting as it would be for others, since the various Mana types simply coiled and spun around each other before coalescing down into one of his two cores...instead of detonating inside of him.

Maybe that was being dramatic, but it was part of the warning Alister and Atar had plied Felix with when he'd told them his plan. Even Zara had called it foolish. She was convinced he'd survive, but siphoning Mana in such quantities had killed people plenty of times, let alone mixing dozens of Mana types together. When Atar and Alister started in, Felix just pointed out that it was they who gave him the idea, back when they'd traded sigaldry notes in Nagast. Back then, Alister had been eager to tell them how pitched, mass combat typically worked for

Guilder forces, how a squad of mages would supplement their Mana for a single ally.

"Yeah but that's all the same Mana type. That's the point. Compatibility is the key, as well as keeping it to a reasonable amount," Atar had pointed out.

Felix had disregarded both of those options, but then he didn't see a way to do it without tapping more power than he had. Sure, the almost nine thousand Mana he had was a *lot*, but Felix ate through half of that just on his first attempt to push up the Low Side of the town. Only by drawing in the Mana of his volunteers had given him enough juice to accomplish an impossible task. He was Unbound. He could handle different Mana types, a butt load of power, and whatever agony got thrown at him.

Boy, had he been wrong.

That sucked. Felix had stopped counting when he'd spent somewhere around twenty thousand points of Mana on the working, instead focusing entirely on perfecting each layer beneath them. The pain was still quivering through his everything, but Felix forced himself to his feet and quested outward with his Perception. *It worked, though.*

He could feel the layers below, the new blue-black stone that raised fully half of Bogfeld by about twenty feet and fully replaced the walls all around the town. Cracks and fissures were everywhere, stress points from where his magic upset the shape of the city, and more than a few empty structures were riddled with similar defects. He also spotted Zara leaning casually against the interior of an abandoned shop to his right.

"You're in a state," Zara said, approaching the empty window frame but not leaning out. "I told you so."

"Yeah yeah. And I told you I could handle it." Felix grunted, straightening his back. "Thanks for getting the water out first, though. Probably would have cost a ton more Mana to do that otherwise."

"My pleasure, and a simple enough task."

"Why'd you do it from hiding, though?"

"It is easier to give you the entire credit that way. I had thought the added display would be beneficial to any future negotiations, since I imagine you plan to trade with the Menders, yes?" When Felix nodded, Zara folded her arms. "I did not anticipate you to sound multiple Skills at once, however. Your Skill with the Chant grows. How is your core? Your channels?"

"Feels like I ran broken glass through them, but I'm still standing." He twisted his head, feeling his neck crack and pop. "But it'll hold, now, whether it's against monsters or tsunami waves."

"I would certainly hope so," Zara said, throwing a glance at the far off walls. They gleamed in the dawn's light, their glossy blue-black surface faintly glimmering with red-gold veins. "You replaced them entirely. Those are the same walls I saw in your Stronghold, are they not?"

"Mhm." He could feel the Knights coming out of their fortress now, as the arrays finally deactivated completely. Gallants and Claw mages alike were panting ragged, and more than half had been laid out on the ground. He could hear their steady breathing, which was a relief. "Damn, I thought—they were more tired from the monsters than they let on."

"They wouldn't let down the Fiend." Zara shrugged. "They are in better shape than you are right now."

Felix couldn't only grimace at that. "They pushed themselves hard. Those Fathom spawn were nasty customers. Oh, did you take a look at the Nettle sample that we saved? What did you think?"

Zara glanced back at the Knights that had started filling the square not two blocks distant. They had no line of sight on her and Zara could make herself all but invisible, even to Felix at times, so she didn't have anything to worry about. "It was corrupted. Manawarped, as your Eye revealed to you. Such a state increases a target's Strength, Endurance, and Vitality at the expense of Intelligence and Willpower. There are stages of the condition, each one worse than the last and just as hard to cleanse from oneself. Manasoaked, Manadrenched, and Manawarped."

Felix recalled the big scorpion in the oasis had been Manadrenched. A slightly foggy memory of that creature's huge claws and tough exoskeleton emerged. "How does it happen? Is it a disease? Or is there a Skill that'll inflict it?"

"It is a condition, but not one that affects the mortal Races, only monster Types. When a monster does not Evolve as it should, the Mana overflows their core and floods their Bodies, leading to unexpected alterations. This can result in the earliest stages and progresses with each botched Evolution or even a refused Evolution, if the monster is willful enough." Both of them could hear the Knights clomping closer, but the steps were slow. Unsure. Zara shifted her stance. "However, it can also be inflicted by a greater creature, one that is in control of a horde and has direct influence over such Evolutions."

"The Fathom."

"I would assume. The dark, mucus-like tendrils on the Draktopi and this Nettle are practically identical. Even the Depthwurm bore a strangeness to it, its aggression far outsizing its ability."

"So, the Fathom is spreading. We need to talk to the Deepking. He should know more about what's going on down below." *The guy was fighting against the Fathom in some sort of war, according to what he told us last time. I just hope the Naga are still okay.*

Zara waved a hand. "Of course. We also need to traverse the gate in Haestus Temple, Felix. Do not forget that."

"Right. Yeah, I didn't, it's just..." He looked over the town of Bogfeld, broken buildings still shiny and wet.

"Worse than this will happen in Nagast, if you do not return, Felix," Zara pointed out.

"I know." Felix sighed. They had to move on, no matter how guilty he felt about flooding the Ghreldan Hills or thrusting this little town into a watery warzone. "I just need to settle up a few things, let our people rest, and we can make our way outta here."

"Very well."

"Prioress Kartez."

The man approached Alessa not twenty minutes after doing the impossible, floating to her position along the Redoubt battlements as if it were as effortless as a morning stroll. Down below, she could make out the Knights that had been sent to bring him back were scrambling across the square, calling for the gates to be reopened. The man had apparently taken off without their leave, or some such. Blue-white lightning crackled from his limbs, but not so much as to appear hostile. Instead, it ruffled his clothes and made his eerie eyes shine.

"Mr. Nevarre. Are you not tired after...everything?" She gestured toward the still-drying expanse of Bogfeld. Words could not do justice to what she was feeling, but awed and small were among them.

"Oh, sure. Who wouldn't be?" The man shrugged away the question and Alessa's curious gaze. He certainly did not look tired. "I know we have not had much time to talk one-on-one, but I do believe we made an agreement."

"Oh?" Alessa asked. She appreciated that the man floated at her eye level, refusing to loom above her very normal Gnomish height. "What agreement was that, Mr. Nevarre?"

"Well, it was with Dahria, actually." He pulled free a glass bottle, within which a bright red liquid sloshed. "Would you like to speak further on it?"

Alessa smiled. "I would, yes."

Dahria watched the Prioress walk down the battlements next to the Autarch, somewhat dumbfounded.

To be alone with such a powerful individual was dangerous in the extreme. She felt as if she should gather all the Menders to walk with the Prioress, or perhaps cajole the Knights into guarding her. Yet none of *them* could raise an entire town from the flood, even if they had all worked together. What, then, could she do?

"You look tense."

"Ah!" Dahria spun, finding a woman with pale hair and fair skin staring at her. "By the Light, you startled me."

"My apologies, truly. I did not intend to frighten you."

"Frighten? No. Of course not. I was simply...otherwise engaged." Dahria drew in her pale robes, similar in color to the woman before he, actually, and lifted her chin. "How might I help you?"

"It is more of a question on how I might help you, dear lady." The woman inclined her head, and Dahria spotted a glinting tiara among her platinum curls. "I am traveling with the Autarch, and I noticed that your Menders are seeing to the sick and injured. Your Skills with Herbalism are quite impressive. I, too, have talents that lie in such an arena, and I would love to extend them to you all during our stay."

"Oh!" Dahria gathered herself at hearing she was a companion with the Autarch. Much as she feared his power, she could not deny it. "That is quite generous, Lady...?"

"Isla. Simply Isla is fine."

"Isla, then. How might you be able to help?" Dahria gestured to the regal woman, and they both started walking down the steps toward the triage tents below.

"Simply show me your worst patients, and we shall take it from there."

CHAPTER FIFTY-ONE

"The deal you are offering is quite generous, Lord Nevarre. Discounted pricing on alchemical products in exchange for our knowledge on herbalism and medicinal practices is tempting. Especially after inspecting this." The Prioress lifted the glass Health Potion and swirled it a bit. "A potent crafting, able to heal over a hundred points of Health. That is enough to bring many warriors back from the brink and into fighting shape."

Felix pulled out two other bottles, one a cloudy yellow and the other blue. "We can also create Stamina and Mana Potions as well. Lesser tonics and salves, too, if potions are too pricey, of course."

"Prize creations. Are these not for your people first? Alchemical creations often take a long while to lose efficacy, so you are putting your own warriors at a disadvantage by trading these treasures away." Her tone was one of a cautious mother, one that saw pitfalls stretching all around her. Curiosity and challenge fluted across the Prioress' Spirit. "Is our knowledge so valuable?"

Felix shrugged while suppressing a wince at the movement. "All knowledge is valuable, which you well know. Anyone with an iota of power here hoards knowledge, and usually it's for their own gain. My goal was always to support my people first, and learning more about the healing arts would go a long way toward facilitating that."

"The knowledge of the Menders is something we have long struggled to keep as ours. As you say, the powerful hoard knowledge. Our ability with herbs and reagents of the Hills has protected us from the...eager hands of Knights and Princes alike. If I were to give them to you, then our power would be greatly reduced within the Hills. Your potions are remarkable, but we cannot bargain away the walls that keep my people safe."

They walked atop the Redoubt battlements still, as far away from the Knights as they could manage, but the fortress was not all that large. They were at least warded for privacy, thanks to a small artifact at the Prioress' belt, just enough to cover the two of them. A few Menders were a respectable distance behind them, as well as four of his Shadows. They had found him during the move and had been stuck to his back ever since.

Felix rolled the Prioress' situation over in his Mind, and even considered once again if the trade he was proposing was worth it. The Menders had proven to have a potent grip on Herbalism, with the Prioress admitting that she was an Adept at the Skill. She was a Journeyman in Temper, of course, but her entire order was such a fount of knowledge, he couldn't pass it all up.

Apart from boosting his Skills in Alchemy and Aria of the Green Wilds, it would help elevate all of his apprentices, not to mention open up new avenues for caring for his growing population. They also had access to rare herbs in the Territory, different than the ones in Nagast, and one of the last places with access since the flood had washed away a lot. Most of all, and the part that the Prioress was bucking against, was his desire for detail on their Titles and Skills. Those were an order's lifeblood...but how to convince her? He cleared his throat. "I can appreciate the need for the hoarding of knowledge and power, especially as all those around you do the same. 'It is a beast of infinite belly, that thing we call self-preservation, one that will eat and eat for survival and never count the cost on those around them.'"

"*The Vicissitudes*. I'm pleased to know you read the book." Prioress Kartez shook her head. "Tern has a great many ideas in those pages, all of them heady with a dream of what could be. That is not our world, however much we wish it."

"Now you sound like my advisor," Felix said dryly.

"They sound wise."

"They are. But I think all of us are stuck looking at the world as how it is, instead of how it could be. We can change the world just by sharing a little information. If we ally together, Prioress, you will be protected by all those who might tear you down. I am willing to swear an Oath on that."

The Gnome turned from the battlements to the waters beyond the Redoubt. They had wandered near the southern portion, where the forests and waves spread until they hit the bases of the Stormeater Peaks. "That is tempting. How would you protect us? Do you plan to conquer this land as well?"

Felix smiled past the ache in his veins. "No. I'm not a conqueror, not if I can help it. But I have connections with Ahkestria, and soon trade will be reestablished. I could arrange for protection for your Priory, absolutely, in addition to selling our healing items at a reduced price."

"Protection. You would leave your soldiers here? An occupying force in Tevis' lands would find themselves accosted in short order. And given the Path you claim to tread, how long before you can no longer avoid becoming the conqueror?"

"I don't have any interest in taking over Territories or fighting in wars. Really. Consider the folks I leave as guards against theft. They would follow your orders, but their primary objective would be to ensure that you and your newfound resources are secure." Felix spread his hands. "That sounds reasonable, right?"

The Prioress didn't answer him immediately, only furrowed her brow and folded her hands. Felix gave her the time to think, instead pressing his Perception outward. He'd been so laser-focused on his conversation that he hadn't realized they were almost directly above the healing tents. The sounds of snoring, wheezing, and pain-filled moans were hard to miss now that he was paying attention, as was the thread of anxious desperation that wafted on the breeze.

"You're pressed thin here," Felix observed.

"We are always pressed thin when calamity comes to our doorstep. Whether it is disease, a hunt gone wrong, or terrible flooding, it is always a fight to gain one single life back from death's doorstep." The Prioress followed his gaze, stepping up onto the elevated rungs atop the inner wall. "My people are dedicated to expanding their knowledge, and putting it to good use. It is our life's work."

Another sound bore along the breeze, one that few could catch but which Felix snapped up in a second. It was music, light and airy and entirely familiar. Flaring his Perception and Affinity stats harder, Felix followed the song to its source, several dozen yards away beneath a tent. He saw the flash of a blue dress and platinum curls—*Isla*—and all around her, the ambient emotions swelled toward euphoria.

"What—what is that? What is happening there?" the Prioress asked. She pressed against the wall, lifting her slight Body just a touch higher.

"Healing," Felix said. "Healing in a way that you have likely not encountered."

Isla moved from one tent to another, this time giving them a far better vantage on her work. Human men, Orcish women, a gaggle of Gnomish children, the Chanter moved between them with skill and poise. A trail of relief and slumber followed her, while her odd magic wove bones back together and eradicated gangrenous flesh.

"How is she accomplishing this?"

"I suppose a conversation with our healer could be on the table," Felix said, rubbing his chin. The Prioress' clutched at the wall, and her

Spirit flashed with a brief pang of greed. "Knowledge for knowledge, perhaps?"

Negotiation is level 38!

The Prioress flared her nostrils, but her eyes didn't leave the flash of Isla's magic. "Keep talking."

The ooze wriggled in its container, even when Vess wasn't poking it with her partisan, like it was trying to escape. All it managed was to slosh a bit in the deep tub of chitin she'd had Beef make, and the sides were so thick that its foul substance wasn't going to burn through it anytime soon. Men and women gave the tub a wide berth—Vess, too—and though she had set it up somewhere a little out of the way near the stern, she could feel the eyes of the sailors on her like the midmorning sun at her shoulders. Her Affinity tagged them as concerned before she closed it off, squeezing her surroundings off from her attention. She had to focus.

Vess leaned over the tub, letting her Elemental Eye flare.

Elemental Eye is level 73!

The ooze exuded a sort of corrosive Mana that reminded Vess heavily of acid, but the color was all wrong. Normally a bright green, this was heavily tinted toward purple, and it coiled on itself in thick streams of vapor that looked far heavier than normal Mana. She stabbed it with her partisan again, and the ooze recoiled. Its material split open, just as before, and Vess watched the thing discharge several bursts of that thickened Mana vapor. The vapor didn't rise up, though, but clung to the ooze's side before congealing back into ooze and patching its own hole.

It was something she would have missed without her Eye Skill. Vess knew that because she had cut it previously, and other than an extensive amount of squirming, nothing remarkable happened before the wound sealed itself.

"That's disgustin'." Evie whispered.

Vess raised an eyebrow and fought to remain unfazed. Her friend had appeared like a ghost, utterly unnoticed. "Ahem. I would advise not placing your face so close to it."

Evie lifted her head, which had just been perched at the lip of the tub. "Ah. Probably smart." She settled back, leaning against the gunwale of the Manaship, and let her thick braid cushion her head. Her armor was scuffed and scratched, her jerkin stained with some dark fluid, and she hastily shoved a piece of bread into her mouth. She chewed, loudly. "Why're you so interested in this thing? It's pretty nasty. Just lookin' at it gives me a headache. When you had them harvest it, I swear those Blades were gonna hurl right into their own laps."

Vess kept stabbing the creature, observing its healing capacity again and again. The ooze crept away from wherever it had last been stabbed, crowding the corners of the tub that were farthest from her spear. She doubted it could feel pain or even actual emotion, being a bundle of blobby Mana, but it had some rudimentary sense of space. "I need to know how this is interacting with the Fathom spawn we keep finding it on. My Analyze cannot get a grip on it though. *Analyze.*"

Analyze Failed.

"How's stabbing it supposed to help?" Evie asked.

"It tells me that it has a sense of self-preservation. That whatever created this...abomination...it was done with Intent." Vess frowned down at the ooze.

"You've the right of it there, Lady Dayne," a new voice announced, and Zara walked up onto the quarterdeck. "That ooze is a vessel of Intent in much the same way your flesh is a package around your bones."

Evie snorted. "Hah, gross."

"Intent," Vess repeated. The Naiad Chanter walked until she was beside her and peered curiously into the thick-walled tub. "Meaning this was created for a purpose. What purpose?"

"Felix asked a similar question. Manawarping is a process that takes time, but after investigating numerous remains and the harmonic traces left by the Slaughter Nettle, I do believe I know how the Fathom is inducing it." Zara pointed an elegant, ochre finger at the ooze. It wobbled, a few small tendrils forming in its mass before losing shape. "This is accelerating the process, introducing a form of dissonance into the weft of harmony."

Evie tilted her head, still chewing. She had gotten a small wedge of cheese from some inner pocket. "Dissonance. Like what Felix talks about. That's Primordial stuff though, right?"

"It is, but it is not exclusive to them. Long before I ever beheld a Primordial, I witnessed threads of dissonance cause mayhem across an entire forest. In its truest form, it is a perversion of the Grand Harmony. This is...a watered down version, atonal strains among the otherwise melodic patterns of true Mana. It acts as a catalyst, I believe, breaking apart the Mana systems inside the creatures it attaches to before it introduces a boost of its own corrupted Mana. This accelerates the

Manawarping process, and, if I am not mistaken, makes them as subservient as any draconic Type."

Vess clenched her jaw. "So this Fathom is gathering a true horde."

"It would seem so, yes."

Distantly, the Redoubt's bells began to ring. Evie popped up to her feet, hand already on her chain. "Oh! I missed the last one. Maybe there'll be somethin' like the Depthwurm again."

"Another attack?" Vess asked. "I thought they said the monsters massed at nightfall?"

"They did say that," Zara agreed, staring into the distance. The Knights were scrambling faster than she'd ever seen them move. "There. Beyond the northern hills. At least ten creatures."

"Yes. I can barely make it out, but..." Vess kicked the lid shut on the thick, chitin tub. Sigils flared along the top, binding it closed. "If those are as big as they seem, you may get your wish, Evie."

CHAPTER FIFTY-TWO

"You are demanding a lot from me, all for some two-bit healers in the back end of nowhere," Isla said.

Felix stood still atop one of the rounded towers in the Priory, having transported Menders and patients alike over to the order's compound for further talks. Isla had been fairly amenable to the conversation when Felix had approached her, and soon was eagerly engaging with the Prioress while displaying a growing familiarity with Dahria and the other subordinates. It had been a bit more than Felix had hoped for, and during the twenty-minute back and forth, he had been waiting for the other shoe to drop.

Isla cocked her head at his silence. "I am still quite surprised at the audacity of it. Offering to share knowledge that you have no claim over. Tsk."

Felix buried his general distaste for the woman and smiled. "It's in the interest of helping others, here and in my Territories. But..." He felt a pulse of satisfaction from the woman, hidden beneath a layer of gauzy anger. Somehow, she had laid a veneer of anger over her true emotions. A curious trick. "You're entirely too happy to be truly mad at me. What did the Prioress agree to?"

He had listened in, of course, though Isla had attempted to make the conversation more private and brought them indoors. That was easy to work around by having Pit fly to a window and listen for him, as the Chanter hadn't bothered to erect any sound wards. Now, she eyed him, and something in his expression must have given him away, because her faux anger turned to disappointment. "You heard?"

Felix just kept smiling.

"Tch. Very well, then. She agreed to your ridiculous terms. Access to their knowledge on Herbalism, their rare seedlings, even Titles and Tempering details." Isla shook her head. "They were willing to pay more for a larger helping of my knowledge, but they did not have enough. They are ready and willing to swear an Oath on the agreement, once you are prepared."

"Great news." Felix had more than enough experience dealing with a conniving creature back when he had the Maw welded to his Spirit, and he'd won that proverbial tug of war. He wasn't about to let someone else derail his plans with their own agenda. "How do you plan to convey that knowledge, by the way? I can't imagine you want to stick around here."

The slight woman paused while she straightened her dress, the diaphanous layers having twisted in the wind. "I have tomes that I would hand over. It would more than suffice for what these Menders require."

"May I see them?"

Isla pursed her lips, but from within her voluminous skirts, she removed three thick books bound in leather and bright green metal. She handed them to Felix. "Three personally scribed tomes, depicting my earliest work with life Mana and the art of healing. They are not Skill Books, but I daresay they'll find enough in there to keep them occupied for several decades at least."

Felix opened the first, flipping page after page as he studied it. The handwriting was fine but far more legible than Pagewright Tern's scrawl, and it was accompanied by a great many sketches and diagrams of various Races and body parts. He kept flipping, letting his eyes rest on each page until he reached the end of the first tome. "This is...wow. This is great."

"As I said. More than sufficient." Isla held out her hand, but Felix did not give them back. Instead, he moved to the second tome, which he moved through just as quickly. Then the third. He could sense Isla's impatience with him, but didn't much care. "What are you doing?"

"Some light reading."

"You've barely glanced at the pages. Even with an astronomical Intelligence, you would be able to glean very little in such a short amount of time."

"Mm," Felix said, pleased as he snapped shut the final book. "These will be great. Glad you were willing to help, Isla."

Her hands twitched at her skirts before collecting the three books from Felix's grasp. "Yes. Well. I did not do so without recompense. You will stick to your end of the bargain? I would not wish to mar our agreements with something so impersonal as an Oath."

"I don't need Oaths to keep up my end of a bargain," Felix said. In order to gain Isla's cooperation, he'd had to promise to answer her questions regarding his home. She was 'compiling information about where the Unbound are summoned from and how' and needed his input. Felix figured she just wanted to know more about him, and any excuse would do.

"Of course not."

"I'll give you my accounting later. Once we're back in Nagast, we'll have plenty of time." Felix gestured to the door Isla had just exited. "Let's go seal the deal with the Menders, and then we can—"

The bells of the Redoubt began to toll. Down below, Menders froze for a second before scrambling up stairs and onto the walls of the Priory. For his part, Felix seized the air and rode lightning up onto the tallest of towers, spinning slightly until he saw the source of the disturbance. Two dozen shapes cut through the waters on the far side of the town, perhaps a half-mile out and heading toward Bogfeld *fast.* He flared his Voracious Eye, enjoying once again the fact that the Skill had no limit except line of sight.

He blinked.

"Damn it." His Perception flagged the Knights amassing along the newly rebuilt town walls. A lot of Knights.

He had to move.

"Steady! Hold your Skills tight!" a Knight-lieutenant cried out, holding their silver-edged sword aloft.

Knights lined up atop the newly built walls of Bogfeld, but the glimmering lights in the glossy stone were ignored for the far more dire threat barreling through the waves. Arrow-like wakes turned the muddy water into foam, and dark, glossy scales were all that could be seen apart from what seemed like a hundred pairs of glowing eyes.

"Aim!"

The writhing shapes lashed forward, propelled faster and faster, until all the sound was dominated by thrashing whitewater. Serpentine maws lifted and jagged crests burst across their wedge-shaped skulls as a thrill of hammer-hearted fear jolted every Knight and Gallant.

The Knight-lieutenant's voice was all but squeezed from his chest. "FIRE!"

Arrows flew like bullets, ripping across space and air with a whine and snap that tore free tendrils of trailing Mana. Glows of blue, white-green, green-gold, and orange abounded, until it was a veritable rainbow that descended upon the advancing horde...only to shatter as a wall of jagged ice ripped up from the waves.

"STOP!" Felix's voice hammered into the Knights and Gallants with a physical force, bringing several of them to their knees. He landed atop the hastily formed ice wall with a crack of thunder, sending more ice Mana down into its base to prevent it from splintering beneath his weight. It burned his already-raw channels, but he couldn't help it. "Stop attacking!"

"H-hold your fire!" the Knight-lieutenant stuttered. "My lord? Do you wish to make the kill?"

"What? No. I wasn't talking to you." Felix pivoted, until he could see down the other side of his icy slope. "Garox? What is going on?"

From the lead of the serpents—the Naga—a serpent like the rest but on a smaller scale and bearing a humanoid upper body–slid from the waters atop his brethren. He wore a shirt of scale mail that gleamed with a purple hue and twin swords at his waist. "Returned God! We are pleased to see you here among the waters of our land!"

Murmurs broke out among the staggered Knights, but Felix ignored them. He focused on not licking his lips nervously. The Naga were no longer Oathbound, and Felix had no clue how this was going to go. "Garox. Why did you charge the town like that? These people thought you meant to attack them."

The Spirit Naga shook his head, though his flat expression was tough to read. "We felt a great amount of power emanating from these waters, and the Fathom have been more and more active of late. Our speed was meant to intimidate our foe. To find the Returned God here instead is a blessing."

"The Fathom spawn have been killed, at least the ones around here," Felix said. "Just hold there for a second." He leaped, collapsing a portion of his ice wall, and hurtled through the air.

Garox seems the same as ever, Oath or not. A knot of tension, building all this time, loosened in his chest. Felix landed atop the battlements of Bogfeld, surprising the Knight-lieutenant once again. "You're in charge?"

The man nodded. "What is going on, sir?"

"Some friends have come to visit. They aren't any threat, so please stand down." Felix reached out to the ice wall with his Mana and Intent. "I'm going to drop the wall now."

"A-ah, right. Yes, sir."

Destroying a Mana construct was always faster than making it, at least for something as simple as elemental shaping. A small pulse of his Rime Shaping started breaking down the ice, and in short order, Garox and his fleet of Naga were treading water only a dozen yards outside Bogfeld's new gates.

"Those are Naga!"

"Monsters—!"

"Can I trust you to calm your people?" Felix asked the Knight-lieutenant, and the man saluted sharply.

"Yes, sir! Stand down! Everyone, put up your weapons!"

Felix hopped back down, landing on a lip of stone just outside the town walls. Pit, resting on the flagship, sent him a worried query, but Felix pulsed safety and reassurance along their bond. "Garox. We don't have much time before a lot of people start showing up and asking questions. Did you really just show up here to fight the Fathom?"

"Of course, my Lord. We wage war against the wretched filth in our waters throughout all hours of the day and night. Normally, they reside within the depths, in the abyss where light cannot reach their vile scales...but the glorious flood that has expanded our demesne has also riled the beasts. Now they not only contest the deeps, but the surface as well." The flat-faced snakeman looked up at the wall, his slitted pupils dilating as he regarded the Knights above. "Something these Humans know well."

"Yeah. We've encountered them a few times," Felix admitted. "They came after us, beyond the mountains there."

Garox drew himself up, his head of brown and tan scales glistening in the sun while the other Nagafolk coiled through the waters, looking at least superficially similar to the Depthwurm. The intelligence in their eyes was a touch unnerving when Felix considered their physical size, even if he was sure he could defeat them all.

"They advanced through to the source of the flood? It must have been in great number, for that is always how they attack. The Fathom grows bold and far more deadly with every passing day, their power waxing like the moons. We...cannot hold much longer in the deeps. Have you returned to lay waste to them?"

Felix opened his mouth, but hesitated. "We've returned, but my people need to pass through Haestus Temple. War is coming, and they are needed back home."

"What of your promise, my Lord? That you would return and aid us against the Fathom?" Garox frowned, and this time, his expression wasn't hard to read at all. Dismay and fear. Anger. "What of our home?"

Broken Oath or not, guilt pulled at Felix, a companion for his feelings toward Bogfeld. The flooding *had* caused the Fathom to grow restless...or perhaps simply bold enough to escalate their conflict. "I'm still gonna help. I promised I would, and I'm not about to go back on that."

"I am pleased to hear that, my Lord." Garox gave him a deep bow, his oversized Body, at least twice the size of Felix's, bending until it was lower than Felix's head. That metal armor glinted again, the sheen on it swirling purple then blue. "There are Dens being formed all over the depths, too many for us to contest. The Fathom spawn are multiplying faster than our noble warriors can beat them back. We need your aid now more than ever."

"Right." Felix frowned, putting all the pieces of his current crises in order. He had the Hierocracy heading to Nagast at some point, the Fathom fucking people over, and his fellow Unbound in trouble across the Continent. Could he resolve the Fathom immediately? "Is there a concentration of them? Some source for where they come from?"

"Yes. Khasma."

"Khasma? What's—" Felix's words were crushed from his chest as a sharp but somehow distant pain ripped through him. In the same second, an alert in red flashed before his eyes.

WARNING!
Your Defensive Array - Mirk Enclosure Has Failed!
WARNING!
The Barrier Has Fallen!

What!

Energy Remains!
Do You Wish To Allocate To The Array In Order To Maintain Perception Occlusion?

It means the fog inside Nagast, he realized. *Yes!*

Mana and Essence both rushed out of him, a tithe he paid directly to maintain at least a part of the Enclosure, and it made Felix's knees wobble and overtaxed channels blaze with agony. He gripped his Inheritor's Will as he stumbled to a knee. "Karys!"

Green-gold light pulsed at his waist. "Felix! The Mirk Enclosure failed! The Stronghold has indicated that a force of six thousand Hierocratic warriors have passed through Setoria!"

"*What?*" He thought he had more *time*. "Where are our people?"

"The majority have made it to Haarwatch, but only just."

Felix's Mind was racing, a thousand thoughts crowding for attention. "Get Cal on. Get people organized. I've kept the fog going in the Territory, so maybe that'll buy us more time. I—I need to resolve things here and—we'll be back soon."

"Please hurry. I fear we will need all of our might to defend against this force."

Felix stood, pushing shakily from his knees. He met the gaze of the Spirit Naga before him, one that was creased with dismay and flashes of anger. "Garox. We...we need to get to Haestus. Now."

"...Very well, my Lord."

CHAPTER FIFTY-THREE

"So you are a Territorial Lord...of *two* complete Territories."

"I am, yes."

"And you defeated Grandmaster Kel'lyv. Personally." Knight Commander Lavin looked at Felix and his retinue, now fully assembled within her command chamber. Alister, Atar, Zara, and Isla all stood beside him, while Pit snuffled around the crystalline pillar at the center of the room. The commander and her second shared a look, and it was one of disbelief and no little fear; echoes of what she'd felt in their previous meeting. This time, however, Felix couldn't keep things in reserve. He had to give them enough reason to believe him, and Authority held a lot of weight.

"And you are allied with the Nagafolk?" she asked. "We know them only at best as a myth and at worst a threat. A tale to frighten children. No," she raised a hand, stopping Alister from speaking. "No, I saw them with my own eyes. I'll not doubt that. To ally ourselves with them, however, feels...dangerous."

"They are sworn to me." Felix paced across the room, and his agitation was not limited to himself. The others were all shifting in place, eager to be gone. He'd explained the basics to everyone only minutes ago, but the Knights and Gallants they were leaving behind needed a little more detail.

"They are also fighting the Fathom, who are responsible for the nastier monsters that have thrown themselves against you. We cleared the Den in the Caleph Pass, but I'm told there are more Dens established throughout the depths. I don't know their numbers, but the Naga claim they're outnumbered. It all points to a dangerous situation, one that I don't think you or your people should wade into."

"Do you expect us to sit here, like a turtle in its shell, until we expire?" Covain asked. She pounded the table with her fist. "We've faced them before. I say we take the fight to them!"

"Peace, Covain," Prioress Kartez said, sitting beside them. The room only had a handful of others, and they were the highest ranking members of the Knights, Gallants, and Menders. "If there are more foes like the Slaughter Nettle in the Fathoms' pocket, then I do not wish to waste our people so needlessly."

"I regretfully agree." Lavin had steepled her gauntleted fingers and was regarding Felix across them. "We must protect our people. Will the new-built walls hold against such monsters, Lord Nevarre?"

"They should. They're about as strong as I can make them. Can you extend your shields to cover the whole town?"

"That is...not possible."

"A shame," Felix said. If he had more time, he would have offered to try and solve that issue. His curiosity still burned about that dead space, after all.

"How far is this Nagast? It is not on any map I have ever seen," the Prioress asked. She was worried, but their recent bargain seemed to bolster her confidence a bit. The crate of healing supplies likely helped as well.

"Far enough that I won't be able to come back and help you. Not quickly, at any rate."

"We will stand strong without you...Lord Nevarre," Covain said, biting off the end of her angry retort. She mastered herself after a second, but Felix didn't much blame her. The lady clearly had a lot of pride tied up in the Knights' capability, and he'd shown them up with his people.

"I truly hope so," he said, then turned to the Menders. "Prioress Kartez, you have a meeting scheduled with my Chancellor in Ahkestria—per our agreement. If you have any needs or messages to send, relay them to him. I'll respond as soon as I'm able, but—"

"But we are not your responsibility, Lord Nevarre." Lavin stood, pressing heavily against the table by the crystalline pillar. The movement carried with it a heaviness echoed in her Spirit. "Prince Tevin is our liege lord, and it is him that we serve in our duties. I admit I agreed to your solution for Bogfeld because I was curious to see how you might fail. Yet you have achieved an impossible thing and proven yourself personally powerful...no doubt that played a role in the acquisition of your Territories. But your duties call you elsewhere, and we must remain. The Knights Ghreldan and the Gallant Lotuses do not require or desire your protection; we shall provide our own."

The woman's words were perfunctory, almost cold, but her Spirit pulsed with a myriad of harmonies that spoke to a tightly controlled fear. He tilted his head, deeper than was proper. Some Knights and Isla in particular sucked in a sharp breath; surprise and disapproval mingling.

"I will respect your wishes. We will be gone within the glass."

Soon after, they were escorted out of the Commander's chamber, led along the covered pathways through their squat towers until they were all deposited in the courtyard and left alone by the Knights. The festival had long been broken down, and the area where there were once tents was now halved as people had begun to return to Bogfeld proper. Felix had seen the Knights advising against it, as they did not know the capabilities of the new walls, but few citizens listened. Most had raced to grab their homes and begin the long processes of returning to normalcy. Felix hoped they were left alone, that his walls would protect them. No one deserved to be uprooted by catastrophe...let alone one that he could have stopped.

Shoving those thoughts down, he gathered the Chanters and mages close, gesturing for one of them to erect a sound ward. Once Zara's blue sigils settled around them, he let out a tight breath. "Did you get anything from the pillar?"

"No," Atar said, and Alister also shook his head. "Not without seeing the interior of the working."

"The pillar is simply a glorified access point," Alister pointed out. "It carries none of the vital sigaldry, just a number of control glyphs and something related to light Mana projection."

"Yeah, I saw that part." Felix put his hands on his hips, looking straight down at the dead spot beneath their feet. "Damn, I thought we could get *something* from it."

"I was able to pull some information from their pillar," Zara chimed in.

"What? How?" Atar demanded.

"Delve deeper into the Harmonics, child, and you will discover a great many capabilities. Felix, they have a Domain Core fueling their defensive construct; you can hear it in the stone. That is the dead spot you have sensed, not because it's warded, but because they've used those same Mana crystals to create a lattice around the core to facilitate their working." She shook her head, seeming impressed despite herself. "There must have been a genius among their order at one point, for it is far more complicated than someone only in the Journeyman Tier could accomplish. This is Master work."

"Can we copy it?" Felix asked.

"We have the raw materials to attempt it, but I'll require time to experiment. This idea of yours has merit, Felix, if we can make it work."

"A big 'if,'" Isla added.

Felix ignored the woman's skepticism. He'd explained his thought process to all four of them on their walk to the Commander's chamber, but she'd never really been part of it. The mages and Zara could handle it themselves. "Good. Focus on that while we travel, and hopefully we'll have something to offer Haarwatch other than just ourselves."

"Don't discount that. Our growth has been great," Alister slapped Felix on the back. "We're far more than we were."

"Not gonna be enough, but hey, I've got more than enough sigaldry to experiment with once we return," Atar said. He wasn't hobbling much anymore, but he still had that extendable stave in his hand. "I'm not going down without a fight, in any case."

"None of us are," Felix said, and walked out of the sound ward, heading toward the Redoubt's gates. "Time to move."

Knight Commander Lavin stood atop her tower as the Autarch and his ten ships sailed off. The sun was still high in the sky, shining almost blindingly off the waves as the ships sped after the wake of its monstrous allies. Her second sidled up to her, and Lavin could almost feel the tension across Covain's shoulders. "Do you trust what he said?"

Lavin sighed. Her gauntleted hands flexed against the parapet, as if to assure herself it was still there, still strong. "I do. He had no reason to lie to us, just as he had no reason to defend us from that monster wave. Or to spend so much of his own power on fixing our town. No. He has earned too much for me to waste time on disbelieving him now."

"Perhaps that was his intent."

"Perhaps. But how long do we hold onto distrust?"

"He is allied with monsters!" Covain pointed out. "He deceived us, infiltrated the Redoubt, and somehow wormed his pet into our Command chamber. If it weren't for his frightful amount of power, I would have charged him with espionage and strung him up."

"Enough. You are right: we cannot oppose them. I may not agree with the actions the Autarch took, but I cannot exert my will against...whatever he is. I suspect a hidden Grandmaster, from the power he clearly contains, and that is in addition to the two *other* Master Tiers among his company. But he made a deal with the Menders—quite the favorable one for him, according to the Prioress—yet in return, he has left her with a substantial amount of potions, tinctures, and salves."

Those were worth as much as their warriors, for without the Menders' talents, they would have been eradicated already.

"What are we to do, ma'am?"

Lavin slapped the parapet and turned away. "The Fathom are not yet here. We will make use of the time given us and prepare. Send the Knights into the boats in force and clear the forest. Have the Gallants prepare the landscape. It may be flooded, we may be surrounded, but we can make the town a nightmare to accost."

"Aye, ma'am. I'll see it done."

It was far faster to reach the Haestus Temple by Manaship, which wasn't a surprise so much as a relief. Felix stood at the prow of the flagship as Garox led the way back, Mind racing as he contemplated his options. His plans were in motion, and though he was flustered and worried that the Hierocracy broke his Enclosure, he was also surprised it hadn't happened sooner. It also meant, however, that there must have been a powerful figure with the Hierocratic army; Karys assured him the Enclosure could not have been breached otherwise—not even by an army of Adept Tiers.

Death and danger lay ahead of them all.

But the plight of the Ghreldan Hills tugged at Felix almost as hard. Nagast was in danger, but the Fathom was here, now, wreaking havoc on the peoples of the Hills...and he had promised to resolve their threat. *That* burned at him, more than a little. He wasn't perfect or all-powerful, and he hadn't even given an Oath or anything, but Felix hated the idea of abandoning the Nagafolk. They might have been giant snakes, but he'd met enough Races and so-called monsters to not question when people were people.

Garox slowed as they reached a portion of the waters that was clearly one of the many lakes, and as one his people dove into the deeps. He lingered behind, saluting Felix before diving himself. Felix called for the ships to stop, and the faint whine of Mana engines faded into the mild, somewhat balmy breeze.

They had reached the Temple, apparently.

What felt like moments later, his Inheritor's Will pulled at his attention like an insistent child. Felix put his hand on the hilt, finding it pulsing with heaviness that was quite unlike when Karys reached out to him. He unsheathed it. A glyph was glowing on the blade, just above the guard, describing a pattern that Felix knew had something to do with absorbing the power of Nymean Temples. Remnant Authority, Karys had called it. The sword had gotten heavier since he'd received it, taking a portion of the Temples he'd claimed into itself.

It flashed, once more, just as the lake ahead of them collapsed into a sudden, roaring whirlpool. Like someone had pulled a plug far below the surface, the water was yanked into a vast, spinning tunnel that immediately dragged their ships toward it.

"Ignite the engines!" Harn shouted. "Full speed backward!"

"No!" Felix shoved his voice as loud as he could make it, all the while staring at his hooked sword. He had no clue how he knew what he knew; he simply did. "No, this is for us! Ahead! Forward!"

The whining engines growled to life, and magic shuddered through the ship's framework like a living creature. Sails snapped taut, and with a lurching dip, Felix's ship surged into the whirlpool's edge.

"You sure about this?" Harn asked, shouting over the roar of the water.

"Yeah! Somehow!" Felix grabbed the railing and held his hooked blade aloft, now glowing with golden and cerulean light. "Take hold of something!"

The flagship traveled once more around the rim before plunging into the depths.

CHAPTER FIFTY-FOUR

Spray shot up around the prow of the ship as it smashed down into the vortex of water, simultaneously soaking and thrilling Felix. His sword sang, bright and high, and the waves answered his unspoken Intent. His fear vanished, for this was the doing of the Deepking; Felix knew it in his bones.

Everyone else was screaming, though.

One-by-one, his fleet descended into the wild spiral of the maelstrom, foam and wave cutting dizzying lines into sea and sky as sailors clambered atop the rigging, and their pilots fought to steady their crafts with desperate strength. Beneath him, the Manaship vibrated *hard*, as if it were ripping through nightmarish turbulence. Flowing down from his blade, knowledge bloomed in Felix's Mind, and he shouted over the roar. "Calm down! Let the ships go!"

"But my Lord—!"

"Do it! Let go! Trust the water!"

The Yttin pilot released the wheel. The ship immediately turned, lurching into the spin of the vortex and tossing the less agile off their feet. The turbulence vanished entirely, and even the roar of the surf became a quiet gurgling.

Harn clapped Felix's shoulder. "Damn. You weren't kiddin'." The sailors started shouting back to the other ships. "What is this?"

"A pathway to the Temple below," Felix said. He nodded at the angled depths before them, where the water churned as it fled further and further from their prow. "The Deepking seems to have grown in power."

"Damn. I'll say." Harn paused, loosening his death grip on the gunwale to peer into the deepening maelstrom. It was getting darker the longer they descended, as if night were setting at midday. "How though? Fightin' the Fathom?"

"I'd have to assume. How else?"

"Hrmm." Harn even grunted when he thought, and Felix could almost see the wheels spinning in the warrior's head.

"What?"

"Dunno. Somethin' feels off. No Skill, just my gut." Harn spat over the railing and watched as his phlegm was spun away.

"Alright. I'll keep it in mind," Felix promised. He wasn't convinced, but Harn was a good friend. If he said things felt weird, then Felix would pay attention. "Get the Claw prepped. I want to start the breakdown the moment we're at the gate room."

"Aye, my Lord." Harn slapped Felix on the back and scrambled back toward the door belowdecks, despite the ship being at a severe angle.

Soon, Felix witnessed the watery tunnel finish its formation, parting the foaming churn to reveal green-tinged alabaster pillars and the crumbling facade of a vast temple complex. It spread out below them like a small city. Buildings that once soared now tumbled and twisted, fallen atop each other like toppled dominoes. They looked small at first, but soon the structures loomed above them, easily three times the height of their Manaships. Fish flashed silver in the limited light, vast schools of them fleeing their procession...or perhaps just the Nagafolk that chased after them with wide jaws.

They have to eat, I suppose. The water was too dark for others to see much, but Felix's gaze pierced the umber depths with ease. He spotted more Nagafolk prowling between the collapsed outbuildings, swimming with serpentine grace among the weathered stone and long, sinuous fronds. They looked like...big, prehistoric snakes really, but their Spirits sang dimly of mingled readiness and fear. *Afraid of the Fathom, that's clear.*

The vortex pressed downward toward one subsection of the Haestus Temple, opening wide when the mouth of it reached the tilted columns and a huge gate. The gate had once been covered in carvings of some sort, but the features were piled with shelled creatures and Ages-deep layers of green slime and dark blue seaweed. Yet, as the water parted and Felix's fleet righted itself within the tunnel, the gate split open, unleashing a brilliant amber light onto them all.

Felix threw up an arm, blocking the sudden flash as he quested forward with his senses, but soon it resolved into an enormous chamber, easily large enough to fit two fleets of Manaships. Ship after ship sailed through the gate, riding atop the waves that extended into the Temple, before weighing anchor near a trio of broken alabaster statues.

Once the last of the ships settled, the whirlpool vanished in a swampy burble, rushing toward them like a waterfall. Before it could flood the Temple, however, the big doors slammed shut with a stentorian boom. Dust rained from the ceiling in such steady streams that had Felix craning his neck upward, just to be sure it wasn't going to collapse. Then, without warning, the walls and ceiling flared with light, and Felix's Perception was hemmed in; no longer could he sense the waters outside the Temple, or even beyond their current room.

"Glory! Glory to the Abyssal Shores!"

The voice boomed across the chamber, louder than the slamming gate. It carried with it a hint of its owner's Spirit, sweeping outward lightly enough that it barely buffeted Felix but sent a few sailors and Claw members stumbling. From the depths of the dome-like chamber, Garox reappeared, along with a number of his warriors. He lifted his hands as he coiled atop the surface of the water.

"The Deepking, Kar'casitrix of the Abyssal Shores has come!"

The water along the far wall suddenly buckled and swirled, and all around them, steam began to rise from the surface. It lingered, thick and cloying as fog, as a shape made from nightmares emerged from below. A head the size of two of his Manaships lashed together lifted out of the dark water, wagon-sized eyes of glowing copper blinking at them all, and a mouth of a hundred fangs opened wide with an intimidating hiss that rippled the waves.

His body was sixty feet in diameter and clad in thick, waterlogged-green scales that changed from smooth at the belly to jagged and armored at the back. Immensely large, powerfully present, and built like an orchicalcum shithouse, Felix still found it a little surprising when the Deepking bowed.

"Be welcome, God of Thunder and Flame," he boomed. "Be welcome, God of our Ancestors, Come Anew."

Right. The god thing. He wasn't sure what made him say the next words, but perhaps it was annoyance; Felix had never liked pretending to be a god. "Hi, Trixie. What's new?"

Silence filled the chamber, so complete that it was as loud as a scream. Then the Deepking rumbled, a sound of confusion rather than displeasure. "Trixie. A curious appellation, my Lord. What does it mean?"

"Oh, uh, I actually think it means 'someone who brings joy,'" Felix said, drawing on a deep memory he hadn't realized was in the vaults of his Mind. *Huh. Neat.*

"Hmm. Would that I could bring joy to all of my people, my Lord." The Deepking's great head bent lower, until he was just a bit taller than eye-level for Felix. His huge eyes flashed, a glimmer of dark color in their depths. "The Fathom are ceaseless in their attacks, and the creature that empowers them has been growing stronger by the day. The flooding has only hastened their plan."

It was supremely unnerving to look into the face of a creature so big. *At least this one doesn't want to eat me.* "I noticed you've gained some potency yourself."

Voracious Eye.

Name: Kar'casitrix, the Deepking
Type: Abyssal Serpent
Level: 901
HP: 65034/65034
SP: 33944/34023
MP: 10498/10498
Lore: Abyssal Serpents are an advanced evolution of the Naga, though their exact nature is not well-known. What is known, however, is that an Abyssal Serpent is a catastrophe when roused.
Strength: More Data Required
Weakness: More Data Required

Felix had only seen the Deepking in action once, where he tore gashes into a necromantic Spirit that had been trapped beneath the Haestus Temple for Ages. Not only was his level insane, but all that experience had clearly inflated his stats. As System designated "monsters," the Nagafolk couldn't Temper themselves, instead having to rely upon Evolutions. An Abyssal Serpent was one of their advanced forms according to his Eye, and everything in Felix urged him to be wary of the Deepking. The big snake was crazy strong then, and likely more so now.

"It is true, my Lord. Those who have survived against the Fathom's constant attacks have flourished...but the cost has been great. We have pushed time and again for their home in the dark deeps, but their numbers overwhelm us every time." The Deepking tilted his head. "Garox says you have an emergency. That you seek the sealed chamber, outside the Chapel of the Eye. Is this true?"

"It is. Can you guide us there?" Felix gestured to the chamber around them. "This place is a maze."

"Of course, my Lord. Garox." The Deepking rumbled again. A thinking noise, it seemed. "We must talk, my Lord. I shall meet you at the Chapel."

Just like that, the biggest Naga Felix had ever seen turned and slipped into the water...vanishing utterly in a span of seconds. According to Felix's Perception, it was like the Deepking simply ceased existing. It was supremely unnerving, but Garox did not let them dwell on it. He soon gathered their attention and led them onward through the half-flooded complex of Haestus Temple.

During the short jaunt, folks in his fleet were a mess of fear and hope; not everyone saw the exchange between him and the Deepking—some were stuck belowdecks—but those that did began whispering fiercely to the others. That the Deepking was a servant of the Fiend, or the snakes owed him a favor. That he had threatened the Naga with death if they defied him. That he was a slave to the Naga's whims.

The last wasn't very popular, even among the families that had come along with the fleet—all of whom seemed to equal parts fear and dislike Felix. Though Felix was only aware of the activity on his own ship, he imagined similar conversations were happening all over. The Deepking was hard to miss.

Felix put it out of his Mind and tried not to pay attention.

Most portions of the Temple complex were tilted at best, and upside-down at worst, with many hallways utterly inaccessible in their ships. Undeterred, Garox led onward, ensuring that every pathway was one the Manaships were able to traverse easily. The rooms and chambers weren't a surprise to Felix, but even the hallways and corridors were vast, cavernous spaces that spoke to Nymean design sense. Stars abounded in the architecture and decoration, carved into stone and out of crystal—though most of that was hidden by the water—and more crumbling statues of armored figures were tilted drunkenly across the submerged paths.

Felix found the Nymean statues fairly eerie. Not due to any supernatural senses or even magic, but by the simple fact that he felt like he recognized them. Only after the tenth or so face sticking out of the dark water did he realize what was going on; it wasn't that Felix recognized the Nym, only that he recognized *himself* in their features.

The sharpness of their cheekbones, the shape of their brow, even the slightly larger eyes. The Nym weren't Human, obviously, but after undergoing so many changes himself, Felix realized just how many subtle differences existed between them both. The last statue they passed had a thick, curly beard, and Felix found himself lingering on it, scratching at his own hairy jaw in thought.

"We have arrived, my Lord," Garox intoned. "The sealed door."

Just ahead was the carved stone door that sat tilted along the wall. Great swathes of black-green moss filled the gaps in the stone, though Felix could also make out the glimmer of ancient, still-active wards. So much of the Temple seemed held together by long-inscribed lines of sigaldry and a deep, strange sort of magic. His sword quivered at his waist when he looked at it all, like a tail wagging.

Felix recognized the moss, too, having seen it adorn much of the room containing the Shadowgate, but here it was almost charred in places. As they drew closer, navigating around the broken statuary and slantwise pillars, he could see why: blue sigils had burned themselves into the door's surface, cutting through the moss and fronds with laser precision. They flared back to life as his flagship came abreast at the ruined tumble of stones just outside the door.

Interestingly enough, from so close, he could *also* make out the presence of a number of scratches in the stone, as if someone had attempted to tear open the door at some point. *Had those been there before?* He couldn't remember looking too closely back then. Perfect recall wasn't so useful if he wasn't paying attention.

"Here you are, my Lord," Garox said, bowing while resting both hands on the twin scimitars at his waist.

"Did...did someone try to break into here?" Felix asked from atop his ship's prow.

"No. It has remained unmolested since you proved your Divinity to us all." The snakeman's face was very hard to read. Even his Spirit was cool as a cucumber.

"Right. Good to hear." Felix jumped out of his ship, setting the entire craft bobbing just a bit. He landed on the stone right before the sealed door, and without questioning the instinct, lifted his left hand and spoke. "Open by my Will."

The blue sigils flared once more then vanished entirely. Ancient hinges creaked as the double doors swung away from Felix into the chamber. Within, the shadows seemed thicker than elsewhere, and not just due to the lack of light. Ahead of him, the darkness writhed as if alive, and all of it was centered on a point on the ceiling.

The Shadowgate.

Much of it was overgrown with the same black and green moss around the chamber. Despite that, Felix could tell it was designed like a set of sweeping mountains, several rows of what he called the Teeth interspersed with malachite forests and thick rivers of sapphire. Along one side was a waterfall, and along the other were a series of soaring towers and humanoid statues that were almost equal in size. It depicted Shelim as it once was, and the landscape as well, all within the ancient Territory of Nagast.

"Beef! Harn!" Both were on his flagship watching him, just in different places. "Break down the ships, like we planned. Pack and store the engines and supplies. I'll get the gate moving."

"Mostly done already. Storage spaces are ready, just got the engines to go," Harn said.

Felix nodded. "Great. Beef, help him get the engines free. Shape them out, if you have to. Do you have a handle on the Shipwright Skill?"

"Yeah. Think so."

Harn grunted. "Better do more than think, son. We're gonna need those ships when we get to the other side."

Beef firmed up his jaw and nodded, hesitation gone. "I got it."

Pit? Felix sent, only to see his Companion hurtle down from above to land with grace on the stones next to him. "Hey, bud. We gotta get the civilians packed up. Can you spread the word?"

"Sure!" Pit hopped, just once, as if eager to fly off again. "Then we're leaving?"

Felix glanced at Garox and the now-approaching mass of the Deep-king himself. Both of their eyes were fixed on Felix, and neither looked particularly pleased. "Go. Spread the word."

"On it!"

"My Lord," Garox said, knuckles white upon his blades. "We need to talk."

"Yeah." Felix sighed. "Yeah, we do."

CHAPTER FIFTY-FIVE

The Chapel of the Eye was named for the three giant Nymean statues that loomed at the top of it all. A purple Belais Crystal had been placed in one of their eye sockets, and its light was a cool amethyst glow across the whole of the chamber. Apart from the other fallen statues and pillars around the wide space, there was a significant amount of blocky stone built up against the tilted door to the Shadowgate, enough that it formed a small island in the water as well as a tiny promontory that Felix stepped across to meet the ruler of the Nagafolk.

Garox had coiled his brown-scaled length across the arm of a fallen statue, his upper body heavy with slabs of muscle and not a stitch of clothing except a golden belt, from which hung his twin scimitars whose hilts he gripped tightly. He did not speak as Felix approached, nor did the Deepking, who had only barely lifted his giant head from the steaming waters.

A part of Felix's Mind noted that they had not been steaming previously, piling together details he'd noticed over the course of his interactions with the Abyssal Serpent. Most of him, however, was concerned with keeping his gaze firm and his resolve firmer.

"My people need to leave," he said. "A threat has announced itself to me, one that could destroy everything we've built. We need to return to my Territory to face it."

The Deepking rumbled, making the water appear to boil all around his massive throat. Garox leaned forward and spoke in a harsh, sibilant whisper. "You will go back on your promise, my Lord?"

"I promised that I'd look into them when I returned from the south.

While I haven't faced the source of the threat, my people and I have destroyed a lot of them, including one of their Nests and the Depthwurm that guarded it." Felix sighed, clenching his jaw several times before continuing. "Those feel like evasions. Quibbling about my promise to you. I don't plan to leave you forever; I will return right after Nagast is defended."

"And what of the threat after that?" the Deepking said through a monstrous snarl. "And after that? This world is not the same one the gods left; it has become wild and unruly, a land of wretches seeking to gobble up all that they can. My people huddle within these Temple walls for safety, where we can guard the hatchery and our future. Out in the deeps, my warriors spend their lives to keep us safe and eradicate the Fathom, but that currency dwindles with each passing day. The Fathom grows stronger as we Naga grow weaker, and soon...even this Temple will fall."

Quest Alert!
Defend The Depths!
The Deepking has outlined a nascent threat to your Authority: the Fathom. Find and neutralize the threat, protect your new people, and seek out the Fathom's purpose.
Purpose 0/1
Reward: Increased Authority, Resources, XP, Varies
Do You Wish To Abandon This Quest?
Y/N

Felix started. He'd never been offered an out from a Quest before. But then...he'd never outright walked away from one, either. Even finding the Shrines of the gods was still on the table; he was just banned from walking near them. Felix composed himself quickly, all too aware of his audience, and mentally refused to drop the Quest. He may have lost their Oath, but the Nagafolk were still clearly invested in working with Felix. "I am not abandoning you or your people, Kar'casitrix. The Fathom spawn are a threat that needs to be handled. But, if I stay, a great many people may die."

"And if you leave us to our fate, God of Thunder and Flame, a great many monsters will die," Garox hissed. "Which, I wonder, do you find more palatable?"

That struck him hard. "Give me a moment, both of you. I—I need to converse with my aides."

"Very well," Garox said, his tone back to being almost aggressively neutral. The Deepking, however, disappeared back beneath the waves.

Felix stepped back, his Mind whirling with new considerations and old guilt. He barely noticed how he walked along the broken stones toward his people, nor the frantic rush of sailors, soldiers, and civilians.

What's the right choice here? Felix looked up, taking in the activity around him before making a beeline through the crowd.

His people had dismantled half of the Manaships already, and the engines and cargo were being steadily removed and placed into rudimentary sleds formed of the same chitinous material. Beef was working his ass off, visibly straining as he grasped planks of conjured matter and reshaped them into the sleds.

As the original casting was his own, Felix knew the Mana cost was considerably lessened than if another were to attempt such a thing—something about one's Intent baking into the construct when shaped made it hard for others to disrupt, even if they had the same Skill—but the Minotaur didn't have a huge amount of Mana. Instead, he was chugging on Mana Potions like they were water, their efficacy slowed with every new quaff, but still a boost to his limited regeneration.

Still, the kid was getting stronger. Already, his Mana vapor was thickening, no longer looking like the wispy remains of a campfire but instead the cloying output of a house aflame. It wasn't liquid like his, but then Beef hadn't even entered the Ring Stage of his core development yet, let alone reached Journeyman Tier. The training Felix had developed for him had paid off, increasing a number of his Skills up through Apprentice Tier and upping several of his stats, and it showed. The kid's hands moved quickly, deftly molding his chitin into rough planks and flat skis. At this rate, they would be ready to go soon.

Felix found Vess talking with Isla, up near the Shadowgate itself. Zara hovered in the air, buoyed by a construct of gleaming aquamarine light.

"—this is how you were able to traverse the Continent?" Isla was asking.

"Yes. Felix...has some unique resources," Vess said.

"But how?" When Vess only shrugged, the diminutive Chanter looked up. "Zara! I know you know. How is this possible? Why have we not known?"

"You will see in short order, dear sister," the Naiad replied, still running her hands over the Shadowgate itself. "We must first find a way to get all of our people through—Ah. Felix. You've returned from your discussion."

"I have." Felix chewed over his words a moment longer before turning to Isla. "The Shadowgate traverses the Void, Isla. I can't really explain how it works except in generalities, but it does." Felix shrugged. "As to its position, I can fix that, I think."

He accessed his Authority.

Authority Acknowledged, Autarch.
Do You Wish To Begin Restoration?
Warning: Stores Of Essence and Significance Are Detected. They Will Be Consumed In The Process.

Limited Restoration, as before, Felix requested. Having accomplished the same thing previously in another part of the Temple, Felix had little difficulty altering the System's desire to repair the Temple.

Limited Restoration In Process!

A hefty chunk of Essence and significance was pulled from his channels, funneled outward into several points along the gate chamber's walls. From there, lights of gold and silver appeared, outlining carvings of stars and time-worn faces in radiance that washed over everything. Beside him, Isla squawked in sudden fear as the ground beneath them rippled.

"What is happening?" she demanded.

Zara chuckled, and her construct lowered itself, allowing Vess and Isla to climb aboard. "Simply watch."

Felix stood still, the slanting flooring flowing away from him like a river, climbing sideways back up the walls. Stone pillars lifted from the deep pools that crossed the space, rising along the walls before connecting seamlessly to the ceiling that was repairing the beams and vaulted shape. Stone lattices rolled across themselves, building upward across a single wall and sharpening in detail. No longer formless, hole-filled rock, now it resembled woven ivy and vines curling with flowers and fruit all crossed by perfect, star-shaped cavities. The entire room shifted, twisting until the floor was level, and the walls had rearranged completely. With the booming sound of a distant gong, it was completed.

"Blind gods," Vess whispered. "Felix, that was amazing."

Isla, on the other hand, had been rendered speechless. She slowly panned her head about, studying the reshaped pillars, the lattice in the shape of vines and stars, as well as the mural formed from a thousand different colored tiles. That caught Felix's attention, too, as it depicted a pastoral landscape of sorts, where people worked fields surrounded by huge trees while a colorful city gleamed in the distance. *Shelim*, he recognized.

"Is this...is this true Nymean art? And the architecture! It is like the Ages have touched none of it!" Isla spun faster, eyes combing the walls until she settled on the biggest and most gorgeous feature. "Shadowgate. I think I understand now."

The portal was now level with the ground, if raised up just a touch on a sloping platform. The precious metals and artistry of its design was untouched, but the plants that had grown across it and much of the chamber had vanished altogether. Now, the wide opening was filled with a swirling darkness, shadows that seemed far denser than merely blocked light, and from its center, Felix could hear a faint...crooning.

Connection Established!
Shadowgate, Designation #5W Is Active!

There was a sudden pull at him, at his center, where his Hunger roused from its easy rest. The crooning increased, and a song he barely recognized but knew perfectly formed in his Mind, before his Spirit and Hunger quivered with a brief but powerful yearning. Abruptly, the connections they had severed were immediately restored. All along the Shadowgate's frame, sigils of gold and silver blazed into being in a grand arc. The swirling darkness turned to thick, liquid tar made of shadow and smoke.

Felix felt a little wobbly, but nothing serious. Losing Essence and significance, even a little bit, always threw him off-kilter. If anything, though, he wasn't nearly as bad off as the last time he'd reconnected the Shadowgate. He cleared his throat. "There you go."

Zara smiled. "Remarkable to see it. The power of Authority and your heritage has proven quite the combination. I imagine that was the point."

"No doubt." Felix grimaced. The idea of the Maw with access to the Shadowgates was horrifying. The Primordial had been doubtlessly aware of their existence; it had come from the same era, after all, when such things seemed to be commonplace. The longer Felix spent on the Continent, the longer he realized just how perfect the Maw's plan would have been, had she managed to force him to be her Vessel.

"The point?" Isla asked, but Felix ignored her.

He walked forward, stepping up to the Shadowgate. The song of it was quieter than he remembered, the space between points a vast emptiness that walked the very edge of the Void itself. It called to mind a great many things that Felix often pushed away, memories that clawed at him. The pirates. The Whalemaw, which would likely prove an issue when they crossed through again. But also Echo's Reach. Bateo. His wife and children and community still stuck in the Void with no way out...abandoned. By him, just as he was going to leave the Naga to their fate while he ran off and did something more important.

"Goddamn it," Felix muttered.

"What is it?" Vess asked.

He turned from the Shadowgate, only steps from passing through its dark surface. "Change of plans. I'm staying."

"What!" Isla and Zara shouted together, before shooting each other a look.

"Felix, why?" Zara continued. "Nagast is under serious threat. We cannot remain here."

"That's why you're not. I'm going to stay alone, and you can lead everyone else back to Nagast." Felix started walking down the ramp, already eyeing the folks who had started to stream into the far end of the chamber. "I'll join you as soon as my Quest here is finished."

"That is foolishness," Isla scoffed. "Vess told me of this Quest of yours. Defeat the Fathom? You may be mighty, but despite what these serpents claim, you are not a god, child."

"No, I'm not. But I'm the best chance the Nagafolk have to survive. You all saw the Den, the Depthwurm, hell, even the Slaughter Nettle. Something is going on here, and the Nagafolk follow me. I can't turn my back on them." Felix clenched his hands, one around his hooked sword and another around the Riposte. "Nagast and Haarwatch will have an army to face the Hierocracy. The Naga will have me."

"And me," Vess said, stepping to him.

"Vess, no." Felix looked at the others, but both Chanters looked surprised, too. "You should go back with everyone else. This isn't your fight."

Vess frowned at him, her dark brown eyes more intense than he'd seen them before. "Felix. You are my friend and ally. And this Fathom, whatever it may be, is of draconic origin. Both of those facts *makes* this my fight. So do not turn me away, or I shall be forced to ignore your orders."

Felix opened his mouth, but any objections he had fled beneath Vess' heated gaze. So he just shut it again. "Fine. You have a point."

"I will stay as well," Zara declared, but Felix shook his head.

"No, you need to help the team figure out that crystal-core shield...thingy," he said. Zara's frown intensified. "Please, Zara. That will save lives. And I need someone to lead them all."

"Zara! You cannot allow this!" Isla said. "He is jeopardizing everything to play hero for some waterlogged snakes?"

"Enough," Zara said, her voice like a whip crack. "You make a fine point, Felix. I...will go and lead your people to Haarwatch...but Isla will remain."

"What?" Felix was not interested in spending more alone time with the annoying Chanter. "She is a healer. She needs to go to the front lines."

Zara held up a hand. "You need a healer at your side to keep you alive. I cannot stop you from risking yourself, that is your own Choice. But your life is far more important than even a Territory full of innocents. If you stay, *she* stays."

Felix gritted his teeth so hard his molars almost splintered. "*Fine.* That's it. No one else stays."

"Stay? What're you guys talking about?" Beef asked, walking up with an armful of metallic parts.

This time, Felix *definitely* felt his tooth crack.

CHAPTER FIFTY-SIX

In the end, Beef, Hallow, Isla, Felix, Pit, and a very insistent Vess chose to stay. The last had been hotly contested by Darius, of course, but something had changed between the two of them. From the time they'd first entered the Shadowgate 'til now, Felix noticed the Hand had kept himself at a distance from the Heiress of Pax'Vrell. He'd busied himself with the training of Felix's forces, putting a ton of his energy into refining their Skills. The two of them had traded a few choice words, some frustrated glares, and it all resolved in the bear of a man stomping off toward the neatly ordered soldiers near the gate.

She had glided toward him, her own emotions in a flurry that Felix could read without even trying. "Vess," he started, before she cut him off.

"Are you going to tell me to go as well?"

"Ah, no. If you want to stay and help, that's your choice. Whichever path we choose right now, we're all headed into danger. And...I imagine this threat has more of a hold on you."

The woman's dark expression faded as he had spoken, until anger mellowed into appreciation. "Felix. Thank you."

"Thank you for wanting to help." He turned to the rest. "That goes for all of you."

Beef shrugged, his big, hairy shoulders jostling the stone and crystal form of Hallow. "I'm interested in finding out the source of this Fathom thing. Plus, as cool as PVP, faction warfare sounds, I'm thinking it'll be better to stick by you. I've gained so many Skill levels these last few days, makes me feel like I wasted so much time."

"Time is not wasted when caution is the watchword. It is merely bided and hoarded, carefully," Isla said.

"I, too, wish to fight. This form has grown much, and while we cannot control as many as before, we can still form a larger force," Hallow said in that strange, multi-throated voice of hers. Her Multipede form was out in the water, swimming cautiously near the Naga that had gathered. "The Nagafolk are intriguing. I wish to claim their dead."

"Oh hey, Hallow. We talked about this," Beef said, looking briefly distressed. "Some thoughts are like, inside thoughts only."

"Ah. Of course." Hallow shifted. "I will keep them inside, then."

"Thanks."

Felix shook his head. She *had* grown. It was perhaps four feet tall now, and its limbs had been refined, looking more and more like bulging muscles, though they were made of rock. However, her personality was still...odd.

"I had intended for you to rebuild those ships when you reached the other side, Beef. Are you positive your...workaround will function as intended?"

"Oh yeah. It's a new Skill, but Zara said that the gate thingy should amplify my control. With the new levels we gained, we can manage one long-range form." Beef scratched his jaw. "For a little bit."

"Hopefully long enough to do what we need." Felix drummed his fingers against the hilt of his hooked blade. "The plan is to get this wrapped up as soon as possible, then we'll be heading through the Shadowgate as well. But, by then, I imagine the main force will be well on their way to Haarwatch."

"I cannot help but feel disappointed I am not experiencing such a wondrous device, but Zara is correct. If you Unbound are staying, then I need to be there for you when you fall." Isla stared at the humming Shadowgate, her Spirit silent but her face betraying her longing. "Then again, I imagine I'll have a chance to inspect it once we pass through, later on. Now, how long do you expect this endeavor to take us?"

"As long as we need," Pit chirruped. Isla shot him an irritated frown, but he only tilted his big bird head, triangular-tuft ears twitching. "Will they be fine?"

Felix followed his Companion's gaze, looking not only at the soldiers that were lining up in rows nearest the Shadowgate, but at the others who lingered behind them. Husbands and wives, mothers and fathers, and children, too. All the civilians who were either related directly to those that joined his army or simply could no longer stand to live in Ahkestria. Many of them huddled close to one another, fear wafting from their Spirits in a variety of flavors. A sharp fear of the Naga, a dull unease around the Frost Giants that loomed above all their forces, and a cloying sense of overwhelming anxiety as they stared at the swirling depths of the Shadowgate.

His stomach lurched just a touch, feeling their worries a bit too fully, before he closed off his Affinity. "They'll be safer in my Stronghold. The Hierocracy will have to burn through Haarwatch before they can even think about attacking there."

"And...that's not gonna happen, right?" Pit asked.

"No, bud. Cal is gonna stomp them into the mud." Felix spread his awareness outward. "Everyone get your stuff and some healing supplies. Stock up. I dunno what we'll need, but it's better than needing it and not having it."

Felix walked off before they could ask him more questions. It wasn't that he didn't want to answer them, but it was a distraction. His Perception flagged the people he was looking for, and Felix pivoted and cut through the mob. Everyone moved out of his way without his asking, which was nice so long as he ignored their expressions. Serpents, giants, and gates weren't the only thing they feared.

"Felix! What's this I hear about you stayin' behind?"

"Harn. Just who I wanted to see. Did Darius tell you?"

"He did," Harn grunted. His helmet was off, and he looked like he wanted to spit, but grimaced instead. "You made these floors too damn nice for a man to have a proper spit, kid."

"Should I rough them up a little?"

"Hrm. Not important." Harn gave him a kind look, his crooked nose and scarred face granting menace to even that. "I appreciate you not takin' Evie. Apart from all the worry she'd cause me, Cal's gonna want to see her when we get back."

Felix nodded. "I wouldn't stand in the way of that. I've already told everyone that I'm not letting anyone else stay. I need Evie and all the rest to go onto Nagast. To lead." He looked around, at the soldiers that were hustling forward with the impromptu sleds carrying Manaship parts. "I need you to keep this army on the right path. You, Darius, and Zara are the commanders of the Claw. The results you and Darius achieved with them so far have been phenomenal, and the rest of the Legion needs the same treatment. Dawnwalkers and Risi Warriors, too."

Harn grunted. "A lotta work, but we'll make do. Having the Fiend's Claw as the spur will help. These kids have grown tremendously in the few weeks we've been gone, and I bet crowns to cores that they've outstripped those who stayed behind."

Felix agreed. Not counting the strange influence he seemed to be having on his allies and followers, the sheer amount of conflict they had encountered and endured was bound to press anyone through the ranks. "Harn, I trust you. Darius, too. Maybe. You'll make it work."

"Ah, he ain't so bad, once you get past all that highbrow bullshit. Kid's a soldier, a warrior. He'll do the right thing."

"Yeah. Yeah, I think so, too." Felix smiled and stuck out his hand. "Good luck, and stay safe."

Harn clasped him hard around the forearm. "Aye, Felix. You, too."

Felix made his way around, speaking with a few select people. As much as Harn and Darius had beaten a sense of unity into his army, they were still fairly cliquey, especially among the Henaari and Frost Giants. He hunted down the Dawnwalkers and spoke to a fair chunk of them, advising them of what he expected when they returned. He did the same with Battlelord Ari, the war leader of the Frost Giants. The reaction was just the same.

"As you Will, my Lord Autarch."

When he reached Alister and Atar, the reception was a bit different.

"What do you mean, you're staying? And you didn't ask me?" Atar paused, tucking his white hair behind his ears. "Not that I would. I'm happy to leave this watery grave behind."

"*I* would like to stay," Alister said, grasping his rapier at the hilt. "I imagine the effort to fight underwater would be illuminating to the application of force magic."

"And I imagine that fighting underwater is a good way to get killed." Atar shuddered. "Besides, there will be plenty of effort in the upcoming battles. Battalions' worth of Inquisitors and Paladins...isn't that what Karys said?"

Felix nodded. "It is. Given Cal's time to prepare and enhance the defenses of Haarwatch, I can't imagine they'll have an easy time of it."

"Depends on what they bring with them." Atar sighed. "Same is true for us, though. You have that Den Core?"

"Gave it to Zara already," Felix confirmed. "Use it. Use whatever you can to fight back, right?"

"Right. You know this battle is going to be harder without you," Atar said, far more gently than he might have, once upon a time.

"Aww, Atar. I'll miss you, too."

"Shut up. I mean it. You're a walking death array; wherever you fight, the enemy finds only Ruin."

"I'll be along as soon as I can. Nagast are my people, but so are the Naga."

"They're *snakes*," he said in a low voice, casting his glance back out the doorway toward where a dozen of the Nagafolk lingered. "They probably eat people."

"So do I."

Atar raised a finger, but his mouth just snapped shut. "Good point."

Alister just gathered up Atar, grabbing both of his shoulders from behind. "Go and fix this issue, and we'll be waiting for you at the front line, Felix."

Felix flashed a relieved smile at the both of them. "Thanks."

Darius found Felix before he'd stepped ten feet from the mages. Had Felix's reflexes not been Tempered with the extreme weight of his stats, he'd have run right into the man. Not for the first time, Felix was reminded of his new height as he stared straight into the once-larger man's eyes. "Oh. Darius. You saved me the trouble; I was going to come find you."

The man's face was...complicated. He had a traditionally handsome face; strong jaw, chiseled chin, all that. But the pieces of it were arranged oddly, or at least oddly to Felix. He'd never seen the man look nervous.

"I know we have not always...seen eye to eye, Felix. I can appreciate what you are and what you are doing for these...people, but the Lady Dayne is important. More than you know. She must be protected, Felix."

"Yeah, man. I don't intend to let her come to harm if I can help it, but she's her own person. With her own choices. I'm not going to make her go through the gate unless she wants to—"

"No, you misunderstand," Darius said, slashing one of his large hands in front of himself. "She has trained to be a Dragoon since she started walking, Felix. She was born for it. No one else has taken so powerfully to the ancient Skills as she has; even I was only ever able to earn the Steps of the Drake."

Darius sighed, and his Spirit let loose a sound like...helpless frustration. Felix almost took a step backward; this was a new side of the Hand of the Duke.

"What are you saying?" he asked.

"I am saying that she is a Dragoon, and your enemy is a dragon...or close enough as not to matter. When I say she must be protected, I mean that it is from herself. Watch her close, and do not let her risk herself for fruitless vengeance. Please."

There was such a depth to the man's plea that Felix had to take him seriously. "I—yeah. I'll keep an eye on her. Why would she want venge—"

"Lord Autarch! We are ready!" Zara shouted at him from across the chamber. The Shadowgate beside her was blurring with its tar-black darkness, now swirling faster than ever.

"Darius, I have to take care of this. Tell me quick—" Felix looked back at the warrior, but found him already halfway through the lines of soldiers. All he did was make a simple handsign in the air.

<Protect.>

Brandishing their array stones once again, a vanguard of Felix's Shadows slipped through the gate ahead of the bulk of their people. Convincing them to travel with the main group hadn't been so much of a challenge as it was painful; ordering his Shadows away from him made all of them uncomfortable. Well, all of them except Felix himself.

Behind the vanguard came the first wave of Claw members with Harn at their head, followed by Alister and Atar, who stepped through the gate with fascination writ large across their faces. After that came more and more of the Claw, and even a soldier in battered red armor and glowing, blackened-green eyes that shambled close behind. Beef's lone Risen. On and on they came, and Felix stood at the side, monitoring the gate along with Zara, watching row after row of his people vanish into inky darkness.

"Felix," Zara said, as the first batch of civilians were swallowed by the Shadowgate. "I'll not mince words: I worry about this splitting of our forces."

"I know it's not the wisest course of action, but it's the *right* one," Felix said, struggling to keep his voice level. He was tired of being questioned about it. "I'm not backing down from it, either."

"And I do not expect you to." Zara turned away from the procession and faced him. "Choice is sacrosanct. You know this. I dare say you have embraced it far more than any other outside my order. I wish only to urge caution, Felix. The Fathom. They feel ancient, yet this Manawarping is newly made. I cannot help but question that discrepancy."

Felix kept watching his people. If he was letting them go without him, the least he could do was see them off. "I'll keep that in mind, Zara. And I appreciate your caring, I really do." He paused, chewing on the inside of his cheek. "But are you *sure* you don't have any other Chanters lying around? Perhaps an enchanted bugle instead?"

Zara smirked before turning back to face the crowd. "You will be fine with her. If you can handle the Archon, you can handle Isla."

CHAPTER FIFTY-SEVEN

"What's next?" Beef asked, plodding up next to him.

Felix had been staring at the Shadowgate, now quiescent, for a couple long minutes. The last of his people had walked through, swallowed up by the tar-like darkness, and the entire contraption had slowed until the sigaldry around it dimmed to a bare glow. Beef's clacking hooves roused him, though. "First, we talk to the Deepking."

He strode away from the Shadowgate, down the ramp and across the polished flooring. A pattern of seven point stars had been worked into the stone, glittering white to contrast the flecked blue-gray of the slabs. An inlay of dull gray metal outlined each star, defining negative space between the white. It was only a single detail among thousands, but it was fascinating. *How did the Nym make these Temples? How can they repair themselves?*

The process took Essence and significance from Felix, lightening the darkness within his core by the tiniest margin. In both senses. The shadows around his cores and Skills were paler, and it all felt just the slightest bit less heavy. Less dense. Sending a quick probe into his core space, Felix took inventory of it all. His Skills shined on, same as ever, and the ribbons that wrapped around his Tempered Skills were pulled taut toward the center, where they twisted ever so slightly. There, at the center, was the major difference that Felix had been working on all this time.

Essence streamed down from the Divine Tree, swirling in streams of light that mingled with the red-gold and blue-white fire of his dual cores. The cores had spread, wider now around the darkness, still there and still blazing with power but mingling more and more. Now all that radiance appeared to bend, lensing around the abyss like a halo, pulsing brighter with each passing second. His abyss, his Hunger, yawned at the heart. Perfectly dark, like the Maw's once-unending appetite. Like the Void itself.

Above arced the Divine Tree, from which the Essence streamed down in countless cascading waterfalls of glimmering vapor. Its trunk was lost among the bending light, an illusion that hid where exactly the growth began, but it was clearly changed as well. No longer a dark, bloody crimson, the Tree now appeared to be fashioned from some opalescent crystal that shimmered a different hue depending on the angle of perception. Its boughs reached up and out, spread wide and filled with leaves of Essence. The branches split countless times, bending back downward toward his cores, filling the dark sky from high to low. A forest made of a single Tree.

Felix's progress had been simple and slow. Small changes, here and there, between training bouts and reading. It was coming together, but he had a long way to go. Longer still, now that he'd spent more of his Essence and significance. The former was easy to measure as they were leaves upon his Tree, but the latter was more ephemeral. It was a feeling, how the core space thickened and weighed against his Aspects. Zara had told him that spending his significance was dangerous and typically reserved for devastating Skills, and that even then, most Grandmasters would rather not. It apparently weakened the stability that was the goal of all advancement on the Continent, reducing a person's resistance to aging and increasing their vulnerability to the actions of others, along with a host of other reasons she wouldn't explain.

Secrets. Always secrets. Those secrets might be necessary so that his advancement wasn't fouled by his own skewed expectations, but it was annoying, always walking in the dark. *Maybe if I leverage my personal information with Isla, I could get more.* Felix considered the slight Chanter as he stepped up toward the others, now gathered near the exit. She was watching Felix like a scientist might watch a particularly fascinating lab rat. *Or maybe not.*

"What are—" Isla started, but Felix swept past her.

"Follow me," he said and strode from the Shadowgate chamber. Was it a little childish? Yes. Was it also satisfying to hear her sharp intake of offended breath? Absolutely.

Felix walked along the broken island of stones, hopping toward the end where Garox still coiled about the alabaster arm of some sunken sculpture. As he did, the water rumbled and roiled, and the Deepking rose from the steaming depths, baring his large, very yellow teeth.

"You have stayed," he said, his voice sending more waves rippling out around his half-submerged throat. It was only from the pleasure that radiated from the Deepking's Spirit that Felix could tell his expression must have been a sort of smile.

Happy Trixie, Pit sent.

"I have. While the rest of my people go to handle the threat, we will remain to help you resolve yours," Felix said. Despite the Deepking's obvious power, he was finding it easier to talk to this guy than any number of non-monstrous authority figures. "I know the bare bones of this conflict; I know that you're on the defensive. Garox has even told me that the enemy is coming from a place called Khasma? What is that?"

"It is the vile center of the Fathom's reign," the Deepking rumbled. "Far below the surface, farther still than this Temple, lies the true depths of the Ghreldan Hills. It is there that the core of their forces lurk, multiplying. Khasma lies there."

Felix put his hands on his hips, thinking. "How exactly can we help?"

Trixie didn't answer, but Garox did. "The Fathom spawn have spread far and wide. The flooding from the south was a boon to us, but to the Fathom, it was far more. It strengthened their reach, allowing their disgusting ooze to spread farther and farther. Far beyond what we can control."

"Their Dens produce Hatchlings too fast to count. Alone, they are nothing, mere snacks for our legendary appetites. I could eat a thousand and still be ready for more," the Deepking rumbled.

"The issue is their Evolutions. They come upon them rapidly, far more rapidly than us Nagafolk or even any natural monster we have ever met," Garox added.

"The Manawarping," Vess said.

"Yes," the Deepking agreed.

"The what?"

"A twisting of the natural process through overexposure to Mana, Beef," Isla explained. "Except, it isn't Evolution these creatures are experiencing, not if they're all Manawarped."

The Deepking frowned at her so loudly, Felix had to clench his Affinity to dim the noise. "Explain."

Isla absently adjusted the coronet atop her platinum curls and continued as if no one had spoken to her. "It is an overflow of Mana when a monster does not Evolve as it should. If it were Evolving, the Manawarping wouldn't take hold. Unless..."

"Unless what?" Vess asked.

Isla bit her lip. "Unless the Mana involved was so potent that the Evolutions happened, and it was *still* flooded with power. But that would require a source that was far beyond Master Tier, and I've sensed nothing like that in these waters." She looked up at the Deepking, every inch of her a queen looking at a peasant. "What leads them? What *exactly* is this Fathom?"

"It is hatred and corruption and dark, vile menace!" The Deepking roared, bellowing a mighty cry into the air that all of his people answered. Felix winced, and his friends all took a step back from the sheer Spiritual pressure of it.

The Deepking lowered his head, and for a moment, a purple-blue radiance surrounded his head like a crown. His voice lowered to a brutal, biting growl.

"It is a Dragon!"

When Atar stepped through the Shadowgate, he was expecting a rendition of the coastal forest they had raced through the last time. What he encountered, however, was a rocky stone island and the endless expanse of a deep, violently surging ocean.

Burning ashes. It's because Felix isn't here. He said that last place was a reflection of one of his Mind Skills. He had looked around, watching as more and more people arrived from what looked like thin air. *But whose Skill is this, then?*

Over the course of a quarter-glass, everyone arrived on the stone island. It was a tight fit, with hundreds of people packed shoulder-to-shoulder and the giants looming over them all. Atar was just about to shove his way to the front, but Alister tapped his arm. "Look."

Above them, Zara flowed across the air on a wave of aquamarine light, arcing over the crowd until she landed at the very edge of the raging surf. The waves were high enough to swallow a Frost Giant, but as she landed, another set of blue-green light burst from her. "Risi Warriors! I shall need your assistance!"

The waves were seized and shoved back, scattered until only a space nearly a hundred strides wide was filled with a framework of aquamarine light. As Atar watched, Zara shaped it into a wide structure of some kind, and the Frost Giants made their way to her side. "Pour your Mantles into the framework before you," she commanded.

The giants shared a few confused looks, but Battlelord Ari nodded sharply. "Tuak fa rasa. Naat!"

Even through the crowd, a blast of cold air hit Atar hard enough to blow back his robes as every Frost Giant activated their Mantle of the Long Night. The stone platform they stood upon was quickly covered with thickening ice, but as it hit the edges of Zara's spellform, the ice was funneled away. Into it, so that its blue-green framework was layered over and over with ice.

"Fascinating," Atar muttered. His eyes danced along the construct, trying to absorb everything. "Alister! She's using Odelkain's Boundary to contain the flow of Mana, and a modified siphon array to pull it from the giants' Mantles!"

"She can't be. That would break the Jasto-Marvane Theory of Displacement. You can't have Odelkain's anywhere near a siphon array, or else it all collapses. It's why they haven't been able to make a lamp much larger than a barrel, not unless you fuel it with monster cores."

"Impossible or not, that's what she's doing. Except," Atar paused, listening. He could hear a strange, multi-toned humming coming from the Naiad. "Damnation. She's using that Chant of hers. She's cheating."

"I would not call it such. Besides, this opens up some options."

"How so?"

As they were talking, the giants gasped and fell to their knees. Their faces were stricken, and several appeared to have passed out, but before them all was a magnificently wide and deep-bellied craft. It appeared to be a Manaship, but not even their modified ships had looked so huge or ungainly. Hundreds of sails had erupted from ice-shaped masts, already rippling in the ceaseless winds.

It's a seafaring ship, like in the ancient tales, Atar realized. He'd once read stories of mariners that plied the farthest reaches of the seas, before the water was turned to acid, and the waves roused to anger. Now, no one dared traverse the endless expanse of the oceans. *It's what the Manaships were based upon. Fascinating.*

For her part, Zara didn't even look winded. "Everyone! Board the vessel quickly!"

A gangplank twenty strides across burst from the ship's side, landing at the edge of the island with a deep, resounding thud. The Claw members closest immediately clambered up the plank, soon followed by all the rest. People jostled a bit, but they were calm for the most part, and the only noise was the sound of boots on ice and the ceaseless roar of the surf.

a paltry conjuration. were you to embrace me, we could boil away the very sea itself, atar.

Quiet, Atar demanded, casting his senses briefly into his core space. The obsidian cage he'd fashioned around his core was intact, though the fire within surged. Flames spread like wings, batting at the glassy stone bars.

release me, and we can do so much.

He looked at the rest of his core space, much changed since his injury. The monoliths were now covered in sigaldry that blazed white and red, while jagged lines swirled around them, connected at the base to his core. The ceiling was no longer vaulted, but instead open to a night sky so dazzling that it hurt his eyes to look at it. Stars glimmered up there, great swaths of them like jewels set into the dark, and brightest among them were a blaze of red-gold and blue-white.

a light that bridges worlds. curious. he is so much stronger than you.

Shut up, Flame.

he dares connect to your inner world, a would-be king. i can show you how to be truly worthy of rule. how to *rise*—

"Well," Alister said, clapping Atar on the back and drawing him out of his reverie. The voice of the Flame was snuffed. "Far easier to examine this up close. Are you coming?" He was already flowing with the crowd toward the craft.

"Yes yes, of course." Atar said, leaning a bit on his staff. He focused on his excitement of the magic before him, content to shove the battle ahead and the whims of a half-dead Urge to the back of his Mind.

He stubbornly ignored the rising heat in his chest and ambled after.

CHAPTER FIFTY-EIGHT

"A Dragon. A true and real Dragon? You are sure of this?" Vess asked. Her voice was calm and measured, but her Spirit flared wildly with strange passions. Anger, for sure, and a touch of hate even, but encompassing all of that was a fierce *hope.*

Felix pulled back, squeezing shut his Affinity once again. It always felt like an intrusion, listening to someone's emotional state. With strangers and enemies, it was a tactical advantage; with his friends, it was an invasion of their privacy. Still, Darius' parting words clung to Felix's Keen Mind, remembered with crystalline clarity.

"...do not let her risk herself for fruitless vengeance..."

Dammit, Darius. Is this what you meant? Felix's attention was recaptured by the Deepking's slow nod.

"We...do not know much. Only that it is nestled deep within the Khasma. Spreading its vile corruption along the tides." The Deepking heaved a rattling breath, a wheezing bellows the size of a city bus. "The dragon *hides*, fearful of our true might. Instead, it sends minnows to nip at us, until we are bloody and weakened."

"The tactics of a coward," Garox said. He slithered off the alabaster arm and touched down upon the surface of the steaming water. He did not sink, and a thin layer of Mana hovered around the scales of his underbelly. "Were we able to push our warriors into its lair, this fight would be over. But it keeps us on the defensive, constantly threatening our Temple where the future of our people resides."

"Well, then. Sounds like we're going to need an idea of the area and a battle plan. Vess?" Felix looked to his friend. "What can you tell us of the enemy? You're the resident dragon expert."

“Yes, yes," Isla said, patting Vess on the arm in a fond manner. "The Lady Dayne and I have had extensive conversations about the matter. What was it you said, my dear? About this Fathom?”

A slight tension pulled back at Vess' shoulders, like a puppeteer's string. She took a breath before answering, her eyes fixed firmly forward. “Only that it seemed clear it is of the draconic Type and quite powerful. The Depthwurm was a corrupted cousin of the Lindwurm, a common and powerful foe we sometimes see in the hills around Pax'Vrell.

“They are leaders in their own right, though you often see them dominating a horde of young Drakes at best.” She shook her head. “This Depthwurm was moving with purpose, as was the Slaughter Nettle. The insight we have into their motivations suggest a greater Mind is directing it. From the signs...I fear it may be a Tidaldrake.”

“What's that?” Beef asked. “Sounds like a detergent.”

“A what?” Isla gave him a look, like she didn't trust him to tie his own shoes.

Hooves, Felix corrected himself. *Whatever.*

“Nevermind,” Beef muttered. “But I dunno what a Tidaldrake is, though.”

“A Threat to any Territory, operating typically at the high Master stage, with the capability to command thousands of its lesser brethren. They hold dominion over the waves and the reed, with a command of magic that is unshakeable.” Isla's face was creased by the smallest of frowns. “The Tidaldrakes died out, however. Hunted to extinction, if I recall, six hundred years ago.”

“That is what the records indicate, yes,” Vess admitted. “So, it could be that we are dealing with something entirely different now. But if you are right, Deepking, then we are facing a foe that is at the very least comparable to a high Master. No dragon could command such potent underlings, were they not far stronger.”

“The past stirs as Ruin descends on us all." Isla patted Vess on her shoulder, managing to appear both concerned and condescending to Felix. “The Grand Harmony will sing what must be sung, and oftentimes, it is the old that resounds within the strains of the new.”

"Uh, yeah. Sure," Beef said. "But like, what's the plan?"

Vess turned to Garox. "Do you have maps of the Khasma and the way there?"

"We do. The depths often shift, but most paths are well-worn. I can take you to them."

"That would be appreciated. My thanks, Garox." As the Spirit Naga bowed, Vess looked at the others. "We need to prepare ourselves for travel and combat beneath the waves. What resources do we have to handle that?"

"I have Sunken Ward," Felix said, and didn't miss the sharp look the

Deepking gave him—he just ignored it. He *had* stolen the spell from them, but he'd stolen a lot of things. "That will protect us from the pressure and temperature of the water. But maneuverability will likely be an issue. I'll be fine, I think, but I don't know if you all will. Pit? You've done some swimming since your Evolution, right?"

"Yup! I had to fish you out of the sea," he chirruped brightly. "It was hard. You are heavy, though, so I think I can do better on my own."

"I think I got Swimming down," Beef said. "Your training got me to Apprentice Tier with it."

"Down won't be an issue. You're almost as heavy as him," Pit said, jerking his head toward Felix. "Up might be worrisome."

"Eh, I'll be good."

"We shall provide you with an escort into the deeps. Twelve of our strongest warriors will accompany you, to carry you into the abyss and fight alongside the Returned God," Garox said. All at once, the crowd of Naga that had gathered let out an undulating, sibilant call. It crawled across the chamber like a thing alive.

"Thank you, that helps. Every advantage will likely matter, if this Fathom is as powerful as you suspect," Felix said. "Anything you can provide is welcome."

"Garox, show them the chamber of the slain detritus," the Deepking commanded. To Felix, he bowed. "I will personally select the warriors to accompany you while you prepare yourselves."

With a final, imperious nod, the unthinkably huge serpent slipped back under the surface.

Vess traded a look with Felix. Her nostrils were flared and brow drawn down. "Slain detritus?" she asked.

Felix looked to the Spirit Naga. "Yeah, no clue. Garox?"

"You are not the first non-Naga to breach the Temple walls. For years uncounted, we have been assaulted by the mad and the foolhardy." Garox gave a boneless sort of shrug. "We have stored all of their effects in our vault."

"Effects? As in weapons and armor?" Beef asked, his voice rising in excitement. "I know a treasure chamber when I hear it!"

Garox gave another motion of his head and shoulders, too liquid to be a Human gesture. "Perhaps. It is of no use to us. But I shall lead you there, if you are ready, Returned God?"

"Yeah. Lead on, Garox."

They left the Shadowgate chamber and the Chapel of the Eye too, quick on the heels of Garox. Before he did, however, Felix noticed a few of the Nagafolk were getting a little too close to the Shadowgate's doors, and he flexed his Authority. The chamber slammed shut, the metal and stone doors locking and sealing with a flare of blue sigaldry. Naga warriors hissed and fell back, startled, while Garox turned to gaze upon them all with a flat-faced glower.

"Attend to your duties," he commanded. The Nagafolk scattered, wriggling off the stone island and back into the water. "My apologies, my Lord."

"Mhm. Let's just get going," Felix said.

He fashioned a boat out of ice, more than happy to let Beef recover his Mana, and they followed the winding path of their guide. Hallow's secondary form, the Risen Multipede, followed beneath them. More labyrinthine hallways met them, all twisted and turned askew, half-submerged in a way that Felix doubted was an accident.

He spotted more than a few places where the stones didn't join so nicely, where thick mortar and smaller bricks had been wedged into place to prevent too much water from entering the Temple. It was clear that the Nagafolk had put a great deal of effort in maintaining their home, not having much magic to hand or even the proper Authority to initiate the Temple's restoration arrays.

In many places, statues were piled together, and holes were burrowed through them, leaving areas honeycombed by porous nests that dripped with some sort of thick, viscous fluid. As they passed one of the many, Felix could sense smaller Naga within, children or adolescents, currently crowded close to larger forms. *Their mothers? Do snakes have maternal bonds? I guess they're not snakes, though, just like Pit isn't a raven or a fox despite his shape. Just more people.*

"Creepy," Beef said as they passed the eyeless visage of a Nymean statue.

"Nests," Isla said. "This is your hatchery?"

"No. Our hatchery is protected on a deeper level. Those outside of it are capable of defending themselves." Garox let a soft, disconsolate grumble rattle through his chest. "Even if all they can do is flee."

"I imagine even your children have teeth," Isla said. She looked at Garox's wide, humanoid back, and Felix saw a sharpness there that he didn't understand. "And scales enough to withstand an Apprentice Tier's strike."

Garox didn't answer for a bit, letting the rush and gurgle of water fill the silence. Felix looked to Isla, but other than keeping her gaze fixed on the Spirit Naga, she gave nothing away. Finally, as they rounded another corner and entered a narrow corridor filled with snapped columns, Garox spoke.

"You fear us, Lady Isla, and our bestial nature. I have seen such attitudes before, and I assure you that you are wrong. My people are predators by our nature, but we do not kill without reason or for the bloody joy of it. I know those on the surface think us monsters; long have I heard the legends they tell of my people. But we think, and feel, and we protect. Just as any." Garox wound to a stop next to a relatively small doorway carved into the shape of a six-pointed star. "We have arrived."

The door lifted, sliding upward into a recessed slot as the water outside the chamber rushed inward, swiftly filling an empty, low-lying area. Beyond the gurgling tide, Manalights bloomed across the room, piles of metal gleaming in the sudden brightness.

"Holy crap," Beef whispered.

"Those are corpses hung upon the walls," Vess pointed out, and sure enough, they were. Chalk-white skeletons wrapped in still-gleaming armor hung from twisted metal spikes that had been driven into the ivy-strewn walls. That ivy also grew across the bodies, and in some cases, fully encased them. "A great many corpses."

"The remnants of all those who thought to hunt our halls for treasure or trophies," Garox said, and this time, there was a guttural growl in his voice. "We protected our own, and now they are part of the treasures they sought to claim."

"That makes sense to me." Pit hopped out of their ice boat, landing nimbly among the piles of discarded armor, coins, and strange objects. He trilled at Felix. "C'mon! I want to look around."

Felix shaped more ice into a rigid mooring around his craft, essentially freezing it all together into a thick shelf and attaching it to the raised stone flooring. Done, he gestured to Vess, letting her exit first. Beef, Hallow, and Isla followed.

"I shall remain with the boat, Michael." Hallow's Multipede form reported, cresting the waters with its blunt face.

"Cool," Beef said, before whispering to Hallow's Homunculus on his shoulder. "Can you stop? I told you, my name is Beefhammer now. Or just Beef. That's cool, too."

"I am sorry, Michael."

"Ugh."

Their group more or less scattered across the chamber, walking through the haphazard paths between piles of cluttered and disjointed loot. It was clear to Felix that the Naga hadn't truly sorted these items, preferring to throw them and their former owners in and let time sort it all out.

"This is a lot of gold and silver," Beef said to Felix. He was whispering, but a whisper from a seven-foot bull-man wasn't as quiet as Beef thought. "Do we just like, take it? We could buy so much stuff."

"We have zero ways to carry any of this," Felix pointed out. "Maybe when we get back, I'll see about taking it with us through the Shadowgate."

Felix's Voracious Eye was going wild as he panned it around the room. Every other item was enchanted, and while many were broken or busted weapons and armor, there were just as many exceptional pieces. His friends started rummaging through the piles, pulling items up to glint in the Manalights. Beef was quick to grab a large, spiked war club made entirely of a green metal called High Serpentine.

"Ooh, this I can use," he said happily. A moment later, chitin flowed across its length, shaping into his usual jagged maul but now adorned with numerous spikes along the back. The kid gave it a few practice swings and couldn't stop grinning. "Awesome. This counts toward my Bludgeoning Mastery, too!"

Earthly steel was a Tier I metal, as far as Felix could tell, and it took high concentrations of different Mana types to push ore from Tier to Tier. High Serpentine, according to his Eye, was a Tier IV metal. Easily better than any materials they had found back in Nagast, though apart from a durability array, it boasted no further enchantments.

Vess moved among the piles methodically, using her spear to sort through the buildup of centuries of invaders. Pit was cooing whenever he found something vaguely magical, but kept flitting around without settling. The Homunculus was moving swiftly among the piles, ignoring the gold and softly glowing artifacts all around them while she hunted for...something. Felix put the creature out of his Mind, focusing instead on what he could find. After some searching, however, he found some good things.

Name: Spikeshot Cuff
Type: Accessory (Enchanted)
Lore: A twice-forged cuff made of Tier III High Steel, it has been enchanted to summon a spiked ball of metal Mana that can be thrown. There are ten charges.
Refinement III - Refines any Mana placed into the Cache, turning it into metal Mana.
Cache II - Retains attuned Mana, enough to provide ten charges.

Name: Pendant of Quick Guard
Type: Accessory (Enchanted)
Lore: Crafted by an unknown hand in an unknown Age, these Pendants create a dense shield around the wearer that has some limited regeneration at the expense of pulling from the wearer's own reserves. The shield reduces damage received, but once it suffers a strike above Adept Tier, it will shatter the pendant completely.
Shielding IV - Generates a shield of unattuned Mana that clings to the wearer's Body.

Self-Repair II - Absorbs ambient Mana to repair itself
Internal Draw III - Absorbs Mana from wearer's core to replenish the item

Name: Bottled Smoke
Type: Container (Enchanted)
Lore: A vial that contains such dense smoke within it, that it appears to be filled with a solid. When opened, the vial will release such a quantity of thick, gray smoke that it will obscure a large area from view. One time use.

Name: Glamulet
Type: Accessory (Enchanted)
Lore: An amulet made of coldforged iron and rivets of brass. Its crude appearance is deceiving, however, as it is packed with dense sigaldry. There are three arrays, all of which form a complicated formation that focuses on illusions centered on the self. Effects last only as long as the wearer can fuel the amulet itself.
Faux Mask III - Generates illusions around the wearer's Body

They weren't weapons or armor, but Felix had little need for either of those things. What he needed were options. The Pendants of Quick Guard weren't even for him, but for the others, though he'd found seven of them in total, so it wouldn't hurt to wear one. He rooted around for more items of interest, but there wasn't much that either wasn't whole or didn't work with his "build."

But a lot of this would be handy for my people. There's a lot here. Bows. Swords. Axes. Armor sets. Some are even complete. Not to mention all the metal we could melt down and repurpose in our Forge. Felix smiled. *Sticking around is already paying dividends.*

After doing a rough catalog of what was there, Felix met his team back near the ice boat. Beef had gotten a red-gold orichalcum helmet in addition to his club, one that apparently molded to his head shape as the metal fit smoothly up and over his horns until they were entirely coated. It even had a neck guard that wrapped around him like a gorget. He gave Felix a thumbs up. "This helmet is so cool. It gives bonuses to Strength and Endurance and even has a Skill!"

"Oh? What Skill?" Vess asked.

"Uh, Madman's Assault. Some sorta headbutt attack."

"I see why the extra Endurance is required, then."

Beside Beef, Hallow stood perhaps two inches taller than she once was; her Body was still rocks and crystals all jumbled together, but a series of new crystals stuck up from her shoulders like spiky armor.

Additionally, a Girdle of Shifting Movement was wrapped around the Homunculus' waist, a strange splash of embroidered black on the otherwise rocky figure. Apparently, it granted a small bonus to Agility.

Vess had found one of the most interesting items. She, too, had ignored the armor and weapons, and instead focused on finding something that would truly complement her fighting style. What she found was a strange metal basket with straps on one side so that it could be worn like a backpack. Inside the basket, slotted cleverly between metal segments, were thirteen dinner plate-sized bronze discs. Each one was thoroughly inscribed with an array, and Felix spotted the similarities to his Glamulet right away, as well as the differences.

Voracious Eye!

Name: Sling Salvo
Type: Thrown Weapon (Enchanted)
Lore: Discs made of High Bronze and inscribed with a duplication array. Each disc thrown will create duplicates that spread out and strike your target. Each duplicate does half as much damage as the original and are destroyed upon impact. Mana for duplication must be metal-attuned and infused into the discs before they are thrown.
Duplication Barrage II - Creates 1-3 duplicates per disc

"Wow, that's fascinating," Felix said, studying one of the discs. He flipped it over, tracing the fine sigaldry that radiated outward from its center.

"It will be of use when we see another swarm of Fathom spawn," Vess said, taking the disc back and securing it in its basket. "Increasing our wide-scale damage seems the wisest course of action at this point."

"I agree. The Fathom is still a concern, but we have to get through his hordes first, right?" A feathery head jutted right into Felix's shoulder, failing to push him back, but still interrupting his conversation. "I'm talking, Pit."

Felix's words trailed off as he saw his friend. Pit had a glass belt dangling from his beak, which he waggled in Felix's face. "Mmph mmmph mph!"

Felix took it from his Companion's mouth, running his hands over the smooth segments of dark-blue glass. "What?"

"I asked, 'what is this?' I don't have Analyze."

"It..." Felix laughed, hesitated, and read his notification again. "It's a belt that transforms your lower half into a 'glistening fish tail.'"

Pit sat back onto his haunches, but his ears pricked forward. "OH! That sounds really useful. Will it make me swim better?"

"Yeah, probably?" Felix's chuckle was cut short by Isla's arrival. She was busily adjusting several pouch-covered belts around her waist, a bandolier, more pouches, and a short arming sword. "Whoa, what did you find?"

"Items of interest. This sword will do nicely if I'm required to expend myself during this outing."

"And what's in all the pouches?"

Isla adjusted the coronet in her hair and smoothed her fine silk skirt. "Contingencies, Felix."

Felix shot a glance at Garox, still waiting patiently at the entrance perhaps twenty yards away. "What does *that* mean?"

"It means I do not trust these serpents, and neither should you." With that, Isla brushed past Felix and returned to their boat. Felix motioned to the others and climbed in after her.

"This discussion isn't over," he promised, before raising his voice. "Garox. We're ready to leave."

"Very well, my Lord."

CHAPTER FIFTY-NINE

"More to starboard! Three big ones!"

Zara heeded the Yttin sailor's warning but did not turn aside the speeding mass of the carrack, and in fact sent a delicate song on high. It stirred the winds into a greater tempest, pressing the ten sails on all four masts to their limit. Yet the creatures were faster, moving through the waters like the shadows from which they came.

"Breach! Breach!" Harn bellowed, just as two burst from the surface of the raging sea. Their serpentine Bodies writhed, clad in dusk-colored scales and festooned with spiny fins that arced like sails. They undulated through the air. "First Talon, loose!"

They were met by fury and dire, deadly thunder.

One of the creatures—Noctnatters—was torn to pieces, its strong flesh pierced by lightning and arrows bearing vicious payloads. The second shielded itself from the barrage with the corpse of its brethren, undulating over its smoking carcass only to run mouth-first into a cascade of brutal magic from the Second Talon.

"Excellent!" Harn shouted, balanced atop the slick, icy gunwale. His impressive Agility was all that kept him from tumbling over the side as the carrack rode down the trough of another wave. Perhaps he'd gotten practice in during their tumultuous journey from Ahkestria. "Lieutenant Pava! Report! Where's the third?"

"Sir!" The dark-skinned Pava sheathed her glowing sword and frowned in concentration. "I—I don't know, sir! The song of it...It's gone!"

Zara shook her head. *Still learning.* She would have been utterly surprised if Felix's strange warriors had so easily mastered their Affinity. That they had grown so fast at all was still a wondrous mystery. She could feel the third Noctnatter easily as it lingered just below their careening ship, hiding in their massive wake. These voidbeasts bore a crude cunning that was on wide display during their many encounters.

Not nearly as dangerous as what we could face, I—She cut off the thought before it could form, quelling the inklings in her Mind with ruthless force. She could not address it, or else their journey would be far worse.

"Focus!" Harn shouted over the crash of the waves. "They don't leave us be, so it's still here. Eyes up, now!"

It burst upward the moment Harn's words left his lips, and none of them were ready. The Noctnatter shot up and over the railing, shattering a large chunk of the ship with its sheer bulk as it flung itself maw-first at the defensive line. Zara saw Harn's leading axe ignite with silver flame, and interesting lines of metallic sigaldry began to scrawl into the air...but he was too slow.

"Bonds of Dominion!"

Instead, a figure in dark leather and flashing metal streaked across the deck. Dark purple chains erupted from the air and deck, snagging the voidbeast across its open jaws and tangling among its spines, giving Evie the moment she needed to bring the full weight of her weapon down.

"Reap the Maelstrom!" she cried out, and just before her chain struck, it accelerated powerfully. Chain hit scales, and voidbeast hit ice deck all at once, sending superficial fissures through the carrack's construction. The Noctnatter twisted, attempting to bring its fangs to bear on the slight girl, but Evie yanked hard. "Rimefang's Wrath!"

Purple-white Mana, already invisibly leaking from the ship, was snagged by the girl's Skill. Twin clawed gauntlets of dark ice manifested around her fists as she shoved the flat blade of her hand into a putrid, yellow eye. Still, the voidbeast would have snapped her up had she not leaped and rotated her entire body upward, light as a breeze, landing astride the Noctnatter's skull. She pulled hard against its skull, dragging those dark, icy claws up through its skull. It twitched once more before expiring.

Impressive. It had taken the girl all of three seconds to restrict and kill the voidbeast. Alone. Zara hadn't expected that. *Perhaps I should be paying more attention to her, as well.*

"That's how you do it, kids!" Evie shouted, lifting a gore-covered gauntlet in victory. More than a few faces pinched in disgust, but others watched with serious eyes and steady, earnest Spirits. "Keep eatin' your vegetables, and one day you, too, could be as stunning as me. Maybe." Evie tilted her head. "Eh. Probably not. But it ain't bad to hope!"

"Alright! Back to battle stations!" Harn shouted over Evie's bravado.

"First Talon, Second Talon, go take a rest. Third and Fourth, you're comin' up here! Move, people!"

"You heard Commander Kastos, no telling when more voidbeasts will come!" Darius bellowed just after, pushing the next group of soldiers up from the lower decks while the others filed below. Zara could sense the soldiers' relief to be in the open air, no matter how tempestuous. The carrack was vast, able to hold all of their people and supplies, but only just.

Darius joined Harn near the mizzenmast, where they began a fierce but quick discussion about tactics. Zara could have eavesdropped, but restrained herself. The Hand would know if she listened, somehow. Zara hadn't quite figured out his trick...and he knew it.

Infuriating man. Within seconds, the voidbeast had turned to streamers of foul smoke, lost to the whipping winds as the carrack continued to sail onward, prodded by her potent Willpower. *Intelligent and strong, surely, but entirely too proud.*

The two commanders returned to their respective posts, this time Harn going belowdecks, and Darius started marching up and down the soldiers that lined up against the ship's sides. Zara busied herself with checking the wards that kept hers and all the power contained. They had lashed the stone wards to the gunwales in all directions, and so long as their people remained within its circumference, they would not draw down the ire of greater and more worrisome beings. Her senses found the array unbroken and functioning as intended. Even still, their very presence within the Shadowgate seemed to signal nearby scavengers.

"Lotta nasties out there, huh?" Evie said, shuffling toward the prow. The deck rolled, but her knees and hips moved effortlessly with them.

"Indeed. It seems these Shadowgates are quite attractive to their kind, if not as permeable as the Dark Passages I've used in the past. Otherwise, our wards would allow us to pass without a trace." Zara examined the sky, which was an unrelieved pewter blue, empty of even clouds. It complemented the slate-gray seas, a calm counterpoint to their swells. "Be thankful nothing worse has noticed us."

"You mean the Whalemaw?" Evie scrunched up her nose. "That thing sounds nasty."

"It was a vile abomination fueled by a dark hunger." Zara shuddered. "If I never see it again, it would be too soon. As it stands, we shall pass through the Shadowgate within another few glasses. Already, we are making greater time than before."

"Huh. Didn't we arrive really fast last time?" Evie asked, shifting her weight as the ship began to climb up another swelling wave. "Like, we traveled for six or seven glasses, but only a glass had actually passed between the leaving and the arriving?"

"Time moves strangely in the Void, and liminal spaces like the Shadowgate tread closely to its influence. The exact conversion is unknown to me, and it very well might fluctuate. Perhaps we will have been gone several glasses, perhaps only a fraction of that time." Zara grinned, baring her sharp teeth to the wind. "I do admit to being quite curious. I have a theory that the amount of space affected influences the temporal dilation, but we will have to use the other Shadowgates to ascertain whether that is viable."

"Uh-huh. Fascinatin'."

Zara's smile swept away with the breeze. She found herself wishing for the company of Atar or Alister; as annoying as their questions had grown earlier, at least they would have been excited by the prospect. "What is it that you want, Ms. Aren?"

"Me? Oh. Nothin'. Me and the Battlelord were talkin' a bit, wonderin' about all this ocean."

Her relationship has improved with the giants. Zara had noticed Evie's attitude toward them had shifted—her Spirit returning to a mellower tempo since the events in Ahkestria—but engaging in friendly conversation was a new turn entirely. *It seems I've more than one reason to be impressed with the girl.* "What is it you are curious about?"

Evie scratched her head, tugging at the braids she'd hastily woven. "Well, is this your Skill? Like how the last one was Felix's?"

Zara tensed. "It is. Like Felix's Bastion of Will, this allows us to traverse the Shadowgate path far faster by providing a medium we may traverse. Without it, we'd be slogging through dense Void-stuff."

Let that be explanation enough, child.

"What sorta Skill is just...an empty ocean? Even with the monsters, this feels way too easy."

Zara sighed as, in response to Evie's words, Zara felt a resonant *click* deep in her core space. A Skill was fatefully engaged. All around them, the water thrummed with a pitch that few could ever hope to hear, and it set the Naiad's heart racing. She knew someone was going to ask sooner or later, and had even managed to keep the mages distracted long enough to forget the question.

She hadn't expected Evie to bring it up, but then, the girl *had* surprised her multiple times. "It is a Mind Skill, the only one that the Shadowgate found a sympathetic connection to, and which I have long Tempered to Master Tier. It is called Guardian's Challenge, a Skill that tests my own limits in order to surpass them."

Ahead, the sound of roaring water was interrupted by a cataclysmic splash. Huge, golden obelisks twice the width of their ship erupted from the surface of the ocean. Each monolith was made of cratered stone that glowed like miniature suns, putting off enough golden radiance to turn the slate seas into sunset waves.

Zara frantically whistled, and the winds shifted them to port, narrowly avoiding the first upthrust stone.

"Noctis' bloody throat! What is *that*?" Evie asked, grabbing hold to the railing as the ship bucked sideways.

"A Challenge," Zara shouted back as more gleaming monoliths ripped from below. The harmonics blazed within her senses, alight with her Intent as she manipulated the ship. "One that only activates when it is acknowledged by thought or word."

"What? Why didn't you warn me! I wouldn't have brought it up!"

"Wouldn't have mattered. That alone would have caused the Challenge to enact. Come, Evie! Harness yourself to the ship and breathe the wild spray!" Zara felt the ghost of old instincts, ones that were native to this Mask, yet almost forgotten. The feel of swimming through chill rivers and endless lakes, battling the tides and the monsters below. "We've no choice now."

The ship raced forward, tempest winds behind, a shifting maze of blazing stone ahead.

CHAPTER SIXTY

After leaving the treasure room, Garox had led their boat down several rivers, each of them flowing over the remains of grand staircases. The water moved far more sedately than the rapids Felix and his people had traversed in the past, moving more like a lazy river than whitewater rapids. It was...kind of pleasant.

In short order, they descended the faux rivers and passed through a high, star-shaped archway which was utterly filled with dangling vines. The vines were covered in pale white flowers, sharply scented in the humid air, and they tingled wherever they touched Felix.

Status Condition: Warm Embrace
Duration: 3 seconds
Warm Embrace
A layer of heat and life Mana clings to your Body, regulating your temperature despite outside conditions.

A warmth followed after that tingle, though it quickly sputtered out and faded for Felix. He glanced at his friends, their faces a range of surprise, excitement, and suspicion. Isla glared at the vines as they passed through before shaking herself. Felix's Manasight caught the faint pop of yellow and green-gold light scatter from her figure, the same Mana that clung to his Companion and friends.

"I would appreciate a warning before inflicting Status Conditions on us all," the Chanter said to their guide.

Garox rolled his shoulders. "It is a boon, to better insulate you from the chill depths."

"I can do fine by myself, thank you."

Felix frowned. His Status Condition had lasted all of three seconds; not exactly useful. He turned to Beef and Vess. "How long does it say it'll last for you?"

"Sixteen glasses," Vess said. "A hefty length of time."

Beef pouted. "Mine's only ten hours. Same for Hallow."

"Three hours!" Pit chirruped.

"The effect is ameliorated by your Body Temper," Isla explained as Garox led them deeper down a winding corridor. "That is why Felix's has already ceased."

"I wouldn't mind it, if it helps," Felix admitted. Water got very cold, after all. "I have Sunken Ward, which does something similar, but a Warm Embrace is nice over top of it."

"Hm." Isla considered their guide through her heavily lidded eyes.

Soon, the corridor opened up into yet another room, this one far more modest than the Chapel of the Eye. It was vaulted and domed, tilted askew but not nearly as badly as some of the portions of the Temple.

A team of twelve Nagafolk were waiting, all of whom were built in a similar vein as Garox himself. A humanoid form sat atop a long, serpentine tail; though that was where the similarities ended. Unlike Garox, they were not Spirit Naga, but something called a War Naga. According to his Eye, it was an Evolution that derived its potency from battle itself—whatever that meant.

Thick scales covered their brows, head, and the majority of their Bodies, humanoid and serpent alike. It gave them the appearance of wearing armor, and they were bulky, where Garox was sleek. Their faces were far less expressive than Garox's, too, which was saying something. Aggression wove through their Spirits, more than any other emotion, even at rest. A variety of weapons were in their hands, from hooked knives to densely woven nets. Each of the twelve also bore a twisted metal trident, each of which gleamed with a dark light. Shadow and lightning Mana flickered among the tines.

The tridents were crude-looking, powerful but clearly confiscated like all of their crafted items aside from the nets. Garox caught Felix's gaze and nodded. "Taken from the more advanced Hatchlings that have assaulted the Temple. They are roughly formed, but the unstable enchantments on them are potent."

"Lightning blast and...something with shadow?" Vess said. "I cannot tell at a glance."

"The tridents have two Skills. One is called Levin Bolt and fires off a single bolt of lightning Mana at a target, while the other is called Inkshadow and releases an obscuring cloud of shadow Mana to hide within. Both are effective if...dangerous." Garox bobbed his head—a distinctly snake-like move. "As I said. Unstable."

"To say the least," Isla said. "A tool that turns against the wielder is one they should cast aside."

"Or, we just make use of what's available to us," Felix said, shoving more than a little annoyance into the words. Isla's mouth thinned, and he hoped that meant she caught the hint. "Introduce us, please, Garox."

The War Nagas were terse but nice enough. Felix thankfully had his Keen Mind to memorize their names, though he only focused on the three leaders: Toa'ut, Rou'd, and Lavix. They were differentiated by painted patterns on their scales; glyphs that designated their positions as leaders, apparently.

While his team introduced themselves to their soon-to-be escorts, Felix felt a humming noise snag against his Affinity. He pressed outward from himself, feeling at the air, the water, the stones all around him. It was the Temple itself, thrumming across the surface of the world. Just like the one in the Foglands, there was a potency in the walls, packed into the stone and seeping into the water.

How much Essence and significance would it cost to restore this whole thing? Likely far more than he had currently. He didn't want to waste either resource; Felix still had to weave his other Pillars, after all. That was one benefit of going into another big fight. Plenty of fodder to feed his core space and finish establishing his foundation.

Eventually.

Felix's core space still wasn't ready for more Pillars yet, and it wasn't just a matter of being a perfectionist, either. The vision he had for his cores and his Hunger was distinct now, his goals solidified—Felix simply had to bring them into being. He was getting better, but it was slow going. Already, Felix had identified a few Skills he'd need to band together, forming several Skill Arrays like the one around his Bastion of Will.

That alone will take time and power that I don't have right now.

He'd made plenty of plans, however. Some confluence of the central Skill's rarity and Tier seemed to influence how many Skills he could include in an array. Bastion held seven now, though it had started at five. It was only Epic rarity.

Apart from being a high level, high rarity, and high tier, each Skill Array had to connect on some level. It was like combining Skills, where the patterns of light and music had to flow into one another, overlapping in crucial parts to lock together. The difference between combining and making an array was the distance; combining fused the Skills as one, and the Skill Array made them into small star systems, each secondary ability rotating around the central one.

Bastion of Will caught his eye. The Skill looked like a collection of intersecting vibrating lines that, if he squinted, could look like a greenish planet. Felix had worked to solidify that impression, retaining the distinct pattern of it while enhancing the idea of each of his Skills as celestial bodies. Around it, the other pieces of his Skill Array floated, orbiting the Bastion like moons...except, unlike moons, they were all nearly the same size. Some even larger. Easy as breathing, Felix named them all.

Meditation, Deep Mind, Relentless Resolution, Skein of Fate, Voracious Eye, Aria of the Green Wilds, and Chthonic Tribute.

Bastion of Will was the Primary Skill or hub of the array. Typically, it should be higher in rarity, level, and tier than the others, but according to Karys, that wasn't a requirement. The other Skills were linked to his Bastion, called Secondary Skills. The Primary Skill would, ideally, provide a measure of meaning and weight to the Secondaries to which it was connected. The meaning and weight had a lot to do with significance, but also the Essences with which folks Tempered themselves. That would generate a slew of benefits for the array, ranging from increased leveling speed, greater efficiency or potency, even range. Each of them would in turn offer a measure of their own potency, but typically far less than the Primary. The actual benefits varied depending on the Primary Skill's purpose.

Skill Arrays, something no one had told him about until Karys, seemed almost too good to be true. Because they were. There was a catch. If any underwent any damage or significant changes, then the Array could unbalance and dissolve. When Oathbinding had become Skein of Fate, it was because of the influence of his Chain-Breaker Title, and according to Karys, that was likely the reason he'd been protected from any real fallout. Without it, the consequences of such an upset could break one or more Skills—or even sunder them completely.

Which meant that he had hesitated on forming any new Skill Arrays. He had the one, but the rest he *had* to be sure. Felix had made a list, though, prodding them all for commonalities in their vibrational patterns.

First among them was Sovereign of Flesh as Primary, which was a Transcendent Skill at Adept Tier, meaning it could hold around *ten* other Skills in its orbit. Cardinal Flame, Green Shaping, Auroral Forge, Rime Shaping, Manasight, Theurgist of the Rise, Invocation, Dual Casting, and Manaship Pilot were all good matches. Each of them dealt with the manipulation of fundamental forces, a through line evident in the song they sang. It was the one he was most sure about and likely the next to be attempted.

Adamant Discord also was begging to be put into an array, and he was almost certain that Wild Threnody, Manifestation of the Coronach, Ephemeral Evocation, Unite the Lost, Last Cry of the Chthonic Host, and Etheric Concordance would function as perfect Secondaries. Felix even suspected that Skein of Fate would work even better in such an array, but the process of removing it from his Bastion and adding it to another was daunting. Karys had suggested it was possible, but it would surely be difficult and painful.

What else is new?

Next was the Song of Absolution as Primary, with Dodge, Blind Fighting, and Armored Skin as Secondaries. Technically, he could add more, but he hadn't any other Skills that sang in quite the right way with Absolution.

Others like Abyssal Skein, Mantle of the Infinite Revolution, Rain of Cataclysm, and Sunken Ward were all about large-scale applications of power, affecting allies and foes alike for good or ill. Felix wasn't certain that was enough of a connection, and the commonalities in their patterns were among the weakest. The absolute weakest were what he considered his standalone Skills: Arrow of Perdition, Shadow Whip, Cloudstep. Even things like Negotiation and Deception. All useful Skills in their own right, but not quite cut out for a Skill Array.

Not unless he started stealing more Skills to match them up.

"Felix?" Vess prodded, and he blinked back to attention.

"Hm?" He drew himself up, realizing the War Naga had been talking to him for the last thirty seconds, detailing the path they were going to take. "Oh. Yes, please let us know more about the terrain."

Toa'ut jerked his head in an awkward bob. "Through the Temple, it is safe. Warriors prowl these stone nests, and few are those Fathom spawn that would dare assault the king. Once we leave the Temple and enter the Tangle, it will be far harder. Ambushes are encountered there on a regular basis, and while the Hatchlings and lesser spawn are trifling foes, in large numbers, they are deadly."

"That shouldn't be a problem," Felix said. The warriors shifted as if restless, but approval washed through their Spirits. "What then?"

"The Tangle goes on for many leagues, descending deep and deeper, until it stops at the edges of the Yawning Mountains. Beyond them and their howling tunnels, we will see the first inkling of Khasma." Tao'ut paused, his Spirit undulating between fear and pain. "The Abyss."

Garox cleared his throat. "The journey into the deeps will take days, a full week at most, and then only if the Dens along the way have disgorged more of their vile brood."

"Dens. Do you know how many?" Vess asked. "And have any progressed into the formation of a Nest?"

"I would be greatly surprised if they have not," Garox admitted. "The Fathom has spread far and wide, thanks to the advancing floodwaters, which allowed its reach to move around us. Once, we were enough to hold them at bay, if only just. No longer."

Grumbles rolled across the twelve warriors, noises that silenced as Garox's tail lashed the water. "Our greatest threat is to be found and overwhelmed. God of Thunder and Flame, I know that you are mighty and perhaps you could lay waste to all of them...but not without drawing the Fathom itself down upon you. I would suggest...caution."

"Wise," Vess agreed. She gave Felix a nudge. "You have gone toe-to-toe with Primordials and gods, but perhaps a quieter approach is best."

"Wait, won't we have to fight our way out, anyway?" Beef asked. "These spawn thingies, they're not just gonna lay down after we kill the dragon, right?"

"That is the double-edged sword of the draconic Type. They pathologically serve those that have a greater concentration of draconic nature, but when those masters die, their allegiance shifts, as well. The Annals of Kehla spoke of a great horde that broke into dozens of warring factions the instant the Firedrake that led them was vanquished." Vess grimaced. "That could lead to a great many more problems, but it would give us ample opportunity to lay waste to as many as we could."

The War Naga grumbled again, but this time, it was an appreciative noise. "I like this one," Lavix announced. Vess grinned.

"The nature of Manawarping may also provide other opportunities as well," Isla said. "It is likely the entirety of its enslaved horde will scatter, and that ooze will break apart, reducing their strength by a great deal."

"Let's hope for that and plan for it all to go wrong," Felix said. "That's always served me best."

"Because it always goes wrong," Pit added.

"Yeah. It does, doesn't it?"

Garox slid forward, still coasting atop the surface of the water unlike the War Naga, who were all half-submerged. "Lower yourselves, warriors." They did. "You are hereby charged with ensuring the success of the Returned God's mission and are to obey him as if he were the Deepking himself."

"We hear, and we obey," they said as one.

Odd wording, Felix thought. *Or maybe I'm just surprised at how much they love their king. Trixie isn't the lovable type, but he is here, protecting their young while they fight in their never-ending war. I suppose I'd like the guy that did that, too.*

"Rise, warriors. You shall leave at the Returned God's pleasure." Garox gestured to the floor, where a circular moon pool could be seen. It was twenty or so feet below water, but once it was pointed out, Felix could feel the warding that covered its open surface. "My Lord, below you is your way out. Leave whenever you are ready."

"Thanks, Garox." To the others, Felix raised his voice. "Recheck all your equipment and supplies. We'll be gone for a while."

Vess, Beef, and Isla did a quick check of their persons and packs, while Pit sat on his butt and nibbled his beak at his forepaw. Hallow, both forms of her, sat perfectly still and staring off at some middle distance.

Felix did a quick examination himself, but before he got much farther than his new magic items, the hooked sword at his waist flared to green-gold life. "Felix?"

"Karys, yes. I'm here." Felix grasped the hilt of his blade and frowned. "What's happened?"

"What's happened is that you are *not* here, my Lord. That is why I am reaching out." Karys' voice was more sour than Felix had ever recalled hearing it. "Zara and a great many others have arrived, but you have not. What has happened?"

Felix smacked his forehead. He'd forgotten to call Karys and tell him what was going on. "I'll explain it all later. For now, get the teams rested and have them start construction on the additional Manaships."

"...As you wish, my Lord. Zara mentioned such a thing already. I am unsure how it shall be done, but I will see to it."

Felix grimaced, disliking the subservient tone Karys had taken. "Can I speak with Zara?"

"Of course. The array focus is easy to shift here."

There was the sound of descending tones before it ascended again and he heard a new voice. "Felix?"

"Zara. Everything went well?"

"It went...as expected. Some injuries, a few complications, but all in all, a solid journey."

"Injuries?"

"As you did not enter with us, the Shadowgate latched onto one of my Mind Skills instead of your Bastion. We made it through without any deaths, and the voidbeasts were only a minor inconvenience."

What sort of Mind Skill does a Master-Tier Chanter have? Felix wanted to ask a dozen questions, but focused on the important things. "The Whalemaw?"

"Unseen. I believe the power-dampening array was far more effective without you along for the trip."

That was good news. The Whalemaw had attacked Zara previously, having been drawn to what he believed was his connection to the Chanter, and the possibility of that happening again was not inconsequential. The dampening array they'd developed had worked, though, which meant that, in the future, they would have to make more for other groups using the Shadowgates... so long as Felix wasn't with them.

"Alright, that's good. It's been only forty minutes since you left here," he said, before correcting himself. "Uh, like three-quarters of a glass."

"Better time than previously," Zara said, a note of approval in her voice.

"We can compare notes on the journey later. For now, can you oversee the construction of the new ships? Karys has one Manaship in dock right now, but we'll need at least three more to accommodate all of our—my—soldiers."

"I'll see it done, Felix."

"And Zara."

"Yes?"

"Thank you. I'll be there as soon as possible."

"You're welcome," she said. "And you'd better be."

The connection died out, and Felix turned to the expectant faces of Naga and Minotaur and Humans alike. Pit had worked his way to his back paws. "Let's go for a swim."

CHAPTER SIXTY-ONE

Days passed.

Felix's team was now well within the Tangle, a forest of massive seaweed fronds and bursts of wild coral. They had passed from the Temple complex on the first day, entering the dense jungle that spread for miles in every direction. The light from the surface did not reach them there, but the fronds visibly glowed with life Mana and the clusters of bright pink and orange coral were filled with luminous plants and animals. Sea life was everywhere, and while most fled from their procession, there were schools of dead-eyed fish the size of small cars that ignored them completely.

<<Cattle,>> Toa'ut said, jutting his thick jaw at the big fish. <<Raised for food, just as the landfolk fatten their birds and hogs.>>

Felix, astride the big War Naga's back, grunted in acknowledgement. Normally, he'd have happily asked more questions, but he was otherwise engaged. Beef rode behind him, both of them secured with straps connected to a harness made of vines and chitinous buckles. Toa'ut had not complained at all, despite their combined weight, and they had covered a ton of distance. The War Naga were *fast.*

Etched onto the makeshift harness, familiar sigils pulsed rhythmically, each beat dragging a portion of Felix's Mana from his channels and directing it into Beef's. Felix had cobbled together a miniaturized version of the array he'd used back in Bogfeld. A considerable feat for him. A perfect memory was handy for such things, but the true difficulty lay in reorganizing all the important parts.

Invocation is level 68!

Theurgist of the Rise is level 84!

<<You good, dude?>> Felix asked, his voice tight and warbling as it wafted across his Sunken Ward. The spell allowed for communication between them all, so long as they remained close by, but the tension was not from the ward but the array. After hours of it, the sensation was awful, like vomiting in slow motion. Every part of his channels felt battered, and he recognized the symptoms of Spirit strain. <<Holding up?>>

Beef nodded, his orichalcum helmet hung at his belt, and his bare face was slick with moisture. The glow of Felix's Sunken Ward covered them all, outlining their forms in faint shrouds of darkest blue and keeping the water off of them, but it did nothing for sweat. <<I'm good.>> He wobbled slightly, and the harness between the two of them went taut for a moment before he caught himself. The kid shuddered. <<I'm good.>>

<<Your Risen is still intact? In control?>> Felix asked. The array was necessary because Beef was funneling his own power through the now distant Risen he'd sent through the Shadowgate. The Skill operated on similar fundamentals as Felix's old Oathbinding, establishing a stout connection between Beef and the corpses he raised that allowed him or Hallow to manipulate directly.

<<Yeah. It feels bad, but I've conjured a ton of chitin planks for the others to use.>> Beef's eyes were distant, staring at nothing as he pressed his Perception through the Body of his Risen. <<It's hard. Every once in a while, the Risen just stops responding, though. Like, they get all slippery. I can't believe Hallow controls so many of these things.>>

<<You're piloting a corpse from across a super continent,>> Felix reminded him. <<The fact that you can do this at all is incredible.>>

Beef did perk up at that, though his eyes were still clouded and distant. <<Thanks.>>

Channeling his magic through his Hallow Rise Skill was incredibly draining, hence the harness to hold them together and on the back of Toa'ut. The ritual fed Felix's Mana into Beef, allowing the kid to continue to provide materials to their distant team as they reconstructed enough Manaships to get them to Haarwatch. According to Karys' reports, the ships were almost complete, thanks to Beef's efforts as well as the Henaari craftsmen on site—a number of them were remarkably good with the vessels.

The original plan was to have Beef make and help assemble the ships through the use of his Chitin Construction and Shipwright Skills, but being able to do it remotely was incredibly useful and allowed the Minotaur to stick by Felix's side. He'd considered refusing Beef's request to stay behind, but honestly, Felix wanted to keep an eye on him. Letting an Unbound loose in a potentially chaotic war was probably unwise when they'd spent so much time retrieving the guy. A little Mana drain and Spirit strain was worth it.

<<Levels?>> Felix asked.

<<Chitin Construction is at 55, Hallow Rise is at 58, and Mana Manipulation is almost at Apprentice Tier.>> Beef grunted as he adjusted himself. <<Shipwright is 32 now.>>

Damn. He'd noticed the kid knocking back a few Essence Draughts during the trip, but to have two Skill rise into Journeyman and another hit Apprentice Tier was great. <<You'll catch up to me in no time.>>

<<Ha! Hope so.>>

Aside from Felix's sigaldry Skills, he'd put his Sunken Ward through the wringer the past few days. Keeping the spell constantly engaged was a bit taxing, especially while also draining his Mana into his friend, but it was necessary. The spell had risen from level 3 all the way to level 19, and all of his friends were coated in its dark-blue shroud. Even Pit and Hallow's two forms both clung to the back of three of the War Nagas.

Felix's gaze sought out Isla. The Chanter sat daintily atop another War Naga, right behind Vess, and the two of them were engrossed in another conversation. Vess wasn't smiling, but then she hadn't since they'd learned about the Fathom being a dragon. Instead, she continued to look intense, and Isla seemed to be explaining something to her based on the Heiress' terse nods.

Tempted as he was, Felix refused to eavesdrop—an easier task thanks to the water all around them. His Sunken Ward needed a certain amount of proximity for their voices to carry along the spell, and while Felix could have probably pressed his Perception, it wasn't worth it. Isla was...he didn't like the lady, but she wasn't a threat, and he refused to treat her like she was one.

With a start, Felix realized both women were staring at *him* now, and he hurriedly looked away. He pretended to be searching the Tangle around them. The jungle of huge fronds was just as thick and obscuring as the Naga had warned. They swam low, nearer the bottom of the lake, navigating the treacherous seaweed forest to keep out of sight. Felix hadn't seen any Fathom spawn yet, but Toa'ut had warned them many times about the ambushes they often suffered in the Tangle. It was better to be safe than to draw undue attention.

The ground sloped downward, and had been since they left the Temple complex. Deeper and deeper they swam, the waters getting darker and colder with every mile they pushed. The sheer size of the lake was incredible to Felix, but then, he'd been told that the Ghreldan Hills was filled with lakes and many of them were connected underground. Not to mention the flooding from the south–from him–that had expanded their borders. Toa'ut had spoken a couple times of the strange new currents from the flooding, speaking of eddies of foreign magic that swirled in the waters.

<<Hold.>> Toa'ut commanded his warband, and every Naga froze among the fronds. <<Den ahead. Lavix.>>

Felix frowned, and this time did press his Perception through the weeds as the most slender of the War Nagas swam ahead. Perhaps a hundred yards away, he felt the familiar, resonant hum of a wide cavern filled with a shimmering barrier. It was well-hidden beneath the greenery, and the creatures that prowled just outside of it were almost as well-camouflaged.

<<Ten Hatchlings and Amphitere,>> Lavix reported, slipping back into their group. <<The Den appears strong. Do you wish to destroy it?>>

The last was to Felix. He was tempted but shook his head. <<No. We can't afford the delay. Can we go around them?>>

<<Yes. It will cost us some time, but not as much were we to fight. Lavix, lead the way.>>

<<Understood.>>

They kept moving, less quickly now that they were attempting greater stealth, but still ate up the miles as they carved a wide circle around the Den. Killing a ton of monsters would have been easily done, had he been untethered from his siphon array. Felix could likely have soloed the entire Den, and judging by the disgruntled expression on Vess' face, she would have gladly attempted the same.

Felix hadn't had a lot of opportunities to talk to Vess, mostly due to the array, but also because of Isla dominating her time. The two of them were always talking; the contents of their conversations were a mystery, but he didn't doubt the Chanter was still mining for information on him. He still hadn't given her a rundown of his life on Earth, but it was clear she wanted to know more. His relationship to the Primordials was of particular interest to her, and while she knew quite a bit, Felix had refrained from explaining anything.

What could they possibly have to talk about? he wondered as they passed through a narrow defile. Two large coral shelves rose to either side, a passage that led them a bit farther from the Den. The oranges and pinks and luminous blues were all beautiful and very eerie in the dark water. He might have been able to see with little issue, but the sheer density of shadow Mana around him was off-putting. By reflex, he flared his Perception...and froze. Just to the west, hiding in the dense coral, were a number of large, sinuous shapes and the glint of sharpened metal.

<<Ambush!>> he cried out.

A great many things happened at once.

From above, sixteen Hatchlings riding thick, web-winged

Amphiteres dove onto them with their crude tridents out-thrust. Over half of them kindled with lightning Mana that leaped toward their group. The War Naga brought their own weapons to bear, rushing upward at the same time, while Vess flashed by them all in a storm of bubbles.

<<The Fang of Havoc!>> she howled, and her Partisan of the Blue-Eyed Dragon ripped into the lead Hatchling just as Levin Bolts tore up the waters.

The War Nagas were there instants later, stabbing and thrashing at the nasty fishmen. Pit was close behind, dark-blue glass belt around his middle having transformed his lower half into a powerful fish tail. Rainbow scales glittered on him now, and it was capped by a wide, powerful fin. His wings and forepaws paddled fiercely, providing streamers of bubbles as air Mana was released from his channels. Thunderwing was clearly hampered by the water, but his fish tail more than made up for it—Pit undulated through the weeds, golden light gathering in his pinions.

No flashy spells, Pit!

Irritation flashed across their bond, but the golden light of his spell vanished, replaced by a dark wavering around his paws. Pit slammed hard into two Hatchlings, and his Hurricane Rasp tore straight through their narrow chests. Their mounts bucked, twisting back after him with their wedge-shaped jaws wide. Pit smacked them with his tail, dislocating one of their jaws and sending the other into an evasive dive.

Chaos reigned.

Hallow swam atop herself, the small Homunculus riding on the back of the chitinous Multipede and unleashing pinpoint barrages of crystalline needles. The needles weren't enough to kill outright, but they were painful and distracting, allowing the Nagafolk to dispatch the Hatchlings or their mounts with greater ease. Isla fought, too, from the back of a Naga warrior, casting green-gold bolts at the advancing Fathom spawn. Where they hit, swathes of strange, fungal growths sprouted from their eyes and mouths and gills, causing the Hatchlings to spasm and tear at their own flesh.

As blows were traded back and forth, four more foes slipped from the other side of the reef, and these were far more intimidating. Where the Hatchlings and their fat fish-mounts were Tier III creatures, these others were far more Evolved. Broodvipers riding atop Drakin, according to Felix's Voracious Eye, the former an Evolved form of Hatchling and the latter an Evolved form of the Draktopus. Both were musclebound and darkly mottled to blend into the terrain around them, and possessing a raw, chaotic power that all but crackled around them as they sped into the fray.

<<Watch out!>> Felix shouted, unable to do much but watch. If he

moved, Beef would expend all of his Mana, and his Risen would crumble to dust. <<Evolved enemies incoming! Tier IV!>>

Without missing a beat, Vess split off from her dwindling foe just as Lavix thundered by her position. She reached out, snagging the edge of the Naga's spine and riding down with her spear held out like a lance. The Broodvipers and Drakin charged, as muscled and brutal as the War Naga, and met Lavix in a furious clash. The odds were in the Fathom spawn's favor, being four against two, but they clearly had never accounted for a Dragoon.

<<Spear of Tribulations!>>

Ten silver Spears manifested around Vess like a kaleidoscope of death, each one manipulated in a different direction. Two sank into a Drakin's side, while three more engaged with the Broodvipers' crooked weapons. They clanged aside, but not before all five Spears detonated. The Drakin fell, its gut torn asunder, and Vess followed its rider down.

<<Draconic Stormfall!>>

Vess, her partisan, and her remaining five Spears all dropped onto the injured Drakin and dazed rider. The reef exploded, filling the water with cloudy debris as a crackling wave of lightning spread outward from the impact. More furious roars and sloshing thrashes spread upward, until everything went still.

You Have Killed A Manawarped Broodviper!
XP Earned!

You have Killed A Manawarped Drakin!
XP Earned!

Felix felt the tiniest trickle of experience feed into him—apparently, just warning people counted as contribution but didn't warrant much in the way of rewards.

Vess rose from the rubble like a rocket, dust, bubbles, and newly conjured Spears riding in her wake. With the aid of Lavix, they fought the last Broodviper and Drakin, though weren't able to surprise it again. It was wary of their tricks, and as the Nagafolk finished off the regular Hatchlings, the Evolved enemy attempted to make a tactical retreat. Before it had swam more than twenty yards, their forms were pierced by frozen lightning, crystalline shards, fungal rot, and two silver Spears apiece.

They did not survive much longer.

<<Finally,>> Beef said with a deep, agonized groan. He reached his arms up, stretching so hard Felix could feel the water ripple with each popping joint. <<Done. Chitin assembled, framework all set. They just gotta hook up the Mana engines and new sails and it should—>>

The kid blinked, mouth agape as he stared at the blood, dust, and floating corpses that littered the waters all around them. <<Uh, what happened?>>

Felix almost groaned himself, all too happy to disengage the siphon array. The return of his Mana felt like blood rushing back into numb legs; a painful restoration. <<Ambush.>>

<<Oh damn. I missed the fun stuff?>>

<<The fun is just beginning,>> Toa'ut rumbled. He nodded with his huge, bulbous head. Beyond the now-broken coral shelf, the large fronds of the Tangle had thinned, and the open waters beckoned beyond. <<We have come to the Mountains That Howl.>>

CHAPTER SIXTY-TWO

The Mountains That Howl were strangely named. While they did howl, they most certainly were not mountains. Where the Tangle ended, the ever-descending lake floor dropped dramatically, resolving into a sheer cliff that opened into dark water. The drop alone was a little unnerving, but what made it worse was the ripping current that ravaged the edge of that cliff. They swam closer, and Felix could perceive a twisted rippling that broke up the dark abyss before them.

<<What am I looking at?>> he asked Toa'ut.

<<Those currents are spinning rapidly,>> Isla offered, speaking over the slow-talking War Naga. <<And there are far more than just one.>>

<<The call of the Sunken Mountains is vast and potent,>> Tao'ut intoned. <<They scream into the dark waters, snatching at anything in their path.>>

Felix focused his Manasight, though it was difficult to separate water and shadow from itself. Slowly, the glowing brilliance of the Mana currents resolved into distinct patterns. They flowed in tight circles, spinning around a central point that was at least thirty yards across. Their mouths were open and undulating through the dark water, moving with the ponderous motion of a whale, and descending somewhere far below that was not so much shrouded in shadow as drenched in a vast distance. *They're massive cyclones,* he realized. *Whirlpools.*

Felix looked out and perceived *hundreds* of them, cutting the emptiness with a furious chaos.

<<Holy hell. That's a lot of whirlpools,>> he said, before explaining it all to his friends.

<<We have to go through that?>> Beef asked. He looked askance at the depths before them and rubbed his arms. The water touched them but didn't at the same time, so the fur along his bare biceps was dry and fluffy. <<Can't we just, like, go around? It's water; there's more than one angle we can take, right?>>

Pit chirruped thoughtfully. <<Is there?>>

Lavix shook her head. <<The Mountains extend the width of the Haestus and Raunen. Perhaps if we ascended, to ride the floodwaters atop the Hills, but that carries its own risks.>>

<<And would cost us a great deal of time,>> Vess added. She leaned forward on Lavix's back, peering into the dark as her own eyes flashed with a prismatic light. <<Not to mention place us squarely in the sights of the enemy.>>

Felix scratched his chin; his beard was growing fuller now, and his claws felt good against his skin. <<They're moving. Do they ever stop?>>

<<The Mountains never cease their howling,>> Toa'ut said.

Great. <<Have any of you gone through here before?>>

<<Yes. It is a path we have swam many times on our hunts, but not since the floodwaters came. The aggression of the Fathom spawn kept us hemmed in our Temple,>> Rou'd said, the third of the leading trio. Pit was nestled nimbly atop his back, fish tail banished, and Homunculus Hallow clung to the tenku's saddle like a barnacle. <<It is dangerous to venture between the Howls. Deadly.>>

<<Why?>> Isla asked.

<<They will drag you down. The currents are too strong to swim against, and the creatures in the down-below are vicious predators.>> Toa'ut shifted, creeping closer to the edge of the cliff. <<Time grows short, and there will be no perfect chance to cross. It will take as long as the Tangle to navigate, so the sooner we leave, the better, my Lord.>>

Felix swept his attention back to the Tangle behind them, unable to spot much beyond the prolific fronds and the overwhelming presence of life Mana. He didn't doubt that the ambush they'd slaughtered would be found eventually, and with the Den so close they'd be swarmed as soon as they were.

The War Naga were already staring into the dark with eager expressions on their dour faces, Spirits apparently alight at the idea of challenging themselves in the wild currents. Vess was right there with them, leaning forward as if she wanted to leap off Lavix and tackle whirlpools on her own. Beef was worried, Pit and Hallow curious, and Isla considered the cliff with something akin to disdain on her face.

<<What is it now?>> he asked the Chanter. There must have been something in his tone, because Vess tore her eyes from the drop to stare at Isla as well.

<<Nothing.>> Isla set about rearranging her skirts. <<A foul sound is coming from these howling mountains, but the—Toa'ut is right. We must move.>>

Felix pursed his lips, but ultimately nodded. <<I agree. Whenever you're ready, Toa.>>

With far more deliberation than Felix had expected, the War Nagas slipped off the edge of the cliff and swam out into the raging current. Immediately, they were caught up, pulled sideways and down as they navigated the very edge of the nearest maelstrom, but Toa'ut and his warriors undulated powerfully, their thick Bodies forging a path through the riptide.

<<Whoa!>> Pit shouted. He had to fight to keep his wings closed against his sleeker Body, something he clearly found harder now that he'd reduced in size a bit. <<These are worse than stormwinds.>>

<<They will take you, if you let them,>> rumbled Rou'd. <<Look, there.>>

The floor of the area was slowly revealing itself, layer by layer as the occluding Mana was thinned and dispersed by the howling currents. Now Felix heard them as well, and there was definitely something wrong with the sound. It was dissonant, though not in the same way as his core space or a cursed Primordial—instead, it was like the Harmony all around them had been twisted ever so slightly out of tune. Soon, Felix spotted why.

The vortex that they rode the edge of was composed of deep water and shadow Mana, all swirling down into gargantuan gaps far below. Those chasms split the earth but were not empty—were, in fact, utterly filled with wriggling growths. They looked slick, like slime given life, the same dark-blue ooze that Felix had seen on so many of the Fathom spawn.

As they pressed farther, slipping skillfully from one vortex to the next, he could see that the ooze carpeted the lake bed. It was clearly not restrained to the bases of the vortexes alone, spreading up and across the rocks like an infection.

<<Manawarping ooze,>> Felix pointed out. His allies looked at it with the same disgust that roiled in Felix's gut, but only Isla seemed to notice the true wrongness of it all. They briefly locked eyes, and the Chanter nodded.

<<This much of the substance...I would not wish to touch it,>> she warned. <<Keep clear of it all. I do not know what would happen were any of us to touch it.>>

<<Doesn't look so dangerous,>> Beef said, just as a school of silver fish flashed past their location. <<Whoa!>>

The fish weren't big, perhaps the size of a football, but there were hundreds of them in the undulating mass that tore overhead. It was clear to Felix that they were utterly caught up in the vortex, and all of their frantic swimming did nothing to slow their swirling descent. Before the Naga could navigate across the currents, the entire school hit the writhing layer of ooze...and was consumed entirely.

Beef swallowed. <<Uh, okay. Don't touch it. Got it.>>

Their progress was slow, as the corridors between the many maelstroms were both narrow and ever-shifting. Often, their guides had to wait several minutes, treading against the ceaseless currents, until two of the vortexes moved far enough away from one another to safely pass. Even then, the sheer Strength and Endurance required to battle the pressure was immensely draining. The War Naga took turns in the lead, rotating every couple minutes so that they could all benefit from riding in one another's slipstream, which reduced the drag of the tides by a decent amount.

More than once, Felix thought of using his various Skills to force their way through, but the dual edge of concern stopped him. The first worry was one of stealth, and the second was a question of sustainability. He could—*perhaps*—push through the Mountains That Howl, could even utilize his Abyssal Skein to hide them from enemy eyes...but after experiencing the sheer immensity of the vortexes, Felix doubted he could maintain stealth for everyone while also shouldering aside what appeared to be hundreds of swirling cyclones of water and deadly ooze. It was better to take the slower approach, he decided, at least for the time being.

It wasn't only the push and pull of the water that hampered them, however. Down between the vortexes, the blue—almost purple—ooze absolutely crawled with creatures. There, enormous things like sea anemones bloomed, almost entirely covered in the ooze and listed as Manawarped Hexanthus. Some sort of monstrous polyp, like the coral within the Tangle, just gargantuan. A variety of the polyps filled the glowing lake bed, from the tendril-festooned Hexanthus to the stalk-like, almost flower shape of the Stolonex. All of them swayed and rippled with the buffeting edge of the vortexes, but more than once, Felix saw them lunge toward another ill-fated school of fish.

The things were *mobile.*

A number of times, the churning maelstroms forced their party low, within a hundred yards of the nasty things, and Felix had *tasted* the sheer, grasping malice from the nearest ones. In fact, they felt remarkably like the Slaughter Nettle.

<<What is the Fathom doing to make all of this?>> Felix wondered aloud. He didn't expect an answer, so was surprised when Vess spoke up.

<<Zara told us that a failed Evolution and overdraw of Mana into a monster's core would cause this affliction. The ooze...it reeks of corruption and ill will. I can only just hear the edges of it, but even I can tell it

is a deadly thing. Look there, where the ooze meets the rock. See the water boil?>> Felix could see that, almost lost among the overwhelming mass of rippling water and heaving monstrosities. <<I don't doubt the Fathom spawn will meet the same fate. Whatever this dragon has done, it has no regard for the creatures that follow it.>>

Beef moaned as he pulled tight on the chitinous straps he'd fashioned around his legs—more than once, he'd almost been pulled out of his seat by the maelstroms. <<Aww, man, I thought dragons were supposed to be cool?>>

<<Dragons are a terror, Beefhammer. They would drive their slaved monstrosities to death, were it to benefit them.>> Vess's voice was heavy and without embellishment. A lead bar hitting hard-packed earth. <<They are not...'cool'.>>

As if the Divines were looking down on him and spitting, Felix felt a tingle at the utmost edge of his senses. Their circuitous route had allowed them to progress perhaps a tenth of the way across the expansive Mountains That Howl, too far for him to feel things with his Perception, but close enough that his Affinity recoiled from a wave of malicious Intent. Back toward the Tangle. Through the black, he could see a mass of darkness that rolled toward them like a storm cloud. He stared, unable to parse it all for several moments, and it was Vess that shouted the warning.

<<Fathom spawn! Thousands of them!>>

<<The Den has roused itself,>> Toa'ut rumbled, a tension rolling through the War Naga. <<They have sent all that they have against us. Why? They cannot reach us without a great many dying.>>

<<Mindless brutes,>> Isla said with dripping derision. <<So few will reach us that it is pointless to try.>>

Yet, as they watched, treading water between maelstroms, the thousands of Hatchlings, Amphitere, and Draktopi advanced. The vortexes took their due, pulling down huge quantities of their numbers, spinning them inexorably into the oozing crevasses, but the horde did not stop. More pushed on from behind, until the waters darkened even further from their sheer numbers.

Bursting from the lead of the horde, not one, but *two* Depthwurms raced toward them, absolutely eating up the distance between them.

<<I don't think they know that, Isla,>> Felix said. <<Toa! Move it, fast as you can!>>

<<Hold tight,>> Toa'ut warned and dove straight into the heart of a vortex.

<<AAAAAAH!>> Beef screamed, echoed by Hallow in both of her forms.

The maelstrom roared as they truly entered its influence for the first time. Felix and his crew all hunkered down close, pressing their bodies as tightly as they could to the scaled backs of the Naga. The currents were monstrous, whipping them faster and faster as they rotated and sank deeper into the dark waters. A hundred feet were lost in a second, just long enough for their guides to reach out and grasp onto each other's tails and jolt forward. They jerked, twisted perpendicular to the spinning tides, and for a moment, Felix felt as if they were going to swing out of control—but the War Naga gave a concerted bellow, and their muscular Bodies thrashed as one.

The entire team rocketed out of the vortex, just as the suicidal Depthwurms thundered into their space. Pit shrieked, absolutely thrilled, and fired off a dozen bolts of frozen lightning. The magic sank into the nearest Depthwurm's hide before bursting into crackling, charring static.

Pit's Tempest Fugit is level 77!

<<Unleash everything you have!>> Felix shouted, mobilizing his Intent and Affinity to send a Chant-enhanced stream of Cardinal Flame straight into the Depthwurm's face. Scale and flesh boiled away, forcing the monster to pull away from its pursuit, at least temporarily. The others sent waves of Skills at the other one; lightning, Spears, crystalline darts, and huge wedges of iron-hard chitin all smashed into its scales. More than a few shattered, ripping open gaping wounds in the powerful Fathom spawn as the War Nagas kept swimming with everything they had.

Between swirling maelstroms, Toa'ut and his warriors sped without time to pause or calculate their chances of getting yanked into the depths. That first incredible dive had given them enough momentum that kept them just out of reach of the Depthwurms, though not even their speed would have been enough had Felix's team not laid down suppressive fire.

Still, Fathom spawn fell upon them. Hatchlings riding Amphitere, Broodvipers atop Drakin, and entire pods of Draktopi survived the culling of the vortexes, too many for Felix to accurately count. Enough that their strange shrieking coalesced into a wildly upsetting chorus that pummeled at Felix's Mind.

A strident, atonal note shivered through the ooze around all of them. Meaning danced at the edge of his awareness, hot and coppery on his tongue like blood. It was violence, stoked and stacked until it blazed in the Spirit of every Fathom spawn arrayed against them. Madness shone in the Hatchlings' wide, white eyes as they thrust their crude tridents after their quarry. Levin bolts sizzled outward, deflected by shields of green-gold luminescence, shields that drove that madness to greater heights.

Chthonic Tribute!

Felix snatched the song out of the air, grasping at the threads he could barely sense among the horde. A connection to a greater Mind, trembling through the ooze that adorned each and every one of the Fathom spawn, and it resisted his grasp. The song was violence and madness, but it was almost automatic, a threat response that consumed the horde entirely, echoing off the ooze upon them as well as below. Felix gathered all of the threads he could, every single one within range of his Affinity, and *pulled.*

Chthonic Tribute!

All at once, the ooze in a three-hundred-yard diameter turned into flashing, bitter smoke and raged toward Felix's channels. The horde faltered and flailed, screaming with incomprehensible pain. They fell into the rolling cyclones, carried mercilessly down below, where even the monstrous polyps were recoiling from Felix's terrible blow.

Chthonic Tribute is level 87!

The Essence and Mana of the ooze hit Felix like a truck, spinning down into his core space like molten glass, just as scalding and twice as bright. He grasped at it tentatively, amazed at the sheer potency that wafted from it all. Connections flourished and thickened, links to the ooze's source that firmed with each passing instant. It sang, a new, strange chord in Felix's ears...that immediately twisted out of tune.

Something *noticed* him.

That Mind shifted, orienting on Felix for the first time. Focusing. A great, bitter rage ripped across their newfound link, as nightmarish as any Primordial he'd encountered. And just as strong.

Bastion of Will!

Felix frantically sounded his mental Skill just as that titanic presence came crashing down on him. It hit with all the weight and fury of a tsunami.

Bastion of Will is level 88!

...

Bastion of Will is level 90!

Blood burst, his Aspects groaned, and something within him smashed and cracked—but his Bastion held firm. A roar of frustration ripped across the stolen connection, detonating along a colossal distance as it raced for Felix's head. Every instinct Felix had screamed not to let that sound reach him, and he flared his Cardinal Flame with all of his might.

Cardinal Flame is level 85!

Grasping the remains of the ooze within his core space, Felix shoved the lot of it into the greedy depths of his Hunger. All of it, all at once.

The connection sundered, torn apart by the force of the dragon's own roar, and Felix recoiled back onto the hard scales of his War Naga ride.

<<Felix! You did it!>> Beef was shouting. His arms were held wide, waving his chitin-shaped war club above him. <<They ran away!>>

Felix suppressed a groan as he leveraged himself back to a seated position and cast outward with his Perception.

The remains of a Depthwurm spun listlessly in the near distance, and the water all around them was clouded with dark ichor and bits of flesh. Most were caught up in the maelstroms around them, sucked down to the lake bed, where the ooze was rapidly regrowing. Two of their escorts were missing—dead, he suspected—and half of those remaining bore weeping wounds that clouded the swirling currents. What's more, they were still well within the maze of howling vortexes, though they'd found a spot of calm. The chase had eaten up several miles perhaps, but they had a great many more to go.

<<Damn it,>> he cursed.

<<Felix? What happened?>> Vess asked as Lavix swam closer. <<I thought...I heard a terrible voice.>>

<<That was not a voice. That was a Challenge,>> Isla stated. She looked at Felix, her hair floating in the water yet untouched by the wet. <<What have you done?>>

With a dim trilling noise, the System shoved a static-strewn notification before Felix's eyes.

<<Huh,>> he said. <<Well that's not good.>>

CHAPTER SIXTY-THREE

The winds above the Foglands were bitterly cold compared to the warmth of the Ghreldan Hills. True, they were flying high among the clouds now, but even within the Stronghold, Zara had felt discomfited by the sudden change in temperature. Traveling so far so quickly was as alien to her as flying through the sky was to the Glitterhogs down below. She could see them over the chitin railing, a herd of the monsters thundering over meadows and ancient, autumnal forest.

A simple life. One that reminded her of afternoons in meadows very like the ones they raced above. Those days were warmer, too, at least in her memories—but heavy and not nearly as simple as she liked to believe. *Tsk. You are far too old to weep over lost things.*

Zara turned firmly away from the gunwale and ran her Perception over the length of the Manaship. The craft was constructed well enough, if slightly slipshod in areas. The Risen that Michael —*Beefhammer,* she thought with a sigh—had sent with them had performed admirably.

The ability for the boy to transmit his Skills *through* his Risen creatures was remarkable, and yet another Unbound accomplishment that had surprised the Chanter. What hadn't worked as well was the Risen's durability; after producing truly tremendous amounts of conjured chitin boards, the already withered corpse had all but turned to dust. That meant, of course, that Beef was not around to aid in the construction of the Manaships.

All that effort to learn Shipwright, only to have his servant crumble. Being so far away, there was no way to summon another. That had been a shock, but less so than the soon discovered knowledge that not one, but *six* different Yttin sailors had a well-leveled Shipwright Skill. A great many more knew enough that they were capable of aiding the construction process. *And such a curious name for it. Vessel Taming.*

The Yttin were known for their mobility in the desert, but it was less known that they built and maintained their own crafts to do so. Designed to capture the wind, the once-diminutive Race had even developed rudimentary Mana engines to supplement their speed. Or, so the sailors told her when they had offered their services. They said little else. The Skill was a secret among their people, one that their various shamans across many tribes had worked to hold close.

The Manaship she rode upon, built to the scale of a true galleon class vessel, was only one of five. Each ship was constructed of Beef's chitin, the craftsmanship of the Yttin, and everyone's blood and sweat. Not to mention, each bore *two* Mana engines that the Yttin and mages managed to jury-rig into functionality. Building them in just a few short days was a challenge, let alone ensuring that they were sky-worthy—yet it was done, and Mana surged through the ships' inscribed channels almost as well as their sails billowed with captured wind.

The Yttin, the Legion, the Frost Giants, and the Henaari filled all five ships to bursting. While many of those that left Ahkestria stayed behind in the Stronghold; there were hundreds now wearing the Burning Eye upon their breasts. They hustled to and fro, many helping with the sailing, while others were caught up in whatever strange training regimen Harn and Darius had devised. The trip from the Stronghold to Haarwatch took a week, and nerves were running high. It was a wise decision to keep them occupied.

Everyone knew that war was just over the horizon.

Two more dawns, and the red-gold Wall will rise before us. And how soon after will the Hierocracy pass through the Verdant Pass? The thought chilled her more than the autumn wind, but she suppressed it. *They will arrive; that is all that matters. All we can do is prepare ourselves.*

Aside from monitoring the piloting and general well-being of the Manaships, Zara had busied herself with working on the project Felix and Atar had started: a shield based on the principles of the Knights Ghreldan's Redoubt, centered upon a Domain core and a unique crystalline matrix. It had proven a fascinating challenge considering the lack of information she had, but with enough inferences, prior experience, and Felix's notes on the sigaldry of the Redoubt, it was surmountable. Barely.

The notes Felix had left them were hastily scrawled and not always entirely legible. Atar could usually make them out—he'd grown familiar with the man's odd shorthand—but he and his other half were entirely too wrapped up in their own special project.

Atar was another one that Zara had to monitor. He had changed since defeating the Highest Flame, and not only in his peculiar new Body—his Spirit was incongruous to his other Aspects. His core was still in repair, but what little she had seen raised more questions than it had answered.

Zara ran a hand along the main mast, letting her Affinity touch on the faint chorus running through the chitin. The song of the Corporeal Realm was wide and varied; as beautiful as it was chaotic. Yet that chaos, when taken on a grand scale, transformed into a majesty so overwhelming that only the gods could hear it in full. Through the decks, Zara could hear the glacial thrum of Mana crystals, slowly expanding in her cabin.

Should I work on the shield further? There was some more sigaldry she could add before the crystal lattice was completely grown, but it would likely not be finished for several days. *Or should I find Atar again? Perhaps this time, he will deign to reveal what exactly has been happening to him.*

A sudden thrill of warmth pulsed through Zara's Spirit, forcing a shiver through her entire Body at once. Her senses flew, expanding outward in a sharp wave from the Chanter, but almost immediately impacted a blade of harsh melody. Sailors and soldiers winced and stumbled, some even passing out entirely as a thrust of Intent echoed all around them.

Child. Attend me.

The call was two steps from stentorian, and Zara clamped her Willpower and Intent around its echoes like a leaden box. Immediately, the pressure vanished, and the people around her looked around in confusion.

"Lady Zara? What was that?" asked a shaken soldier. Olia, she recalled. One of the Fiend's Shadows. "It felt as if a spear had been driven into my chest..."

"Your newfound Affinity opens you up to many new sensations," Zara explained, more than a little distracted. "Have you been practicing your exercises?" Olia nodded, and Zara gave her a smile. "The benefits are slow to accumulate, but soon such a thing will not bother you in the slightest. You must only stay the course."

The Dwarven soldier saluted, fist to chest. "Aye, Lady Zara. We will."

Zara left the soldier and a gathering, dizzy crowd, hustling across the deck and down several flights of stairs. The galleon class was not as big as the carrack she'd formed in the Shadowgate, but that had been more of a memory of a ship than a true vessel. Still, she descended three entire flights and squeezed through a hundred strides of narrow corridor before she reached her cabin. The moment she did, Zara secured the door and conjured a series of spiraling wards with nothing but the Chant and a thread of her Mana.

Only then did she unveil the small copper basin that stood atop an elegantly carved wooden stand. She touched the sides of the hammered metal and felt a harsh blaring as her Mana was seized by the contraption. The bowl was immediately filled with the aquamarine glow of her liquid Mana, spinning rapidly in a counterclockwise motion.

Zara sang a single, reverberating note. Blue and gold briefly flashed in her vision as the System noticed her song, and the swirling Mana rose out of the copper basin. All at once, it formed into the shape of a skull. It was followed by tendons and muscle and skin forming over the skull, layering over itself until it formed a facsimile of a floating, withered head.

"Mauvim. You should not have called. Things have changed—" Zara started, before the withered head let loose a scoff.

"How long should I have held my tongue, girl? After I sensed you departed from the open water, it was all I could manage to convince the others to wait on you. But that was days past, and still there was only silence. We have unrest boiling across the Continent, not the least of it is in the Dwarven strongholds—" The wizened face of her mentor frowned. "What do you mean, things have changed?"

Zara swallowed her annoyance at Mauvim's incautious blade of Intent, and tried to listen to her mentor with an open heart. It was true, she should have reached out to the Cantus as soon as they had returned to the Stronghold. Yet, there were countless tasks that ate into her time, and, were she being honest, she did not wish to report on recent events. "Felix Nevarre has destroyed a captive Primordial and defeated a Grandmaster in a duel for Authority."

"*What?!*"

"He has also claimed the Seat and Seal of Ahkestria, restored an ancient sea to the entire Territory, found and secured both Isla and her Unbound, and," Zara took a breath before continuing. "And the majority of the soldiers around him have somehow gained access to at least one Harmonic stat."

Silence reigned for longer than Zara had ever experienced with her ancient mentor. Mauvim's tiny simulacrum of Mana appeared stunned, wrinkled jowls twitching in a mixture of confusion, disbelief, and outrage. "Truly?"

"All of it is true. I would hazard a guess that almost all of them heard your call, and it nearly deafened them."

Mauvim tutted her tiny tongue. "They are not properly trained? What have you been doing since they awakened to the Harmonics?"

Zara repressed a sigh of annoyance. "The standard exercises for all of them. But when I say the majority, I do mean that. At least three hundred have unlocked Affinity and Resilience, by my last count."

"How?"

"Felix's influence, we believe," Zara said.

"That is not possible. I *know* that is not possible. A single man's presence cannot affect the Grand Harmony in such a way."

"I cannot offer explanations. Not yet. And perhaps not for a while. We ride now to war." Zara winced as Mauvim's small projection swelled, more than doubling in size as Mana was drained from the copper basin.

"*WHAT?* You are bringing two Unbound into—*what* war?" she demanded, before realization set in. "The Hierocracy. They have finally dispatched an army, haven't they?"

"They have. Several thousand strong, and among them at least one capable of shattering the Enclosure array."

Mauvim's eyes closed. "Dissonance and Damnation." Slowly she deflated, returning once more to her original size. "The world is in an uproar. All of it is balancing on the edge of a blade, Zara. All of it." Mauvim breathed forcefully from her nostrils. "Bring them to me. I would speak with them both."

Zara opened her mouth, shut it, and opened it again before she managed an apologetic grin. "Ah. About that."

CHAPTER SIXTY-FOUR

Sunken Ward is level 22!
Adamant Discord is level 83!

When the last of the chaotic maelstroms released their party, a full two days had passed, and all of them were exhausted. The War Naga had taken the brunt of the punishment, of course, but even clinging tightly to their backs had proven a real challenge. At a certain point, Felix and Beef had been forced to fashion harnesses and saddles for all of them, if only to allow them some modicum of rest.

So now, as the roar of the riptide faded and the wild chaos of water Mana was tamed into the steadier currents of the deep, their party descended to the pockmarked and pitted stone shelf just beyond it all. Toa'ut groaned as they came to a stop, while Beef and Felix dissolved the constructs with a brief flaring of their Skills. Isla and Vess slid gracefully from their Naga's back, while Pit and Hallow flopped somewhat ungainly onto the lake bed.

<<My legs are numb,>> Pit complained. He wobbled in the water, afloat but unable to stay properly upright. <<They feel all tingly!>>

<<I cannot feel my limbs at all,>> Hallow added, her voice reverberating more than usual through the Sunken Ward.

<<You're a rock,>> Pit pointed out.

<<Yes.>>

Felix slipped from Toa'ut's back with less grace than usual, still feeling the all-over feeling of strain to his Aspects. He stifled his groans, however; he'd had worse. The exhausted Naga settled themselves onto the thin layer of silt atop the stone shelf, their scales grinding audibly against the grit. Toa'ut let out a tired, hissing grunt. <<We need true rest, my Lord. A time to recuperate will allow us to press farther, faster.>>

<<That's fine. You folks went above and beyond back there.>> Felix turned so he was including all of the War Naga in his statement. <<Without you, pressing through those whirlpools would have been impossible.>> Toa'ut, Rou'd, Lavix, and all the others bowed, their heaving chests and haggard expressions easing now that they were at rest. <<You have been here before. Where would you normally take a break?>>

<<There are caverns. Hidden. Follow us.>> The Naga propelled themselves from the lake bed, tails lashing with the dregs of their Stamina.

Felix and his team followed.

Outside of the Mountains That Howl, the water was easy to move through, especially for people with their stats. The rocky shelf soon split, fissuring until they were surrounded by a network of cracks that grew larger with every hundred feet they swam. Thin canyons formed, within which more and more plant life began to swell, until it was like flying over a miniature jungle. Felix kicked his legs and knifed his arms through the water, his Endurance and Strength more than enough to keep up with the tired War Naga. Easy enough that his Mind wandered, turning over the problem he still hadn't resolved.

After the fight against the disturbed Den, Felix had propelled them onward with all of the force he could muster. Adamant Discord yanked aside currents and grasping plant-monstrosities, hauling their party in its thunderous wake, but he could only keep that up for so long. The tendrils of connection he'd established with the Fathom twinged with every casting, almost calling out to him from the shimmering ooze far below. Once he'd established enough distance from the site of the battle, Felix had ceased using his Skill, instead trusting the War Naga to lead them through as before.

There was a large part of him that was afraid of establishing contact with the Fathom again. It was powerful, of that there could be no doubt, but more than that: it was *familiar.*

He just didn't know why.

The familiarity was even more upsetting than the sheer, rampaging power behind the Fathom's roar. When it had turned its focus on him, it was like a burning brand that twisted and writhed, a living thing of fire and heat and pain. It was the writhing, the sense of chaotic disorder, that allowed Felix the time to erect his Bastion of Will. Without that beat, the Fathom could well have blasted through Felix's Mind and more. Instead, he'd been able to cut it all off in time, feeding the potency of the ooze to his ever-hungry abyss.

More, it rumbled at him.

Quiet. Felix wanted to rub his temples and lay down for a week, but instead he had to focus on the notification that still floated in his periphery.

Attention!
A Challenge Has Been Issued!
You Have Been Challenged For Your Authority!
Child Of The Nym! Do You Accept?
Y/N

He'd shown it to his friends and followers, hoping for someone to pipe up with an explanation, but all of them had stared at it in confusion. <<Is this anything like how I Challenged the Grandmaster of Ahkestria for Territorial Authority?>>

Isla had been the first to respond. <<There are many kinds of Challenges, Felix. Some are System-born, but others will find their genesis within Skills. Those are often self-focused, Skills of the enhancement category meant to improve your Aspects directly, and are exceedingly rare. The more dire the stakes, the greater the rewards.>> She had pursed her lips in that way she had, adding a severity to her face that seemed to add decades to her deep eyes. <<This one is System-born, that is clear...and somehow, this Fathom holds enough Authority in the Ghreldan Hills that he can access such an option.>>

<<But that should be impossible,>> Vess had said. She looked just as shaken as Felix by the roar, but rage was catching up to her fear. <<A ruler cannot Challenge a visitor, only the opposite.>>

Isla had only shrugged. <<A wrinkle in the System's rules is not outside the realm of possibility. There are many depths to the Grand Harmony that we are not privy to.>>

Vess had frowned at her before regarding Felix, concern briefly winning against her battle fury. <<What will you do?>>

<<Ignore it? For now. I've no need to challenge this thing.>> Felix had paused. <<I *can* ignore it, right?>>

<<You can,>> Isla had confirmed. <<And I would suggest it as the best course. Even rejecting the Challenge would give this Fathom an answer from you...ignoring it will keep them guessing. As the Grand Harmony's progeny, the System demands a willing choice. Consent must be given for this to have any effect.>>

<<So why issue it?>> Beef had asked. <<That's kind of a waste.>>

<<It is a Dragon. Dragons are arrogant and willful; they will always expect their foes to act as they do. And no Dragon would shy from a Challenge.>> Vess had explained.

The notification glimmered at Felix, bright gold and deep azure. There had been no further sign of pursuit by the Fathom spawn since their battle. The brief connection Felix shared with the Dragon was not enough for it to pinpoint their location; how he knew that, Felix was unsure. Yet it sat within him regardless, solid and certain, like the knowledge that such details would change were he to choose either "yes" or "no" on the Challenge. He closed it again, without choosing.

Below them, the crevices had split open into large gorges, and the proliferation of frond and wriggling vine continued. In the hazy distance, the cracks in the lake bed only grew wider and wider. He wondered how far they went, when the Naga dove down into one of the thinner crevasses. Felix and his team followed.

Toa'ut led them deep into the verdant canyon, past narrow lips of pockmarked stone and among the twisted sea grasses, thick bundles of crimson algae, and luminous, gelatinous orbs. Those floated in the invisible currents, glowing golden and warm, tethered to the cliffs by knobbly tendrils and thick roots. The foliage was deep and varied and surprisingly colorful for so far beneath the surface; Felix would have expected muted greens and pale whites, but he supposed the light that emanated from the odd bioluminescent orbs helped with that.

The path wound farther and farther, eventually hooking a sharp turn around a ridge that completely hid it from sight. Toa'ut swam ahead, whipping through the waters with renewed energy as he entered a dark cavern. <<We may rest here, for a time, my Lord.>>

Felix coasted to a stop just outside the mouth of the cavern, pressing his Perception forward into the dark hole. As far as he could tell, the cavern was relatively shallow and completely free of monsters or other threats. He nodded to Toa'ut. <<Looks good.>>

The other War Nagas arrived seconds after him, and his friends just behind them. As the giant serpent people settled in, Felix realized they all carried bushels of crimson algae, fronds, and even a pair of those gelatinous lights.

Vess floated to the ground beside him as the others swam past, each hurriedly claiming a portion of the sandy floor. She held her hip with her left hand, partisan floating effortlessly beside her, and was grimacing. <<What is the plan?>>

<<First is rest, like I said. We all need it, even me.>> Felix nodded at her hip. <<Are you okay?>>

<<Simply saddle sore.>> Vess waved his concern away, but her cheek dimpled with a half smile. <<Let me fight a monster horde, and I will not complain, but set me on an Avum for a few glasses, and I shall ache for days.>>

<<Careful how you talk about them. I said one of the Naga looked like my friend Jimmy's pet iguana, and he got real bent outta shape.>>

Beef float-stepped his way toward them. He was quite heavy, but still his small hooves were having trouble finding purchase in the thick layer of sand underfoot.

<<I shall be sure not to offend them,>> Vess promised, her soft smile turning wry. <<But...rest sounds good. I had thought myself ready to keep pressing on, but this swimming has revealed a few aches I would be a fool not to address.>>

<<Uh yeah, what she said,>> Beef added in. <<I could sleep for days, I think. Wait. We're underwater. How does that work?>>

<<My Skill will continue to provide for us, even if we sleep,>> Felix assured the teen, and Beef let out a loud sigh of relief.

<<Oh, thank god.>>

Felix could use the rest, too. According to his memory, he hadn't slept in six entire days. That was entirely too long to go without sleep, even if his Endurance and Vitality made sleeping more of an optional thing. <<Zara and the others will reach Haarwatch in the next few hours, I think,>> he said.

<<Hopefully to find things as calm as ever,>> Vess added. <<Has Karys sent any word on how things are progressing in the Verdant Pass?>>

Felix shook his head and tried to ignore the sensation of his long hair wafting in the water. It was weird. <<No.>>

Karys had stayed behind in the Stronghold, but he had direct access to Cal, and as Lady of Haarwatch, she would have reported if the Hierocracy had shown up. Felix supposed he would call his Chancellor in the morning. The old Nym still wasn't particularly pleased with Felix for staying behind, so the conversation was unlikely to be comfortable, but it'd set some minds at ease.

<<I hope the ships are working well enough,>> Beef said as he came to a wobbling halt. His fingers toyed with the haft of his war club. <<Still can't believe my Risen just fell apart like that.>>

<<Failure is a constant companion, Beef. What you choose to do after is what matters.>> Vess patted the Minotaur on his bicep as she swam away. <<I believe I will attempt to get some of that rest. Much to do tomorrow.>>

The two Unbound watched Vess leave, both lost in their own thoughts. Felix couldn't stop thinking about his friends heading into a dangerous battle, which looped into his concern over their own coming fight. Beef, on the other hand, seemed to be worrying at another issue entirely.

<<Wasn't anything I could do,>> he said. <<The thing turned to sand, and Hallow and I lost control immediately. We're still not sure why it happened.>>

<<Life's a learning process,>> Felix said. <<Only thing you can do it keep moving forward.>>

<<Yeah, I guess,>> Beef said, more than a little sulkily. <<I just wish I didn't have this ringing in my ears all the time now. Would've been way easier to maintain the connection if it hadn't gone squealing.>>

<<What?>> Felix glanced at the young teen in the enormous bull-man Body. <<What ringing?>>

<<Oh, it's so weird. Ever since I got a new Title for sending my Risen so far away and maintaining control, I've been hearing the worst stuff. Like music, but it makes no sense.>>

He unlocked at least one Harmonic stat. It was likely to be Affinity as well, considering what he was hearing. <<What was the Title?>>

In response, Beef just swiped something at him. A blue window rolled into existence before Felix, displaying an impressive new Title.

Congratulations!
You Have Earned A Title!
Puppeteer of the Dead (Epic)!
You have learned to operate your servants from a great distance away, while still maintaining precision. Increases Endurance and Agility of all Risen by 5%. Increases control limit by 5.

<<Oh wow, that's a great Title for you,>> Felix said.

<<Agreed. Except for all this ringing, I'd have actually enjoyed it.>> After the battle, Beef had spent a good portion of his time trying to capture and Rise one of the Fathom spawn. Control limit aside, the new Risen had been too weak and ungainly to navigate the pressures of the Mountains That Howl. They were ripped down into the vortexes, time and time again.

<<It sounds like you unlocked your Affinity. Is that it?>> Felix asked.

<<Affinity and Resonance, it said. Honestly, it's been freaking me out. I know about them, right? You told me. But that ringing isn't the only thing I'm hearing. The whole time we've been swimming, it's like something's been *singing* to me.>> Beef shuddered. <<Like something hiding in the dark water.>>

Felix immediately knew what he was talking about, though at this point, he'd unconsciously tuned it out. <<That's the water itself.>>

<<What?>>

<<Well, remember what I said? About the Grand Harmony? Everything has a vibrational frequency, and all of it sings out to us all the time

—>> Felix started saying, but a slender pile of platinum curls and flowing blue gown cut him off.

<<Michael! You didn't mention you had unlocked your first Harmonic stats! That is excellent!>> She flowed through the water with more grace than Vess, her movements clean and natural-seeming, as if she routinely walked along the bottom of a lake. <<I shall take any education from here, Felix. I am, after all, his mentor.>>

Felix tried not to frown. <<I was simply telling him what I knew.>>

<<And that is appreciated. Now, Michael—>>

<<Beefhammer,>> the Minotaur corrected.

<<Michael, what you need to know about Affinity and Resonance is that they can both be trained. What are your values right now?>>

<<Um, 34 and 22.>>

<<Excellent. Plenty of room to grow. Utilizing a few specialized exercises will aid in training your technique, though it is hard.>> She sniffed. <<It takes *far* more work than lifting heavy things and setting them back down again.>>

Felix repressed a sigh, letting Isla take over the conversation. He'd get with Beef later and tell him what he knew; there were other things Felix needed doing. <<Beef, Isla. Make sure you get some rest.>> He kicked off the lake bed, sending up a small cloud of sand and silt.

<<Felix! We'll talk later, yeah?>> Beef shouted after him.

Felix gave the kid a thumbs up as he shot away, deeper into the cavern to where Pit and the others were settling down around food and impromptu beds of sand.

CHAPTER SIXTY-FIVE

Felix tried to sleep. Really. He wanted to blame the lack of pillow or blanket or bed, but he'd grown used to such things a long time ago. He also wanted to blame his stats and Temper, which made sleep almost unnecessary in most cases, but that wasn't true this time. After the brief contact with the Fathom, his strained Body was begging for rest. It was his racing Mind and still aching Spirit that were not having it.

After tossing and turning on the oddly squishy sand, Felix got up and prowled about the cavern. The space was wide enough, but each of the War Nagas had burrowed the long serpent portion of their forms deep into the sand. Their overly muscular humanoid top halves were splayed out on top, most of them fast asleep. That left a relatively small portion where Isla, Beef, and Pit were bedding down.

Isla and Beef were both asleep, the latter's snores almost deafening through the Sunken Ward, despite the muffling effect of the spell. She was posted up beside his sprawled form, somehow in possession of a small sleeping mat and blanket, her platinum curls bound up in a delicate sleeping cap of some sort. Felix snorted and moved on.

"...been fighting for a long time." Two of the War Naga were up and chatting, keeping watch while the rest slept. "This is nothing new."

"Maybe," another said, rubbing her jaw. "But it's not been this bad since before the king went to Khasma himself."

"The Deepking?" Felix asked. The War Naga pivoted toward him smoothly, putting their fists over their chests, and Felix waited for them to sit up again. "He went to Khasma before?"

"He did, Returned God. It was in the old days, before Haestus was a haven of our people. Before the Deepking *was* the Deepking." The heavier-set male had a fevered look in his eyes, as if he were imagining some glorious battle. "He took a small war party and descended on the Fathom spawn, all the way to the edge of the Breach itself."

"Until the Fathom bested him and killed all of our warriors," the other said, a different sort of heat in her gaze. "It was the first time he had ever lost, and the last, too."

"He Evolved into the Abyssal Serpent after that," said the male with pride. "Since then, he has kept his vow to keep our people safe and to fight back the Fathom spawn. Until now, we'd only managed to fight them to a standstill. We have not been to Khasma in force ever since."

"Until you, my Lord."

They bowed again, this time going so far as to press their blunt snouts into the sand. When they returned to an upright position, Felix nodded in a way that he hoped conveyed his...something. His resolve? Felix wasn't sure, but it was enough. The War Naga returned to their watch, and he gratefully moved on.

Out of the corner of his eye, Felix saw that Pit and Hallow were cuddled together. The horse-sized tenku was wrapped around the small rocky Homunculus in the way of a big dog around a favored toy. It was cute. Wrapped around *them* was Hallow's Multipede form. That was... less cute.

But where's Vess?

The cavern was wide, but Felix hadn't sensed much depth to it when they had entered. So he stepped outside, through the curtain of fronds that the Naga had wedged into the crags to further hide their hideaway, and into the narrow crevasse just beyond. Yet as his Perception spread outward, Felix could not spot his friend there, either.

His thoughts raced, spinning through possibilities, most of which were either ludicrous or unbelievable. Had she left? Felix worried at that like Pit with a bone before a soft exhalation and flash of metal Mana broke against his anxious thoughts. To his left, where the walls of the gorge tightened until they were barely more than ten feet across, there was a split among the stone. Silver and white-green vapor curled through the waters, gone in an instant.

He slipped forward, through the broken entrance and the crooked passage beyond. It rose and dipped, less a path than it was a fissure cracked open by ancient tidal forces. Inside, Felix found a space that had, at some point, collapsed within the rocky shelf. A small cavern had formed and was strewn with rocks that ranged from hand-sized stone to boulders taller than him.

Some of the brittle iron in Felix's spine softened as he saw her, alone among the rocks. Vess kicked and spun through the resistance of the water, floating at apparently random speeds as she shot up and down through the boulders. Her partisan was out, weaving forward as if it were liquid itself, and not a solid pole of arcane metal. The dragon that Rafny had carved into the haft seemed half-alive, writhing with a serpentine grace that was superior to their brutal guides. As he watched, she missed a strike and cursed to herself, grinding her heel into the grit and marching backward.

<<Up late training?>> Felix asked.

Vess looked up at him in surprise. She'd been focusing hard, that was clear. <<Felix. Is something wrong?>> She half-stepped toward him. <<Was there an attack?>>

<<What? No. We're fine. I just...couldn't sleep.>>

<<Ah. I, too, cannot find it in me to rest.>> Vess sighed, the sound almost totally lost among the ward's muffling. <<I should. It has been a trying few days.>>

<<It has. What are you training?>>

<<Movement, for now.>> She waved a hand through the water, and despite her Strength, Felix could see the drag on her limb. <<Battle beneath the waves is proving more difficult than I anticipated. I need to account for the water's resistance when I am maneuvering or attacking.>>

Felix nodded. He'd noticed it, too, the floating when he leaped or attempted to change direction rapidly. <<Mind some company?>>

Vess smiled. <<I would be delighted.>>

The heiress of Pax'Vrell began her movements again, leaping rock to rock in a pattern as she thrust and spun her partisan. Felix joined her, keeping away from her path but attempting to copy her choices around the perimeter of the room. Relentless Resolution flared with every kick and step, his Body and Mind communing with lightning quick efficiency as he darted through the water.

Moving as if he were in the air was very hard in the water, and it only increased the sense of floating between his bigger jumps. What's worse, bubbles and silt swarmed him with each kick off and landing, clouding his immediate surroundings. It was like television static for his senses; not so terrible he couldn't see past it, but an extra layer that Felix had to learn to anticipate. Often, Vess would swoop past him, lapping him as they ricocheted off boulders and the frond-infested walls, smiling bright and victorious. Felix grinned right back, putting fresh energy into the exercise.

They raced.

The hours passed wordlessly, both of them visibly improving as they opposed one another, attacks and feints to keep their guard up, and all the while their path grew more and more labyrinthine. Their movements sped up with each revolution, eyes on each other as well as their next step. Felix copied Vess, twisted his body so that his fall cut through the water like a knife instead of a stone, and Vess copied Felix, her spear cleaving the way forward much as his flattened hands pushed liquid around himself.

She was elegant in the way she moved, as sleek as anything in her white-enameled half-plate, but she moved slower than Felix expected. Her deceptive footwork was not on display, or any Skill that he could spot. Perhaps that was to acclimate to the water faster? Or another reason only evident to people who had trained all their life for battle.

For his part, Felix utilized as many Skills as he could keep active at once. Which was a lot, truth be told. Platforms of blue-white Mana appeared beneath his feet, allowing him better traction between boulders, while vines and thick pillars of ice were shaped from the walls to redirect him with increasing accuracy. Vess strained, shattering his constructs with her partisan when she could, but Felix only made more. A lot more.

Relentless Resolution is level 80!
Manasight is level 74!

Dual Casting is level 57!
...
Dual Casting is level 62!

Cloudstep is level 51!
...
Cloudstep is level 58!

Blind Fighting is level 60!
...
Blind Fighting is level 63!

Dodge is level 71!
...
Dodge is level 73!

Rime Shaping is level 64!
...
Rime Shaping is level 66!

Green Shaping is level 63!
...
Green Shaping is level 65!

Soon, Felix left her behind, lapping her as he pressed every advantage he had, the water in the confined space flowing after him. It roared almost as loud as his heartbeat pounded in his ears, the sound of screaming surf so familiar after days of the same howling. Felix felt a giddy laugh bubble up in his chest as he knifed forward, smashing through boulders now and relying entirely on Cloudsteps wrapped in frozen vines to move *faster*.

<<Stop, stop before you bring this cavern on top of us!>> Vess shouted at him.

Felix did, dropping from the dizzying pattern they'd been following. Silt and sand exploded outward, already half-torn up by the whirling waters, but his relentless momentum was barely interrupted. He was forced to conjure Cloudstep after Cloudstep, shattering through them until the last was enough to arrest his velocity. He bounced off the last, blue-white barrier with a gentle grunt. <<Jeez, I didn't realize how fast I was—Whoa.>>

Around them, the small chamber had become a miniature version of the Mountains That Howl. A riptide flowed around the perimeter of the cavern, stone and silt and debris dragged in its slowly dying wake. A few of the bigger stones had even shifted, lifted from where they were sunk deep into the ground.

Vess swam to his side, her braided hair now slightly undone. Several dark brown locks rippled with the current, strong even here at the outside. <<Yes. Whoa, indeed. Did you not notice?>>

<<I uh, may have gotten caught up in the race,>> Felix admitted, sheepishly. With his Perception no longer so hyper-focused, he spotted several bleeding cuts on her face. <<Oh! You're hurt.>>

<<Simple scratches. A few splintered stones caught in the force of your maelstrom.>> She waved off his concern, and Felix had to admit she didn't seem particularly hurt. She did, however, seem tired. <<I had not expected that result, I'll admit.>>

Felix scratched at his neck, embarrassed at how hard he'd taken the training. <<I shouldn't have gone so hard.>>

<<No. That was fine. I need to improve, Felix, and you are someone I do not need to hold back against. I need that, too.>> She shook her head. <<I wish I could afford to spend my Mana in this place, but with air Mana so far away, my recovery is greatly reduced.>>

Felix could understand the first part. He usually had trouble training with the others for that very reason. This had been the first training session in a while to garner him so many Skill levels. The second part, however, was foreign to him; he could recover the same anywhere he went except the Void. <<Ah, I didn't realize.>>

<<Why would you?>> Vess waved off his concern. <<I shall be fine. We brought many Mana Potions for just that reason. Just perhaps not so many that I could unleash my Skills with impunity.>>

He chewed at his cheek. <<I'll admit, it was nice to let loose. I think

I can go faster, too.>>

Vess laughed, the tiredness retreating. <<I would like to see that. Preferably from several hundred strides away.>>

Felix grinned. <<Oh. I've been meaning to tell you: I've been using your visualization technique.>>

<<Truly? Felix, that is wonderful!>> All the frustration fled from Vess' face as she grasped his hands. <<I was convinced you could make it work!>>

<<It took some...creative thinking, but it turns out if I can get close enough to the Hunger inside of me, I can just...>> Felix went to gesture with his hand, but realized he quite liked where they were at the moment. <<Well, I can make it work. I've started on my way toward a more focused core space, though I think it'll be a bit longer before I can finish all the changes.>>

<<That is excellent news, Felix. I am truly happy that you could make use of my family's technique.>> Vess' smile didn't crack so much as slowly fade. Her hands slipped free of his. <<If only my dilemma had such an easy solution.>>

<<Your Skills?>> Felix tried to ignore the ghost of warmth that lingered atop his palms. It was spoiled a bit by the guilt that rose in his chest. <<The dragon-themed ones?>>

Vess laughed again, more bitterly than before. <<Yes.>>

That guilt lanced through Felix. <<For what it's worth, I'm sorry. Again.>>

She frowned at him. <<I told you already. It was my choice to take that Essence, Felix. You are not responsible for my actions.>>

<<No, but I am responsible for mine,>> he shot back. <<I could have chosen not to share it with you at all.>>

<<And would you have survived?>> she asked, her voice quiet. Felix hesitated, and she nodded. <<I thought not. I could feel your desperation in that moment, Felix. We all could. We would not leave you when you had need of us. I would not.>> She straightened. <<I did not, and I bear the consequences proudly. But I do have a path forward, or perhaps backward is the correct phrasing.>>

<<You do?>> Felix was experiencing some emotional whiplash. <<How?>>

<<I have been speaking with Isla at length. When she heard of my situation, of how it came to pass, she proposed a method to return my Skills to their states before the Primordial's Essence changed them.>> Vess settled back against a half-broken boulder with a fatigued groan. <<That is the *other* reason I was not using my Skills tonight. Keeping my evolved Skills from leveling will aid the process, I am told.>>

Isla. What are you doing? Felix wasn't a fan that she was mixing into the situation and wondered at her motivations. <<Are you going to sunder

them? Start over? You're nearly at Adept Tier. Won't that ruin your...everything?>>

<<My foundation is still strong, still secure with prior Skills before their unfortunate evolution. That will be retained after the process is complete, Isla assured me.>>

<<How?>> he asked. <<What exactly is she going to do?>>

Vess tilted her head, nose crinkling. <<Why do you fear her?>>

<<I don't,>> Felix said, perhaps too forcefully. <<I just don't trust her, or any of the Chanters, with the possible exception of Zara,>> he said, stepping closer. <<They have both been hiding things from the moment we met, but at least Zara has come forward with the truth. Isla...she gets under my skin.>>

<<As I said before, I do not blame you, Felix. I chose to aid you, knowing that unexpected consequences were likely. I just...had not considered this as a possibility. When Isla informed me of a path forward, dangerous or not, I planned to meet it head on.>> Her gaze firmed, fixed upon the tip of her spear. <<I will not shrink from this battle.>>

Vess' face turned up toward his, and her eyes pleaded with him. <<If you cannot trust the Chanter, then trust me, Felix. As I trust you.>>

Uncertainty ate at Felix—doubt in Isla, but also in what he felt he had to say. <<Look, Vess. I trust you, I do. But how much of this is you picking the right way forward, and how much is you chasing after your parents' expectations?>>

<<Excuse me?>>

Affinity held back or not, the disbelief and anger flowed from Vess in waves more dense than the depths around them. She stood, bristling with it, but Felix plowed ahead anyway. <<All I mean is—>>

<<I know what you mean,>> Vess said, her voice like a whipcrack despite the muffling ward. <<And you cannot understand, Felix. It is more than the weight of expectations. It is an honor. The Dragoons protect our people from monsters, but they are also a bulwark against the Hierocracy itself, keeping their Paladins and Inquisitors away from our borders.

"Without a strong, unified front, they will use our weakness as an excuse to occupy our towns and villages. The leader of Pax'Vrell must always be a Dragoon or married to one. It is a tradition that I cannot simply abandon, Felix. The Dragoons protect my people, and without them, I would be nothing."

She kicked off of the sand, pure Strength and Agility catapulting her through the water and toward the crooked exit, leaving only dust and cloudy water behind.

Felix sighed. *Great job, idiot.*

CHAPTER SIXTY-SIX

Felix trained alone for a time. He pressed his Skills, conjuring shapes out of the limited light in the closed cavern, or summoning fists of acid to sizzle and sputter against boulders. His heart wasn't in it, however, not like before.

Auroral Forge is level 28!
Auroral Forge is level 29!

The gains ended there. His Aspects ached, but far worse was the realization that things were spinning out of his control. The anxieties that had been burning at his Mind were inflamed by the one-two punch of Vess' risky plan and the Fathom's contact. His team was limited, featuring a kid and his pet rock, a manipulative Chanter, and an uncertain warrior. Beef was a good egg, but he was too young—he'd fight, Felix didn't doubt that, but the Minotaur's skillset was limited. Hallow would follow Beef, of course, but its Risen weren't strong enough to face down a Depthwurm let alone the Fathom itself.

Pit, he could trust, of course. Isla, however, was apparently working to drastically weaken Vess. Perhaps she meant well, and perhaps the timespan was not as immediate as Felix feared—he doubted Vess would be so foolhardy as to introduce a glaring weakness into her core space right before a fight. A fight, he reminded himself, that she desperately wished to take part in.

Then again, maybe she is *willing to attempt this mysterious process soon,* he mused. Vess was very dedicated to eradicating draconic Types, and the Fathom most of all. Worse than her going after the supposed dragon directly was the idea that she would do so after damaging her Aspects and Temper. At the very least, the Fathom knew of them, and depending on what it gleaned from Felix in their brief connection, it might even know they were coming.

Felix's training soon lapsed into a long, quiet bout of thinking.

The water flowed around him as he sat in the center of the small cavern, sloshing in time with the pressure that fed inward from the crevasse. Silt and debris settled, until the water was crystal clear, and Felix could hear nothing over his Sunken Ward except the beat of his own heart.

I can't do anything about Vess and Isla, not without pushing them away. If she chooses to go through with something like that, it is her *choice.* That decision hurt him to make, but it was the right one. *Focus instead on what you can affect.*

Felix dove into his core space.

Down among the crystalline tree, burning dual cores, and dark, endless abyss at the very center, Felix regarded his Skills. They glimmered, masquerading as celestial bodies, and he sought out one in particular.

Sovereign of Flesh, he thought, isolating the Skill among the revolving multitude before crooking his finger at a number of others. *Cardinal Flame. Green Shaping. Auroral Forge. Rime Shaping. Manasight. Theurgist of the Rise. Invocation. Dual Casting. Manaship Pilot.*

All of them were caught up in Felix's inextricable Willpower, pulled into the orbit of Sovereign of Flesh. As a Transcendent-rarity Skill as well as one he had Tempered with multiple times, it was far larger and more complex than the others. Cardinal Flame and Theurgist of the Rise came close, while Manasight and Dual Casting were the smallest. Yet even the less complex patterns of those Uncommon Skills were hellishly convoluted, each trough and crest within them a unique vibration. Felix flared his Affinity, confirming once more the threads of commonality in the songs of every single Skill that he gathered around his Primary—and once he did that, he got to work.

What little Essence Felix had was drained by the process, and his Mana, too. His regeneration fought to keep up, pulling more and more Mana from the environment around him to fuel his cores. Chthonic Tribute also flared over and over again, almost an instinctive reaction at this point, consuming boulder and sand and thick bedrock all around him, but the Essence of inanimate objects was so thin—it was all Felix could do to keep up with the demands of the formation of a Skill Array.

Felix focused instead on weaving the delicate rhythms and chords together, tying the edges of one Skill to another. It was a process that was similar to combining Skills and somehow distinctly separate. Where combining was subsuming multiple abilities into a unified, often totally dissimilar whole, a Skill Array was about working in concert. Like his

Bastion of Will, Sovereign of Flesh soon drew the other Skills closer and closer to itself, until each one rotated around its glistening shape like tiny moons around a swirling gas giant.

The closer the Skills moved, the more Felix could feel the invisible connections between them solidify. It was like utilizing his Adamant Discord or Skein of Fate: as each Secondary Skill joined the Array, a pulse of power flashed between it and the Primary. It moved too fast for anyone normal to be able to perceive it, but it was there, a wrist-thick cable of relevance.

The cable repeated, Skill after Skill, a strobing connection that seemed to grow more brilliant with each additional addition to the Array. It grew heavy, a solidity that weighed on his core space with incredible pressure until everything abruptly pulled inward, and a surge of vigor shot outward in all directions, ripping Felix's awareness up and away.

Felix sucked in a ragged, wet breath and opened his eyes.

Sunken Ward!

Instinctively, he fumbled a Mana Potion to his lips, before flaring his ward again, and the deep blue barrier flashed back into place. It had almost lapsed, stuttering over an incredible lack of Mana within his channels, something that hadn't happened to Felix in a long, long time. He coughed. <<What in the world—?>>

Around him, the little cavern had been worn down. The boulders, even the ones he hadn't smashed, had crumbled into chunks, and the water itself was oddly still. Lifeless and listless. The sandy ground had been leached of all color where it wasn't missing entirely—Felix sat at the base of a pit, the sides steep and smooth, and beneath him was only thick, lifeless bedrock.

*I absorbed this pit with Chthonic Tribute, sucking what Essence I could out of it, but the rest...*He spread his Perception outward, alarmed at how dead everything felt. *The rest was drained by my Mana regeneration?* It was the only thing that made sense. Mana regeneration pulled power from the environment, converting it into usable Mana depending on the attunement a person settled on. For Felix, that meant *anything* was fuel for his fire...and he'd used a lot while constructing his new Skill Array.

He stood up, and apparently that was entirely too much for his obliterated cave; the water trembled and flexed and the walls of his pit, of the cavern beyond, sloughed away. In an instant, Felix was inundated by a rain of blinding, dead dust as it all crumbled. Holding back a cough, Felix swam upward through the dark, cloying debris and slipped out of the crevasse.

Outside the little cavern, life returned to the environment. Currents pulled at him, plants undulated across the walls, and small crustaceans scuttled across the sands. His regeneration kicked back in now that there was Mana around them again—it was strong enough that Felix felt a sharp pressure at each of his Mana Gates for a few seconds. The wide cavern where his team slept was just ahead, and Felix's flared Perception caught most of them still within.

Hours had passed while he'd established his new Skill Array, hours where he'd slowly drained the world of vital Essence and animating Mana. It was strange to Felix, knowing he could accomplish such a thing. Stranger still to think of how far it might have spread, had he more time. If his regeneration got any stronger, how much more could he siphon away? Would it affect living creatures too? The idea of it frightened him a little, but Felix shook himself. *Don't dwell. Just be more careful next time...and make sure no one is close by.*

He swam back to his team.

Felix inspected his new Skill Array as he parted the fronds at the front of the cavern. As his Bastion looked almost like Earth surrounded by a number of colorful orbs, his Sovereign of Flesh was an ebony and ivory gas giant. It loomed, Jupiter to his Bastion's Earth, and all of the Secondary Skills in the Array spun at various speeds around its circumference. Cardinal Flame was red-gold and burning, like a miniature sun, it and the glowing Theurgist of the Rise half the size of Sovereign.

Manasight and Invocation hung closely about the latter, each the size of small moons comparatively, both shimmering with shifting, mutable writing in silver and gold fire that was echoed in Theurgist. Manaship Pilot was near as well, though it hung slightly apart from all the rest and rotated with a slower confidence. All of the other Skills glittered like jewels around the rest, spinning in rapid revolutions around one another.

Felix whistled. In the same way that his Bastion Skill Array felt stronger and more stable, this felt poised on the edge of frenetic activity, like an engine waiting to be ignited. Or a bomb about to go off. It was equal parts thrilling and terrifying.

Let's just hope it works as advertised. Karys had claimed they would strengthen one another, and Felix needed all the boosts he could get.

Within the cavern, he found the War Naga still buried in the sand. Still asleep. Beef and Hallow too, though they were tucked back against the far wall. At some point, the Homunculus and Multipede had moved to the bulky Minotaur and were now draped around him like the world's worst pair of scarves.

Pit, however, was awake.

One of the glowing sea plants had been secured to the craggy wall by clumsy, if industrious paws, and it cast a faint light over the pile of Pit's saddlebags. Their contents had been spilled out onto the fine silt, potions and rations cast about without much care. Thankfully, Sunken

Ward extended to their personal effects, operated by Felix's Intent rather than a strict bubble around each individual.

Perhaps if he relied on System Intent, the codified assistance baked into the Skill's pattern, perhaps then it wouldn't allow the ward to cover such things. The why of it all was lost on Felix; who knew why the System had developed the way it had? All he knew was that having conscious control of his Intent, being able to utilize the Chant, meant he could boost the Skill in ways both obvious and subtle. In this case, Sunken Ward covered all of them and anything on their person, from food to baubles. All it cost was a truckload more Mana, but he had it to spare now.

Felix blinked. His thoughts had felt a bit sluggish since emerging from his long meditation, but now his Mind struggled to accept what was in front of his eyes.

Pit had a book in front of him. He was *reading*.

<<Since when can you read?>> Felix asked, putting his hands on his hips.

Pit looked up, trilling a happy greeting. <<Learning. It's hard.>>

<<I'll say. Wait,>> Felix peered at his friend. In the low light,he'd almost missed it, but as he flared his Manasight, Felix could see the bright sparkle around Pit's eyes. <<What are you wearing?>>

<<Spectacles.>>

Voracious Eye!

Name: Spectacles of the Fledgling Scholar
Type: Accessory (Enchanted)
Lore: Designed and inscribed to enhance the reading speed and comprehension of the wearer, these spectacles are tools used by the mages of the Lucent Towers on their more promising students. They are rare creations and quite difficult to create, the secrets to doing so kept hidden among the gleaming spires of Levantier.
Improved Cognition I - Reading comprehension and knowledge retained is increased a minor amount.
Leaf On The Wind I - Reading speed is increased by a minor amount.

He *was* wearing glasses. Little circular lenses of gold crystal had been cut and set into a frame made of thin silver. They were perched atop his beak, unwavering despite Pit's movements. <<Where did they come from?>> Felix asked.

Pit tilted his head, paw held over the page he was reading. <<Same place as the books. The Grandmaster's old library. He had a couple pairs of them, though Zara told me they're extremely rare things. I

wanted to learn to read, like you and Atar and the Dangerous One—ah, Vess, I mean.>>

<<Huh.>> Felix wasn't mad or anything, just impressed. He *did* wish that he'd had glasses like that, back when he'd had to learn to read from scratch. <<What are you reading? God, that's a weird thing to say out loud to you.>> Felix crouched down and read over his Companion's shoulder. <<'A good general will know when to deploy her mages and when to pull them back for recovery. Recovery is the greatest concern in battle.' What is this?>>

<<*Notes From The Blastlands.* It's a book on war strategies and stuff.>> Pit looked a little embarrassed. <<Now that I'm faster and have more power, I want to know how to use it best. When Zara mentioned reading to learn, it made sense. So...so I got these out.>>

Next to him were six more volumes, all thick and inscribed with sigils declaring them memoirs and treatises. <<Pit, that's amazing.>> The tenku warbled in delight, his feathers and fur ruffling. <<I'm proud of you. Keep it up.>>

Felix looked around. <<Where's Isla and Vess?>>

Pit gestured with a paw back toward the hanging fronds. <<Out. Sparring, I think.>>

<<Sparring, huh?>> *Or were they proceeding with their plan?* His worries returned, but Felix pressed a portion of himself closer to his Hunger. The emotions were pulled away, devoured by the abyss within him. <<Finish up your reading, bud. I need you to wake up the Naga so we can get moving.>>

Pit groaned as if he'd been asked to climb a mountain and run a marathon. <<Why? Where are you going?>>

Felix had already started swimming forward, back toward the fronds. <<Get them up. I want to leave in ten minutes.>>

<<*Fine.*>>

CHAPTER SIXTY-SEVEN

Perched atop the crow's nest, Evie was the first to see the gleaming, red-gold Wall of Haarwatch. As the call went out, and the commanders shouted down the cheers until they "got their blighted asses moving," Evie watched the city grow nearer.

It wasn't home. Few places had earned the title since she lost her parents, back when Magda had dragged her ass over hill and dale in search of their next meal. But Evie had lived in Haarwatch longer than many other cities, she had friends there, and her other sister ran the place. It wasn't home, but it was close.

Some of the mages released pulses of Mana into the air ahead of the leading ship, little more than flares of colored light. They were answered in turn by figures down on the gargantuan wall, ants far below that threw their own sparkles. It was a code, and a familiar one at that—she could recognize Yan's handiwork there. He'd used similar codes with little flags back then. Evie smiled at the memory as their ship passed uninterrupted over the Wall...only noticing the shimmering shield of yellow-white energy as they sailed harmlessly through it.

Whoa. Was that always there? Evie hadn't ever flown in a Manaship before. Memories tickled at the back of her Mind, something about those bug monsters that had attacked the city once. *Right. The Wretches were mostly blocked, but they broke the shielding. Got through.* Evie leaned out of the gray-brown chitin basket, peering downward. *Huh. They fixed the Rent. Cal must've upgraded the defenses. Wonder how much that cost.*

The Wall had once been torn through by some giant, fuck-off Arcid—the Abigail or something—and it had stomped a path of devastation across the entire Quarter. Now, that huge hole had been repaired so well that Evie couldn't spot the seams. Cal had even managed to sheath the whole thing in orichalcum, the same metal that made up the rest of the Wall. *That* was rare. What's more, as they flew over the city, Evie saw rubble-free streets and vanishingly few structures that weren't in the midst of a full repair. *It's almost like the Archon never attacked.*

The rest of the city looked the same, rebuilt and repaired. Improved, judging by the new construction and proper stone roads in the Dust Quarter. As the Manaship banked into a turn, Evie could just make out the bare rectangle where their warehouse headquarters had once been. She shook her head. That didn't matter much.

Cal had built a much better one.

The air shook as all five Manaships steered toward the airdocks at the top of Haarwatch Manor. It was almost as high as the Eyrie once was, yet contained none of the snooty gilded edges. Instead, the Manor resembled a massive mansion and fortress all in one, a place intended to represent safety and security for the city. At the top of the structure were three cylindrical towers, each one a third as wide as the Manor itself and equipped with a ringed platform around the topmost levels. The ships pressed onward, slowing as their chitinous bulks approached the designating landing spots among the platforms.

"Talons, present!" Darius Reed bellowed, just as mooring lines were tossed down to the docks.

Claw members hustled forward, assembling into orderly lines that the Hand had drilled into them. Each one wore Apprentice Tier armor and bore at least one newly gleaming weapon, not to mention long, black cloaks emblazoned with Felix's "burning eye" crest. Most of them, anyway. A core group bore dark purple cloaks instead, a badge of honor for those who survived the conquering of Ahkestria. The pride that wafted off of them stung her ears something fierce, but even Evie had to admit, they looked sharp.

Damn Affinity is more trouble than it's worth, she groused. *Ugh. Reed's giving a speech.*

The Hand—Commander Reed, as the soldiers called him—spoke about journeys and sacrifice and...other things, probably. Evie stopped listening after the first few words. The man liked to hear himself talk. Instead, Evie climbed up onto the lip of the crow's nest and balanced precariously on the edge, staring out over Haarwatch.

This has been the most boring week of my life. Vess and Felix go off to wage a private war on some sea monster, and I get to bunk with a clutch of mages that stay up too late. Reading *of all things.* Evie scowled. At least she had plenty of time to keep refining her core space, as well as grow more acclimated to her new Skills.

Didn't quite hit full Adept Temper yet, though. I'd kill for a fight right now. A bit more practice, and I can push my Spirit over the edge, I know it—

The morning sunlight caught on something to the east, once, then again. Evie squinted, flaring her Perception for all it was worth. In the distance, just beyond the edges of the Sunrise Quarter...the flash of metal. Below, the gangplank dropped, but Evie didn't notice—all she could hear was the hammering of her heart.

"They're fightin'," she whispered, before pitching her powerful voice downwards. "They're fightin' at the Sunrise Gate!"

Soldiers were filing down the gangplank, streaming quickly off all five Manaships, but Harn and a few of the others were still there. They swiveled to follow Evie's frantic jabs.

"Burn me, they are," Atar said.

"You!" Reed shouted at a man in Haarwatch blue that was walking quickly toward their ships. "What's happening at the Sunrise Gate?"

The officious-looking man took several stuttering steps, his eyes wide before he collected himself. "I...am here to speak on that exactly: the Lady Haarwatch sent me to fetch all of you. If you would come with me."

Without waiting for their response, the man turned and reversed course toward the center of the air docks, where a large structure housed a sturdy guard house filled with blue-jacketed men and women. The whole thing was swarming with guards and the faint glimmer of inscriptions. Evie was impressed. The Manor was a damn sight more impressive than it had been when she left.

Harn grunted. "I'm goin', Reed. Keep the troops on standby; I have a feelin' we're gonna be goin' into the shit today."

"Better than standing here talking about it," the tall warrior agreed. Evie noticed his hand flex, like he wanted to grab that barn door he called a sword off his back. "I'll locate the rest of our soldiers as well."

"Doubtlessly at the Sunrise Gate," Zara said, practically floating in from the captain's cabin. She was resplendent in a gown of black and deep green, setting off her ochre skin brilliantly. "From what I can sense, they are fighting a pitched battle. Not yet desperate, but intense."

"All hands on deck then, I imagine," Alister said, his face a bit pale. "Shall we go see the Lady Haarwatch, then?"

"Indeed." Zara gestured to them all, along with twelve of those guards that always hung around Felix. Evie thought they called themselves the Shadows or something equally silly. "Captain Pxal and his crew will take care of the ships while we visit Calesca."

Evie groaned. She'd rather they head right to the fight. *But I should greet Callie. I guess.*

The little man in blue had waited for their party near the guardhouse. The moment the lot of them approached, he bowed and opened a wide set of doors, which led inward to a foul-smelling chamber. It was empty, filled only with hay and the sharp stench of excrement, but Evie spotted the reason for their passage.

"Are those...giant birds?" she asked.

Large, winged creatures stooped at the edge of a sudden drop. Men and women in blue hustled about, many of them fitting large saddles and harnesses to the birds, eliciting long, lazy screeches that echoed painfully off the stone interior. The birds were feathered brilliantly in blue and green and yellow, and had wide, bulbous beaks that looked more useful scooping up kelp than stabbing at prey. Crests of feathers surmounted their heads like colorful fans, opening and closing with every cinch and pull of the attendants.

"What is this?" Zara demanded. "I thought we were to meet with the Lady?"

"You are. The Lady Haarwatch is currently at the Sunrise Gate, directing the battle there."

Harn growled in annoyance. He singled out the Shadows. "You. Go find Commander Reed and tell him to change plans. Meet us as fast as they can at the Sunrise Gate."

"Aye, sir!"

As the Shadow sped off, Harn turned his harsh glare onto the unctuous official. "You could've said where we were goin' earlier."

The official swallowed, and Evie noticed a sudden flop sweat on the man. "Um, ah, the Lady did not wish for her current location to be bandied about. We have had a number of assassination attempts. I—I apologize for the inconvenience it may have caused you."

Harn frowned so hard Evie was certain she could hear his face crack. "Assassins? How many? Who was responsible?"

"That is all information for the Lady Haarwatch to pass on," the man insisted. "Please. Claim a mount from these Eiders, and I shall take you to her."

An ochre hand laid atop Harn's shoulder, gentle but with clear command. "Questions can wait for now. Let us move quickly to the battlefront."

Harn grunted.

<More Sworn?> she handsigned to the man.

<We'll see. If it is, I get to kill them this time.>

Evie smirked at the banked inferno within Harn's Spirit, a sound she didn't mind at all. The moment she heard the word assassinations, her core had gone into overdrive, and her hands ached to draw her chain.

"Mount up," Zara commanded.

Bright orange eyes regarded Evie as her group approached, most of them placid except for one or two. Those she could hear a squealing from their Spirits, like a tea kettle left on. It stabbed at her Mind, aggressive and unpleasant compared to Harn's clean anger. "Enough of that," she said, grabbing the reins. The Eider bucked its head, but she flared her Born Trait, borrowing the weight of the stone at her feet. The bird squawked in surprise, and before it recovered, Evie was already astride its back. "I'm in charge, see? In the saddle, holding the reins. You're listening to me now, yeah?"

The Eider bucked once more, but Evie held tight and grabbed clumsily at her Intent. That she meant no harm, that she was in charge. It was unfocused and weak, but Evie balled it up with her limited Willpower and shoved it at the bird. It squawked again—a low, upsetting noise—before falling silent and still.

You Have Gained A New Skill!

"Avet's teeth, what?" Evie cursed as a System notification blared into her senses.

Fauna Handling (Uncommon), Level 1!
You have proven your ability to wrangle and control fauna.
Minor increase in simple control over fauna per level.

"Evie? What's wrong?" Atar asked, fighting to stay upright on his own mount. His bird kept rustling its large wings. "You—are you alright?"

"Fine, fine...just learned a Skill, is all," she said, still a little flabbergasted. "Never learned a Skill so easy before."

"The Chant and Harmonics affords a greater understanding of this world," Zara said, wheeling about her own Eider with apparent ease. "I am impressed, Evie. You have kept up your training."

Their guide cleared his throat, his voice or perhaps the echoes strong enough to cut through their conversations. "Esteemed guests, please follow me."

Without another word, he and his mount fell from the ledge, diving into the open air like a damn fish. Evie watched with wide eyes. She had gotten used to Manaships, but this was something else entirely.

"C'mon. Let's go kill somethin'," Harn shouted, before he, too, dropped into the sky.

"That is...is this safe?" Atar asked.

"Safe is overrated." Evie kicked her heels, somehow knowing that was the best way to move the Eider. It clambered awkwardly toward the ledge and tipped over. Despite everything, her guts churned with fear. "Blind gods and burning, bloody ass!"

She and her dumb bird fell like a rock.

CHAPTER SIXTY-EIGHT

Fauna Handling is level 2!

The Eider snapped its wings open, catching the roaring winds between its absolutely ridiculous wingspan, and jerked upward as it caught an updraft. The cantle of the saddle jabbed Evie's middle as she was splayed out onto the Eider's back, her hands clutching desperately to the reins.

"Ouf!" she wheezed. The sheer force of their arrested descent had bypassed her impressive Body, forcing her own bodyweight against herself. "That'll leave a mark." The Eider flapped onward, eager to fly...but it was heading in the wrong direction. Evie sawed at her reins, Strength against Strength, as it squawked defiantly. "No, no! You're listening, remember?"

Fauna Handling is level 3!

Evie squeezed her legs, holding herself in the saddle as she once again balled up her simple Intent and shoved it down at the big bird. The Eider threw its big, horse-sized head, its noodle neck whipping to the side as it fought back...before it let out a harsh quack. The reins went a bit slack as it responded to her commands, pulling into a banking turn that brought her level with the rest of the team. The Eider flapped hard, catching up.

"Where'd you go?" Harn shouted over the wind.

Evie made a rude gesture, and the grizzled warrior laughed.

Something about flying as a group was easier, because Evie barely had to guide her dumb bird once they settled into formation. The official led the way, his mount draped with blue cloth bearing the image of a castle on a hill, while the others were arranged in a large V behind him, each on their own mount. Even the two Giants who were a part of the Fiend's Shadows were slung atop birds, though these were far, far larger and had huge beaks like water pitchers.

The city center vanished behind them all, the stepped levels of the richest merchants and nobles still somewhat bare. The old Eyrie tower had collapsed on them, when Evie and her friends had fought in the Domain, and they were among the first places that Callie stripped to build the Manor. Quite a few of the nobility had been pissed about that, but Callie didn't much care; Evie's heart felt full at the thought.

Just what those leeches deserved, she thought. Only a few nobles she'd met were worth the trouble to get to know, and one was on a giant duck twenty strides to her left. Alister was also looking back at the center of the city, his eyes fixed on one particularly empty stretch of town. *Shit. He had a family here, didn't he?*

Strains of spiraling melancholy drifted on the air, but Evie shoved it away. *Not now.* She glanced at Alister again, but he was staring forward now, and his face was carefully blank. The music pushed at her senses. *Blighted ass, not* now.

"Ho, look at that," Harn called out.

They'd approached the Sunrise Gate far faster than Evie had realized, and now she could see far more clearly over the fortifications. Beyond the wall, where there was normally a wide plain of grasses, was instead *filled* with enormous mushrooms.

"What? Where'd *those* come from?" she shouted back.

"Lamellans," Zara announced, and her face was grim. "They're mobile and tough, but their spores are far worse."

"Wait, wait. What are Lamellans?" Atar asked. A moment later, as their Eider all dove toward the Gate, he cursed as his Analyze got into range. "The *mushrooms*?"

"A common foe in this area. But rarely so numerous," Alister said.

Evie frowned as they lost sight of the monstrous horde, their mounts coming to a speedy landing. All of them grunted and groaned as the Eider's webbed feet slapped into the flagstone thoroughfare that had been cleared for such arrivals. Evie pulled on her reins, the big bird finally listening without issue.

All around them, Humans, Hobgoblins, Orcs, and others hustled about in blue uniforms and sturdy steel armor. Carts full of arrows were racing across the street just ahead, pulled by two sweating porters, joining a brace of similar carts atop a wide platform. Shouts and odd, meaty screams could be heard, emanating from over the wall itself.

Everyone was moving with purpose and speed, intense but measured. Evie winced. The pressure of emotions was too much for her to hold out against, and she was inundated with a mess of crashing cymbals and squalling strings. Magda had dragged her to an amphitheater once, and it had sounded very similar, just messier. Now though, Evie could pick out meaning from it all. Anxiety and excitement and fear and the sharp tang of bloodlust all wrapped around her, pushing against her skin like a physical pressure.

Eugh. She shoved it all down, reducing its noise if not muting it entirely. *Feel like I need a bath now.*

AFI +1!

Huh.

"So, what changed?" Atar asked. He wobbled a bit as he dismounted, but the mage barely needed his stave anymore. He still used it, though, bracing it against the flagstones as he stepped away from the colorful plumage. His new Body was almost as exotic as the Eider, especially his bright white hair and red eyes, drawing more than a few glances from the soldiers around them.

"The Hierocracy did."

Their guide and the Haarguard all around them came to a sharp salute before parting ahead of a small procession. A wiry man with a tall spear walked beside a woman in robes with short blonde hair and a man with dark skin and huge build. At the front of them all was a woman in blue-dyed leathers and a wide, dagger-sharp grin. Old friends. Kelgan, Portia, Bodie, and...

"Callie!" Evie shouted, leaving her mount in the hands of some young Beginner Tier.

"Evie." That smile grew a lot wider. Callie opened her arms just in time for Evie to crash headlong into them. "Oof, watch that chain, girl."

"Sorry," she mumbled into Callie's—her *sister's*—shoulder. Some of that melancholy song rose up again, and no matter how much Evie shut it out, she couldn't silence the sound. It took her too long to realize it was coming from her own Spirit. "Missed you."

Callie stroked her hair. "Me too, kiddo."

They just held each other a moment. Perhaps, if they'd been alone, they would have stayed that way a while, but eventually Evie coughed twice and stepped back. Behind her, Atar, Alister, Harn, and Zara were arrayed before the twelve Shadows. The two Giants among them stood out like sore thumbs, and more than a few of the Haarguard were glaring with hands on their weapons. Yet all of the Shadows stood proud, their purple cloaks stirring in the morning breeze.

"Zara, Harn. You've returned at last." Callie swept both of them in an embrace, perfunctory and lingering, respectively. "I had hoped you would make it in time."

"Did we?" Zara asked, eyebrow raised. "What of the fungal forest just outside your gates?"

Callie pushed a hand through her tawny hair. "Yes, well. Monsters alone won't breach these walls, and we've been sure to cut down any fungus that grows too high. The Hierocracy is clearly pushing the monsters ahead of them, but they are not a true threat."

"Lamellans are hearty beasts, and crafty, too. I would not underestimate them," Zara cautioned.

"We are aware. The far bigger threat are the spores that they release, but our mages and the wall itself have kept them at bay." Portia, the short-haired woman in the flowing robes said. "If they get into your lungs, they take root and are quite costly to remove. Impossible, if enough are breathed in."

"How do they handle fire? I—" Atar asked, and Evie felt a fierce heat from him before it vanished. Veins in his neck stood out, as if he were straining against something. "I can help, if fire is of use."

The dark-skinned Human let out a boisterous laugh. "They hate it! Well, they hate lightning, anyway. Not much of fire attunement around here, anymore."

"What Bodie means is that Felix's influence has most of our mages attuning to lightning," Kelgan explained, tucking his spear into the crook of an elbow. "We could always use some more ranged help. Can't get close-up, in case we breathe those blighted spores."

"That's why we're here," Evie said. "Right?"

"Right," Zara agreed. "Darius is on his way to us as well. We've brought some reinforcements from Ahkestria."

"Truly?" Callie shook her head. "No, no I believe you. Karys told me as much. It is just rather miraculous. Ahkestria might as well be across the world, and here you are, only a few weeks removed from its sun."

Evie shrugged. "Ain't nothin'. Killin' in the sand weren't much different than killin' in the forest." She paused, thinking. "Hotter, though."

"You got ranged attacks now, kid?" Kelgan asked, giving her a once-over. "You don't look much stronger."

"I'll dance circles around you, old man," she shot back, grin in her voice. "I'm practically Adept."

Kelgan tilted his helmet back, an odd conical thing, and scratched his forehead. "No kiddin'."

"Fighting alongside the Autarch has its benefits," Harn grunted. He reached out and grasped Kelgan's forearm. "Good to see you, spear-boy."

"You too, axe-face."

Greetings went around the group. Friends and allies meeting again after entirely too long apart. That warmth Evie had felt upon seeing Haarwatch had redoubled, a glowing coal just beneath her ribcage. It felt...nice.

"My, you've grown." Portia came up to her and embraced Evie before holding her out at arm's length. Her smile was wide and kind. "You've filled out a bit."

"Speak for yourself," Evie returned, gesturing to her belly. It had been hard to tell at first, but up close, her condition was all too obvious.

"Ah, can you tell already? I had hoped the robes would hide it better." Despite the complaint, Portia was positively beaming.

"How far along?" Evie asked, excited despite herself. She'd never seen a baby, not from someone she knew, anyway.

"Only a few months. Yan is beside himself."

Evie screwed up her face. Of course it was Yan's; the two had been thick as thieves, but not knowing had kept the inevitable mental image at bay. "Right. That's good, I figure."

Portia laughed. "I figure so, as well." She looked around. "Where is Vessilia?"

"Someone said somethin' about killin', right?" Evie cleared her throat and looked to Callie. She had no intention of talking about Vess, not then. "What're we standin' around here for?"

They rode up the wooden platform Evie had seen carrying all those arrows. It was empty now as their group piled on, and she gave a dubious glance at the waist-thick ropes and the sheer size of their team. Harn was a heavy man, but all of them, including the Frost Giants *and* Bodie? She was half convinced those cables would snap, or at least the big pulleys would fail, or the avum wouldn't even lift them.

Despite it all, they ascended. When the handler cracked a whip, the whole thing lurched upward like a primitive version of the crystalline lift in Ahkestria. It wobbled, requiring everyone to adjust their balance, but not even the Shadows were so low in Dexterity that they'd blunder off the sides. Still, Evie much preferred the silent and steady version in the Leviathan Depths. *Tch. They should make somethin' like that here. Bet Zara and the wonder boys could do it, given enough time. We got the crystals, anyway.*

The Sunrise Gate and its fortifications were way higher than Evie remembered it, half as high as the Wall to the west, and the lift wasn't moving very fast. They had plenty of time to stare at the red-gold metal as it passed by.

"Orichalcum," Alister said, his voice catching. He was drinking in the sight of the Sunrise Gate. "This costs several hundred gold per pound!" Alister was agog, but he kept his words quiet. "Where did they *find* it all?"

"Mines?" Atar said, uncertainly.

"The mines produce quality iron ore and some few others, but not this. Not for a very long time," Alister said. Something pinged in her memory, bouncing off an old conversation. She remembered his family was heavily invested in the mines.

Guess he'd know, she thought. Callie probably had an answer, but she was talking in quiet tones with Zara. "Eh, who cares so long as it's here and workin'?"

"Because...well, I—" Alister deflated a little. "I suppose it doesn't matter much, in the scheme of things."

Atar gave her a sharp look, made sharper by the wave of heat that accompanied it. A mote of something stabbed at her, not to harm, but it unfolded inside her Mind like a blossoming flower. Thoughts not her own came flitting outward in random patterns, accompanied by a burst of blistering heat that filled her Mind with a sizzling agony. *Alister's family...mines...his father's dream—*

be quiet, girl.

Evie flinched back. "Did you just shove your Intent at me?" Evie demanded, grabbing the white-haired idiot by the collar of his robes. She could barely see through the pain that still scorched away at her thoughts. Even her vision was stamped with the afterimage of some weird flame. "Did you?"

For his part, Atar looked as surprised as she was angry. "Ah, uh, I didn't—I didn't mean to—"

"Don't ever do that again." She let go of the mage and stalked away, just as the lift reached the top of the Sunrise wall. Evie quickly stomped off, weaving nimbly through the press of bow-wielding warriors and potion chugging mages. She didn't stop until the sounds of Atar's apologies had been drowned by the impact of arrows on meaty fungal flesh.

Stupid damn mage. She slipped up to the parapet, still cursing. *Stupid damn harmonics. Stupid damn—Noctis' tits, that's a lot of mushrooms.*

Spread out before her was the forest of huge mushrooms, their caps as big as houses and twice as tall. There was a gap between them and the wall, but it was narrowing as she watched. Spores floated on the wind, moving with apparent aimlessness, but wherever one of them landed, a new fungus would sprout. Soon after sprouting, they were taller than her, nearing a Frost Giant's height only heartbeats later. Arrows laced with flame and acid rained down on them in waves, splitting and sundering the disgusting things before they ever got tall enough to top the wall.

Where the fire and acid touched, no fungus grew.

Damn, a rain of acid sure would be nice right about now, Felix, Evie thought sourly. Maybe she *was* a little bitter at not being involved in their dumb fish hunt. *I'd be more use there than here.*

She didn't have any ranged attacks, not ones that could hit from such a distance. There was perhaps a hundred-stride gap between the wall and the fungal forest, a churned wasteland of mud that looked to be scorched with fire and sizzling acid. Pockets of it still bubbled, likely all that prevented the spores from taking root again. Sharpened pikes had been placed throughout the area, increasing as they came closer to the wall, likely to prevent charges. *Charges from what, though?*

Frenzied Vigilance is level 68!

Odd reverberations jumped out at Evie's vision, almost as loud as the notification she only half acknowledged. Her eyes felt...strange, burning but cold as Mana surged up from her core and into her head. The thick shadows among the fungal caps suddenly clarified, filling with stirring swirls of...something Evie couldn't identify. What she could tell, however, was that there were creatures moving out there.

"What are they?" she asked aloud.

To her side, someone apparently heard her. A young man shoved his sweat-slick hair back with a skeletally thin hand. "You see something?"

"Huh? Yeah, I do. There, under the eaves, like three hundred strides out." Evie pointed, and the Haarguard leaned forward, squinting.

"I don't see anything."

"Well, I ain't lyin'," she snapped back. "It's a big...mushroom man. And a bunch of tiny crawly things."

"You didn't learn Analyze?" he asked, incredulous. "All Haarguard are expected to—"

Evie waved him off. "I was busy that day. They're comin' closer."

"What?"

"Mushroom man and, oh, Twin's teeth," Evie said, grimacing. "Those're spiders. A lotta spiders."

A horn sounded somewhere down the line, soon picked up all over the wall, as the spiders burst from the canopy. They were the size of small avum and just as fast, scuttling over the muddy terrain with unerring strides. The Haarguard next to her shouted in alarm. "Spiders! Spider charge!"

Other shouts came as well, filling the air before being drowned out by the whine of Skill-laden arrows. The spiders were various shades of dull green and brown, almost impossible to see individually, but easy to hit due to their sheer numbers and the fog that only affected the intruders. The muddy field was covered in them, and they let out high-pitched shrieks as explosive arrows blasted them apart. When the first volley ended, another began, but it wasn't enough.

The spiders reached the wall.

"No you don't. Bindings of the White Waste!" Evie hurled Mana from her palms, skittering it down the surface of the wall with all the force she could muster. Chains of purple-white ice burst from where the wall and muddy field met, entangling dozens of the monsters in an instant. Most kept coming, but now their jagged legs stabbed and pierced their fellow spiders, killing many under the sheer weight. "Bindings of the White Waste!"

Binding of the White Waste is level 73!

More chains, again and again, lashed outward and trapped the spiders. Arrows and bolts of fire, lightning, and jaws of shadow tore into the restrained foes. She even got a few swipes in with her spiked chain, reaping a half dozen at a time with each careful swing. Sweet, sweet kill notifications filled her vision. The spiders weren't much before her powerful Skills, but even the largely Apprentice Tier Haarguard's volleys were making short work of them.

Not everywhere, though. Farther down the line, some of the creepy bastards had made it to the crenellations. Warriors jabbed spears and pikes with practiced motions, focused and only slightly panicked. Evie was impressed. She made a note to give Kelgan and Bodie less of a hard time when she saw them next.

"Lamellan Crofter!"

Those mushroom men, at least thirty of them, plodded out of the fungal forest, their beefy bodies stumping at a far slower pace behind the spider horde. Their heads were giant mushroom caps, wide and thick, shining darkly beneath it with swiveling eye stalks that made Evie want to throw up just looking at them. She didn't, though, because she was a professional.

"Why're they called crofters?" she asked, but that skinny man was hiding behind the parapet, both hands covering his mouth and nose. "What're you doing?"

"Get down!" he hissed, before covering his face again.

Evie looked back at the mushroom men, then down the line. Almost half of the Haarguard were covering their faces, and the rest were furiously firing arrows and spells at the lumbering Crofters. One of them fell, cut down by arrows and spells, but that left far too many still standing, and they raised their thick fists into the sky. Jets of gas shot out of their giant caps, streamers that speared across the battlefield, directly at the wall.

At her.

"AH!" Evie shouted, before stoppering up her mouth and nose and whirling her chain. The spores hit, but Evie spent the last of her breath to shout. "Reap the Maelstrom!"

Mana and Stamina fled in equal measure, fed into the spinning length of Evie's chain. Spores scattered, dragged into the path of her dancing weapon as a relentless current was stirred into being. She borrowed mass from the wall beneath her, feeding it into her Body and chain to multiply that force, lungs burning as she tried to banish the pressurized jet of foul fungal seed. Screams echoed down the line, but Evie couldn't spare the Perception it'd cost her to know what was going on; everything she had went into Reap the Maelstrom and keeping the spores from touching those around her. And it wasn't enough.

Evie fell as a fist the size of a battering ram hit the wall, setting the weakened stones to quivering just beneath her. Her concentration slipped, and her Born Trait dropped, sending mass right back into the wall and forcing her chain awry. Reap the Maelstrom still spun, but now the cone of wind she'd forged was gone...and the spores rushed toward them all.

"Incendiary Vortex!"

A cyclone of flames ripped through the spore cloud, igniting it, feeding it as it howled down the wall. The Lamellan Crofters nearest Evie were caught up in it, too, their fungal flesh turning to desiccated char within a heartbeat. If they could scream, she was sure they would have, as more cyclones manifested along the red-gold fortification, until the air was filled with only smoke and brutal, furnace heat.

"Are—are you okay?"

Evie looked up, and Atar hobbled through the smoke, a scarf draped across his face as his white hair shone in the firelight. He reached down for her, and she took his hand. "Yeah, I—"

Her gaze caught on the skinny Haarguard, who was curled into an agonizing position. Fungus grew atop his face, and he was very, very still.

"I was too late," Atar said, sadness and anger floating through his Spirit. "Cal said the Lamellans are being controlled by the Hierocracy somehow. I should have started with that damn spell instead of my Stars. I thought—I fucked up."

"Yeah. Me, too." Evie coughed. "You got more juice in you?"

Atar nodded, not taking his eyes off the fallen guard.

"Good. 'Cuz I wanna rip that forest apart," she spat.

"Let's **burn it all**," Atar snarled.

Evie couldn't tell whether the crimson glow in Atar's eyes was a reflection or whether she actually heard that strange whispering.

And frankly, she didn't care.

CHAPTER SIXTY-NINE

<<That's it. Breathe deep and slow, exhaling on the third count each time,>> Isla said. She gestured to her diaphragm. <<Breathe from your belly, from your core itself.>>

The heiress did so, pulling a deep draw of air through the Sunken Ward. Part of Isla marveled at that spell, though it was a simple enough working; the spell essentially generated sheathes of air Mana to circulate around and between targets that the boy chose. It was remarkable that Felix could maintain such a spell for so many and as long as he had, even on the two of them, who had retreated some three hundred strides from their cavern. Remarkable and terrifying.

To have such deep wells of Mana within him...how is it possible? Isla had long known that the Unbound were not subject to the same System-enforced restrictions as others. When the summoning was still a whisper among the Hierocracy, she and her sisters had delved into ancient records that hadn't been perused in centuries, digging up every fact, rumor, myth, and legend they could find. Among those living, Isla considered herself a premier scholar on all things Unbound...and she found herself stymied by them, time and time again.

<<Is this right, Lady Isla?>> the girl asked, eyes still closed as she breathed.

<<Yes, yes. You are breathing properly, but you must remember to maintain the flow of that breath down into your core space. A flexible, cleansing wind. Do you feel it?>>

<<I believe I do.>>

<<No.>> The Chanter swiped her hand through the water, sending ripples of force splashing into Vess. The girl gasped before blinking at

Isla in surprise. <<You cannot simply believe. You must know each step is completed with absolute certainty. To do less is to invite calamity that you will not survive. Do you understand?>>

Vess squared her shoulders and inclined her head—every span of her an echo of the duchess she would one day become. <<I understand.>>

<<Very good. From the top, then.>>

The heiress went back into it, beginning with the visualization exercises Isla had laid out. The process for Temper recomposition was not a simple one, and it was—at best—an extremely dangerous task. Luckily for the girl, Isla had specialized in healing for a very long time, and her expertise had led her down numerous experimental roads.

The Chanter supposed that there were others capable of guiding one through a Temper recomposition, but none of them were trustworthy. Exposing one's core space was both extremely personal and dangerous, after all.

Isla considered the girl once more, eyeing the flow of Mana through her channels and her deep, steady breathing. As dangerous as the process was, it required utter conviction in the subject. Without conviction, the endeavor would fail, and reconstituting her original Path would become impossible. Temper recomposition was exactly what it sounded like, reverting pieces of your Aspects to a previous state to reclaim where your formations went awry. Typically, it was done to back someone off an unwisely chosen Skill, a sort of extreme version of sundering a Skill. The difference from the frankly crude sundering process was that the Skill would not be lost, simply reverted.

Still, Vess' situation was unique. Her Skills did not evolve through her own actions, but that of another. A foreign Intent was tangled among her core space, visible to those with the senses to see, and it was unnerving to see how deep it had spread. This "Tier IV Link" that the girl bore was new and strange to the Chanter, but its effect was obvious. With every Skill level gained, Vess would be bound further to her new Path...and the Unbound boy as well.

Isla drove a sharp breath from her nose, irritation followed close by fascination. She had made a deal with Felix for information on his Earthly origins—truly a silly name for a land—but they had not yet had time to speak. With Zara unwilling to divulge his secrets, Isla had been forced to take matters into her own hands. She was still surprised that he had come to her for aid, but was pleased that he agreed to her request. Knowledge was what she needed most of all, and perhaps with more details, she would finally have a handle on the fledgling ruler's nature and motivations.

Understand, so that they might be managed. A light hand compared to the slavery of the Hierocracy. Isla steadied her breathing again. She could not risk the

Unbound turning against the Continent. Isla had spent too much time researching their histories to underestimate the danger they posed individually, let alone as a group. If the Unbound could not be corralled, they could prove to be just as devastating as the Ruin itself.

She already had Michael in hand when she first encountered Felix. The boy had listened to her, heeded her wisdom...but that, too, had changed. Now the child was following Felix around like a lost hound, aping the would-be king's training. Felix was even influencing Michael's Skills, teaching him brand new ones and pushing Michael into a punishing regimen. It had not missed Isla's attention that Michael was growing far faster in Felix's presence, too. Had he established a "Link" with the Autarch, as well? Michael denied it, but his rapid growth needed an explanation.

Or is it simply the strange aura that Felix seems to exude? The one that affected the fates of hundreds of his soldiers with his mere presence. Zara had downplayed the enormity of it when she'd spoken to Felix of the phenomena. It wasn't just rare for someone to unlock their Harmonic stats, it was nigh unto impossible, especially for those of such...simple origins.

Isla was not a pagewright, toiling in their towers with their numbers and their aborted attempts at the etheric arts. She was a Chanter, a Sorcerer. A healer steeped in the Grand Harmony. The Chant enhanced one's capabilities, whatever they were, offering a direct tapping into the greater mysteries of Creation. If what Felix was doing could be replicated...it would ignite a paradigm shift on the Continent. A handful of peasants with their Harmonic stats unlocked had the potential to overturn nations, if given the right guidance.

What would happen if there was an entire Territory of such people?

What could the Cantus Sodalus achieve, then?

Yet another reason to hold tight to these children. Felix cannot guide such a kingdom alone.

Ripples through the water all around them alerted Isla to Felix's approach only a heartbeat before he arrived in a burst of bubbles. He kicked into the room, passing through the narrow aperture of their ravine with enviable grace and speed. He came to an abrupt halt so as not to bowl them both over, but the pressure of his approach hit Isla and Vess like an invisible pillow the size of a wagon bed. The both of them braced but skidded backward an entire stride. Felix looked to the girl. <<Vess. Sorry. Are you—?>>

<<No. This is merely preparation,>> the girl said, and there was a coldness in her tone that Isla had not heard before. Not directed at the fledgling Autarch. That was interesting. Almost as interesting as the manner in which he was baring his Spirit, something he usually kept tight control over.

<<Oh.>> Relief was evident in his Spirit, but her show was over. Felix cleared his throat, and his Spirit was pulled tight and veiled once more. <<We're leaving in five minutes. Got a long way to go.>>

<<Of course. Isla, if you will excuse me?>> The girl stood up at Isla's gracious nod and swept back down the thin canyon, toward their group. She didn't even glance at Felix.

<<Five what?>> she asked.

He ignored the question. <<What have you said to her?>>

Isla raised an eyebrow. <<I have simply answered her questions.>>

<<And offered to break her Skills?>>

<<If she so wishes.>>

The young man turned to her, exasperation clear on his face if not his Spirit. <<And did you tell her the consequences of that?>>

<<She's not a fool, boy. She knows her own Mind, and Body, and Spirit. She is aware of the risks; I made sure of that.>>

<<Oh.>> He paused, clearly unsure what to do with the righteous anger she'd just cut short. Then the boy surprised her. <<Can you tell me how it works?>>

Isla stood. <<No, I cannot.>>

<<Why not?>>

There it was, the anger's return. Isla shook her head. <<This is not knowledge to be spread to all and sundry. It is dangerous.>>

Felix's nostrils flared, and she wouldn't have been surprised to see the water boil around him. <<That's my problem. I've partially sundered my own Skills before, and that left me a mess. You're not planning to do this now, in the middle of the enemy, right?>>

Isla picked up her satchel and slung it across her chest, making sure to carefully adjust her robes. She didn't answer.

<<What are the chances that she can't handle this? That changing things doesn't help at all, but just weakens her?>> he demanded.

<<It is a procedure I have done before, with a perfect track record of success. You needn't know anything else.>>

Isla kicked forward, floating across the narrow ravine toward the exit. Felix interposed himself, hand out. <<No. That's not enough. You're interfering with one of my team. I need to know what to expect. Now.>>

The Chanter pursed her mouth. <<I am doing what is best for the heiress, Felix. If you wish to know more? Ask her yourself.>>

She swept past him, moving through the water like a fish by virtue of Skill and stat. Felix did not stop her, though Isla could sense he wanted to; that frustrated rage had pushed against the boundary of his control, and it was clear he wanted to make use of it. Yet he didn't.

Good, she thought as the ravine closed around her. *That boy needs to learn to heel.*

Pit swam up to him the moment Felix returned to the group. *What's going on? You're angry.*

Felix patted his friend atop his metal barding, the sound of scales on metal dull in the water. *I'm fine. Just an argument.*

His Companion gave him a long, disbelieving look but didn't pry. *Are we leaving now?*

Immediately.

The War Naga were up and about, their bulky Bodies twisting in the waves in what looked like warmup exercises. Pit advised him that they were still a bit tired, but more than ready for the trip ahead. Felix quickly got everyone organized on their respective Nagas, weaving more saddles out of plants so that everyone could sit securely. Other than Beef and Hallow, there was little conversation going on beside affirming grunts.

When everything was set, Felix turned to the leader of their guides. <<Toa'ut. Where to next?>>

The massive War Naga pointed up and out of the gorge they'd hidden within. <<The Fathom resides in that direction. Within the heart of Khasma.>>

<<Khasma. What can we expect?>> Vess asked. She didn't meet Felix's quick glance. <<What is the terrain? Do the spawn have a heavy presence there? Are there more Dens or Nests?>>

<<The terrain is as you see, but the gorges deepen and widen until the very bottom of the lake falls into endless darkness,>> Toa'ut said.

Cheery, Pit muttered.

<<The Fathom spawn...it is unknown. Few of our patrols have reached beyond the Mountains That Howl, and those that tried never returned. Prior to the flooding and the Fathom's sudden surge, Khasma was the primary area where our forces would meet. Fathom spawn abounded. I can only imagine it has grown far worse.>>

<<Alright. Then we're heading into the real enemy territory now,>> Felix said. <<But time is of the essence. We are going to move fast and hit hard. Mount up.>>

The Naga were by far the better swimmers than the majority of his team, and riding atop the serpentine warriors had been their own idea to speed up their journey. Now that they were out of the vortexes, and he no longer needed to maintain an array, Felix had no intention of riding as the rest. As the others strapped themselves down to the serpentine backs, Felix kicked off, just behind Toa'ut so the guy could lead the way.

They skimmed the tops of the ravines, high enough that they could spot approaching threats but low enough that a quick dive into the greenery was possible. It was long and boring and filled with several false alarms, leading to them hiding for several minutes from what amounted to a very large fish. At the very least, however, it afforded Felix time to think.

Skill Arrays. That had been the topic he'd focused upon. If he could get strong enough, combine enough Skills, then he could take on the Fathom directly. He was slowly coming to terms with the fact that he couldn't stop Vess from altering her core, but he could try to keep her from hurting herself needlessly. With one Skill array down, Felix plotted out his next.

As the hours passed, the way ahead deepened. The greenery spread as the trenches widened and dropped, the water around them growing murkier with every mile. The walls of the ravines thinned, but in some cases they rose higher, until they formed spires of improbable, water-smoothed shapes.

Often, plant life would festoon these spires, turning them into flags of fronds that whipped in the direction of the shifting currents, and provided food for a bevy of smaller creatures. Fish, crustaceans, mollusk-looking things, and more filled the trenches and the waters near the spires. If nothing else, they were an excellent cover for the team's approach. Which was needed, because as the fifth hour passed, Toa'ut informed them they had finally reached the true outskirts of Khasma.

It was swarming with pockets of Fathom spawn.

Schools of Hatchlings and Amphitere swarmed through the waters. Many of them chased the silver glitter of prey, and others swam in wide, convoluted paths that the War Naga identified as a patrol. They had immediately hid upon seeing the first group, and Toa'ut informed them that moving would be slower going. Too fast, too careless, and they'd get spotted and bring down a whole swarm.

<<No,>> Felix said. They were in distinct pockets, moving in groups of only two dozen or so, which made things a bit easier.

Green Shaping!

Soundlessly, the patrol was immediately caught up in nets of knotted tangleweed. Felix pulled back, altering the Intent he threaded through his Affinity as his Resonance shook across his Skills. The tangleweed dropped, shaped back toward their group, until the still-alive spawn thrashed before his team. The spawns' mouths were bound with sharp nettles, screams and bugles of alarm throttled as they trembled with restrained madness and fury.

<<We do this carefully, with precision, but I'm tired of sneaking around. The Fathom knows we're somewhere close by, but the less spawn he has the better. We all need to be stronger.>>

Rime Shaping!

Felix gestured, his Intent now woven through a second Skill. Spears of ice flash froze the restrained monsters, stabbing through each of their chests with a sudden, terrible finality.

You Have Killed A Fathom Hatchling (x13)!
You Have Killed A Fathom Amphitere (x13)!
XP Earned!

<<We need to grind.>>

CHAPTER SEVENTY

The Hatchlings roamed over the edge of Khasma, prowling the currents that roiled around the Wedges. The massive, rocky protrusions were how they marked their positions, their wide eyes fixed on the water as well as the fronds that rippled like delicious eels off the stone. Those not mounted atop the serpentine Amphitere, the lowest, molting Drudges among them, burst forward as they closed with a Wedge. Fish and crustaceans scattered, but they were not fast enough to dodge the spindly claws of the Drudges and were soon speared through and brought back to the mounted spawn on rapid flippers.

Hunt.

The leader, a dark-scaled Broodviper, stared at the Drudges as they returned with the swarm's feast. The moment one was within range, it stabbed one of its two tridents outward, spearing the Ironside Crab from the Drudge's dull fist. "*MINE,*" it burbled, before the words were eaten—along with the crab—with a tremendous chomp. The Drudge kicked away, its eagerness cowed, as the Broodviper intended.

Dominate.

The rest of the riders feasted, stealing the bounty from the Drudges while leaving only floating scraps for their wriggling mounts. The Broodviper cared little for the Drudges or even the other, brighter-scaled Hatchlings in the swarm. While they bore the scales of their betters, the Hatchlings were not blessed with the majesty of true power. It only cared for its liege, and for the bundle of instincts that drove the Broodviper to lead the swarm.

Patrol. Hunt. Dominate. Kill those that approach.

The Broodviper knew that it had once been weaker, that it had

Evolved through their liege's magic, but thought was a dim shadow. It felt a burning Need to obey its instincts, its capacity for malevolent violence only tempered by its liege's Will. The Broodviper wished to stop, to strip the Wedge bare and suck the life from the very stone...but it bugled to the swarm. They advanced as one.

Patrol.

They moved as one, their many Needs blurring into a singular whole, and the dark trenches spread out around them. Eyes wide, they watched in every direction. At the front, a large Pyroclastic Shrimp tore through the water, bolting backward, and six tridents thrust forward. Lightning blasted the creature to bits.

A dark pleasure coursed through the Broodviper's limbs, and its Drakin twisted in savage glee beneath it. It was good to follow its Need. The pleasure, the food, all of it was a spur that drove them onward. "Forward. Patrol," it ordered.

"Patrol," the swarm repeated, their voices barely able to fit around the word. "Patrol."

Their Need had them in its grasp, as it always did...and the Broodviper did not see the spear until it was too late.

"*Heurk,*" it managed, before incredible pressure burst from within it, and its frustrated Need was the last thing it felt as the waters turned to inky black.

Hu-unt...

The others took to Felix's plan fairly well, and each patrol of Fathom spawn died by a cavalcade of chitinous spikes, conjured spears, icy spears, crystalline darts, and lances of water. The last was from the War Naga, who, aside from their prodigious Strength for their Tier, had the ability to shape water Mana into wide bolts that increased their range. The bolts couldn't be thrown and were manifested in the Nagas' hands, but the warriors were so fast at swimming that it was a moot point.

The patrols were utterly destroyed in moments, every time.

It was great, though Felix was slightly worried they'd run out of enemies. It was a silly fear, as each new trench brought new groups into Felix's senses, and he would lead their team forward at a rapid pace while holding Abyssal Skein around them all. Ambush after ambush, silent and undetected, save for the brief flashes of their Skills, their Skills began to grow.

Abyssal Skein is level 71!

...

Abyssal Skein is level 73!

After the twentieth patrol, Felix began changing tactics. He would open up a restraining salvo, knotting them in Green Shaped weeds or bands of solid ice or simply lashed them with his split Shadow Whips until they were easy pickings for the team. Hammer blows, spear thrusts, talons and crystal darts would hit almost all of them, and as they drew closer to the center of Khasma, the patrols grew in level and durability. Soon, a quick ambush wasn't enough to eliminate an entire patrol, requiring Felix to hold them all the tighter as they squirmed with a wild, aggressive madness. Sometimes, he ripped through the monsters himself, his patience for his team's Skills growing thin.

His ice, rigid wooden spears, and even thin needles of light were enough to end them all, time and again.

Rime Shaping is level 67!
...
Rime Shaping is level 69!

Green Shaping is level 66!
...
Green Shaping is level 69!

Auroral Forge is level 30!
...
Auroral Forge is level 35!

His team was far more ungainly in the water than the land, especially Beef and the Homunculus. Thankfully, the Multipede was adept at maneuvering through the water, and both chitin spikes and crystalline darts had a decent range on them. The teen was also using Hallow Raise to bolster their numbers, and soon they were trailing a long line of half-rotting Fathom spawn. They weren't as fast, which necessitated them to ride atop the War Naga like a bunch of gross zombie-troopers, but it worked. Their claws were sharp enough to deal with their brethren, and there was little need for Agility when Felix held them all for the slaughter.

At least it helped him workout his Void Skill.

Abyssal Skein is level 74!

Vess fought well. Her training in the water showed as she all but flew through the water, each kick and thrust assisted by the conjured silver spears that hovered just below her feet, like tiny platforms. Felix noticed that she never used her other Skills, relying almost entirely on basic movements and her Spear of Tribulation to maneuver and kill the

Fathom spawn. He had no doubt it involved her Temper recomposition, but Isla refused to answer his questions even when he choked down his pride and asked a little more nicely. He tried to ignore them after that.

Felix soon found the patrols growing larger and larger, until the deep undersea canyons were flush with Hatchlings, Amphitere, Broodvipers, and Drakin. Pods of Dractopi swam past them, nearly brushing the edge of his Abyssal Skein. In the murky distance, Felix even sensed larger creatures, things that rivaled the Depthwurms in sheer size. These were creatures that were beyond his team's ability to easily dispatch...but Felix didn't intend to slow down.

Fight? Pit asked across their bond.

Oh you know it, bud. <<Stay here,>> he ordered aloud.

<<Felix?>>

<<Boy!>>

Ignoring their protests, Felix and Pit both kicked off a Cloudstep, in perfect tandem. Abyssal Skein followed, leaving his team huddled beneath an outcropping as another pod of Dractopi headed their way. Felix and Pit met it, fist and claw first, tearing through one then the other, while spears of silent, frozen lightning embedded themselves in the other six. The Draktopi twisted their eel-like bodies while their goopy, ooze-formed limbs paddled at the water in alarm. Crocodilian maws opened wide, primed to release a bellowing cry into the depths...and were immediately filled with molded blocks of ice. They gagged, writhing in pain and fear, only to have their target among them.

Brimming with acidic Mana.

Rain of Cataclysm!

Some of his Skills worked differently underwater, mostly by nature of physics and the Mana itself. Rain of Cataclysm, which normally produced clouds of acid Mana that rained upon a large area, instead spread out from Felix like a fog bank. The dark water was stained a virulent green as the potent magic flooded outward, enveloping every single Draktopi in an instant. They were strong, durable, higher-leveled than the creatures he had faced in the Leviathan Depths...but their hide was no match for the potency of Felix's magic. When the fog bank cleared, there weren't even bones left over.

You Have Killed A Draktopus (x8)!
XP Earned!

Rain of Cataclysm is level 73!

Pit chirruped, happy at the influx of experience. <<Just a little more, and I level.>>

Felix nodded. <<Let's get after it, then.>>

The two of them ranged ahead, Abyssal Skein singing its dark chorus over their forms as they hunted the Fathom spawn. Felix had intended on simply clearing the way for his team, and they did follow at a discrete distance—but with each successive grouping of monsters, Felix found new reasons to keep going. Keep pushing toward that next Skill, that next level.

Your Companion Pit Has Gained 1 Level!
He Is Now Level 70!
+10 to STR, +9 to PER, +4 to VIT, +11 to END, +7 to INT, +10 to WIL, +20 to AGL, +20 to DEX Per Level!
+10 to AFI, RES, REI Per Level!

Pit's level up notification came and went, yet neither of them slowed down. Pit's magic belt had him swimming better than a dolphin, while Felix's Relentless Resolution was just as tireless beneath the waves as above them. Shadow Whips, poisonous flames, conjured vines, weapons of ice, and arrows of blue-gold light all were summoned and expended upon the hordes they conquered. With each swarm, the Fathom spawn grew more cautious, more fearful. Felix could hear it in the water, a modulated whine among the placid, basso tones all around them. Spirits strained by that foul, noxious ooze were leaking fear into the world like a punctured oil pan, slick and telling.

Still, Felix didn't stop. His primary concern was to get strong enough to handle the Fathom itself. He had a vague grasp of its strength from their aborted connection, and it was crazy powerful. Yet it had only been a glimpse between moments, and Felix did not entirely trust the impression. If the Fathom were a Tidaldrake, as Vess assumed, it would have been at least hundreds of years old to have escaped the extinction of its fellows. A creature so old would surely have gathered a remarkable amount of Skill levels and stats.

Some time later, Felix took a ragged breath, scaled hands coated in dark ichor that just wouldn't wash away. The remnants of another patrol was around them, with Pit tearing through the last Amphitere with a beak that crackled with captured lightning. They had managed to corner this group between the narrow walls of another greenery-filled trench, well out of sight of any passing swarms, but still Felix signaled Pit to disengage his Mantle of Tumult.

Pit's Bloody Gnaw is level 75!
Adept Tier!
He Gains:
+7 VIT
+7 AGL

+7 STR

Pit's Hurricane Rasp is level 75!
Adept Tier!
He Gains:
+7 DEX
+7 AGL
+7 STR

Pit's Etheric Concordance is level 84!
Pit's Tempest Fugit is level 78!

Pit's Mantle of Tumult is level 75!
Adept Tier!
He Gains:
+10 WIL
+10 END
+10 STR

Pit's Thunderwing is level 71!

The distant song of the System thundered through his Companion, sending brief, paralyzing paroxysms across Pit's frame, yet it was over quickly. Such gains barely phased the two of them now. In fact, Felix took the moment to check out his own growth in the hours since beginning their embattled advance.

Dodge is level 74!
Blind Fighting is level 68!

Corrosive Strike is level 75!
Adept Tier!
You Gain:
+10 STR
+10 END
+10 PER

Wild Threnody is level 81!
Armored Skin is level 81!
Relentless Resolution is level 86!
Manifestation of the Coronach is level 72!
Voracious Eye is level 82!
Dual Casting is level 71!
Etheric Concordance is level 84!

Abyssal Skein is level 75!
Adept Tier!
You Gain:
+10 PER
+10 EVA
+10 FEL

Cloudstep is level 66!
Rime Shaping is level 72!
Green Shaping is level 71!
Auroral Forge is level 47!

Sunken Ward is level 32!
Apprentice Tier!
You Gain:
+5 WIL
+5 INT
+5 END

Mantle of the Infinite Revolution is level 55!
Arrow of Perdition is level 49!

Quest Complete!
The Proving!
Advance Five Spells To Adept Tier!
You have proven yourself as an Adept Magus!

You Gain The Following:
Title: Adept Magus (Rare)
You have shown you can rise above your peers, becoming a true force upon the Continent. Power is yours. Wield it well.
+Increased Authority

...Rewards Increased Due to Advancing 2 Spells of Legendary Rarity
...Rewards Increased Due to Advancing 1 Spell of Transcendent Rarity
Accessing Options...

Please See Your Stronghold Seal To Receive Rewards!

Felix grunted. That Quest had been hanging open for months, and now that he'd completed it, he couldn't claim any reward until he got back home. *Couldn't give me an edge against the Fathom, huh? Figures.*

It wasn't that he was unhappy with his Skill levels or even stat gains, but none of his Skills had pushed into an evolution by themselves. There was growth everywhere, but it didn't feel like enough.

Chthonic Tribute!

The remains of the Fathom spawn reversed course, no longer spreading in dark clouds of viscera but tightening and thickening into a gaseous slurry before pouring into Felix's open maw. Essence and new Mana flooded him, refilling the steadily depleting stores inside his cavernous core space, and fueling the surge of his Sovereign of Flesh.

The Skill amplified his healing, allowing all the cuts and scrapes across his Tempered Body to revert to unblemished flesh. The Fathom spawn continued to get stronger the closer to the center of Khasma they traveled, and now the Broodvipers and Drakin were the predominant enemies. They had wicked claws and jaws that could penetrate his skin, even if just a little bit.

Can we do this? he wondered. Felix had fought down the shadow of two Primordials, weaseled out from under the gods, and he'd sucker punched an already weakened Grandmaster. The only true challenge that he'd taken head on—and succeeded at—was the Archon. If the Fathom was as strong as a Primordial, they were likely done for, but he doubted that was the case. Otherwise, the Naga would be smears of blood across the collapsed ruin of Haestus Temple. No. The Fathom was likely around the Grandmaster Tier, and Felix was all out of tricks.

We can, Pit affirmed, his feathers ruffling and his silver-scaled fish tail waggling. *Or we can run.* Felix gave his friend a sharp, accusatory look, but Pit only shrugged his fox-like shoulders. *It's an option.*

It isn't. Not if we're going to live up to our end of the Quest. Felix sighed. *Where are—ah.* He sensed his team now, perhaps a hundred yards away and advancing on their spot at speed. Felix squared his shoulders. *We should keep—*

Felix's gaze alighted on one of the stone spires, a sight that had become basically background noise to him by that point. Yet, among the normal proliferation of greenery and clustered life, the stone had.... <<Pit? Does that look like—>>

<<Oh. Yes.>> Pit tilted his head, quizzically. <<Why?>>

Felix didn't know.

Why *would* there be a carved metal door there?

CHAPTER SEVENTY-ONE

Felix swam forward, Pit at his heels, but they only made it as far as the edge of the ravine before his team finally caught up with them.

<<My Lord, you have stopped your glorious slaughter. Is something wrong?>> Toa'ut asked, arriving first with twin tridents held in his meaty fists. He and the other Naga were breathing heavily, the gills at the sides of their scaled necks fluttering with each heave of their beefy torsos. <<Are you injured?>>

He said the last with hesitation, as if he could barely express such a thought. Felix shook his head, amused. <<No. But—>>

<<Felix Nevarre!>> Isla hissed, sliding off of Lavix's back and ripping through the Green Shaped vines of her saddle in the process. <<How dare you plow ahead! We could barely keep up, not to mention all of the monsters you left alive in your wake! We had to spend more and more time subduing them before they could call for aid!>>

<<That was the point,>> Pit said, swimming in a circle around the chanter. His magical fish tail lashed the water into near-invisible currents that buffeted them all. <<We were helping!>> he added, cheerfully.

Isla scoffed. <<Helping?>>

<<I am stronger than all of you, with the possible exception of yourself, Isla,>> Felix said. He didn't quite believe that, but the woman was deceptive and clever; Felix didn't doubt that she had tricks to try and bring him down. <<I cannot grow if all I am doing is helping everyone else. This was my best solution.>>

<<Small fries for us, huh?>> Beef asked. He, more than anyone, looked exhausted. His huge shoulders were drooping as he treaded

water, requiring Hallow's Multipede form to prop him up from beneath. <<You underestimating us?>>

Felix clapped the teen on the arm. <<Never. If you're up for more, I'm happy to have you fight at my side, man.>>

The Minotaur perked up at that, and his big, bovine eyes widened. <<You mean it?>>

<<Of course I do.>> Felix let his gaze pass around them all. <<I would have any of you at my side...but the enemies are growing stronger with every new swarm we encounter. These last ones were nastier and even managed to drop my Health a bit.>> He followed Vess' gaze, which was fixed on his unmarked skin with a raised eyebrow. <<I heal fast. But all of you don't, and unless you're willing to waste all of our limited Health Potions, it's easier for you to follow in my wake.>>

<<But you are uninjured?>> Vess asked, her eyes lifting from his torn shirt and jacket to his face. His eyes.

Felix nodded. <<I am...Are you?>>

<<I am perfectly fine, Felix.>>

<<Good.>>

<<Yes. Good.>>

<<Boring,>> Pit warbled in annoyance as he swam in a tight circle around the group. <<Look! We found a tower.>>

Everyone turned their attention to the stone monolith, but Isla swam closer to Felix, her skirts swirling about her legs like diaphanous clouds. <<You should have told us what you were planning, boy.>>

<<Not having all the information grates, doesn't it?>> he asked, leaving his tone low and his Spirit carefully bottled up.

She snapped her mouth shut, lips thinning and jaw clenching as if chewing over what she wanted to say. Yet she said nothing, merely pushing past Felix with another swish of her skirts.

Felix was being petty; he could admit that. Admitting it didn't mean he regretted it, though.

He swam after his team, all of them careful to stay within the deeper shadows of the ravine, where the increasing patrols couldn't spot them so easily. The big stone tower-thing was above and ahead of them, rising up into the open plains above the greenery-strewn chasms.

It was very similar to the hundreds they had already passed, festooned with weeds, algae, and a thriving colony of coral. The one difference was a suspicious recess at its base. This may not have been telling to most, but to Felix's Perception, it was a red flag he couldn't miss. Among the wild fronds, crimson algae, and vibrant anemones clinging to the base of the structure, he could spot the tell-tale signs of carved metal.

Careful to stick close to the cover of the fronds and weeds, Felix swam past everyone with a few swift kicks and stopped right before the recess.

Green Shaping.

He summoned his Skill, once more refusing to rely on the System itself and plying it with his Affinity and Intent. Using the Chant to access his Skills was the task Zara had put to him so many months ago, and Felix was finally approaching a point where it was almost instinctual.

Golden green Mana poured from his palms, bathing the overgrown recess in front of him and taking root. A flex of his Willpower sent all of the plant life cascading outward, not dying or wilting, but rapidly growing *away* from the metallic door beneath. In seconds, an eight-foot-tall doorway made of carved silver was revealed, glimmering dully in the faint light around them.

<<Huh.>> Felix ran his hand across the surface, his short talons clicking against grooves and whorls. Someone had carved the door into beautiful, swirling designs that were dotted with finned shapes and serpentine creatures. There was no handle or latch, no hinges or any apparent way to open the door. <<Someone clearly built this thing.>>

<<But who?>> Vess asked, looking up. The rest of the stone monolith was covered in algae and rippling weeds, offering nothing to her sight. <<Who would build something at the dark bottom of these lakes?>>

<<Someone not much bigger than us,>> Beef said. When Isla and Felix looked at him in surprise, he all but blushed. <<What? If they were smaller or bigger, why make the doorway this size?>>

<<No, no, that's good reasoning,>> Felix said. <<Good job.>> This time, the Minotaur *did* blush, a darkening just around his eyes and snout. For the kid's benefit, Felix pretended not to notice.

<<It is likely the tower, if that's what it is, fell from above. Perhaps in the same event that sank Haestus Temple,>> Isla suggested.

<<That would make sense,>> Vess agreed. <<Are we aware of what caused such a thing?>>

Isla was studying the door as she answered. <<I am not, but I doubt it matters. The past is strewn with great battles and terrible, natural disasters that have shaken the Continent many times. It would not surprise me if this was a result of something like that.>>

<<I want to know more, though. So...>> Felix placed his hands against the door, placing himself directly in front of Isla's view. She scowled at him, but he was getting pretty good at ignoring her, too. The door didn't have a handle, so Felix was ready to heave the whole thing open with sheer Strength.

A buzzing deep within his chest halted him.

Before he could even think the words "heart attack," a notification leaped into his vision, startling him with the sound of a loud, tolling bell.

Authority Recognized!
Seal Breached!
Inheritor, Autarch Of Nagast, King Of Ahkestria, Lord Of The Leviathan Depths, Be Welcome!

The door before them split in half, releasing a riot of bubbles in all directions as the tarnished silver opened on hidden hinges. Around them, the deep water of the lake surged inward, pulled by an inexorable suction that very nearly yanked Felix off his feet. Instead, he slammed his hands into the six-foot wide doorway and planted himself, grunting as he felt Beef, Hallow, Pit, and all the rest slam into his back.

<<Felix!>> Beef hollered in his ear, and Felix only had an instant before every single War Naga came barreling toward them. They were going to be crushed.

Felix let go.

The lot of them plunged inward, a tangle of limbs, claws, and serpentine tails that rolled through the rushing waters. Inky darkness filled the chamber beyond, and before Felix's Perceptions could expand beyond the chaos of his tumbling team, a series of brilliant, golden lights flared into being.

Detecting Authority Bearer...
Manalights Ignited.
Do You Wish To Seal The Door Of Waves?

Yes!

With a boom that vibrated his bones, the silver doors slammed shut once more. Felix whipped around, watching traceries of Mana zip up from the silver lintel and into the flat ceiling, where it split, tracing the outlines of a thousand tiny, four-pointed stars before it hit a wide, circular depression in the ceiling. The Mana filled the depression before flashing a brighter shade of blue, the color of force, and suddenly the water around them went utterly still. Each of his friends slowly righted themselves in the ten feet or so of water that filled the very wide room.

"What the hell is happening?" Beef shouted, water dripping from his suddenly sodden fur. "Did you drop Sunken Ward, Felix?"

"I did." Felix looked around them, tracking more Mana as it flourished all around them. "We won't need it in here. Look."

"Air Mana," Vess said, breathing deeply. "Far more than your Ward generates."

"All of that air Mana was pouring out into the lake, too. Something might have spotted it," Isla pointed out. "Opening this place was a mistake."

Door Of Waves Sealed.
Cleansing In Process.

"Brace," Felix warned, moments before a pulse of force emanated from the circular depression above them. All of them winced as a shock-wave hit them all like a dense mattress to the face, forcing Vess, Beef, Pit, and both Hallows down into the water. The Naga flinched, but their Bodies stayed afloat, while Isla and Felix ignored the blast completely. More of that light blue Mana raced outward, along the carved stars and down into dozens of discrete points below the water line. Felix spun in place, splashing, as he tracked what they were doing. "It's draining the room!"

It was fast, too, because the chamber—that Felix estimated at around two hundred feet in diameter—was soon empty. Small grates had opened up at the base of flaking buttresses, shimmering with the same force Mana that had activated them, but pulling instead of pushing. Felix walked over to one, squatting to watch it work, and marveled at the design.

Sigils are hidden in the walls, he noticed, flaring his Manasight so that the dense fabric of stone turned at least somewhat transparent. He could make out some of the formation, but certainly not all of it. *A lot of it follows the pipeworks extending down from here.* Force *and* water *are here, but so is* earth, *forming the secondary sigil of* mud. The sodden silt and debris was sucked up along with the last vestiges of puddles in the chamber. *Damn. This is efficient. It doesn't feel like it used a lot of Mana at all.*

"Wonders of the ancients," a voice said from beside him. Felix glanced up to see Lavix looming over him, but her blunt face was tilted upward, toward the stars. They were still faintly glowing, but that was fading quickly. "Another temple of the gods, my Lord. The mighty Nym."

"Maybe," he said, standing up as he rubbed his dirty hands against his trousers. He put a hand on his hooked sword and focused his Intent upon the first glyph in its blade, the one that siphoned power from Nymean Temples. Yet it didn't buzz or flare with light at all, not like it had in the presence of previous Temples. "But I don't think so."

"Then who?" Toa'ut asked, his scales rasping against the now-dry stones. Most of his team had drawn closer, though Isla and Beef were poking at different ends of the room. "Who would dare copy the gods?"

"Who indeed," Isla remarked, loudly enough that her voice carried perfectly. She eyed the ceiling before humming a few notes. The sound thrummed across the chamber, a pitch perfect cascade that was as clear as any bell. "Whoever built this place knew what they were about. The acoustics are impeccable."

"Does that affect the Chant, Lady Isla?" Vess asked.

Isla crouched and ran her hands across the smooth, seamless stone flooring. "Everything affects the Chant, as it is the key that unlocks the mysteries of Creation." She looked up, sharply. "Felix. Do you hear that? Chords keep pressing through the Harmony of this place."

"I hear them." Felix gestured, and another large notification appeared, blue bordered by gold. He spun it so that it was suddenly visible to his entire team. "It seems this place respects my Authority."

Cleansing Complete.
Do You Wish To Open The Door Of Green, Autarch?

"Whoa," Beef whispered. "The building is talking to you?"

Pit puffed up his chest. "My Companion is very talented."

"Michael is very strong, too," Hallow said, both of her Bodies clinging close to the sopping wet Minotaur. "And tough."

Pit nodded solemnly. "He is."

Felix smiled at the three of them and caught Vess doing the same. Her smile stuttered, fading. Felix cleared his throat. "Whatever this place is, we should check it out, at least for a short time. Then we can get back on the path toward the Fathom's home."

Toa'ut bowed his head, and the rest of the War Naga followed suit. "If you wish, my Lord."

"Open the Door of Green," Felix commanded. At the far end of the chamber, opposite the Door of Waves, the Door of Green stood twice as tall at sixteen feet high. Sigils flashed in a strange, rapid combination across its surface before opening right down the middle with a drawn-out hiss. It, too, was made of metal, but this one was tinted an emerald color and carved with lifelike renditions of tangleweed, algae, and those orb-like light plants.

"Door of Green?" Pit asked.

"I dunno." Felix shrugged. "The other one was the Door of Waves. Why name them at all?"

"Strange. Wait here." He trotted through the door, ears perked forward and golden eyes wide. "It's just a hallway." Pit sniffed. "Smells bad."

The team followed, Naga and Multipede included. Luckily, the hallway beyond the Door of Green was huge, at least thirty feet wide with ceilings twice that in height. More seamless stone covered the floor and walls, all made of pink stone lightly marbled with white. The ceiling was patterned with groin vaults, pockets of archways supported by rows of thin, rounded pillars along the length of the corridor. Light was everywhere, burning from sconces that looked nothing like the Manalamps Felix had seen in Zara's old mansion. The pillars themselves glowed with a subdued, faintly blue-green light that called to mind the waters they had just left.

"Thematic lighting," Beef said. He was leaving a trail of water and plant debris with every clopping step he took. "Neat."

"The hall stretches in two directions," Felix said.

"So I noticed," Isla muttered.

Felix ignored her. He was getting very good at it. "So, we're just going to pick a direction." He squinted into the distance. "I can't see the end of the corridor. That can't be right."

"I...hrm," Isla planted her hands on her hips. "I cannot see the end, either. What is this?"

Just as the words left her mouth, a thick fog rolled through the hallway, rising from the floor itself. It spread, fast, until everything was covered in thick, impenetrable mist. Felix flared his Perception as best he could, but it was like running directly into a stone wall, as if nothing existed beyond the haze at all.

"Damn it," Felix muttered.

CHAPTER SEVENTY-TWO

"What the hell is all this?" Beef asked. He jostled into Felix, bumping off of his back like a wall. "Sorry. It's freaking me out."

"Is it a defensive array?" Vess asked. She, too, crowded close, pressing her shoulder against Felix and Isla's. "You said it recognized your Authority, Felix. Can you clear it?"

Authority, clear the fog, Felix ordered, but there was no response from the bundle of command within him. *Authority?*

"Of course not," he muttered. Whatever part of the tower that had been communicating with him had gone just as silent as the room they were in. "Seems like this is a feature, not a bug." He waved his hand through the fog. It was so thick, it barely moved at all. "If it's an array, then it's well-hidden. Perception, even Manasight, only picks out water vapor...and the floor."

"The Grand Harmony is strangely muted...the fog is...woven of silence itself," Isla said, her voice catching with something Felix couldn't quite parse.

"Isla?"

The small blonde Chanter started before busing herself with wiping her hands on her skirts. "It is simply disturbing. The Grand Harmony should not be silenced."

Felix reached out with his Affinity, finding much the same as Isla. The room was utterly quiet and still. It felt like the Void in some ways, though not as complete. He could hear the faint rumble of his team, after all, not to mention the small stretch of pink stone at his feet. It was less a sound and more of a pressure or presence, a vibration very unlike living creatures.

Inanimate objects didn't have a Spirit, not that Felix had ever seen, so while they were composed of Mana and Essence, they were also made up of a lot of other ill-defined "stuff" that didn't sound the same to his Affinity. Felix had noticed it a long time ago, when he'd been practicing with his Hunger. A chair or bedframe didn't contain much Essence at all, a decent amount of Mana, and a lot of nameless filler he'd never been able to identify.

Significance, maybe? It was a question he should have asked Zara when she was around, and Felix breathed sharply from his nose in annoyance. There was never enough time, and for all his vaunted memory, Felix was too distracted by...everything he had on his plate. He risked a look at Isla. *Should I ask her?*

Felix's breath turned to a snort. *Pass.*

In any case, the silence was almost complete. It made everything feel close and intimate, made a touch worse by how everyone was crowding him. Vess and Pit were both visibly unnerved, their heads on a swivel as the fog swirled thicker and thicker around them. Hallow was impossible to read, as usual, and Beef...Beef's open book of a Spirit was relieved, of all things. "Beef, you good?"

"Huh? Oh yeah. Yeah." The Minotaur took a breath so big it made the leather straps on his breastplate creak lightly. "It was freaky at first, but now it's like...nice. It feels like home, kinda."

Felix blinked. "Huh. You're right. It does."

The silence was like those late nights back on Earth, when everything was asleep, and the quiet was so loud. It reminded him that on Earth, Felix had never once heard the mysterious sounds of the Grand Harmony, even by accident. *Is that because Earth doesn't have the System? Or does it mean...that Earth doesn't have the Grand Harmony at all?*

"Toa'ut? Lavix? Are you all feeling okay?" Felix asked.

The War Naga were vague shadows in the mist, towering well over Beef's head before one of them leaned in close. The familiar features of Toa'ut resolved from the fog. "We are well, but it is hard to hear you, even from so close. I would suggest we do not split up, my Lord. I...do not trust this murk."

Felix nodded "Let's take it one step at a time. Everyone, behind me. Weapons at the ready." If the place wasn't going to listen to his Authority, then who knows what the hell they could expect.

He led the way, stepping cautiously down the hallway. Felix focused, attempting to force his vision through the cloying fog in every way he could conceive. Nothing seemed to work. They walked slowly, cautious step after cautious step, but the end of the hallway never materialized. Felix was starting to feel a little annoyed, and even Beef's contentment soured to the tune of anxiety. "No one's observation Skills are working, right?" he asked.

"Nope," Beef answered, a bit too quickly. Pit, Hallow, and the War Naga all answered in the negative.

"Elemental Eye is drawing nothing but the earth Mana directly beneath our feet. Everything else is—" Vess swallowed. She had faced slavering monstrosities without batting an eye, and fear was coming off her in waves Felix couldn't help but sense. "Everything else is blank. Like there is nothing out there."

Nothing out...there. Hm. Maybe I'm doing this backwards. Felix, still walking, pushed his Affinity not outward, but inward. He pressed at his Manasight, sounding the depths of its pattern before focusing the vibrations back outward with the shape of his Intent. It rose, riding along his channels until the song of power welled at the back of his eyes, just as it always did.

Manasight.

The world immediately around him sprang into chaotic disarray as vaporous whorls of Mana became visible. At this point, Felix could always see the hidden world of Mana, but he had to focus to see in further detail. This was that, but amped up to eleven. And *still*, there was nothing beyond the small circle of his team, and even the long tails of the Naga faded as if slowly erased from existence itself.

"What are you doing?" Isla asked, irritation clear in her voice. "You're so close, I can hear you fumbling around at the Grand Harmony like a courting farmer."

Felix raised an eyebrow at the comparison. In his opinion, he was pretty damn good at using the Chant to enhance and activate his Skills without the System. "I'm fumbling?"

Isla sighed, that irritation turning inward, much as his Affinity had done. "I won't say you're unskilled, Felix. We both know that would be a lie. Instead, you are simply not as refined as you can be. Accessing the songs of Creation encompasses so much more than simple Skills."

Hm. Zara had never said that, but it made sense. The Grand Harmony was supposed to be the underpinning of all things, everywhere. To have it be limited to Skill activation would be silly. "Are you offering to teach me, Isla?" he asked.

The Chanter picked an invisible speck of dust from her shoulder and flicked it away. "Perhaps. For a price."

Of course. "What price?"

"Nothing onerous, boy. Simply answering a few questions."

"What questions?" Felix asked, his mood souring again. *Anything to dig up some secrets. This lady...* "I've already agreed to tell you a bit about my time on Earth. What else could you need?"

The Chanter smiled. "It is less a matter of need and more a matter of inquisitiveness. I wish to understand those that would save us from..."

She looked around at the Naga before emphasizing her words. "...the *threats* that are coming."

That wasn't entirely unreasonable, he had to admit. The woman drove Felix up the walls, but getting to know him wasn't the worst thing that could happen.Yet, his stubborn nature reared its head. "I'll figure it out myself, thanks."

"You—aah!"

Whatever Isla was going to say to him was suddenly lost as she let out a high-pitched shriek and began to tumble. Felix reached out, easily snagging her around the shoulder with his large, scaled hands. For a brief moment, the Chanter clung to his arm, held out at a forty-five degree angle over a sudden, sheer drop. Felix only entertained the idea of dropping her a little.

He reeled her in.

"Siva's Grace. The stone simply stops," Vess said, kneeling at the edge of the pink marble. Ahead, the fog swirled and eddied in various directions like a landbound cloud, but through it, they could finally see more than unrelenting mist. Trees rose from it, thin trunks filled with branches and thick, green leaves. Fruit hung from a few of them, white and red *kelaar* and purple *galgan*, a stonefruit the size of Felix's head. "Why is there a forest in a tower built at the floor of a lake?"

"I wish I knew," Felix said. Though he couldn't see the ground, Felix had seen the *kelaar* trees many times in his travels across Nagast. Based on the rough height and age of the trees, Felix estimated the drop around twenty feet. Nothing that would hurt any of them, even if they had fallen. A high-pitched song wafted up from his core space, a lilting melody that smelled of growing things and deep, fertile loam. In a way Felix couldn't explain, the song drew his eye around the sudden forest, and he spotted more plants he recognized. "I'm more interested in why all of these plants are from the Foglands."

Aria of the Green Wilds is level 87!

"Food," Pit said with a warbling growl. "C'mon! I'm gonna eat every fruit I find!"

The tenku leaped outward but let out a strangled gurgle as Felix snagged the back of his barding. Pit's wings flapped ineffectually twice, before Felix yanked him back to the ground. "Pit! No eating until I figure out what's going on here. This isn't just a forest under the lake, it's the Foglands. See?"

Felix gestured into the swirling mists, and slowly the forest around them was growing lighter, until he could make out the shape of a distant cliff, upon which hung a gargantuan tree that dwarfed the crag it clung upon.

"The Spirit Tree," Vess said with wonder. "How?"

"An illusion. It must be. I do not know this Spirit Tree you speak of, nor have I ventured into the Foglands, but this is all impossible." Isla pivoted, taking in as much as possible. "The exterior of this structure was quite large, immense even, but not so large as to contain a horizon within its walls."

"Illusion?" Beef said, just as a pale blue wisp of light landed on his finger. "I can feel this thing on my hand, though. How's that work?"

"Careful," Felix warned. "Those things can be nasty."

"It's a lightning bug, Felix. I think I'm strong enough to—OUCH!" Beef slammed his hands together, crushing the weak Body of the wisp. It flashed once before going dark. "That thing bit me!"

"Wait 'til you feel a horde of them," Felix said, eyes panning the forest. "If this is an illusion, it's the most convincing one I've ever seen. Manasight is working again, but it's picking out the flows of life, earth, water, and shadow from the forest. I don't see how this is being made," Felix finished with a growl. He did not want to be stuck in a hallway for hours or days while they tried to figure it all out. "What is the point of this place?"

"Wherever the illusion is originating from, it is invasive. It is no coincidence that we see the Foglands, Felix. Zara told me you have a mental defense Skill. Do you sense an intrusion with it?" Isla asked.

Felix frowned. Of course. Why hadn't he thought of that? Now that Isla said it, it was obvious that he should check his Bastion of Will...and immediately seized upon a spiraled thread of Intent that was meddling with his thoughts. It attempted to get him to ignore his Bastion again, but Felix's powerful Mind grasped the Intent and followed it down, deep into his core space where he fell into the blue-green world of his mental defenses.

Bastion of Will!

He landed among the towers of his Bastion, the glassy stone shining in the bright midday sun. With a flex of Affinity, Intent, and Willpower, Felix flared the normally-passive defenses of his mental fortress. His thoughts clarified immediately, able to now trace that first thread of foreign Intent to a dense pattern of distraction that huddled close to the exterior curtain wall.

Felix shifted it, pulling the bulk of the pattern away from his walls and holding it tight. His cleared thoughts pinged upon further threads, each vibrating to a subtle, intricate melody that led him all around his Bastion's interior. Each length of Intent he bundled into an ever-widening mass in his hands, but it never seemed to end. Each handful seemed to produce another somewhere else within the walls. However, the buzzing touch of the Intent sent a sober realization hurtling through Felix's consciousness.

"It's scraping my memories," he said as he returned to full consciousness. His team looked at him questioningly. "The tower slipped a bundle of Intent into my Bastion of Will, bypassing my defenses and accessing my Mind. All for this." He gestured to the forest ahead of them. "To fabricate the Foglands from my memories."

"Foul magic," Toa'ut rumbled.

"Cool," Beef and Pit said, in tandem.

"Did you see its source, boy?" Isla asked.

"No, but I can do this," Felix said, before closing his eyes in concentration. Mana and Essence flooded his Bastion, drawing out the gorgeous song of its pattern from the Skill. He pressed his Affinity to find the connections still lingering within, while his Intent flared his mental defenses to their utmost. The Skill Array sang, spinning like a top as several Skills engaged all at once.

Bastion of Will is level 91!
Skein of Fate is level 48!

Like the slamming of a door, the illusion of fog and forest vanished with a puff of illusory air, the hall returning to its pink marble glory. Felix panted. The effort to exorcize the invasive touch of the working had tired him out more than fighting Fathom spawn for hours...but he wasn't done.

"It's gone," Beef said in wonder. He reached out and touched the wall that was only a few feet ahead. "That was so *real.*"

"Felix, there is something else," Isla warned. "I hear it—"

"I know," he grunted. "There."

Among the pillars, those that glowed with a soft aquamarine light, there twined dozens of those threads of Intent. Felix could hear an atonal buzzing from them all, but it was their pattern more than their noise that drew his attention. They twisted and tangled like waves of sound turned inward on each other and were emanating from the pillars themselves.

Felix strode up to the nearest one. He could smash them all with ease, but he had no clue just how much they were supporting the ceiling. Bringing a tower down onto their own heads wasn't something Felix had any desire to experience, so he did the next easiest option. He grasped the pillar and reached outward among the tangling threads of Intent with his own, tracing it from one pillar to the next. Then again, and again, over and over until Felix was straining to grasp the gossamer thin threads at all.

Chthonic Tribute!

Intent burned like a lit fuse, sparking back toward Felix in a wave of combusting smoke. A slurry of Mana and Essence poured into Felix, diving through the base of his skull and directly into his core space. All at once, the pillars went dark.

"Look," Vess called out. At the far end of the corridor, now only a short distance away, was a set of spiral staircases that led up and down. "The illusions are fully broken."

"Yeah," Felix panted, ignoring the very interested look in Isla's eyes. "The whole room was a big illusion array."

"But why?" Vess asked.

Ephemeral Evocation is level 2!
Ephemeral Evocation is level 3!

Target's Power Has Been Fully Digested!
You Have Gained A Memory!
Would You Like To View Or Save?

Felix licked his lips. "Let's see if I can find out."

CHAPTER SEVENTY-THREE

"What are you on about?" Isla demanded. "Did you *eat* the array? That was a complex working that deserved to be studied, not demolished."

"Speak up faster," Pit chirruped at her.

Isla glowered at the tenku, hard enough that the horse-sized Pit took a step back. "If I had known his intentions, I would have. Now. Explain. What are you trying to do, Felix?"

Felix simply sat down at the base of one of the dull pillars and closed his eyes.

"Boy," she warned.

"He has most likely consumed a memory and will review it. The process is quick," Vess explained.

Felix cracked an eye, frowning first at Vess and then Isla, who appeared intrigued. He could almost see her jot the detail down into some mental list she kept of him. "Vess..."

The spearmaiden had the grace to look a little ashamed before she frowned right back. "There is no point in hiding that detail, Felix. Too many know, and hiding it now would only decrease the trust among this team."

He considered that a moment, attempting to hold his Spirit as close as possible. He was mad that Vess revealed another of his abilities, but then, he'd never explicitly told her not to, and she was right: all of his friends knew. He was pretty sure Darius and some of the Claw knew. The Fiend's Shadows definitely did. Keeping secrets was impossible once more than a few people knew the truth. Felix grunted something vaguely agreeable and closed his eyes again.

"How does this woooooo—" Isla began, before her voice warped into a wobbly tone that bled in every direction at once. Time, or his perception of it, slowed to a crawl as the world was leached of color. A ripple undulated from within him, spreading outward in a dramatic slow motion...before all things shattered.

———

This time, there was no hall of possibilities or chain of moments. It was strange that he'd been able to steal a memory from an array, of all things, but perhaps that was an effect of his Ephemeral Evocation, which increased his chances of gaining Memories from his targets. Ideas for future uses flashed across his Mind, before the shattered darkness resolved into something more.

Felix stood in the same place, upon the same pink marble floors, yet chunks were missing. Beside him, four creatures the same size and fur-to-skin ratio as a grizzly bear struggled with a large pink slab of marble. They wrestled it down, setting the slab into the flooring with far more grace than Felix expected from their wide forms. They laughed as it settled in, big breathy guffaws that revealed short, pig-like snouts and tusks the size of daggers.

"I am always impressed with their Strength."

The voice was light and appreciative, belonging to a waif-like figure in white robes and a deep hood. In fact, all three of the people behind Felix wore the same robes, a formal sort of thing wrapped around their torsos and draped from their shoulders. It let them cut a striking silhouette while allowing it to remain free flowing. Three of the four wore the drapery tucked back, clipped somehow to their belts of woven vines. The small figure was staring through Felix as if he weren't there, presumably watching the boar-like laborers lift another slab from a hovering wagon.

"The Orken are mighty warriors and even greater craftsmen. I am more impressed that they agreed to come down here at all," said a large, brawny man with the head and hooves of a stag. Bronze and silver adorned his antlers, with several chains strung among the tines. "I have heard they are not fond of the depths."

"And the Theron are? I seem to recall you bleating in alarm at every bump and jostle during our descent, Lovarius." The diminutive figure laughed gently. It did not sing of cruelty or derision, but of simple, friendly jokes.

"That is beside the point," Lovarius the Theron said with a snort. "I simply abhor the tight confines in which we find ourselves."

"The sea is but another frontier to forge our Paths," said the third and final figure. They stood head and shoulders above the deer-like Theron but shy of the Orkens' bulk. Familiar appendages tensed along their back, each one clad in a white, chitinous shell that left their tips surprisingly delicate-seeming. A Yttin. "Within these walls, a new Path beckons us all. I am eager to see where it leads."

"As are we all, Tlxa. It is why we came down here, after all." The smallest of them lowered their hood, and Felix goggled. It was a Geist, the same Race as Vvim. They scratched at their cheeks, while overly large eyes the color of cloudy skies looked wistfully at the pillars that were now glowing. "Well, with this construction, the confines won't seem so onerous, I think." She patted the nearest pillar, the one Felix had previously settled against, and a puff of aquamarine vapor wafted outward. "An entire hall dedicated to soothing illusions and sprawling vistas, keyed to that which brings you the most comfort."

Felix clenched his jaw. He tried not to think about what it suggested, that the array had called up the Foglands instead of his apartment back in Fort Lauderdale. Or even his mother's house. Tried, and failed. What did it say about him that the most stressful time in his entire life was his comfort?

The array is definitely broken, he decided. Yeah. That had to be it. Otherwise, he had some trauma he needed to unpack and approximately zero time to do it in. *Think later.*

"..comfort, hah. You think this array will truly keep our Minds away from...from that *thing* we watch?" the Theron asked, shuddering. His fur bristled all along his shoulders and exposed arms, like rippling waves. "How could it?"

The trio of robed folks had continued talking, and Felix was lucky his Mind was so resilient. The pace of his thoughts could ratchet up to considerable speeds, and all that existential worrying had taken up only a couple seconds at most. The Geist was still talking about the "Hall of Green Pleasures" as they dubbed the chamber, describing the convoluted process in which they spun out the array itself.

Similar to the process in which Karys was put into his Eidolon form way back when, the array utilized Memories themselves in glyph-strewn formations that twisted across one another with a mathematical precision that made Felix's head swim. It was incredibly complex, and he didn't understand half of the terminology that the small, ferret-like Geist used, but Felix smiled despite his earlier misgivings.

Knowledge, after all, was power.

"...and that's why it works so well," they finished, looking proud of themselves. The Geist gave a sharp little grin to the Theron. "Did you follow that, Lovy?"

"Did I follow it? I created half of it. I only—I only asked you about your half to be polite," the deer-man said before glaring at the others, as if daring them to call out the hitch in his voice. "I do not need reassurances about our work. It is pristine."

"Of course."

Shit, so I'm missing half the details? Felix wanted to shake the information out of the stag-looking Theron, but it was a Memory, and Felix couldn't exactly interact with it like that. The rules were hazy and shifting, much as any dream might behave, but Felix knew it with a cold certainty. This was a snapshot in time, somehow captured by the array as it was formed, an additional Memory among its glyphs. *But could I rewind it? Review it again? Maybe then I could pick out some more.*

Ephemeral Evocation is level 4!

He tried, earning himself another Skill level, but the best Felix could manage was pausing the Memory in mid-stream. Even that took an extraordinary amount of mental strength, and in mere seconds, Felix was panting with renewed exhaustion as his Mana and Stamina both began to bottom out.

"Gah!" he exclaimed, releasing the Memory to flow freely. There was a stutter, as if he were watching an old movie, and the film had been jostled on the reel. Just the slightest hitch before it resumed, the three white-robed individuals jerking in place as their words tumbled senselessly over one another. But in that moment, Felix spotted a tall, lithe man standing in the stairwell not twenty feet distant, wearing robes almost identical to the three others. The man's face was sharply angled, like a Human but more severe, with eyes just a touch too large. He hadn't been there before.

He looked directly at Felix—not through him at all, but *at* him—and crooked his finger. Before Felix could do more than take a step, the man vanished, striding up the staircase with a preternatural speed.

No, he realized with a jolt of fear and curiosity. *Not a man. A Nym.* Felix hesitated. *Wait. What did they say about a* thing *they watch?*

The Memory unspooled, rippling before it burst once more.

"Can he not hear me while he's like this?"

"No, as he has described it to me, it is an intensive process. Lady Isla, please. Do not touch him."

"I was simply—"

Felix jolted to his feet.

"Whoa, you move fast!" Beef burst out, his meaty hands reaching out to grasp Felix by the shoulders. "You okay, Felix?"

Felix blinked away the rippling world, finding the color restored and himself missing a small chunk of time. Everyone stood in different positions around him, with the War Naga guarding them from both directions. "How long did that take?"

"Uh, like ten minutes?"

"Damn, used to be faster," he muttered. His new Skill was to blame.

Ephemeral Evocation is level 5!

...

Ephemeral Evocation is level 8!

Speak of the devil, he thought. The Skill allowed him to maintain greater fidelity in the Memories he stole, as well as facilitated a larger chance to get them in the first place. In exchange, it meant he had to be under for a longer period of time. *Did it also allow me to see that Nymean guy there? But how did he see* me?

Isla snapped her fingers before his eyes, disrupting his train of thought. "Felix, I will let slide the particulars of where you learned such things, and instead ask you the more pertinent question: what did you learn?"

Felix scowled. "Do *not* snap your fingers at me—"

His stomach *heaved.*

"Felix!" Vess cried out, and he could very distantly feel his body falling to the ground. Distantly, because Felix was already dropping down, delving into his core space like an arrow loosed on a target. He arrived, blasting through the Essence-strewn branches of his Divine Tree...to find the black hole at his center was boiling.

That can't be good.

Felix! Pit was suddenly there, flapping his enormous wings to stay level with Felix's visualized Body. *Felix, what's going—oh no.*

That's what I said. Felix nodded into the boiling black, a constant stream of Essence and Mana the only thing that limned it against the greater dark of his core space. *It feels like I'm gonna throw up, but with everything. All of my Aspects, somehow. Can a Mind puke?*

Below the black hole that represented Felix's untamed, Primordial Hunger was a cauldron of foul bubbles and forces that Felix couldn't quite make sense of; when he looked too closely, it felt like he was sliding sideways off of a ledge. With a sickening lurch that nearly made him eject from his core space altogether, the black hole...burped.

Gross.

It certainly looked disgusting as a large, ichor-strewn bubble expanded upward at incredible speeds. Felix drew Pit away just as it burst, releasing a massive, glowing sphere of screaming energy.

Whoa! Felix reversed course, reaching out to bobble the thing in his visualized hands. It burned him even before he touched it, scorching through his faux flesh so deeply that only his incredible Willpower and Intent could grapple with it.

Armored Skin is level 82!
Armored Skin is level 83!

The thing was a screaming bundle of chaotic noise. Dissonance came off it in waves, and it was that which burned him. Rapid-fire realizations cascaded through Felix, his Mind struggling to categorize the sensations he was enduring. It didn't burn so much as killed a piece of his visualized Body with every pulse, every off-tempo beat. It strained his already exhausted faculties, scoring deeply into him.

"Why. The hell. Did you spit this out?" Felix shouted down at his Hunger, frantically searching for a place to put it. Usually something so dangerous would be thrown into the black hole to be swallowed up safely...but clearly that wasn't going to work. "Take it back!"

TAKE. GIVE.

Even through the searing pain, Felix was surprised enough to suck in a stilted breath. "What?"

EQUAL.

"Equal? To what I've given you?" Was his Hunger...*repaying* him for feeding it? That was so out of left field that Felix couldn't parse it.

WATCH.

Without more warning than that, a great shift occurred in Felix's outstretched grasp. As if it were unlocked, the burning sphere expanded, growing and spreading outward in a bundle of swirling noise and patterns. Chaos tilted, twisted, realigned.

It surged from Felix's grip, rocketing downward into the revolving rings of his core space. The ones that spun ceaselessly around his dual cores and the event horizon of his Hunger. It landed, bobbing once, before blooming in a shower of heavenly light.

New Skill!
Illusory Double (Rare), Level 1!
Illusions are but lies made real. Create an illusory double of yourself for a moderate Mana cost. You can perceive through the double with a percentage of your Perception. Double cannot interact directly with the Corporeal Realm. Fidelity of

illusory self increases slightly with Skill level. Percentage of effective Perception increases slightly with Skill level. Number of illusory selves increases with Skill level.

"You gave me...a Skill?"

His Hunger was silent once more. Felix stared between his new Skill and the black hole that sat at his center. It had never given up the meals it took from his Essence and Mana.

This was new.

He watched the Skill spin, waiting to see if it soured or turned caustic again. It did not, and in fact, the chaos of its song had stilled to an elusive, phantom melody. Unsure what else to do, and still massaging his visualized hands, Felix stepped back into himself to find Isla complaining.

"—he won't talk to me."

"If you tried speaking to him civilly, then perhaps he would, Lady Isla."

Still got my back, he thought with an inward grin. "Okay. I'm good now."

"Felix! What was that?" Beef asked. He looked shaken, like he'd seen something horrendous.

How bad do I look? "I'm fine, man. Just had to do some...housekeeping."

Isla raised her eyebrow skeptically. "And what of this Memory you consumed? I presume it told you the purpose of this place?"

"It did," he admitted. He thought about everything the Geist, Theron, and Yttin had said. "I think...I think this is a research facility."

CHAPTER SEVENTY-FOUR

"Felix, your hands," Vess said, reaching to grasp his wrists gently. She turned them over and, much to his surprise, Felix's palms were burnt through. Charred meat and bone could be seen, though much of the wounds had already repaired. "How did this happen?"

"Huh. It affected my actual Body?" Felix hadn't expected that. His Song of Absolution was so strong it usually negated a ton of damage...but in this case, it seemed it only negated his pain. He still couldn't really feel it other than a faint ache, easily mistaken for simple fatigue. "More new things."

"What affected you?" Vess asked, gently. She tilted his hands, inspecting them even as his regeneration patched up more of the worst parts. It was a bit gnarly to see, even for Felix, but Vess didn't blink until she was satisfied he was healing well. "What could do this to an Adept Body?"

Felix was intensely aware of Isla standing nearby, waiting for them to walk up the spiral staircase. He carefully extracted his hands from hers. "Just some quirks of being an Unbound, I think." He gave her a smile. "I'll be fine."

Vess was too close to hide her emotions from Felix, and he was too tired to hold back his Affinity as much as he wanted. So he felt the conflict of disbelief and annoyance at his clear lie...but then she glanced at Isla, who stood only a few yards away, talking to Beef. Begrudging acceptance rolled across her, a timpani's decrescendo. She smiled, very slightly, and they moved to the staircase.

The stairs were formed in a familiar pattern, one that Felix had seen before in Shelim. Larger on the outside, the inner portions were carved to accommodate creatures of a smaller stature. Geist, Felix presumed.

"How amenable," Isla remarked.

"In the Memory, I saw many different Races here, working together. Only makes sense to shape the structure to their needs," Felix said. "Same was true in Shelim."

"An inconvenience for us, forced to either side as we are. Still, there seems to be quite enough space to let us pass single file." The Chanter looked to Felix then the Naga. "I assume they shall go in the lead? To ensure our safety."

"What? No." Felix stepped forward himself. "I chose to lead us into here instead of swimming through the ravines. I'll lead the way and handle whatever dangers come our way. Beef, Isla, and Vess, you can take behind me. Toa'ut, you and your people take the rear along with Hallow's Multipede form. Pit, with me."

"Yes, my Lord," the Naga said, all of them bowing at the waist.

The rest of his team shuffled about until they more or less assembled into the order he had defined. There was plenty of room on the staircase, despite Isla's weird complaints, though with Pit's big horse size and wings—even folded—he was a bit in the way.

"Felix, could you not have let the illusion go on?" Pit asked him. His voice was pitched low, which wasn't saying much for the tenku. His words always sounded more like a child or preteen than an adult.

"What do you mean? It wasn't real."

Pit scuffed a paw at a stone stair, pushing through a layer of mealy dust. "I know that. You said. But it was...nice. To see home again."

Home. The breath caught in Felix's throat, unsure whether he was sighing or gasping. For all its faults, the Foglands—Nagast—was Pit's home. His Mind touched on old memories of his own home, on Earth. Felix was hesitant, fearing an ache that was far less than he expected. It also didn't feel like home anymore. "Yeah. I guess it was."

They began their climb along the spiral steps, though it was only two rotations before Pit grew annoyed at managing his bulky form beside them all. With a chirruping call and a whump of air, Pit shrank down into his Dire Hound form and bounded in Vess' arms.

"Siva's Grace, but you're adorable!" Vess cooed, holding the puppy-shaped tenku in her arms. Pit's tongue lolled from his mouth, a doggy grin stretching his jowls as Vess scratched him vigorously along his head and ears.

"Pit can turn into a dog?" Beef said. He, too, reached over and pet Felix's Companion, laughing happily when Pit started kicking a hind leg. "Oh, that's cute. I always wanted a dog. Dad always said no."

"Should I find a small dog to Raise, Michael?" Hallow asked, leaning out from his back. Her small, uneven rock head/face tilted with the sound of grinding stone.

Beef stared at the Homunculus. "Uh, What? No, it's fine. Pit's a dog; that's enough."

"...Very well."

After another few rotations without relief or landing, the walls and stairs themselves began to show signs of weathering. Specifically vines and roots that crept along the stonework, clinging to seams that were almost invisible to the naked eye, even Felix's. The mealy dust that coated portions of the stairs seemed to be shed from the vegetation, a pulpy remnant of a cycle of growth and decay. Felix's Aria of the Green Wilds burned in the back of his core space. Giving him that particular nugget of wisdom, as well as others. Its song danced among the vines, leaves, and mossy tendrils that soon hung from every available surface. The Aria and his Voracious Eye worked to identify everything, some of which he'd seen in the ravines outside, while many, many others were growths he'd never before seen.

"These vibrant orange blossoms...what are they?" Vess asked, looking closely at a waterfall of blooms that covered the interior wall of the stairwell.

"Irumi Vett, otherwise known as the Sting Flower," Isla answered, before Felix could Eye the plant. She grabbed Vess' arm before the spearmaiden could reach out and touch it. "Dangerous to touch. They have barbs within their stamen that release if jostled too quickly."

Felix read the information his Eye presented to him. "Whoa. They can pierce Master-Tier Bodies. That's a strong-ass flower."

"The penetrative capabilities of the barbs are less concerning than the odor they impart. It induces an instance of the Paralyze Status Condition." Isla walked carefully around the flowers, never stepping closer than required. "Avoid them whenever you can."

Blanching, Vess stepped back, following Isla as they proceeded upward. Felix lingered. *Think I could get some seeds of these to bring home?*

Can you get them without getting everyone paralyzed? Pit asked.

Felix opened his mouth before shutting it almost immediately. *Maybe? Any chance you want to risk being paralyzed for some seeds?*

Pit just looked at him over Vess' retreating shoulder as a deadpan melody plucked across their bond. Felix sighed and trudged after.

Soon, the profusion of flowers and vines gave way to a root-clogged doorway. It, too, was made of a silvery metal, much like the others, but this one was jammed open by the thick growths of rugged roots. They crawled from every direction, across the floor, the walls, the curved arch near the ceiling, all of it. As the others hesitated, Felix approached, feeling for the Authority that had been so responsive to him in the tower.

It was there, but strangely truncated like a radio station that kept repeating a message before cutting out to an incessant rain of static.

Authority Det—
You—

Felix peered through the door.

Inside was a curving corridor, split off into a number of smaller rooms that were each separated by a door of silvery metal. One of the nearer chambers was propped open, leafy vines and rugged roots having grown through its entryway as well. He couldn't see much from the angle outside, so he stepped inside, walking carefully on the uneven root floor. The hallway was tall, and in addition to the chambers on that level, there were two others above them that contained similar-looking rooms and doors. *The hall is like a long, open-air courtyard. Or like a cheap motel with outside entrance rooms.*

He stepped up to the closest open room, casting about with all of his senses. Immediately, he spotted the lumps of broken and rotted out furniture. A chair, a couch, or something like it. Even a small table. A thing that might have been a stovetop, but probably wasn't, had been perched in the corner and was surrounded by the fruiting branches of a small tree.

"Look, Manalamps," Vess pointed out.

Beside his head, a type of Manalamp was hung askew on the wall. It was made of Crescian Bronze, of all things, and despite the flora that hung from it, seemed perfectly serviceable beneath a patina of ancient grime. Felix placed his hand on it, guiding out a streamer of Mana with Cardinal Flame. The Manalamp flickered once, twice, before fully igniting on the third attempt.

Interesting. As he watched, the Manalamp burned away the detritus that clotted its surface, until it was returned to a nearly pristine artifact. It still hung sideways, but he fixed that with a gentle lift and twist. "They still work."

"Of course they do. Crescian Bronze takes enchantment so well, an artifact made of it would last interminable Ages," Isla said in a matter-of-fact tone that struggled to hide the awe in her eyes. She reached up and stroked the Manalamp. "A find worth more than some small cities. And there are likely hundreds more."

Beef whistled. "Can we take them and sell them? I like being mega strong and all, but being rich sounds really nice, too."

"Maybe on the way out," Felix said, though part of him twisted at defacing the tower. "Let's keep moving. These are apartments or dorms or something. There's more here, I know it."

That Nym in the Memory had looked at Felix and beckoned him up the stairs. That wasn't normal, even for the Continent. There had to be something to find in the upper levels.

They moved on, inspecting the rooms that were open or broken by the unremitting advance of greenery. The rooms became more desolate and not less as they progressed, but Felix didn't let anyone break down the doors that were sealed shut. A sense of urgency laced across his Mind, both for their task at hand and the world beyond. The Fathom was still out there, doing who knows what, and his people were fighting for their lives in Haarwatch. Or would be, soon. A jittery restlessness sank into Felix's limbs, a sensation he had grown all too used to since waking up on an acid beach.

He pressed ahead, careful not to disturb the riot of greenery all around them.

It was clear that plants had run amok, filling every inch of space along the floors and walls of the living quarters, as well the wide staircase beyond them. The team followed those steps upward, another six rotations of what was basically jungle vegetation, before finding the next silver door so full of vines and roots that it spilled outward like a river of green. That door was fully wedged open and, impossibly, sunlight streamed through it.

"What the hell?" Beef muttered. The sunbeams bounced off the Minotaur's orichalcum helmet like a mirror. "How's that possible?"

"I'm gonna go out on a limb here and say 'magic,'" Felix said, before ducking into the room. The others followed, though the War Naga had to almost fold themselves in half to fit. Lucky for them, they were insanely flexible, being mostly snake. Felix pushed his Perception outward, feeling at the space before his Voracious Eye and Aria of the Green Wilds began cataloging everything in sight.

Voracious Eye is level 82!
Aria of the Green Wilds is level 88!

The same sorts of flora abounded in the cavernous room, absolutely filling the space until there was little evidence to the naked eye that they still stood in a man-made structure. The walls looked to be made of rough, striated wood, with dizzying networks of roots clinging to them, each proffering a bevy of leaves out into the bright light. The sun-dappled foliage soothed Felix more than he expected, though he suspected it was...yes, he spotted it through the haze: a crystal carved into a near-circle and brimming with golden light Mana.

Almost perfectly hidden, however, was an absolutely massive tree. Felix stared at its crown as he followed the golden light back down toward the floor, tracing its huge, dark, blue-green leaves and thick branches. They all met along a trunk that was around forty feet in diameter, if he had to guess, and was further covered in vines and moss that entirely obscured its bole and thick roots. More than that, Felix's Voracious Eye struggled against it, almost failing before it triumphed in a blaze of trilling notifications.

Name: Abundance Anima
Type: Spirit Tree
Lore: Spirit Trees are a rare and powerful organism imbued with elemental Mana dependent on their growth cycle. Due to its location and growth, the Spirit Tree before you has chosen its attunements. The Abundance Anima is attuned to Water, Shadow, Earth, and Life.

"A Spirit Tree?" Vess said in surprise.

"A Spirit Tree!" Isla exclaimed. She stared at the glorious shape of it with glee on her face. "Beneath the waves, no less. How could it thrive down here?"

"It's huge," Beef said, and Pit cooed in appreciation while Hallow tilted her little stone head.

Felix stared as well. Unlike the other one he'd found in the wild, this one seemed to be thriving...almost...undulating.

Authority Detected.
Welcome Au—

ERROR!

Ouranic Override.
The Seeds Have Been Turned.
Beware.

"That can't be good," Felix managed, just as the foliage around them began to rustle. Within instants, rustling turned to cracking branches and quaking leaves as a dozen creatures let out shrill bellows. "Weapons up!"

The attack began.

CHAPTER SEVENTY-FIVE

Voracious Eye!

Name: Moontouched Wickerjak
Type: Plant (Manawarped)
Level: 84
HP: 6844/6844
SP: 26831/26899
MP: 4323/4323
Lore: Born of wood and earth, Wickerjaks are mercurial spirits of nature. Similar to Sprites, they often embody the unconscious Will and Intent of the natural world. Moon-touched Wickerjaks have been perverted by an outside source, increasing their aggression and physical stats in equal measure.
Strength: More Data Required
Weakness: More Data Required

The glimpse Felix got of the monsters in the moments before their attack flooded through his Mind, absorbed even as he raised his hands and called upon the Grand Harmony.

Stone Shaping!

A nine-foot wall of smooth rock burst from the earth around them, just in time to be peppered by the explosive impacts of the Wickerjaks. Cracks immediately formed in the stone, and Felix devoted more Mana to shoring them up. "Vess!"

"On it." The woman leaped up into the air, easily clearing his wall as five silver spears and five discs of burnished bronze unfurled around her like wings. The spears held their place, but the five discs blurred forward and down, out of Felix's direct sight. He felt the impacts, though, pressure against his Perception, and it was far more than five as the discs duplicated themselves. Fourteen concussive, metal-on-wood collisions rang out. "They are strong! I am doing damage, but not enough."

As the five discs returned to her side, Vess' Spears shot outward, hitting and exploding with far greater force. Beef growled, chitin already covering his body and weapon. "Open the wall, Felix. We can take 'em!"

Mind whirling through options, Felix sounded Stone Shaping again. The wall before them melted away, leaving their front exposed, while the stone flowed backward to reinforce the wall on their sides and rear. They were surrounded, but he could shape the battlefield.

The impacts behind them decreased yet did not stop, while the sounds of furious rustling rose to a fever pitch. Wickerjaks ripped through the brush before them, heedless of the Spears that rained down, blasting off pieces of their wooden forms. They looked like bundles of sticks, vines, and thorns bound and animated with a dark purple light. It shone from the gaps between their limbs and from their thorn-lined mouths as they screeched in a primal rage.

"Relentless Charge!" Beef bellowed, zipping forward to intercept the first line. "Seismic Shatter!"

A cone of earth Mana ripped up from the ground, churning vine and frond and root into a malevolent morass. Wickerjaks fell shrieking, torn by their own thorns and bursting debris. They did not stop, however, as many returned to their feet or slipped through the churning strike.

"Uh, Circle of Smash!" Beef brought his hammer down as they advanced, and the area around him for twenty feet was suddenly pressed violently flat. "Circle of Smash! *Circle of Smash*!"

"Tempest Fugit!" Pit cried out, shedding his puppy form and flapping up into the air with the sound of thunder. Frozen bolts of lightning dropped from his outstretched wings, spearing down into the concentrated mass before bursting free. Although the lightning seemed to do little to harm them, the initial piercing strike was doing significant damage. The plant monsters already smashed by Beef were laid low, no longer possessing the limbs or power to move much at all.

Behind Pit came Hallow in both forms, the Homunculus riding atop the agile Multipede. Crystalline darts sprayed outward, pinning their foes to the ground in places, while the Multipede ran roughshod over them all. Its sword-sharp legs stabbed and sliced with every movement.

The War Nagas roared, rampaging to the fore with tridents and claws bared. Their powerful, sinuous Bodies wove among the scrabbling Wickerjaks, smashing and clawing at the monsters and stopping their advance cold.

Yet more were on their way.

Felix pumped a bit more Mana into the stone wall around them, sounding Green Shaping and Rime Shaping for good measure. The stone turned dark blue and glassy, with glowing red veins throughout its surface before he cut it off. "That should do the trick for now."

He focused forward, beyond the chaos of battle, to where the Spirit Tree rose above them all. That same purple glow suffused its trunk, beneath the matted tangle of vines and clinging plants, and it pulsed brighter and brighter every second. The light among the Wickerjaks pulsed in time, and Felix saw the fishing-line-thin threads of connection between them all.

Skein of Fate is level 49!

Is the light in the Tree itself, or in the vines that are choking it out? Felix cannot tell, but he also cannot delay any longer. His friends were fighting a dangerous battle, and while individually the Wickerjaks weren't overpowering any of them, en masse was another story. The War Nagas were stopped dead by the onrush of twiggy aggressors, and Beef was having a hard time swinging his hammer as Wickerjaks piled atop his arms.

Rain of Cataclysm!

Streamers of liquid Mana poured from Felix's Gates, until his hands and elbows were all but consumed in violently green power that shunted upward into the air. He sounded Cardinal Flame at the same time as his AOE acid spell, shaping the torpid cloud that formed far above him into something that kept clear of his allies and focused on the Spirit Tree itself. Much as he didn't want to destroy it, he would if it meant his friends survived.

As the spell built, Felix kicked and stomped on any Wickerjaks that made it to him, but they were few in number. His team and the semicircular wall behind them were holding the lot of the monsters at bay, though they all suffered for it. Knife-edged branches sliced bloody gashes in arms and legs and faces, an onslaught of wounds that wouldn't kill them, but were slowing them all down.

Yet as Felix watched, somewhat helplessly, Beef, Vess, Pit, Hallow, and even the War Nagas suddenly blurred. Their forms bled into one another, hard to pin down and harder to hit, as the Wickerjaks soon found out. More of them tumbled back, struck by weapons and Skills that they never saw coming. Manasight flaring, Felix could spot the augmentation Mana, a shade of purple that was distinct from the virulent light of the monsters. *An illusion.*

The Mana flowed in liquid streams from a single source: Isla. The Chanter stood back in the safety of the walls, hands outstretched and a song on her lips. Felix couldn't hear it over the din of battle, but he suspected it was more than that; he shivered as a massive weight shifted in the air, intangible to the physical but immensely vast to the Spirit. She met Felix's gaze and gave him a small nod…before her eyes widened in alarm.

Felix spun, following her line of sight, and found a new creature entering the fray. His Eye named it a Moontouched Wickerjak Elder, and it was far, far stronger than its lesser brethren. It was also five times their size, reaching somewhere around fifteen feet tall and covered in vicious thorns. A head made of twisted vines and glowing purple eyes swiveled until they landed on him. It stomped through, flowing past its allies in a beeline toward Felix.

Relentless Resolution!

Felix charged forward, zipping past his allies faster than they could track. Wind roared at his back, hurling several Wickerjaks in his wake, and Felix sounded Sovereign of Flesh.

Sovereign of Flesh is level 82!

Bones cracked, and flesh swelled, splitting and turning to diamond-hard scales the color of midnight. He expanded in size, muscles ballooning as he grew four feet in a span of moments. Felix's Garment grew along with him, but still, his rapid increase in size was too fast for its magic: he tore it apart at the shoulders, chest, elbows, and knees. Brilliant cyan spikes of bone jutted from his joints, his claws shone with a crackling light that sparked through a spectrum of red-gold and blue-white, while his jaw was overgrown by a half-mask of dark scale and monstrous, massive fangs.

Felix met the Elder fist-first. The creature's thorny hide buckled and snapped, and the monstrosity's immense momentum was arrested and overcome. It flew backward, smashing sideways into the ground before rolling through the underbrush and dozens of its Wickerjak allies. But the thing wasn't so easily defeated. New limbs grew from its body, pressing into the earth and shoving it back to standing before it ran at Felix once again.

Corrosive Strike!

Cardinal Flame!

Sounding his acid punch Skill, Felix didn't stop there. He grabbed at his semi-complete Rain of Cataclysm, the cloud of liquid Mana that hung among the leaves, and shaped it down into his strike. Cardinal

Flame burned bright in his core space, its song hauntingly beautiful as Felix wound up and jabbed forward with all of his Strength. Acidic Mana trailed after the punch like a comet's tail, and the raging Wickerjak Elder met his punch with its own…and was immediately overcome.

The Elder split and shattered, bark, wood, and resin rendered to mush with a deafening sizzle. Resilient, wooden flesh fought back but was no match for Felix's unconquerable Willpower, nor the force of his Mana and control. Cardinal Flame aided him, sending the acidic Mana in spiraling, explosive flows through the Elder's frame, eating it up from the inside out.

You Have Killed A Moontouched Wickerjak Elder!
XP Earned!

The Elder fell to pieces, still sizzling and popping, but the magic didn't stop there. It lashed outward in a circle guided by Felix, a spinning storm of acidic Mana that ripped into all of the lesser Wickerjaks that tried to attack him.

You Have Killed A Moontouched Wickerjak (x56)!
XP Earned!

They were torn to shreds, instantly.

Skill Evolution!

Felix stood stock still among the sizzling dead as the notification overcame him. *What's this?*

Due To The Massive Influx Of Acidic Mana, The Influence Of Rain Of Cataclysm, Wild Threnody, Cardinal Flame, And Skein Of Fate, Your Skill Corrosive Strike Can Evolve!
WARNING!
This Will Consume An Extreme Amount Of Energy!
Failure To Provide Requisite Energy Will Result in Death Or Worse.
Do You Wish To Evolve Corrosive Strike?

Abso-fucking-lutely.

Stand By.

Essence and Mana fled Felix by the boatload, but he had more than enough. Unlike previous evolutions or combinations, the pain was barely palpable, and existed only as a sharp pressure in his middle for a brief handful of seconds.

Congratulations!
Corrosive Strike Has Become Hand Of Calamity!
Hand of Calamity (Legendary), Level 1!
Your affinity for destruction is only matched by the nature of acid itself. Consumption and corrosion, you hold calamity in the palm of your hand. Beware. Control of acid Mana increases per Skill level. Amount of acid Mana controlled increases moderately per Skill level.

"Another shaping Skill," Felix said, his armored mask grinning with him. "Hell yeah."

Felix stumbled as he felt the Spirit Tree shake the very earth. It took him a heartbeat to realize that it wasn't the earth that shook, but his Spirit. A massive, oppressive weight slammed into him. Into all of them. Once he realized that, Felix marshaled his own powerful Adept Spirit and slipped free of its influence, but the Tree's Spirit was persistent. It wasn't just an oppressive weight, but a myriad of wild impressions that forced his senses into disarray. Felix's vision blurred at the edges, while a high, atonal note sheared through his hearing.

Above, Pit shook it off, too. He shared in Felix's Spiritual potency through their bond, but the others were all wincing or had fallen to their knees on the ground. Wickerjaks surrounded them, lashing their flesh with arms of sharpened bramble and thorn. Their offensive was entirely broken, and it was all his team could do to defend themselves.

Without warning, vines tore outward from the Spirit Tree, criss-crossing the air like a net. "Pit!"

"I see it!" His Companion dodged the spearing vines, twisting and spinning through them with an incredible grace born of Agility and Dexterity.

Pit's Thunderwing is level 72!

Yet he could not avoid it all, and the vines were too restricting. He dropped back to the ground, reverting to his puppy form as he landed. His Mantle of Tumult crackled around him, a tiny, savage storm among the leaves, and he tore into the Wickerjaks with tooth and claw.

Pit's Mantle of Tumult is level 76!
Pit's Bloody Gnaw is level 76!
Pit's Hurricane Rasp is level 76!

Pit's Howl At The Dark is level 69!

Wickerjaks were frozen in place, stricken with a brief stun status as Pit protected their friends.

"Kick their asses, bud!" Felix cheered, wincing at the deeply upsetting sound of the Spirit Tree's offensive. It kicked up a notch, increasing in volume and tempo as more Wickerjak Elders emerged from beneath the Tree's great roots. Mud squelched and popped, birthing these goliath abominations, flooding them with a sticky liquid light. An ooze.

"Goddamn it. The Fathom's been here, too?" Felix turned to face the approaching horde, staring down over a dozen of the Elders now as they slowly worked themselves into a charge. There were too many for him to handle alone, not if his friends couldn't evade or properly protect themselves. If he was too slow, they would die.

The tone of the Tree's Spirit shifted, pitching higher than it ever had before. From behind Felix, Beef screamed out. "It's the Tree! It's in my chest! Kill the Tree, Felix! I—I got this!"

Blades of chitin sprang from the earth, shearing through Wickerjaks in great swathes as Beef demolished those nearest him. Hallow was just behind him, stampeding the creatures as they were mowed down by crystalline darts the size of short swords. The teen Minotaur bellowed, his voice a pressure all its own that somehow pushed back the Spirit Tree's presence. Pit ran to them, ears flopping within his lightning shroud, and the War Nagas were free, their foes scattered by the combined assault.

Felix turned back to the stomping Elders and took a measured breath. Thanks to Beef, the Tree had lost some of its grip, and that atonal buzzing resolved into something he recognized. It was the opposite of the strident melody of Harmony, a sound he heard with every revolution of his cores. In that song, Dissonance sang strongly, accompanied by additional elements he hadn't been able to parse out. However, now that he found it, Felix could track the sound through all of the plants around him, back to the Spirit Tree itself…and a spot upon its bole that resonated in distorting whorls of energy.

Adamant Discord is level 84!

Skein of Fate is level 50!
Adept Tier!
You Gain:
+20 RES
+20 REI
+20 FEL

There.

Felix blasted forward, dirt and plants ripping up in his wake. He slammed into and through the lumbering Elders, who were just now getting up to speed. They tried and failed to stop him, but when Felix passed through their grips like oiled smoke, they gave up and continued their charge. Toward his friends.

Felix put it out of his mind, focusing wholly upon his task. More Elders were crawling from the root-muck, and more would keep coming if he failed.

Dissonance was a piercing pain through his ears now, both physical and metaphysical, but Felix did not stop. He kicked off a bulging root, launching himself into the air as flowers the color of gold and dark purple split and bloomed, shooting darts the size of javelins at him.

Adamant Discord!

He grabbed at them, their trajectory forming brief connections to him that Felix could repurpose. Claimed, he swung his arms, still in flight, and hurled the darts into the bark of the Spirit Tree. Lightning snapped, discharging in their wake as they sank into the bark, and Felix landed atop them.

"Can't stop me so easily, Tree!" Felix grasped the craggy bark and hauled himself upward with a mighty thrust and a blast of Adamant Discord to the ground below. Felix landed among the tangled vines at the curving apex of the trunk, where the first several branches spread outward. He screwed up his nose at the sudden, foul scent. "Eugh. That's nasty."

Before him, nestled among the bole, was a reservoir of the Fathom's bubbling ooze. It felt perhaps a touch weaker than the ooze in the chasms, but his Skein of Fate and Adamant Discord could see thick cables racing into the distance…connecting it to something far greater.

If I absorb it, the Fathom will see us again. It could find us before we're ready. Felix hesitated, worrying at the possibilities. And, he could admit, a little fearful of the vast presence he had felt the last time he'd attempted consuming the ooze. *But if I eat it, then immediately burn the power I take… will that be enough?*

It didn't matter. It had to be.

"Sorry Abundant Anima. This isn't going to feel good." He shoved his arm into the ooze, immediately feeling its vile bite. "*Chthonic Tribute!*"

Ooze turned to wretched smoke, flooded with purple, and it raced toward Felix so fast that it threw him bodily from the Spirit Tree itself.

He couldn't speak or scream, because the world flashed and twisted. Shattered.

Unbidden, without even a warning, a Memory consumed him.

CHAPTER SEVENTY-SIX

Ephemeral Evocation is level 9!

As with the Memory he'd stolen from the illusion array, Felix was deposited directly into the action. He dropped to the floor, skidding atop a layer of loam that had been scattered across dark marble. Felix stood as soon as his feet found purchase, quickly realizing his Body had returned to its mostly-Human appearance. He flared his Perception hard, attempting to take in everything at once.

It didn't ask me to view the Memory. Didn't even warn me that there was *one.* Felix's cores spun, grinding against one another as if to mimic the agitation that filled him. *What's going on?*

Typically, when things went weird, it involved forces that were far beyond Felix. He was more than prepared for the Fathom to suddenly appear before him, monstrous and huge...but the chamber remained silent. Perhaps too silent. The foliage that had overrun the vast room surrounding the Spirit Tree was mostly absent. In its place was a series of glass-lined enclosures, inscribed with sigils to seal and strengthen them.

Almost every one was shattered.

Plants were scattered in all directions, but not as it was in the present. No dense network of roots had taken hold, nor had vast mounds of earth built up in discrete hills and valleys. Felix could still see the marble flooring, inlaid with gold and precious stones to form half-glimpsed sigaldry. Free of vines and foliage, the walls were lined with arcane instruments that glowed with various forms of Mana vapor. In the very center, unhindered by invasive growths, was the Spirit Tree.

And it was dying.

Felix took a concerned step forward before stopping. *Just a Memory,* he reminded himself. *See where it leads.*

Blue ooze had already made its way into the chamber, pooling around the Tree's roots on the left side. He watched thin tendrils slap outward, slowly squelching higher. As they did, the ooze took on a distinct purple hue that bled through its form like dye in water.

This Was The Last Day.

Felix jolted, his attention snapping outward from the crawling ooze. There was no one in the room with him, however. No one but the Tree itself. "The Last Day?" he asked.

Watch, Inheritor. Beware.

Without warning, Felix was hurled from the Spirit Tree's chamber, rushing along some tight corridor at breakneck speed. His Body had vanished, rendered into a simple set of eyes that slipped up through the oozing walls of the hallway, past flashing sigaldry and into the vast, dark pressures of the deep waters beyond.

Roots, he realized. *I'm traveling along the Spirit Tree's roots.*

Indeed, as he flashed through the water, he rose, granted a new vantage of the shattered terrain. The water was more clear than it was in reality, and Felix's vision spread for what seemed like miles. Roots branched out in all directions, but the largest and thickest followed a curving arc across the unbroken earth, until they reached another lone tower in the depths. Cast to a far distant time, this tower looked nothing like stone, but a living thing of wood and wavering fronds. A familiar aura hung around it.

Another Spirit Tree? They're connected?

Not others. One.

Felix's eyes widened at the voice, just as his blistering progress through the waters blurred into unfathomable speeds. Roots spread out, the thickest still describing a curving arc as tower after tower interrupted the roots at set intervals. The aura was always the same, resplendent and proud…and filled with an ineffable sense of loss.

The Spirit Tree was there, spread among the waters like a massive network of coral. A single organism that had clearly been grown deliberately, based on the precise way the roots were laid out. Those spoke volumes once Felix noticed them, twisted and bending in whorling designs. In fact, the longer he sped around the Abundance Anima's network, the more he saw. Patterns grown into root and branch and leaf.

No. Not a pattern. An array. A huge, hundred-mile-long array that branched through the entire area that he knew now as Khasma. The ground was still shattered in the vision, but it seemed healthier, with even more greenery among the ravines and chasms. At least, until Felix spiraled out far enough that he could see the whole of the Tree's growth. The roots and Trees grew around a center, and there, far below him, Felix perceived a hollow shaft big enough to swallow Ahkestria with room to spare.

An abyss.

Words fluttered back to Felix, recalled from a previous Memory, as if the deer-man himself whispered them into Felix's ear. *"You think this array will truly keep our Minds away from...from that* thing *we watch?"*

Look.

Dark hands grasped Felix's shoulders, then his jaw, guiding his vision with a gentleness he couldn't refuse. Suddenly possessing a Body again, Felix was wracked by the gelid crawl of something visceral inside him. An instinct, a message from his hind brain that had nothing to do with the System or Skills. It stalked through him, a twisting chill across his spine and heart and lungs until he realized he couldn't breathe. The sound of discordant chaos speared up at him, driving barbed hooks into that crawling, primal fear.

Below, in the dark depths, something shifted. Writhed. Like a moon slipping free of eclipse, a vast, pale face fixated upon him.

And it grinned.

"Got you!"

Felix was aware of rushing wind and the sensation of falling when a pair of huge, hairy hands grabbed at him. Felix's Mind stuttered and shook, still consumed by a pale visage he could not unsee...yet one he could no longer envision. Its features melted and sank, dropping down into the eternal dark like a hole in the world itself. He landed, uncontrolled and heavy, as someone screamed beneath him.

The scream brought him back, and Felix blinked to find himself splayed across the lumpy earth and staring up into the dim outlines of wide branches and deep blue leaves. Everything felt unmoored and wobbly, but Felix twisted until he saw Beef writhing on the ground only ten feet away. Tears poured down his face, and his arms were twisted into two extremely unnatural positions. Guilt and worry thrummed against Felix's Spirit, but they were as distant as Isla's sharp words.

"Hold still, Michael! I need to reset your shoulders! Damn fool, trying to catch him! You are not strong enough!" The Chanter was practically on top of Beef, her hands weaving liquid strands of Mana into a complex net around the Minotaur's arms and torso. She looked to Felix, and rare concern was etched across her features. "Felix. Are you alright? What happened when you consumed the corruption?"

Felix didn't answer, because the ooze inside of him took the time to remind him of its presence. It roiled—a barely contained storm that wracked his core space with tempestuous winds. That wasn't all, however, because Felix could also feel a vast presence shifting its attention toward them all, as if all the music around him had dropped several octaves.

For a brief, terrifying moment, he feared it was the sunken *thing* in his Mind...before recognizing its familiar cadence.

Fathom. He panicked, jolting to his feet so fast that the earth depressed all around him as he sped off.

"Felix! What are you doing?" Vess and Isla shouted after him, almost in unison.

The Wickerjaks, small and large, reached trembling claws out at him as he blasted by, but their strength was gone. Felix's clawed feet smashed across their brittle bodies, now entirely devoid of that purple light. He paid them as much attention as his friend's queries. He'd been thrown farther from the Spirit Tree than expected, but the distance vanished swiftly beneath his heels.

What's happening? Do you need help? Pit sent, trying and failing to keep up with Felix's mad dash.

"Just stay clear, bud!" Felix skidded to a stop at the base of the Abundance Anima. The vines and fronds upon its surface had withered to husks, and the Tree itself was little better. A thin dirge threaded through Felix's Affinity, pinging against his Aria of the Green Wilds to bloom into knowledge: the Tree was dying, fast.

Grasping all of the churning potency within his core space, Felix seized it with the twin pincers of Intent and Willpower, before sounding the resplendent strains of his most mysterious Skill. "Unite the Lost!"

Essence, Mana, and significance surged forward, spun through the oscillating pattern of his Skill before metabolizing into something *more.* Beneath Felix's outstretched palms, the Spirit Tree quivered and quaked, rippling like the constricting surface of a massive serpent. And just like a snake, the desiccated vegetation shed from it like a second skin, its bark peeling in great strips wherever the flood of Felix's Skill washed over it.

A concussive blast ripped through him, forcing Felix to dig in his heels as a wave of pressure savaged the underbrush in all directions, devastating the Wickerjaks that remained. Their Bodies were mowed down, the little animation left in them torn loose before becoming rooted where they stood.

The Abundance Anima was waking up.

Another blast flowed from the Spirit Tree, hurling the shed detritus from its bole as life took hold. The Green Wild sang, an enkindled chorus of destruction and rebirth, a bright, glorious violence alongside a deep and verdant tranquility. Flowers bloomed from the corpses of the Wickerjaks, and the dimming crystal above them surged to newfound radiance, until sunbeams shone along the dancing branches far above. Creation followed destruction, hand-in-hand; two sides of the same coin.

Harmony and Dissonance.

There was no warning as the Skill cut off, only a mountainous weariness that sat atop his back, and a sudden, unnatural silence.

I...Am Whole.
Thank You.

Felix sat, almost but not quite crushed by his exhaustion. He patted the thick root next to him. "Don't...don't mention it."

"Your sacrifice will not be forgotten, Felix Nevarre."

It was a mark of his fatigue that Felix didn't immediately summon a hailstorm of acid or lightning or do much else but turn his head toward the deep, smooth voice that had spoken. A man stood beside him, well-shadowed by the branches of the rejuvenated Spirit Tree. He was tall, somewhere between Felix and Beef, but slender with fine, angled features. His long hair was pulled back into a series of braids, and his skin was almost the exact brown as the Tree's bark. Were it not for the white robes that hugged his lean frame, Felix supposed the man could be lost among its surface. The man stared at Felix with eyes that were entirely blue, without whites.

"Sacrifice?" Felix asked, tensing slightly. He might have been exhausted, but he still had a little left in the tank. His Mana and Stamina were already refilling. "I hope that's not a threat, stranger."

"Not a threat, not to one who possesses Unite the Lost. You have expended so much of who you are, the stolid foundation upon which your Aspects balance. Giving such a bounty away will kill you. A life for a life." He shook his head, and a sense of deep regret and sorrow rang out from him. "You have restored a piece of my Companion. Were it in my power, I would save you. As it is, I will ensure that you are not forgotten."

Felix chuckled. "Oh, that." With an effort that sent a quiver of strain across his cores, Felix pushed himself to his feet. "Just give me a couple minutes, and I'll be alright."

The man blinked, his thin brows furrowing on his dark face. "I do not understand. How is this possible?"

Felix wasn't sure how to answer that. "Well, I didn't really use my own significance, at least not a lot of it. Are you actually here, or is this some sort of spiritual projection or something?" He reached out, flicking his hand through where the man stood. There was nothing there, though the man's form didn't waver or anything. "Yeah. I thought so."

"Wha—?"

"Unf, my head hurts," Felix said, wincing as his thoughts tried to jump at the *thing* he'd glimpsed in the Memory. He forcefully wrested his Mind free of it, but it cost him. "That's not going away anytime soon. Wait. You said Companion?"

The illusory man regarded Felix with curiosity, alarm, and a considerable amount of sudden fear. "You're Unbound."

"And you," Isla shouted, shoving her way through the flowering underbrush. She was followed by Pit, Vess, Beef, and all the rest. "You are Nymean, aren't you?"

CHAPTER SEVENTY-SEVEN

"Everyone can see him?" Felix asked, surprised.

"Yeah," Beef grunted. He was being supported by two Naga, shoulders seemingly repaired but still in clear pain. "He kinda looks like you. Sorta."

"Nymean," Vess said with an awed whisper. The Spears behind her tilted back, away from the white-robed figure. "How?"

"A detail that concerns me as well," Isla remarked, before arching an eyebrow. "You still have not answered my question, spirit. Are you Nymean?"

"I am of the Nym, yes," the dark-skinned phantom said, though he did not address Isla directly. His strange eyes bored into Felix's instead. "How...how long have I slept, Unbound?"

"If I had to guess...it's been something like several Ages?"

The phantom's head rocked back like Felix had punched him, and he reached out to press his long-fingered hand against the restored bark of the Spirit Tree. "So long. From the looks your allies are giving me, I fear the answer, but I must ask this as well: how fares the Empire?"

Pit let out a trilling cry, no longer in his puppy form. "Bad news there."

"A Chimera. I am honored," the phantom bowed to Pit as the tenku ambled forward. "Please explain this 'bad news.'"

"Uh." Pit gave Felix a look, clearly unsure how to proceed.

"That's a long conversation, and I need to make sure of something. Hold on," Felix said. He stepped closer to the Abundance Anima and laid a hand upon its trunk. Life Mana thrummed beneath his fingertips like rivers of rolling timpanis and bright, crashing cymbals. Felix pressed deeper, flaring his Affinity. Blue-white lightning crackled from his shoulders, and a rush of sublime music assaulted his ears as Adamant Discord and Skein of Fate were both activated.

Yet Felix felt nothing more than the Tree itself. The connection to the Fathom was no longer immediately present. "Whew. Okay, good."

"What was the purpose of that?" Vess asked, cautiously sidling up to Felix. She hadn't banished her Spears, and still watched the phantom like he would vanish at any moment. "Are you alright?"

"Just peachy. I had to eat the ooze infecting the Spirit Tree, and that left me open to the ooze's connection to the Fathom." Felix gestured vaguely into the distance. "I did it before, and the damn thing notices every time. If I hadn't burned it up to restore the Tree, then we'd be facing down the monster boss already."

"So it knows we are here?" Isla asked, her voice sharp.

"No. Well, sorta. I've gotten its attention enough that I'm sure the Fathom knows about me, but it's never been able to pinpoint my location." Felix tapped right below his sternum. "The connection in me is gone as well. What little I didn't use up, I devoured."

"Devoured," said the Nym, tilting his head. Combined with his all-blue stare, it came across as alien and a little unnerving. "That is the province of beasts and monsters. Unbound, what Race did you choose upon arrival?"

"Oh." Felix scratched his jaw. "That's a complicated answer."

"Were you not guided to a suitable choice?" the phantom asked. Felix could hear the man speak, the rustle of his robes and where his hands rubbed nervously against his thighs...but the Nym's feet made no sound upon the ground, nor bent a single frond below. "An Augur should have consulted the Omens during your reception. What did they say?"

Felix laughed. It was easier to do now, across the gulf of months. "That would have been nice. But no. No Augur. No answers at all, really."

"What fools would summon the Unbound and not follow the Path of Arrival? Who performed the summoning?"

"Someone you wouldn't know, I'd wager. Listen, all this is great to learn and all, but we're pressed for time. What is your deal? Wait, no. What's your name, first?"

"I was once called Paxus, Chanter of the Green Wilds and Companion to the Abundance Anima." The Nym's voice deepened, ever so slightly, as if he were used to giving his full title as part of a ceremony.

"Chanter?" Isla asked. Her voice, by contrast, slipped higher and filled with an uncharacteristic excitement. "You are a Nymean Chanter? Of the Grand Harmony?"

"A facet of it, yes. Specialization is the heartsblood of potency, after all. Harmony itself asks for it, and for all pieces to work together as one." Paxus frowned. "This, too, should have been explained upon your initialization into the Harmony's pattern."

"Right." Felix would rather avoid having to rehash his unorthodox arrival to the Continent. If not for brevity's sake, than for Paxus'; the man's Spirit was all but unguarded, and Felix could hear it shaking like a leaf in autumn. He was more affected by their revelations than he let on. "The facet you're talking about is the Green Wilds, right? What is that, exactly?"

"The Green Wilds? They are the verses of the great song that brings life from death and death to life. All things that grow must also perish, in order to fuel more growth. The Green Wilds are a cycle that never ends but will always flourish once more."

"I have a skill called the Aria of the Green Wilds. Is that related?"

"Ah yes. I had thought I detected some resonance within your Spirit. Following the path of the Green Wilds is a popular choice among us, even among the Unbound. Or, so I have heard."

"Right. That Path." Felix cleared his throat. "You mentioned being a Companion. To the Spirit Tree?"

"Of course. Not all of us are found worthy of a Chimera's attention, after all." Paxus once again bowed to Pit, who took the opportunity to preen under the attention.

Isla strode right up to Paxus and stared up at him. She was over a foot shorter than Felix, let alone the taller Nym, but still her gaze was steel. "Answer swiftly. We haven't the time to waste. What is this place? What is its purpose, and how was it perverted by this strange ooze?"

Paxus frowned, but he did not back down from the small blonde woman. "You stand within my Companion, the Abundance Anima, spread round the floor of this sea after the Convocation of the Sundered determined it must be studied."

"Sea? Thought this was a lake," Beef muttered.

Felix nodded. "I was right, then. It's a research facility."

"Researching what, exactly?" Vess asked.

"The Breach."

Felix's Mind scrambled for a moment upon hearing the word, as if someone had sent ten thousand volts coursing through his spine. A darkness spread outward, a great abyss of water and shadow that raged with invisible currents...and a face that drove unthinking terror into his limbs. Doors of stone slammed shut, massive gates that cut the image away from his Mind, sealing it within a tomb of glassy blue rock. Felix blinked, suddenly staring at his own hands. Both were crackling with blue-white lightning and crimson-gold flame, and the ground at his feet was charred to ash.

Title: The Call Of Defiance Is Active!
+25% Willpower When Contested By A Foe Of Divine Or Greater Advancement!

Bastion of Will is level 92!

"Felix, it's okay," Pit cooed at him. His big head pressed down into Felix's hands, and the song of his Skills cut out. "Focus on me."

He looked up, swallowing to clear the bile from his throat. "What—what did I do?"

Isla stared at him as if he were someone she had never seen. An animal, perhaps. Beef, Hallow, and the War Nagas had all fled back about twenty feet; well outside of the ring of charred earth. Vess stepped forward, just a hair behind Pit. "You screamed something and hit the ground. Felix...Felix what did you see in that Memory?"

Felix licked his lips and met Vess' gaze. It was soft, but her brow was taut with worry. "Something awful. It...it lives in the Breach—" He tensed, feeling his thoughts stutter, but this time, he was prepared. "There's a hole in the world, and my Mind keeps skipping back to it."

"The Creature," Paxus said. He remained nearby, his white robes untouched by the devastation Felix had wrought. "You have seen it?"

"Only in a Memory I took from your Tree...or from the ooze, maybe." Felix stood up with Vess' help, and he did not push her away. "I saw the Abundance Anima spread wide, all over the bottom of this lake, connected by huge roots to other Trees. All of them surround this...hole in the center. Inside it...inside it is something I can't describe."

"You have seen it, then. All of the magi who worked within my Companion were tasked with viewing the Creature at least once. It slumbered for a great many centuries; an entire Age, we think. The facility, the array we grew, all of it was an effort to contain it within the Breach." Paxus ran a hand over the thick root of his Companion Tree. "Together, our efforts were enough, and the magi were allowed to focus on exploring the unique flora and fauna within the trenches."

"Breach," rumbled Toa'ut. The War Naga had remained silent all this time, his brooding profile watching without expression. Now, however, Felix heard the quiver of alarm in him. "The Breach is where the Fathom resides."

"The center of Khasma," Lavix said, her voice almost as deep. "The stronghold of its spawn."

"Are you suggesting the Fathom is this Creature they're talking about?" Isla asked.

"I do not know. Only that Khasma's center is where we are headed, and if this Creature is there, it will prove troublesome." Toa'ut's brow furrowed more than usual. "Deadly, perhaps."

Felix had finally mastered himself, flaring his Bastion to greater heights as he cut off the intrusive thoughts. "They're separate. I've felt the Fathom's influence, and it was *nothing* like this. The Creature or whatever, it triggered my Call of Defiance Title."

"I thought that only occurs when you are contested by a Divinity?" Vess asked. Isla and Paxus both gasped, sounding nothing alike yet united in their surprise.

"Divinity or greater, according to the Title." Felix looked around, meeting his team's gazes and nodding. "Yeah. That's what we seem to be up against."

The Nym studied Felix, his open Spirit vibrating with surprise, delight, and a constant measure of fear. The fear hadn't subsided, not since the guy had put together Felix's identity. "You would face the Creature, Unbound?"

Aiming for nonchalance, Felix shrugged. "If I have to. I'd rather not, though, so anything you can tell me would be golden."

Paxus straightened his spine, and his braided hair swung in time with his sudden bow. "As you wish, Unbound. What do you wish to know?"

"Let's start from the top. Is the Abundance Anima here and all over the lake bed? They're all one organism?"

"Correct. My Companion agreed to securing the Breach in return for her cuttings to be planted all over the Empire. Her root systems have been grown intentionally to form a seal over the Breach, one that was fueled by the Spirit Tree's power. It was, we thought, impregnable."

"And how did you come to be in this...form?" Isla asked, gesturing to his immaterial body.

Paxus pressed an arm through a bright pink blossom, not even shaking the dew from its new-grown petals. "The how remains a touch hazy...but I recall the why of it." The corners of his mouth tightened into the shadow of a grimace. "One of the Abundance's Trees fell to the Creature's corruption. That ooze of which you speak, the substance that clogged this very chamber, it bored into the seal and created a flaw. That is the only thing that would have caused the cascade of failures we saw that day.

"I...We gave ourselves to the seal, to keep the Creature below." Paxus touched the tip of his tongue to his teeth, his expression cycling between so many emotions Felix found them hard to track. "My Body was sacrificed. My Mind and Spirit live on within my Companion's Trees. When you revived her, you revived me as well. From the depths of my heartsong, thank you, Lord Unbound."

"You're welcome." Felix looked up at the spreading branches of the Tree. "I assume the other Trees are still corrupted, then?"

"Indeed. We are connected, but the sensation is muddled and sour. I can feel more of those Wickerjak monstrosities prowling the root tunnels, filled with foul light."

"Wait, wait," Felix said, holding up a hand. "What root tunnels?"

CHAPTER SEVENTY-EIGHT

Paxus led everyone back down the stairs of the tower, and Pit goggled at the changes that had taken place. Where the chamber had been chock full of tangled vines and choked-off soil, now it was a cultured path lined with pink blossoms and the thick, rugged roots of the Spirit Tree.

This is much nicer, Pit thought at his Companion. Felix flashed a tight smile at him before returning his attention to the Nymean phantom. The tall ghost was speaking, talking about trees and roots or something. Pit didn't care to pay much attention. His primary concern was potential threats.

Pit snuffled at the ground. He smelled loam and violence, muted by thick sap and the rotting tang of sweet petals turned foul. The Stickmen had fallen, many killed by Pit and his team, but the rest had been felled by Felix's use of Unite the Lost. When the Spirit Tree returned to its senses, a great wave of spiritual pressure and Mana had shot outward from its trunk. Pit recalled the feel of it rippling across his fur and feathers. It had tasted like springtime rain and winter's chill ice, all at once.

Mana Digestion In Process...

For the first time in a long while, a Skill was brewing within Pit's core. Recently, he had only gained minimal stat points from the various cores he devoured, and even that was giving diminishing returns. He'd long since lost the Gourmand Title that he and Felix had shared—responsible for Pit stealing things like Cold Resistance and Poisonfire from his enemies. Things were different now, though. He wasn't sure if it was due to his Etheric Concordance or simply to the fact that Pit was now also a Primordial, and he didn't much care.

I wonder what Skill it might be? The possibilities filled him with excitement. Seeing Felix learn his new illusion spell had him champing at the bit for new abilities. *Hopefully it isn't some plant Skill. That'd be boring.*

They pressed down the stairs and through the network of ruined quarters. Many of those rooms were free of clogging plant matter, and Pit immediately wandered through the unblocked chambers. They all smelled so tantalizing, like old pungent moss and grubs under wet logs, and he followed his nose through as many as he could enter. Sadly, he found little other than rotting furniture, the ground up shells of big beetles, and, in the last chamber, Isla pulling some of those Manalamps off the walls. Pit huffed in annoyance.

"What?" she asked, small face pinching around her tiny nose. "These are wondrous artifacts from another Age. They need to be preserved."

Pit cocked his head. "Have you found any food?"

"...No."

The tenku groaned and walked back out.

They moved on quickly from that space, the big Slithers carrying sacks that bulged with more of those lamps. Pit swore he saw a half-crumbled chair leg, too, but he didn't care. He smelled a new flavor on the air. Felix, clearly sensing his Companion's distress, produced a number of large fruits that he called "Hot Watermelons." The sense image that came with the description was confusing, as the watermelon Felix recalled was green with stripes instead of a bright yellow with swirly black spots. Still, it tasted almost exactly like Pit expected: juicy, watery, and very spicy.

Pit ate all of them.

The team pressed on, down the next set of stairs and beyond the broken hall of illusions, or whatever Felix called it. The stairwell went deeper, as the phantom informed them. Round and round and round, their team drilled down into the rock below, the stone walls giving way to uneven bark. Pit was forced to shift back into his Dire Hound form, shrinking until he was the size of a puppy and more able to navigate the tighter confines.

"Tell me, spirit. Why do you remain visible? Is it due to the Companion bond?" Isla shuffled down the steps, boots splashing in worn grooves or clambering over uneven roots. Her face, however, remained impassive and steady, as if she were taking a stroll across a manicured lawn. Pit watched her, confused as to why she was putting such an effort into looking unaffected as she dogged the heels of the phantom.

"In part," he replied, his two-tone voice sounding more than a little bored.

"Does the Chant play into it?"

"The Chant plays into all things. It is the Chant. A practitioner of your Tier should be intimately aware of that."

"Of course. I am simply attempting to determine where my knowledge and your own intersect and diverge. A great deal of information has been Lost in the Ages since your kind dominated the Continent—"

"We did not dominate," Paxus said, more forceful than Pit had ever heard the spirit. "That is the *point.*"

Paxus left her, floating downward faster than the Chanter could keep up while maintaining her dignity. Pit trilled a light laugh at the anger on Isla's face, but scurried down the steps when she turned the expression on him. Thankfully, he was quite fast.

"Honored Tenku."

Pit looked up. Everyone was a lot taller than him when he was a Dire Hound pup. "Hello, Nym."

"Call me Paxus, please. I would be honored if I could call you by your given name as well."

Pit shrugged. "I'm Pit. Nice to meet you, Paxus."

"You as well." The spirit walked with Pit for a while longer, silent but in a way that Pit actually liked. Since the Void, quiet was something that left Pit feeling more than a little unnerved. This silence didn't feel empty, however, but hummed pleasantly. It reminded him of Felix. "Might I ask for your Path?" he asked after another turn of the stairs.

"I walk the Path of the Guardian Beast." Pit lifted his beak and thrust out his chest. "I was offered others, but it's what I do. I keep Felix safe, in my own way."

"Truly? I know little of the Chimera myself, so I cannot say if that is uncommon or not, but I can understand the desire to protect those you care about." Paxus ran an insubstantial hand across the bark, his skin and bones shifting as if he were really touching it. "I am a protector as well. Path of the Verdant Warden."

"To protect your Tree?"

"Indeed. While she has a plethora of defensive measures, her nature limits her ability to remain free from all threats. I have raised Abundance since she was no more than a seed, gifted to me by the Empyrean Halls. She is more family to me than those of my blood."

Pit nodded. He understood that completely. "Felix...Felix can protect himself. He's Unbound, and a strong one. He protects the team, his army, even his enemies, if they let him." Pit snorted, wrinkling his soft snout. It was always a little odd to not have a beak. "He protects everyone, but no one protects him. That's *my* job."

Paxus smiled, and it was a handsome thing, despite the all-blue eyes.

"I commend you, Honored Pit. Defending those you love is a noble Path. To speak frankly, it is the only reason I still live."

"Oh?" Pit hopped over a thick root. "What happened?"

The phantom waved off the question. "The Creature's final strike should have killed us all and broken the seal. I cannot remember the details, but the power in that abyss is not to be underestimated. Yet somehow I stand, not whole, but cognizant of my own existence. That is more than I can say for the magi who once lived here." The spirit looked up, back toward the living quarters, perhaps. "I doubt they ever saw true daylight again."

Paxus sighed. "It was quite nice, my Body. Formed during my training in the Empyrean Halls and touched by the magic of that place. Not as sturdy as some of your folk, perhaps, but I miss it. Perhaps I will grow used to my new circumstances after a while, but I am finding it...frustrating to be unable to touch."

Pit blinked. "My Companion is good at getting new Bodies for people. We have a Karys in a big metal shell, now."

"A Karys?"

"A friend," Felix interrupted, appearing from nowhere to rub one of his big hands over Pit's crown. Pit let out a bark of surprise before it devolved into an uncontrolled growl of contentment. He only barely listened to the rest of his friend's words, focusing more on his sharp claws and the wonderful scratching. "Are you...able to move to a new Body?"

"I am unsure. I clearly sacrificed my original to retain even a shred of my other Aspects here in my Companion's demesne. Pieces of me, of my Companion, are locked within the corrupted seal. Were the other Trees freed of the Creature's influence, I would know more." The big gardener clenched his jaw and shook his head. "That, I fear, is too much to ask of even you, Lord Unbound."

The scratches stopped, and Pit blinked. Felix looked pensive as the phantom floated on ahead of them.

They kept walking. There were no vines or tangled growths, but the roots themselves split and multiplied, all the same color as the Spirit Tree itself. Eventually, the temperature dropped, and the stairs grew wet beneath Pit's paws.

"We are here," Paxus intoned. His voice continued to sound strange to Pit's ears, as if he were speaking in two voices, each in perfect sync with one another. "These are the lowest levels, and that," he said, gesturing his white-sleeved arm forward. "Are the root tunnels."

The landing at the bottom of the spiral stairwell was not particularly huge, but it was more than enough for three times their number to stand comfortably. The bark-covered walls flowed and split here, opening up into three separate doors that were easily double the dimensions of the silver ones above. Pit sniffed, tasting the damp in the air.

"They go out into the water?" Felix asked.

"Yes, but they are—were—quite safe. The root tunnels connect each of the Abundance's Bodies, allowing our people to travel swiftly between the stations while observing the Breach." The phantom approached a golden door inlaid with polished blue gems. The door depicted a huge tree with wide branches that spread outward across a wavering landscape. "I can feel through her that the other Trees are still injured and possessed by the Creature's foul touch. Abundance's Perception beyond this tower is limited, but she warns that there is no guarantee of safety in these tunnels."

"Better this than swimming through the open water," Vess said. "The spawn are too many here. Do these tunnels draw us closer to Khasma?"

Paxus inclined his head. "They do. Lord Unbound, you saw Abundance's Memory. Do you recall the layout of her Bodies?"

Pit felt a twitch from inside Felix, but it was swiftly suppressed before his Companion spoke. "I do. Based on the direction we were headed, that'd make us south of the Breach by a good margin."

"Thereabout, yes. We are six leagues from the Breach itself. The seal we grew was a complicated one, requiring a great many offshoots to provide stabilization to the array." Paxus held out a slender hand, and blue-green light kindled above his pale palms. "The Trees at the very edge of the Breach carry the greatest of the load. Even now, they're still maintaining a piece of the seal. She can feel that much."

"The Dragon's in the big hole, right?" Beef asked. The big bullman was still walking pretty gingerly and had discarded his conjured chest armor. "What's the plan, then? Just...just jump in and duke it out?"

"That would be foolish," Isla said. "The Fathom is Master Tier at least, and if the ooze is indeed a hallmark of this Creature you speak of, then we must anticipate that the Fathom has gained strength from it."

Paxus' dark blue eyes widened. "A Dragon has fallen to the Creature?"

"I don't think so. You said the seal is still working, right?" Felix asked.

"It is. Barely."

"Then, at worst, the Fathom has found some use for the ooze. Maybe this...Creature..." Felix barely stuttered this time when he said the name, and Pit sent a pulse of support along their bond. "Maybe it releases this gunk passively, and the Fathom is using it. Why else would it be here, in a prison made for some nightmare monster?"

"That is unlikely. All those that attempted to use the Creature's power died, whether they meant to strengthen themselves or simply cleanse it from an area." Paxus gestured to Felix. "Only the Lord

Unbound here has ever survived such an occurrence, through a confluence of Skills and capabilities that I cannot believe. That you have Unite the Lost is an astounding thing, and I do not expect even a mighty Dragon to claim the same."

"We need to talk about that in a second," Felix said. "But you're right. I do have a set of abilities that are custom-fit to take the Fathom down a notch. If we can get close enough, I might not need to step a foot into that Breach at all. These tunnels will be our ticket in and out, if we're lucky. Everyone ready?"

Shoulders squared up, and spines straightened as Felix panned around the room. Pit trotted up to him to receive a set of vigorous scratches. "I'm ready. Let's go eat some monsters."

"Damn right."

CHAPTER SEVENTY-NINE

Authority Recognized!
Inheritor, Autarch Of Nagast, King Of Ahkestria, Lord Of The Leviathan Depths, Be Welcome!
Unsealing The Northeast Root Tunnel.

Warning!
Northeast Root Tunnel Is Compromised.
Threats Detected.
Threat Designation: Moontouched Wickerjak
Threat Designation: Moontouched Thornvald
Threat Designation: Green Wild Distortion

Do You Wish To Unseal The Northeast Root Tunnel?

Thornvald? Green Wild Distortion? Felix squared his shoulders. "Yeah. Open up."

The massive golden doors split, releasing a rush of thick air that smelled of wet rot and slime. It blasted their hair back, rippling Felix's jacket and leaving the Nymean spirit at his side completely unaffected. As the gap between the golden doors expanded, he could make out a wide space lined by rugged roots, hanging vines, and muddy floors that were pocked by pools of dark water. A song like bubbling sludge percolated through the air, and lurching among it all were *hundreds* of Moontouched Wickerjaks.

Felix motioned to Pit. "I'm gonna need the Fang, bud."

Pit shifted to his tenku form, silver barding appearing from nothing to reveal the massive sword strapped just under a wing. Yet before Felix could grasp the hilt, Paxus held up a hand. "Please, Lord Unbound. Allow me."

Felix blinked. "Uh, sure. Go ahead."

With a snap of white cloth, the Nymean phantom stepped forward just as the golden doors boomed into the open position. Wickerjaks shrieked, a reedy scream that echoed through the tunnels like an amphitheater before they bounded forward. A rolling sea of twig and violet light.

"Are we...ugh...are we just standing here?" Beef asked, leaning heavily against his chitin maul. Vess and the War Nagas were beside him, tridents and spears held at the ready. "I hate the pressure down here. I feel like my head is going to pop. Can we get moving?"

"I will only be a moment," the spirit said.

The Wickerjaks were only feet away from them when Paxus lifted a single finger. That sour, slow-bubbling song was immediately overcome by the dulcet strains of woodwinds and the rolling thunder of deep drums. The tunnel itself shook, trembling and shifting just as the nearest Wickerjak came within clawing distance...and was promptly snatched back by a vibrant blue-green vine. The entire tunnel swelled, blue-green overwhelming the withered, sickly purple and gray that predominated, until the entire space was twenty feet smaller in all directions as whip-cord vines and car-sized thorns ripped through *everything*.

"Oh shit." Felix scratched his head. "You weren't kidding."

Paxus turned back to them, his form silhouetted by the spray of ooze-infected Wickerjaks as they were crushed and diced into mulch. Righteous victory roared across his Spirit, still utterly bare to Felix's senses. "I retain some control this close to my restored Companion. While it continues, please allow me to clear the path."

Felix grinned and unsheathed an eight-foot length of carved bone—a tooth from the mouth of a baby Primordial. "Sounds good to me. Move out, people. Those who can't keep up, mount up!"

Paxus proved his worth a hundred times over. The scope of his influence crushed the life out of every Wickerjak they encountered for the next hour, even at the pace at which their team moved.

After that first hour, Paxus relented, his power waning as they sped farther from the Abundance Anima's sphere of influence. Still, his manipulation of the very tunnel itself was able to slow the flood of monstrosities that dwelled within, including Thornvalds, creatures with enormous thorns sprouting like swords from the ends of their arms. The Wickerjaks grew more dangerous as well, changing from diminutive humanoids to four or six-legged variants. These were far faster than the previous incarnations, though they appeared to share similar stats.

As the phantom's dominance over the battlefield receded, Felix and his team picked up the slack. Without Elder Wickerjaks to threaten them, even the Thornvalds and speedy animal variants were deftly handled. Felix exercised his muscles, wielding his Blade of the Fang with sweeping abandon. Monsters fell before him, split like logs beneath the whirling blade until they were little more than splinters. Pit flew above, the tunnels wide enough that his aerial maneuvers could be managed, hurling frozen lightning bolts and shimmering crescents of cutting light by the dozen.

Beef and Hallow charged forward, Homunculus atop Minotaur, and bovine warrior atop a charging Multipede. He claimed to be tired and a bit woozy from the pressure in the tunnels, though that didn't stop him from swinging his maul at anything that came within arm's reach. Every monster they felled was soon surrounded by the blackened green glimmer of necromantic Mana, becoming Risen that fought against their purple-hued brethren. Most of the Risen died soon after, their Bodies too brittle or broken, but Beef was nothing if not tenacious. He kept at it despite the constant groans of pain the kid let out. From Hallow, crystalline darts flew with unerring accuracy, shattering joints and pinning stumps to the earth, allowing the calamitous cavalcade of insectoid legs to trample those who remained.

Vess fought alongside the War Naga, weaving deceptively through the lightning thrown from stolen tridents and clearing the field in forty-foot bursts as her Spears detonated. She still refused to use her other Skills, but there was little need; she was a force of nature, a whirling hurricane that left only devastation in her wake.

The Naga relied mostly on their brawn, the lightning only half as effective compared to conventional foes, but their claws did serious damage. Ten enormous half-snake warriors were not a force to be underestimated.

Isla wove faint illusions, workings of the Chant that enhanced their defenses enough that, had the enemy been less numerous, would have proven incredibly effective. As it was, the sheer mass of the Wickerjaks and Thornvalds had nowhere to go except right into Felix's team.

They were cut into kindling.

Miles vanished beneath their feet, blurring the dripping tunnel walls into a procession of swift violence and experience points. There were so many monsters that the War Naga, Beef, Hallow, and Vess all leveled at least twice during the fighting. Pit and Felix, of course, were far from such gains, sadly. Isla didn't share.

Another hour passed, their steps slowed by the advent of an even greater number of plant monstrosities. Their levels and strength did not increase, however, and Felix's team advanced without a hitch. The one thing that did change, though, was the slow bubbling riot that was the Green Wild Distortion.

It took him a second to figure out what the System had meant by it, but after Paxus used his influence to replace it with a cleaner, more vibrant melody Felix had pieced it together. The Green Wild—the aspect of the Grand Harmony that seemed dedicated to life and growing things—was being bent out of true by the Wickerjaks and their ilk. More specifically, it was the blue and purple ooze that created that distortion.

No. Not distortion, he thought. *Dissonance.*

Buried under it all was the same buzzing, atonal noise that Felix had been hearing since his arrival. Dissonance, he was coming to realize, wasn't only within things like the corrupting ooze or a Primordial's being...but within everything. The Green Wild Distortion grew like white noise in his head, a wall that tried to blot out all other things, but Felix's Affinity had grown too much for that. Steeped in the confluence of Dissonance and Harmony for months, it was all too easy to pick out where the two grew into one another, like weeds between slabs of concrete. Dissonance was hidden in the spaces between notes and chords, a jarring cacophony to the heroic accord of Harmony.

Two sides of the same coin.

The realization wasn't a thunderbolt to his Mind, or a shock to his Spirit, merely an understanding that had been accumulating for almost a year. It blossomed inside of him, resonating with the grinding of his dual cores until every inch of Felix felt baptized in sound and light.

Above, Pit jerked in mid-air, wings hitching strangely before dropping thirty feet with a dull crash.

Pit! What's happening? Felix sent, a seed of panic germinating in his heart. Pit landed amid several Thornvalds. The Mantle of Tumult around his Body was more than enough to drive the creatures back, which was relieving for Felix, as Pit remained crouched. The tenku shook his head, as if dizzy, and Felix heard noise rolling from deep within his Companion. *Pit, what am I hearing?*

New...Skill, Pit sent, before he threw his head back and shrieked.

Thornvald (x9) Are Stunned!

Mana Digestion Complete!
Your Companion Pit Has Learned A New Skill!

Breath of the Wild (Legendary), Level 1!
With a mighty exhale, you create a zone of air, life, and light Mana that infuses all within it with might and durability. It

travels with you, lasting as long as you can continue to exhale, boosting the Health regeneration of those within its bounds and increasing their Strength and Vitality scores by a fixed amount for as long as they remain within it. Zone increases slightly in size per Skill level. Bonuses to regeneration, Strength, and Vitality increase slightly per Skill level.

Adamant Discord!

Felix rushed forward, blasting outward like a semi shearing through Sunday traffic. Cords of connection turned to steel bars, slamming into Wickerjaks and Thornvalds, smearing them into paste as he ran to Pit's side. His Companion was on his belly, panting into the mud, as sparks of effervescent azure-gold energy spat out of his wings and paws. "Bud!"

I'm okay, Pit sent, his beak clamped shut against a spasm of pain. *Does it hurt this much when you learn new Skills?*

"Only sometimes," Felix said, pressing a hand against Pit's neck despite the flare of Essence and Mana that singed his sleeve.

"Michael!" Isla screamed.

Felix's head whipped back up at the same time a massive surge of malevolence rolled across his Affinity. Back at the line, right where Felix left, a thick, spike-riddled pseudopod of blue-purple ooze lifted from a crevice and slammed downward into Beef. It moved too fast, giving the kid zero time to react before he was launched from his seat atop the Multipede. The muddy stone floor cratered as he hit.

"Ten Tribulations!"

"Levin Bolt!"

Silver Spears hit and burst at the same time six separate lightning bolts cracked into the oozing appendage, obliterating it entirely.

It was too little too late.

Beef went into sudden convulsions, his mighty limbs smashing deeper divots into the stone as every single one of Hallow's forms—Homunculus, Multipede, and various Risen Wickerjaks—fell limp to the earth.

CHAPTER EIGHTY

"What happened?" Felix shouted, before yelping as Pit Converged with his Spirit.

Go to them! Pit sent, along with a flurry of anxiety and pain. *I need a second!*

Got it! Felix crashed through the few plant monsters that tried to intervene as he sped back to Beef's side. "Beef! Hallow?"

The War Nagas circled up, keeping their thick tails between the fallen and the enemy. "My Lord! What do you wish of us?"

"Just keep those plants back!" Felix crouched beside Beef, finding Isla already leaning over his giant face. "What's going on? Is he okay?"

The Chanter was singing beneath her breath and removing the magical helmet from Beef's head. It popped off with the sound of pressurized air, the orichalcum retreating from his horns like liquid metal before forming into a dense sphere. Isla dropped it into the mud and pressed her fingers rhythmically alongside Beef's jaw and temples. "His Aspects are rebelling against an external force. He's retreated into his core space, which will protect him for a time but not forever."

"The boy has been feeling ill since we began our journey," Paxus said. He stood close, concern etched onto his face and broadcasting from his open Spirit. "His Aspects seem strained."

"Because of his arms?" Felix asked. Cold guilt wormed into his chest.

"No. Your associate healed him of that injury. This feels like more." Paxus' left eye twitched. "He swells with a foreign vibration."

"Let me in, you stupid stone!" Isla's song broke, and she thumped a fist down onto the muddy earth. "His blighted Spirit is defending against my delving."

"Hallow?" Felix looked at the various Bodies around them. At the Multipede, Wickerjak Risen, and the crude rock Homunculus. "He's reacting to the ooze, right? Is it the Dissonance?"

"You know…of course. Lord Unbound, the underpinnings of the Grand Harmony do not lightly reveal themselves. They are hallmarks of foul creatures and those that have pushed too far." Paxus met Felix's eye as shrieks and splintering wood grew loud all around them. "I can tell you speak of Dissonance with the cadence of familiarity, Lord Unbound. Your existence is, by its very nature, counter to ours, but you must also tread carefully around such power. There is a reason it is hidden."

"A little late for that," Felix said. "Isla, step back. I have a way in."

She did so, settling back onto her heels with a dissatisfied snort. "I told you. His Hallow Spirit is blocking all delvings. You cannot reach him."

Felix thrust a hand into the middle distance, where a thick thread thrummed at right angles to the world. A Tier IV Link between himself and Beef appeared, made of dusty brown and blackened green threads that were more than Mana and less than physical. "Watch me," he growled, and Pit crowed in his Spirit.

The Link *sang*.

The world around them winked out.

Very briefly, in the moment that Felix's awareness was consumed, he felt inundated by a faint, rigid presence. The presence lost all rigidity the moment Felix flared his Willpower, and suddenly he was freefalling in the black.

The darkness soon resolved as Felix's booted heels hit a plush surface. He flexed his knees, his landing softer than he expected, and cautiously looked around. "Beef?"

He was in a small room, just big enough for the bed, desk, and dresser that it contained. Two of three walls were plastered with posters of various cartoons and anime, all of them featuring barely-dressed heroines with swords that rivaled some of his in size. Felix wasn't familiar with any of them, but he'd never made much time for TV once he'd started working.

Dotted among the posters were shelves overflowing with seven-inch statues of the same scantily clad characters and more than one cheap plastic axe. Piles of laundry, stacks of papers, and empty, slightly greasy containers were scattered all over the bed and dresser, but the desk was immaculately clean. It was a wide affair with plenty of space for the three monitors and large tower unit.

"That looks more expensive than my last apartment," Felix muttered. "Pit, you in here?"

I am. With a flash of light, Pit manifested on the bed in Dire Hound form…and promptly fell over, big ears flopping as he slid between the bed and the wall. "Gah!"

Felix snorted. "You okay?"

"Yeah. Ooh! There's food back here!" Harsh crunching filled the room. "Salty! Tastes like onions!"

Stale flavor filtered across their bond before Felix could cut it off. "Weeks-old chips. Eugh. I don't think you should be eating someone's core space."

A sense of stubborn incredulity and sarcasm accompanied the taste of ancient chips. No words, but with more than enough Intent behind them to suggest the phrase: *Really?*

"Shush." Beef had been very reluctant to show Felix his core space before. *Is that why? Because he's a slob?* The comforter shifted on the bed as Pit wormed further down beneath, revealing a long body pillow with a printed cartoon lady on it. "Oh, no wait, I get it now."

The sound of muted thunder drew Felix's eye to the third wall, the last one. Just beside the bed and desk, it was dominated by a large, eight-pane window. Now, Felix was pretty tall—around six and a half feet since his transformation—and this window was taller still. It extended from the floor all the way up to a few inches shy of the ceiling, which Felix estimated at about ten feet. That alone was interesting, but not nearly as fascinating as what he saw beyond it.

There was a storm outside.

"What's that?" Pit asked, wiggling out from under the bed.

Felix only stared, letting his Companion join him at the window as rivers of rain coursed down its panes. The rain itself seemed to fall slowly, and lightning traced a bright line through the distant clouds that seemed to be locked in place. Directly outside were the pebbly shingles of a sharply-pitched roof, and farther out, the hazy silhouette of a suburban neighborhood. Skeletal trees waved in the wind as if they were underwater, their slow-shifting branches changing the shape of the houses Felix couldn't quite make out. The storm and the dark concealed it all, even from his Perception.

"Beef? Are you here?" Felix asked again. The place was clearly the teen's bedroom from Earth, now functioning as a core space of some kind. The anime statues, the posters, the cheap, fake weapons, even the general unkempt disarray of the place spoke to it. "Beef?"

Where was he?

Apart from the window, the third wall was also covered in knickknacks, but these were framed instead of stuck up with push pins and packing tape. Awards for academic achievement were dusty and crooked, hung with old, tattered-looking ribbons and tarnished medals. The glass was so smudged that Felix couldn't make out the subjects on the placards, only that there were at least sixteen, with half as many medals, ribbons, and tiny trophies on tinier shelves. Below that was the computer.

"What's that thing?" Pit asked, sniffing up into the air with his small nose. "Smells like magic."

"Probably is," Felix said, casting his Perception outward. The room was throwing him off, for some reason. It felt like there was an itch he couldn't scratch, a feather touch behind his eyes. He wrinkled his nose, smelling only the onion funk from his Companion.

"Everything is magic here. It's all visualized internal Mana. And, if I had to guess…" Felix reached out and jiggled the dark shape next to the keyboard. Lights immediately flashed from the optical mouse, racing across the keyboard in red, green, and blue shimmers before ascending the tall, black tower of the PC. "This must be Beef's core."

The three monitors flickered to life, a little too bright in the dark room, but soon resolved into a long desktop image of a rolling, golden field lit by a gorgeous setting sun. Brilliant pinks, oranges, and faint greens streaked the clouds and mingled among the rows of grain. It looked photo-real, almost as if Felix could reach through the screen and into the scene. The only thing that broke that illusion were the numerous icons that cluttered all three monitors.

"Skills, if I had to guess," he muttered. Experimentally, Felix took the mouse and guided the cursor—shaped like a small hammer—toward the nearest icon. It was shaped like a big, green beetle and had the name "Chitin Construction" appear as he hovered over it. "Oh yeah. Skills for sure."

The icons were placed around the three monitors in no particular order. Where Felix would have grouped them all by type, or maybe by function, Beef had them in an arcane pattern. Felix was certain it meant something, so after hovering over the one Skill, he let it be. He wasn't here to fiddle with the kid's core…not yet, at least.

Look.

Felix froze, still bent in half before the computer keyboard. He didn't hear the word so much as feel it as a basso thrum through his middle.

The Floor.

He looked to his metal greaves. They were half-buried in the thick carpeting…and directly next to a set of black cables that dropped from the desktop before snaking up toward the—

No. Look. See!

The room stuttered, skipped, as a snippet of screeching static tore at Felix's ears. He was standing at a wall, toes touching it. It was the fourth wall. *There are four walls? How? How'd I miss that?*

It was made of stone. Two-foot square blocks were stacked atop one another, undressed and rough, but fitted together so cleverly it was hard to find the seam. In the center, just next to the computer desk, was the door. A crack traversed its beveled face, one that very nearly bisected it. The crack was just wide enough to allow a chill wind to whistle through it, and to allow the cables to pass into the darkness beyond.

Felix kept his eyes wide, not daring to shift his attention at all. Something was trying to make him forget this wall and door existed, and if he looked away, Felix wasn't sure he'd know to look back again. His middle rumbled, no longer a voice but a deep, throaty growl.

Open. Eat.

He pursed his lips. Felix should have known the voice was his Hunger. *I'm not eating anything here. This is my friend's core space, understand?*

"Felix, who are you talking to? And why are you staring…at—" Pit shook his head, jowls flapping. "Weird. What are you doing? You're staring…"

"Don't worry about it, bud. Just stand back," Felix warned, still refusing to blink or shift his gaze. He pulled a fist back as far as he could. "Beef! Beef, I'm coming in!"

There was no answer, but Felix didn't expect one. He threw his arm forward, a demolition charge of flesh and scales, and the entire stone door *exploded.*

Pit squawked with surprise. "Wow! What did you—Hey! A wall! Where'd that come from?"

Felix was already through, shoving past the two-foot thick remnants of the door and stepping out onto a flat expanse of…nothing.

"Is this the Void?" Pit asked, and for the first time since they arrived in the core space, a trace of fear crept into his Companion's voice.

"No, but it feels like it," Felix said. At a right angle to his senses, the Link between him and Beef thrummed insistently. It quivered once, then again and again, each time rising in pitch until it sent a cascading series of ascending notes. "Beef! Bee—Oh."

The room looked infinite and cavernously empty at the same time.

Unrelieved black extended in all directions, which made it very easy to see the crude granite platform, plinth, and poorly designed throne. The teen Minotaur was slumped there, head lolling as drool poured from his wide mouth.

A set of wavering lines wrapped around the platform, shining with a multitude of flashing colors. They slipped onto the platform, snaking through the plinth and throne in concentric circles. A set of three thick cords that connected back through the broken gate and directly to the desktop PC.

"What is this?" Felix asked as he burned his Agility. The distance between him and the platform vanished in an instant. He pointed at the glowing lines. "Stealing internet from this place?"

Beef's head didn't move, but his shoulders shook ever so slightly.

"You can hear me," Felix said, looking around. There was nothing but the platform, plinth, and throne. He kneeled down at the edge of the platform, running his dark hands above the braided cords of light. "Good. Hold onto your butt while I rip this whole thing apart."

"W...wait..."

Beef's voice was a faint rasp, and he still couldn't lift his head. Felix hesitated, about to touch the strange light that seemed responsible for holding his friend hostage. "Beef? What's going on? This doesn't feel like it's just Dissonance."

"My...my Spirit..." he hissed, and a measure of power pulled the tendons in his neck taut enough that Beef met Felix's sharp gaze. "Hallow..."

The plinth beside them burst into an indescribable, transcendent song, nearly throwing Felix back. Through the din, however, he heard a single word from Beef.

"Regalia."

CHAPTER EIGHTY-ONE

You Have Killed A Moontouched Wickerjak (x13)!
XP Earned!

Spears and discs reformed and returned to Vess as she bounced back from her attack, while the only remnant of her foes—a mist of sap—scattered in all directions. One of the bronze discs briefly shoved up beneath her leading foot, allowing the spearmaiden to launch off of it, leaping high enough into the air that she could plant her partisan deep into the wooden ceiling. There, she assessed the situation as her Stamina began to slowly recover.

Elemental Eye is level 74!
Analyze is level 71!

She looked down at the defensive bulwark her allies had made around Beef's prone form, now with Felix kneeling over the Minotaur's chest. Pit had vanished into Felix's Spirit, and Hallow's Risen were laid out beside their master. Without either Unbound, their team had to rely on the War Nagas' sheer physical bulk for the majority of their protection, while Lady Isla slung strange magics that fuzzed at Vess' senses. They did worse to the plant monstrosities, turning them against one another or sending them sprawling over imagined terrain. It allowed Toa'ut and company to follow up with punishing trident thrusts and that strange Nymean spirit to attack with lashing vines.

Mana swirled everywhere. Shadow, lightning, and poison Mana snapped from the War Nagas, and Lady Isla spread liquid streams of life and augmentation. The spirit was a conduit to a large reservoir of Mana—water, shadow, life, and earth predominantly—but very little of it escaped the Nym's Mana Gates. The spirit had claimed he was losing potency the farther they traveled from his Companion, and Vess tried not to curse their luck. Her own air and metal Mana dotted the field, faded now and not nearly as dense as the Chanter's power. She had been the only one to take the fight outward and attempt to cut back the horde. It wasn't working. *No matter how many we kill, there are always more on the way.*

Vess had trained for battle her entire life. It *was* her life, in many ways, but she had rarely been so challenged as she was recently. Part of her efforts to change her fate involved not using her new, very powerful Skills. That had forced Vess to focus wholly on utilizing her basic movement techniques and her summoned Spears, both of which were untarnished by the Primordial's touch. It greatly limited her capabilities, restricting her fluid movements and eating away at her Stamina. She had forgotten how much her On The Wing reduced her Stamina expenditures, not to mention The Fang of Havoc, which normally assisted her costly leaps.

What's more, her Skills yearned to be used—crooned at her, almost. That had been something the Lady Isla had not warned her about; her escalating Affinity had only made it harder to ignore her evolved Skills.

She had been relying entirely on her Spear of Tribulations and her newest weapon: the Sling Salvo. The High Bronze discs were devastating when used in conjunction with her Spear Skill, floating them with a greater control than the weapon naturally offered. That they duplicated themselves mid-flight was an even greater boon, spreading a lesser damage with every pass. But, like her movement techniques ate through her Stamina without a proper Skill, the discs and Spears burned through her Mana at a prodigious rate.

I am so close to advancing my Spirit. If it were Adept Tier, perhaps then I—no, she shook herself before resetting her feet against the tunnel roots. *I need to rectify my Skills before I can advance again.* Lady Isla had told her it would be a risk, but Vess was willing to face down every danger that stood between her and where she needed to return. Where she *must* return.

A piercing noise cut suddenly through the shrieking din. Vess nearly lost grip on her partisan as a wave of darkness bubbled out of her chest, heard from outside but somehow emanating from within. She cast it aside, squeezing tight on her Affinity until the sensation departed with a dizzying whorl of sensations. Vess blinked away the stars from her eyes to see the battlefield below...and it was changed.

Gaze of the Unseen Hunter is level 72!

All around the War Naga, the Wickerjaks and Thornvalds had been blasted to frozen kindling, their bodies shattering to pieces as those farther back moved up with halting steps. Her Gaze allowed her to view living creatures as collections of colors representing the heat their Bodies gave off, and now it only showed her the darkest of colors. In some places, those closest to their allies, it was utterly black.

What in Siva's name was that? Did Felix do that? It looked nothing like Rime Shaping. A gasp tore from Vess' throat as her Gaze of the Unseen Hunter found a mound of blackest night sitting at the center of her allies' bulwark. Felix, Beef, and much of Hallow were covered in thick, opaque layers of ice. "Felix!"

"I'm trying to thaw it, Lady Dayne!" Lady Isla shouted. That wave of frost had hit them all, leaving hoarfrost on the Chanter's sleeves and hanging thick on the War Nagas' backs. Twin orbs of green-gold liquid were congealed on her palms, bright with heat. "Focus on *them*!"

Pinging among the horde were a number of shapes that stood out in her Gaze as if they were burning. Dozens were slipping in through strange crevasses in the root tunnel, streamers of dark water following them, but they didn't need it to navigate. Their Bodies were *soaked* with that vile ooze, and dripping fins the size of wings morphed out of the muck. They twisted into the air, eel-like monstrosities straddled by savage fish men, blackened and slimy while their eyes burned with a raging malice.

"Broodvipers and Drakins." Vess said, a very Felix-like growl rolling from her throat. *Dangerous to face alone,* a part of her warned. She did not care.

Spear of Tribulations!

She hurled herself down, Born Trait amplifying her jump as ten Spears manifested in a swirling cone of death before screaming off ahead. She bellowed, with all the strength of her Body's lungs.

"Ten Tribulations!"

A wave of chill darkness rolled outward, centered upon the glowing plinth. However, it got caught up in the shimmering light show, failing to penetrate and reach Felix. Instead, it bounced backward off the cords of power, which multiplied until they were a small wall of furious noise and illumination. The dark power was funneled immediately toward the throne Felix's friend was sitting upon.

The teen Minotaur screamed.

"Beef!" As the darkness vanished, it left behind thick slabs of frost on the platform, throne, and Beef's legs. If Beef had been capable of getting up previously, Felix doubted he could even make the attempt now. The kid was flash frozen to the chair.

Beef let out a lowing groan. "Regal…ia. The…echo…"

"What do you mean? What about the Regalia?" Felix asked. The transcendent, multicolored storm still raged around them, and it was only getting louder. His friend wasn't responding, but Felix could see that Beef's wide chest was still moving. "Hold on! I'll get you out!"

Felix licked his lips, nervously casting around the featureless Void. Pit stood nearby, braced against the swirling, multi-hued winds. *Converge with me,* Felix sent. *I think we'll need our combined Harmonics on this one.*

On it! Pit vanished in a flash of light, instantly appearing as a heavy weight within Felix's Spirit. *He said Regalia, right?*

He did. Felix cast his Perception and Affinity outward, trying to get a handle on what was going on.

Pit warbled in concern. *Didn't he carry that thing for a while? Didn't he say that it kept trying to control him? Is that the echo?*

Shit. More darkness and ice blasted up and inward, splashing against the maelstrom of light ineffectually. More ice built up and over his friend. *Pit, you're a genius.*

I know.

Fiendforge!

Focusing his attention, Felix listened instead to the whirling cacophony in front of him as his Skill activated. It clamped onto everything around them—a feeling like a vise squeezing his entire body—and fed a stream of general information to him. *This clearly isn't the Void…but it does feel like the liminal spaces around cores.* Like where he had stepped in order to traverse the Links between his friends' spaces. *But…we're not outside of Beef's core. I can feel that through Fiendforge. But that means…what?*

Felix hadn't a clue. The storm of light sounded like the Grand Harmony and was just as overwhelming, but it afforded him little insight. Except…at the edge of the spinning light, there was a bouncing to the tone. A wobble that didn't make sense. That tremendous, melodic roar was too large, too complex and layered to prance with staccato notes—yet it was there.

The echo.

Felix followed it, tracing the rippling patterns as they expanded before his Affinity. Threads of light tangled and flexed, forming and dissolving into lattices and knots that didn't so much as vibrate as *breathe.* Felix's Born Trait tugged at him, insistent, and he recalled the last time he'd heard such a song.

Yeah. That sounds like the Regalia. He could almost feel the rush of cold waters and a vast, impossibly distant doorway somewhere just out of sight—like a familiar voice two rooms away.

The inside of the platform bloomed with dark energies again, and this time, Felix's Fiendforge felt the full force of it. Icy death crawled across his Skill, strange and eerily familiar in the way of nightmares.

A face like a sunken crater stared at him out of the darkness.

"Gah!" Felix leaped back, clamping down with Fiendforge and Bastion of Will even as his arms ignited with red-gold flames.

The face was gone.

"I hate that thing," Pit whimpered, and Felix realized his tenku had leaped from Convergence and was huddling behind his leg in puppy form. "That's what you saw in the Breach?"

Felix swallowed. "Yeah. And it seems that is what's affecting Beef inside that ring." He licked his lips before tentatively pressing his Willpower back into place, shoving the memory of its too-wide grin somewhere deep behind his Bastion's walls. Beef's core space tightened and flexed, ever so slightly with the pressure of Felix's Fiendforge. "Okay. Okay. The Creature is in the ooze. Or the ooze *is* the Creature. Unclear. That stuff is putting out waves of something like Dissonance, and it got to be too much for Beef. Not sure why."

Felix's Bastion gained ground as he spoke, the fear and confusion the Creature instilled in him fading with each word. Pit seemed to be reacting too, because he had shifted back into his Chimera form.

Pit nudged the ring of light with a dark paw. It passed harmlessly through the energy. "Right. Then what's all this? It's keeping the ooze-stuff inside. How?"

"I think that's related to Beef. To me, too." Felix pointed at thick flows of dusty brown and blackened green in the spinning lights. "That's Beef's particular brand of Mana, or at least what his Skills lean on. But he's Unbound, like me. That means he can use all kinds, and his core should reflect that. That ice," he said, pointing inside where layers of hoarfrost had coated Beef up to his hips. "That's something to do with the ooze, and Beef is keeping it from overwhelming the rest of him."

"He is?" Pit asked, stalking forward. He tilted his head, beak poking into the wall of light. "I don't think he's doing anything."

"What?" Felix stepped closer as well, and through the increasing flows of Mana, he spotted the wide, two-foot-high granite plinth. There was no column atop it, just a rough and broken surface, as unfinished as everything else appeared. Except, from this angle, Felix spotted a depression in the vertical surface, the one facing Beef's throne. "What is that?"

The granite plinth had a sizable chunk of it missing, as if something had scooped out a massive chunk.

Fiendforge is level 33!

He could feel an imbalance all around him–flaws in the surface of

Beef's core space like cracks in the surface of an egg. Yet somehow, it did not collapse as Felix tightened his grip, shifting the pieces of it until they revealed the hole that had been bored out.

"He is missing his Spirit."

Felix and Pit both whipped their heads up, away from the damaged plinth to a feature that had not been there before. A woman was bound against the invisible ceiling, seated in a throne all too similar to Beef's save that it was upside down. She had long red hair streaked liberally with gray, and it hung down around her kindly, age-lined face. She wore a thick sweater and jeans, the fabric pressed against bands of dark chitin that seemed to rivet her in place.

"Who are you?" Pit chirruped in alarm. "Why're you upside down?"

The platform, throne, and plinth was a perfect mirror of Beef's, down to the bands of swirling Mana and layers of dark ice. The woman smiled at them, but it was touched with sadness.

"Hello. I fear we haven't properly met." All around her, the empty black seemed to stretch and wobble as that echo redoubled in intensity. She winced, but the sad smile returned soon after.

"I am Hallow. And all around you are the emptied remnants of Michael's Spirit."

CHAPTER EIGHTY-TWO

"Emptied Spirit." Felix narrowed his eyes at the inverted woman. Not far from his side, Beef seemed to have fallen fully unconscious. "You don't sound like Hallow, and you certainly don't look like her."

The beautiful older woman shifted her shoulders, her smile fading a bit more. "The voice you normally hear is filtered through Beef's core space and my own power. I am capable of inhabiting multiple Bodies by my very nature, after all. The form before you is one that Michael found the most comforting when he created me."

"Comforting?" Pit asked.

"I am a near-exact replica of his mother, Helen."

Felix traded a glance with Pit. "Alright. That's…well, I can't fault him for missing his mom. But how?"

The emptiness shook around them as a burst of chill shadow once again suffused both platforms, above and below. When it cleared, more ice layered over Beef and Hallow in almost identical patterns of frost.

The woman who claimed to be Hallow grimaced, stretching her neck so that the ice cracked and snapped. "Though I wear this face, I am unaware of Michael's beginnings. I only know snippets of the time before my creation. Michael was brought here, summoned the same as you, Lord Autarch, and dumped into the heart of the Scorched Expanse. There, he fought beasts and monstrosities, changing his Race in order to survive, yet coming closer to death with every passing moment." Her eyes were bright and colorless—like empty glass orbs—yet her gaze bored into Felix's. "I am a result of that trauma."

Felix could understand that. The first few hours of his arrival had gone badly, too. "What are you, Hallow? I thought you were a Skill that Beef had learned, but what you're saying is suggesting something else."

That smile returned, still sad but now somewhat impish. "In an effort to extract the magic he required to survive, Michael did the impossible. He wrenched free his nascent Spirit by some virtue of his Unbound nature. Me. I am his Spirit, whole and completely separate from his Body and Mind."

"Whoa," Pit said, beak agape. "You're not a Companion. You're a Beef."

"Hallow, please. Michael gave me that name shortly after I inhabited the corpse of the first Sandwolf he killed."

"Not Helen?" Felix asked.

Hallow frowned, her expression turning dark for the first time since she'd started speaking. "I am not Helen. I only wear her face for Michael's sake."

"He *makes* you look like his mom?" Felix asked.

"Unconsciously. It was a form he chose when he began to visualize his core space, and he first found this empty chamber."

"Right. Empty because you weren't here any longer."

"Exactly."

"This light…this is Beef protecting the rest of his core space from the ooze?" Felix asked, pointing to the barrier around both platforms.

"Incorrect. This is *me* protecting the rest of Michael's core space. He is trapped, as I am, and barely holding on. I do not know why it is resonating so deeply with his Spirit, but I fear that even this solution will not hold for long." Another burst of darkness, worse than the last. Thick ice crawled up Hallow's chest. Her face twisted in pain, but her voice was steady. "Not long at all."

Felix heard the increasing violence woven in the dissonant expulsion of ice and shadow. Whatever the ooze was doing, it was getting stronger. For the briefest of moments, Felix sent his awareness outward, back along his Link toward consciousness…and found his Link slam into a solid wall. Felix drew in a sharp, angry breath. "What the hell?"

The door out of Beef's core space had closed.

"That is dire. The ooze is touching more of Beef's power than I anticipated." Despite the bitter cold, sweat beaded along Hallow's pale forehead. It dripped off, turning to icy slush before vanishing into the dark. "My barriers are failing, and it is…it is claiming him."

Felix whirled toward his friend, the teen Minotaur who just wanted to have a fun adventure. Ice had crawled up onto his jaw and around his face, locking his square, bovine head into a menacing snarl. Beef's eyes were open, but inside there was only a deep, terrible darkness.

Hallow panted with wide eyes. There was no sad amusement, just a mounting panic. "Lord Autarch. Felix. If it takes him, I do not know what will happen. I am its point of entry into his core. You must destroy me."

"Absolutely not." Felix spun from Beef to glare at Hallow. "You think I'd just roll over and kill an ally—a *friend*—because some eldritch ooze wants to start calling the shots?"

"A friend?" Hallow asked, quietly.

"Yeah! We're all friends!" Pit agreed with a bright chirrup. His wings spread, beating at the dark and crackling with sudden lightning. "And we fight for friends!"

"Damn straight." Felix glared at the two platforms, Mind whirling. "Okay, what do we have? Barrier. Echo of the Regalia. Ooze. What's the deal with the broken plinth there?"

Hallow seemed unable to speak for a few seconds. "Uhm…that–that is one of the few extant pieces of his Spirit. All the stone you see before you is such. A chunk was required—a piece of himself—when he formed my Homunculus. Primordial power or not, such a creation was beyond Michael's abilities without a piece of who we are."

"Primordial power…" Felix grinned. "Of course. I knew I recognized it."

Fiendforge!

The multicolored lights, the flashing hues of multiple Mana types and System power, all of them stopped swirling as Felix closed his Will and Intent upon them. His grip around Beef's core space tightened until the emptiness around them shivered.

"What are you doing?" Hallow shouted, and this time there was no mistaking the fear in her voice. "If that barrier is broken, you'll doom him entirely!"

"If I do nothing, either you or him will be killed or worse." Felix reached his hand out, letting the stilled light mingle among his fingers. "Those are not options I can accept."

He shoved his hand through the light and right into the darkness as it burst.

"Chthonic Tribute!"

Isla witnessed wave after wave of the dark-scaled Drakin and Broodvipers pouring through the root tunnel. Thick ooze followed them, clinging wetly to their slick hides and pouring over the ground like a tide of onrushing blood. The War Naga fought against it, tridents and heavy muscles claiming their due from the monstrosities, while the Lady Dayne danced among them in explosions of air and metal Mana.

Yet they were flagging. Stamina and Mana were depleting faster than any of them could recover, despite their various potions. The numbers of the Fathom spawn only increased. For every beast killed, another three took their place, and now something else tore at the root tunnels. Something very, very large.

They could not hold.

Their only saving grace were the thick blue roots that had lifted and swelled, a thorn-lined bulwark against the monstrous advance. Holes in the tunnel were patched and filled, stemming the flood of water and ooze even as large talons clawed at it from outside. It had worked, giving them a brief reprieve, but the Nymean spirit that fueled them was likewise rapidly waning in strength.

"This is not enough!" Paxus cried out. His shape flickered in and out of visibility, much as Isla's own illusions might when she was pressed to the edge of her power. "You must all of you run!"

"Can you bottle them here?" Trained as a healer, Isla was all too familiar with making hard decisions. Even with the Chant, there was only so much one could do before the dire truth must be confronted. Sometimes the limb must be amputated to save a life. "If we run, retreat to your Companion Tree, can you keep them back?"

"Not for long. My influence over these tunnels has dwindled to almost nothing. All that I command now is my own limited potency." The spirit's dark blue eyes, completely without whites or pupils, stared down at Isla with a vast swell of soft sadness...one that swiftly transformed to hardened conviction. "Your Autarch gave us our lives back. I will repay that, no matter the cost."

He inspires such loyalty in mere hours. Isla could not help but marvel at Felix's abilities, separate from his Skills or Temper. To Paxus, she only gave a nod and raised her voice. "Lady Dayne! Toa'ut! We must retreat! Is the ice broken?"

"It is!" Lavix shouted back. The Naga had been tasked to break the increasing layers of ice off the two Unbound and their Companions. "I can pull them out!"

"Take the Unbound and go!" Isla summoned up her power, humming just beneath the cadence of her words. It was a complicated technique, but one she had mastered after many long centuries. A defensive construct wove into place, shaped of green-gold, faint purple, and oily brown Mana; an illusion to aid their phantasmal defender. It was the least she could do. "Fall back!"

The Lady Dayne barely made it back to the fold when the battle changed.

"The ooze!" the spearmaiden cried out, still mid-air. She landed with a flex of her knees. "It's moving!"

Isla whipped around, just in time to see that the ooze indeed was moving. Where before it had flowed like a restless sea, now it congealed, rising up less like a wave and more like a behemoth. The ooze formed a mass of twisted tendrils that resolved into the gaping maw of something far from natural, a shrieking abyss filled with a blistering cold.

"Brace yourselves!" she cried out, activating her defensive working. All of them blurred in place, sending the Fathom spawn stumbling around their forces, but the wave of gelid shadow hit them like a tsunami.

Isla hastily hurled her power into another shield, but it was not her strong suit. The shield detonated, doing little to blunt the cacophony of screeching chaos that encompassed them all.

Beefhammer blinked.

Wha—where am I?

All around him was a white expanse, empty and sterile. Beef lifted his hands. They were just as dark and blunt as ever, the backs of his hands covered in a brown pelt shot through with red and tan. He was also totally naked. That was weird. Other than that, though, he felt...normal.

Until he looked up.

"Jesus!" Beef dropped to the ground, just out of range as a massive tendril of monstrous *goo* thundered inches above his head. "What the hell is that?"

"She does not like you, Michael."

Beef twisted awkwardly, his huge Body unencumbered by his chitin armor but still not made for these sorts of movements. He ended up throwing himself to his feet, brow furrowed and head ducked low. A hard lump formed in his throat. "Mom?"

"No," Hallow said, and Beef watched a complicated twitch cross her face. "Just me."

"Oh. Yeah." Beef swallowed, but the lump didn't vanish. He looked up, where the endless white expanse was stained by skittering, blue-purple shape. He had trouble focusing on it, like he was staring at buzzing static through a rain-soaked windshield. Ropey strands hung from it—that much Beef could make out—striking out in every direction like they were swatting at flies. If it was as huge as the appendage that swung for him, then the thing was absolutely monstrous. "What... that's the Creature's ooze?"

Hallow nodded, and recent events flooded back to Beef's bruised Mind. He recalled feeling ill and unsteady and the long fight down the root tunnel. He remembered falling.

"Bastard sneak attacked me," he muttered. "What do we do? How do I fight this thing? Am I in my core space?"

"You are. The Autarch stepped into it to save you."

"Felix is here? He saw my core space?" *Oh god, that's embarrassing!* Beef suddenly wished he hadn't dodged that massive tendril. At least then he'd have been at peace. "What—what did he say? Anything?"

Hallow leveled a look at him, so similar to one his mom would use.

"Yes! Yes, that is what I'm worried about, right now!" Beef swallowed. His fur felt too hot, and his hands were sweaty. *What did he see?*

"Beef. Focus. Felix needs you now."

That stopped him. Beef lifted his eyebrows. "Felix...needs me?" Pride swelled in him, and he puffed out his chest. "What does he need? Wait, where is he?"

Hallow pointed. Up.

Beef followed her finger, gazing up into the fuzzy mass of monster that seemed to be slowly expanding. Or getting closer. Except parts of it were whirling this way and that, slapping outward at the endless white like gooey frog tongues only to be batted away violently. Beef focused, straining his Perception, and could barely make out another shape beyond the blue-purple blob. It, too, was massive, like the shadow of the moon itself, lit with flashes of blue-white and red-gold. Too fast to truly see.

"Wha—what does he want me to do?" he asked, staring up at his friend who was battling the behemoth.

"He needs you to embrace the storm, Michael," Hallow told him. Her voice was quiet, but the words almost boomed in Beef's ears. "We both know what that means."

Beef's breath caught in his chest, tangling around the vast riot of power that still waited within his core space. "I have to?"

Hallow's colorless eyes were soft as she looked at him. His mother's eyes had been brown, and sometimes it was all Beef could use to assure him that Hallow wasn't his mom. "You have been delaying the storm for weeks, Michael. Perhaps, in another time, you could have avoided it entirely. But you were given a choice. You chose to be selfless. To help, uncaring of the costs.

"Now it is time to pay."

Beef looked back up where the white nothing had begun to fade. It was a shell, his Mind whispered to him, a protection, keeping him away from the monstrous battle that was occurring beyond his senses. Felix was there, Converged with Pit, scales darker than the black around him, whorls of cyan glowing upon his chest and arms in an echo of his haunting eyes. Wings made of scale, claw, and feathers spread outward, hurling lightning from them with every stroke.

More than that, shapes seemed to manifest and vanish all around him, flickering and fading like ghosts. The ooze attacked, and he savaged it, consumed it with teeth that shone like red-gold fire. He moved...he did not move like a Human. He was an engine of violence and power, brought to bear against the undulating monstrosity the size of a skyscraper.

And he wasn't backing down an inch.

"I'm afraid, Hallow. What if I…what if I lose the room? It's all I have left."

"Felix is strong. Perhaps he can fight the ooze alone, and perhaps you can stay on the sidelines and remain unaffected." Hallow shrugged, but anger churned under her too-familiar features. "Change will always happen. But it is better to embrace it than to let it run you over, right?"

"Beef!"

The cry came from above, from somewhere impossibly distant. Felix had become a whirling vortex of lightning that was devouring pieces of the ooze. "Your core!"

A tendril slammed down, along with a second, but they were deflected by summoned shields of ice and stone. "It's cool! Sick gaming rig!"

More came, spearing outward from every direction. It shrieked and charred as Felix breathed out red-gold flame. "Now—hah!" He caught another protuberance and ripped it in half. "Let's kick some ass—together!"

Beef took a big, shaky breath. He closed his eyes. Everything twisted as Beef took command of his core space. He returned to his core, to the replica of his old room back in Texas. The storm outside was raging harder than ever before. Trees whipped hard enough to uproot themselves, and the foggy shapes of houses were tearing apart beneath the titanic winds. The storm, the Primordial's Essence he'd held off for so long, it was coming.

"Hallow?"

"Yes, Michael?" She stood at his back, as always.

"My name is Beefhammer."

With a savage cry, Beef kicked open the window.

CHAPTER EIGHTY-THREE

Fiendforge is level 34!
Fiendforge is level 35!

Felix felt it when the storm rolled in. Primordial Essence—previously all but frozen just outside the bounds of Beef's core space—now raged with all the pressure of once-dammed river.

He floated outside the space, viewing it from above like a diorama spread out on a table...all while he dodged the relentless appendages of the ooze beast. It was amorphous and grabby, a puddle made of pseudopods that were both sticky and incredibly dense. A single hit was enough to lower his Health by a whole percentage, and the thing struck a dozen times a second. It screamed constantly, a single atonal note that hissed and buzzed at the edges, meant to tear him down. But Felix had heard far worse from inside his own core space.

Hand of Calamity!

Hand of Calamity is level 2!
...
Hand of Calamity is level 15!

Slipping through its whirling attacks, Felix ripped through the ooze with an acid punch, liquid against liquid in a sizzling explosion of blue-purple gore. The creature's screams increased in volume, if not pitch, but it didn't retreat. It was just as tireless as Felix.

He never realized how annoying that could be.

Felix could have eaten the ooze—had even tried at first—but the tangle of connections he had perceived within Beef's core space had halted that thought at conception. The ooze, whatever it was, had knotted itself so deeply with Beef, the Mana of his core, and even the echo of the Regalia that Felix wasn't sure what he could just tear out. More worrisome were the threads that spread outward, beyond the core space to somewhere very close by—and when he brushed against them, Felix was afforded a grim look at the outside situation.

Everyone was in trouble.

So now he was fighting a multi-pronged battle against the ooze, engaging it away from Beef…and elsewhere. If nothing else, he could strengthen his friends, giving them all the space to save themselves.

And if Beef can work through this, he'll be strong enough to clear this up on his own.

Smart!

Thanks, Pit. Just keep us flying as best you can. We need to keep this blob's attention for as long as possible.

Easy! Pit dropped them, fully in control of their shared wings while Converged. They swooped low before twisting into a cyclonic corkscrew. An expulsion of ice Mana manifested blades on both hands, turning themselves into a living blender for a few moments. *Oh, that was effective!*

Pieces of the ooze were flung in all directions, but the majority were quickly reabsorbed into the main mass. Their attacks hurt it, Felix could tell that much, but it barely slowed the thing down. The best they could hope for was to occupy its attention until Beef was finished.

The storm flashed, lightning chased by a hot, dry wind that tore apart trees and buildings. A hurricane condensed into a city block, filled with rain and debris that burned as it hit. It sizzled over the sound of his fight, a rising, sputtering hiss that almost drowned out Beef's panicked shouts.

"Felix!" the Minotaur cried. "What do I do?"

They dove, Pit tucking their wings tight to their Body as Felix seized upon the myriad connections around him, juking in a dizzying flow around the ooze's tendrils. Felix could see Beef, standing stock still at his window, hoof still upraised from when he'd booted it open. His hands trembled on the frame while Hallow—still at his side—clenched harder than a fist. They both sang with dread, a bellowing crescendo that was far louder than Beef's words.

Thundering toward them, the storm did not stop. Flows of wild, desiccating dust and violent heat advanced, changing in the flashing lightning from a deluge to a sandstorm and back again. Lights flickered among the core space, the pieces of it loosening even further than before. The entire thing was collapsing under the incredible pressure. Beef had to take action immediately, or else he wouldn't survive.

"Beef! You—" Unbidden, a flurry of lights ripped from below, splashing into Felix as if they were a flock of suicidal birds. His words choked off as a Memory flitted across his Mind, a half-glimpse gleaned from the casual contact: a bed, machines, and a woman with red hair holding a small boy's hand in his childhood room.

The Memory vanished, fled into the dark, and Felix floundered. The woman had looked the same as Hallow.

Helen, Pit said.

The Primordial storm had been held back by fear. He heard it in both Beef and Hallow, a bitter, tentative song that wore long notes into their collective Spirit. Felix didn't know why, not fully, but it didn't matter. He knew what Beef needed to hear; what Felix had needed to hear, during all of his worst moments on the Continent.

"Embrace the fear, Beef!"

Felix didn't shout it, but he didn't have to. His Intent was transmitted to everyone within and it reverberated with Beef's core space. Things shook, rocked by it, softening ever so lightly around the edges as it all destabilized.

"Use it!"

Rime Shaping!

Stone Shaping!

Illusory Double!

"Fight!"

Isla could not believe her eyes.

"That…that is impossible," she managed through a gasping breath. "To cast while fully unconscious? While actively delving into another's core space?"

Mere strides from their faces, the monstrous ooze pulsated and writhed, held back by a legion of stone and icy spires. More arose as they watched, bludgeoning and slashing into the tacky mass with brutal abandon.

"He is Felix," Lady Dayne said, shrugging her shoulders as if that was all the explanation needed. Her knuckles were white against her partisan's haft—a sign of the rage and aggression that thundered in her core—-but her expression appeared utterly self-possessed. "The true question is: do we take advantage of this to flee or to fight back against this…Ooze Leviathan?"

"Fight," Toa'ut and Lavix said, almost in unison. Their dwindling compatriots agreed unanimously.

"We cannot risk it. We must flee," Isla insisted.

"I find myself emboldened," Paxus said, almost cutting her off. She sniffed but eyed the spirit. Indeed, he seemed to look more solid than before, the pattern of his phantasmal existence somehow more vibrant to her senses. "But I am concerned. What is that, precisely?"

Isla wasn't sure why she kept being surprised by the utter strangeness of Felix's company, but her eyes widened nevertheless as she perceived a single, strange, featureless shadow dancing among the erupting elemental blades. It flitted around the Behemoth, moving faster than she could properly track.

An illusion!

It was a suggestion of a person, a silhouette framed only by the flickering of blue and red near its chest. Yet, as it continued to move, deftly avoiding the heavy impact of the Ooze Behomoth's slamming tendrils, its shape clarified. Until its tall frame, scaled profile, and blazing blue eyes were unmistakable.

"That's…that's the God of Thunder and Flame!" Rou'd said.

"Has he claimed Shadow for his demesne as well?" another War Naga rumbled in awe.

The boy fights even while delving. That is truly unfair. Isla shielded her people from a stray burst of goo, but the Behemoth was well and truly distracted by Felix's display of power. The Broodvipers and Drakin behind the ooze were another thing entirely. They flowed forward and through the Behemoth's limbs, intent on fighting them all.

"We fight!" Lady Dayne howled and blurred forward along with ten shining Spears. The Naga were at her heels, crashing into the line of Fathom spawn like a slithering cavalry.

"Ruinous fools! We should flee!" Isla shouted after them, but it all fell on deaf ears.

A few still got through, despite it all, and Isla played defense around the still-unmoving forms of the Unbound. Vines whipped nearby, plants swelling with a sudden influx of life Mana before bursting in all directions in ropey tangles. Nets to disrupt and delay, and the Nymean phantom stood behind each burst, dark hand outstretched.

Despite it all, Isla feared that they would not last. Even if Felix continued to fight, the rest of the team was on borrowed time; they each were scraping the very bottom of their Stamina and Mana in this fight, pushed to their limits by the endless waves of monstrosities. She even resorted to hurling vials of bubbling green and electric yellow liquid from her bandolier, spreading swathes of crackling light and burning flame across the horde.

I cannot believe I must waste these here! Isla fumed. Her plans were collapsing with every grain of sand that fell. *We cannot fight this much longer!*

Abruptly, the boy's illusory double was there, standing next to the Nymean spirit. During the fight, the boy's control of the Skill had grown. In the low light, it was almost like Felix was standing beside them. The double nodded and pantomimed something to Paxus, who laughed.

"Aye, I see what you intend, Lord Unbound. Let us try," Paxus lifted his arms, his wide, white sleeves falling back to reveal dark forearms. "Or perish in the attempt!"

The illusory double lifted a single finger as if in protest, but then shrugged and lifted his own hands.

"Wake the Green Wild!" Paxus shouted into the Ooze Behemoth's shrieking maw.

All around them, the root tunnel walls burst into vibrant, deadly life.

Illusory Double is level 4!

...

Illusory Double is level 19!

Maintaining concentration on both fights at once, Felix was all but rooted to the spot. He could perceive enough through his Illusory Double to cast his Skills beyond his supine form, though things were far more hazy than he was used to. That cleared with every level gained in the illusion Skill. But it was taking everything he had—while with Evie and others, he had chosen to remain passive as they solved their own problems, now Felix found himself with little left to give Beef.

Fiendforge is level 36!

...

Fiendforge is level 42!

He held on tightly, clasping the trembling bits of Beef's core space together as the teen embraced the chaos. Tides of power surged below, tearing at his control and Willpower even as the ooze tried to rip his projected Body into pieces. Pit defended up, decoupled from their shared transformation, now strafing across the vast expanse of the nasty goo. Frozen lightning and crescents of golden light hit its jiggling mass like bombs, tearing holes that healed over only seconds later.

It was enough.

Hold on, Beef! Hold on!

Beef fell.

It was only two stories, but it felt like an eternity as the stormwall raged. A hot swelling was taking place, somewhere deep in his chest where his heart and lungs all tangled about; it hurt, but it felt like it was supposed to hurt. The heat of the oncoming tidal wave was immense, baking him with its proximity as it swept down his street. That was a different sort of hurt, but one he was forcing himself to accept.

He screamed, terror and jittery enthusiasm all bound into a knot. "You with me, Hallow?"

"Always."

He landed moments ahead of the wave of dust and water and lightning. A handle materialized over his shoulder, a post as thick as a telephone pole, but he knew what it was without conscious thought. He hefted it, lifting a maul so heavy his knees buckled, and the asphalt splintered in concentric circles all around him.

"Hey! Primordial jerkass!" The maul was the size of a damn house. His entire core space—his small, cramped room on the upper floor of a suburban home. All of it bound to the end of his maul. "This is *my house!*"

Beef brought it down *hard.*

The tidal wave split and crashed, and Beef laughed as it swallowed him up. Burning assaulted his limbs, soaking into his fur and ripping into his mouth just as it pervaded the end of his impromptu weapon. Images flashed across his vision, things he'd seen and things that no one should ever see. Airplanes flying low over his house. A Sandwolf hunting him in the dark. Lightning storms above the Gulf. Cursewinds filled with undead intent on eating his skin.

A face of bones.

It spoke.

BEEFHAMMER. UNBOUND. CHILD OF HEALERS.

"Get outta my head!" Beef swung his maul again, but it had become unmoored in the swirling storm. The telephone pole dissolved in his hands. "What? My room!"

YOU RUN. YOU HIDE. WHY?

"Because you're a creepy bastard!" Beef scrubbed at his eyes, but the bone face never vanished. It was there, before him in the storm, too large to be real and too visceral to be fake. Sand tore around them, turning to water that faded into desolate dust once again. "What do you even want?"

I WANT TO ILLUMINATE THE TRUTH, AS I HAVE FOR THE OTHER ALLIES OF FELIX NEVARRE.

"That tells me exactly jack-shit, dude!"

I WAS THE PRIMORDIAL OF THE WITHERING DUST. MY ROLE WAS TO BREAK APART, TO WEAR AWAY. I AM THE CHILD OF A CARDINAL BEAST, ONE OF THE LAST. TRUTH IS NOT MY ROLE, BUT IT IS WHAT MUST BE. The bone face split, its too-large features becoming more and more inhuman as it spoke, until it bore several sets of jaws and far too many eye sockets. **BEAR WITNESS.**

Impossibly, the tempest around them grew more frenetic. From the whirling dust came motes of light that screamed in Beef's limited senses. He wasn't so great at the Harmonics stuff, but even he could hear that they were *filled* with a nasty noise.

AND BE CHANGED.

The lights hurtled at him, but Beef lifted his arms and caught two of them in his massive, bare hands. Hallow caught the last, though it very nearly buckled her thinner frame. "I'm not letting you hit me with some crazy magic lights, man! Ugh, what are they?"

A LIE, A TRUTH, AND A WAY FORWARD. IF YOU ARE STRONG ENOUGH.

"Fuck you, I'm plenty strong!"

"Beef! No!" Hallow screamed, as the Minotaur teen took both howling lights and slammed them into his own chest.

CHAPTER EIGHTY-FOUR

From above, the light within Beef's core space was blinding, even to Felix's powerful senses. Essence and Mana congealed, the storm now centered upon a point immediately below him as he floated in the space between.

Is he doing it? Pit asked, still dropping deadly magic on the writhing ooze abomination.

He's doing something, Felix said.

Is it working?

He had only guesses, all based on the friction he felt against his Fiendforge. Felix still wasn't entirely sure of all that the Skill could accomplish, but he knew, without a doubt, that if he stopped maintaining it, Beef's entire core would collapse. Or explode. And it grew harder to hold by the second, especially as Pit grew tired of his battle.

Felix's Illusory Double was also having issues. Though his way out of Beef's core space was cut off, blocked by the ooze, it was not a perfect seal. Felix was still able to channel his Skills out of his Mana Gates, a detail he used to wreak havoc on the monsters above. It turned out, Illusory Double allowed him to utilize a tiny percentage of his Perception, providing dim flashes of events as they happened.

That was how he had been guiding his shaping Skills around; otherwise, Felix would have certainly killed his own people. Thankfully, as Illusory Double gained levels, the percentage increased bit by bit, until he could see and hear a reasonable amount of what was occurring in the root tunnel. His team was alive, but things were looking more and more dire.

Rime Shaping and Stone Shaping were effective at driving the

Fathom spawn back—even killing them—but they were of limited use against the Ooze Behemoth that raged above. The thing shattered the barriers and spikes he manifested like they were made of glass or paper. His team was pulling their own weight, but the Behemoth was too tough. Beef wasn't the only one who was brimming with fear.

Do like you said, dummy. Felix shook himself. *Use the damn fear. Fight!*

Felix couldn't do anything about Beef's struggle, but he damn well could bring the pain on a monster.

The phantom and shadow sprinted around a jiggling mass of tendrils as it smashed down onto the earth. From their channels, Vess could make out streamers of dense liquid—all of it colored green-gold—that fed into the floor and walls of the root tunnel. Vines, roots, and thick fronds burst from the earth, fat and vital. The tunnels choked with it as they expanded and grew just beyond the Ooze Behemoth's advance. Fathom spawn crashed into the swelling greenery and were rent asunder by the deadly thorns the size of swords or held fast by the rivulets of viscid sap.

The roof of the tunnel shook, pieces torn apart before life Mana repaired the damage. *Something is trying to get in.* Vess' eyes cast across the curved root tunnel ceiling, noting the cracks and splits where ooze and geysers of dark water were still finding a way through. *Can they hold against it and the Behemoth?*

Isla was hurling jars and vials from the bandoliers on her chest and pouches at her hips. She cursed every time she did so, but it was so musical, so potent, that Vess was unsure whether it was part of her Skills or not. Enemies went up in swathes of emerald flame before being blasted with tiny projectiles that bounced among them all while the plants grew ever faster. Whatever Isla had taken from the Temple treasury, she knew how to use it.

The War Naga, now down to nine, fought tooth and nail at the front. All of them were doubled up with stolen tridents, trading blasts of Levin Bolts with the Broodvipers. The crossfire was astounding, and only the strange nature of their enchantment kept the lightning relatively contained.

Which was just as well, as Vess moved among them all.

She spun through the enemy in the only way she knew, relying on the Seven Steps of the Dragoon. Not a Skill so much as a technique, a kata, the movements of the Seven Steps were fundamental to Vess' training as a Dragoon and formed the foundation for what would later become Dragoon's Footwork. *Which then mutated into On The Wing,* she reminded herself grimly. She took great care to ensure she wasn't activating the Skill itself, relying instead on her muscle memory, Stamina, and Agility to move in the proper way. She would not sacrifice her people's history for some twisted, malformed Skills—even if they were more powerful.

Vess had more than enough power for these foes.

Everywhere she stepped, Fathom spawn were cut to ribbons. The Bodies of the Broodviper and Drakin were strong—ridiculously so, considering their levels—but Vess had grown stronger. Her partisan and Spears were like surgeon's tools, slashing here or thrusting there, always moving, always spending the least amount of Stamina and Mana she could manage.

But the Fathom were *everywhere.* Paxus and Felix's shadowy double managed to choke off the far end of the root tunnel, but it left plenty more on the battlefield. They swarmed the sky, too, swimming through the air like water. Vess leaped, cutting down Drakin by the handful and raining down vile blue ichor.

More eel-beasts swarmed, snapping their double jaws with malicious revelry. Madness swirled in the Fathom spawns' eyes, burning bright enough to glow with a white-red intensity. Vess sent silver Spears into them all in a whirling cluster.

"Ten Tribulations!"

The Drakin exploded, many torn apart by the release of her Skill, and others dealt a crippling blow. Others pushed into the gap, though, even as a jagged blade of ice cut across them with a spray of dark ichor. Vess spun toward an outstretched, shadowy hand.

"I have this, Felix! Focus on the Behemoth!" She shouted at the illusion, then noticed the tremendous ooze bashing apart pillars of ice and stone, while vines tried unsuccessfully to bind it in place. The creature simply pushed through all obstacles and bonds, as hard to restrain as it was to injure. "What…what is happening?"

The Ooze Behemoth was bristling with Fathom spawn. Broodvipers carrying crooked tridents and shields made of large shells clung to its back and limbs, intervening bodily whenever an offensive Skill approached it. Another blade of ice thrust upward, but it was met by a wall of Drakin that blunted almost all of its savage edge.

"Vess! I need you to open a path!" Felix shouted, not from his shadowy double, nor from his physical body, still collapsed over Beef's broad chest. It was a voice she felt in her chest and Mind—across their Link. "This thing is in here, too!"

The insubstantial hand of Felix's double touched her forehead, faster than she had time to react. For a brief instant, Vess saw what Felix saw.

A mass the size of a small mountain burst all around her, tendrils moving faster than her eye could trace, there then simply gone. She did not move, but lifted a clawed hand and stopped the appendage cold, not so much as shifting from her spot. A blurring bundle of lightning and howling winds ripped by, neatly severing the oozing tendril and sending out an arc of frozen spears. Felix didn't move—couldn't, she realized. The ooze monstrosity, dozens of times larger than the Behemoth, was being fought to a standstill by *Pit.*

Her—his—eyes shifted downward, and for the first time, Vess made out a burning ring of light. It seared into their vision, a spot of brilliance in an endless darkness.

Abruptly, she was back. A Broodviper thrust a crooked trident at her face, but Vess batted it aside with barely restrained surprise. Rallying her senses, she caught a bolt of lightning from another Broodviper on her partisan, sending it whirling down into the dirt. Vess spun, partisan slashing as two more silver Spears manifested at sharp angles to her foes. She struck.

You Have Killed A Manawarped Broodviper (x2)!
XP Earned!

Felix's double still stood there, shoulders shifting as if it were breathing hard. His voice still transmitted crystal-clear through their Link. "I am holding Beef's core space stable, and we are holding the majority of that Behemoth's power here. My strength is split among it all, but I can muster an effort against the bastard, if you open a path. Those Fathom spawn need to drop, all at once."

"Beef can't handle it himself?" she asked.

"Maybe. And maybe he'll burn up, if I release my Fiendforge." The shadow shook his head, and thin skewers of stone ripped upward to take another several Fathom spawn in the gut. It was a wild shot, badly aimed. They didn't die, but they were stuck for a moment. "I can't take that chance, and I can't maintain precision without sacrificing power. Can't even use Chthonic Tribute through this thing."

Damnation. She had been hoping Felix would finish and wake soon, solving this issue for them, but she understood. He couldn't escape…not until the Ooze was destroyed.

"I only have one Skill that can do that," she whispered, and it felt like a weight on her soul.

"I know," he said. "Find another way, if you can. But we're running out of time. *I'm* running out of time."

Thoughts and ideas flashed through her Mind, tactics and maneuvers she could employ. The Ooze Behemoth was surging forward, its Body still covered in clinging spawn—each time they killed one, another took its place.

"GAHHH!" She thrust through the skull of a Drakin as it dove for her, killing it instantly. The eel-beast whipped its body around in its last moments of life, and she kicked it free. "Felix!"

The Fang of Havoc!

She rocketed into the air, powerful, gale-force wind at her back as she ascended to the peak of the tunnel and flipped, mid-air.

On The Wing!

"Do not miss!"

Draconic Stormfall!

She landed atop the Ooze Behemoth itself, and a ring of powerful lightning exploded from her feet. It blasted outward, ripping apart the nearest Fathom spawn with air, metal, and lightning Mana. The sheer volume of it seared flesh from bone, and the rest were hurled backward by the concussive impact as tempestuous winds whipped outward from her position. The Behemoth shrieked with its bubbling mud voice, pain and rage contained in a buzzing howl that made her vision fuzz.

Yet, worse of all, within her core space, she felt the clouds parting as a dark sky bloomed in the heavens, and a metallic dragon bellowed out a dark, melodic challenge.

Matriarch's Lament!

An identical cry ripped from Vess' throat, a sound that was both amplified by her Journeyman Body yet did not originate in her lungs. It was primal, a sound not of fury but of loss.

Of sorrow.

You Have Inflicted Enervation On Your Targets!
Status Condition: Stamina Drain!
Status Condition: Vitality Drain!

Every Fathom spawn for fifty strides around the Ooze Behemoth collapsed to the ground, unable to maintain their movement as their Stamina dropped to almost nothing. Their Health maximums, determined by their Vitality, shrank incredibly fast, until it was all they could do to keep breathing.

But the effect only lasted so long.

Felix! Now!

Vess felt it as not one or two, but *five* different Skills activated within her friend's core space. Stone rumbled, ice cracked, vines creaked, a thick core of virulent green surged and, surrounding them all, a brilliant torrent of red-gold flame swirled from Felix's core space. Again, her vision doubled as a vision of Felix's channels supplanted her normal sight, and she witnessed the horrifying flood of power as it ripped from Felix's unconscious Body…

…straight into the Ooze Behemoth itself.

"Now!" Paxus yelled.

Lightning, shadow, life, air, and metal Mana all hit the creature at once. Fathom spawn went up in a flash of smoke, their unresisting Bodies no match for the might of all of them together. The Ooze Behemoth bubbled a final, caterwauling screech as it swelled up and up, stretching to impossible, bulbous proportions.

It burst.

You Have Killed A Moontouched Ooze Behemoth!
XP Earned!

The Fang of Havoc is level 73!
Draconic Stormfall is level 72!
Matriarch's Lament is level 69!
...
Matriarch's Lament is level 72!

A rush of System power flooded her channels, rolling in from across her visualized horizon like the dawn itself. It thundered into the metallic dragon at her center, her...core...where it spun and spread, rippling outward in targeted gales and shimmering waves. Her Skills grew, their peaks becoming more detailed in an instant, more real. And all Vess could do was grit her teeth against it all, feeling the rawness inside her Aspects that she could not fight or prevent. She felt tainted.

Even so, a version of the Lament welled up from deep inside her changed temple, a chant that brought traitorous tears to her eyes.

Felix's shadowy double stepped up to her, cradling her hand in its insubstantial grip. A face that was a bare suggestion of features—save for the burning eyes—smiled sadly at her.

"I know. I do not blame you. It...had to be done." She straightened. "Now wake up, so we can fix this tunnel and continue onward."

"Yeah, give me a second—"

"Run!" Paxus shouted again, and this time, he was looking straight up. "I haven't the power to stop it! Run!"

Roots snapped above them, louder than any explosion, as claws larger than some buildings ripped down into the tunnel ceiling. Dark water dropped from those rents, a deluge so powerful it blasted new holes wherever it landed, and more water rushed inside. Vess leaped just as Felix's shadow double was torn apart, attempting to grab the real Felix from the still-frozen earth.

The water found her first.

CHAPTER EIGHTY-FIVE

FELIX!

The ooze burst all around him, rendered into stinking vapor before streaming down into Felix's gullet. Below, Beef still blazed too brightly to look at, but all around Felix, the once-omnipresent ooze had gone. His core space was stuffed full to bursting, but he couldn't think on it. The way out was open, and that voice was Vess. She was in trouble.

FELI—

"Pit! To me!" He barely paused as their visualized forms Converged once more. Felix hauled on the Link back to his Body. Blinked open his real eyes.

Just as an entire lake fell on his head.

Sunken Ward!

The spell ripped from Felix's channels, slipping across his allies with the ease of long practice, even as panic gripped his Mind. Pressure and icy darkness rolled him and Beef together, limbs smashing into root and stone hard enough to rip them asunder. Direction became meaningless, the world nothing more than the howl of roaring waters, furious spray, and the shadow of something vile and gargantuan bearing down on them all.

Sunken Ward is level 33!

...

Sunken Ward is level 37!

The sheer force of the water on him and his allies pushed Felix's spell to the limit, instantly consuming all of his Mana. If it weren't for the ooze's overwhelming energy, that would have been it; his friends would have been smeared along the tunnel's walls.

Sunken Ward is level 38!

...

Sunken Ward is level 42!

The ward held, cold and pressure held at bay, but it did nothing against the shadow in the waves. Claws tore through the tunnel, ripping more of it apart with arms the size of the Abundance Anima's branches. Felix's Perception was awry, too overwhelmed by everything to piece it all together, but he definitely noticed as the padded paw of a huge monstrosity seized him by the torso. He was hauled up as ice burst across his chest, through the broken tunnel and into the wide expanse of the lake bed.

This isn't good, Pit murmured inside his Spirit. *This isn't good at all.*

Felix had to agree. Pulled up into the greater dark, Felix's Perception finally had a chance to catch up. His senses spread outward, pinging off of countless shapes in the murky water, many of them familiar. Voracious Eye confirmed it, noting hundreds—perhaps thousands—of Broodvipers and Drakin. No mere Hatchlings, each one was strong—at least on par with a high Journeyman-Tier warrior—and in their eyes was a maddened glint that could have lit up the waters with its intensity.

Far more pressing, however, was the creature that had its claws around Felix's chest.

Moontouched Lindwurm. Just as the first Depthwurm he faced, it resembled a mix between a snake and wurm, except this one had sprouted a dozen arms, each tipped with two-foot-long talons. Their body was a mix of scales and swirling, faintly luminescent fur, most of which framed a wedge-shaped face and a pair of stunted horns. The monster was absolutely massive, twice as big as any Manaship and strong enough that his Voracious Eye struggled to read their details. *Dammit. Tier V. That's equivalent to a High Adept.*

And there were *six* of them.

"*This* is what has our monarch so worried?" one of them rumbled. Its voice shook the water like a subwoofer, all but slapping Felix in the face. "It is but a single morsel. I could end it with nothing more than the snap of my jaws."

"Careful, sister. He maintains a spell, one that keeps his fellows alive." Another Lindwurm shifted their Body, the waves of their undulations enough to make Felix tense his neck muscles to keep from having his head snap back. "See?"

The creature held up three of its appendages, showing Beef, the Multipede, and Vess captured in its claws. Felix easily made out the white-green light that limned their forms, as well as the dark ice that bound them. Beef and Hallow were down, but Vess stared daggers at the draconic-Type Lindwurms. A bizarre feeling swelled within Felix's core space, like a drum being slammed far away, one that he felt vibrating in his gut. It was pure and simple violence.

Vess. Don't, he sent across their Link. He'd managed it somehow earlier, and it was far easier now. *Wait for my signal. Please.*

Fine, was all she sent back. Her gaze did not waver from the Lindwurms for an instant.

"How did you survive the rending of the roots?" crooned the Lindwurm holding Felix. They tilted their wedge-shaped head at him, a single yellow eye the size of a mid-sized sedan blinking languidly. "What spell is it you cast, little morsel?"

Felix grinned. <<Come closer and find out.>>

The Lindwurm's head rippled forward on its long, sinuous neck. It was a disturbing undulation as it left the rest of their Body unmoved, as if their neck were somehow detached or independent of their thicker trunk. The creature opened their jaws, revealing a black tongue within a bright pink mouth. They stopped only inches from Felix's face, and somehow he could feel the stink on their breath.

"I would know what I am to destroy for my monarch. I feel a danger to you which cannot be true for one so meager." Their black tongue tapped against a set of fangs taller than Felix, and all the water around him felt suddenly too warm. "Explain."

Felix licked his lips and took stock of his situation. Vess was ready to fight, though she was practically hobbling herself thanks to her Temper recomposition efforts. Isla, held by one of the other Lindwurms, was fully unconscious and bound in more dark ice. The War Naga were likewise captured, and Felix only counted six of them remaining. Three had died since that morning. He shoved that fact away. *No time to deal with that now.*

Of Paxus, there was no sign.

Beef is still fighting, Pit added.

Felix could feel that as well. The teen was still resolving his core space, evidenced by many things, not the least of which was Felix's continued hold on his Fiendforge. The effort of it was immense, and it was burning up a significant chunk of the Ooze's stolen Essence and Mana. So long as he held Fiendforge, Felix would be limited in what he could do—unless he was willing to sacrifice his team.

If Felix were to tangle with the Lindwurms, the sheer amount of Fathom spawn would bury his friends.

"The spell, gobbet," they demanded. That eye returned, tilted downward to stare at him balefully. "Or I shall eat your allies one-by-one."

The cool rage that was pooling in Felix's chest stoked hotter at those words. His cores sparked, throwing thunder and flame in wild bursts of shrieking melody. <<You want to fight, you fight me. You're not gonna touch a hair on their heads.>>

"You make demands, little nibble? That our monarch sent us to deal with you is already too much glory for such a small thing. You," they said, squeezing Felix for emphasis. Ice cracked and spread, crawling up his shoulders and neck. "Do not make demands of us. Answer me. What spell is this? Why does it not fail against me?"

It took a considerable measure of Felix's insane Willpower to keep himself calm. The pain was one thing to shrug off, but the casual threats against his team—against those he cared about—that was too far. Yet, before words could spool up in his Mind, whispers caressed the edges of it, as if drifting on a roving current. *Seek the center. Strengthen the Tree.*

Paxus? There was only a brief pulse, something Felix could take for confirmation or simply a coincidence. *Well, who else would be worried about the Tree right now?*

"Too late!" the Lindwurm cried out, and its tail moved fast. It whipped through the water and smashed into one of the other Lindwurms…except they swam backward, leaving behind three of the War Naga floating helplessly in their frozen cages. For a brief, horrifying second, Felix met Toa'ut's stoic gaze and heard terror.

All three were shattered.

<<No,>> Felix whispered. Toa'ut and two of his warriors were simply…gone. They left behind only frozen chunks and thick, swirling clouds of misty crimson.

"Their deaths are on you, mage," the Lindwurm rumbled. Its tone of delight was unmistakable, even if it had bothered to veil their Spirit from Felix's senses. "As are your other companions, if you do not heed my words. The spell!"

<<Right,>> Felix hissed, Mind whirling as he fought his rising emotions. Images and impressions flitted about, organizing themselves in a wild, almost incoherent order. Red-gold flame escaped from the corners of his mouth, turning to boiling bubbles where it met the water. <<New plan.>>

Adamant Discord!

Lightning erupted in a perfect circle around Felix, the connections he had established with the water and even the Lindwurms themselves serving as battering rams for his Intent and Will. The Lindwurm squawked in surprise, its paw blasted open along with shards of its own icy spell.

"You dare! I will freeze the blood in your bones!"

Rime Shaping!

Felix pointed at the Lindwurm and unleashed a Chant-boosted ice

Mana spell, conjuring a huge, blunt chunk of ice to crash into the beast's chest. The draconic Type was huge, bigger by far than anything he'd fought recently, but it was still in the water. Leverage was hard to find. The Lindwurm was blasted back, a look of reptilian outrage on its face.

<<I wanna talk to the Fathom. Now,>> Felix said as the spell faded.

The outrage on the Lindwurm's face turned to a deep amusement. Their laugh was deep and throaty, enough to send chills up Felix's spine. "You cannot make demands of us, morsel. You are prey, and we are predators!"

It lunged forward, wedge-shaped jaws agape as if to swallow him whole.

Sovereign of Flesh!

The song of it wobbled, its Transcendent pattern too large and complex while he was also still maintaining Fiendforge. Immense familiarity and burning far too much of the Ooze Behemoth's Essence did their magic, however, and the Skill stabilized. Before the Lindwurm could even reach him, Felix hurled his Willpower against it.

"N-no!" the Lindwurm cried. "Release me!"

With a scream of effort, Felix laid claim to the Lindwurm's very flesh. The moment he did, skin, scale, muscle, and fat were flensed from its bulky frame. Sovereign of Flesh sang within him, a ruthless melody that surged with buzzing atonal beats.

Felix ripped their fucking bones apart.

Sovereign of Flesh is level 83!
Sovereign of Flesh is level 84!

You Have Killed A Moontouched Lindwurm!
XP Earned!

Chthonic Tribute!

<<Let's try this again,>> he said, letting the ichor and offal flood into his channels before turning to the Lindwurm that held Vess and Beef. <<Take me to your leader. Now.>>

CHAPTER EIGHTY-SIX

The Lamellan Titan stomped, and the earth itself heaved. The battlements of Haarwatch shifted, jolting beneath Atar's feet in an eerie rendition of a ship at sea; he stumbled and was only saved from tumbling off the wall by his stave's sharpened end. With a desperate twist, the claws hidden in the tip latched tight to the rock, and he threw his free hand over the crenelation to steady himself.

pull with all your strength, child! you will not perish here, not to these fungal weaklings!

"Quiet, Flame!" Atar hauled himself back to his feet, yanking his stave from the dressed stone with a weary grunt. "These damn Lamellans are bad enough. I don't need you in my Mind as well!"

All around him, Atar saw evidence of the Titan's stomp as well as its spores. Where they hadn't ripped into lungs and burst from chests, they had inflicted a sort of euphoric daze that was quickly followed by a brutal berserker rage. Haarguard fought against Haarguard where the spores still hung thickly, the mages dedicated to burning them from the air having fallen victim.

"Damnation and Ruin," Atar cursed. "Incendiary Vortex!"

A significant measure of Mana ripped from his channels, bursting alight as a streamer of white and crimson flame before coalescing into an air-borne wheel. The wheel raged, a truncated, spinning cyclone that pulled the spores from the air and burned them to a crisp. Haarguards fell, partially burned, but alive. Free.

Better to be dead than a slave to some vile Condition.

join us together, and we may burn them all from the face of the continent, atar!

"I said, quiet!" Already, the last Titan was standing from its catastrophic stomp, readying itself to charge the wall like all of its fellows once had. Despite being taller than the wall itself, the thing was shaped vaguely as a man, but with a wide mushroom top for a head and thick, stunted limbs, all made of slick, fungal flesh. Most importantly, it was covered in wounds—evidence of their bitter battle. Atar stabbed a finger at the recovering guards and Claw members, all of them spread out atop the wall. "There's only one left! I plan to sleep for two days after this, but we have to end it first! Mages! On my signal!"

A weary chorus of shouts met his words, not nearly the same enthusiasm Felix would have engendered, but it was enough. The forest and fields before them were aflame, merrily burning with the consequences of their protracted battles. Their little army, ragtag and mostly underleveled as it was, had put up a savage fight these past few days. The mushroom monsters had eked out some wins, but only for a dire price—and for the most part, the wall had done its job. The spiders had swarmed them, too, but they had been dispatched as of that morning, the last of their disgusting Orb Weavers turned to putrid goo. The field of battle was a ruin, a blasted wasteland filled with the smoking remnants of Lamellan Crofters and huge Orb Weavers, with small conflicts bursting up and down the wall. Here, however, they had one last hurdle to overcome.

"One more, and we can rest," Atar muttered to himself. He barely knew where his friends were, only that Alister was off down the wall, while Zara, Harn, and Darius were leading regiments in other sections. All he knew was the forty-stride section of the Sunrise Wall where he and the mages had made their stand.

The Titan started moving, tromping toward them on its wide, fungal-flesh limbs. Its wide-brimmed head wobbled with every quaking step, but its movements belied its astonishing speed. It would reach them in a few heartbeats only.

"Steady!" he shouted.

The Titan sped up, its Body blurring suddenly at the edges, and Atar held his breath. The creature stumbled, but its center of balance was too low to be outmaneuvered so easily. It tossed its cap-head, releasing another cloud of fetid spores. Atar burned them out of the sky just as a figure leaped from the shadows at its feet.

"Bindings of the White Waste!"

Purple-white chains of Mana tore across the last Lamellan Titan, binding its trailing arm with a deep, bitter frost. It didn't freeze so much as desiccate, withering down even as it became locked in place. The

Titan bellowed in its windy, wheezing voice, confused and angry as Evie landed atop its head, chain whirling above her.

"Ugly as you are stupid! Tooth and Claw! Bonds of Dominion!" Evie brought her chain down, its edge turned to vicious blades and spikes that dug deep into the Titan's cap—driven far deeper than such a slight girl seemed capable of. Its ridged gills rippled, the inside exposed to the air as the Titan screamed anew and tried to move...and found more chains somehow binding it tight. "Atar! I can't hold it for long!"

"Mages! Fire!" The word left his mouth and the world lit up in a deluge of flame, acid, and lightning.

"Astrum Revelation!" he continued, pulling at the Flame in his core for more and more power. It gasped in delight, a white patch of fire that danced in his center, before pushing a tide of Mana through his channels. Atop his head manifested flames in the shape of a crown with nine prongs on it and a single, tenth shard floating at its peak. The spell was dangerous, as it increased the potency of his fire magic but infused him with...reckless emotions. Atar gritted his teeth as the giddiness of the Flame suffused his Spirit and Mind, stoking the readily available emotions of aggression and disdain inside of him.

finally. finally, you have listened to reason, the Flame purred at him. **only together might we beat back such a harrowing enemy. only together can we dominate this land.**

Atar laughed. He couldn't help it. The power felt too good. "Stars of the Sovereign!"

White, four-pronged motes of flame appeared all around him, at first a handful but soon twice that and twice again. And again. Until Atar felt himself suspended in a sea of stars, each burning so hot as to melt Untempered steel by their sheer proximity. To him, under the influence of his Revelation, they were a gentle breeze on a warm spring day.

He pointed right at the Titan. "Go."

The Stars, every single one of them, ripped outward at once. What once might have looked like rainfall had become a torrent of flame, a river of Stars that sought out the Titan with unerring speed. Sparkbolts and Levin Bolts that had torn more holes in the Titan's flesh were consumed, burnt up by Atar's power. As was the weakened and trapped mushroom beast.

"YES. BURN," Atar laughed, though part of him struggled against the feeling of giddy superiority. His Willpower clashed against the Flame itself, which had bloomed within his core so that it filled all of its obsidian cage.

no! it must die before us, atar! i will show you how it must be!

Atar didn't speak, merely hurled the rest of his impressive Willpower and Intent at the Flame. He envisioned it dwindling, fading, the look of embers and ash at the end of a long, cold night.

stop! stop!

The fire mage ignored its pleas, pressing his Will against the Flame's until the winged shape buckled and broke. The Flame collapsed upon itself, spouting dark ashes and flurries of molten embers. It shrieked in annoyance and frustrated ego, like a deflating bladder of hot air.

"I…said…quiet," Atar panted, fully back to himself. The crown had vanished, along with the passive boost it gave his fire magic. He snapped his head up, panning the field of battle before sagging against his stave. "Highest Flame, it worked."

You Have Killed A Lamellan Titan!
XP Earned!

You Have Earned a New Title!
Champion of the Fungal Forest (Rare)!
You have proven yourself in extended combat against the legions of Lamellan, and have even bested a Lamellan Titan!
+15 to VIT, END, and WIL!

Stars of the Sovereign is level 81!
Astrum Revelation is level 74!

Only one more level, and I can complete my Spirit Temper into Adept. Atar waved the notifications away, barely taking a moment to enjoy the boost of clarity—both mental and physical—that came to him upon gaining forty-five stat points from his new Title. He'd already earned Warrior of the Fungal Forest, as had everyone else who fought against the damnable Lamellan. He wasn't concerned with Titles.

"Evie!" he shouted into the waning afternoon light. For the first time in days, the fields just outside Haarwatch were quiet. Soldiers all down the line were regrouping, quaffing potions, getting healed, or otherwise staring out into the empty stretch of blasted terrain before them. The last Titan lay among the mud and muck, far closer to the wall than Atar had expected. Its huge, fungal body was now a charred ruin. The withering of her cold magic had primed the monster for his flames, allowing them to eat through its wounded hide without impediment. "Evie, are you alive?"

"Unfortunately," came the answer. Her voice was a bit muffled until a chunk of ashen fungus was hurled away, revealing Evie covered in soot and something viscous. "I didn't think these things had guts."

Atar grimaced, scrunching up his nose. He was unable to smell the girl, but that didn't mean he had to take chances. "Foul. Must have liquified its insides during our combination of magic."

"Right. Right. The Frostfire Combo. Worked again, eh?" She whipped her hair back, which had come loose from its elaborate braid atop her head and started plaiting it again. She paused, then looked up at him with a grin. "Wait. Were you worried about me?"

"What? I merely did not wish to waste our combat resources," Atar said and made a show of fixing his robes. He pointed farther afield. "We still have that Matriarch to worry about!"

Evie's grin didn't fade. "Admit it, Sparky. You like me. We're *friends*."

Atar rolled his eyes, and in doing so, saw the gaggle of mages that had gathered around him. A number of them were stifling smiles, but most just looked confusedly between the two of their commanding officers. *Ugh. People are the worst.* "Focus up. The field might have gone quiet, but the Weaver Matriarch is still in those trees."

"I thought we killed her," said a Half-Orc Atar couldn't remember. Loogans or something. He was dressed in the armor and distinctively marked cloak of the Claw, so Atar knew the boy had followed them to the desert at least. "I saw her take a full barrage to her chest."

"She lived," Evie said, suddenly among them. Several of the mages jumped and the girl grinned like a damn cat. "Saw her scuttle off myself."

"But sir, you said we only had the Titan left," one of the younger mages said.

"I lied," Atar admitted. "But maybe we'll be lucky, and the Hand or Harn will take care of her."

"SKREEE!"

The shriek tore through the long shadows at the edge of the forest, revealing the ten-stride-high Weaver Matriarch, now covered in mud and muck but exuding an aura of fury. She lifted her forelegs up in a clear threat and clacked mandibles large enough to snap a tree in two.

"Speak and summon her," muttered one of the mages, but Atar ignored them.

"All hands! Fall in and end this!" A deep voice bellowed from down the line. It was Reed, and he hefted his door-sized sword to point it right at the Matriarch. "Fire ranged attacks on my signal!"

"Line up!" Atar ordered, a touch shrilly. "Line up now!"

His mages rushed to listen to him, while Evie still crouched atop the crenelations. Watching. "Seems strange. Thing is just standin' there, all puffed up. Why's it not movin'?"

"Fire!" Reed shouted, and they all unleashed their basic attack spells. Many fell short, the distance too far. "Again!"

"I do not know," Atar admitted, keeping his spells to himself. He drank down another Mana Potion. Half as tall as the Titans, the Matriarch had proven impossible to target due to the trees, the fungal warriors, and the plethora of her children. Of course, all the spiders were dead, killed earlier that day, causing the Matriarch to flee behind the last of the Titans. Now even that meager protection was gone, and she was exposed within a web of silken threads.

Threads, he realized. *A trap!*

"Watch the threads! Do not get close!" Atar hollered above the roar of flames. Atar wasn't the only one with fire-attuned cores, and they had not been shy about using it on the forest.

But the warriors were already advancing, and as the Matriarch pulled her massive legs downward, several trees began to fall. Threads flashed, connected to the trees, and the bulky trunks careened toward the rushing warriors. The soldiers dodged them or leaped aside entirely, but the trees splashed down, fouling the ground further and cutting into their speed.

I need to do something, Atar thought furiously. "We need to—"

Quite suddenly, the Weaver Matriarch stuttered to a stop…before sloughing into two, roughly equal parts.

"What?" Atar said, mouth agape.

"Noctis' tits," Evie cursed. "Avet's teeth and Yyero's ass!"

"What?" Atar repeated, still confused. The Weaver Matriach's body had immediately begun to dissolve, though it was shining far brighter than he'd ever seen. Almost…golden.

A sword lifted, one that was easily the match for Reed's, but made entirely of golden light Mana.

Evie clenched her jaw and chain. "Inquisitors."

CHAPTER EIGHTY-SEVEN

"I thought we had more time," Atar said, his voice barely above a whisper. Only Evie could hear it, and she simply grimaced. "Everyone! Health, Stamina, and Mana Potions, now! Top off!"

His mages had been conditioned by the long, grueling hours of war, and none hesitated. They pulled free a trio of vials at their waists. Atar and Evie did the same. His Mana was slowly recovering, as was his Health and Stamina, but none were far past fifty percent—far from optimal. They were going to need every edge they could afford.

In the distance, that golden sword was raised in a massive, golden gauntlet that was connected to a hulking, translucent suit of conjured armor. Ten feet tall and almost as wide, it was a suit of plate made entirely of hardened planes of light Mana, containing within it a red-cloaked Inquisitor. With the hundred stride distance between them, Atar could not make out all the details, but the redcloak floating at its center was manipulating its limbs like a sort of puppet. The Inquisitor drew the massive sword back to their side, hefting a huge slab of light Mana formed into a tower shield.

"I thought that was a hard Skill to learn!" Evie hissed, her jaw still clenched. "They've got thirty of 'em!"

Atar had noticed that as well, as more brilliant conjured suits of armor stepped from behind the tumbled trees. He'd never encountered the Skill he was witnessing, but plenty of others had told him of it. Evie had once recounted her fight with a golden-armored Inquisitor down in the sewers. It had taken her, Vess, and Felix to defeat their opponent, and he had been one of the lower-ranked redcloaks. "Those don't look to be Apprentice Tier, either," he said.

The distance was too far for Analyze to function, but Atar had fought enough strong combatants to identify the air of someone who had advanced beyond the limits of Apprentice. Perhaps even Journeyman.

As he considered that, the woods were ignited by the concussive shout of Tempered lungs as rank after rank of redcloaks appeared from the withered fungal thicket and web-tangled trees. Fire, bright and gold, licked across logs and invisible threads, appearing, for an instant, to form a wild, strange array in midair.

Evie rolled her shoulders. "This is gonna be bad."

Behind the golden giants, rows upon rows of redcloaks marched in perfect synchronized steps, their white-enameled armor half-hidden by their blood-red capes, but showing enough that the golden sunburst on their chests gleamed. At least a thousand, by Atar's count, they might have been manageable for the Haarwatch defenders, until a second shout rocked the air.

"Paladins, halt!"

Dwarfing the count of Inquisitors were the bulky, crimson-armored hulks of the Pathless' Paladins. Banners were held high, depicting a rippling standard that was echoed on every blood-red breastplate: a sword and clenched fist over a golden sunburst. Atar's eyes danced across their details, their rank and file, trying to sift through what he knew about their organization.

That's…that's two entire battalions of Paladins and a single battalion of Inquisitors arrayed against us. The numbers chilled him. *Blood and burning ashes. They truly did bring an army.*

they must die.

Atar pursed his lips but didn't respond. He wouldn't lie, but the last thing he desired was to admit the Flame was right.

A deep thrum echoed across the Verdant Pass, and the smoking trees rippled as three Manaships rose from their depths in perfect synchronization. They were easily larger than the galleon-class ships Atar's people used, perhaps twice the size, in addition to being covered in heavy metal plating and thick bronze stabilizing wings. Sigils festooned their hulls and sails, flashing briefly as tree branches impacted the glimmering traces of wards, before the ships settled a touch higher than the Sunrise Gate wall. These, too, were over a hundred strides away, but Atar could make out the hundreds of white-enameled soldiers that stood atop their decks in neat, red-cloaked rows.

The Hierocracy had finally made their move.

"Gotta be another battalion of those bastards on the ships, too,"

Evie muttered. The strains of fury rolled from her like waves, but her eyes were wide and worried. "How're we gonna fight all this?"

"We just will," Atar said, though something was wrong with his voice. It came out entirely too high. "We just will," he repeated.

better that time.

Atar curled his lip, his mustache bristling against his nose. "Mana levels?" he asked.

"Eighty percent at the lowest, sir," said Lazlo the Half-Orc. Lightning crackled between his fingers. "What shall we do to them, sir?"

"Do to them?" Atar raised an eyebrow. "We'll be lucky if we can penetrate their shielding."

"But we have so many mages, not to mention our warriors. The Claw alone—"

"Won't stand a chance if those inscribed wings on the ships are what I think they are," Atar said, his voice sharp as any knife. "And stop discharging Mana. That's a waste of power that we *will* need."

"I—the Fiend—fine." The idiot stopped leaking immediately, clenching his fists hard over the Mana Gates in his palms. "If the Fiend were here—"

"He isn't! And he damn well should be!" Atar snapped, puffing air through his nostrils like an overblown Avum.

burn them all.

"Attention, vassals of the Hierocracy! Attention, all those who would uphold the truth and glory of the light!"

Atar pulled himself away from Lyle the Half-Orc lightning mage with great difficulty. His hand had knotted into the man's robes and was starting to smoke, but Atar put it out with a wave of his Will. He tried his best to ignore the look of fear in the mage's eyes—in all their eyes—and turned instead toward the new voice that was booming across the battlefield.

"I am Sword, of the High Guard," said the figure, before pausing as if to drink in the gasps of astonishment from Haarwatch. They were indeed prevalent, and even Atar couldn't hold back from flinching from the name.

The High Guard. Atar looked him over, hoping to spot the lie but unable to find any flaws. A man, judging by the timbre of his voice, for his face and body were entirely covered in a milky white armor of smooth, interlocking plates. He stood atop the leading Manaship, at ease with his hands folded behind him as if he were simply a soldier at parade rest. At his side were others in similar armor. *Four of them. They sent executioners to quell us.*

"My associates and I were sent here, not to kill you, but to prove to the Hierophant that you are innocent of the dire accusations that have been leveled against your city. Accusations of treachery, tyranny, and treason."

The man's voice boomed at the last, not so much loud as it was pervasive. The trees thirty strides below his ship flailed as if shaken by a terrible beast. The man—Sword—continued.

"We would ask that all those who are innocent of those charges, who are simply caught up in the wiles of the vile and wicked, to return to your homes. To stand aside and let us confront those who have truly wronged our great nation. You are not our target." Sword took a single step forward, and suddenly a sword made entirely of red-gold orichalcum was in his uplifted hand, blade bare to the sky. "We have come for Felix Nevarre, who is charged with fomenting civil unrest, for usurpation of Territorial rule, and with the murder of several prominent members of the Pathless' clergy."

More gasps arose from the man's words this time, and to Atar's surprise, almost none were fearful. They were *angry*.

"Liar!"

"Hierocratic dog!"

"The Hierophant can kiss my ass!" Evie hollered from beside him. "Felix did nothin' wrong! Autarch! Autarch! Autarch!"

Her voice ripped across the battlefield, among the loudest, and soon the silly chant she'd taken up had spread. Up and down the walls, soldiers screamed and shouted along, uncaring as the High Guard watched them with their featureless helmets and rigid body language.

"Felix Nevarre!" Sword shouted and released a piece of his Spirit. It fell on Atar like a wet blanket, heavy and cloying and restrictive, and the chanting faded to nothing. "Felix Nevarre is a petty tyrant! He has claimed Territory under the purview of the Hierophant, a responsibility given to her directly by the Pathless Himself! Your *Autarch* is but a *thief*."

Their faces were hidden, but in that moment, Atar felt a tingling, buzzing jolt along his Affinity. A raw aggression and hatred flashed from Sword's Spirit, and though it was gone an instant later, Atar found it pressed indelibly into his memory. The sheer depth of it was a shock that almost knocked the lungs from the mage's chest. *That man will kill us all.*

The High Guard leaned back and slowly replaced his namesake in a sheath at his waist. "My conflict is with your leader. You fine soldiers have proven yourselves more than capable against the beasts of this wretched valley, eliminating them before they could multiply too greatly and threaten the lands beyond.

"The inaction of your leader has led to their overpopulation, an issue that you have corrected here, once we gave them a bit of a push. That is commendable." Sword spread his hands wide, a stance that screamed of calm, rational acceptance. "Lay down your weapons, and bring to me your Autarch. We shall end this without more bloodshed."

Quiet. Atar watched with bated breath as the entirety of Haarwatch looked at the horde of Hierocratic soldiers. Then the silence was broken.

"Hold!" Reed called out, his voice no quieter than Evie's. He was still down there, among the warriors that had started to charge the Weaver Matriarch, and he had rallied their attention. They weren't too close to the enemy, but they were far enough from the wall that getting back might prove too difficult. "You sent those monsters to test us?"

"A test any city beneath the Hiercracy should be able to pass." The High Guard paused, leaning over the railing of the Manaship and peering downward. "Do I know you, Adept Tier?"

"Loose!" Reed commanded, and in an instant, the sky was filled with light. Balls of fire, bolts of lightning, spears of earth, and sharp, spinning blades of air Mana all hurled up at the lead Manaship. All of it converged upon a single, exposed target.

All of it for nothing, as the wardings absorbed the entirety of the attack.

The High Guard, their ship, and the hundreds of Inquisitors behind them all looked down upon Haarwatch's defenders, utterly unharmed. "A lesson must be taught, then," Sword said. He raised up his sword once more, and this time it burst into brilliant, emerald flame.

"Blessed of the Pathless," he cried, and his booming voice turned hard as Adept Tempered steel. It was as pitiless as the man's smooth, featureless helmet. "Advance."

CHAPTER EIGHTY-EIGHT

<<You had better know what you're doing, Felix,>> Lady Isla muttered as bars of iron and stone closed around them all.

Vess couldn't help but agree. The survivors of the root tunnel had been tossed to earth after Felix's violent display, and while the largest part of her cheered for him, the rest was keyed up with twitching anxiety. Too many Fathom spawn surrounded them, not to mention the enormous Lindwurms that held each of them in their clawed grasps. Yet the draconics had released them all, choosing instead to bundle them together in a cage they summoned from below.

Felix had held the glare of the Lindwurms through the entire process, and though the terrifying beasts bared their teeth and curled their lips, none drew close to their group until the cage was finished. Even then, they hesitated, until the largest forced the smallest to swim over and seize the top of the cage. With a lurching rush, they all rocketed off into the dark.

Now they were traveling across the blasted terrain at the bottom of the lake, moving fast enough that the ground beneath them was rendered a blurred, murky haze. Vess sat atop the crude, twisted bars, her Mind ignoring the discomfort to focus on the trouble they were facing. Lady Isla, Beef, Hallow, and Felix were beside her, sat or laid out in various states of consciousness.

The War Naga were arrayed around them in a protective circle, filling up the majority of the cage with their weapons propped outward. Lavix was nearest the heiress, her scaled length trembling along with her grieving Spirit. The loss of Toa'ut and other warriors was hitting them hard, though their weapons and furious gazes were steady.

Vess placed her hand on Lavix's warm scales and caught the Naga woman's frayed attention. She said nothing, but Lavix's Spirit quietened just a touch. The Naga nodded before turning back to the monstrosities that surrounded them.

There were so many.

The Fathom spawn spread out in all directions, a horde as uncountable as any she had encountered. *Reminds me of the Domain under Haarwatch, right before it burst.* The Archon's servant had collected all of the monsters in one spot, and it had been a nightmare to handle even the tiny portion they had faced. Felix had been right to surrender, though it soured Vess's stomach.

<<What is happening with you, child?>> Lady Isla said. Beef was unconscious, as were the two remaining Bodies of Hallow. The Chanter cradled Beef's big head in her lap, hands intermittently glowing with green-gold Mana as she attempted to wake him.

<<Don't bother. He's…working through some stuff,>> Felix said.

<<What have you done?>> she demanded.

<<Saved his life, probably,>> Felix muttered. Vess frowned. He looked strained in a way she had seen before, likely when he had faced another too-powerful opponent.

He split himself between aiding Beef and us, she reminded herself. Vess still couldn't understand how he had accomplished such a thing. *Small wonder he is injured.*

<<Felix,>> Lady Isla said, her voice low as she gazed at the undulating masses around them. The Lindwurms were watching, likely listening, too, and it was clear the Chanter was choosing her words carefully. <<What is your plan?>>

<<You think I have one?>> he asked, flashing a sharp, handsome smile.

<<Felix.>> This time Lady Isla's tone was a rumble that somehow shook Vess' inner ear. As if the Grand Harmony was bleeding through her voice.

Felix simply raised a finger to his lips. <<Wake me up when we get there,>> he said…before collapsing backward in a heap.

<<Fe—!>> Vess cut off her own scream with a titanic effort of Will. She floundered for that feeling in her chest, the one that had been growing above her core space. The Link thrummed, skittering away from her grasp

Felix! What is going on? Are you alright?

Vess? Oh right, the Links. Yeah, I'm fine. I just have to—ugh—I just have to handle some things. He paused, and all Vess could hear on the line were the sounds of a distant thrumming.

That is not a good explanation. We are trapped and headed toward the Fathom,

Felix. Vess took a breath through her nose, the magic of his Sunken Ward tickling against her sinuses. *Tell me you have a plan.*

The thrumming increased, becoming more and more chaotic as strange, half-heard notes flitted through their connection. Oddly, Vess could almost perfectly visualize Felix, as if he were standing inches from her—he looked surprised then guilty. *Yes. Sorry, I was—the sarcasm was for Isla. I have a plan. Mostly.*

Vess' irritation melted—a little. *That is a relief, because I simply wish to tear into these monstrosities with all that I have. Does your plan include destroying the Fathom and its kindred?*

The image of Felix solidified completely before her, and he flashed that handsome grin again. *Make sure Isla doesn't wake up Beef. He's putting his core space together, and he needs all the time he can get.* He took a breath, but the smile didn't fade. *Me, too, actually. Wish me luck.*

Before she could respond, the connection vanished. Vess opened her eyes, only to find Lady Isla staring daggers at her.

<<Well?>> she asked. <<I could tell you were communicating with the boy, somehow. That smile on your face tells me as much. What did he say?>>

Vess let the smile—one she hadn't known she was wearing—fall away. <<I do not appreciate your tone, Lady Isla.>>

The Chanter jerked backward, as if Vess had slapped her, but the surprise faded quickly. An expression of repentance flooded over the woman, though, as usual, Vess could feel nothing of her Spirit. <<My apologies, Lady Dayne. I overstepped myself.>>

<<Indeed,>> Vess said with a sniff. Her eyes flickered outward, taking in the rushing waters and shifting mass of spawn that surrounded them on all sides. <<Felix is simply recovering from his fight, as is Beef. I would insist that you leave both of them alone. Now. There are more important things than Felix.>> Vess settled her partisan across her lap while she attempted to pull her concerns away from the slumbering Unbound beside them.

<<Such as?>> Lady Isla asked, her voice more deadpan than her smile suggested. <<We stand at the brink of disaster, Lady Dayne. We are being carted to the Fathom, announced no less, without any assurances that we will survive the encounter. Is *that* the boy's plan?>>

<<The boy has a name and a title,>> Vess said, her voice hard. <<You shall use it as you choose to use mine.>>

This time, Lady Isla's smile dropped fully into a grimace. <<Very well. Autarch Nevarre. What could be more important than his intentions?>>

Vess idly rolled her partisan in her lap, fighting the urge to grip it tight. <<That we be ready for their consequences.>>

Felix set aside the Link with Vess, hiding it away from himself. As much as he wanted to tell Vess everything—to reassure her—he didn't have the time. Reassurances would have been lies anyway. Felix only had scraps and inferences to work with, after all, and now they were being carried to the Fathom at speed.

He had to work quickly.

Drifting down toward his dual cores, Felix let his Mind settle. Tried to, at least. The pain of his recent exertions as well as the bundle of howling song that was his Fiendforge were twin knots in the fabric of his consciousness. Here, within his core space, the latter even had a physical presence.

The pattern of Fiendforge was huge and complex, as befitting its Unique rarity. At first glance, it appeared to Felix as a massive planet streaked liberally with dark clouds that blanketed its shape in shadow. Blue-white lightning flashed among them, as if the surface were suffering under a single, world-spanning storm.

It wasn't, but the only places where there was a break in cloud cover featured angry, magma-spitting volcanoes. It was a world that looked to be still forming from scratch, as Earth would have looked billions of years prior—except, unlike Earth, this celestial body was sparking with ripples of red-gold and blue-white energies that escaped its bounds and speared outward…to vanish into the dark.

Yet the ripples weren't vanishing, but traversing the strange pathways between internal worlds. Slipping across the Link with Beef, the Skill sounded its pattern again and again, maintaining the connection over the chaos of the other Unbound's core space. The whole of the Skill was drawn taut, a vise turned tight. It was a constant drain on Felix's mental acuity, not to mention his slowly dwindling supply of Essence and Mana.

That was the other reason for the tension and pain. Felix had consumed the Ooze Behemoth and, for the first time, had not immediately divested himself of its power. It was one of several reasons why he'd demanded a meeting with the Lindwurm's master—he needed the Ooze's potency, and that meant risking the Fathom's attention. Yet, the moment the Lindwurms had agreed to take them into the depths, the mystifying attention of the Fathom had dropped away, as if satisfied or perhaps no longer quite so curious. They were a known entity now.

Killing the one Lindwurm was a risk, and Felix had briefly sensed the Fathom's renewed interest after its death, but it was necessary. If they were to make it out of Khasma, then Felix needed to make a few gambles. Thankfully, their master's attention had drifted away once again, as something like reassurance had puckered the waters between Lindwurm and Fathom.

That had been interesting to witness, and he filed it away for later.

The closer he drifted to his cores, the more the pain and tension faded. Down past the branches of his Divine Tree, a crystalline formation that glittered with stolen power and spread over nearly the entirety of his core space. It sparked along his senses, the Lindwurm and Ooze's repurposed strength sizzling as it hung in stasis as bits of it were siphoned off and into his Fiendforge.

Down the immense trunk, thicker than any skyscraper back home, until the coiling roots vanished into the splashing waves of melodious Harmony and crashing Dissonance as his [Thundflame Core] and [Cardinal Beast Core] ground eternally against one another. He let both wash over him, a background radiation that Felix had long since learned to ignore. Eventually, even that faded, *everything* faded, and Felix stepped onto the edge of a yawning abyss at his very center.

"Hello there, Hunger."

FEED?

Felix could feel the thing's attention shift to the swirling clouds of Essence and Mana that festooned the Divine Tree. Its attention was a bared blade, an open maw, but it was oddly calm. Felix was still uncertain what his Hunger was, other than some piece of his Primordial nature, but for all its danger, he felt a certain empathy for it. All it knew was its own needs. Plus, it had helped him before.

He hoped it could do so again.

"I'll feed you after this, but for now, I need that for what I'm planning." Felix stepped a bit closer, feeling more of his core space go silent. "I need your help to focus. You down for that?"

A profound silence met his words. The looming black at the center of all things did not answer.

And then it did.

...DOWN.

Felix blinked. "Uh. Alright. Cool." He took a bracing breath, though this was a visualized Body. "Then let's start now."

He stepped into the abyss.

CHAPTER EIGHTY-NINE

The forest felt weird, and Pit was worried. He padded silently through the underbrush, tail swishing through fronds and scattering droplets of early morning dew. His internal world, the forest of his home, was quiet…save for the rattling thrum that emanated from the tree at his center.

"What a strange noise," he muttered, stepping closer to the spiraling roots. Branches hung low, heavy with the fruit of Pit's Skills, each one a glimmering pattern to the tenku's eye. These were not the source of the sound.

The trunk reached upward for a great distance, weaving around itself in a tight knot of wood and bark. It was composed of several smaller trees, bound tightly around one another and leaving space for a curious gemstone, pulsing with an intermittent beat and shaped as a four-pointed Nymean Star.

This was the source of the sound, and it ratcheted to a higher volume the moment Pit's attention fell upon it.

"Why?" he asked no one. His friends were on the outside, and not even Felix could hear him. Not when he was submerged in that nasty Hunger. Pit's tufted ears drooped. He had entered into his core space to help Felix with his *efforts*, if only by passively boosting his Companion's Harmonic stats, but that left Pit with a ton of time to sit here. *Thinking.* It had been enough to drive him to explore his core space, and only the noise had brought him back.

It sounded like a rockslide but far too heavy, and an echoing howl that lifted his hackles. The gemstone at Pit's center, his core, emanated the sound as if from down a long and narrow chasm. Pit's gut lurched, the noise triggering something in his Mind that half-convinced him he wasn't on solid ground, but free-falling. It wasn't the giddy rush of flight, or the aggressive drop of a leap, but a terror that gripped him as shadow swept out from all directions to swallow everything that he was—

"Felix?" Pit gasped. He sent his thoughts scurrying across their bond but, as before, felt the message dissolve against an invisible barrier. "This doesn't feel like Felix. It should. It should!"

Their connection was strongest at Pit's center. In fact, the fruit of Etheric Concordance, their bond Skill, hung closest to the four-pronged gemstone. The feel of Felix was normally here, like a cloak thrown over everything, but it was being choked away by that sensation of plummeting descent. The sound of it tasted cold and stale, an echo across an endless expanse, reverberating like the ghost of something that was once natural.

Is this...is this the Hunger?

Pit knew the plan, knew what Felix was attempting, but this—

Everything shook.

"Squawww!" Pit cried out, spreading his paws and wings for balance as the entire forest was jostled. "What?"

Again. The earth heaved, and trees swayed, ripping from the dirt and toppling. Savage pain lanced across his breast, a deep, icy ache that compounded with every fallen branch. Pit stumbled forward, eyes fixed on the woven trunks of his core and on the gemstone that was still vibrating with a rumbling detonation. It quivered, harder than the forest around him, as if it were trying to rip itself free of his core space.

"Stay still!" Pit demanded, throwing his Willpower and Intent at the thing. Vines and branches grew across it, lashing over the four points of the glowing gem and binding it tight. They immediately began to wither, splintering almost too fast for Pit to keep up.

Felix! What are you doing?

"Oh crap, this hurts way more than you said, Felix!"

Beef shouted into the light, his mouth burning every time he opened it. He'd been all but blinded once the stormwall of Primordial Essence had hit him, flooded with an incandescent, burning radiance that shined *inside* of him as much as outside. Closing his eyes did nothing against it, and Beef hadn't ever been all that good at shutting down his Perception or that weird Affinity stat.

His everything was vibrating, and holy balls was that the worst.

Beef's core space had been rendered down to soup once the

stormwall had hit him, turning even his central most area into molten light. It swirled around him now, his old, familiar room indistinguishable from the maelstrom, and Beef tried to stop being sad.

It's just stuff! It wasn't even real! Beef lifted his trembling arms, empty save for the light that burned against his skin and singed his fur. *Focus! Corral it, like Felix said!*

He pressed the potency around him. Not just the Primordial Essence, but the pieces that made up his power. Even Hallow. His oldest friend on the Continent had vanished the same moment the Primordial Essence engulfed them, with neither a word or a cry. Just—just gone. That had hurt a lot, and Beef was putting a lot of effort in not thinking about it too hard.

Focus! he reminded himself. *She'll come back, if you do this right! Spin it and compress!*

Felix had gone over this process, the elevation from Actualization to the Ring Stage of core development. He'd said it was painful, and he hadn't lied, but Beef felt the guy had left out some crucial details. The power he was wielding was so vast that it was slipping from his grip with every second that passed. It still was contained in his core space, such that it was, unable to flee the bounds of his Aspects, thanks to Felix's special Skill; but condensing all of the Primordial Essence and Beef's own remarkable strength was beyond him.

I need a foothold. A funnel, where I can create some, like, leverage. Beef's memories flashed back to his gaming days, when he'd pull mobs in SwordLore using doorways and boulders to limit the numbers that could assault him and his team. *I need a choke point!*

Easier said than done, but Beef threw himself at the issue. With his core space rendered into Primordial soup, he had the rare chance to rebuild it as he wanted. That was easier said than done, however. Despite repeating it to himself as a mantra, focusing on a cohesive vision for his core space was way harder than anyone had told him it was—the last time, he'd just sorta made it. The process had been almost complete by the time Isla had started teaching him more about it all.

I bet Felix had visualized his core space the right way in two seconds, he groused, attempting to order his thoughts. His Intent squirmed away from him like a fish. *Bet he didn't have to turn his first, lame attempt into slurry and start over.*

Beef hadn't seen his friend's inner world, but he was sure it was cool. He was called "the Fiend," of course it was gonna be cool. The way Evie had spoken about hers—even Harn's—had convinced Beef that he had to have something just as fantastical. He wanted something awesome, something befitting the person he'd become.

Minotaur. Whatever. He bet Felix didn't have posters on the walls of his core space, or anything from his home. The guy never talked about Earth unless Beef brought it up—for all that Beef threw himself into this new world, Felix was the one that was actually totally engrossed in life on the Continent. By comparison, Beef was skimming the surface, barely even making an impression—Unbound or not. So he tried not to talk about his home, to be more present in the magical world around him. After all, no one wanted to hear about growing up in the suburbs of anywhere, let alone his dumb town.

"...it's fine if you want to play games. I was just hoping you could take a break sometimes. Come outside? I wanted to go on a hike this weekend..."

The moment the voice started speaking, Beef whipped his head around, but there was no source. No one was standing beside him in the light.

That's...that's my dad. "Dad?" he said, not caring if the light burned his gums. "Dad, are you—are you here?"

A voice—his *dad's* voice—emanated from the whirling chaos. "...I saw this cool beetle in the field yesterday! Look at its shell!"

"Oh, wow. That's really shiny," said another voice, one that Beef was horrified to realize was his. It sounded so incredibly high and small.

"It's called iridescent, meaning it shows different colors when viewed from different angles," his dad said.

Dad... Beef remembered these words, this conversation. As he recognized that, the brilliant madness swirled and formed into the shape of his old dining room table. Seated at the table, his dad was leaning over and showing a younger version of Beef—of Michael—a shiny bug. And behind his back was a plastic bag, hidden at the edge of his chair.

"It's cool," Michael said, pretending not to be interested at all. Beef frowned at that. "I guess."

"Glad you think so. But I know you don't love my job stuff. So, here," his dad said, pulling the plastic bag open and handing a white cardboard box to Michael.

"What! Dad!" Younger him ripped into the box, going absolutely feral as he unwrapped a several-piece statue of his favorite character from SwordLore, his favorite MMO. It was a heavily muscled woman wielding a battle axe, one of the story mentors. She was also really pretty, but Beef had never admitted that. In fact, Michael blushed when he realized his dad was watching him stare at the figure, but still leaped to his feet to hug the man. "Thank you, thank you, thank you!"

"I know you wanted to start your collection," his dad said with a laugh. "You like this one, right?"

"I do! She's my favorite!"

"Good!"

Beef was smiling, the memory bringing back so many other things.

That had been three years ago. He could ignore the pain while looking at that scene, the memory made into a movie, but before he knew it, the tableaux vanished.

"Hey!" he protested.

A LIE.

That face of bones reformed in the maelstrom, looming so high that Beef had to crane his head back to see it all. Its voice was like the light; so utterly pervasive that it vibrated inside his chest and head.

"Gah! You again! What lie?"

THE LIES WE TELL OURSELVES.

"I repeat, bone man: what lie?" Beef gritted his teeth against the burning agony. "That was a memory. A good one, too! It wasn't a lie."

LIES ARE MORE THAN WHAT IS SAID, BEEFHAMMER.

The memory came back, resummoned from the storm, but this time from a different angle. This time, Beef saw the stack of papers sitting on the table, half-hidden in another plastic bag. Divorce papers.

The memory flashed, changing to show Beef's old room. It was days earlier, and Michael was huddled on his bed, listening to his parents fight somewhere downstairs. Tears streaked his little face, but it was half-buried in his oversized pillow.

Beef grimaced. "So, maybe not the best memory. What's your point? What does this have to do with anything?"

The bone face of the Primordial was alien. Disproportionate and possessed of bizarre expressions, it still conveyed a sense of emphatic sorrow. A heaviness that threatened to smother Beef entirely.

LIES CONTAIN TRUTHS. YOU MUST CONFRONT YOUR LIES TO SEE IT.

"See what?" Beef asked, his agony only half due to the light. "What lies? That my parents were, like, shitty at being married? Duh. I don't need a bone face to tell me that. Ugh," he grunted, the storm wobbling out of his grasp once again. "Damn it! I just need some help! Can't you help me figure this out? It's your power going crazy in here!"

I AM HELPING YOU, CHILD. YOU MUST ONLY LISTEN.

Beef paused, the memory of his room shifting. It moved closer to his window. To the latch that had, at the time, held the thing shut. Beef shook himself, and the memory scattered. "Can't I just make a core space and be done with all this cryptic bullshit?"

CAN YOU, UNBOUND?

"Again," Beef said through his teeth. "Fuck you. Yes. Yes I can."

CHAPTER NINETY

They descended again, a sickening lurch as powerful currents tore at them before the Lindwurms wriggled their way through.

Cold Resistance is level 22!

Vess shivered between the bars of their cage. Felix was still maintaining his Sunken Ward, which had warded off all sense of chill, pressure, and even moisture—but as the Lindwurms swarm farther into the depths, its power began to wane. They had personal shields, thanks to the Pendants of Quick Guard Felix had given them all, which had prevented many injuries thus far, but their magic did nothing against the dangers of the deep. She could still breathe, thankfully, but the effects of the rest were mounting.

<<Take this.>> Lady Isla handed her an open jar. It was made of clay and covered in complicated sigaldry. Inside were pale white flowers, glowing faintly to her Elemental Eye. <<Place your fingers within.>>

Vess did so, and immediately felt a thrill tingle across her skin.

Status Condition: Warm Embrace
Duration: 3 Breaths

Warm Embrace
A layer of heat and life Mana clings to your Body, regulating your temperature despite outside conditions.

The sensation of cold vanished, and though it did little for the pressure, Vess was immediately grateful.

<<Keep your fingers within that pot, and it will help ease the burden,>> Lady Isla said before handing out similar jars out to everyone else, including the War Naga.

<<Where did you get this?>> Vess hadn't seen the woman harvesting plants, though her pockets and pouches bulged.

<<From the Temple, before we left. It was too useful a plant to leave alone, not when we were heading so deep.>> The Chanter forced a smile. <<Leaning so heavily on Felix alone was never a part of my plans.>>

Vess inclined her head in thanks, and the Chanter returned her focus to the Minotaur in her lap. Lady Isla had put most of her focus on Beefhammer these past few hours, and for good reason. The Unbound was still sporting a nasty gash across his forehead, bruises on his forearms, and broken knuckles—all courtesy of his frequent thrashing spasms. It had gotten so bad that three of the War Nagas were draping their heavy snake bodies across the boy. Even that was only barely enough to stop him from careening across the cage. He twitched again, but thankfully stilled beneath Lady Isla's hands. A long, continuous note was hovering about the woman, a ribbon that swirled through Vess' Affinity with a green-gold radiance.

<<The seizures are getting worse. Is there any sign of Felix waking?>> the Chanter asked.

Vess looked to her right. Felix remained in the spot he'd taken up at the start of their incarceration, seated with his legs folded beneath him and arms loose at his side. He was breathing easily, but sweat beaded upon his brow. She knew that, if she were to touch him, the man would feel as stone; a detail they had discovered when Beef's first spasm had launched a wild fist at Felix's face. The Autarch had not budged, but Beef's fist had broken instead. <<No. He is the same as he has been.>>

<<I suppose if Michael's blow did not awaken him, nothing will,>> Lady Isla muttered.

Vess agreed. Nothing was going to wake Felix but Felix himself, much to her chagrin. Beef's haphazard attack hadn't even smudged Felix's cheek. However, the force of Beef's punch had spread, splintering the iron and stone beneath them. The Lindwurms had not appreciated that, threatening them all with death and worse…but they shied away from Felix as they reinforced it, until Vess could barely see between the bars at all.

They fear Felix, but not us. Vess tried to swallow her bitter anger at the draconic monstrosities, and found herself unsuccessful. It stewed in her gut, an alchemist's potion of bile and frustration. She gripped her partisan. *Not me.*

The chill increased again, and Vess realized she had taken her hand from the pot. She released her spear with a single hand, getting her fingers to the edge of the lid before hesitating. *Cold Resistance is a useful Skill…and I cannot level it if I do not let it flow through me.* Vess capped the jar once more, tucking it into her belt pouch. *I can handle more than this. I barely feel it.*

A corner of her Mind recognized that for the lie it was—it wasn't that she didn't feel the cold. Vess felt it in her bones now. No, merely that the stewpot of bitter bile inside her was boiling hard enough that she simply didn't care.

Cold Resistance is level 23!

We need every edge we can procure. Soon, I will reach Apprentice Tier, she thought, channeling her anger toward productivity. *Just a little longer.*

By Vess' estimate, it had been at least four glasses since their capture, and there was no evidence of their stopping yet. Distance had become rather murky for the heiress, as their caged journey had blended into a chill uniformity, and time itself felt strange. She was positive of its passage, but the dark waters and undulating Fathom spawn blocked all view of passing landmarks. Time was unmoored—mutable, where once it was held in lockstep with the world.

Beef shivered again, but the War Nagas tightened their coils atop his legs and chest. The warriors on loan from the Deepking were stalwart despite the strains of fear and anger that sang from their Spirits. Vess felt a kinship with them as never before. They traded only a few words, but they were unified in their hatred of the Fathom spawn.

Vess shivered but kept her fingers clenched tightly around her partisan. She fought against the cold, stoking up the fires of opposition in her heart. The Lindwurms and their lesser brethren were exactly what the Dragoons were founded to fight against; vile, murderous, and without remorse. Among draconic Types, they were among the strongest she'd ever encountered. Save for the Depthwurms they had already faced, Vess had not even heard of a draconic Type that approached Tier V—what would be a Master Tier for monsters.

These Lindwurms…each one held the weight of a Tier VI. Vess burned to kill them, to bring them low with the thrust of her spear, but she knew she would fail. Felix might have been able to rip one of them to shreds alone, but it was an impossible task for her…especially as she was restricted to using only her Spear of Tribulations and stats.

She needed the Skills of a Dragoon.

Yet those Skills were beyond her, locked in the Skill books that were still strapped to her pack, rendered untouchable by the eldritch influence of a Primordial. If she were to stand a chance against the Lindwurms, let alone the Fathom itself, Vess needed to reconstitute her Temper.

<<Have I progressed far enough?>> she asked the Lady Isla. <<Is my core cleansed?>>

The Chanter did not look up from Beef's horned head, her hands constantly moving. <<That is a question only you can know for certain, child.>> She looked up, and Vess couldn't help but notice the deep lines beneath the small woman's eyes. <<I told you. To proceed with less than utter conviction is to invite disaster.>>

Vess pulled a breath through her nostrils, trying and failing to cool her emotions. She had never felt so agitated, but she had also never had her people's enemies so close, and her so helpless to fight back. <<How can I be ready faster?>>

<<That is entirely up to you, Lady Dayne.>> The Chanter broke eye contact as Beef twitched again. <<Or you can press your luck once more. Use your tainted Skills and perhaps risk never recompositioning again.>>

Vess stood, suddenly and furiously. <<I—>>

<<You used them to good effect, child. I cannot fault you for bringing us out of a dire situation with the tools at your disposal. But each use simply strengthens the roots of those unwanted weeds.>>

<<I know,>> Vess whispered. <<I will not use them again.>>

True, they had been so...useful, earlier. But even that short usage had pushed them closer to tiering up, and their visualization within her core space felt firmer than ever. It filled her with dread, a fear that was one part anger and two parts nauseous anxiety. Felix had asked her, but she'd done it knowing the consequences. Removing them would be that much harder now, just as Lady Isla said.

Beef kicked out a leg, drawing a pained hiss from one of the War Naga. Lady Isla grasped his horns, gripping them and wrenching with more Strength than Vess expected. Beef's head twisted, and a burst of eerie, burning liquid forced itself from his mouth. It curled on itself and faded into dusty sand moments later, but not before Vess' Elemental Eye identified a great number of Mana types infused within it.

<<It grows worse,>> Lady Isla said, her voice somber. The long song of her Chant faded from hearing, and she let go of the Minotaur's horns in frustration. <<We will see this Fathom soon, and I cannot wake Michael or even budge his core. It's simply madness within him. I do not understand how he still lives.>>

<<They will both be fine,>> Vess insisted, pushing beyond that boiling brew within her. <<I am certain of it.>>

<<And what of us?>> Lady Isla asked, her coronet askew. <<Will we survive to see them wake?>>

Vess brandished her partisan, and in a flash of silver, summoned a single Spear to hover beside her. <<I am a Dragoon, Lady Isla. We do not fall to Dragons.>>

No matter what, Vess would be ready.

Down, down, down.

The Lindwurms carried them further and further afield, down into the black depths. So far below the surface that Vess had to clench her abdomen so that her spine wouldn't compress. The cold increased again, so frigid now that it felt like fire in her veins. It was a brutal, terrible test of her Endurance and Willpower, but Vess did not set it aside. Anything and everything she could hold to fight against the Fathom, she would sharpen to a razor's edge.

Spear of Tribulations is level 81!

She stood, pacing herself through the Steps of the Dragoon and maneuvering one other Spear in addition to her partisan. It was all there was room for within the cramped confines of the cage. But Vess did not let it stop her from extracting every inch of value from their time in transit. The cage, her allies, even the thickening gelid waters surrounding them became obstacles to overcome. Training partners she tested her mettle against as she pressed her Agility and Dexterity to its limit to avoid them all.

Time passed. Her initial count grew unreliable, until Vess no longer worried about estimating it at all. There was only the moment. There was only the Spear.

When she grew tired, she rested. When she was hungry, she ate from their stores. She flared her Skills, those that would not risk her fate, cycling through them whenever she had the stores of energy to afford them. Slowly, they rose.

Spear of Tribulations is level 82!
Analyze is level 73!
Diplomacy is level 67!

The last was a strange result, which Vess soon attributed to the looks of admiration she garnered from the War Naga. Her unflagging diligence had earned her more than one mute nod of appreciation.

She felt…not ready, but honed. Primed for a battle that she might not win, but would fight until the last breath left her Body, her Mind went dark, and her Spirit returned to her ancestors.

The cage shook.

<<What was that?>> Lavix asked. She slithered to the bars before gasping. <<The spawn! They are retreating!>>

Vess strode to her side, peering through the miniscule gap between rock and iron. The Naga was right. The flood of Fathom spawn had vanished, leaving only the five huge Lindwurms guarding them. They were more than enough on their own, but Vess took heart. <<A fortunate turn of events. It seems the Lindwurms are escorting us alone.>>

<<Truly? Do they no longer fear the boy?>> Lady Isla asked. The Chanter looked more than tired, but a measure of strength entered her voice at the prospect of change. <<Felix was able to rend one of their number into pieces. They must hold great faith in their master to dismiss their army.>>

Lavix grunted, clutching at her head. <<Or the spawn simply could not withstand this,>> she said through clenched fangs. <<Oh, it is agony!.>>

Vess felt it, too, as the water rapidly increased in chill and pressure once again. And again. She managed to release a single, high pitched exhale before falling to her knees in pure pain.

Cold Resistance is level 24!
Cold Resistance is level 25!

You Have Reached Apprentice Tier With Cold Resistance!
You Gain:
+5 END
+5 VIT
+5 AGL

Cold Resistance is level 26!
...
Cold Resistance is level 35!

The moment her resistance exceeded Apprentice Tier, the majority of the mammoth pain vanished, replaced only by the hideous sensation of live coals replacing her bones. Vess bit off her screams, fumbling with her pouch to retrieve the jar she'd gotten earlier. The Warm Embrance Status Condition alleviated the worst of the cold, enough that her vision unfuzzed, just in time to see the retreating lip of a great cliff vanish above them.

<<Is that ice?>> she asked, her voice worn thin. It came out far quieter than she expected, and Vess swallowed twice to no avail. Her throat was raw from the screams.

<<We are inside the center of Khasma,>> Lady Isla said. She was hastily smearing a thick unguent on the War Naga before turning to

Vess. <<The Fathom is close. I can feel it distorting the strains of Harmony. Here.>> She laid the paste onto Vess's forehead, and her throat immediately restored itself as aches and minor wounds from her mad training faded. <<We will need our strength, and this is all I have. Make it count, Lady Dayne.>>

Vess nodded mutely, her gaze pulled uncontrollably to the world outside their cage as her heart hammered wildly in her chest. The dark had receded somewhat as a purple-blue glow suffused the waters, highlighting the lightning-like patterns of ice that crawled up the walls. Soon, far more quickly than she anticipated, they reached the bottom, and Vess looked on in amazement.

Vessels of all shapes and sizes littered the deep silt, most encased entirely in ice, and all clearly of Ages long since past. They sat scattered among the frozen, half-mutilated corpses of titanic beasts, each one a rival for the Lindwurms.

<<Remnants of an ancient battle,>> Lady Isla whispered. <<Beasts so old that my Analyze does not recognize them.>>

<<A war of the gods,>> Lavix said in a horrified hiss. <<How do we fight something that did this?>>

You don't.

The voice rumbled above them, utterly calm yet as loud as any scream. The cage shook itself apart beneath that voice, the stone and iron turned instantly to a fine dust that swirled once around them before whisking away in an invisible current. Vess stumbled, but only slightly, her stats and training allowing her to level her blue-white partisan in the direction of the voice. She nearly dropped it in horror, however, as she beheld the twisted monstrosities that surrounded them all.

The voice chuckled.

You beg.

CHAPTER NINETY-ONE

Shadows shifted, moving like liquid among the freezing waters as they revealed the figures around them to be not monsters at all, but statues. Vess swallowed, eyes flicking between the hideous, unmoving shapes. They were built of ice-coated stone, utterly terrifying but crafted with a deft hand. They were scattered around them, set between the frozen roots that interrupted the otherwise flat plain there at the bottom of the Breach. Uniformity was their antithesis, but most were larger than the five Lindwurms that still surrounded their diminished party.

They are statues of... Urges? However, there was no sign of whoever—or whatever—had spoken.

<<You will not frighten us with children's games,>> Vess said after working some strength into her voice. <<Reveal yourself!>>

Come. Closer.

The voice rumbled again, and still Vess couldn't track its source. It emanated from all directions, omnipresent and so powerful it disturbed the sands. After Vess had shifted her weight, it was clear how much power it would take to simply move her body, let alone shift sands with simple words.

<<Tread cautiously,>> Lady Isla warned. Her hair hung down around her face, pressed out of its careful coif by the relentless pressure atop them all. Vess nodded.

APPROACH.

A wave of sand rose behind them, catching their entire group in its flow. Vess shouted in alarm, reaching down to grasp the still-immobile Felix, but all of them were carried forward through the forest of hideous statues, hurtled through the icy waters to a large, broken colonnade. The wave stopped there, and Vess nearly fell to her knees while Felix, Beef, and the dual Bodies of Hallow were deposited without respect or care.

A snarl from behind them alerted Vess to the arrival of their jailors. The Lindwurms pointed clawed hands toward the colonnade. "Enter. Beg for your lives, mortals."

Beyond the tilted columns, it was as wide as any Temple construction in Haestus, built on a scale that Vess could not understand, as if giants had worshiped before the raised dais she saw beyond the tilted columns. There was another statue there, just as big as the Lindwurms but far more angular, showing little sign it had been carved at all. As the others, this was covered in the purple-blue ooze. The entire structure before them was all but dripping in layers of it, and free-floating globules of the stuff sat unmoving in the heavy, dark water.

Vess traded glances with Lady Isla and Lavix, the latter of whom was trying to unsuccessfully lift Felix's immobile form. <<Lavix, please stay here with the War Naga to protect Autarch Nevarre, Lord Beefhammer, and Hallow.>>

Lavix assented with a deep bow, which was copied immediately by all the rest. <<We shall guard them with our lives.>>

A thick, scornful laugh ripped from the Lindwurms' throats, their long snouts crinkled with amusement. Vess paid them no mind and instead offered her arm to the Chanter. <<Lady Isla?>>

<<Of course,>> she said, looping her arm in Vess' own. <<Let us see this Fathom.>>

The ooze coiled around their feet with each and every step—sticking to their footwear like foul mud—and it only grew thicker. They were a scant three strides into the ruined structure before their feet were completely engulfed by the ooze. Vess hesitated, but the foul thing did nothing but attempt to root her in place.

A few swings of her partisan cleared them up, scattering the foul thing in all directions. That taught her two things: the ooze was harmed by her weapon, and simply swinging her spear was incredibly difficult at such depths. It felt ponderous and weighty, almost too heavy to control, but Vess' Strength was up to the task. Barely.

She cleared the way, one heavy blow at a time, until they stood before the dais. Vess craned her neck, looking to the shadows that swirled constantly around the columns and half-broken walls. Distances were obscured, thrown into chaos by darkness, rippling currents, and the undulations of the seemingly sentient ooze.

<<Reveal yourself,>> Vess demanded, fighting to keep the quaver out of her Spirit. <<We will not ask again.>>

You do not give demands, mortal.

<<Blind gods,>> Isla whispered and stumbled backward out of Vess's grip. Vess whirled, following the Chanter's gaze, only to find the monstrous statue on the dais blink at her.

Siva's holy Grace. Vess hefted her spear, shoulders burning as she realized she was staring at an enormous *head. Those are eyes, nostrils, and* horns.

The head, wedge-shaped and angular, lifted up in the water on a long, plated neck covered in ooze and shadow. A mane of writhing tendrils—purple-blue and glistening—hung from its head and neck, just behind two enormous sets of horns that branched like a stag's.

Vess craned her neck up and up, following the monster as it kept rising to its full height. If she had to compare it, the closest thing in her memory was the Ravager King—and just like the Ravager King, this creature was a vile hybrid of scales and malformed flesh. More ooze dripped from it, floating in spherical globules and rigid tendrils that merged with the utter dark.

That body stretched back into the sand and water, serpentine and festooned with tendrils that came to life as its head lifted from the dais. The very ground shifted, ice cracking with stentorian reports as some of what Vess had mistaken for frozen roots were actually the scale-covered length of an impossibly long body. Its mouth opened, strings of ooze stretching between gaping jaws as a tongue the color of midnight wriggled like a worm.

It *laughed.*

Such delicious fear.

Lady Isla swallowed, her breath coming faster. <<Blind and bleeding. What are you?>>

<<Analyze,>> Vess spat.

Analyze Failed.
ERROR!
Ouranic Override In Place.

Ouranic…? Vess couldn't control her breathing. Her gut twisted, the boiling brew bubbling until it overflowed into her veins, until her arms quaked with repressed fear and hate and rage. She didn't need Analyze to recognize the monstrosity before her. It was the Fathom.

It was a *Dragon.*

Yes. I can feel you recognize it. I am a Dragon, one of the last on this pitiful Continent.

That huge mouth snapped closed, tossing gobbets of ooze in all directions. They did not fall but remained suspended around the Fathom's face, like raindrops frozen in time. **And you…you have a familiar scent upon your Spirits. Dry and dusty, it tastes of failure and death. What is it? What is it?**

Vess raised her eyebrows. <<We come recently from Ahkestria. Over the Stormeater Peaks.>>

Ah. The word was thunder on its lips, and the ooze at their feet trembled with a strange…glee. Vess could feel it, plain as day, a joyous satisfaction that quivered through the foul carpet around them. **You have seen the Withered One. I can sense his touch on you.**

<<The…Primordial,>> Vess said, flexing her fingers along the haft of her spear. <<What do you know of him?>>

I know much, mortal. I was his downfall, his curse. I! Not those wretches among the waves, those armored cretins!

<<The Yttin?>>

Vile children that refused my worship. They were shown glories never known to them, power and Skills beyond any they could hope to learn, and they cast it aside. The Fathom snarled, baring its massive fangs that curled across its jaw like the miniature tusks of some great boar. **You smell of them. Of the Withered One. You…** The Fathom stopped sneering, its huge, alien face twisting toward something else. **Oh, this is delightful.**

Chuckling, the Fathom slithered its long neck down, until it regarded Vess and Lady Isla through large, sea-black eyes. Several pairs opened and closed in the gooey mess of its face, vanishing and manifesting over and over. **You carry his Boon but have discarded it? Hah! Not only discarded, but *disdained!***

Vess wanted to reply to that, but a wave of incredible pressure followed the Fathom's laugh, knocking both of them back several steps. Lady Isla barely seemed to notice, muttering as she was beneath her breath. It was all Vess could do to keep the Fathom in view—something about it distorted her vision.

What a worthless death. Ill-fitting a Primordial. He should have accepted the inevitable and joined with me. The Fathom shook his head, the oozing mane swirling behind his horns. **Now he is rendered back into the dust from whence he came.**

Vess had heard the story enough times to answer that truthfully. <<I—yes. The Primordial of Withering Dust is dead. At our hands.>>

HAH! A pitiful end, to be killed by mere mortals! How did you do it? The Fathom's eyes popped open, all of them at once, boring down on Vess. **You are...weak. Rejected Boon or not, you could not have faced the Primordial as you are. You—**

It stopped, flaring its nostrils. Water pulled into them so hard that Vess could see the momentary riptide. Innumerable orbs appeared and vanished from its ever-changing face, and its tongue lashed viciously.

You...you are not the one that caught my eye. The one that *burned* in the night. The Fathom's huge head snaked to the side, tilting as it stared beyond the ruined structure. Vess didn't have to ask where it was looking...except it shook its head, as if suddenly confused. **No. Where is he? I—you! Where is he? Where is the beast that ate my children?**

Is it confused? Vess was unsure, but she wouldn't let the moment go to waste. She had to buy time. <<I *am* the one you seek. I lead this party, and we have come to discuss with you terms of your surrender.>>

There was a moment of utter silence, before the Fathom's booming laughter filled the waters. Vess hunkered low, buffeted by the powerful currents the creature generated in its mirth, and had to drag Lady Isla down with her. The woman was still muttering something in a distant, melodic rhythm, but Vess hadn't the time to ask her what she was doing.

The Fathom stomped forward, a single, thirty stride-wide claw landing among the ooze-coated stones and shattering them all. Its head snaked forward, until its vast, dribbling maw was next to their tiny, Human heads.

You Have No Idea What You Face, Child. The thing's voice was no longer the same as it was before, now layered with notes that screamed at her Affinity in strains of pure chaos. Vess fell back under its onslaught, her braced partisan the only thing giving her the strength to stand at all. **Where Is The Beast I Seek?**

A shadow had fallen across the Fathom, one far deeper than the black of the dark waters. All Vess could see was the Fathom's curving fangs and its midnight tongue...but somehow still, shapes writhed in her periphery. That shadow filled with unnatural angles, limbs distorted and bent, and the sound of a vast and unending silence roaring from all directions—

<<Do not look, child!>>

All at once, a muted song cascaded from her ally, as Lady Isla lifted a pale hand before them both, trailing visible strands of violet and green-gold Mana. They spun, weaving into one another as the harmonies grew too complex for Vess to follow, until they formed a hexagonal lattice that Lady Isla immediately grasped and *twisted.*

<<Here!>> she cried.

ERROR!
Ouranic Override In Place.

Grand Harmony Detected.
Ouranic Override In P—
ERROR.

The Fathom jerked back, not hurt, but suddenly briefly *less* in some indefinable way.

Information filled Vess' vision, caught between the latticed panes of Lady Isla's strange working. Health, Stamina, Lore, all of it filled with blanks, but one thing contained information. Vess's breath caught as she stared up at the Fathom. It had a Race.

No. No, that is impossible. Vess reached up to her own throat, as if she could pull the words out of her mouth. <<You...are a Dusk Dragon? >>

CHAPTER NINETY-TWO

Name: Fathom
Race: Moontouched Dusk Dragon (Manawarped)
...

The rest of the information washed over Vess, too much to absorb. Vast quantities of Health, Stamina, and Mana—indicators of a powerful set of Aspects that Vess couldn't care less about. Before her was the physical embodiment of why the Dragoons existed, a Race of creatures that her mother had all but worshiped. The unstill shadows had assaulted her senses, but the revelation of its provenance set dire winds loose within her chest.

Vess' core *howled.*

I Am Fathom, the immense creature said, but only a faint echo of whatever had inhabited it remained. Vess flinched, all of it too much. There were *things* within that darkness. **And You Will Answer The Question, Chanters.**

<<You know us,>> Lady Isla stated, her hands still toying with the edge of her woven lattice. It glimmered while slowly compressing beneath the immense pressure the Fathom was giving off.

Chanters. Sorcerers. Meddlers. Dabblers In Mysteries That Are Beyond You. The Fathom—the *Dusk Dragon*—scoffed, releasing a wobbling bubble from its maw that immediately collapsed. **I Know Your Kind. I Know Your Tricks. You Hide Behind The Primordial's Noise. Clever.**

<<Moontouched,>> Isla whispered, eyes roving across the Lind-

wurms behind them. The craven creatures huddled just beyond the portico, surrounding their allies, but otherwise taking shelter.

<<What?>> Vess asked. She was still reeling from the sight of the writhing shadows, let alone the revelation of the Fathom's true Race. <<What are you talking about? Isla, that is a *Dusk Dragon.* I—I cannot—->>

The woman wasn't listening. She regarded the sneering Fathom with eyes that almost burned with a vivid curiosity and no small amount of fear. <<I had hoped the phrase was a coincidence. Something to do with the Trees.>> She shook her head. <<Can you not hear it now? It has been so faint that I convinced myself it was not there. But it is.>>

Vess clenched her jaw, bracing against the echo that still pressed against her senses. She...heard something. Her Affinity flagged an atonal buzzing that set her teeth on edge and made her skin crawl—Dissonance. The rest was a jumbled mess that made no sense to her, as if chaos had been forged into the mockery of a tune.

<<The touch of the Divine,>> Isla explained, and veins stood stark against her forehead as if she, too, were resisting something immense. <<This thing is incredibly powerful. Far more than we anticipated.>>

<<You are a Dusk Dragon...how have you come to this?>> Vess asked. Isla's words made little sense, save that the thing was powerful. <<I was told you all perished in a prior Age.>>

You know of us, the Fathom said, its voice losing all but the barest hint of its haunting echo. **You—of course. That spear. That armor. You are a Dragoon as well. A Betrayer.**

<<What?>>

Not all of us perished in your pogrom, Dragoon. Some survived the Slaying Skies. Some fled. The Fathom's primary eyes lightened, shifting from abyssal black to something glimmering. Its voice rose in volume with every word, until it was roaring thick bubbles into the heavy water until it seemed its face was boiling. **Some took flight! Some survived, Betrayer!**

<<No! The Dragons betrayed us! They turned on the mortal Races!>> Vess gnashed her teeth, the howling in her core space growing to a fever pitch. The Fathom was lying. She was sure of it. <<You—!>>

<<Enough,>> Isla interrupted, grabbing Vess by the pauldron. The would-be Dragoon hadn't realized that she had advanced several steps toward the Dragon, and let herself stumble back. <<It may have started as a Dusk Dragon, Lady Dayne, but it is tainted now. Corrupted—>>

Hold Your Vile Tongue, Sorcerer, the Fathom demanded, cutting the distance between them to nothing. In an *instant.* Its dripping snout was a finger-span away from their faces, the smell of it somehow pervading the Sunken Ward as that echo returned in full force. Its primary eyes had returned to abyssal pits in its face. **I Am More Than A Paltry Morsel. More Than This Vessel, No Matter How Potent.** The Fathom took in a deep, burbling snort. **And I Have Found My Beast.**

All at once, the Fathom was beyond them, slithering its immense length across the ruined structure and through the wide gaps of the colonnade. Vess felt frozen, its speed barely within her capability to perceive, let alone match. Still, she tried, rotating her Body and partisan in the direction of the Dragon—but it was too late. It reached their friends, Beef and Hallow and Felix lying still among the guarding War Naga, and lifted its gargantuan head like a serpent about to strike. Ooze and scale and fang fell in deadly, meteoric speed.

Your End Is Here!

The Fathom struck.

And was met by a storm of beak, claw, and feathers.

<<Don't touch them!>> Pit shrieked.

The Fathom's head snapped to the side, bashed in the jaw by Pit's Mantle-draped form. It screeched, bubbles boiling from its cavernous maw, before quickly sweeping its serpentine form to the side. Columns snapped like twigs, collapsing on themselves as the Fathom's Body crashed through them. Vess made it just in time to deflect a falling entablature. She sliced through it, splitting the stone so that it fell to either side of the cowering War Naga.

<<Beef! You must wake!>> Isla said, reaching the team only moments after Vess. She gripped the Minotaur and shook him.

What Is This? The Moontouched Dusk Dragon reoriented itself, more of its impossible length drawing forward into bulging coils of oozing shadow. It touched a long claw to its jaw, where the ooze and scale had split. A miniscule drop of ichor floated out, hovering before the Fathom's unblinking eyes. **A Chimera. How...Novel.**

<<There's more where that came from!>> Pit promised, flapping his wings to reorient himself in the water. A silvery fish-tail had manifested on his hindquarters. <<You...smelly slime worm!>>

What A Shame, the Fathom rumbled as its wound stitched itself closed. **That The First Chimera This Vessel Has Seen In Ages Should Die So Soon.**

There was no more warning, as this time the Dragon moved far beyond Vess' ability to perceive it. There was only a deep, crackling cacophony as stone shattered, water blasted, and mountainous jaws snapped shut.

On...nothing?

Vess stared in almost as much confusion as the Fathom spat out a mouthful of silt and stone as it planted its feet and pulled back. Blue-white lightning crackled off its head and mane, which was scorched free of its ooze in several places. Vess' chest tightened as the howling quietened within her. In its place was a strident, joyous shout.

Status Condition: Rallying Cry!
Regeneration Doubled!
Reduced Chance Of Frightened Status Effect!

<<Back off,>> Felix said, floating above them all. Ice cracked off his Garment as it shaped away his jacket and loose pants, leaving him in a form-fitting tunic and breeches. <<That is your only warning.>>

The Beast, I Presume, the Fathom said, working its jaw as if it had been punched. Judging by the fading lightning, Vess supposed it might have been.

I couldn't see the attack at all.

<<Everyone keeps making that mistake,>> Felix said, but there was no smile on his angular face. A quiet strength rolled off him like a palpable pressure. <<You didn't answer me. Will you back off?>>

Why Would I, Child?

"Master! He is the one!" one of the Lindwurms cried out from some distance away. Vess had noticed them fleeing once the Fathom started attacking, but hadn't expected them to linger nearby, sheltering behind the various statues. "He is dangerous!"

Is That So, Child? The Fathom sneered. **Do You Have Claws, Little Human?**

<<You have no idea,>> Felix said. <<Last chance. Back off. We can resolve the issues between you and the Deepking with words.>>

A piece of Vess cheered for Felix, even as the rest of her knew his words were fated to fail. *All of those lessons in Diplomacy, and he uses them on* this *creature, of all things!*

Vess was almost relieved when the Fathom simply laughed.

I Refuse.

The Fathom and Felix vanished. Vess couldn't bear to blink, but still she missed all but the clash, as blue-white lightning, red-gold flame, and virulent green acid burst outward in a corona of frenzied energy. They appeared above them all, hundreds of paces up, and both Felix and the Fathom were knocked back.

A shriek tore through the waters, rippling the heavy liquid in a tidal wave that smashed Vess and all of her allies flat. Stone splintered, sand was hurled in a concussive wave, and that echo of terrible chaos…vanished.

<<The Dissonance! Her touch!>> Lady Isla cried out. Her lip was bleeding, and her eyes were glazed as if the Chanter stared at something no one else could see. <<He…drove it away.>>

Vess leveraged herself to her knees, the stone crumbling beneath her, and felt at her chest. The howling winds within her core hadn't settled, and indeed had only intensified. <<Whose touch?>>

Isla blinked, refocusing. <<The Goddess of the Night,>> she whispered. <<Noctis.>>

<<...What?>>

All at once, a thrumming chord rippled through Vess' chest, sending her back to the ground as Mind, Body, and Spirit buckled.

<<Lady Dayne!>>

<<Spearmaiden!>>

The cries of her allies vanished, subsumed by the raging windstorm within. Vess fell, cast down into her internal skies, as that chord vibrated across her very soul.

What is this?

Above, sky darkened to night, and the glimmer of red-gold and blue-white stars shone with a gemstone brilliance. *My Link to Felix.* The vibration continued, originating not from that Link, but to her core. *My...temple.*

The center of her core space—that once-immaculate temple turned into a dragon of gold and stone—stretched wide its wings. The mountain cracked, splitting beneath claws that freed themselves from the rock, and clouds spun in a hurricane of stormwinds. The Skills around her stood as shrieking sentinels among the cyclone, pieces of them ripped off to feed the churning pandemonium—a grinding morass that did nothing to alleviate the paralyzing song that inundated everything.

The chord deepened as she fell, plummeting faster than any Skill she bore, utterly unable to stop herself. The temple lifted its vile, draconic head, and Vess was assaulted by a volley of uncontrollable emotions.

Sorrow. Rage. And a deep, abiding despair.

Jaws spread, fangs glistening in the fading light, and a voice spoke. A voice she had heard once before, back on that day in Ahkestria. One that she refused to acknowledge.

WITNESS THE TRUTH, VESSILIA DAYNE.

The maw of her own core closed on her.

FIND YOUR PATH FORWARD.
OR PERISH.

CHAPTER NINETY-THREE

Vess fell into the dark, blind, until a field of bones spread out below her. She twisted, pulling on her Agility and Dexterity to at least get her feet beneath her—yet it didn't matter. She hit the field of bones and smashed right into them, the spread collapsing beneath her boots as easily as shifting sands.

She grasped a huge femur as she sank, desperate for something to slow her mad descent. Yet the moment her hand came in contact with the bone, it was held fast.

"Let go!"

The bones refused, and instead piled atop of her in a mad, rumbling cascade. Ribs, spines, and small bones she had no name for clung to Vess' skin and armor, wrapping around her flesh as if they would squeeze the very life from her Body. Her fear resurfaced, even as she fought to do the same—and instead sank ever further.

Just as the bones enveloped her face, she perceived a vast, alien face clatter together. It was made of those bones that had not yet overwhelmed the heiress, and its expression could not be read, but its lips moved.

YOU DO NOT HAVE LONG.

The bones blocked out sight and sound, leaving only the grinding sensation of her continual fall. Until even that faded.

Until there was only the thread.

Vess blinked. The thread existed beyond her mortal senses, much in the same way her Link to Felix persisted; immaterial yet inexplicably tangible. It hummed with a threnody of despair, the same emotions she had felt before falling into her temple's maw. The song of it clung, vibrating against her with all the alarming insistence of a buzzing hornet in her ear. While nothingness reigned, it dominated her being, growing until it consumed every bit that was once Vessilia Dayne.

Until, all at once, the darkness cleared—and the world had changed. She had changed.

As if the howling maelstrom from her core space had manifested into reality, a wild tempest filled the sky, whipping clouds and debris in all directions. Far below, a distant series of bumpy smudges sped past in a blur.

Where is this? The word thundered through her Mind, too loud, and Vess winced… only to find that her head moved in the strangest of manners. The wind tried to catch it, turning her head sideways before she flexed her long and powerful neck muscles in order to keep from being folded in half. Her hands flexed, most of them grasping at the thin air and *pulling* at it to stabilize herself, all while she twisted her lithe Body through the raging currents of the storm.

I am flying. What—what am I? It came to her all at once, a fully formed realization that hit her like a bucket of ice water. *I am—I am a Dragon!*

Horror and fascination surged through Vess in equal measure as she flowed through the skies, a double-time beat that accompanied that foreign song of despair. A warmth flowed from her breast, a gemlike weight that soothed even as her nerves frayed. She could feel the connection there, a vibration that shot off into the depths of her soul, holding it close to this strange new reality.

This is a Memory, Vess realized. *A Dragon's Memory. How did I—the Primordial. It was that Primordial that did this to me.*

"Yini. Yini… Where are we?" a voice asked from behind her. It was a guttural grunt, but weaker by far than the crash of lightning around them. Still, Vess heard them as clear as a bell, as if the voice were speaking through her very Spirit.

She tilted her head back, careful to tense against the winds, and beheld a small, musclebound form clinging to her white mane as it fluttered above golden scales. It was an Orc, green skin so dark it seemed shaded purple, and covered in plates of enameled armor that did nothing to hide the dark streaks of blood that covered it. The Orc woman spoke again, but she barely moved.

"Yini, where are you going? We have to go back… the children…"

"I carry them with me," Vess said, but it was not her voice, nor her Mind that compelled the words. They sprang from her draconic throat of their own volition. "All that I could save is here, little Rana. Please rest. You need to conserve your Strength."

For the first time, Vess became aware of a weight in one of her claws. A container formed of woven trees hung from her grip, dragging down their flight speed almost as much as the storm around them.

"We know… we know I do not have much left." The words hit the Dragon hard, a blow that turned the thread of despair toward a sorrow so deep it defied words. Vess floundered, unable to cope with the depth of such feeling. "That last attack… the Grandmaster caught me by surprise."

"A pitiful Grandmaster? Hurt you? Little Rana, a Paragon could not fall to such a creature."

A mane. Fur rippled from atop her head and down the length of her back, surmounting her thick golden scales and powerful limbs. Heavy, branching horns swept back from her brow. She was not just any Dragon. She was a Dusk Dragon. *The Fathom?*

The Orc shuddered, and it took Vess a moment to realize that she was laughing. "You have seen the War brewing, Yini. Even the gods are not safe. Do you think… do you think I am above the gods?"

"Curse the gods! We are not part of the War! We—"

"Yini, you must flee." Rana coughed, and more dark blood spread out onto Vess'—the Fathom's—scales. "You cannot let them find you or the children. Keep them safe. Hidden. No matter… no matter the cost."

A warmth rose from that thread at Vess' center, a heat so intense it rivaled the sun as Yini—the Fathom itself, nodded its head. "It shall be done, little Rana. But you shall live to see them hatch yourself. You must only hold on."

Silence and the storm were all that met those words.

"Rana?"

The Orc, and the deep connection Vess had felt with her, had vanished.

"RANA!"

Unnamable fury consumed their connection. Emotion so raw and potent that the Memory twisted under its onslaught. The skies blurred, and the landscape far below swelled and burst, becoming verdant plains dotted with deep, black-water lakes.

Vess' consciousness was sliced by a strangled cry that echoed backward and forward through Memory, splitting her perceptions. She saw the Dragon drop, hurling itself into the waters as *something* attacked it from behind. And she witnessed Rana's bleeding body in the courtyard of a vast mansion, stabbed by a glimmering spear made of pure air Mana.

A Spear? Vess recognized the Skill instantly, though it was leagues beyond her own ability. *She was killed by—*

A figure stepped into view, wearing enameled armor nearly identical to Rana's. A second Spear of air floated beside him, and a sad smile was all she could see of his face. "You chose the wrong side, Paragon Rana.

They can't be trusted." The Spear shot out, too fast to trace, and Rana threw up an arm.

"All Dragons must die."

The Spear sent the Memory sprawling sideways, jolted by a burst of incandescent pain. Flashes of a pale gold dragon poking through a thick, metallic shell. Of a dark green hand, clutched at the belly of a wyrmling as it purred to sleep. Of battles won and lost. Of blood that filled the skies and muddied the ground, as lightning and fire razed the mountains of her home.

Vess screamed, unable to process the chaotic jumble as her time and reality became unmoored. She couldn't parse any of it, not until the roil was subsumed by an endless eternity beneath the waves of countless rivers and lakes. The black depths became everything, sinking deeply into the Fathom's scales and bones that little else mattered but eating, protecting, and continuing to move forward.

Away.

Until, finally, the Fathom stopped. It had found a hole to hide within, one so deep that nothing could ever find it again. Not monster or mortal, enemy or ally. A silence of darkness and pressure, where barren sludge smoothed the passing of Ages, and the Fathom slept. It slept without dream or hope of waking, save for the clutch of eggs held instinctively to its breast.

From that darkness, a face. Not of bone, but of collapsing darkness, a tunnel of flesh and bone that stared at them as if from a vast, incomprehensible distance.

It struck.

All at once, Vess returned.

She gasped and fell to the shattered earth, partisan abandoned as she clenched the split silt with her hands. It ran from between her fingers, puffs of smoke that quickly collapsed. Crashes shook the water all around her, and voices shouted a dozen different things. She heard none of it—she was too consumed by the now-fading connection between her and the Dragon named Yini.

The ground shook and the faintest impression of a face appeared, etched into the sand. *What I saw—*

THE TRUTH.

Then, the Creature is—

YES. CHOOSE YOUR PATH, VESSILIA DAYNE.

Mother. Father. Vess pulled in a breath as deep as she could, drawing it around herself like armor. And, for a moment, her core space stilled. *Please forgive me.*

Vess threw out her Intent and Affinity, a spear cast into the abyss, and grappled with the thread of connection. Its fading line thrummed to new life, burning, screeching—and deep inside Vess' core space, her temple did the same.

Felix dodged backward, avoiding another clash as the Fathom lashed out with two enormous claws.

Impudent Whelp! Cease Your Fleeing!

The Fathom was so big, but it was equally fast; a combination that bothered Felix a lot, and not only because he'd taken several awful wounds from the beast. *Seems kinda unfair, doesn't it?*

It cheats, Pit suggested. *Its shadow is cheating.*

Felix grunted in agreement. He'd noticed. They might have been facing a Dragon—a goddamn Dusk Dragon, according to his Eye—but it was being controlled. *The Creature,* he sent at Pit. *We have to break its connection.*

Pit shot another handful of radiant crescents at the beast, slashing through its oozing hide but leaving the scales beneath unharmed. *How?*

Felix met a lashing tendril of purple-blue ooze with his rending claws, Sovereign of Flesh expanding his hand and forearm to unreasonable size for just a moment. The ooze split and exploded, liquid shadow and crackling ice Mana surging randomly around them all. He dove again, flaring his movement Skill to its utmost. The damn Dragon took up so much *space*, it was hard to avoid all of its gelatinous appendages. *I need to get past the ooze on its scales. The stuff is insulating the Dragon inside from my attacks. I felt something when I hit its bare snout, but it's totally covered now.*

Pit whipped past, more tendrils following him as well. Feathers hung loose from his wings, and blood trailed the tenku, but his Spirit was grimly determined. Both of them were hurting, but Pit couldn't bounce back as fast as Felix. *What if we—?*

Without warning, the Fathom went rigid, its serpentine Body and the ooze upon it convulsing as if hit with an electric current. Felix had tried that, though, so he knew that wasn't happening. The Fathom's maw gaped open, ooze and air bubbles pouring upward in a vile gush. Felix swam backward, avoiding the cascading mess, but not before noticing that the Fathom's eyes had turned a brilliant, shining gold.

NO! The shadow behind the Fathom writhed and bubbled, but it was flailing ineffectually for the first time that Felix had seen. **NO! HE IS MINE!**

Vess. Felix saw her, far below them, now shining with a radiance that matched the Fathom's eyes. Harmony swelled, as beside her, Isla reached out and added *something* to the effect. The Creature bellowed, the sound distinct from the roar of the Dragon, and it surged down and away from Felix.

<<No, you don't! Pit! Get her out of there!>>

Pit shot off, fishtail speeding him in a curving descent, while Felix blasted after it, boiling the water in his wake.

Adamant Discord!

A ten-foot-thick lightning bolt blasted into the Fathom's curving bulk, arresting its momentum for the barest of moments. This was far different than simply punching the monster in the face. This was about leverage. Felix kicked, summoning a stack of Cloudsteps beneath his feet as he hauled back harder than he ever had before.

Cloudstep is level 67!

...

Cloudstep is level 71!

It wasn't enough. The platforms of solidified Mana splintered and burst as the mountainous Fathom hauled Felix downward. All at once, the tether of lightning surged and *snapped* in two.

<<VESS!>> Felix shouted, kicking off once again.

Below him, the Fathom roared as its shadow expanded to consume everything.

CHAPTER NINETY-FOUR

Within a maelstrom of burning sands, Beef stood with arms outstretched and eyes clenched shut.

"C'mon," he muttered, ignoring the burn of heat on his tongue.

The fury of light and heat around him shifted, sands and golden radiance pulled into alignment by the slightest of margins. They shone, the sands turning red hot as they ground each other into molten glass, and the light flashed through it all, a corruscating circle of wild, untamed potency.

A ring.

"C'mon!"

All at once, it collapsed back into a chaotic roar of power. Beef fell to his knees, hands slamming into the bones that lined the ground and letting loose a frustrated scream. "Damn it!"

The bones scattered, blasted by his pummeling fists, sliding away from him even as more rose from the ground beneath. An endless, churning supply. Knee caps clattered and spread, arranging into the lipless mouth of his least favorite person. Beef hurled a handful of joints at the face as it formed. "Screw you, too! Leave me alone! I gotta finish this!"

YOU MUST—

"Nope!" Beef shoved himself to his feet. He set his hooves in the shifting bones and reached out once more with his Intent. "Felix can only hold this for so long, Boneman. I don't have time for your stupid visions!"

YOU SEEK TO BEAR MY POWER. YOU CANNOT ACCOMPLISH THIS ALONE.

"Watch me!"

Yet no matter how Beef threw himself at the storm of light and sand, it did not budge. The light failed to bend to his Willpower as it had, and his Intent felt almost bruised. He gasped, several minutes later, sweating profusely and cursing.

"Don't look at me like that!" he half-shouted through his panting. The Primordial's bone face had not twitched since it last spoke. "I can feel your judgy eyes."

MINE IS NOT TO JUDGE. MINE IS TO SHOW.

"...Show what?"

TO BEAR MY POWER. YOU MUST WITNESS THE COST OF ENTROPY.

"Entropy? Like rotting stuff? Hard pass." Beef steadied his breathing once again and felt tenderly at the edges of his Intent. It wasn't a physical sensation so much as a mental one—there was nothing to touch—but the comparison felt appropriate. His Mind was sore and strained, and his Body and Spirit weren't far behind. The light and heat still baked and boiled his skin; it was fighting constantly to repair itself. "It's not more memories of my parents, is it?"

I AM THE POTENCY. YOU ARE THE FILTER, UNBOUND.

"Doesn't really answer anything..."

WITNESS.
AND CHOOSE YOUR PATH.

"I choose this!" Beef said, flaring his Intent with all the strength he could muster. Felix had instructed him back on the boats, but reality was far different than practice. "I don't need to see anymore dumb, cryptic things about my dad or my old life! All I need is to focus! On! Now!"

The liquid light surged, swirling faster and faster, burning the world. Burning him, as sand turned molten once again, joining into bands of brilliant glass.

Don't force it, guide it.

The words seemed to drift from somewhere beyond, but Beef couldn't be bothered to source them. They felt right, so he pulled back, letting the maelstrom rage. It surged, spinning faster and faster, propelled by its own momentum. The bone face beneath him stared blankly, but Beef swore he saw a frown cross its weird eye sockets. He ignored it, just as Felix would have; he didn't have to give in to some spooky face just because it offered him power. The power was *here*.

He just had to take it.

There!

The voice spoke again, just as a mote of something flashed by—it shone only slightly brighter than its surroundings. Beef seized it, guided by instinct and the ineffable pressure of that whisper. His Intent snagged it within fingers of steel and chitin, drawing it close.

You have it! Hold tight and visualize!

"That's Felix—!" The moment the words escaped Beef's lips, the energy around them shifted to show his friend poised as if diving through deep, dark waters. Beef sucked in a lungful of scalding air.

Don't visualize me*!* The vision's eyes flashed a cyan-blue so bright it overwhelmed the golden dust, and the entire vista collapsed. *Visualize your new core space!*

"O-oh! Right!" Beef bore down, flinging the remnant bits of his Intent and Willpower at the mote that, even now, the maelstrom was attempting to pull away. "Visualize!"

The chaos tightened again, more sand compressing into molten glass with every heartbeat, shimmering into an unstable, liquid ring of riotous color. The golden light, the yellow, and the orange were overtaken by a veritable rainbow of hues. Mana types surged, drawn from somewhere deep inside of Beef's scattered core—the unchained potential of an Unbound warrior.

I can't be everything. His skin was blistering, and his fur had caught fire in three very uncomfortable places. *But I gotta be something! Visualize!*

Thoughts skipped through his Mind, too fleeting to catch, but he bore down on them anyway. The colors flashed, throwing up spikes of solidified Mana around him in random shapes. This one a blue beam, that one a yellow shelf. Again and again, it happened faster as Beef caught onto his own thought process, his own desires. Colors shifted, muting and turning earth toned and mundane as the shapes solidified. Flash. A chair. Flash. A bedframe. Flash. A tall window casement, lock rattling as a storm brewed outside.

Flash.

Beef fell to his knees, and for a moment, could do nothing but breathe. But...the pain was gone. Beef felt at his arms, his chest—his burns were healed as if they never were—but he clutched at himself in sudden, terrible fear.

He wasn't a Minotaur anymore.

"No no no!" Beef stood in a panic, but not nearly as tall as he used to; instead, he was barely five and a half feet tall, which threw him off as he tried to run. His feet tripped over themselves, the ground far closer than before, and he fell, just barely catching himself on the edge of his desk. He lifted himself with a grunt and stared into the blank glass of his computer monitor…where he could see a small, freckled face with big, chunky glasses hanging off the edge of his too-large nose. "I'm… Michael again."

A knock at the door. "Michael? Can I come in? I brought another beetle."

Thunder accompanied those words, along with a flash of light that nearly blinded him. Beef stood up, pressing his thick glasses up his nose with the knuckle of his forefinger. "Dad?"

WITNESS.

Beef walked from his computer monitor to the door of his room. Yet, before he could reach it, the door burst open and his dad stumbled inwards. "Did you…did you block the door with your figurines? I—Oh." His dad's face fell as he looked into the room, toward the bed. "Oh, you saw them."

"Yes," said a defiant voice, seated atop the twin bed. Beef blinked in surprise to find himself there too, a perfect replica of his current—old—form. "Leave me alone!"

No. No, I don't want to see this. Beef backed up, eyes flicking between his dad and his own form huddled atop the bed. *I thought I said no visions!*

YOU MUST WITNESS THE TRUTH.

"Mikey, I didn't want you to find out like this." His dad had something clutched in his hands, apart from another taxidermied beetle. *Papers*, Beef remembered. "Your mother and I were gonna tell you tomorrow…"

"You lied to me! You said it was gonna be alright!" Beef shook, not wanting to see this but riveted to the spot as his younger self quivered as well—only it was in anger, instead of fear. "You said!"

"Mikey, listen—"

"You said!"

Beef couldn't blink, though he wanted to howl and turn away, as his younger self lunged forward. Small hands hit his dad's slight paunch, shoving with all the strength he had in his teenage arms. Surprise registered on both their faces at the same time as his dad's feet hit one of Michael's vinyl figures on the ground.

"Dad!" Beef and Michael screamed together.

His own memories and the vision before him collapsed, crossing paths until Beef was Michael, hands outstretched, staring in abject terror as his father tripped into the window. The broken latch snapped, giving way beneath his dad's bulk, and the whole thing flew open…and his dad fell.

Beef ran out into the rain, which was coming down sideways at that point, driving into his skin like freezing needles. The small stretch of roof outside his bedroom window was empty, but Beef remembered this entirely too well. *I tried to forget!* He spotted his dad's hands hanging at the very edge. "Dad! I'm here! Hold on!"

Lightning forked in the sky, illuminating the twenty-foot drop to the ground below. His dad clung desperately to the gutter, eyes almost totally closed due to the rain. "Mikey! Mikey, get back inside! Call 911!"

"No! No, I can help this time!" Beef shouted. His other self was gone. It was just him now, and he wasn't going to let it happen again. "Reach out to me! Gimme your hand!"

His dad grunted, shifting his bodyweight to reach up—only for the gutter to give an alarming groan. It lurched, dropping away by several inches, and his dad let out a startled yelp. "Mikey! It's okay! It's not that far, a-and I'll be fine! Just get inside!"

Beef knew he was lying. Twenty feet might not have been a lot back on the Continent, but people died from less on Earth. Beef got on all fours, reaching out over the edge. "Gimme your hand! Please!"

Finally, his dad did it, leveraging enough of his weight up to grasp Beef's hand…except he wasn't a Minotaur anymore. He was just a kid again, and when the gutter tore away from the house, Beef—no, Michael—couldn't hold on.

His dad slipped.

He fell.

Lightning speared down from the sky, brighter than before and far more liquid than it had any right to be. Beef remembered this, too, but he could barely see it through his tears. His dad fell in slow motion, falling into the wet shadow of their yard, as Beef was seized by the lightning. With an awful, definitive lurch, Michael had been taken away.

Beef blinked. He was back in his room, and the window was securely latched…but his entire body was soaked through with rain. "Did he survive the fall?"

A LIE.
A TRUTH.
A WAY FORWARD.

"That's not what I asked, you bone-faced idiot! Did he live?"

WITNESS.

The room flickered, becoming a vast, endless expanse of water. Beef floated, listless and increasingly angry, as huge creatures frolicked through the depths around him. They looked like whales crossed with dinosaurs and were entirely too big as they swam around a huge, floating mass of bones.

WE CANNOT GO BACK.

The whale-things—leviathans, he somehow knew—twisted in sudden pain, dying by the hundreds. Their corpses turned to a sick, purple-blue ooze that instantly stripped them to the bone, before spreading to the next. And the next. The mass of bones waved an appendage made of femurs and skulls, turning them all to dust.

WE CAN ONLY MOVE FORWARD.
ALL THINGS DECAY.

The waters themselves turned to sand and hot, fetid wind. Bones were scattered, and dunes rose up to swallow any remnant of the majestic creatures.

BUT.
ALL THINGS RISE.

In the distance, a blaze of power split the sky as an image of a sword was lifted in a hand of black scales. Water burst from the sands, swelling to fill the desert once again. The ocean returned, and storms dominated the heavens.

ALL THINGS MAY CHANGE, IF WE CHOOSE.

The face of bones vanished, as did the water and the sands, leaving Beef alone with the storm outside his window. In his old room that he crafted from Primordial Essence and his own Willpower. There was a knock at the door.

"Michael? Can I come in? I brought another beetle."

WHAT DO YOU CHOOSE, UNBOUND?

CHAPTER NINETY-FIVE

For a single beat, the world before Vess hung between measures. A hundred competing rhythms congealed into a single, frozen caesura as the world itself inhaled.

The Fathom was dropping as its ooze-coated mass flared with horrid darkness. Pit swooped low, too far away but pushing forward valiantly, beating mighty wings that crackled with tempestuous fury. The War Naga stood guard over the ice-coated Beef and Hallow, their tridents and claws lifted toward the descending cataclysm of cold shadow.

Isla clenched Vess' shoulder, hard enough to buckle the Journeyman metal of her armor, and a nameless melody spun from her throat. It bolstered the moment, the pause of the world's breath, spinning glory into the radiant harmonics that burst wild from Vess' core. That, above all else, was what stretched the spearmaiden's Perceptions, turning instants into hours as a riot of light and song tumbled forth from the connection within. It was pure, majestic, and for a moment, a riotous cacophony of hope.

Vess fed her all into it, letting the hurricane within her breast run wild.

She let it sing.

Fathom! Wake! she cried into the connection. *You must!*

Its primary eyes flashed golden, bright as the conflagration around her, and a razor-sharp sense of despair curdled the melody. Vess weathered the inchoate agony that blasted down from the Fathom's rousing Mind, head unbowed as she bore its unbearable fears.

The Creature! Free yourself!

Yet all at once, the Dusk Dragon's eyes flickered and faded, the golden light in them extinguishing just as the thread of connection fizzled. The frozen, umbral aura of the Creature's abominable Spirit was too much—and growing stronger. Divine or worse, whatever it was, Vess could not fight it any longer.

As the world began to breathe again, Vess heard only a scornful laugh.

Fathom—!

Harmony and unchained Dissonance hit, a cymbal crash upon the skin of the world as the shadow-wrapped Fathom hit a wave of cyclonic power. Heat and dust spun through the torpid water, boiling it, buffeting the ooze-coated coils of the corrupted Dusk Dragon and throwing it back from its calamitous descent.

<<Step off, turd missile!>>

A colossal, chitinous leg unfolded from between the huddled War Naga, lifted up as if it were a spear.

<<Core…Manifestation?>> Isla gasped in clear disbelief. <<Impossible!>>

<<Don't touch my friends!>> Beefhammer shouted, standing tall among his allies. Vess gaped at him, almost unable to see his form among the swirl of Mana and the towering insectoid leg that seemed to extend directly from his chest.

Pitiful Thing! Your Power—!

The leg's tapered end flashed upward on those currents of heat, dust, and fetid decay—right into the Fathom's surprised skull.

<<Eat a dick, dude,>> Beef grunted.

The attack struck through ooze and scale and flesh with ease, striking not the Fathom's Body, but its Spirit. The impact blasted outward from its forehead, a concussive wave that cracked the earth fifty strides below the Dragon. The Fathom roared, but it was nothing compared to the screech that wracked the shadowed Creature.

<<AAH!>>

<<Close your ears—!>>

<<Eugh!>>

Reality lost all meaning as a shearing, atonal tumult ripped through them. It was more than the Dissonance Vess had experienced before, more than the Grand Harmony, even—it felt as if a fundamental piece of Creation was shrieking in torment. Vess cast her Perception upward, toward the Fathom and the grappling Creature; the waters boiled and fuzzed before the onslaught of that scream, but she could make out two things. The Fathom was alive…and the Creature had all but pulled free of its flesh.

Fathom! Fa—no. Vess shoved a hand to the shattered earth, pressing herself up to her knees. Echoes of the Memory unspooled within her Mind, faint things that thinned their dwindling connection. *Yini. Yintarion of the Cerulean Skies.*

Vess lifted her hand, fingers splayed. *WAKE.*

<<Matriarch's Lament!>>

<<Lady Dayne! No!>>

The hurricane that raged inside her burst free as a mountain peak within her split in twain. Rocks and moss fell, caught up in the spinning maelstrom, revealing an open, draconic maw—identical to the spectral one that formed atop Vess' physical shoulders. It raised its long, fanged snout into the air and let loose a deep, mournful cry. It was a lament of unremitting loss and terrible, inconsolable grief.

The Fathom reacted as if it had been set aflame.

No! Silence! Silence That Caterwauling!

Vess neither knew nor cared if the Creature was speaking to her or the Dragon; she did not stop, but poured more of her power into the Skill.

Matriarch's Lament is level 73!

Already, she could see it working. The connection between them thrummed with new vitality, a thread into a streamlet of golden light. Above, the shadow was thrown back as the Fathom bucked in agony.

Remember, Yintarion! she urged. *Remember and throw that parasite off of you!*

I—

A single syllable tumbled through their connection before it was smothered, but Vess would not relent. She committed, even as she knew that doing so would ruin all of her chances at recomposition. Vess released her warrior's fury and embraced the long sorrow and deep compassion her father had instilled within her—the hallmarks of a ruler.

Within, the maelstrom of Primordial power kicked up another notch. Mountain peaks crumbled—On The Wing, Draconic Stormfall, and The Fang of Havoc all breaking to pieces, their once-twisted facades shattered beneath the tearing wind. Batlike wings, coiling tails, and even a gargantuan tooth were laid bare, stripped of the stone that hid their metamorphosis, revealing the glimmer of gold and a rich mosaic of harmonies. They joined in, the vibrations turned to music turned to song, flowing among the roar of winds and clouds as all of it was focused upon the Matriarch's Lament.

Matriarch's Lament is level 74!
...
Matriarch's Lament is level 79!

Congratulations! You Have Reached Adept Tier In Matriarch's Lament!
You Gain:
+15% END
+15% AFI
+...

Vess fumbled with a Essence Draught, pulling it free of her belt and pouring it into the spectral jaws of her draconic head, and pulling it down into her core.

Legendary Essence Detected During Formation!
[Essence Draught of Atlantes (Air/Metal)]

Choose A Feature:
Sorrow
Wrath
Triumph

System energy blasted down through Vess' core space, filtering through the night sky that reigned above. More than that, the twin lights of red and blue stars grew, becoming something far more than distant motes. Red-gold and blue-white radiance illuminated her core space, somehow resonating with the System's energy as all of it hit the Primordial-forged temple at her center.

She chose the only option that would break through the Creature's guard.

Congratulations!
You Have Absorbed The Essence Of [Triumph]!

An explosion of light and sound ripped from her temple doors, forcing a wave of pressure that scattered the clouds, revealing depths Vess had never known existed. Heat and something far more primal emanated from below, but Vess flinched away—for behind that pressurized wave, a brilliant, gleaming light raced outward. It clung to her new-formed peaks like liquid gold, coating her Skills with a power she had never experienced.

The Fang of Havoc is level 74!

On The Wing is level 78!
Draconic Stormfall is level 74!

Among all of it was the Grand Harmony woven into a Dragon's roar.

Vess poured all of the Mana and Stamina she had into the strident call of her Lament, a Skill designed to inflict the grief and anguish of an ancient Dragon upon her enemies—grief that spun visions of burning skies, frozen mountains, and the betrayal of kin. Vess recognized the visions, and she pressed them all along her strengthening connection, all of it tinted by the Essence that flared within her Skill.

Remember, Rana! You are not yet Lost!

Their connection suffered through a devastating quake as the Fathom—Yintarion—blinked open shining golden eyes.

Yintarion roared. Ooze stripped from his snout, revealing dull golden scales and a tongue the brilliant red of blood and flame. Yet the ooze stopped just beyond the Dragon's snow-white mane, as the umbral waters cracked into near-ice.

You Shall Never Be Rid Of Me, Vessel. It had been cast off, but now the Creature's faceless head swam in the spectral depths, drawing closer and closer. It grew, as if one of the moons were falling atop them all. **You Have Failed All That You Hoped To Achieve. Lost All That You Loved. There Is Nothing But My Worship For You. Nothing But Me.**

You Are Mine.

A hopeless gloom swallowed the Dragon, engulfing the thready strains of Vess' Lament as if it were nothing. Yintarion's eyes fluttered, gold flickering to black and back again.

Enough Of That, Dragoon.

Vess stumbled, Aspects stricken as her Skill was forcefully cut off.

"Dragoon…run," Yintarion whispered, but he bellowed through the waters like a bugle.

The Creature laughed, that same slow derision curdling its faceless essence. Its oozing tendrils sank into the Dragon's flesh, crawling up his neck and jaw once more, as the Creature's shadowed, faceless form hovered just beyond and outside. **Enough Speaking, Vessel. Yours Is Not To Think.**

<<Divine or not, you are a monster,>> Vess said through her hitched breath. Her Mind felt scrambled by all that had occurred, and her Spirit and Body weren't far behind.

That chuckle again, as deep as the lightless pit of the water. **I Am More Than You Could Ever Conceive, Little Chanter. I Am The Sliver Of The Night Itself.**

<<Moontouched,>> Isla said, her throat hoarse and her scalp leaking blood into the listless water. <<Noctis.>>

<<Wait, what?>> Beef asked, lifting his bovine head.

The Most Clever Of All The Gods. Destroyer Of The Ten Thousand Ships. Breaker Of The Undermount. The Creature swelled, its faceless visage overtaking everything within view as it spoke. The voice of it scraped at their eardrums, raw and discordant yet containing stentorian notes that commanded every ounce of their attention. **Yes. All Of That, And Far More.**

<<And yet you are trapped here,>> Vess said, fighting through the deafening noise and drawing herself to her feet. It hurt. It hurt so very much. <<Bound by the Seal. Even with the Dragon, you cannot get out, can you?>>

A growl shook the water and earth like an earthquake. **I Will Enjoy Devouring You, Girl. You And Your Worthless Allies Will Be The Fuel I Require To Overcome This Prison.**

<<You will choke on my spear,>> Vess promised. The anger was easy to summon, and it burned clean in her Spirit. <<I will free Yintarion, and he will tear you to pieces himself.>>

Fool. The Dragon Is Gone. There Is Only Fathom. Somehow, even without a face, it sneered. **The Paltry Power Of A Dead Primordial Cannot Overcome The Might Of The Divine. All Of Your Tricks Achieved Nothing, Girl.**

<<Overcome?>> Vess panted, wincing through the strain she felt across her Mind. <<I…simply bought time.>>

What?

A bolt of lightning hit the Creature, screaming through the water itself as silence bloomed into a new chaos.

"Chthonic Tribute!"

CHAPTER NINETY-SIX

Adamant Discord!

Skein of Fate!

The world bloomed open to Felix, a haze of connections that spread like spider's silk in every conceivable direction, but he rocketed down toward the depths upon a thread the size of an ocean liner. The water boiled behind him as he all but became the lightning he rode upon.

<<Chthonic Tribute!>>

The shadow bubbled and shrieked, flaring outward in jagged spikes toward Felix's outstretched claw. He ignored them, focusing all his might, all of his Hunger upon the Creature's Essence—and the spikes and claws of shadow dissolved.

No! Impossible! the Creature howled, while the Fathom's body contorted into spastic knots.

Below, a glorious golden light filled the waters as Vess lifted her hand one last time and sounded the connection between her and the Dragon. Felix still couldn't believe that, but it had given his Hunger time to mobilize itself, and beyond the surprise, all he felt was gratitude.

I Am A Sliver Of The Night Itself! Heretics! Anathema!

A Willpower contested his—something ancient and terrible and stronger than any mortal combatant Felix had ever faced. The cavernous face of the Creature loomed in every piece of the shadow Felix was devouring, and it raged. It bucked his Skill, refusing the pull of Felix's Tribute, but he had an answer for that, too.

Title: The Call of Defiance Is Active!
+25% Willpower When Contested By A Foe Of Divine Or Greater Advancement!

Title: Born of Will Is Active!
What Is Beyond You, If You Have The Will?

Like the slow bend of heating steel, the Creature's Will warped under the steady increase of pressure. It may have been Divine, it may have survived countless Ages, but it was no match for an Unbound forged in the harshest of flames.

Your Will! How?

Felix offered no answers, only bore down harder, his Hunger roaring against the Fathom's unthinking pain. Shadow, ooze and Creature stripped from the Dragon's hide, piece by foul piece, revealing soiled golden scales and a mane that floated limply among glittering, crystalline horns.

Release Me, Heretic! Whatever Pact You Have Sworn To The Primordials Will Not Save You From The Wrath Of The Divine!

"You think I care?" Felix shouted into the water, his Adept voice so powerful it blasted through his Sunken Ward. "Chthonic Tribute!"

The pressure redoubled, peeling the Creature from the Dragon to the sounds of shattering stone and snapping wooden beams; its hold on the Fathom was deep and thorough. Felix grimaced through the pain as his core space filled, packed fuller than ever, and still there was more. The Creature, sliver of Noctis and whatever else, felt endless.

Do I even have the space?

I DO. EAT! his Hunger roared, and Felix could only oblige.

A deal was a deal, after all.

Foul Little Thing! Begone! The Creature hauled on its stretching tendrils, still bound around the Dragon's forelimb, and slashed toward Felix. A clutch of searing, icy crescents formed, launching through the water at breakneck speeds, and Felix regarded them with his Eye.

Engaged as he was, he could not eat the attack. Nor had he any intention of tanking it. *Only one thing for it.*

Strained and struggling with devouring the Creature, Felix still managed to force Mana outward and into the first glyph on the blade at his hip. Surging up into his left hand, the crooked blade of his Inheritor's Will slashed upward, igniting the glyph with power as the crescents hit—splitting water, ice, and the darkness itself on the razor edge.

A cataclysmic reverberation tore through the water as empty space was carved into the wake of Felix's sword. Harmless, unshaped Mana split to either side of his weapon, the spell rendered into harmless vapor. The cavitation collapsed on itself, booming in every direction as the Creature stared at the sword in horror.

Herald. The word echoed from its empty face like a tolling bell, final and undeniable. **Nym—!**

A brief, staccato howl of panic sounded...and the Creature was consumed.

Felix recoiled from the last smoking tendril and, for a time, simply tread water.

<<You did it,>> Beef said, breathlessly, before his eyes rolled into the back of his head, and he collapsed onto the shattered ground.

"Master! No!" The Lindwurms cried, their Bodies twisted up as if in terrible pain. Their limbs had started to burn, somehow, their scales igniting as if from within as smoke poured in bubbling coils from their mouths. "Heretic! What have you done?"

<<Silence!>> Vess shouted, conjuring her Spears around her like a halo of violence. <<Be careful how you speak, draconian!>>

<<I'll give you the same chance I gave the Creature,>> Felix said, forcing his voice to resound in the too-still water. <<Surrender to me, and that'll be it. No more killing.>>

"You–!"

<<One chance,>> Felix interrupted, lifting a single finger. <<One.>>

The Lindwurms stared at him, not only pain but fear scrawled across their Spirits. One by one, the remaining five Lindwurms snapped shut their jaws and banished the heat from within their breasts. Then they surprised him.

They bowed their heads, and words flowed from their lips.

"We surrender to your strength, monarch. We are yours, bound by Oath and Power. Upon our honor shall we serve, or else upon our honor shall we die."

Congratulations, Autarch!
You Have Vanquished A Threat!
The Lindwurms (Moontouched Lindwurms) Have Joined Your Fledgling Nation!
+25% To All Positive Relations With Draconics!

Still Moontouched, huh, he observed. He shoved down his concern over this new and clearly Divine-afflicted group of followers. He had worse things to handle now. "Good," Felix said to them, before grunting in sudden, sharp pain.

<<Felix? Are you alright?>>

<<Fine. Beef. Is he okay? Did he—>> Felix bent, his Body wracked by a splitting, tearing pain within his gut and chest.

<<Boy! What have you done?>> Isla said, kicking off the broken ground to swim toward his floating form. Pit beat her to him, flowing to Felix's side like iron to a magnet.

<<Must be something I ate,>> he said, scratching at his friend's ears. Pit warbled, and his wings spread around the two of them.

Isla stared through the feathers, aghast. <<That monstrosity…you allowed it inside of you?>>

Felix grunted again. The force of the Creature's release from the Fathom had been like a cable under tension; the moment it snapped, it clattered down through his channels and into the wide abyss of his core space. It was running wild now.

He didn't have enough time.

<<Get Beef up. And Hallow. Everyone.>> Felix forced a breath from his lungs, and a crackling miasma of Mana and Essence poured from him. <<Get back, for your safety. Pit?>>

With you. Always.

<<Atta boy,>> Felix said through a rictus grin. <<Time to finish it.>>

<<Finish what?>> Isla demanded. She dodged away from the sputtering mass of Mana and Essence. <<Please. Felix. Tell me something! I need to know what's happening, so I might assist you!>>

Pit vanished in a flash of light, adding the weight within Felix's core and yet lightening it at the same time. Felix breathed back in, sucking back the clouds of Mana and Essence that had escaped. "The Creature isn't dead. It's not even contained, really."

<<What?>>

Spikes of agonizing pressure stabbed through Felix's gut, as if something were trying to tear itself free. "It's not happy. Run, or I can't be blamed for what's about to happen."

Felix didn't wait for her response, and was only dimly aware of Vess shooting upward toward them on a pair of huge, spectral wings. *Oh. Cool.*

He dropped into the dark.

His core space was under assault.

From within the nebulous clouds of Essence that hovered above his Divine Tree, masses of endless tendrils had sprouted. It gathered the

Essence and Mana together, congealing it into huge appendages that lashed about in all directions, snagging on Skills and his cores with equal measure. Each hit was a fissure of savage pain that nearly blinded Felix as he descended...but then, he'd felt worse.

Felix bore the torment as he drifted to a stop within his core space, his small form floating before the cloud of stolen Essence that was once the Creature...and what was swiftly becoming the Creature once again. A horrifying skull pressed against the formless clouds, faceless and crumbling, just as bad as it had been in the Memory he'd experienced—Felix's Mind stuttered for a brief moment before his Bastion of Will clamped shut.

Nymean.

Felix forced himself to watch the oozing, faceless skull of the Creature pull itself from the muck of its Essence. His Bastion blazed, burning down below within its array like a distant spotlight, and Pit's thrumming voice soothed his straining Mind.

You are strong! Fight that jerk!

Teeth formed among the wreck of a corpse, perfect and too-square within that shattered visage. They snapped and clattered, a jaw testing itself as words tumbled from its unformed throat.

Foolish, Foolish Child. Release Me, And Perhaps You Will Be Allowed To Live.

"I gave you your chance," Felix said. His Perception flitted over the whole of his core space, feeling at the layout. Assuring himself. "You refused to take it."

And So You Brought Me Here? To The Center of Your Power? Clueless, Overconfident Nym! I Can Feel My Power Growing With Every Passing Heartbeat As You Draw In More Of My Essence! I Am A Sliver Of The Divine! I Cannot Be Bested By Nyms Nor A Primordial's Heinous Plots!

"You're not getting out of here," Felix said, his voice calm. He probed at several spots of his core space as surreptitiously as he could. "That Dragon is free of you."

Dragon? Do You Think I Care What Shape My Vessel Takes? No. No, You Shall Do Nicely In His Stead.

The Creature spread itself wider, clinging to his Skills now instead of tearing at them. Seeping over the celestial bodies and toward the spinning rings of his core.

Two Cores? Quite Novel. And Potent, Despite The Rickety Foundations, it said as it avoided the black void at his cores' center. **And A...Tree...What Is—**

Felix spoke up quickly. He couldn't let it inspect things so closely. Not yet. "You control with flesh and Dissonance, Creature. I can hear it."

The Creature tilted its vast skull toward him. The gaping hole where its face should have been conveyed no expression, but it seemed amused by his clear attempts to stall.

Yes. The Primordials Might Be Anathema, But They Do Have Their Tricks To Teach. To Steal. The Creature stilled, and a vast quiver overtook its formless Spirit. **I Do Not Understand. I Have Your Cores Within My Grasp! None Can Withstand Me Once I Have Taken Hold Of Them. You Should Be Afraid. You Should Be Angry!**

"Oh, I am," Felix said. "Your kind makes me downright furious."

My Kind? I Have No Peer But The Arc Of The Heavens Themselves, Whelp!

"No peers?" Felix snorted, and the trembling in his Mind faded, just a touch. "Every petty dictator and wannabe tyrant is just the same. Every guild elder, city lord, and mad god. I'm sick of it."

For the first time, the Creature hesitated. **What Madness Do You Speak Of, Nym?**

"You want to know why I brought you here? Why I let you, a big blob clearly designed to possess the beings you get hold of?" Felix felt the pain in his Mind fade entirely before the clean burn of his fury. Pit screeched in harmonizing agreement.

What Madness? The Creature demanded, its questing tendrils forgotten. **What God?**

"I did it because you made a mistake." Felix bared his teeth, and at his center, his Hunger roared.

Relentless Resolution!

Cloudstep!

Felix hurled himself from his core space to find his Body already moving. Kicking off shattering platforms of Mana, Felix rocketed the last fifty feet to the bottom of the Breach, where hill-sized hunks of ice wove between the twisted statuary. He hit one of those hills, his landing blasting silt and rime in a floating explosion of debris, revealing the desiccated husk of an ancient root.

He grasped it and hoped his friends had gotten far enough away.

Unite the Lost!

A gargantuan surge of Essence and significance flooded out of him, pouring not just from the Mana Gates in his palms, but from all of them. He lit up, a torch of power in the darkest depths, while within him, the faceless Creature screeched in sudden terror.

The Seal! No!

The Seal! Yes! Pit rejoined, bugling his joy.

Felix couldn't pay attention to their cries—he could only focus on hanging tight to the root. Power overwhelmed him, energies that he hadn't the first clue how to wield, but which were bridled and tamed by the soaring pattern of his Skill. Harmonies swelled, accompanied by the atonal rasp of Dissonance that curled through melodies and rhythm, seemingly without rhyme or reason.

The root between his fingers swelled, flooded with sudden vitality as time itself sloughed from its ancient bark. Gold and silver sigaldry etched themselves to life, formations that looked grown rather than created by the hands of a person, and a vast blaze of once-hidden light burst forth from the floor of the Breach.

The Abundance Anima Has Been Restored!
Restoration In Progress!
30%!

Felix screamed, the flow of Essence and Mana and significance burning bloody furrows inside of him. Scorched and raw, his channels spat red-gold radiance and blue-white wrath as the weight of countless enemies and the mighty power of the Creature itself—from the Ooze Behemoth—was depleted.

70%!
85%!

The words of their phantom friend echoed through Felix's memories. *Seek the center. Strengthen the Tree.*

95%!
100%!

Congratulations!
The Abundance Anima Has Been Restored!

A sudden chorus sang out from high above them, and Felix fell back with a ragged groan. In the dark waters, far up at the edge of the frozen

Breach, a glorious electrum ring burst to life. The chorus rang out, higher and more pure than anything Felix had heard before—as if the Grand Harmony were extolling its very existence.

A flickering, too-tall man in white robes appeared beside Felix. His face was split in a broad smile, and his Spirit sang with astonished joy. "You did it!" Paxus cheered.

"Not done yet!" Felix shouted back.

"Of course! Press on, young Autarch. I'll follow your lead!"

Felix stumbled forward, his legs suddenly refusing to work. Pit shrieked in terror as flashes of red sparked in Felix's vision. The Creature was going wild inside him. "Not much time!"

Green Shaping!

The Skill sputtered and failed, Mana sizzling through the riotous haze of power that still cloaked the Spirit Tree's roots. *I don't have the Mana to force through the interference...that* I *created.* Felix laughed, incredulous, as the Creature tore through something inside of him, and blood poured from his nose. *Gotta touch it!*

Felix threw himself forward, powered just by his arms, but fiery, Mind-numbing pain made his Body spasm. He landed, inches too short of the root, but Felix stretched as a paroxysm of agony rippled across his entire being. He reached out his hand...and someone took it. Felix blinked up through bloody, floating tears to find Vess grasping his hand and elbow.

<<I am here,>> she said simply.

Nothing more was needed.

Together, they lunged forward, and Felix's hand made contact with the root.

Green Shaping!

Theurgist of the Rise!

Theurgist of the Rise is level 85!

He shaped the wood, inscribing an array he'd made a thousand times before. In battle, to raise a town, and to support a friend. Now, he scratched it out to save himself and everyone within the Territory.

Siphon.

The Seal thrummed, the chorus rising to a fever pitch as the Abundance Anima sang out a paean to its glorious rebirth. Beside him, Paxus laughed, understanding swelling through his Spirit. The phantom laid his incorporeal hands upon the root as well, and the swelling chorus spun, pivoted on its head as the pitch and cadence flowed in a new direction.

The siphon array lit up, bright as the sun, and the waters boiled around them all.

Paxus shouted into the churning, turbulent waters. "As without, so within!"

The power of the Seal of the Breach flipped, turned inward. Into Felix himself.

He screamed, and Vess screamed with him.

CHAPTER NINETY-SEVEN

Felix grappled with the power, his screams not abating in the slightest as he rode the current down into his dark core space. The process, which was normally as simple as breathing, was now fraught as he teetered on the razor's edge of burnout. Not since the Ravager King had he felt so bloated with power.

I'm here! Pit cried out.

Just as with the Ravager King, Pit was a steady presence in his Spirit. The tenku siphoned pieces of the Abundance Anima's power, rotating it through his whirling star before sending it back down into Felix's core space.

It wasn't enough. Unite the Lost had brought back more power than it had cost to enact the Skill—from a standpoint of conservation of energy, it made no sense to Felix. Yet he hadn't the time to waste, figuring it out. He fell, emanating gold and silver trails that burst from him like solar flares. He was the sun, carrying a light that threatened to burn everything within him to dust.

I—I too—am here!

Vess appeared, her hand upon his physical shoulder transferred, phantom-like to ripple beside Felix's descending form. She flickered and resolved into a brilliant Link, a cable made of solidified silver wind. It flowed and flashed, grasping at the power that spun off of Felix and nearly buckling…but she held on.

I have it! Vess' words spilled out between stifled screams. *I can*—a guttural growl tore through their Link—*I can shoulder the burden!*

Goddamn, he was impressed.

Felix was filled with the might of the resurrected Abundance Anima, its power, and a portion of its truth. Its significance. The screech of a tenku and the roar of a dragon ripped through his consciousness as Felix emerged into scintillating chaos.

What Have You Done! Nym! What Trickery Is This?

Light blossomed among his core space, igniting the expansive dark with the light of a hundred orb-like particles and illuminating the sprawling, congealed mass of writhing purple-blue tentacles at his center. It flinched from the light, as if the gold and silver radiance hurt, and indeed its Essence-flesh charred and sizzled away into embers where it tried and failed to cross the boundary of Felix's core space.

This Thing Hampers Me! You Should Not Be Able To! What Fell Artifact Has The Withered Given You?

The Creature let loose a bellow like twisted horns descending into basso fury and atonal, squealing violins. Waves tore through his core space, puckering the very fabric of his inner reality before it rebounded from those glimmering orbs in a cascade of golden-silver sparks.

Felix landed among the branches of his Divine Tree, and the crystal branch rang like a bell. The Creature might seem trapped, but it wasn't foolproof. He needed to buy time.

The Spirit Tree's power still bloomed from Felix's visualized form, still poured in from the seemingly endless font of the Abundance Anima. Pit flickered into being beside him, a dazzling collection of lightning caught between wings of ice. Vess, too, though she was a mere whisper, a cord that could have been a silver spear thrust through the nearby branches. Loops of golden-silver connected them to Felix, a constant flux of energies that threw his overgrown hair into a wind-blown mess.

"You're as stupid as you are ugly," he said.

The crumbling, collapsing sinkhole that served as the Creature's skull swung toward Felix's voice, and its jaw hung open in a wordless, malevolent hiss.

With a flare of Felix's mighty Intent and Willpower, he shoved his borrowed power down through his feet. The Divine Tree beneath him rang again, and this time, the bell felt like it was the size of a planet. All that time preparing, Felix had built up his Divine Tree, and now it blossomed. As if fruit upon a galactic tree, nebulas of swirling golden-silver swelled into gaseous giants, spreading in an almost perfect circle around Felix's entire core space.

The Creature spun, its skull tracking the sprouting trees with alarm.

Tendrils lashed, rebounding from the Skills below as it was hedged in from all directions. **This Is Impossible!**

Crystalline roots rose from the shadows, bursting with opalescent shoots as their too-thin sapwood swelled into enormous, twisting barriers. The wood grew thick, rugged bark, turning vibrant with the thrum of newfound energies as Felix fed rivers of vigor into his Tree. It wasn't just power and vitality, though. It was Essence and Mana—and a portion of the Abundance's very being. It was significance, matured and turned back around to the hand that brought it from the edge of Ruin's oblivion.

All at once, across his entire core space, saplings erupted straight up from the barrier of roots. The baby trees thickened and grew, turning to adolescent copies of the Divine Tree itself, as sigaldry revealed itself across the expanse of crystalline root and branch.

The Creature spun, its broken skull hurling at the risen barrier of light and branch. A chorus of vibrations met the Creature's substance and cast it back, burning its questing tendrils into spasming husks of charred Essence-flesh. **How?** it roared. **How Have You Done This?**

Felix bit his lip, drawing a rivulet of visualized blood that he knew was trickling down his actual chin, too. "I've got a really good memory."

The Creature moved.

Pit shrieked in warning, and Vess' dimming presence flared in alarm, but Felix didn't flinch. The tendril snapped out, almost too fast for him to perceive it, and splattered against a shield of opalescent light around the perimeter of his Divine Tree.

The Creature howled, withdrawing in pain as its appendage turned to ash. **What Foulness? The Seal Cannot Accomplish Such Harm To Me!**

It peered closer, its enormous, eyeless skull pressing cautiously toward Felix and the huge expanse of his Divine Tree. The Creature easily matched it in size, though its form ebbed and flowed like the tides of a cursed sea.

This Seal...This Tree—! How Did You Obtain This?

Felix pressed his Intent further than ever before. He had pushed himself during his long meditation, further than he'd ever pushed himself before, but it hadn't been enough. *The Seal is active, but it's not enough!*

Vess and Pit were shadows of their former presences—they could handle no more, and the streamers of potency ripped through Felix's veins like barbed lightning. He bore down on it all, channeling everything he could into the Divine Tree.

Answer Me, Nym! How Did You Steal A Piece Of My

Beloved? Its voice was a constant cacophony of Dissonance, threaded with only the patchiest of melodies. Rage suffused all of its Essence-flesh, turning its amorphous hide the color of a bloody bruise. **What Have You Done To Vellus?**

"Like I said," Felix grunted. "You gods are all the same."

This time, there was no clever planning or deceitful sleight of hand. This time, the Creature didn't hold itself back. It threw all of its might against Felix and his Divine Tree—the one he'd grown from a sliver of Vellus' power, and which he had used Vess' visualization techniques and his Hunger's Mind-numbing effects to forge into a near-perfect replica of the Seal of the Breach.

It wasn't perfect, but it was goddamn close. Close enough that a sympathetic connection between his Seal and the one in the Corporeal Realm could be established. A Link.

A phantom voice echoed through him. *As without, so within.*

The barrier flared, turning to a solid sheet of golden-silver as the Creature's colossal bulk hit all of it at once. The new-grown trees around his core space swayed with the impact, flashes of liquid, prismatic light flowing down the roots in wild streams.

I Will Destroy You, Nym. You And All That You Love. Your Empire Will Fall, And No Matter What Aid The Withered Has Given You, It Will Not Be Enough.

The Creature's voice boomed, louder than anything Felix had experienced, even the Maw. The pressure of its unhinged words drew more sparks from the barrier, which had begun to bend ever so slightly outward. Every muscle in Felix's body was tense as he moved caustic flames through his pathways as fast as he could.

I Stole The Withered's Very Power! A Mere Sliver Of Glorious Godhood, And I Bested The Scion Of Misrule Itself! I Claimed The Powers Of Flesh, Even Dissonance—The Warped Echo Of Harmony! I Shackled Them To My Will And Laid Low All That It Cared For! Just As I'll Do To You, Nym!

The barrier bent further, a steady buckling that was turning the golden-silver light to a distinct, bloody crimson. Felix could see the gnashing teeth of the mountainous Creature, biting at the light as parts of its Essence-flesh turned to charred dust. It was driven to the brink.

He Called Me The Treacherous One. Ha! I Was To Make This World Better! To Remove The Dross! Yttin, Primordial, And

This Seal Are Nothing More Than Temporary Delays Of That Fate. You Cannot Run From The Inevitable, Nym!

"Holy shit, do you ever shut up?" Felix snapped as the barrier impacted the crystalline branches of the Divine Tree. He was so close, as golden-silver sigaldry spread in complicated patterns beneath his feet—patterns that bore a distinct similarity to those in his Stronghold.

For Even Daring To Touch My Beloved, I Will Not Stop Until You Have Fallen Before Me! For Stealing Her Potency, I Will Puppet Your Flesh And Force You To Hunt Down And Kill All That You Love! I'll Cut You From The Grand Harmony Itself And Feed You The Twisted, Anemic Strains Of Dissonance!

"You idiot," Felix stepped forward, his feet splashing among pools of liquid light. Sigaldry spun out farther and farther. "I said you made a mistake, and you never once asked what that was."

The barrier shrieked, pressed to its utmost limit by the Creature's furious assault…but it was utterly subsumed by the tolling sound of ten thousand chiming bells and the stentorian peal of a crystalline tree the size of a town. Golden-silver sigils connected, finally connecting the last bits of the sprawling design Felix had worked into the Seal.

"You said you claimed flesh and Dissonance. That you controlled them." Felix bared his teeth, revealing a mouthful of bristling fangs. "Those are *mine*."

Sovereign of Flesh!

Though it was not a true Body, the Creature's Essence-flesh was more than valid as far as his Transcendent Skill was concerned. Immediately Felix's Willpower locked over the Creature's, and its writhing form was hauled bodily from the edges of his core space. The barriers faded back into quiescence, their waterfalls of sparks gone, as Essence-flesh was pressed and packed into a far more restrictive space.

You Cannot! Nym! This Is—I Am Above You!

It fought, tooth and nail, but it was useless. All of its strength seemed to fail before the Title-boosted onslaught of Felix's Will and the fury of his sovereignty.

Sovereign of Flesh is level 85!

…

Sovereign of Flesh is level 88!

Tendrils of Dissonance and Harmony spat outward from its

collapsing form, waves that tried to send fissures of pain and torment through Felix's Mind. They met instead the stone-fastness of his Bastion, flared as hard as he could manage. The Creature's assault battered into him, shaving stone and sending cracks through his modified Mind Skill.

You Cannot Hold Me! Your Body May Be Mighty, But Your Mind Is Weak!

More cracks spread through his Epic Skill, and pieces of his reforged walls began to shear away. Felix screamed as lances of pain cut through his resistances like red-hot pokers. The Creature howled with mad laughter.

Yet, he dared to turn away from his Bastion entirely, putting everything on the line as he pressed a massive chunk of his Mana toward the Seal itself.

Cardinal Flame!

The Seal ignited, bathing the endless dark with a dome of impassible light and the overwhelming strains of a concerto so complex it beggared the imagination. It was the music of many things. Dissonance and fury, expansive hunger and aching silence as the Creature rebounded from the threshold of his Bastion. The Creature reared back, struck suddenly dumb as everything hit it at once.

Very distantly, Pit trilled in triumph.

You Cannot Contain Me! The thing's head pivoted within the cage of Willpower Felix had forged, and its pulsating Essence flesh twitched in unresponsive outrage. **I Am Eternal And Elemental! A Goddess!**

"Fuck the gods," Felix growled. "Hunger!"

The tiny solar system around him shuddered, the light of the Tree and Seal dimming as if an object suddenly cloaked them all. The Creature stared down at the darkness it had so far ignored. A darkness that was bending the light and sound all around it into a halo of shuddering, inescapable Need.

"Sic 'em."

CHAPTER NINETY-EIGHT

His Hunger began to feed.

The discarded ash that had fallen from the Creature's damaged limbs was pulled in first. It had collected within the spinning halo of his Hunger, and for the first time, Felix felt a thrill of power as it was consumed. There was no number—no counter within his notifications—but each morsel of Essence-flesh seemed to bolster something deep and primal within his cores.

FINALLY! his abyss thundered. It roared, matching the pitch and timbre of the Creature's savage howls. **FEAST!**

The Creature rebelled with all of its available might. Essence-flesh lashed outward, flensing edges meant for Skills and cores, yet missed. Each attack met the unyielding bulwark of Felix's Will, and though it cost huge measures of Mana and Stamina, he remained standing. Unbowed.

"You're *mine*," he hissed.

Fool!

Shouting its defiance, the Creature's skull opened like a blossom, its collapsed face a sudden quivering tunnel into someplace else. Noise ripped free of it, knocking Felix back a step and setting his Divine Tree to ringing. His Mind, Body, and Spirit shook as if each were under the sway of a hurricane's wrath.

It was a blast of sound snatched from the tapestry of Creation itself, torn and flipped upside down until its atonal burr rasped against the fabric of all things. Dissonance, captured and weaponized in a way he hadn't felt since the Maw. It surrounded him, tearing at Felix's form like hungry wolves and he the vulnerable lamb. Yet their snapping jaws brought forth nothing but dazzling pain and sizzling discordance, a shower of red-gold flame and blue-white lightning. His vision was white with the agony of it all.

"Is that it?" he asked, forcing his voice to remain level, despite the pain.

Impossible! The words tumbled from the Creature's maw as its skull snapped closed. **You Withstood The Malignant Disarray Of Creation Itself. A Mortal...The Withered One Must Have Inured You To Its Corruption.**

"What? No." Felix ignored the pains in his everything and forced himself to take two more steps upon the main branch of his Divine Tree. Each footfall rang with a deep, soulful knell. The Creature's attack was still caught up around him, swirling and clawing at Felix.

It hadn't drawn blood, but instead pieces of his Essence. They flared around him, the colors of his cores, arcing between his limbs and the array at his feet. "At best, the Primordial of Withering Dust gave me a power boost. Compared to that, this is nothing."

Inch by inch, the Creature sank further, hauled down by Seal and Sovereign of Flesh, until its edges hit the widening, glowing halo around his cores and Hunger. It screeched, its voice splintering into a thousand echoes that overlapped one another.

***You* Are Nothing! Release Me Or Suffer The Wrath Of All The Gods! You Are Crossing A Threshold That Cannot Be Returned From, Nym! War Or No, The Elysian Halls Would Never Condone Such A Foolish, Childish Attempt!**

"You're behind the times," Felix said, voice thick. "War's been over for Ages."

The Creature flinched. **What?**

Fiendforge!

Felix ignored the sliver's confusion, and instead marshaled his Unique Skill, grasping at the Dissonance the Creature had hurled his way. He gathered it up around him, pressing the vicious attack between the grip of his ability and the anvil of his Will until it shone with a red-gold radiance—yet he didn't stop there. He also pulled at the refined vibrations that haunted his dual cores.

At the junction of his [Thunderflame Core] and [Cardinal Beast Core], the liquid-seeming flame of both rings ground into one another like flint and steel, producing sparks of Harmony and Dissonance. Those sparks had filled him for months, a constant flaring of cacophony that had baked into every inch of Felix's core space.

He'd felt it before, when he'd sunk deep into his Hunger and visualized his evolving inner world, but he'd never known just what to do with it. Now it came to him, an idea born of the Creature's ruthless attack and his own desperate invention.

Felix forged a weapon.

A fist, clawed and scaled, formed among the branches of his crystalline perch. It sizzled with red-gold flame and sparked with blue-white lightning, yet its form was dominated by a vivid purple glow that seemed to be pulled from the edges of his Hunger itself.

Fiendforge is level 43!
...
Fiendforge is level 54!

Journeyman Tier!
You Gain:
+Decrease Significance Consumed In Forging!
+5% WIL
+10% INE

Waves of power flowed from the fist like a tsunami, yet it did not move. It was all Felix could do to hold it there, manifested within his core space by the sheer, unlikely combination of Unique Skill and a Willpower that exceeded a sliver of Divinity. The Creature recoiled from it, its Essence-flesh jumping and scattering like oil from soap, or like sand atop a vibrating metal sheet.

You Wield Dissonance And Harmony...Together? How? No Mortal Can Shape Dissonance! None!

"Yeah, didn't I tell you?" His Hunger roared, and its pull grew into a vast, inescapable tide. Felix flashed his brilliant fangs. "I'm real special."

The immense, conjured fist opened, revealing a massive, burning blue eye in the center of its palm. A sapphire radiance filled Felix's core space as a swell of magnificent music filled every inch of him. He lifted off the ground, held in place by vibrations so refined that he no longer knew where he ended and the world began.

Holy shit! Felix was drowning in the sensations, his Perception and Affinity so filled that he could barely tell up from down. *What* is *this?*

There was no new Skill notification, only the reality quaking presence of his bonkers new ability. Dimly through the rising swell of a glorious, sublime concerto, he heard the Creature's fury.

Yyero! Siva! The Twins! Even Dark-Eyed Avet Would Come For You If You Dare To Consume Divinity!

Huge swathes of the Creature fell into the halo of his Hunger, disassembled by its titanic forces to join the river of sparks, Essence, and Mana that flowed around it. Nevertheless, it fought, skull and the majority of its bulk straining above its inevitable fall. Felix strained, too, sweat pouring off his false brow as readily as his cores shed their flickering song—he leveraged everything that he was into the effort, pitting Mind, Body, and Spirit against the Creature's own. For all his confidence and the potency of his Willpower, even within the cocoon of his own raucous symphony, he was only barely holding his own.

Stupid. Damn. Divinity! Each thought punched through his Mind like a hammer blow, driving the Creature ever lower. *Just! Die!*

More Than Nym. Primordial...No. You Cannot Be. They Are Not Allowed!

Of all things, that pierced the transcendent song Felix was wrapped within. "Wh—what? What isn't allowed?"

But the Creature was beyond words now, its bored-through skull collapsing in truth as the intense dual pressures of his Hunger and Sovereign of Flesh pressed and pulled at it. The thing could only howl, wordless and primal. Sounds sharper than any blade, as Harmony and Dissonance were woven together so quickly Felix could barely register it, let alone stop it.

Anathema! The words burst from the crumbling skull, born on the notes between his rising song. **A Sliver Or The Whole, All Of It Is Divine! I Am Noctis! I Am Queen Of The Night!**

The Creature's last words escaped the crushing grip of his Hunger, a gasp that nevertheless hit Felix like a bucket of ice water down his back.

I Rule The Space Between The Light...

Its Essence flesh vanished.

...And The Dark—

Then it was gone. Consumed.

New Title!
Devourer In Darkness (Unique)
You have descended into the depths and returned with another foe vanquished. Your Hunger grows ever stronger.

Loose your maw, Primordial Ascendent! Fiendforge can now directly access the resources your Hunger has consumed but not digested!

As if a cord had been cut, the massive hand above him failed. The song it carried faded so abruptly it was like a physical pain to no longer hear it, while the entire construct dissolved into streamers of incandescent light. Felix was left kneeling atop his Divine Tree, grasping at the opalescent crystal of its branches to steady his trembling.

"What the hell was that?" he asked—and, because the Continent had a sick sense of humor, Felix felt a new, deeply upsetting note rip through his senses. "Oh come *on*."

The world outside rippled, a sensation Felix—soaked in the innumerable vibrations of his recent battle—could detect even from within his core space.

Felix! Something bad is happening! His sense of Pit returned full-bore, now that the Creature was gone.

"Yeah." Though his Affinity was almost deafened by the profusion of recent events, he could feel Vess' sharp spike of awe and fear. "Of course it is."

Felix! Wha—something is---damn, my head! Something is attacking us!

Beef. If he was awake again, then his core needed to be checked on, not to mention whatever was out there. Felix cast about, trying to take in everything in his core space that had changed; to see if there was even a trace of the Creature remaining. He sensed nothing, but his ears were still ringing. He hadn't gotten a kill notification, but his Hunger had consumed the Creature. Right? *Damn it!*

He took a gamble. Felix hurled himself out of his core space and into his physical Body, finding himself surrounded by a complicated array carved from solid roots and glimmering golden-silver light. His friends were nearby, gathered at the edge of the array and staring with pale faces off into the distance.

Pit flashed out of his Spirit, landing next to him in the still waters. <<Those shadows don't look right.>>

<<They aren't.>> Felix peered through the blazing lights of the Abundance Anima's roots, Seal of the Breach fully active again for the first time in Ages. But…the Spirit Tree had sacrificed some of its potency to Felix in order to trap the Creature, and the Seal wasn't perfect. Out there, between the gleaming sigils and glyphs, perhaps a hundred yards away, the shadows roiled. Bulged.

Split.

Darkness poured from those rents, a substance that far surpassed the gelid shadow of the deeps, as shapes slithered from it. Deep within, Felix felt the familiar reverberating ache of a silver cord, now severed. The figures were limned with a terrible purple-blue light, filling their eyes and outlining their forms so effectively that Felix didn't have to use his Voracious Eye to identify them all.

<<Naga?>> *The broken Oath. Shit.* He looked back to where the War Naga were staring in confusion at the army of serpentine folk that emerged. <<Did you know? Was this planned?>>

Lavix's blunt face was a mask of horror. <<No. No, my Lord. This cannot be.>>

It was a portal through the shadowed liminal spaces and was the Creature's final act of rebellion. So, when an absolutely massive serpent emerged, eyes burning like purple fire, he wasn't surprised. Instead, the sight of his frenzied animation, so like the Fathom itself, drove a spike of deep, terrible guilt into his chest. *How did this happen?*

<<God Of Thunder and Flame!>> the Deepking roared, his Sunken Ward connecting with Felix's. An aura of writhing tendrils surmounted the Abyssal Serpent's head, a halo of vile ooze that was the Creature's calling card. <<Your reckoning has come! Children! The roots!>>

All at once, the literal army of Nagafolk scattered, heading for every glowing root they could find. Scimitars and tridents slashed and stabbed, drawing sparks from the powerful roots that nevertheless hurt the Spirit Tree. He could almost feel it.

<<I told you!>> Isla hissed. <<Traitorous snakes!>>

<<We must stop them!>> Vess said, flexing her legs as if to kick off after them…when the War Naga next to her convulsed.

<<My king?>> Lavix said just as she let out a surprised gasp of pain. Every single one of the War Naga doubled over, their humanoid portions gone suddenly, vividly purple. When they rose, their eyes burned with a mad purple flame.

<<Lavix?>> Vess asked, knuckles white around her spear.

<<We serve the Deepking, the Vessel of Noctis!>> They spoke and moved as one, flashing toward Vess with nothing but murder in their Spirits.

CHAPTER NINETY-NINE

<<Down!>> Beef warned and Isla leaped aside. Vess conjured Spears beneath the unmoving Bodies of Hallow and dragged them along, just as the War Naga rushed in. <<Keratin Conception!>>

Before Felix could move, a flood of dark energies spooled outward from the Minotaur, manifesting into giant, segmented legs of chitin. They crashed down, clasping around each of the War Naga with bone-shaking impact that briefly drove the breath from their lungs and trapped them against the lakebed. The serpentine warriors wriggled and raged, mouths foaming and tridents stabbing, but Beef screamed something unintelligible, and more constructs appeared to trap their weapons to the ground as well.

<<What the hell is going on?>> Beef asked, voice tight and breathless. He was shaking like he'd run for hours in a dead sprint. <<Why is the Deepking attacking us now?>>

"He is under control of the Creature," a voice rumbled from farther back.

Felix blinked in surprise to find the huge form of the Fathom laying limply in the sand. He was smaller than before, since he had been stripped of the Creature's oozing bulk—but not by much. His voice sounded strange at first, but Felix realized that he simply hadn't heard it before. It had always been the Creature talking through the Dragon.

"I...remember pieces. That Naga came here a long time ago, chasing power and prestige—" A dark, rusty laugh was forced through the immense Dragon's snout, ejecting bubbles that were quashed by the pressure of the water. "He made the same mistake I did. He entered the

Breach, an army at his back. They did not survive, and he…was changed. Sent away with a piece of the Creature left dormant in him."

The Dragon coughed, and pale, honey-colored fluid spattered into the water like smoke. "Nym…or whatever you are. You may have stopped a piece of the Creature, but it is as wily as any Dragon. My Mind has been soaked in its plans for too long. Its contingencies hold hidden facets that it has arranged for centuries." It rolled a single, great eye at him, too tired to lift his head. "You must flee."

<<Ridiculous,>> Vess stated. Hallow's forms were settled some distance away from the trapped War Naga, and she planted herself before the great beast. A child before a mountain. <<Felix defeated the Creature once. Together, we can do it again.>>

<<Yeah,>> Beef echoed, his voice just a touch too thin. <<A whole army of Naga? Psh. That's—that's like, a normal Tuesday.>>

<<You are all children playing with power that you cannot comprehend,>> Isla said, but her heart wasn't in her words. Her face was drawn, had been for some time, and she stared at the glowing Naga with blank eyes. <<There is only doom here.>>

"The Chanter is right. Doom." The Dragon closed its eyes. "Only doom."

Felix didn't respond to any of them, too busy sorting the mess of inputs that fought for his attention. His Affinity was still ringing painfully, but it was recovering fast. Strands of connection and meaning were weaving all around them in a chaotic storm that only he seemed to be aware of—but he was more than certain they weren't random. *Cause and effect. The choices we've made are all poised at the edge of a cliff, hovering above the drop. The Naga…*

He looked up. The Nagafolk, all of them limned in that purple-blue radiance that was the Creature's hallmark, were busy savaging the roots of the Abundance Anima. The Deepking had not moved, nor had Garox or his elite guards. They were watching Felix. Waiting for…something.

<<Why'd they even come here?>> Pit asked. <<They're trapped now. Couldn't the Creature have just run free in the Deepking's Body?>>

<<I don't know. I think—,>> Felix shook his head. His thoughts dwelled on the strange fist he had manifested within his core space. The Creature had been overcome by its power, but he had almost zero clue what it actually had done, only that the technique had driven it to desperation.

<<I do know they're trying to break the Seal on this place by eating the roots,>> Felix pointed out. He could feel the strength of the Abundance Anima waning slightly with each snuffed out sigil, but it was also

growing new roots for every one that the Nagafolk severed. <<If they do that, they'll be free again.>>

<<We cannot have that,>> Vess said, hefting her partisan. <<Shall we fight, then?>>

"You must," Paxus appeared beside Felix. This time, he looked far more present than before—even the sand beneath his feet seemed to dimple. "Ignore the snakes at the roots. Focus on the Vessel. They cannot break the Seal, but that is not their goal. We can sense it. Another presence, hidden—"

<<**SILENCE!**>>

Kar'casitrix, the Deepking, roared across the Breach, and space itself seemed to fold and buckle for the briefest of flashes. When it cleared, Paxus was gone.

<<What the hell did you just do?>> Felix asked. He scanned the mess of connections for evidence of his phantom ally, but there was only the Spirit Tree.

<<Swatted an insect. Nothing more,>> he said. Behind him, the Dark Passage finally closed, and what looked like thousands of Naga warriors had flooded the Breach, all of them intently hunting the sands. His voice took on the manyfold echoes of the Creature, finally putting to rest the hope that the Deepking was in any sort of control.

<<Felix Nevarre. False God of Thunder and Flame. You have chosen the wrong path.>> The possessed king of the Naga did not advance. He barely moved, in fact, aside from the writhing mane of tentacles around his enormous head. <<Where have you trapped the rest of me?>>

<<Creature. You think I'd let something that dangerous live? Let Trixie go.>> Felix patted his stomach. <<Cuz I've got plenty of room for dessert.>>

<<Impossible,>> the Deepking scoffed. <<Whatever bolt hole you have hidden my greater self within, I shall find it. I split off a fraction of my power into this Vessel to prepare for threats far more dire than you, Nym. You may have brought the Seal back to life, but it cannot hold, not when every lake in this Territory teems with my spawn. Not when the thousand Dens I have formed come to fruition. My victory is only a matter of time.>>

<<Why even bother to return, then?>> Felix asked, leaping atop one of the Abundance's roots. Felix spread his arms, claws black as the waters around them. <<Why not watch the Seal fall from the outside? I think I know. You're afraid. What scares you so much, Creature?>>

<<You—>> The Deepking roared, lunging forward before something hauled it back. The tendrils atop its head slashed at its Body.

<<Yeah,>> Felix said. <<Me.>>

Relentless Resolution!

Adamant Discord!

Felix launched like a comet from the earth, riding a bolt of lightning as thick as a city bus and cratering the lakebed behind him. He pulled, flashing toward the Deepking so fast that the water felt like fire against his exposed skin.

<<Warriors!>> The Creature drew itself up and snarled into the Breach. Eyes of mad purple gleamed from the darkness below. A field of fury. <<Kill him!>>

As one, the Nagafolk surged from below, serpentine bodies lashing for speed as their wide jaws opened in mad hunger.

<<No. I'm not killing them,>> Felix said, switching his focus. His connection to the Deepking and his people was strong—Felix had taken up a Quest for them at the cost of the escalating conflict in Haarwatch. It was a potent link between Choice and Consequence, the metaphysical bonds that seemed to govern this world.

But it wasn't his only one.

<<I'm just here for you!>>

Adamant Discord!

The Creature's eyes widened.

A surge of blue-white electricity vaporized the dark, a hundred feet wide and sizzling with compounded meaning. Consequence. Felix grabbed hold and didn't so much pull as hung on as he left the scattered Nagafolk warriors behind.

Hand of Cataclysm!

Rime Shaping!

Green Shaping!

Auroral Forge!

Cardinal Flame!

Felix hit the Deepking in the face, blasting forth with every shaping Skill he knew. The combined might of his spells ripped the layers of ooze from the Deepking's visage, splitting backward under the relentless deluge of acid, ice, life, light, and flame. The Creature's ooze-body flinched, peeling up from the blackened scales of Kar'casitrix's maw, writhing and undulating as it screamed.

<<You lost your connection to the Naga weeks ago!>> the Creature protested.

<<Not by choice!>> Felix snarled and finally jammed his hand onto his ally's snout. <<Trixie, if you're in there, hold on tight.>>

The mane of ooze-flesh snapped forward, Dissonance screaming from each and every tendril as it rushed for Felix's throat. They were too late.

Unite the Lost!

Felix reached down, grasping not his own significance to fuel the

Skill, but relying on his new Title, Devourer In Darkness, he plunged his hands into the spinning halo of his Hunger.

MINE!

Not yet, it isn't! Felix hauled back, pitting his Mind against the stubborn sapience in the black...and it relented. He surged back up and hurled the lot of it like gasoline into a fire.

The Deepking ignited.

Or rather, the ooze that surrounded him did, erupting in red-gold flame that forced it off the king of the Nagafolk, back into the cold waters of its prison. But Felix wasn't done there. He bore down on the connections amassing all around him, woven threads like silver chains between king and his people, and sent Unite the Lost racing along them. Red-gold flame erupted in a swelling wave, spreading from Felix outward into the thousands of Nagafolk. They lit up like torches in the night, screaming in sudden, excruciating pain before all of them went suddenly limp.

Not dead. Free. For perhaps the first time in a very long time.

Sovereign of Flesh!

The moment Unite the Lost ran its course, the ooze pounced. It leaped over the unconscious form of Trixie and surged for Felix's throat—only to be caught by his undeniable Will.

Foul Nym! How? You Cannot Hold That Skill! The Creature rippled and writhed in Felix's grasp, held at bay only feet from accomplishing its murderous intent. **That Is The Province Of The Gods!**

<<Really? That's interesting,>> Felix said, trying not to pant too hard. His clawed hand was steady, at least, as he held back the sliver of Noctis, Goddess of the Night. <<Because I got it by becoming a Primordial of the Unseen Tide.>>

The ooze's Spirit all but froze. **You Cannot Be.**

He hauled it closer, peering into its bubbling mass with eyes that he knew were burning blue. <<Explain.>>

Teeth of black formed atop the purple-blue goo. It snarled at him. **I Shall Die Before Revealing Anything To You.**

Felix clenched his jaw. <<Fine.>>

Chthonic Tribute!

<<Have it your way.>>

The Creature's scream tangled Dissonance and Harmony and wrapped them into baleful chords, but Felix weathered it, flexing the shaking walls of his Bastion to their utmost. It clawed and tore through his channels, his core, but it could not escape.

The Seal within caught it, then his Hunger.

The Creature was gone, once more.

YUM.

Quest Complete!

Defend The Depths!
The Deepking has outlined a nascent threat to your Authority: the Fathom. Find and neutralize the threat, protect your new people, and seek out the Fathom's purpose.
Purpose 1/1

XP Earned!
Authority Increased In The Ghreldan Hills!

<<Is everyone alright?>> Felix asked as he floated back down to his friends. All but Vess were huddled away from the still-trapped War Naga, who had fallen just as unconscious as the rest of their people when Felix had removed the Creature's influence. Of his spear-wielding friend, there was no sign. <<Isla. Injury report.>>

The Chanter looked up at him and frowned. <<We are all at full Health, with only passing Status Conditions, though some of us have expended an unwise portion of our Mana and Stamina.>> She shot a mild glare at a sheepish-looking Beef. He was sitting on the ground, tired as hell and holding the head of his Multipede in his lap while the Homunculus hung off his back. <<And others have crossed unwise thresholds.>>

Felix had noticed that. <<And yourself?>>

Isla's eyes widened imperceptibly…to all but people like Felix, at least. That had surprised her. <<I am simply tired.>> She gestured brusquely to the glowing rim that marked the distant exit above. The edge of the Breach. <<Will this Seal allow us to leave?>>

"It will not. You are all trapped, as I have been these many Ages." The voice of the Dragon boomed around them, a feeling Felix still did not enjoy while immersed entirely in water. He could feel it shake his entire Body, though it left him unmoved. Others, like the stirring Nagafolk, were tossed back several inches. "You cannot defeat the Creature, Nym. No one can."

Felix traded glances with Isla, who shrugged her shoulders. He stepped toward the mountainous bulk of the Fathom, passing by Beef with a simple pat on the shoulder. <<You good, dude?>>

<<Y—yeah. I'll be alright,>> the Minotaur said, but he was still pretty shit about veiling his Spirit. Felix felt a hard-edged sorrow at his

center, but it was bolstered by a steady pulse of what he could only describe as conviction.

<<We'll talk soon,>> he promised before swimming ahead.

<<Yeah. Okay.>>

Felix was worried for his friend. He had no idea how well he'd been able to reconfigure his core space, or whether he'd been able to use the Primordial's power to push into the Ring Stage. Beef certainly felt stronger, but there was no gauge or readout that his Voracious Eye could display. Felix wouldn't be sure until he could delve into his core space again.

Focus. You have Dragons to talk to, he told himself. As if he needed to be reminded as he swam up to the huge, wedge-shaped head of the Fathom. *Former Fathom?*

This was the first time Felix had been able to inspect the Dragon since he had been freed of the Creature. He was covered in scales of varying size, shape, and ruggedness, from the small, smooth scales around his eyes and nostrils to the large, ridged ones that coated his neck and back. All of him was dull gold, dirty and smudged and scarred, like the ancient jewelry of a hoarder, and a mane of dirty white fur surrounded his head and back, caught up between branching antlers of what appeared to be crystal.

And at his side, sitting and staring daggers at him, was Vess. With Pit at her side.

"The Devourer in Darkness," he rumbled, and the voice was even worse up close. Felix had to sink to the ground to banish the worst of its vibrations. "A fitting Title for such a warrior. Now, tell me, slayer of monsters—if I entreat you—" The Dragon opened its giant eye. It was all gold within, though there was an iris and pupil present, all of it so close in coloration that the Dragon's eye seemed a solid whole.

"Would you kill me as well?"

CHAPTER ONE HUNDRED

<<That's—that's a heavy ask.>> Felix managed to keep his tone level because he could feel the weight of the Dragon's Spirit behind the words; he was serious. Buying for time, he adjusted the Garment around his shoulders. Mana flowed into it, restoring its torn appearance into a short jacket, tunic, and loose trousers. He looked to Vess, but she was still staring down the languid Dragon and was shaking a bit. Pit shrugged but stayed huddled at her side, one wing over her shoulders. <<Why would I do that? I put a lot of effort into not killing you in the first place.>>

"You—" The great, golden eye blinked. A loud *whumph* pulsed through the water, followed by a second and a third. The Dragon was *laughing*. "You stayed your hand?"

Felix raised his eyebrows. "Well, yeah." He flared his Voracious Eye. "You're strong, remarkably so, even without the Creature attached to your hip, but I gave the Creature a chance to stop its actions. It chose not to listen. But you weren't in a place to be making any choices at all."

Another giant, golden blink. "Choice," he rumbled. "Words of the Nym."

<<Are they? That makes sense.>>

"You are…Nymean?"

<<More or less,>> Felix said with a shrug. <<Does it matter? The System might mock me with the slogan, but it's not wrong. Everyone is entitled to choose their path, and all choices have consequences. The Creature was blind to that—and now it's gone.>>

"Gone…I do not believe that, but you have come closer than any other, Child of Nym." The Dragon's nostrils widened, snorting in a great lungful of water and silt. "You smell of Authority. A great deal of it. Claim mine as well, then. These old scales hold potency yet. Let my death be the catalyst to advance you beyond your enemies."

<<You will not be dying, Yintarion.>>

The golden wyrm jerked his enormous head, the largest movement yet, as Vess floated down before him. "Dragoon. An offshoot of the Betrayers themselves. Do not think that you have a say in my fate."

It was Vess' turn to flinch at that, and Felix found himself lost. Something had gone on between the two—Dragon and Dragoon—and it had something to do with their connection. There was a great Link between the two of them, though Felix didn't think anyone else could see it. The chain of meaning was bright gold, different from the Links he held with Vess, Beef, and the others. In fact, it reminded him mostly of his bond with Pit, were it not lacking something intrinsically vital.

<<She saved you,>> Pit pointed out, zooming around the Dragon's snout on his enchanted fish's tail. He turned in lazy corkscrews through the water, his wings cutting bubbling trails in the languid liquid before landing in a heavy burst of cloudy sand. <<She cut the gap into the Creature's hold on you. Without that, Felix and I wouldn't have been able to separate you.>> Pit let out a low, throaty trill. <<We'd have eaten you, too.>>

Yintarion seemed at a loss for words in the face of this entire experience. Felix felt for him; he'd been there before. Vess, however, pressed her advantage.

<<The Primordial of the Withering Dust, it,>> she hesitated, licking her lips. Her dark brown eyes were locked to the Dragon's golden one, but everything else about her, from the twist of her lips to the set of her folded arms, demonstrated a frantic urge to be *away*. With what seemed like monumental effort, his friend forced her hands to her sides and squared her shoulders. <<A connection was established. A Link. I can no longer feel it, but it let me glimpse into your Memories. The Primordial—it gave me Skills, powers that no Dragoon has ever held, which bridged some uncanny gap between our Minds.>>

"Primordial? You cannot trust the touch of them. They are cursed."

<<I am aware. This one was..." Vess looked to Felix, who nodded. "This one was cleansed of its curse. Its power was pure, simply too much. It changed many things within my core space. My movement Skills, spearwork Skills, even my specialized taunt. Now—the Lament, it—>>

"The Matriarch's Lament was one of the evolved Skills of the Dragoons who reached Adept Tier." Yintarion's mouth twisted, much the same as Vess', as if he tasted something sour. "Rana bore that Skill."

<<Tr–truly?>> Vess asked. The stoic anger in her Spirit had been

wavering, but now it collapsed entirely. In its place was a glimmer of distant silver light. Felix smiled as he identified the vibration.

Hope. Huh. Where's this gonna go?

"I…am aware of your aid, little Dragoon. But our…connection… does not give you power over me or my decisions. As the Nymean said: choice is paramount."

<<Then I choose not to kill you,>> Felix said.

Yintarion gave a frustrated huff, and his breath alone toppled several of the nearby statues. "Authority or not, you will not stop me from this, boy."

<<I will.>>

A cold silence stretched between them, punctuated only by the uneasy groans of a slow-waking army of Nagafolk, and the faint, almost inaudible cursing of Isla.

"You ate the Creature."

<<I did.>>

"How?"

<<Trapped it.>> Felix waved his hand. <<Not really important, but it is gone. Or will be, in time, anyway.>>

"Impossible. It was a sliver of a goddess. You cannot eat a god."

<<Who told you that?>> Felix asked. He was genuinely curious. <<Everyone is always so confident about that.>>

The Dragon narrowed its one eye, the only one he could see from his vantage point. The thing's head was so huge, Felix would have had to swim thirty feet over its snout to see the other side. "You claim to eat gods and cleanse horrors beyond knowing. You burn brightly with power, so-called Nym. Too much power. What are you, really?"

Felix grinned. <<I—>>

Just as the words formed on his tongue, Felix's core space gave a sudden, dizzying lurch. A sizable chunk of the Creature's potency fell beyond the event horizon of his Hunger. Not only devoured, but digested. Yet his world quaked with a cataclysmic murmur of discontent.

MORE. FE-LIX.
MORE.

A great suction pulled at his insides, like a vacuum had been shoved into his veins. All of the swirling impurities, the sizzling bits of char and purple-blue haze of uncaught Essence-flesh was seized and hauled wholesale into his Hunger. The blockage around his Perception and Affinity was snatched away, replaced by a keenness that set his Divine Tree to ringing. Felix stumbled to his knees, and the messy chaos of his senses snapped back into abrupt, intense focus.

FELIX!

The scream cut across time and space, rippling through his core like a dozen messages in a bottle. He could feel how old they were—how urgent. Days, hours, minutes, all of it colliding at once as visions of fire and fury filled Felix's Mind like a bucket beneath a waterfall.

Someone was screaming.

Men and women in blue coats and purple capes were falling, severed by blades of golden light or obliterated by flame. Ships rose from dark forests, and figures in milky-white armor stood imperiously upon their decks. Executioners.

<<Felix?>> Vess was saying, attempting to pull his too-heavy frame up from the ground. Pit was under his torso, doing the lion's share of the work. <<Felix what's happening? Is it back? Has the Creature returned?>>

<<Haarwatch,>> he gasped and almost fumbled Sunken Ward in his disoriented state. <<We need to get to Haarwatch. Now. They're dying.>>

Vess let out a strangled sound. <<Across the Continent? We would first need to get back to Haestus, and then from your Stronghold to Haarwatch. It is weeks of travel!>>

<<We've already lost too much time.>> Felix blinked, gaping at the rising amount of clarity that digesting a chunk of the Creature had afforded him. He still felt the connections of things, vivid as ever, but now there was a twisting he could feel, like a wind made of cool glass. It hid from things, tucked into the fabric of deepest shadows, places where the realm had been worn immeasurably thin. The renewed Seal thrust it into sharp relief, but it wasn't a function of it. <<Too much time has passed. Weeks. And yet…how long have we been down here?>>

<<Days—>> Vess said.

<<Three weeks in the Breach alone,>> Isla also said, with the same amount of confidence. The women traded surprised looks before the Chanter pursed her lips.

"Time moves strangely within the Breach," the Dragon said. It was staring at him again, his curiosity more apparent than ever. "The Creature's nature bends it, and it has been here for a very long time."

<<Noctis. Goddess of the Night,>> Isla said, swimming closer. <<But not only the night. Her power held sway over the liminal spaces. The Dark Passages were her demesne.>>

Felix's head swirled with ideas. Some…riskier than others. *Paxus? Paxus, are you still alive?*

Faintly, as if from an immense distance away, he heard the phantom's voice. All of them did. *A tricky question, that.*

Fuck, Felix sent in relief. <<You weren't blasted apart. Can you open

the Seal here? The Abundance is getting stronger, and I don't want to hurt it.>>

No.

<<Huh. Do we chop down the trees, then?>> Beef asked. He had his maul slung over his shoulder and an uneasy smile on his face. <<Doesn't seem right, honestly. The Abundance has been like, top-tier support this whole time.>>

<<We're not doing that,>> Felix agreed. <<Paxus. Any other ideas? We need to get out of here and to Haarwatch immediately.>>

Look below.

All sensation of the phantom Nym vanished after that, and even the Abundance Anima would not respond to Felix's inquiries, other than to indicate it was recovering.

<<Below? What does that mean?>> Beef asked, already looking into the deep cracks they'd driven into the lakebed. It offered nothing but shadows and sand. <<We're at like, bedrock right now, right?>>

<<Spread out! Look at anything you can!>> Vess commanded, then was swift to act. She soared through the waters, lightning crackling from her partisan as readily as spectral dragon wings formed atop her back. She hit a nearby column hard enough to snap it in half and send the base tumbling aside.

Beef ran after, chitin spikes thrusting from the earth like pry bars, tossing apart the broken remains of the Creature's odd temple. Homunculus Hallow, still uncharacteristically silent, hung about his neck, while the Multipede clattered behind like a loyal dog.

<<Pit,>> Felix said, finding his Companion already at his side. <<What do you think?>>

The tenku sniffed the air, then turned fully around, just as a rumbling voice spoke.

"Nym-Who-Is-Not."

The Dragon had been quiet during the entire exchange, though it was clear he heard it all, even Paxus' messages. Now Felix looked at him and realized he'd reared up, just a touch, so that his head was no longer resting on the broken earth.

"My time enslaved to the Creature's Will is hazy, but I retain scraps, as I said." He took a deep breath that was still shaky, for all its terrible heaviness. "If I aid you, will you grant me peace? I cannot go on as I have, not after Ages of torment. Not after losing all that mattered."

Felix and Pit watched the Dragon for a long, measuring moment. Unsurprisingly, their Spirits were united in their opinion of the former Fathom, and Felix nodded with every earnest bone in his body. <<I will.>>

The mountainous Dragon almost deflated, his Spirit sounding as a gong of ancient sorrow and tired triumph. "Very well. The statues. I can feel a piece of the Creature hiding in the one I just knocked over."

Felix's clarified senses felt it too, once he focused on them. It was extremely faint, as if only a fraction of a fraction had been invested into the monstrous sculptures...but there were a *lot* of them around the Breach.

<<Wow. Talk about contingency plans.>>

"Gather them up, as you did the Creature itself. Provide the fuel, Nym—" Yintarion bared his teeth, and the shadows fled from his golden gaze. "I shall pave the way."

<<Oooh!>> trilled Pit. <<The fun begins!>>

CHAPTER ONE HUNDRED ONE

"Mervin! Above!"

Without conscious thought, Mervin Cors lifted his shield, Mana sizzling atop it in a sporadic show of blue light. Thankfully, the Skill—or more likely, the thick slab of steel on his arm—was enough to stop the gleaming Fire Arrows.

Shield Mastery is level 32!
Force Barrier is level 22!

It did not stop the charge of another Initiate, in whose hand glowed a conjured sword of light. "Diurnal Rupture!"

"Drilling Thrust!" Mervin cried out in response, and the sword in his hand lit up with streamers of blue and bright yellow, forming a whirling, buzzing cone. Force and heat propelled his strike farther, skewering the Initiate's broadsword near its tip. The blade shattered, and Mervin pressed his advantage, batting aside the pieces and committing to the attack. He thrust, and soft flesh and hard bone split, but not before the bastard stomped on his boots.

You Have Killed An Initiate Of The Inviolate Inquisition!
XP Earned!

Drilling Thrust is level 42!

Warning!
Stamina Is Less Than 10%!

Health Is Less Than 50%!

Status Condition!
Broken Foot: Severe!

Mervin shoved the dead Inquisitor off his sword and fumbled for a yellow and red potion at his waist before biting off the corks and quaffing them together. They tasted like sour piss, but Mervin was beyond caring. The battlefield around him was a mess of dirty armor and flashing Skills, too wild and incoherent for him to parse much, but his team had cut out a moment of silence. He breathed and flexed his grip as he fought to ignore his broken foot.

Things were going poorly.

He was surrounded by Blades, Bones, Fists, and the blue-coated Haarguard by the dozen, but they had been met by overwhelming numbers. After the initial volley from the Hierocratic forces, the warriors led by Commander Reed had been in trouble, and Commander Kastos had ordered them onto the muddy battlefield to bring the lot of them back to the wall.

Explosions ripped across the field, blooms of fire and ice and shadow, and Mervin barely ducked. How long had he been fighting?

Days prior, Mervin had started off eager to prove himself. He hadn't passed muster months back when Lady Aren and Commander Kastos had tested the Legionnaires. Before the Lord Autarch had vanished. He'd figured it was his time to show off the Skills he'd sharpened to a killing edge in the Foglands, clearing that Domain and hunting the various monsters in the thick forests. With an entire city's powerful defenses to fall back on and an army bigger than anything he'd heard the Guilders ever fielding, Mervin had been confident. This, he had thought, was to be his chance to be noticed.

It had devolved into a horror almost immediately.

First had been the spiders—Orbweaver Minions—whose legs were sharp as daggers and whose fangs dripped with Apprentice-Tier poison. Then came the Lamellan hordes and their nightmare spores. Mervin had seen too many people die, choking on blood and vomit as mushrooms bloomed upon their soon-to-be corpses. He had cheered the loudest when the mages had burnt the last of them.

Now, the Hierocracy had attacked, and Mervin was learning what a *real* army was like. The orderly ranks of the Inquisitors and Paladins were like freshly oiled gears, moving in perfect sync as Skill after Skill was lobbed at his head. In comparison, all Haarwatch had was enthusiasm, and that was a dim copy of the enemy's zealotry.

Pathless...why? Why send your armies against us? Order rules us, gives us

Strength. And our Purity of purpose cannot be denied. We have survived! Would you rather us die?

Mervin's prayer went unanswered, as it always did. Yet the entreaty was all he could do as his Stamina refilled, and his foot throbbed like mad. The Status Condition wasn't going anywhere. He simply had to endure the pain.

In the opening blows, Commander Reed's prowess had stymied the Hierocracy's attacks, slapping them out of the air with contemptuous ease before cutting through their rank and file. The Legion and Haarguard had rallied behind the man, roaring their defiance at pristine armor and bloody cloaks. It was thrilling, until the numbers of the redcloaks overwhelmed the Commander's ability to cover.

The fog that was their ally mattered less in close combat and broad, sweeping volleys of sizzling light magic. Commander Reed's retreat to the city walls had been stymied by Inquisitors in huge, summoned armor—armor that shrugged off all but the mightiest of magic and physical blows. With the armored Inquisitors at their back and the advancing army at their front, their band of warriors was trapped. All they could do was fight for their very lives and hope for a miracle.

City shield's still holding, Mervin thought. His Mind felt numb and sluggish. He hefted his sword and shield, tightening the straps. *Just gotta get to the wall. Get through the Inquisitors. Get them back. Do it, now.*

As Mervin lurched forward, one of his fellow Blades fell with a cry, brought low by a burning arrow to his eye. Flowing over his twitching corpse, two Initiates bared their glowing swords, edges aimed at Mervin's throat.

"Force Barrier!" Mervin threw up his shield behind the flimsy layer of force Mana, but the first sword only skittered off its surface before falling limply to the ground. "Uh?"

You Have Killed An Initiate Of The Inviolate Inquisition!
XP Earned!

"Hoo, they almost got you, there Mervin!" Thaddeus Thangle stepped from between the two collapsing Initiates with a long, curved dagger in his grip. Holes had been neatly punched into the backs of both of their necks. The Gnome looked a bit singed, but better than most. "You okay, kid? Need a morale boost? I got a few Rallying Cries left."

"Keep it in your back pocket, Thad," Mervin said, dropping his shield with a relieved sigh. Chaos reigned all around them, separated by only a few ranks of their fellows. Mervin set his jaw and moved toward the gap. "Do you have enough Mana to do an Obfuscation on me?"

Thangle grimaced, fingers playing with the empty jars at his waist.

"Not for a while yet, even with that Mana potion at your side. Got enough to keep myself a bit foggy, but it wouldn't do much for a Human, even one that's your size."

"Damnation."

A sharp whistle caught their ears as a man with a flame-red beard leaped over their heads. His woven leather armor flowed with him as he spun, performing an incredible roll in mid-air as he loosed his bow. Green-gold arrows flashed outward, striking the earth only paces from the nearest redcloaks. Vines burst from their impact point, filling the sodden earth a dozen, thorn-lined snares that tangled legs and weapons. The orderly forces fell, trampling one another, and the archer landed among them, breathing heavy.

"Mervin! Thangle! We're making the push! Go now!" Karp lifted his bow, manifesting more arrows upon the bowstring. "We'll hold them off!"

Sentinel's Regard is level 49!

Mervin could hear others spreading the same word, and his Perception Skill snagged on the vague details only strides away. Bodie. Vivianne. Kelgan. Yan. And here, Karp. Companions of Lady Boscal, who trained with the Autarch himself. Warriors ran past them like rocks in a stream, fleeing the final strides to the city gate as walls of sand, vines, steel, and sigaldry put pause on the Hierocracy's advance.

"Karp? You're staying?" Thangle blinked his big eyes at the Human archer, as if he really were just some old man who had gone too deep into this war. "You'll die, boy!"

"Maybe. Or maybe I got the Fiend's own luck, eh?" Karp grinned before letting another six arrows fly in the span of a breath. "Now run!"

The field had cleared, their forces having fled and the redcloaks and Paladins held for a few moments longer. Thangle started moving toward the city but stopped when he noticed Mervin had not. "Kid, now's not the time to play hero. Get to the gate; we can make a difference on the wall!"

"No. I'm not getting far on this foot, and even if I did, I'm no mage or archer. I've got my sword, and that's it." Mervin stepped forward, standing next to a surprised Karp. "I'm with you, sir."

The man's flame-red beard split in a wild grin. "Good on ya! Just aim for the ones I miss!"

Mervin heard a pained groan, and Thangle stumped forward to stand at his side, hair wild and unkempt. He snapped his fingers. "Gimme that Mana Potion, then." He grabbed it from Mervin's outstretched hand and chugged it down in three hearty swallows. "Eugh! The things I do to keep you kids safe."

The sand wall burst apart, vines snapping and sigils blown out as six Inquisitors in golden armor charged through it. Behind them, the orderly ranks of the Hierocracy followed in a terrifying rush, a wordless cry upon their lips.

Mervin raised his sword. "For the Fiend!"

Sword watched the battle unfold below them through heavy-lidded eyes. A chair had been brought to him, and though he didn't need it, he lounged indolently. The enemy could not see his face through his smooth helmet, but they could certainly read body language, and Sword wanted all of the heretics to know that they weren't a concern. Not to him, nor by extension the Hierophant.

Truthfully, he *was* bored. The battle—if one could call it that—raged in sputtering volleys and wan Skills. Few hits landed from the Inquisitors, thanks to the accursed fog, though the Paladins were having better luck up close. Fewer still were actually reaching Haarwatch's walls. There, though he could barely see it, ancient wards rippled with every stray attack, a patchwork shield that seemed dredged from some ruin. It was holding, though, despite the assault by spiders and mushroom monsters his people had urged before them. Sword clucked his tongue, his boredom easing by the smallest of increments. The weaklings were, no doubt, fueling their wards with cartloads of monster cores and would run out sooner or later.

The entire battle was a farce. He wanted nothing more than to end it, but they weren't here to murder the trash. They were here to teach them a *lesson.*

To defy the Hierocracy was to defy the Pathless Himself.

Yet the heretics refused to back down. Worse, they were picking off the weaker among the orders, slaying them through cowardly tactics and Mana Skills that were flung from the walls with little regard for conserving their energy. He had counted at least two hundred mages there, and more must have been rotating in—or else these children had more Mana at their disposal than was possible.

They've clearly trained to fight in large groups as well. The heretics possess a meager amount of skill. More than that, the salvaged monster cores indicated they had able alchemists and inscriptionists to hand. Recovering enough usable cores to run an entire city that had been stripped of its defenses only months prior?

Sword wouldn't be surprised to learn that every warrior was trained in the recovery of such things, foolish as that was. Few would waste their resources in such a way. To teach disposable meat shields how to craft was akin to instructing an Avum to dance; all the bird was required to do was run when commanded.

Tome hummed to himself, flipping a page in his overly large book. The silver filigree flashed in the afternoon sun as his long-time ally peered over the prow like a curious bird. "They are strong, but not strong enough. Were we to concentrate our efforts, I predict a five percent chance of our loss."

"That's too high." Spear asked. "I could end this with a single spell, Tome. There's no chance of us losing, if we were actually allowed off this damn boat."

"Explain, Tome," Sword demanded, not bothering to look away from the battle. Together, the four of them could best any Grandmaster —and they had the record to prove it. Spear had the right of it; were they to apply themselves to this paltry conflict, it would soon be over.

"Because we haven't seen their leader yet," Mace growled and Tome chuckled in that languid way of his. She gripped the thick weapon at her side and leaned against the thick span of her tower shield. "He'd better show soon. I want to see how this man likes the taste of his own blood."

"Patience," Sword ordered.

"This Autarch is a coward. Hiding behind his fog and his walls while his people fight." Spear sniffed, her voice faintly metallic behind her helm. "This would be over already, were he simply to surrender."

"The lessons must be taught," Tome said before looking at Sword. "But perhaps we can speed up the process?"

Sword tapped his chin. "Very well. Arm the Mana Cannon."

Mace yanked her huge shield from the deck with a single hand. "Yes! Let loose the cannons!"

"Target, my Lord?" asked an Inquisitor with an exacting bow.

"Ahmm." Sword leaned further back, stretching his back needlessly. The image was all that mattered. "Aim for the gates."

"As you wish, my Lord."

CHAPTER ONE HUNDRED TWO

Volleys of arrows filled the sky, erupting in tangling vines and thorn-spitting plants as a mace made of compacted earth smashed the redcloaks back. Erupting spikes of steel stabbed through boot and greave, hobbling the lower-leveled Initiates, while sizzling acid burst from hastily inscribed sigaldry.

The Hierocratic forces led with their weakest at the fore, and that was all that allowed Mervin's allies this moment. Had they sent their strongest, the battle would have already been over. Mervin couldn't spare the portion of his Mind needed to understand such ruthless tactics, other than a phrase echoed by his trainers time and again. *Forged in battle.*

Shield Mastery is level 36!
Force Barrier is level 24!
Sword Mastery is level 36!
Drilling Thrust is level 44!

You Have Learned A Skill!
Pain Resistance (Uncommon)!

Pain Resistance is level 2!
...
Pain Resistance is level 6!

His leveling Skills were all that had saved him as, time and again, the hampered redcloaks came within a finger's-breadth of killing him.

Mervin wove among the encroaching redcloaks, his foot nothing more than a red-hot lump of pain at the end of his leg. He spared a glance back, just in time to see the last of their warriors retreat behind the Sunrise Gate, and felt a sharp exhale of relief.

They'd accomplished the mission.

Yet Mervin found himself fighting on, stabbing at nearby Initiates with newfound rage in his veins. He could have made a run for it, perhaps even made it to the Gate while Karp and the others fought on…but no. Mervin was done with running.

He fought on, sword and shield stabbing and parrying with every ounce of technique and Skill he could muster. He hamstrung tangled opponents, blinded them, even drove their own burning blades into one another while Thangle blurred about, stabbing groins with his curved daggers.

It was chaos, and they were being beaten back.

Flaming swords of steel and armored bodies filled his vision as magic and brawn was brought to bear against their limited number. Bodie was knocked back by a behemoth of golden light, while Kelgan was all that stood between Karp and the burning blasts of crimson-armored Paladins. Mervin could no longer see Vivianne nor Yan. The press of bodies and Skills was too much.

Above the shouts and noise came an odd whirring sound so loud that Mervin fouled his riposte, nearly slicing his own hand off. That was nothing, however, compared to the almighty scream as the world was suffused with golden radiance.

"Mervin! Get down!" Thangle yelled.

It was an unnecessary command; the passage of the blast was so great it threw the entire battlefield to their faces as it tore above them. Past them. Directly at the wall.

"The gate!" Mervin tried to stand, but his foot twisted between the legs of a dead Initiate, and he collapsed with a cry. "The gate is—!"

"Fine." Karp lowered his bow, for just a moment, as he stared in wonder back toward Haarwatch. "Just fine. Look!"

A sizzling dome of crystalline power had coated the gate—the entire wall—and pulsed with a swirling brown and green-gold radiance. The faintest of cracks shimmered, strides from the gate itself, but even they closed before Mervin's wondering eyes.

"She did it," Thangle said with a heavy breath. "Lady Zara did it."

Sword sat up.

"What in the Light is *that*?" he demanded.

"Ah, uhm, it would seem that the heretics have utilized some form of crystallized Mana to generate another shield layer," stammered the attending Inquisitor. The man was sweating beneath his enameled plate, and his eyes flicked between all four members of the High Guard as they crowded him and the railing. "One th–that seems able to withstand our Mana Cannon."

Mace laughed, and Sword looked at her sharply. "What?" she asked. "They don't have Dragon's claws, but damn it'll be fun cracking that turtle's shell."

Sword grabbed the Inquisitor by the breastplate and lifted him bodily until they were face to helmet. The man's Spirit almost broke beneath a spike of sudden fear, but Sword ignored it. "Fire the Mana Cannons again. All of them."

———

Atop one of the four towers on the Sunrise Wall, a figure in flowing black robes stood upon a crystalline plinth. In her hands was what seemed like a piece of the sky itself, raised up and pulsing with rainbow waves of power. Ochre hands clutched the blue orb, now covered in crystals like a fine netting, upon which those rainbow waves rippled.

Crystalline Matrices Is At 78%
More Mana Is Required!

Zara blew a frustrated breath through her teeth, fighting against the scouring of her channels. The shield had not yet been ready, not for a battle of this scale, but Zara had been afforded few other options. She was barely holding it together with sheer Willpower, Intent, and her small store of Might. The Grand Harmony sang around her, through her, into the crystalline matrices that housed the Domain Core.

As did the modified siphon array they had centered upon her.

Zara's awareness encompassed all of them, some three hundred volunteers who were now writhing under the pain of the array. The working was not refined, built as it was in the field, and aside from Felix, it had never been used by anyone on such a scale. Perhaps the boy and his unique abilities allowed it to work better for him, but Zara strained to keep the array from immediately ripping the magic out of her people. Slow and steady, she repeated, bending the Grand Harmony to slow the transmission until she needed more—if she gave it free rein, the array would extract every spare ounce of Mana on offer, leaving her people unconscious at best.

"You may choose to act at any time, Mister Knacht!" Zara shouted.

"It's not ready yet!" Alister cried out from the wall below. Zara couldn't see him directly, but her Perception encompassed him and his tarp-covered project. "I need another quarter glass!"

"We haven't the time!" Zara warned, just as the massive Manaships began to hum once more. "They are firing again! Avet's teeth…they're charging all three! Brace yourselves!"

Particles of Mana swarmed the three large cannons that hung from the bottoms of the crafts, each one a marvel of milky-white steel and crimson-gold sigaldry. Fractions of a heartbeat later, the particles coalesced into a spinning lattice of living light. Zara saw it all as if through eternity's lens, one moment flowing into another as each Manaship charged their weapons. The lattice spiraled in on itself, until it collapsed entirely, leaving only a bar of gleaming, golden light that tore through the sky.

All three of them hit at once.

A blazing pain speared through Zara's Mind, Body, and Spirit as her shield was ripped apart entirely. Gleaming, crystalline facets burst under the combined salvo of Hierocratic might, and a bloodthirsty cheer sounded from the field. Their Tempered lungs easily overcame the cries of terror and sudden injury of her defenders.

Crystalline Matrices Is At 2%
More Mana Is Required!
Failure Imminent!

Zara hurriedly disengaged the siphon array, releasing her volunteers with a ragged gasp. Those who still remained standing stumbled away, hands to head or guts as Mana drain set in. The Chanter could not spare attention for them.

Crystalline Matrices Set To Standby!
Mana Siphon Disengaged!

The Manaships began to charge yet another round, but far more concerning was the figure in milky white armor that leaped from the flagship. They landed with a sound that split the very earth.

"This bores me! Heretics! Let me test your mettle myself!"

"Mace!" Sword growled, but the woman was already charging forward, shield and namesake weapon held high. A brace of Journeyman warriors formed up to meet her, but they would stand no chance. "Spear. Get down there. Bring her back."

"Perhaps she will draw out this reclusive Autarch," Spear mused, fingering the edge of her weapon. "At any rate, I imagine our odds—how do you say it, Tome? Our odds of sustaining minimal losses have increased by a significant margin."

"Go. *Now.*"

Still chortling, Spear leaped from the deck.

"She is not wrong, you know," Tome said.

"Quiet. You," Sword snapped. "Fire the cannons as soon as they recharge. I want that wall sundered."

"Pitiful!"

Mervin stumbled back, horrified by the mountainous woman who had trampled her own army, shoving even fully Tempered Paladins and Inquisitors from her path, before punching through Bodie's wall of sand with a single, off-handed strike.

The man was bloody and barely standing, his huge muscles unable to stop the descent of the armored woman's huge, red-gold mace. It smashed into his pauldrons, ripping through them and into the meat of his shoulder. Bodie fell.

"You dare wield a mace with a Strength so low?" she said through a disdainful snort. "You must be joking."

"Nnng, sometimes it's not about personal strength," Bodie said, spitting out a few teeth. Mervin paled, hand barely able to hold onto his blade. "Sometimes, it's all about finding the right sorta friends."

"Pike Field!"

"Span's Edge!"

Steel spikes ripped upward, thick as swords and as tall as any man. Behind them came Kelgan, spear thrust out to catch the gap between the woman's elbow joint. Meanwhile, the bald, mustachioed Yan slid down low, brandishing his twin short swords like a pair of shears.

The huge woman in smooth, white armor moved too fast to track.

Mervin blinked, and the spikes were shattered, then both Kelgan and Yan were in the dirt. Bloody and unmoving.

"Who else?" the woman roared, her voice carrying like a giant's roar. She tore off her helmet, revealing a square, ruddy face filled with freckles and a cascade of thick, auburn hair. "Who else can this pathetic city throw at me? Hm?"

Something tapped Mervin's leg, almost making the young man collapse in fright. "Shh! It's just me!" Thangle said. "We have to run! We can only die against the likes of her."

"What of the others?" Mervin asked, looking to the sigils that erupted around the mace-wielding monster. Acid splashed up against her armor and failed to even blemish its polished surface.

"The others will do as they will! You proved yourself to them already. Run, boy!"

"I'll not leave them behind!" Mervin insisted.

"No one gets left behind today," another voice said, loud enough that it made the mace-wielding maniac pause. An armored figure landed in the dirt strides away from Mervin, short and stocky but wide with muscle and steel. Twin axes were alive with silver flames.

Commander Kastos, Mervin thought with profound relief.

"High Guard!" the Commander bellowed. "I've come for your head!"

Behind him came a fresh group of warriors, at least a half battalion, the lot of them bearing the purple cloaks of the Fiend's Claw. They lifted their weapons as they ran from the Sunrise Gate, all of them shouting. "For Nagast! For the Fiend!"

"For Haarwatch and Lady Cal!"

The woman stopped her weapon mid-swing, moments from cleaving Kelgan's head from his shoulders. Her face split with an eager, joyous grin. "Oh? A little army and an…Adept Tier. How unexpected in this backwater, but hardly enough for me to waste my time."

Commander Reed landed, his half-cape whipping about upon a gust of air Mana. He leveled his huge sword at the woman. "Face me as well, then."

"*Two* Adepts, and one approaching the middle stages of their Temper. This fight intrigues me now." She gripped her oversized mace in both hands, the metal almost glowing in the fading afternoon light. "I had hoped causing a ruckus down here might have lured your leader out of hiding, but…I suppose you will do. For now."

Mervin didn't see them move; he only felt the aftermath as a wave of pressure blasted him off his feet. He flew, tumbling head over heels into mud and rock before fetching up against the legs of the Claw members. Rough hands grabbed him and held him tight, while Mervin craned his neck to see.

Silver fire filled a crater the size of his old farmhouse, filled with sharp-edged holes that still glowed with heat. The white-armored High Guard stood in the center, feet barely moved from her starting position, and both Commanders were bloody on the ground.

Mervin felt more than heard the intake of breath from the soldiers around him. He couldn't believe it either. "H–how strong is that woman?" he asked.

"Master Tier," someone said.

Master Tier. Thangle was right. Mervin closed his eyes. *We're all dead.*

"Look!"

Mervin cracked open his eyes again and, amazingly, he saw the commanders stir.

"Hearty Bodies on you two," the High Guard said, her voice seeming a touch annoyed.

"Ain't dead yet," Commander Kastos groaned. His famous armor had broken apart from his leg, revealing a bloody calf and foot. "Not by a long shot."

Commander Reed didn't say anything, but he braced himself on his huge sword and stood, too.

"Looks like you need help, Mace!"

Before the mountainous woman could act again, another figure dropped from the sky. She was armored similarly in milky white plates and an obscuring helm, but bore a red-gold spear in her hands that was twice the height of an average Human. "These Adepts too much for you to handle?"

Mace gripped her weapon. "Shut your mouth, Spear."

"Come back to the ship."

Mace snorted. "And miss out on going wild against these fools?"

"They're *children*, Mace."

"Fight awful hard for children. Besides, they already tried to kill me." Mace grinned. "It's personal now."

"Fine," the woman known as Spear said, and she lifted her too-long weapon into the sky. "I will remove the temptation."

"Stop!" Mace shouted, but it was too late.

Something whipped from the red-gold weapon, something fast and invisible that shot directly into the sky. A sense of overwhelming dread sank into Mervin's stomach as he witnessed it, which was only compounded by Commander Kastos' frantic shout.

"Retreat!"

In the sky, hundreds—no, *thousands*—of shapes manifested. Mervin gaped at them as he was carried back, the Claw running with every ounce of Strength and Agility they could burn. *Spears of…air?*

The High Guard thrust her weapon upward, as if piercing the heavens themselves…and every single conjured spear fell.

"You ruin all my fun!" Mace screamed, almost as loud as the air and metal Mana that hurtled toward Mervin's face. He closed his eyes.

Pathless preserve me…!

Ouranic Override In Place!
ERROR!

Mervin fell, again, as a wave of pressure threw him and the Claw members off their feet. Yet, as he blinked his eyes open, he wasn't greeted by a conjured spear or the bloody remnants of his fellows…but instead, his vision was dominated by the sky turned mad.

"What is that voice?" Mace shouted.

"I don't know!" Spear replied. "It's in my *head*!"

Storm clouds had gathered in the late afternoon sky, dimming the light and spilling whipping winds and a deep, horrifying darkness across their shapes.

Ouranic Override Removed!
Chthonic Authority Recognized!

At the very center, the sky itself ripped open into a huge, fanged maw of shadow that bellowed a chorus of defiance into the heavens. The High Guard flinched, and the Manaships swayed in the aftershocks.

Karp, who had somehow gotten next to Mervin, clapped him on the back. He was laughing so hard he was crying. "The Fiend's own luck!"

An army of huge serpents burst from that dark maw, and at their head was a creature too big to be allowed. A mountainous monstrosity of golden scales and crystalline horn, and upon its back rode a man in black, surmounted by a blaze of red-gold and blue-white power.

"GET OFF MY LAWN!"

CHAPTER ONE HUNDRED THREE

Ouranic Override Removed!
Chthonic Authority Recognized!

The words repeated in Felix's head, but he hadn't the time to figure them out; he was too busy laughing like a madman as he and his friends rode through a gap in the world atop a *freaking* Dragon.

Title Evolution!
Voidwalker (Epic) Has Become Chthonic Traveler (Divine)!

New Title!
Chthonic Traveler (Divine)!
You walk in places not meant for mortals, skipping through Dark Passages that skirt the empty Void. You hold within you a seed of veiled potential. Do you choose to let it blossom?
In addition to the benefits of Voidwalker, you gain:
+Increased Accuracy When Utilizing Dark Passages Or Shadowgates
+Increased Stability When Utilizing Dark Passages or Shadowgates
+Reduced Cost Of Initializing Dark Passages or Shadowgates

That's not half bad, either. Felix watched as the Mana Cannons on the underside of the three ships oriented on him and fired. The Dragon pulled up, shielding Felix and his friends from the blast.

"Yintarion!" Vess shouted, aghast.

The Dragon screeched, agony rolling through the sound, but he did not stop flying from the Dark Passage they had navigated. "I remain!" he declared.

"That was their one chance," Felix said, mostly to himself, but he knew his friends could hear him. He saw the cannons charging again. "No more." He pressed a hand to the Dusk Dragon's skull. "Now, Yintarion!"

"This is my final service to you, Autarch, for I shall hold nothing back!" Yintarion howled as shadow and thunder split the sky. "Begone!"

Bursting forth from the Dragon's scales came a tidal wave of water Mana, formed and shaped into the likeness of a dozen monumental Dragons. They opened their jaws and dropped onto the battlefield like a hammer. Each draconic wave twisted and turned, spinning over themselves as they avoided Felix's allies and curved toward the advancing line of the Hierocracy. Teeth of solidified water ripped wide, rending the lesser Inquisitors and Paladins like a knife through paper, until the waters ran as blood.

"Trixie, Garox! Go!" Felix commanded. A deep, bowel-shaking call sounded as the Abyssal Serpent and his army of Nagafolk rushed into the waves, their own jaws, claws, and Skills brought to bear. The sound of it was almost as loud as the riot of shame and anger from their Spirits.

"Lindwurms! Now is your chance to prove your loyalty!" Felix roared. "Follow the Nagafolks' lead!"

Five of the draconic-type monsters slipped from the sky, their wedge-shaped heads and horns a faint echo of Yintarion's majesty, but not before giving Felix a fearful stare.

Manifestation of the Coronach is level 73!
...
Manifestation of the Coronach is level 77!
Adept Tier!
You Gain:
+20 FEL
+30 RES
+20 AFI

Rallying Cry Is Active!
Double Regenerations For All Allies In Range for 45 Seconds, Reduce Chance Of Frightened Status By 60%

Willpower Check Successful!
All Enemies In Range Are Affected By A Crisis of Faith for 3

Seconds!
Willpower Is Reduced By 60%!

Felix felt the Skill catch among his people, his range extending well over the battlefield and onto the wall itself. It was like a spreading wildfire, counterpoint to the deluge of draconic waves, and it bolstered flagging Spirits until their collective song soared.

"Rally!" someone cried. "The Fiend has come!"

"Autarch!"

"The Blue-Eyed Fiend!"

The city and battlefield rejoiced, and their weapons lifted into the sky as they charged into the fray.

At the moment, Felix couldn't be concerned with them; he was entirely too preoccupied with the failing Dragon beneath his feet. "Dude! Pull up!"

"Yintarion!" Vess shouted again, and Felix felt her connection with the Dragon spike and sound—Yet the Dusk Dragon was unresponsive. He plummeted from the storming sky, carrying all of them with him.

Adamant Discord!

Felix snagged his friends—Isla, too—and hauled the lot of them straight up just as the mountainous Dragon hit the battlefield below. New waves surged, earth and water flowing as one to bury the front lines of the Inquisition. Their choked-off screams were drowned by a piercing, draconic cry, and Vess leaped from Felix's grip. He let her go, spectral wings forming atop her back as she arced down to the Dragon's massive head.

Don't die, Yintarion.

"Gah! This—hey Felix, this hurts!" Beef yelled, flinching whenever lightning zapped along the lines of their connection.

"Right." Felix eyed the ground that was slowly approaching them all. "Hold onto your butts!"

Vess had amazing leaping abilities—the others weren't so fortunate. So Felix chucked them.

"Feliiiix!"

"Sorry, Isla," he shouted after her, watching her splash down on his army's side of Yintarion's Body. He'd done it as softly as he could. Beef, meanwhile, also hit with a deep-sounding splash, along with both of Hallow's Bodies.

Felix couldn't pay them any more attention, though—they'd have to fend for themselves. He had a Territory to defend, and he was already riding the razor's edge. Deep inside his core space, a screaming ache was tearing at the ribbons of light and power between his Skills and cores. His Pillars were trying to form—had been, ever since he'd entered the dark rift between Realms.

The added pressure of the Creature's stolen power called to something deep inside of him, and the endless jaunt through liminal space had catalyzed it, turning the already nightmarish ride through the Dark Passage into a marathon of applied Willpower and Endurance.

Though Yintarion had taken much of the power Felix had claimed from those ugly statues, he'd left plenty behind when he had punched a hole through the Realms. Apparently an accomplished Sorcerer himself, the Dragon had tapped into the Grand Harmony, utilizing the fraction of power Felix had stolen from Noctis, Goddess of the Night. The Seal offered no resistance, for Paxus had cleared the way, and the liminal space had opened like a doorway into the Void.

Felix tried to push it all from his head, the struggle through relative days of dark travel, skirting the Corporeal Realm atop the back of a golden Dragon, even the burning need at his center to advance himself. He surged through the air, riding upon flows of lightning and streamers of incinerating fire, only to land on the far side of Yintarion's unmoving form. The waters hissed and steamed, burning to nothing where they touched his potent aura, while electricity branched outward in grasping claws to jolt every nearby Inquisitor and Paladin.

You Have Killed A Initiate Of The Inviolate Inquisition (x35)!
XP Earned!

You Have Killed A Paladin Of The Pathless (x 23)!
XP Earned!

Kill notifications flashed by his eyes relentlessly, and Felix accepted them as he took in the scene around him. Inquisitors in golden armor stomped through the calming waters, huge swords leveled against Felix's Claw members.

"No. That's not allowed here," Felix muttered and lifted his hand. The Spikeshot Cuff at his wrist thrummed, stored Mana quickly manifesting a basketball-sized orb of metal covered in cruel spikes.

Ten shots, he reminded himself.

Felix summoned and hurled the spikeshots one after the other, so rapidly that his arm never stopped moving. Each spikeshot hit a breastplate of hardened light Mana and shattered it to pieces, driving deep into the Inquisitors within. Each redcloak fell, chests ruined and blood fountaining from them as the metal ball first broke through then was trapped inside the golden armor. It turned all of them to slurry.

You Have Killed An Inquisitor Of—

Felix accepted the kill notification as his Nagafolk and Lindwurms drove their forces deeper into the Hierocratic forces. His Claw was not far behind, familiar faces dotting their number, including dozens that bore additional limbs upon their back. The Yttin fought alongside Henaari and Human, Half-Orc and Dwarf, while even the Frost Giants stomped atop rapidly freezing sections of flooded earth. All of them wore cloaks emblazoned with a familiar crest: a wide eye that looked to be burning.

"For the Fiend! For Nagast!"

The battle was only beginning, though. There were far too many enemies left. Felix looked up, straight at the Manaships.

"You're next," he muttered.

Beef waded through the water that now swirled powerfully around his thighs, wincing as the muscles in his left arm and back healed. At seven feet tall and way too many pounds, it hadn't been nearly enough to cushion his fall. Apparently, his dumb Pendent of Quick Guard didn't consider fall damage as an attack. "Jesus, Felix. You're lucky I'm so sturdy."

His regeneration was fixing his injuries, and his right arm was working just fine, which was good because he had landed in a clutch of Paladins that were none-too-happy to see him. Beef had killed three of them in quick succession, his maul proving far too much for even their impressive armor, but more were coming. He lifted his left arm, ignoring the twinge of abused tendons. "C'mon, then! Let's dance!"

The four Paladins spread out, looking to encircle him, but Beef snorted in annoyance. "None of that. Shatterwheel!"

Shatterwheel is level 45!
...
Shatterwheel is level 48!

As a replacement for his old Circle of Smash, the evolved Legendary Skill Shatterwheel was impressive. It blasted the ground around him with an immense gathering of earth and force Mana, combining the two in a concussive press as devastating as his falling maul. The Paladins were crushed to the earth, and the water itself was pressed outward in a ten-foot-tall wave.

You Have Killed A Paladin Of The Pathless (x4)!
XP Earned!

"I like your moves, little bull!"

Beef whirled toward the voice, planting himself against the water that surged back into place as his Skill dissipated. Chaos surrounded him, shouting and clattering, metal on metal, magic burning the air until it smelled like ozone.

"Over here."

Aboot kicked Beef in the back—right where he was still healing. Barely able to gasp, he stumbled forward a half-dozen steps, recovering far too late. Yet, he found his attacker had simply stood and watched him reset. Beef looked her up and down, noting her fancy white armor and tumble of copper-colored curls. "You look important," he said.

A mace that was as big as his own maul was hefted atop the warrior woman's shoulder. It was red-gold, just like Beef's magic helmet. Doing the mental math, he wasn't too confident his helmet would be any protection against it.

The lady grinned, like she could read his mind. "Oh, I am. Question is, are you?"

"I'm strong enough to kick your ass," Beef said.

"Journeyman Tier, and freshly baked, too. But strong. Too strong." The woman quirked an eyebrow. "What're your stats?"

Beef lowered his stance, maul held in both hands and shoulders up—ready to use his horns if needed. "Wouldn't you like to know."

She blinked. "I would. That's why I asked, you idiot."

Beef snorted. "Come and find—"

Your Pendant of Quick Guard Is Shattered!

A savage thrust caught Beef square in the jaw, ringing metallically off of his magical helmet and throwing him back onto his ass—which meant half underwater. His pendant burst in a shower of sparks, the enchantment overloaded with a single, powerful strike. Beef spluttered, vision swimming as much as his arms, and was only barely able to avoid the disdainful downward slash the woman delivered.

"Tough enough. Not nearly fast enough, though." She lifted her mace, which dripped with water and mud and blood.

Beef touched his face and hissed when he found his chin split to the bone. "I wasn't ready," he spat.

"My apologies, little bull. I'll give you a moment to gather yourself."

Before the words even left her mouth, the woman appeared at Beef's side, a wild wake of water and mud cresting behind her as she swung low with her oversized mace. Beef hollered, his words muffled by splashing water, barely able to summon a wall of chitin from his reserves. The mace blasted through it and took him hard in the gut.

"Ooof!" Beef grunted, driven up out of the water in a dizzying arc, only to land twenty feet away with a tremendous clap of water. He blinked, half-submerged and unable to stand up. His Mind spun, unable to grasp onto solid concepts like ground or how to bend his knees. Urgency drove him to flail outward, hand still clenched around his chitin-covered maul, but he did little better than splash about.

Status Condition: Concussion (Major)
Status Condition: Bruised Solar Plexus (Minor)

"Hm, dazed, but still nothing broken." The words were muffled, and Beef couldn't make sense of them; their meaning tumbling around his Mind without answer. Something grabbed the remnant of his hauberk and yanked up back above the water, and all Beef could make out was a curtain of tangled copper hair. "A Minotaur. Never heard of someone like you. Are all your people this tough?"

"Are—are all…are all you zealots…stupid?" Confused or not, he felt a surge of glee as rage passed through her green eyes. *Gottem*, he thought.

"Fine." The woman's hand dropped from Beef's hauberk, but he managed to get an elbow up, at least. She stood back up to her full, impressive height. "You aren't worth the trouble, anyway. Die, trash."

The mace moved, and Beef hadn't even the time to flinch before sparks of red, gold, and green burst inches before his face, instants before a wave of water and mud all but bowled him over. He gawked, Mind catching up, as he beheld a glowing, crooked sword that had fully stopped the mace's descent.

"Oho, and who're you?" the woman asked, her tone surprised and delighted.

"Get away from my friend," Felix said, before hesitating. "Mace? Your name is Mace?"

"That's only name you need to know, boy," Mace said, putting what looked like her entire weight behind her weapon. Felix's sword didn't budge an inch. "Who in the Light are you?"

In response, scales rippled up Felix's shoulders and neck, and Beef felt a physical pressure push him backward through the water. "Ow!" he gasped as lightning zapped his face. "Felix!"

"Stay back, Beef."

"Felix," the woman said, a grin splitting her freckled face. She pulled her mace and retreated several steps in a blink. "Autarch. Finally!"

Felix reset himself, hooked blade to the side and his clawed offhand empty. "Who're you supposed to be?"

That smile grew wider, until Beef could count her teeth.

"Your executioner."

Whoa, that's a good line, he thought, just as the two blurred toward one another.

CHAPTER ONE HUNDRED FOUR

"It's injured," an Inquisitor pointed out, staring at his own broken sword in annoyance. Behind them, well away from the downed Dragon, their lessers surged around the impediment on their way toward the front-lines. All was wet, squelching mud and a splashy din among the clattering armor and shouted Skills. "Now's our chance. Kill it now!"

"You kill it," another Inquisitor shot back, while blood seeped from a gash across his forehead. "I'll not risk my life in jaws large enough to swallow half a city block."

"Get out of my way, you cowards," said a voice like rolling shale. The Inquisitors turned to see a seven-foot-tall giant in platemail push through the press of Hierocratic bodies. The crest of the Paladins shone like gold upon his crimson armor, and his unsheathed greatsword glimmered in the failing light. He grunted, igniting the length of steel until it burned like a torch. "I'll end the monstrosity, then we can focus on the real enemy."

"Draconic Stormfall!"

The clueless Hierocratic dogs were driven into the mud as a woman in blue and white armor hit the Paladin spear-first. Water burst upward and away, blasted out by a ring of crackling lightning that swept through it and into the Inquisitors. Their screams were high and short before they ended on their backs in the shallow water, and the Paladin's shout was a gurgling rush of blood and returning waves.

"You heinous, heathen dogggglhgh!" he said, before Vess put all of her considerable Strength behind her partisan and twisted.

You Have Killed A Paladin Of The Pathless!

XP Earned!

"Eugh! You!" One Inquisitor rose to his feet, swiftly followed by another. "Diurnal Re—!"

"Spear of Tribulations," she hissed, and ten silver Spears dropped from the sky onto their armored heads.

You Have Killed An Inquisitor Of The Inviolate Inquisition (x2)!
XP Earned!

Vess yanked her partisan free and whipped it to her side, wicking the blood away as the waters rushed back around her feet. Her eyes found the humongous head of the golden Dragon and went wide. "Yintarion."

She leaped into the air, her legs carrying her right to the Dusk Dragon's giant eye. It was closed, but a heavy rasp bubbled the waters around his lips, and her presence seemed to stir him further.

"I have upheld my bargain, little Dragoon," he rumbled, and the water frothed. "Leave me to die."

Vess' brows drew down. "That is idiotic. You can help, still! Fight with me!"

"No." A flash of blue and white, and a status screen rolled before Vess' eyes.

Health: 240/244,349,003

She paled and felt a cold sweat spring across her back. For a creature his size, so little Health was like clinging to the edge of death itself. If those Inquisitors had managed a proper strike, they truly could have killed him.

Yintarion rumbled as if agreeing with her frantic thoughts. "The Creature held me too long. It wore me until I became so thin that little else remains. I've not even the strength to shift my tail. I am a shell of scales, all but empty."

Vess pressed a hand to the Dragon's jaw, feeling a chill that had not been evident during their wild flight. "We can heal you. We have Chanters and…and Felix! Felix can help, I'm sure of it."

Something flickered in the Dragon's Spirit, there and gone. It was too dim to be hope and too stern to be joy. It felt…like mulish obstinance.

"Little Dragoon, I—"

"A Dragon…a *Dusk Dragon*?"

Vess spun toward the new arrival, partisan lifted between them. She was a woman, wearing some sort of high-Tier armor all in white; her face was bare, revealing a sharp chin, aquiline nose, and piercing amber eyes beneath a tight bun of raven-black hair. Her gaze did not waver from the dull golden bulk of the Dragon. "You, girl. It called you Dragoon, and I see the hallmarks of apprenticeship upon you. Explain this. How is this possible?"

Vess stared at the woman, her Mind still piecing together the scenario from the chaos of war that surrounded them. It took Vess too long to recognize the shape of the woman's armor from her father's old tomes on the Hierocracy. An old book she studied long ago, but one put diligently to memory. After all, it was important to know your enemy. "High Guard."

"I said: explain. Now. How does our greatest foe still live?"

"Our?"

The strikingly beautiful woman cocked her head before lifting the gleaming orichalcum spear in her hands. It was taller than Felix and tipped with a wide, hooked blade meant for rending and tearing. "Do you not recognize me?"

Vess shifted her stance, letting a deep music begin to flow within her. A dance she could almost remember flitted across her senses, distracting her from the High Guard's words. "I have never seen you before in my life."

"Tch," the woman said, her neutral face turning to a sneer. "Does the order truly keep such poor records? A hundred years ago, my name was on the lips of anyone who dared hold the spear; a prodigy the likes of which the Dragoons have not seen since before the Betrayal. I am Spear, named for my mastery." A gleeful light swelled from the woman's features, and Vess had to lock her knees as an almost casual pressure tried to shove her to the ground. "And I shall be the first in Ages to slay a Dusk Dragon. Step aside."

The music rose in her veins, a steady, vibrant sonata that set her pathways alight and slipped around the High Guard's Spiritual pressure. Her Body wished to move, to step upon the Tempered path that lay before them, oh so tantalizingly close. All three of her Aspects were on the cusp, and they were reminding her of that fact. Vess' Perception took in Yintarion's closing eyes, already rolling back as his breath dropped into a hitching gasp. She clenched her jaw. "I do not know you, and you will keep away from this Dragon."

The High Guard paused, and her face morphed between surprise and anger so seamlessly that Vess felt a touch dizzy—or perhaps that was the notes that rolled through her chest and belly, all but driving the air from her lungs.

"Childish rebellion," the woman scoffed. "Did the Dragon promise you riches? Power? That is their way, apprentice. They entice and tempt, until they have you in their grasp…Out of respect for our shared order, I shall ask this once: step aside, and I'll let you live after I've killed this monstrosity."

That rush of strings sounded again from within Vess' core. This time, it was not just the sonata that drove her to move, but a piece of Harmony that sang of sorrow, cold rage, and a burning compassion that surprised her. Yet it was being crushed by the weight of buzzing interference, a knot that mangled that Harmony until all the heat and passion faded into a stolid, bitter acceptance.

Yinterion…

Vess could feel more than just Yinterion's Health. Their Link was still there, faint but far more noticeable outside the Breach, and she could feel the damage to his Mind, Body, and Spirit. Irreparable damage, perhaps. As he'd said, the Creature's possession had taken a terrible toll.

"Girl," Spear growled. "Move or die along with it."

The power the Dragon had embraced and rejected had changed it. A choice had been made. Vess felt at their Link, the bond that had been forged by a Primordial and her own heritage, felt where that faint music swelled—where it melded with the song in her veins, becoming something deeper and swifter. Something more.

Do You Choose To Save Him?
Yes/No

Forgive me, Yintarion. You are not yet done.

"What is—!" The High Guard threw her arm up as a gold, blue, and white-green radiance exploded all around them.

Fine, little Dragoon.

A Choice Is Made.

Vess was hurled from her feet, lifted by a streamer of Mana and Essence that stabbed through every single one of her Gates at once. She rang like a bell, her temple roaring into the nighttime sky as a Dragon screamed its last.

All Choices Have Consequences.
Bear Your Burdens Well, Vessilia Dayne.

"Put it there! There!" Alister said, jabbing a greasy finger toward an array. An Inscriptionist ran to where he pointed, robes flapping and stylus outstretched as they began to sketch sigils. "Keep it in balance!"

"Alister! We need that ready now!"

"Soon, Zara! Soon!" The force mage shouted back, sparing a single glance for the battlefield that had descended into utter madness. A hole in the sky, the return of their friends, and a blighted *Dragon* had descended on them. The battle had changed in an instant as the field flooded, and Nagafolk seized Hierocratic soldiers in their powerful jaws, while some sort of draconic monstrosities surged deeper behind enemy lines.

Now people were going wild on the walls, many of them rushing down the battlements to join the next wave of combatants. Nevermind that many of them bore deep wounds or flagging Stamina; men and women in purple cloaks ran up and down the parade ground, long flags waving in the winds. Flags that depicted a burning eye upon a field of blue. And all around them, a chant.

"Nagast! The Fiend! Nagast! The Fiend!"

Yet all of that was meaningless, as the three Manaships still retained their cannons. They had blasted apart Zara's cobbled-together shielding, and the next volley should have annihilated them all where they stood…but it had never arrived. Instead, the cannons had trained themselves upon a riotous display of violence that dominated the battlefield, shooting several times and pockmarking the terrain but failing to stop it. Alister couldn't make out the details, but he'd seen Felix in action enough times to know his handiwork.

Just keep them busy, Felix. Just a little longer.

Sigladry is level 70!
Focus is level 68!
Siege Weapon Mastery is level 13!

Alister put his stylus to work, inscribing another set of sigils beneath the stability array. The weapon was so close to finished, yet so far. Each time they'd attempted to use it, something else had failed, and most recently, the backlash of offloading so much Mana had set the entire frame swaying backward alarmingly. "There's a leak on the collection array! Stop feeding it!"

"On it, sir!"

The mages around him hustled just as fast as Alister, each scrawling lines of smoking light onto the weapon while another mage stumbled back from the collection plate, his palm red and in clear pain.

"Step back until we fix this," Alister said to the Apprentice Tier, but they weren't listening. Instead, the mage was staring out into the distance, mouth open and eyes wide.

"How will we survive this?" the mage asked, only to receive a sharp slap on the back that nearly jolted him out of his boots.

"Don't worry. Didn't you hear? The Fiend is returned," Atar said, out of breath. The Apprentice Tier stuttered something, but Alister didn't pay much attention, his eyes riveted on Atar. The fire mage had hollow cheeks, blood crusted to his face, and he was leaning heavily on his stave, but his Health was high enough.

"Atar. Your team?"

"Down at the gate. The fools can't target anything with that Dragon in the way, so they're lining up to get onto the field."

Alister paled. "It's a meat grinder down there."

"They'll be fine," Atar said, gesturing beyond the crenelations. "See?"

Alister glanced backward in time to witness the flooded field begin to rapidly ice over. Behind that front of frost came the fifteen-stride-tall Risi Warriors bearing axes and hammers taller than most Humans. The Frost Giants crashed into the Inquisitors and Paladins that had struggled closer to the city walls, smashing them flat before a slew of Sparkbolts, Ice Arrows, and Shadow Jaws followed. Atar's team of mages flowed behind, led at the front by a slight woman with a whirling chain.

"Evie and the Frost Giants will provide them with the cover they need," Atar continued. He smacked the weapon beside them with his stave. "While they do that, I'm here to help. What needs doing?"

"Right."

The two of them leaned in, Alister completing his work on the frame while Atar ran his Perception across the whole of the weapon. With swift, sure strokes of his stave, the fire mage corrected several unnoticed imbalances in the complicated network of arrays. "Here, the crucible wasn't pulling the right amounts from the collection array. I've patched it, but it'll pull a lot all at once."

"Will it work?" Alister asked, sweating as explosions rocked the wall. "Will it fire?"

Atar grimaced. "One way to find out."

The fire mage reached out to grasp the inscribed handles on the weapon, just above the standing platform, but Alister stopped him. "I've got this side. Take the other one, Glyphmaster."

Atar smirked. "Fine. But you drop it the moment you feel Mana drain, right?"

"Right." Alister set his jaw and grasped the handle, feeling a jolt as the array initialized and began pulling on his channels. His other hand twisted in the tarp that covered the front of his creation, and he took a deep breath. "Ready, my love?"

let us rain fire upon our foes and lay waste to their grandeur.

"Who was—?" Alister began, but Atar's pale face stopped his words.

"I'll tell you," Atar said, teeth bared. Not at Alister, but at something else entirely. "Later. For now, unveil your masterpiece."

Alister ripped the tarp away, revealing a weapon that only nominally resembled a ballista but was formed more like a massive scorpion's tail. Sigils and glyphs lit up along its frame, lines that sizzled and popped as more and more power flooded through its collection array, until the curving barrel blazed with blue and orange spirals. A discordant hum shook the air, forcing the other inscriptionists back, hands over their ears.

Atar laid his hand over Alister's, lacing their fingers and shouting above the din. "Together!"

"Together!"

together! and let the world burn!

CHAPTER ONE HUNDRED FIVE

Dodge is level 75!
Adept Tier!
You Gain:
+20 DEX
+20 AGL
+30 PER

Felix dodged the High Guard's weapon, feeling the edge of a whirlwind flow in its path as System energy flooded him. The increase was relatively minor for him, but in the heat of the moment, his muscles loosened, and his joints bent a fraction of an inch more as the colors around him crept toward unknown shades.

He could see the sweat dangling from Mace's squashed, freckled nose, count the faint, downy hairs on her cheeks, and even perceive the prismatic light as it filtered through her frustrated spittle as it caught the last glimmers of the setting sun. "You move well, usurper."

Dodge is level 76!

"Too well," she growled. "Titan's Ward!"

A thrumming half-sphere of metal and earth formed before her, releasing a sudden sonic blast that sent Felix skidding backward through mud and water. He held his feet, the force of it not enough to knock him over, even if it did shave five percent of his Health away. "That all you got, lady?"

Mace smirked, now well over thirty feet away. "Hardly."

FOOD, his Hunger rumbled.

What? Felix asked, a heartbeat before a riot of golden violence landed where he stood.

Dodge is level 77!
Armored Skin is level 84!
Blind Fighting is level 69!

Mana Cannon! his Mind screamed at him, moments too late. Thankfully, his Body had been forged in the crucible of a thousand life-or-death battles. As the beam of gold, orange, and yellow Mana tore into the battlefield, Felix just barely evaded its strike.

Garment half-burnt, he was panting as he came to a rest just feet from what was now a glowing pit of molten stone. The waters rushed in, hissing like ten thousand angry geese while steam billowed like land-borne clouds. He looked up just in time to see the second Manaship train its cannon directly at him.

"It's like that, is it?" Felix asked, flexing his grip on the two blades he held. Inheritor's Will and Skyslaine's Riposte felt light as feathers, but Mana swirled around them like wind. "Fine."

He thrust his Riposte out, feeding the weapon an absolute torrent of Mana. The dagger's blade lengthened rapidly, blasting forward for an incredible distance straight toward the Hierocratic ship…and the tip crashed with resounding force against a shell of multi-colored energy.

"A fancy dagger, Nevarre, but it's not gonna penetrate those wards," Mace said. She spun her weapon casually, but her eyes never left his figure.

"And your cannon won't catch me," Felix shot back.

"True." Mace scratched her jaw. "But can you say the same for everyone else?"

As if waiting for her words, the nearest ship pivoted its huge Mana Cannon as energies gathered in its blossom-like barrel. It locked into place with a distant crash, aimed now at the struggling soldiers on Felix's side. The two others followed suit, slowly turning toward targets down the line.

"Don't turn your back on me—!"

Mace's words vanished as Felix exploded from his stance—not toward the High Guard, but sideways, into the fray.

Relentless Resolution!

Adamant Discord!

The earth cratered beneath him with each step. Stone and dirt, mud and water flung into the air as he passed, and lightning spun around his limbs.

The first cannon fired.

Stone Shaping!
Rime Shaping!
Green Shaping!
Cardinal Flame!

Felix thrust Mana from his feet as he flashed through the battlefield, his Willpower guiding it as his Intent shaped it all together into a familiar form. Curving ramparts of blue-black stone erupted from the earth, startling both sides as their confrontations were stymied—but not so surprising as when the first massive beam hit. A concussive wave followed Felix as he ran, earth and water and stone transmuting beneath his heavy tread, as golden light and terrifying heat washed across the far side of his construction.

The second and third cannons fired, and Felix was there to meet them. Red-veined ramparts rose like breaching whales, water and mud erupting in every direction, only to be met by the evaporating might of the magic cannon. Everything shook—even Felix's stride was thrown off as he slid to a crashing halt and looked back.

Smoke and fires filled the center of the field, but that soon faded… leaving only a thirty-foot wall of unbroken stone.

Manifestation of the Coronach is level 78!
…
Manifestation of the Coronach is level 80!

Rallying Cry Is Active!
Double Regenerations For All Allies In Range for 50 Seconds, Reduce Chance Of Frightened Status By 60%

Willpower Check Successful!
All Enemies In Range Are Affected By A Crisis of Faith for 5 Seconds!
Willpower Is Reduced By 60%!

Holy shit, that worked. Something unclenched in his chest, and he exhaled deeply. There were still cracks in the ramparts, but those were fixable. The battle had halted, whether from surprise that the cannons had fired or from the surprise arrival of his walls, Felix was unsure. Either way, it was an opportunity.

He channeled his power, forcing more Mana down into the earth and toward the interconnected walls he'd crafted. His Mana dropped, but it was nothing to his regeneration, after all. Stairs and crenelations formed, arrow slits and murder holes above barred gates.

"Everyone! To the ramparts!" he shouted, and the battlefield came alive again.

In the distance, Felix's call was taken up by Reed and Harn, and he could even see Evie and a score of Frost Giants rush to the cover of his new fortifications. Figures in robes hustled to the tops and began hurling spells from on high, blasting back the Inquisitors and Paladins that were scrambling to recover.

"SKREEAH!" Pit cried out, rushing above the battlements. A cloud of flashing Mana vapor poured from him with that cry, a mingling of life, air, and light that sank into the bodies of every warrior and mage. Men and women straightened up, weapons lifted as new vigor shone from their eyes.

Pit's Breath of the Wild is level 2!

Keep at it, bud.

Farther down the line, the great bulk of the Dragon suddenly and gloriously ignited. Like a second sun had risen, the battlefield was briefly transformed into midday before it vanished…taking Yintarion along with it.

"Damn it," Felix cursed. A wave of potent emotions surged through the Spirits around him, lifting the already chaotic atmosphere to greater heights. "Hope you took some with you, Yintarion."

"HOORRAAAAAAH!" another familiar voice bellowed, followed by the sound of shearing metal and rumbling earth. "Keratin Conception!"

"Titan's Ward!"

Shit! Felix shot forward, flaring his movement Skill to all but fly down the line. Hierocratic soldiers tried to take pot shots at him, but Felix didn't even dodge them. Those that actually hit did nothing to pierce his Armored Skin, let alone the scales along his arms and legs.

"Form up! Fire!" shouted a man with a vibrant plume atop his helmet. Three dozen Paladins gathered before him, each one leveling their flaming blades at Felix's oncoming form.

"Bad idea!" he shouted.

Adamant Discord!

He rammed through the clustered Paladins, scattering them into a bloody scrap heap as lightning leaped between his outstretched hand and a young Minotaur. He pulled, and the thick connection turned to steel as the world whipped past his ears.

Ahead, he saw Mace charging down a wounded Beef as he and Hallow tried to desperately fend off her attacks. She was too strong, batting away his maul with a contemptuous swipe of her own weapon.

"You're a child playing at war! I'll teach you the only lesson you will ever need." Mace smashed the Multipede into the mud and batted the

Homunculus' crystalline darts away. She lifted her orichalcum mace in both hands. "The lesson of true strength."

Felix blasted into her, feet first. A jolt of galvanizing lightning tore through her, but more than that, her precious armor crumpled before she was hurled bodily into the distance. He landed lightly, his momentum all but absorbed by the High Guard that tumbled helplessly through water, mud, and her own soldiers.

"Beef. Hallow. You both okay?"

"Unf. Yeah." Beef leveraged himself up, clambering from his knees to his hoofed feet. "Hallow?"

"F-fine." The Homunculus was clinging to Beef's shoulder armor, which was hanging by a thin leather strap. "I have not regained my former strength."

"It is…disconcerting," the Multipede said, the feminine voice deeper and laced with echoes. Water streamed from its rounded skull as blackened green lights blinked through its carapace. "And that woman is not yet dead, Felix."

"I know." Felix unsheathed his Inheritor's Will and Skyslain's Riposte again, the latter back in the form of a large parrying dagger. He looked up. "She's not even my main problem."

The cannons had repositioned once again and were gathering energy. The hum was faint but growing stronger. All three were aimed at a single point of his newly-built wall. Together, they were sure to punch through it; not even his shaped fortifications could withstand that much firepower.

"I could use my chitin to—" Beef started to say, but Felix waved him down.

"Don't waste your strength." He eyed the distance between the ships and adjusted his footing. Orange, yellow, and golden Mana gathered at the three separate barrels like radiant eggs, ready to hatch their destruction at any second. "I have to take this fight to them. Step back, I—"

Without warning, the cannon to the far right exploded in an eruption of incandescent flame. Blue force Mana rippled across the incendiary cloud, ripping through metal and stone like hot knives through butter, as smaller explosions followed the first.

"Holy balls!" Beef cried out. "What was that?"

Felix spun back to Haarwatch, and his eyes immediately landed on a construction of steel and stone and complicated sigaldry that was at least fifteen feet tall…and two robed individuals at its base. A crown of magma hung in the air around the entire construction while bright blue pillars rose and fell like the pistons of some huge machine. "Son of a bitch. He got it working."

"What? Who?"

Frenetic orders were coming from the field as the Hierocratic forces surged toward Felix's fortifications, just as the far right ship began to tilt and fall. Fire was consuming it at a rapid pace, the sigiladry once hidden within it now taken to flame as Mana backed up and burst across its many, many arrays.

The Mana Cannons on the other two were also moving, pivoting toward the new threat when a second shot blasted out of Alister's creation. Fire and force mingled into a white-hot beam that was far smaller than the Mana Cannon's, but it punched through the Manaship's shields like they weren't even there.

Another cannon was engulfed in a firestorm.

"Impudent children!" bellowed a figure in stocky white armor. Mace was back up on her feet, but instead of charging Felix, she headed toward Alister, Atar, and the giant magic ballista.

"Oh, no you don't!" Felix kicked forward, scattering water and mud behind him as he raced to catch up. Within his core, he sounded the patterns of a spell he used too infrequently.

Shadow Whip!

A flexible tendril of darkness surged from his right palm and immediately tangled with Mace's trailing leg.

Adamant Discord!

Alongside it, the wrist-thick cord of connection between him and the High Guard flared into life, becoming steel in his left hand as Felix was dragged forward several yards before planting himself and hauling back.

"Get over here!"

A wordless shout of alarm and dismay cut through the air as Felix's power proved too much for the Master Tier to handle, and Mace was pulled backward into the soupy remains of Yintarion's last and greatest attack.

"Felix!"

He turned, disengaging his two Skills as Beef called for him. The flagship, the last craft still standing above the forest, fired its Mana Cannon.

Relentless Resolution!

Cloudstep!

Adamant Discord!

Felix leaped through the sky, flying up Cloudsteps that shattered beneath blurring feet, as lightning danced along his every nerve ending. His Link to Atar shone, thicker than his entire body and made of white speared with bloody crimson, but it was drowned out by the screaming approach of the Mana Cannon's beam.

Chthonic Tribute!

Gold, orange, and yellow Mana—just inches away from his outstretched hands—boiled and buckled, turning in on itself as its incredible momentum was snatched away. The beam *turned*, and slammed right into Felix's open maw.

"Fire!" Atar screamed in a panic, but Felix didn't hear him as he was slammed into the soggy earth beneath the tumult of a momentous fusillade. The stone burst and broke, heated to molten slag while the water steamed into invisible vapor.

All he felt was the energy that raged in his channels and core space, filling him with such immense heat that it felt as if his blood were boiling. The urge to form his Pillars became an all-encompassing need, as the potency forced his Skills to spin faster and faster. The cannon's discharge wasn't a straw, but a lead weight upon the camel's back, forcing the wild combination of Mana, Essence, and stolen Divinity into an inevitable conflagration. Ribbons of light spooled inward, roots of crystalline might thrust down, through the dark and the flames as his dual cores ground out their unique song.

All he heard was the roar of his Hunger, the vast black hole that seized the flood of power and claimed it, blunting the edge of what he had to do…but it changed little. Too much swirled within him, compacting into a density that even his Hunger couldn't take apart. To refuse the call again—he knew he wouldn't survive. The time had come to form the rest of his Pillars.

I am on the way, Felix! Pit sent to him. *I am coming to help!*

He couldn't wait. There, at the bottom of a crater of molten stone and steaming earth, Felix began.

CHAPTER ONE HUNDRED SIX

burn them! shatter them!

Atar shoved the molten crown away, dropping the rage and arrogance that stifled his Spirit whenever he used it, and fell to his knees. His sudden burst of mental and spiritual stats helped, but more was the surge of potency that accompanied his fall.

Stars of the Sovereign is level 85!
Lens of the Magus is level 79!
Incendiary Vortex is level 77!

Astrum Revelation is level 75!
...
Astrum Revelation is level 79!
Congratulations! You Have Reached Adept Tier With Astrum Revelation!
You Gain:
+50 WIL
+100 ALA
...

"Atar!" Alister shouted. A glass vial was pushed against his lips. "Drink!"

Legendary Essence Detected During Formation!
[Essence Draught of Atlantes (Fire)]

Choose A Feature:
Epiphany
Constellation
Evoke

As with his previous Temperings, Atar was out of his depth. His rate of growth had rapidly accelerated in the last year, and the pattern of his future was far different than once assumed. He had no map, no guide to inform him of his choices. He was blind.

constellation has promise, but epiphany is the province of madmen and charlatans. naught but smoke. choose evoke.

What? Atar clutched at his head. The wall was spinning around him, and it was only Alister's steady hands on his back that gave him any sense of grounding. He felt as if he were going to fall into the sky. *What are you talking about?*

evoke. choose it, or be relegated to mediocrity for all of time.

Nonplussed and frankly out of options, Atar listened.

Congratulations!
You Have Absorbed The Essence Of [Evoke]!

3 of 3 Mind Essences Formed!
Tempering Has Begun!

Atar convulsed as System power filled his core space, while Flame shouted in glee.

yes! yes! expand our spark into the inferno from whence we were born!

He hadn't the space to curse at his Flame, though he wished he could, instead focusing all of his Willpower on simply not passing out. "A-Alister. Did we—?"

"The Manaships are…they're down." Alister's hands shifted on Atar's back, moving to lift him up. "And we need to move."

the…blue fool is correct. a great fury is building upon that field of slaughter. those in white are coming, fast. we are exposed here. flee, atar!

Pieces of what the Flame was sensing fed into his already quaking Spirit, and Atar gasped. He seized the front of Alister's robes. "We need…to go to Zara! The shield!"

"The shield? Atar, what are you on about?"

danger, boy!

Alister swallowed. "There. The voice. Atar, what is that? What is happening?"

Atar bit at the inside of his cheek, drawing blood and pain just to focus as energy rampaged inside of him. "Later! It's right! There's no time to run! We need to power up the shield, or we're all dead!"

The energy dwindled, fading from a blinding glow to something moderately less. Vess fell to her knees upon the baked ground. The water was gone, evaporated in a wide ring around her body, but it was trickling back through hardened furrows of earth. Wind still whipped around her in a frenzied cyclone, snatching away the now-empty glass vials at her feet as motes of Yintarion's energy coursed upon the currents—tiny serpents of gold, deepest blue, and white-green almost invisible against the whirlwind itself.

Vess shook, within and without, as she was remade.

3 of 3 Body Essences Formed!
Tempering Has Begun!

3 of 3 Mind Essences Formed!
Tempering Has Begun!

3 of 3 Spirit Essences Formed!
Tempering Has Begun!

Her core raged, the interior of her golden temple now flung wide open. A whirling, molten ring of air and metal danced with increasing fervor around the sinuous strands of water and light. Vess bore down on it all, compressing it even as it tried to fly out from her control.

Only absolute certainty will let you stay the course.

Isla's words echoed through Vess' Mind, chasing her consciousness as she held on for dear life to her rampaging core. She had chosen her Essence Features, bound them to her Skills. Now she only had to survive the consequences. Her core spun, and she squeezed, until all her world was molten power and blinding light.

"Where is it?"

Instincts screaming, Vess threw herself into a side roll as a gleaming, red-gold spear thrust for her heart. The ground bucked, rippling outward before the hardened earth blasted apart and threw Vess into a wild sprawl. Spectral wings tilted and flapped, righting her without conscious thought, just in time to duck beneath the High Guard's sudden follow-up.

"Tempering? While we fight? Bold of you, apprentice!" The woman's eyes flashed, white-green Mana spreading around her head like a halo that combated the whirlwind around Vess. Her pristine armor was crazed with glowing cracks, and her face was bloodied. "But this… this is no mere Tempering. What are you playing at, girl?"

Vess' core tightened, flowing faster and faster, until vibrations ran through her chest and limbs like waves of weakness—mimicking the whirlwind that spun around them all. She clenched her partisan until her knuckles split. "Come and find out. Spear of Tribulations," Vess spat. Silver Spears manifested around Vess, ten of them, as the High Guard looked on in contempt.

"An apprentice's Skill, not yet evolved into a higher form. Pathetic." The High Guard flourished her orichalcum weapon, ending with the long blade pointed directly at Vess' heart. "I do not know how you did it, but you stole that Dragon from me, girl. I'll take the price out of your blood."

"You will try."

Before the final word left her mouth, Vess dodged. Her vision narrowed, the edges crowded with darkness, as the orichalcum spear came within a finger-span of her neck. On The Wing burned within her, spectral wings adding force to her steps that had never been there before.

It was all that saved her head.

On The Wing is level 79!

The High Guard's spear sliced sideways, shearing a hefty lock of Vess' hair as it descended to the earth. Vess bent and flowed around it, kicking backward hard and launching herself twenty strides into the air. "Hah!"

Silver Spears flashed forward, dive bombing the High Guard.

"Ten Tribulations!"

The explosions of wind and metal tore apart rocks and roots with abandon, churning their battlefield into dust that blocked Vess' view of events. Still, she knew the woman lived. There had been no kill notification.

"Azhdaha Ascent!"

The words reached Vess the same time the High Guard did, and she drove a white-armored elbow deep into Vess' abdomen.

On The Wing is level 80!

Those spectral wings saved her again as Vess' body was hurled backward from the High Guard's strike. She'd taken damage, if her flashing Health bar was any indicator, and her Status told her of two broken ribs—but she'd survived. Had she taken the full brunt of that attack, Vess was positive she would have perished.

She landed, skidding atop the ankle-deep water at the edge of their blasted battlefield. Chaos surrounded them, and the noise of death and destruction battered Vess with a thousand clawed fingers. She shut it out as the High Guard landed gracefully only a dozen strides away.

"Impressive, apprentice. You show uncommon promise for one so young." She leaned forward, spear held closer to her side as she lowered her stance—a great cat eager to pounce upon a mouse. "A pity that I should end it."

"You—you have yet to prove—you can," Vess said between hitching breaths.

Spear's beautiful face soured. "I will enjoy this."

Spear flared forward, propelled by Skill and stat, as Vess danced away. She pressed her Tempering Skill for every bit of grace it could provide, slipping through the edges of most attacks—but not all. More than once, Vess took glancing blows to her shoulders, bicep, even thigh as she fought a desperate, defensive battle. There was no strategy, only blind instinct to stay one step ahead of the Master-Tier High Guard. Her Health dwindled as her wounds increased, her armor split and cracked, until it was all Vess could do to hold onto her own weapon.

The wind, she realized. *It is…aiding me?*

The whirlwind had intensified, pulling closer and closer as they danced across the battlefield. Twice it fouled the High Guard's footwork, even as it sent Vess soaring into a graceful leap. Those serpentine tendrils flashed among the winds, flitting among her partisan and limbs like curious beasts—they jolted her, more than once propelling her arms to lift her weapon and parry a savage thrust.

Vess' eyes widened as she met the High Guard's gaze, and revelation swept through her.

"What is this?" Spear growled. Her hair tangled in her eyes and mouth as those serpentine tendrils slid across her face. "What are you doing?"

"Teamwork."

You Have Gained A Companion!

Yintarion of the Cerulean Sky, level 1

Congratulations! You Have Earned A New Title!
Pactmaker (Rare)!
You have formed a pact with a Dusk Dragon, gaining benefits even while binding your life to theirs. +40 AGL, +30 DEX, +40 PER

You Have Learned A New Skill!
Companion Pact (Uncommon), Level 1!
You have formed a pact! Increasing Skill Level and Affinity will net larger gains from the pact, for both you and your Companion.

Calculating Prerequisites.
Standby...

Congratulations! Companion Pact (Uncommon) Has Evolved Into Draconic Bond (Legendary)!

Draconic Bond (Legendary), Level 1!
By mutual agreement, you have formed a deep connection with a Dusk Dragon! The skies quake before you, and the horizon stretches ever onward. Increasing Skill Level and Affinity will net larger gains from the pact, for both you and your Companion.

Congratulations! As A Pactmaker, You And Your Companion Share Level Benefits!
Overlapping Bonuses Do Not Stack.
You Gain: +20 PER, +32 VIT, +22 AGL, +13 DEX Per Level!
Companion Gains: —

ERROR!
Level Too Low To Provide Bonuses To Companions!
Advance To Master Tier Or Higher To Progress Further!

Notifications flowed through Vess like wind and water, absorbed into her awareness before she could fully understand it all. All at once, the whirlwind around them collapsed into a point of incandescent glory, forcing Vess backward once more as it exploded.

The High Guard was hit far harder. The armor along her left arm was shattered completely by phantasmal claws and teeth as Spear's entire body was sent skidding across the ankle-deep water.

Vess watched in mute awe as those serpentine tendrils of power shimmered around a single radiant shape, no bigger than a housecat and perched delicately at the tip of her partisan. Gleaming golden scales covered its sinuous form, its four limbs tufted with the same downy white fur that sat between two small, crystalline horns. A distinct head opened its draconic jaw and ate the tendrils with increasing ferocity.

Yintarion of the Cerulean Sky is level 2!

...

Yintarion of the Cerulean Sky is level 72!

In moments, they were gone, and there was only the tiny dragon on Vess's spear tip. She goggled at him, voice forgotten, thoughts scrambled by the Tempering still ravaging her Aspects.

"Yes," Yintarion rumbled. "I am fearsome."

"Wyrmling!" the High Guard cried, rushing forward at incredible speed. "Die!"

"You are not welcome here, Dragoon."

"Illuyanka's Coiling Gar!" A river of white-green energy snaked around the High Guard's spear, until its tip ripped open into a snarling maw of manifested fangs.

Yintarion lifted a four-fingered claw. "Adherents of Ophidia."

The water at Vess' feet lifted in thick streamers that resembled dragons the size of horses. They shot forward, spiraling into a roaring column of force that met the High Guard's attack…and ripped her attack to pieces. The water dragons continued onward, dragging the furious woman off her feet and to the sodden earth.

Yintarion panted, his small chest heaving breaths between his bristling lips. "I do not know how many more attacks I have left in me. I am not what I once was, little Dragoon." His all golden eyes turned onto Vess. "I shall require…your assistance."

Vess smiled. "You have it."

A vortex of air Mana erupted nearby, ripping the remains of Yintarion's Skill to pieces and leaving a bloody High Guard in its place. "Dragon!"

"Let us show her the might of a true Dragoon," Yintarion growled.

CHAPTER ONE HUNDRED SEVEN

Thunderwing is level 73!

Pit shot through the sky, ignoring entirely the spells and Skills that shot at him from below. He was far too fast to be hit by the few that noticed him, and all Pit had eyes for was the glowing stone crater near the city wall.

Felix! I am on the way!

There was no response from his Companion, only a thunderous crescendo of chaotic song. Pit recognized what was happening—it had happened before, after all, back in the Omen Path. He was too far away to Converge with his friend's Spirit, but glimpses flashed along their bond, and the sheer magnitude of Felix's struggle was overwhelming. All Pit could do was get close enough to merge—then, at least, he could help.

Pit was so intent on his flight path that he wasn't entirely sure what made him look aside, except perhaps a dire instinct passed down from his ancestors. A frisson of phantom terror stole up his spine and tingled across his limbs, and Pit's golden eyes swept around. *What is*—?

Ahead, three figures in white armor strode through the battlefield. Directly toward Felix.

A warble of anger gathered in Pit's throat, but it died away as the High Guard met resistance. Six Frost Giants fell, split in half by a single blow. A dozen Legionnaires were crushed beneath an immense slab of stone, as if the earth had folded them up, while three dozen Haarguard clutched their throats and simply fell limp to the ground.

Never once did they stop.

Felix won't be done when they reach him! That thrill of fear clutched at his voice, but he shoved it aside with his iron Will. *He needs more time.*

Gloaming Shroud!

Pit would buy all he could.

Fiendforge is level 55!

Felix had descended into his core space, through the Essence-laden branches of his Divine Tree and across the shining expanse of his slowly rotating Skills. Farther down, past his grinding dual cores, the root-formed sigils and Seal, and into the glittering darkness beneath it all. There, in the shadows of his core space, two woven Pillars resided. Made of thick, gleaming cables formed from his Skills, each Pillar was threaded through by opalescent roots plaited into a nightmarishly complex weave.

Cables of light descended from above, where each of his Tempered Skills were tethered to his spinning dual cores. They had been gathering for months now, waiting for when Felix was ready to make this attempt. As Karys explained it, he only had one shot—and to weave them before he was an Adept would have risked his foundations. Fear and caution had kept Felix from pursuing the weaving, even after he'd reached Adept. Now, however, as the ache of it echoed throughout his core space, Felix had little choice.

His Willpower and Intent were firmly grasped around those colored cables, his Cardinal Flame flared for fine control. His Fiendforge clamped atop the entirety of his core space, for good measure. He was relying on his perfect recall to weave the cables together, twisting and braiding them as he had once done before with his first two Pillars, until they were trunks thick enough to support all that resided above. Within each glowing cable, Felix could feel the song of his Skills change with every pass, the texture of the weave altering the timbre, tone, and pitch.

Fiendforge is level 59!

The visualization techniques Vess had taught him were paying off, as was his Hunger's ability to numb his senses. He floated within his personal void, and he worked.

Willpower and Intent were the hands by which the weaving operated, but it was his Affinity, Alacrity, and Perception that kept him ahead of the ever-changing patterns. Dissonance and Harmony sang sweet chaos into the dark, pressing deep within the Third Pillar as he went, flickering and flashing at their centers with red-gold abandon and blue-white freneticism.

As before, the opalescent roots of his Divine Tree intermingled through the Pillar—unlike the last time, however, the roots were far more responsive to his touch. He called them roots, but the System called them Veins, and they were not alone. First, the opalescent roots of his Divine Tree were seated deeply in the Pillar, anchoring his Skill cables with a solidity that could not be denied. Then, slipping through the gaps that Felix had not noticed, was a drumming Need whose rhythm hung like background radiation across his core space.

FEED.

Leave them alone! Felix warned. *These are not for you!*

The presence retreated, but it did not flee. His Hunger sat like a fat spider at the center of its web, watching and probably drooling while Felix braided power into physical marvels. The cables grew thicker and more potent the farther down he constructed them, their bases anchored by the heaviest and slowest-moving portions of his Skills' songs. Each revolution and twist deepened their potency, until the working became so monstrous that even his Willpower could not fully encompass it. The Pillar snapped from his control, thrumming with a note so pure it shivered the entirety of his core space. Harmony and Dissonance chased after one another, note and counter note fitting together like the pieces of some teeth-grinding jigsaw puzzle.

The Third Pillar was done.

Six more to go.

He lost himself in the process, retracing his steps time and again. The deluge of Essence, Mana, and significance threatened to crush him as it piled through his hands, but he did not stop. He couldn't. The weaving was unrelenting and tireless, too fast and heavy for him to halt. All he could do was guide it.

By the end of the Fourth Pillar, his firm grip turned to a precarious balancing act atop a blade that sliced him even as he strode forward into the breach. Yet, to fall off meant certain destruction. It sped up, the weaving moving faster and faster.

Fiendforge is level 64!

The Fifth Pillar was next. Then the Sixth.

Power was gathering, trapped inside the cables and crystalline Veins that threaded through them all. It was growing, multiplying with every new Pillar he forged, but it was held at bay. Karys had mentioned this part as well; while the first Pillar had granted a bonus immediately, all nine would have to form before he could reap their full benefits.

Three more remained, but the implacable advance of power had slowed to a trickle. Above, his Divine Tree was barren, bereft of its Essence just as Felix's cores were sucked dry of Mana as soon as he regenerated it. Even the halo around his Hunger, the Essence and power it had not yet digested had faded to almost nothing.

Still, just barely, a Seventh snapped into place.

Cardinal Flame is level 86!
Fiendforge is level 71!

Felix was so close to hitting Adept Tier with Fiendforge that he could taste it. A little longer, and he could harvest the System energy that would flood his core as it Tiered up...but no. Not yet. He might have been almost out of energy to fuel his weaving, but he knew other ways to get more.

Chthonic Trib—

A Link closest to his chest spiked with sudden fear, anger—and far more terrifying—agony. Felix's focus broke. *Pit!*

If he left his core space, the Pillars could foul themselves as they continued to try and form. Karys had warned him of that—leaving things undone could have catastrophic consequences on his core space.

But his friend was in trouble.

There was no hesitation, no blink of the eye to weigh consequences. The knowledge of what could happen flitted through him, but Felix was already moving, rising back to his Body. He leaped from a twenty-foot deep crater and landed on the still-hot ground beyond.

Just in time to see an orichalcum sword chop off Pit's wing.

Status Condition: Spirit Damage 15%
Status Condition: Curse of Flame!

Curse of Flame
When this Masterwork weapon deals an injury, the curse born by its blade ensures that said injury is permanent. The curse of flame is to burn forever.

"Oh, he is awake," said a thin, almost skeletal looking fellow. He wore the same milk-white armor, but he carried a large, silver-chased book. His expression was curious but also very bored. "He is angry."

"You should have stayed in your hole, Autarch," Mace said. "You can't fight all three of us at once."

Two other High Guards advanced along with him, all of them

without their smooth, featureless helms. The wild-eyed Mace stared with a manic glee, and the man—the man with the bloody blade glared with an expression of utter serenity.

"The Autarch finally graces us with his presence. Good." Casually, as if mailing a letter, he sliced off Pit's other wing, and his Companion writhed in utter agony. It echoed through Felix's core, a debilitating pain that threatened to topple him. "Let us end this."

Status Condition: Berserk
Berserk - Increase Damage Output By 20%, Increase Damage Taken By 20%

White-hot rage surged through his veins, unlike anything Felix had ever experienced. It evaporated the pain like it never existed, even as the Spirit Damage ratcheted up another fifteen percent. There was no thought.

There was only violence.

Mace charged forward, her namesake weapon lifted high.

Sovereign of Flesh!

Relentless Resolution!

Felix's Will seized her Body, even as his morphed into a deadlier form. Scales ran the length of him, and his hands became tipped with vicious talons—talons he used to rip at her shoulder joint. For the tiniest fraction of a second, Mace's Body resisted Felix's Skill and Strength, but then it failed. She fell, screeching in pain and gushing blood, her momentum ruined as Felix held up her severed arm.

Chthonic Tribute!

And he fucking ate it.

"Blessed Pathless..." The sword bastard whispered, his calm broken. "What *are* you?"

Felix's eyes blazed, staining his vision blue-white and red-gold. "Your executioner."

CHAPTER ONE HUNDRED EIGHT

"A–affliction of Deprivation!" Tome stuttered.

A flock of purple and green-gold birds flashed toward Felix, but he was faster. His clawed hand found the skinny book-bearer's head and drove Tome into the dirt.

Hand of Cataclysm!

Acid burst across Tome's face, and he let loose a harrowing, burbling scream, his silver-chased book falling to the side.

"Rancor's Blade!"

Dodge is level 78!

Felix leaped aside, narrowly avoiding the descent of Sword's fiery blade. Tome had not died, and regret boiled inside of him even as his vision was still stained with the light of his fury. He rounded on the presumptive leader of the High Guard, closing the distance without a thought.

Stone Shaping!

Green Shaping!

Huge, blunt rods of stone smashed into Sword from below, taking him hard in the midsection while flowering vines erupted to tangle his feet and ankles as Felix slipped inside his guard. The man did not stop his swing, however, and it came down atop Felix faster than he could move—which was when Felix seized the fire Mana that coated his sword.

Cardinal Flame!

Flame bent to Felix's Will and sprayed Sword in the face.

"Gah!" The High Guard shouted in alarm more than pain, before tripping backward over the thick vines. His exposed face was beet red, but seemed unharmed. "You're dishonorable as well as a thief. I should have known."

Felix looked beyond the man to where his friend was bleeding into the muddy water. A large, golden eye caught his, and shame vibrated across their bond.

Status Condition: Berserk (Major)
Berserk - Increase Damage Output By 40%, Increase Damage Taken By 40%, Willpower Reduced By 10%.

Status Condition: Spirit Damage 30%

Convergence!

Close enough now, Pit vanished in a flash of light. Sword frowned, eyes flicking between the two of them. "And full of dirty tricks as well."

Relentless Resolution!

Felix closed the distance with Sword again, meeting orichalcum blade with his Inheritor's Will. Sparks flew, showering the landscape as their arms blurred through too many sword forms to count. The High Guard was strong, but enhanced by his rage, Felix was stronger—yet he couldn't manage to land a solid hit on the bastard.

"You," Sword panted. "You're a brute without an ounce of technique. A monster."

"And you don't shut up!" Felix growled. Stone tore from the ground, ice crackling atop it in jagged spikes, but the High Guard flowed around it all. His footwork was sure and incredibly adept, moving with far more precision and grace than Felix. It was infuriating.

"Behemoth's Collapse!"

"Searing Attrition!"

The water folded beneath Felix's feet, metal and earth Mana surging in a wide expanse as the ground opened up like a trap door. A massive slab of rock swung upward and arced down atop him like a closing lid, sprouting with purple and green-gold flames along its falling face. Felix did nothing but lift his scaled arms and let loose an unhinged cry.

Wild Threnody!

Stone Shaping!

Green Shaping!

Dusty brown and green gold surged into his hooked sword, a colorful counterpoint to the brilliant glyph that showed near the hilt. A vibrant, liquid light ignited along its length as he slashed four times in quick succession. Channeled through his Wild Threnody, through his weapon, his two shaping Skills caught and seized the Mana that was descending upon him. It burst, splitting over his head as it was reduced to shapeless vapor.

Wild Threnody is level 82!
Stone Shaping is level 86!
Green Shaping is level 73!

"That...was remarkable," Tome said. His face was melted and bloody, his breathing ragged, but his one remaining eye was fixed on Felix as if he were a particularly interesting bug. "Was that...the weapon or him?"

"Doesn't matter!" Mace shouted, her weapon held out accusingly in her remaining hand. It gleamed with red-gold light. "This heretic owes me an arm!"

"Then come and get it!" Felix bellowed and rushed toward the woman.

Bird constructs flashed by him again, a far larger flock than previous, forcing Felix to pull ice from the water into an arcing shield. It lasted all of a half-second, but he was moving much faster than they expected. Mace's eyes widened as his clawed hand reached out—and was stopped by the flat of an orichalcum blade.

"Lord's Ire!" Sword cried out, and a concussive, golden blast took Felix full on in the chest.

"Oof!"

Lifted straight off his feet, the condensed explosion of light threw him backward more than thirty feet—right into Tome's flock of birds. A dozen tore through him, shredding his Garment and bursting against his midnight scales before Felix landed with a splash.

Chthonic Tribute!

The birds flickered, and some vanished, but his Willpower, normally so dominant, felt wan and thin as it ran against the High Guard's. Felix was afforded a moment of pure, unadulterated shock before purple and green-gold flames erupted all around him.

Status Condition: Searing Attrition
Searing Attrition - Reduces your Health and Stamina at a rate of 50/sec for 300 seconds. You are more vulnerable to heat and fire Mana for the duration.

What? Felix stood, glyph burning atop his Inheritor's Will as it sliced the birds around him into Mana vapor. *How is my Willpower so weak? Ah, shit.* Rage burned in him, so bright that it made darkness pulse at the edges of his vision. His heart was racing in his chest, and his skin felt scorching beneath his hand. *Berserk Status. Fuck!*

He had no more time. Sword, Tome, and Mace rushed him, their Skills and spells and techniques hammered at him from every angle. All he could do was move. Fight.

Stone and metal came at him, ripping apart the sodden ground with each attempt, while curses in the shape of birds and locusts swarmed him. Through it all, Sword was there, his long blade shining in the gaps between his allies' attacks—and each time the man landed a hit, Felix's fury grew.

Status Condition: Berserk (Severe)
Berserk - Increase Damage Output By 50%, Increase Damage Taken By 50%, Willpower Reduced By 20%.

He met them. Blow for blow.

Dodge is level 79!
Armored Skin is level 85!
Relentless Resolution is level 87!
Stone Shaping is level 87!
Rime Shaping is level 74!
Green Shaping is level 74!
Wild Threnody is level 84!

The High Guard was gaining ground. Felix's Health dropped point-by-point with every strike that bypassed his defenses. Berserk gave his fist and swords greater power, but increased his injuries by substantial amounts. Searing Affliction, meanwhile, turned Sword's fire attacks from annoyances to agonizing threats, worse each time Tome managed to hit him with another stack of the Skill. And for the first time in—months?—his Stamina recovery was slow enough that he had to be cautious about his movements.

For all his stats and Skill levels, Felix could not fight them off.

Inside his chest, his final two Pillars called to him. They were an open wound that he'd managed to ignore, clamping down on them with Fiendforge while he fought. But as his Willpower fell before his increasing unthinking rage, the interminable ache of his unfinished efforts further blunted his edge in combat. His strikes were off, his Mind dulled, and his Spirit heavy with the whimpering sounds of his injured Companion.

I need...to calm...down!

"Plague of Multitudes!" the gangly Tome shouted, just before shoving a gauntleted hand over his silver-chased book. Another flock of green-gold locusts shot into the air, all of them swirling around the other High Guards before swooping directly at Felix.

Chthonic Tribute!

Compromised Willpower or not, Felix pitted it against the bastard's spell. He wasn't the only one suffering, and the High Guard mage flinched as their Minds clashed against one another. Barely, just barely, Felix won. He opened his maw and pulled, until every single mote of Mana was consumed.

"He ate it, too?" Mace shouted, her voice on the ragged edge of panic. The bleeding had stopped, but she was very pale.

"Focus!" Sword commanded. "He is only an Adept!"

"It should not be possible—" The words barely left Tome's lips when another white-armored figure crashed into his legs, followed by a deluge of blasting water shaped like—

"Dragons?" Felix's confusion turned to joy as Vess dropped from the sky, her spear stabbing at Tome and the newcomer with thunderous intensity. "Vess!"

Status Reduced!
Status Condition: Berserk (Severe) > Berserk (Major)

Huh.

The newcomer High Guard, still prone, swept an orichalcum spear at Vess' legs and unleashed a wave of cutting wind at them both. Vess leaped backward, and Felix stomped his left foot, summoning a wall of stone and ice from the ground that shoved all of the High Guards away from him and his friend. Still, the Skill hit his barrier with the sound of screeching metal, but it didn't penetrate.

Vess landed beside him, hair fluttering around her as if in a constant breeze. She smiled, and her cheek dimpled beneath a streak of blood. "Hi."

"Hi." Felix blinked, Voracious Eye flaring as he spotted something on her shoulder. "Is that—"

"I am Yintarion of the Cerulean Sky," the little golden Wyrmling rumbled, voice almost as deep as it had been before. He lifted his cat-sized head, and his tiny mane rippled in the breeze. "We have formed a bond, the Dragoon and I. Little else needs to be said."

Felix closed his mouth, not only at the reduction of his Berserk Status, but the sheer surprise of it all stymied the heat that had built up in his chest. "Right. Help me kill these idiots?"

"It would be my pleasure," Vess said.

"Beware," the Wyrmling murmured. "They have…changed."

Felix whipped his head around, Perception tagging on the High Guards that had retreated. A short distance away, blocked from his direct vision by the walls of stone and ice, they had begun to glow.

"That cannot be good," Vess murmured.

Felix sank his barrier back into the shallow water and saw the armored warriors had gathered close together. Sigils flashed across their armor in a complex display that Felix couldn't comprehend.

"They are joining their strength!" Yintarion warned.

Felix charged.

Hand of Calamity!

Rain of Cataclysm!

Arrow of Perdition!

Wild Threnody!

A torrent of acid and gold-azure radiance gathered up into his sword and dagger as he tore forward, water and mud spraying behind him in his wake. None of the High Guard moved, but the sigaldry around them flared until it was blinding.

Chthonic Tribute!

Maw open, Felix tried to snatch the power away from the bastards as it crackled about their armor, but it was like trying to drink an entire ocean. His Willpower failed, the Skill screeching in recoil—but he wasn't done. He struck twin slashes with Inheritor's Will and Skyslain's Riposte.

Hand of Calamity is level 20!
Rain of Cataclysm is level 74!
Wild Threnody is level 85!

Arrow of Perdition is level 50!
Journeyman Tier!
You Gain:
+50 STR
+40 VIT
+30 DEX

The flood of violence threw every single one of them from their feet, though Felix couldn't tell who—the light was so bright, it was all he could perceive. That is, until it cut off abruptly, and Felix watched them stand, one after the other, as acid Mana evaporated from their forms. The cracks in their milky white armor were patched with lines of golden light, and a complex, multi-layered array had formed across their chests and limbs...and trailed from their backs like cloaks of gold.

"We are your judgment, Felix Nevarre," Sword said, his voice deeper and far more resonant.

For all his anger, Felix wasn't so far gone he'd forget his Voracious Eye. Aside from their Health and Mana, it caught little else but the impression of their Tier...and that was rising rapidly. Felix blinked, looking between the High Guard, but it was the same for all four of them. Whereas before his Eye acknowledged the threat they posed... now it all but screamed at him.

"Grandmaster," he whispered. "All of you together—"

"Smart, boy," Spear growled. For the first time, Felix noticed she was missing an eye. She had looked haggard before...but now a flaxen radiance poured from her wounds, just as it did her armor. "Too smart."

"Perhaps I should have taken your tongue instead of your eye," Vess said from behind her leveled spear.

"Deceiving wench—"

"End this. Now," Sword ordered. His impassive face had returned, but Felix could feel a trace of the man's Spirit; he *burned* that Felix had seen his fear. "Kill him."

As one, the High Guard advanced.

Sovereign of Flesh!

Consuming the dregs of his Essence stores, Felix's Body swelled with muscle, scales, and claws as he met the warriors' attacks. His eyes blazed and crackled, lightning trailing from them as he blurred forward.

Relentless Resolution is level 88!

Felix danced at the edge of their attacks, though it cost him several wounds. Spear, Mace, and Sword struck again and again, each aiming for a different part of his body; he couldn't avoid them all, so long as he was attacking. Felix screamed, a horrendous noise that blasted water from their feet from the sheer volume, and put everything he had into attacking. Inheritor's Will was a cudgel in his fist, while the Skyslain Riposte had become a heavy machete. Rock and water scattered around them, shattered beneath their collective tread or evaporated by bursts of their power.

Yet the High Guard were too fast. They hit Felix twice for every blow he landed, penetrating his Armored Skin and midnight scales with an ease that staggered his Health and depleted his Stamina at a rapid pace. In the short seconds after their collective Tier advancement, Felix was sliced and burned and bashed until he trailed blood like crimson streamers.

"Wending River!" a deep voice shouted, and Vess was suddenly there. Felix gaped, the blaze of his eyes flickering out as he witnessed a millisecond of her speed and grace while Yintarion stood ramrod straight on her pauldron. "Binding Light!"

Water Mana glittering with golden light Mana flowed around them both, deceptively slow in that split-second viewing, but it punched into Mace with the force of a monstrous waterfall. Grandmaster array or not, the one-armed warrior was hurled back and away.

A tendril of the same magic also hit Felix, though far more gently, and he was hauled back nearly forty feet before he cut free of it. "What the hell!"

"You are not thinking, fool king!" Yintarion shouted back. They dove between the High Guard's attacks, spectral wings flaring atop Vess' back—she was moving *very* fast. "Your rage! Eliminate it!"

Felix gritted his teeth, more than ready to show the Wyrmling what he could do—when he felt a frisson of utter agony tear through his core. He gasped, clutching at his wounded chest, but it did nothing to dilute the torment that twisted inside of him. His Pillars were demanding their release, the power contained inside of them pulsing as if eager to escape, to soak into Felix like a balm…yet he couldn't touch any of it. Not until all nine were formed, and he had nothing left to spend on them—not without sacrificing what little combat potency he had left.

Fiendforge is level 72!

It was taking all he could just to keep the process halted, and even that felt like a gaping wound in his chest. The pull of his Skills and cores as they tried to spin was incredible, enough that he was only holding on by his fingernails. One wrong move, one slip, and his Pillars would start up again—only this time, Felix wouldn't be there to guide them.

B-be calm, Felix. I—I can do it.

Pit! When had he roused? *Are you—your wings were—Don't waste your energy!*

Be calm! A wave of images flashed across their bond, Memories the two of them had shared in the rare quiet times between conflicts. As if they were a key turning in a lock, Felix felt his rage abate, soothed.

Status Reduced!
Status Condition: Berserk (Major) > Berserk

I can do it! Don't stop me!

Fuck. He was still so angry, but the feeling of his friend descending into his core space made the fury falter. He had no other real options. His final two Pillars had to form—quickly. Pit could more actively direct the situation, but without Felix there…

HELP.

What? Felix's eyes finally left the dizzying battle between Vess and the High Guard, one that he feared was going to end badly. *How?*

UN-FEED.

Un—what the hell are you talking about—!

"Focus on me, would-be king!" Sword said, brandishing his blade at Felix's head. Somehow he'd escaped Vess' distracting onslaught, and Felix kicked backward, out of range entirely. "You're too weak to ignore us!"

Fine! Whatever it is, do it! Pit! Keep the other guy in check!

Felix set himself, letting his oversized, scaled form deplete. Unused Essence swirled back into his core space before getting sucked up by his Pillars. He spat out blood before baring his flat, Human teeth. "Fine. You and me, Sword. Let's dance."

CHAPTER ONE HUNDRED NINE

"Nevarre," Sword said, as if weighing the name. They stood, separated by churning water as fire and light and stone rained upon them all. He adjusted his grip upon his overlarge blade. "That is Wyvarren, is it not?"

Felix felt sweat or blood trickle down his back. A hollow ache pulsed at his center, but he forced it from his thoughts. "What?"

"Yes." The word was drawn out. Savored. "Wyvarren. Perhaps after this, we can go find your family. I daresay our treaties with Wyvarr would make the matter simple."

"We could find them, yes," Tome said in a distracted voice. His face was half melted and bloody, but he looked as detached from their conflict as if he were reading a research paper. "Easily. A House that produced such a powerful combatant could not hide from us."

It was a distraction, clearly. Felix had no family on the Continent—but he was more than happy to play it up for time. "You'll never touch them," he said and let the truth of that sentence ring through his Spirit.

"Perhaps. Or perhaps we shall parade your corpse through Isindr, and take them when they cry for our mercy."

Forcing himself to disregard the disturbing imagery, Felix split his attention for the briefest of moments. His inner songs rang loud and bright and he clamped tight with Fiendforge before spinning his cores as fast as he could—even as he ducked beneath the horizontal swipe of his enemy's weapon.

He took Sword's sudden strike against his blades, and despite the numbing shock that ran up his arms, he took a single, easy breath. The internal pressure eased...before swiftly turning to a hot, searing pain.

Dissonance and Harmony raged, unleashed from their enforced stasis and eager to swell up inside his core space.

"Rancor's Blade!" Sword shouted, and fire erupted across their crossed weapons.

Cardinal—!

The Skill slipped from Felix's grasp, and fire washed over him, uncontested. He clenched his teeth against the agony, rolling into the water and pulling a shield of ice from below to blunt its hungry edge. In the split-second respite, he felt at his Skill…only to find it fully active and aimed inward instead of outward.

Sorry! Pit cried, his lilting voice filled with pain, pressure, and urgency. *I need it! And this!*

Fiendforge vanished from Felix's control as well. He could still hear their songs, still feel the vibrations through his Aspects…but the physical and mental strain of them both vanished entirely. Unbidden, a bead of hope accumulated in his heart, and it grew larger and brighter with each muted strain of sound—even as he desperately danced away from a barrage of flaming darts.

"Do you not have the courage to face me, Navarre?" Sword scoffed at him, following up his volley of projectiles with a horizontal swing. A crescent of orange flame licked outward…only to meet a curtain of half-formed ice. With an explosive hiss, it turned into a cloud of superheated steam. "Hiding now? My Perception is far too sharp to deceive, Nevarre."

Within the sudden cloud bank, Felix floundered. Delight chased after the hope that fluttered within him, joy that his Companion could do such a thing. A half-dozen darts of stone shot toward him, but he slapped them out of the air with his Riposte. He sensed the onrush of Mace, weapon lifted high with her remaining arm—yet Felix couldn't help it.

He laughed.

Status Condition: Berserk
Status Condition Ended!

"You've broken him, Sword." Mace said, uncaring at the noise she made in the shallow water. She appeared from the fading steam with a fervent light burning in her eyes. "My turn, yeah?"

Her strike was fast, and the loss of his Berserk Status Condition was like dropping a heavy weight from Felix's neck.

He lifted his left arm, too slow before her heightened stats, and her attack was like a collapsing building in its descent. Undeniable and bone-crushing. The bladed flanges gouged a bloody furrow in his shoulder, and Felix felt something snap just above his elbow. "Hah! That's just the start for repayment on my arm, boy!"

Her triumphant grin froze, however, when instead of crying out, Felix seized her weapon. "I'm not done," Felix hissed. "*Mine!*"

Chthonic Tribute!

The orichalcum mace fought back—all things wished to remain as they were, whether they were a rock or a magic weapon. But neither stone nor orichalcum could match his unfettered Will. Felix wrenched it hard, yanking it free of the High Guard's grip...and it blasted apart, dissolved to liquid Mana and smoky Essence that poured into Felix's gullet.

Claiming what he needed with Sovereign of Flesh, his arm snapped back together in a rush of pain...and the rest he sent skittering into his depths. *Pit! Take it!*

"Wha—my Masterwork weapon!" Mace cried out, falling back. "You—he—!"

"Do not gawk! Kill him!" Sword commanded. "And these pests, as well!"

Felix spotted Vess and Yintarion leaping through the air at the same time as the High Guard. He bellowed a warning and ripped a thirty-foot tall wall of stone from beneath their feet just in time to meet the slash of Sword's blade. The crescent of flame cut through the two feet of stone like melting wax, only to hit a swiftly woven shield of wind and water. The Wyrmling roared, and the explosive impact sent the pair hurtling to the ground.

"Vess!"

"I am—fine!" she gasped upon landing. Her left hand and shoulder were charred, the white enamel in her silver armor spiderwebbed with cracks.

"But we are at our limit," the golden Wyrmling said. "I have held them all that I could. We must rest! The Dragoon is not meant for this battle."

"Then go!" Felix ordered, worry and anger warring within him. If they couldn't fight, he needed them out. Safe. "Now!"

It was too late. Spear and Tome joined the others, each bearing a dazzling golden cloak. Joined by sigaldry and some arcane process, their combined Spirits pointed at them all. More dangerous by far than any mere weapon.

The High Guard charged as one.

Stomps that shattered stone and thrusts that split the very air rained down on him, but Felix held on. He devoured spells and Skills but could only grasp the barest edge of their power—at best blunting them before he was forced to dodge aside, and many came on entirely too fast. Their strange array was too potent. Yet, it wasn't just the array—their Skills seem to mesh and intermingle, Spear's wind working in tandem with Tome's lightning and Mace's earth and metal. Sword, flaring with fire Mana, was apart, a flourish to each concerted attack meant to upset the rhythm of the fight.

Vess and Yintarion gave their all, but they were exhausted, and she had barely enough Stamina to last another few minutes. Felix was their wall, building barriers of stone and ice and greenery where he could… and interposing his own Body where he could not. His scales took the brunt of those attacks, Armored Skin acting as backup for his already mighty Body, but they took a savage toll.

Wound after wound accumulated on Felix, and his Health plummeted. Sovereign of Flesh hummed through him, fed by the glancing feedings he took from their Skills—enough to maintain his Health and Stamina, but not nearly enough to feed Pit's efforts. The roar of his Hunger had increased, seemingly angry at a lack of sustenance, and the hollow pang of Pit's efforts was a dull knife dragged along the insides of his bones.

Felix knew how this played out. He'd done it twice before, weeks prior, when he'd faced the Grandmaster of Ahkestria. He may have won in the end, but that gray-skinned bastard hadn't been at his peak; when he had been, Felix had nearly died. Now, fighting four Masters somehow joined into a Grandmaster was like battling a tempest. Attacks came from every angle, at every moment, until the world was reduced to him and them.

"Adherents of Ophidia!"

Thin dragons of water spun upward and around, splashing ineffectually against the golden haze of the High Guard's power, but succeeding in making all of them flinch backward. All but Spear, that is.

"She flees!" the woman cried, before throwing out an empty hand. "Howl Aphson!"

A fleet of air spears manifested and launched all in one motion. Felix's Perception tracked backward, even as Sword advanced on him. *Vess!*

His friend and the Wyrmling blurred across the ground, sped by strange air magic and the ghostly wings she bore. Yet Spear's Skill surged across the shallow water with unerring accuracy.

Relentless Resolution!

The ground exploded. Mud and water cascaded over the High Guard, and Felix was abruptly elsewhere, his hands reaching outward to grasp at the air spears. "Chthonic Tribute!" he howled.

Air Mana and smoky Essence flooded his pathways, dimming the Skill's glow, but he couldn't pull it all.

Stone Shaping!

Rime Shaping!

Green Shaping!

Blue-black walls erupted from below, curving around his friends in the split seconds before the spears hit…and punched right through.

Vess screamed, and Yintarion roared in piercing agony.

Felix made it there a half-heartbeat later, to find his friends bloody on the ground. *Still alive,* he realized. *Barely. One more hit…*

The High Guard were closing in.

Pit! I need those Pillars done!

I need more Essence! You have so much Mana, but we're all but out of Essence to weave these things!

Four warriors tore up the water almost as fast as Felix had, their steps thunderous as the sky was painted a bloody crimson by the setting sun. He did the only thing he could think of; the only thing that had worked for him time and time again.

He ate.

Chthonic Tribute!

Felix pitted every ounce of his restored Willpower against everything around him but Vess and Yintarion. The water, the mud, the stone and drowned grass, even the air itself—he devoured them all.

Chthonic Tribute!

The world dissolved around him into a miasma of loose Mana and Essence smoke, spreading farther and farther until he reached the edge of his power. The air buckled, and the ground evaporated, until they were inundated within a writhing curtain of dark smoke. It alone wouldn't do…because Felix was going to eat it all soon. So, he uncorked a bottle at his side, and let flow a deep, thick fog from within. The Bottle of Eversmoke from Temple Haestus spewed forth an impenetrable cloud around them all, and Felix and his friends were concealed.

Spells and Skills launched at the perimeter of his externalized hunger, attacks that nearly caught Felix head-on despite their concealment. Before he could address them, however, a vibrant light flowed from behind him. Felix turned in time to catch Yintarion lifting a shaking claw and breathing out deep flows of darkest purple tinged by blue.

"You are not—the only one with tricks, Felix Nevarre. Sever The Eye!"

The miasma of released Essence and Eversmoke were inundated by Yintarion's Skill, and it seemed all of the golden Wyrmlings swirled around them. To Felix's eyes, it was a storm of Mana that crackled as it met the magic of the Eversmoke…and let it expand into strange, whirling dimensions. Distance and space suddenly upended as a hurricane of chaos was born.

"An illusion, and all I can spare," Yintarion said. His voice was thin, and the glow from his golden scales dimmed, as if he had truly pressed everything into that Skill. "It will not confuse them for long."

"Thank you." Felix turned back toward the roiling fog around them. Chewing on ideas as water rushed around them, filling in the sudden hole he'd taken out of the earth. Rock, soil, air, and water had little in the way of Essence compared to a person, but it was enough that Pit had begun weaving again. *What else can I do?*

Skills fired off, but this time they spun away from where Felix, Vess, and Yintarion huddled atop their platform of stone. Boulders arced over, birds of green-gold light swirled, and air spears stabbed down at erratic angles—all of them far from hitting. Distantly, he heard them curse.

"You finally face us truly, and now you run?" Mace said, the wrath in her voice as clear as the derision—and the buried pain. "Pathetic! You are not fit to be a Territorial Lord!"

"He is not," Sword affirmed. Felix's skin crawled just to hear the man's voice. *He* was the one that Felix was worried most about, and there was a weight to the man's voice he could not place. "And so I challenge you, Lord of Nagast, for your Title!"

Attention!
Territorial Lord Autarch Felix Nevarre Has Been Challenged For His Authority!
The Challenger Is Master Callum D'or Of The High Guard!

Shit. Apparently, Felix didn't get a choice to refuse the matter. Even the Grandmaster of the Desert's Flame got a choice. *What sort of Authority does he have to force the issue?*

Begin Challenge!

"Judgment's Squall!" Sword's words boomed through Felix's concealing cloud. His Perception caught the High Guard lifting his weapon above his head...only for it to ignite into a tower of flame, hundreds of feet into the air. "Face me with honor, Usurper Nevarre! Or your people will be punished for your cowardice!"

The firestorm coiled upward, an inferno in the guise of a cyclone, high enough that, were it to fall, the flames would reach Haarwatch's walls. Through the haze of illusion and fog, Felix could tell how powerful it was, and that it would savage the entire wall—and set the Sunrise Quarter beyond ablaze. Thousands would die, unless he acted, and if he acted...Felix licked his lips. He looked behind him, where Vess lay unconscious on their narrow stone platform, and the wan light of Yintarion all but guttered out.

"Very well!" Sword cried out, and his voice boomed twice as loud as before as he addressed the entire battlefield. "Your Autarch has abandoned you! He refuses to face a lawful Challenge! As such, he has condemned you and your city to death!"

"Run, fool king," Yintarion rumbled.

Felix took a single, steadying breath. "Yeah, that'd be smart."

Pit, he sent. *Prepare yourself.*

A warble of strain was interposed with confusion and—as Pit sensed Felix's Spirit—fear. Swiftly followed by a fierce determination. *I stand ready.*

Felix stood up.

"It's time for something stupid, though."

CHAPTER ONE HUNDRED TEN

This is pathetic. Sword let the thought linger in his Mind, tumbling about the font of condensed might that coursed through his Aspects and Twelve Point Array. The firestorm in his grasp bucked and twisted, but he held firm. *Cowardice. Huddling within a fogbank.*

The swirling, folding illusion before them infuriated him. Quite apart from the damnable Territorial mist, it was even more impossible to peer through. Sword had tried to cast it aside with the light of the Pathless, but it remained. Somehow, it was a spell that was beyond their Twelve-Point Array. While the array did not provide true advancement, it joined them in such a way as to mimic the power of a Grandmaster, and few things could withstand their direct attention.

He is full of tricks. Aloud, he spoke with all the volume afforded to him by his artificial Temper. "You are strong, but to hide yourself before a Challenge? I find myself disappointed in your weakness, Felix Nevarre."

Admittedly, the Autarch of Nagast had pushed them this far—the use of the Twelve-Point Array was not one the High Guard engaged in casually, and brandishing Judgment's Squall was something Sword had not done in many decades. The firestorm continued to fuel itself above them, raging from the tip of his orichalcum Masterwork blade. It was a whirlwind of pure destruction, a Skill he had last used in the conquering of the northern wilds. The moment it touched earth, the firestorm would raze the city of Haarwatch as if it were no more than kindling, and nothing would remain.

"Ugh, just release it already!" Mace shouted, her voice thin and strained. "You're using more power than you need, Sword! The wretch is gonna die soon, anyway!"

"This isn't for *him*," Sword corrected her, turning his Perception upon the wounded warrior. "This is a demonstration."

"For who? You'll kill 'em all."

"For all heathens," Spear snarled. Her one remaining eye was fixed on the confusing cloud of potent illusions, and her free hand clenched reflexively, as if she wished to hurl more of her air spears into it.

"Fine. Fry the city, for all I care. Just be done with it!" Mace shouted the last, and it did not escape his notice that she was bleeding anew. The wound at her shoulder was not healing, and her contribution to the Twelve-Point Array was wan and feeble.

"A few more moments will not halt anything," Sword said as Judgement's Squall gathered the force it required. *A shame.* A faint regret twitched at his heart, but he let that go, feeding it to his flame. Certainty replaced it. He would need to kill Mace soon. Without an arm, her effectiveness in battle was greatly reduced, and whatever the boy did, it was interfering with her Body's protections. Such a situation was unfortunate, but they must remain strong. For the Hierophant. For the Pathless. *Truly a shame.*

He put that out of his Mind. Mace, for all her flaws, was right.

We must burn the heretics from the earth. Scorching fire, cleansing light. As it always must be.

The firestorm roared, a sound beyond noise that pummeled the battlefield with a physical pressure. Dozens of warriors had attempted to rush them in the time it took to gather its momentum, but the Twelve-Point Array had elevated their Spirit so far above them that it was a simple matter of flexing their Spiritual presence. Most fell, beaten to the ground, while the sheer heat stopped the rest.

"Should we order a general retreat?" Tome asked. He was sweating, his face bruised and bloodied by the usurper, but his expression was as calm as always.

"Hm," Sword said. He was fighting to hold onto his Judgment now, forced to flare his array-born Strength to simply keep it steady. "Do so."

Tome sent a whisper of his Mana back toward the battalions, but Sword ignored it. The firestorm called to him, pulled his power—their power—into its all-consuming whorl. Instead of opposing it, Sword encouraged its flames to howl with all the ferocity he could muster.

"I call Judgment upon you, Nagast! Murderous thieves will be paid in kind!" Sword's voice boomed outward, the force of it toppling warriors hundreds of strides away. Men and women scurried atop their wall, raising barriers and shields, as if a soap bubble could stop a boot. He tightened his grip upon his blade. "Haarwatch ends because of you, Felix Nevarre!"

Sword swung down. The firestorm roared and kicked, the momentum and pressure fighting back, but it succumbed to their combined might. Judgment fell upon Haarwatch.

"Bad idea, douchenozzle."

Sword's Perception spiked in alarm as a figure garbed in black scales appeared out of nowhere. His compatriots flinched, equally surprised, as the vile Autarch lifted a clawed hand.

"Adamant Discord!"

An eruption of incandescent lightning tore from the man. All four of them were sent skidding across the sodden earth, forcing Sword to twist his stance to avoid collapse. A simple thing, normally, but he bore in his hands the weight of a falling mountain. His strike was turned, but he pressed on—it mattered little where the blade would land, for Judgment's Squall would raze the city regardless.

In fact, his surprise turned to glee as the others recovered near-instantly and assaulted the lone Autarch. Skills flew, bright and fast, and the scaled man vanished beneath their impact. Sword bore down with all his might upon his blade, and his Judgment screamed as it hit the city's barrier.

The glimmering, faceted shield screeched beneath the pressure of the inferno, before paneled sections popped and shattered entirely. Flames swept outward, above the wall and rooftops beyond, a field of unstoppable, elemental heat.

"Rime Shaping!"

A wall of ice hurtled skyward, meeting his firestorm and bursting into blinding steam. Behind it, a figure flew from the illusory ward, trailing lightning and fog like a stormcloud, garbed in a short jacket and black, midnight scales.

"What?" Sword's astonishment swiftly turned to indignant rage. "Illusions!"

Felix Nevarre's hand met the firestorm, and it bent away as something atonal and horrendous screeched from his unnaturally fanged maw.

"Chthonic Tribute!"

Illusory Double is level 22!

His illusion Skill had cut off as soon as the High Guard destroyed his double, but it had served its purpose. Just as his other Skills served theirs.

Mantle of the Infinite Revolution is level 59!

Rime Shaping is level 75!
Adept Tier!
You Gain:
+50 INT
+30 WIL
+30 VIT

Ice crackled as his Mantle spun in slow, inevitable courses, and he drew that ice up and around his body like armor. It snapped and melted almost the same instant he formed it, but Felix wasn't deterred as the firestorm dropped.

Chthonic Tribute!

Felix's Hunger yawned wide, opening itself as the flames of apocalypse fell atop him. Fire turned to Mana, surging into his mouth and the Mana Gate at the base of his skull. Flames crashed against ice and the greedy grasp of his most useful Skill.

Chthonic Tribute is level 88!

It did not stop the flames from scorching him. Searing Affliction increased the damage he took from fire and the heat it produced, but Felix refused to stop. Ice formed and steamed, superheated by the sheer potency of Sword's Judgment—it was a thin shield, but all he could muster. Felix's Health dropped, sinking with every second he endured beneath that whirling storm, but he refused to relent. Blue-white lightning crackled at his back, propping him up against the earth far below. His Will was all that stood between Haarwatch and total destruction.

Warning!
Your Health Has Dropped Below 10%!

Pit! Felix could have taken the Essence and Mana from the Skill and fueled his Sovereign of Flesh, but there was only one chance for them. He gave it up, pushing it deep, below his core space and into the great dark beyond. *Take it!*

Darkness flashed across senses inundated with light, and the phantom sensation of soft feathers met his charred, brutalized flesh. Felix screamed, pulling with all of his might as the firestorm cascaded over him.

Chthonic Tribute is level 89!
Chthonic Tribute is level 90!

The Judgment collapsed around him, unraveled by someone other than Felix. Great chunks of Essence, Mana, and trickles of significance sank into his channels, but not enough. Still, a sound like ten thousand harps strumming stoked the chaos in his soul, and Felix's Eighth Pillar snapped into place.

He fell to the ground, hitting the dehydrated earth so hard it crumbled like lifeless sand beneath him.

The inferno guttered out. The High Guard were screaming something Felix couldn't understand. The word rang like a bell, or perhaps that was his own head. With heavy, ponderous motions, Felix pressed himself upward. The world swam as if he were back underwater, and he tried to focus.

His Health was low. Too low. Less than 5%, according to his interface, and his Stamina wasn't much better. The Essence he'd stolen was already gone, woven into his Eighth Pillar, with none left over to even start the Ninth.

Felix. You need to heal!

Can't. Felix shifted his legs, gathering them underneath his body with all the speed of a tortoise. *I need more Essence. Gimme a sec.*

No!

Felix got to his feet, though it cost him more blood. His skin was burned all across his face and chest and arms, the scales turned to flaking ash and wet, weeping sores. If he were being honest, it didn't feel great.

The High Guard closed in.

Felix regarded them through a dribble of blood from his scalp. Offhand, he realized his hair had burned away, and his Garment was little more than a patchwork rag on his back. "Damn," he croaked. "Bit off more than I could chew, there."

Sword did not reply, but swung his weapon for Felix's head. Reactions baked into him by long months of training lifted his crooked blade up, parrying the blow. It was a testing strike, something one might do to a new opponent to determine their abilities. Even so, it drove a spike of pain through Felix's shoulder and numbed him to the elbow. He bit back a curse and reset, waiting.

Sword sneered. "You are spent, usurper."

"Maybe," Felix said, shrugging without thinking. It tore something in his chest, and warm spread down his torso. He winced. "Still gonna kick your ass, though."

The High Guard laughed, but it never reached his cold eyes. "Admit defeat, forfeit the Challenge, and leave your people in our hands. It is the only way forward that doesn't end in the slaughter of thousands of innocents."

"Slaughter by you."

Sword inclined his head, conceding the point. "Semantics. It is you who brought this down upon them all. Had you not proclaimed your triumph those months ago, we would have taken far longer to find your wretched lies." His brows drew down, and golden cloaks flared around all of them in time with the sigaldry on their chests. "Had you faced me as a warrior, your people would not suffer."

Felix laughed, and it hurt. "You think I'd believe you? You guys just tried to drop a megaton bomb on my city because I didn't come out and play when you wanted me to. Nah, I think I'll fight."

"You can barely stand," Tome said. "Let alone lift your weapons."

"Yeah." Felix wet his lips and tasted the copper tang of his own blood. "You still haven't made a move, though." He looked at them all and let his Mana flare through his pathways. His eyes *burned.* "Who's the coward now?"

Mace screamed something incoherent and rushed forward, stone flowing around her outstretched fist. Felix pivoted, stepping into the hole in her attack where her other arm once resided, and kicked as hard as he could. He caught the back of the woman's knee, tripping her, but his blunted Strength wasn't enough to break through her armor.

C'mon Pit! One more Pillar! We have to have something else!

The lumbering woman stumbled through, and Spear took her place, stabbing forward with her namesake weapon in a series of rapid thrusts that moved incredibly fast. Felix wove between them, not so much seeing them as feeling their placement in the air, but still he took two hits to the chest and hip. He barely had time to recoil in pain when Sword stepped up, long blade dancing in his hands, and took a solid chunk out of Felix's bicep.

I AM READY.

His Hunger had been so quiet since its offer of help that Felix had discounted it entirely, and now, without warning, the empty darkness within his core space *convulsed.* A ripple of pressure spread from Felix, enough that even the High Guard took notice.

"What is he doing?" Spear demanded.

"Kill him! Kill him!" Mace cried out, still getting up out of the mud.

Sword thrust his weapon and Skills kindled upon outstretched palms…only for all of them to abruptly slow, as if the world itself was stretching like taffy. Heat burned in Felix's core, his Perception stretched to its utter, unnatural limit by that rippling pressure before it was all yanked inward. Consumed by the insanity within. He was hauled into the dark to witness Essence and Mana pour from his Hunger in cascading showers.

What is this?

UN-FEED.

Power that his Hunger had consumed fell in great heavy streams, yet none of it was useful. The Essence, Mana, and significance his greedy passenger had offered was all solidified into elaborately-formed star shapes. Four-point, six-point, even twenty-point formations shot into the lower dark. Not only that, but a red wash of pain accompanied each regurgitation, as if his Hunger was harming itself in the process. Felix felt it as much as heard it. It was the pain of loss, of rejected Need...yet it did not stop.

Pit shrieked, happiness and savage anger baked into a singular sound, and suddenly red-gold light filled his core space. Cardinal Flame sang from its place above, its vibrations latching onto each crystallized morsel of power and heating them up.

Pit, you absolute genius!

Fiendforge blared into the dark, redoubling the heat as crystal melted like ice, releasing vast streamers of liquid potency—potency that Pit seized upon instantly. Cords of power formed, woven in an instant as Felix joined the process, braiding them together faster than all those that came before. Opalescent roots flashed down among the blue-white and red-gold centers, reinforcing his final Pillar with an infinitesimal portion of the Divine.

MORE!

A darkness gushed from his Hunger, fully liquid but writhing as if alive. Fear spiked through Felix as he recognized it—the Creature's power, in all its Stygian glory. It shot downward like an arrow, splitting into nine equal parts before landing upon his Pillars...and sinking within.

MORE!

The unused power the Hunger had given up, the shards of crystallized potency, all of it sank to the base of the Pillars, coating their bottoms with gleaming facets and connecting each of them to another in a dizzying array of crystalline lattices.

ENOUGH!

The crimson heat of it all cooled instantly, hardening into an opalescent shine. Immediately after, a glorious chord swept through Felix's Aspects as if the essence of pleasure and triumph were being channeled through every nerve.

The Ninth Pillar had completed.

You Have Formed All Nine Pillars!
Congratulations!

Due To Vein Of Divinity (x2), All Skills Woven Into Your Pillars Gain Seven (7) Levels!
Sovereign of Flesh is level 95!
Relentless Resolution is level 95!
The Song of Absolution is level 94!
Bastion of Will is level 99!
Chthonic Tribute is level 97!
Voracious Eye is level 89!
Adamant Discord is level 91!
Cardinal Flame is level 93!
Theurgist of the Rise is level 92!

New Titles!
Champion's Convocation (Legendary)!
For weaving all nine Pillars before level 100 and before reaching Master Tier, you may weave further still! A tenth Pillar awaits you, if you've the courage to face it!

Weaver of Destiny (Epic)!
You have woven all nine Pillars within your core space! +50 DEX, VIT, PER!

Artisan of Divinity (Mythic)!
Your Pillars contain significant elements of not one, but two Divinities. The strength of your foundation is the stuff of legends! +100 WIL, INT, MIG, ALA!

Shaper of Chaos (Primordial)!
You have successfully woven Harmony and Dissonance into your Pillars! +75 STR, END, INE, RES

Infernal Appetite (Legendary)!
You have immersed yourself in a Grandmaster's flame and lived to tell the tale. Not only that, but you have consumed a piece of it and incorporated it into your own power. You will now find consuming sources of fire and heat to be far easier than previously.

You Have Gained 3 Levels!

You Are Now Level 62!
+60 to STR! +66 to PER! +66 to VIT! +78 to END! +72 to INT!
+84 to WIL! +78 to AGL! +87 to DEX!
+60 All Harmonic Stats!
You Have 45 Unused Stat Points!

Power coursed through Felix with a ferocity he hadn't experienced since his Omen Path. It raged across his senses and core space, filling up until he was sure he would burst, until his Skills and cores and Pillars were all soaked in brilliant potency.

Distantly, almost reflexively, Felix threw his unused stat points into Endurance before he was carried out of his core space by the wave of it, thrust unceremoniously back into his Body just as his heightened Perception faded. The High Guard came at him, blindingly fast. Riding the edge of that brilliance, however, he knew what he had to do.

Last Cry of the Chthonic Host!

Essence and significance fled his replenished core space, fed into the rarely-used Skill as his Health and Stamina were abruptly replenished back to full. Felix spun, catching Sword's blade upon his Inheritor's Will while the other two were blocked by an elongated Riposte. The High Guard leader stared at him, a brilliant spark of shock singing in his Spirit.

"What in the Light?" he gasped.

Felix grinned, and his skin didn't split. He was whole again. "I haven't been keeping track. Round three, right?"

With a surge of Strength, Felix threw all of them back before closing with Mace. He sounded Stone Shaping within him, singing its pattern until it burst from his channels with a domineering potency that merged the woman's stone-coated fist to a pillar of summoned rock.

Sovereign of Flesh!

"You—!" she cried, but that was all. Felix's clawed fist latched onto the jagged edge of her armor and wrenched it, Strength and Willpower opposing her Endurance, Vitality, and her shaken mental faculties.

It was no contest.

The milky white armor bent and shattered in a burst of caustic, golden light. Mace screamed…until Felix's claws took off her head.

Chthonic Tribute!

You Have Killed Tabit Wikkard of the High Guard!
XP Earned!

Essence by the truckload flooded his channels, fueling his Sovereign of Flesh even further. Felix's full-body scales returned, coating him in midnight armor and blazing with cyan swirls across his chest and arms.

It was a pattern that, now that he thought of it, resembled the High Guard's. Perhaps, with effort, he could—

Focus, Felix!

Right. Felix blinked himself back, almost lost in the welling of new Intelligence as his thoughts spun faster and faster. The High Guard were only just reacting, lifting weapons and firing spells at him despite the golden flames that burst upon their chests. Their Grandmaster-faker array flickered and sizzled, not failing completely, but reducing them to something lesser.

I can deal with that.

Green Shaping!

Birds of green-gold and purple Mana flew toward him on liquid wings, but Felix seized the life portion of their composition and scattered them to the winds. Tome barely had a chance to gawk before Felix landed a kick on the mage's knee that shattered the joint. He screamed, only to have Hand of Cataclysm tear through his throat, leaving a glut of acid to sizzle through the man's spine.

You Have Killed Davin Kincaid of the High Guard!
XP Earned!

"How?" Spear screeched, diving at him from above. Felix spun, grasping her weapon and kicking her full in the chest. His metal boot deformed around his foot, but the damage was far worse against the High Guard. She tumbled backward in a rapid roll, head over heels, kicking up a spray of water in all directions.

Relentless Resolution!

Adamant Discord!

Felix blurred forward upon a bolt of lightning, catching up with Spear's tumbling form just as her remaining eye opened in desperate disbelief. It was her last expression, as his Inheritor's Will cut off her head.

You Have Killed Esre Teel of the High Guard!
XP Earned!

Felix stood in the ankle-deep water, breathing hard and quivering with what felt like lightning in his veins, when an orichalcum blade descended on his back. He spun around, meeting the sword with his dual weapons and stopping it cold.

The last remaining High Guard grimaced at him beneath the light of three moons above. "What you have done is worthy of legend and song, false king. But you are an abomination under the light of the only true god, and even my death will not save you from the Pathless' retribution!"

The man twisted, breaking Felix's guard and launching into a series of Sword Forms that wove a dazzling net of offense and defense. Felix's weapons could not penetrate it, no matter how he moved and pivoted, and even his sudden increase in Strength was not enough to bypass it. The force of his strikes was deflected, again and again, energy scattered to either side of the man's body and only served to propel the High Guard into faster and faster speeds. Sword had mastered his weapon, earning his strange name, and there was little chance of Felix beating him in such a contest.

So he didn't bother.

Felix walked into that blender, no longer dodging or parrying, but flaring the potent song of his Sovereign of Flesh. Some hits struck off his scales, but most bit deep, drawing dark blood from his veins and dropping his Health like a stone. Sword struck faster and faster, until Felix's blood rained down like water, but he kept closing, forcing the High Guard to move.

"What—what are you doing, you heretical oaf?" Sword slashed at Felix's shoulder, and he lifted his forearm to take a nasty gash there. "You will die long before I burn through my Stamina!"

"Will I?" Felix asked, advancing yet again. His footsteps shattered the earth, launching him forward in response to Sword's nimble retreat. "Are you sure about that?"

"You—!" Sword jolted as his back bounced off the gray expanse of stone that was Haarwatch's Sunrise Wall.

Relentless Resolution!

Felix blurred forward, putting everything into the simple act of acceleration, and finally slipped just inside the man's guard. Skyslain's Riposte stabbed forward at the same time—but was caught by Sword's cross-guard.

"You still missed," he sneered.

Felix reached out and grasped the man's forearm before flooding his Riposte with Mana. The blade grew explosively from dagger to the brutal blade of a broadsword in a moment.

Sword gasped, blood pouring from his mouth as he scrabbled against Felix's iron grip. "You—st-stand beyond the Light, Felix Nevarre." The man put all the disgust and condemnation he could into his words, and it coiled like a physical weight against Felix's Affinity. "You are—nothing before the—the Divine!"

Something shifted in the air seconds before the High Guard's skin burst alight. Flames ripped outward, engulfing both of them in a conflagration of flesh, steel, and Mana.

Cardinal Flame! Pit shrieked.

The flame Mana was seized until it split around Felix's body like a boulder in a river. It was all over in a half second, leaving him standing alone against a half-melted wall, blinking against the desiccating heat.

F-forgot to give that back, Pit panted. *Sorry.*

You Have Killed Callum D'or of the High Guard!
XP Earned!

I forgive you, bud.

Challenge Complete!

EPILOGUE

"Run, or by the Light, I will skewer you myself!"

Blood and mud soiled their armor as they stumbled along, fouling cloaks until they dragged behind them like leaden weights. The man at the lead wore the insignia of a full-fledged Paladin, and his crimson armor hid all but the worst of the blood that soaked its face. Behind him trailed nearly two hundred soldiers of the light, though the Paladin hadn't bothered to count. All that mattered was escape.

The High Guard were dead.

That string of words echoed in his Mind, relentless and repeated, until he thought he would go mad. It was impossible. When he had been dispatched from Amaranth in the company of four of their number, he had felt invincible. No foe could face down the High Guard and live. Even when their army had been met by stiff resistance by the heretics, the Paladin had been sure of their victory. The Hierocracy was as inevitable as the rising sun.

Now they fumbled through the dark, breath heavy and brows wet with sweat. None of their Stamina remained hale, and most had bare dregs upon which to draw despite their Skills with Heavy Armor and Marching. Their Health was no better, ranging from untouched to those who bore savage wounds from the vipers that had assaulted them.

Quite aside from the heretics, the monsters that had broken through the sky had hunted his brethren with a ferocity he had never seen before. Now, he flinched from the craggy bark of a fallen tree, thinking for a moment that they had found them again.

Keep moving, he chided himself. *Trust in the Pathless' light.*

He could not shake the image of that man, covered in midnight scales, as he lifted one of the High Guard in his claws. *No man. A monster.* He shuddered, recalling the nightmarish maw upon the enemy's face. *A demon.*

The army had broken as a strange fissure of doom settled upon them all. For a time, the Paladins Willpower had been affected by the terrible event, and though he knew it to be a Status Condition, that did not change his decision. He fled, gathering what soldiers he could as he ran into the dark forest. A monster such as that *thing* would not stop with the High Guard. It would descend on them all until they were all food in his unholy belly.

I must tell them. I must warn the Hierei! The thought was the small light in his Spirit that goaded him onward, that kept him from wailing and gnashing his teeth at his fellows' death. Good men had died that day, and the Autarch of Nagast would see retribution. *Upon my power and Temper, I swear it!*

Twigs snapped as a slender shape dropped from the trees above. The Paladin skid to a halt. "Brandished Sun!"

A storm·of daggers erupted from the Paladin's fist, each forged of holy light and aimed with a surety born of a thousand uses. They met the thickening shadows and flashed, scattering into the woods where they weren't shattered outright. A woman in leather armor stepped forward, around an axe blade made of luminous ice that had interposed itself. She was small and slender, but the Paladin and all those around him froze in place as he felt the weight of her Spirit.

"That was rude," she said. "Almost like you meant to kill me."

"Because they did," said another voice, this one far deeper. The incongruous axe head was lifted up into the blue-skinned hands of a Frost Giant.

"I know," she said, and seemed...exasperated.

More giants emerged from behind the trees, at least a dozen of them, all topping ten strides tall. The woman's chain uncoiled, and huge serpents slithered from the shadow of the giants. *Nagafolk.* The thought was fear and despair rolled into one. *I thought we left them behind. How did they get ahead of us?*

"Try better this time," the woman said, and the Paladin could not miss her wolfish grin in the moonlight. "Let me enjoy this."

The Paladin clenched his jaw. There was but one thing to do, before fear unmanned all those behind him. "Order. Purity. Strength. We will not bow to you, heretic! We reject your path of shadow!"

The woman scrunched up her face and glanced at one of the blue-skinned monsters. "What?"

"Children of the Pathless!" he called, ignoring her question as he lifted his sword. With a flare of his stalwart Willpower, one of his holy Skills activated, transforming his blade to golden flame. "Attack!"

The remnant might of the Hierocracy surged behind him, and for a moment, golden light suffused that dark forest. It was glorious.

Until the dark consumed him.

The sound of warfare had vanished and been replaced by the triumphant cheers of the warriors on the walls. Felix had followed them, for a time, ensuring that the majority of their living opponents were captured. A few had gotten away, scattering into the night-dark forests of the Verdant Pass, but he left their return to others.

For now, Felix rested against the half-melted wall, simply breathing.

Full night had fallen on Haarwatch, and darkness would have cloaked the blasted battlefield had someone not set a seared sigil of light in the sky. A new, glaring sun, it served its purpose as Inquisitors and Paladins were shuffled into makeshift prisons. He'd made those, too, forming them from the ramparts he'd pulled from the earth—they would suffice for the moment.

He adjusted his position. No matter how Tempered his Body became, he doubted he'd ever enjoy sitting on rubble. Felix swept the ground clean and plopped back down with a sigh. *Pit? How're you feeling?*

Inside him, huddled within his Spirit, Pit muttered something groggily. Sense images fluttered across their bond, of cozy mattresses and warm fires juxtaposed by searing heat and lightning-bright pain.

Just about the same, huh? Neither of them had been eager to end their Convergence, due to his friend's injuries. In his Mind's eye, Pit's wings were simply bloody stumps on his back, and though his Health had stabilized, they were both still suffering Spirit Damage. *Focus on resting. I'll...I'll figure something out.*

Of the others, Vess and Yintarion were already within Haarwatch's walls, getting treated for their injuries by Isla and the other healers. Felix had carried them in himself before he'd even cared about hunting down redcloaks. Beef and Hallow had joined up with Harn and some of the Fiend's Claws and were out there with Evie and the rest, fighting.

"Karys? You there?" he asked. His hooked sword crackled once before radiating a green-gold glow.

His chancellor's deep, worried voice emanated from the sword. "I am, Felix. Is the battle done?"

"Yeah. It's done."

A sigh like wind through metal pipes echoed across the sword. "Thank the Ancestors. How did you return to Haarwatch? I could not reach you for a long time, and when I sensed your return, you had already returned to the Territory."

"A Dragon did it."

"A Drag—This isn't a time for jokes, Felix."

"Life's funny sometimes," Felix said, his eyes roaming the battlefield.

Corpses were everywhere. Friend and foe alike. An icy spike settled somewhere in his gut and would not leave. "Sometimes not so much."

"Felix?"

Zara. He didn't so much as turn his head, but Felix lifted a hand in greeting. "Hey there, folks. How's it going?"

Alister, Atar, and Zara walked down the pile of slagged stone toward him, and none looked their best. Blood had stained Alister's blue robes, turning them into a gruesome purple in the dark, while Atar's gray hands appeared as if he'd tried to cook them. They were charred from the fingertips all the way to his palms, but were otherwise unblemished. Together with Alister, they looked like they could use a long nap.

For her part, Zara's sea-green hair was frazzled and her black chorister's robes torn as she let her Spirit sing with a touch of disgruntled anxiety. "Could you not have rested *atop* the wall, Felix?"

"I like the way the High Guard melted this portion," he said, wiggling slightly. "Fits my back nicely."

Zara just stared at him, but Atar's red gaze all but glowed as satisfaction poured off his Spirit. "You killed them all?"

Felix inhaled before letting out a heavy breath. "Yeah. Ate them, too, for good measure. Kept this, though."

He tossed something at the mage, who had to fumble with his stave and the oversized object. "What in the—You don't just throw things at people, Felix! I should—What," he said, realization dawning on him. "What is this?"

"One of the High Guard had a big magic book on them. It's packed full of sigaldry." Felix shrugged. "Figured you could make use of it."

"I—I certainly can," he said, opening the pages. His expectant face fell into a sour grimace. "Eventually. These are warded against those less than High Adept."

"Oh. Makes sense why I couldn't read it yet." Felix reached back toward the mage. "Well, if you don't want it—"

"No!" Atar said, clutching the book to his thin chest.

Alister smiled. "He means, 'thank you.'"

"Yes," Atar nodded. "That."

"Are you…well, Felix?" Zara asked. She settled upon another rounded chunk of stone and arranged her black robes about her legs. She paused mid-adjustment when she saw the other orichalcum weapons next to him. "Facing the High Guard alone was an unnecessary risk."

"Everyone else was busy," Felix said, and he didn't even glance at the Masterwork spear and sword that held her attention. "Or hurt."

Redcloaks were marched past, some distance away. More stragglers, dragged in chains of ice by a contingent of Frost Giants. They were taken to the crude, mass holding cell, same as the rest.

"What are we gonna do with them?" Alister asked.

burn them.

Felix raised an eyebrow as he caught Atar's eye. The mage cleared his throat and tucked the silver-chased book beneath his arm. "Ah. Would it not be safer to…remove the threat they pose?"

"And against the Accords of Elysium, as well as any shred of decency. I would not be party to such contemptible action." Karys said from Felix's waist.

"Oh. *You're* listening. I didn't say you had to do it." Atar raised his hands up, catching the look in Felix's eye. "Fine. So we hold them. For how long?"

"Until a better option presents itself," Zara said. She turned to Felix. "I need materials for the construction of a better barrier. Given enough time, we could truly defend against the Hierocracy."

"Then you'll have it. Include Hector and Atar's people. See if you can combine that Domain core barrier with this." Still sitting, Felix pulled up a System window and tossed it to all three of them.

Mirk Enclosure - Ritual, Defensive Array, Tier IV
***Effect*: Encase your Territory in an impenetrable fog, invisible to your people within, but a physical and sensory barrier to all those without.**
***Initial Cost*: 10,000 Mana/5,000 Essence**
***Ongoing Cost*: 5,000 Mana/2,500 Essence Per 12 Hours**

"Your defensive fog wall?" Atar said. "But that failed already."

"Yeah. But it was strong enough to require a few masters to break it. We need it to be stronger by far." Felix lifted the orichalcum sword, letting the false light of the burning sigaldry play across its glossy surface. "I want to send a message to the Hierocracy. We are not meant to be trifled with. I'm the sword, but we need a shield, too. Can you do it?"

"Perhaps." Zara frowned. "They will come regardless, Felix."

"I know," he said, and stood. Lightning played off the Masterwork blade, and his vision was stained by the flare of his power. "But I've got plans."

Felix could feel the connections all around him, and between the people of Haarwatch, his friends, even the enemies that were huddled in fear a couple hundred feet away, the world was awash in them. Standing out among them all, however, were those that connected him to the other Unbound.

"Together, we'll be ready for them."

ABOUT NICOLI GONNELLA

Nicoli Gonnella spent his formative years atop a mountain, breathing deep of the world energy and expelling impurities from his soul. Also he went to school and stuff. He always wrote but now he's abandoned everything to do it full time. Readers give him strength, spirit bomb style, and there's no telling how strong he will become. This isn't even his final form.

He lives with his wife, two kids, and a corgi named Cornelius.

Connect with Nicoli Gonnella:
NicoliGonnella.com
Discord.gg/sqQvJQhY8F
Patreon.com/Necariin
RoyalRoad.com/fiction/30321/Unbound
Facebook.com/Nicoli-Gonnella-Author-347428719693359

ABOUT MOUNTAINDALE PRESS

Dakota and Danielle Krout, a husband and wife team, strive to create as well as publish excellent fantasy and science fiction novels. Self-publishing *The Divine Dungeon: Dungeon Born* in 2016 transformed their careers from Dakota's military and programming background and Danielle's Ph.D. in pharmacology to President and CEO, respectively, of a small press. Their goal is to share their success with other authors and provide captivating fiction to readers with the purpose of solidifying Mountaindale Press as the place 'Where Fantasy Transforms Reality.'

Connect with Mountaindale Press:
MountaindalePress.com
Facebook.com/MountaindalePress
Twitter.com/_Mountaindale
Instagram.com/MountaindalePress

MOUNTAINDALE PRESS TITLES

GameLit and LitRPG

The Completionist Chronicles,
The Divine Dungeon,
Full Murderhobo, and
Year of the Sword by Dakota Krout

Metier Apocalypse by Frank G. Albelo

Arcana Unlocked by Gregory Blackburn

A Touch of Power by Jay Boyce

Red Mage and
Farming Livia by Xander Boyce

Space Seasons by Dawn Chapman

Ether Collapse and
Ether Flows by Ryan DeBruyn

Dr. Druid by Maxwell Farmer

Bloodgames by Christian J. Gilliland

Unbound by Nicoli Gonnella

Threads of Fate by Michael Head

Lion's Lineage by Rohan Hublikar and Dakota Krout

Wolfman Warlock by James Hunter and Dakota Krout

Axe Druid,
Mephisto's Magic Online, and

High Table Hijinks by Christopher Johns

Skeleton in Space by Andries Louws

Dragon Core Chronicles by Lars Machmüller

Chronicles of Ethan by John L. Monk

Pixel Dust and
Necrotic Apocalypse by David Petrie

Viceroy's Pride by Cale Plamann

Henchman by Carl Stubblefield

Artorian's Archives by Dennis Vanderkerken and Dakota Krout

Vaudevillain by Alex Wolf

www.ingramcontent.com/pod-product-compliance
Lightning Source LLC
Chambersburg PA
CBHW032247020726
47495CB00001B/3
* 9 7 8 1 6 3 7 6 6 1 8 1 9 *